JANET DAILEY

The Great Alone

WARNER BOOKS

A *Warner* Book

First published in Great Britain in 1986 by Michael Joseph Ltd
Published by Sphere Books Ltd 1987
Reprinted 1987, 1988, 1991
This edition published by Warner Books in 1992
Reprinted 1992, 1994

ISBN 0 7515 0390 8

Printed in England by Clays Ltd, St Ives plc

Warner
A Division of
Little, Brown and Company (UK)
Brettenham House
Lancaster Place
London WC2E 7EN

'You bitch!' He slapped her across the face.

The force of the blow knocked her to the floor, briefly stunning her. She was conscious of the ache in her arm from the wrenching he'd given it. One whole side of her face felt as if it was on fire. She propped herself up on one arm and gingerly touched her cheek and jaw, tasting the blood from the cut in her mouth.

'You lied to me!' he bellowed at her.

'I didn't.' She hurried to her feet, anxious to appease his temper. 'I swear I didn't, Gabe.'

'The whole damned town knew I took a breed for a wife – everyone except me! You left out that little piece of information.'

'You never asked.' She cowered from him, shielding her throbbing face with her hand. 'I love you. I wanted to be your wife and help make all your plans and dreams come true.'

'You've ruined them! You've destroyed every chance I had! Don't you see, you stupid slut! They'll never appoint me governor when this becomes a territory! I'd be lucky if they'd give me an appointment as a postmaster – not a man with a wife who's part Indian!'

Also by Janet Dailey

*Were you ever out in the Great Alone, when the moon was
    awful clear,
And the icy mountains hemmed you in with a silence you 'most
    could hear;
With only the howl of a timber wolf, and you camped there
    in the cold,
A half-dead thing in a stark, dead world, clean made for the
    muck called gold—*

Excerpt from the poem
'The Shooting of Dan McGrew'
by Robert Service

GENEALOGY

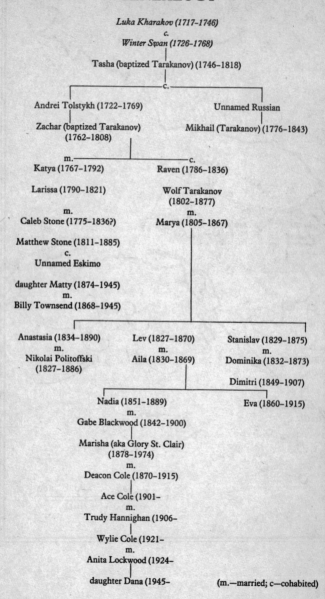

Luka Kharakov (1717–1746)
c.
Winter Swan (1726–1768)

Tasha (baptized Tarakanov) (1746–1818)
c.

Andrei Tolstykh (1722–1769)   Unnamed Russian

Zachar (baptized Tarakanov)   Mikhail (Tarakanov) (1776–1843)
(1762–1808)

m.   c.
Katya (1767–1792)   Raven (1786–1836)

Larissa (1790–1821)   Wolf Tarakanov
(1802–1877)
m.   m.
Caleb Stone (1775–1836?)   Marya (1805–1867)

Matthew Stone (1811–1885)
c.
Unnamed Eskimo

daughter Matty (1874–1945)
m.
Billy Townsend (1868–1945)

Anastasia (1834–1890)   Lev (1827–1870)   Stanislav (1829–1875)
m.   m.   m.
Nikolai Politoffski   Aila (1830–1869)   Dominika (1832–1873)
(1827–1886)

Dimitri (1849–1907)

Nadia (1851–1889)   Eva (1860–1915)
m.
Gabe Blackwood (1842–1900)

Marisha (aka Glory St. Clair)
(1878–1974)
m.
Deacon Cole (1870–1915)

Ace Cole (1901–
m.
Trudy Hannighan (1906–

Wylie Cole (1921–
m.
Anita Lockwood (1924–

daughter Dana (1945–   (m.—married; c—cohabited)

Introduction

While America was being settled by westward expansion, Russia was expanding its territory by moving east. Throughout its early history, the one commodity Russia had in abundance to trade to both Europe and China was furs – sable, ermine, fox, bear, and other valuable pelts. Everything was computed in furs; taxes, salaries, penalties, and rewards were paid in furs.

It was the *promyshlenik* – or *promyshleniki* in the plural – a breed of *coureurs des bois* comparable to American mountain men, who exploited this natural resource. While serfdom prevailed in the rest of the country, forcing people to work the land for the nobles, these men were free to go where they pleased, traveling in bands, electing their own leaders, and sharing the profits from a season's hunt among themselves and the merchants financing the expeditions. When they had hunted out a fur grounds, they moved to a new area – ultimately confronting the vast wilderness of fur-rich Siberia.

The *promyshleniki* scouted, and the Cossacks followed to claim. A warlike people from the steppes above the Black Sea, they were a social rather than an ethnic class who robbed as frequently as they traded, and prized their freedom highly. They had reached the Pacific in the 17th century and heard rumors of a "great land" across the waters to the east. At the same time, European scientists were speculating that Asia and America were connected at some northern point.

It was Peter the Great who ordered the first expedition to explore the uncharted North Pacific and Arctic Oceans and to ascertain whether the two continents were joined. In July of 1728, Vitus Bering, a Dane serving in the Russian navy, sailed the newly built packet boat *St. Gabriel* from the shipyard he'd constructed near the mouth of the Kamchatka River onto the sea that would bear his name. Two short months later he returned, satisfied that no land mass connected Asia and America, but bringing no proof.

A larger, more comprehensive exploration was ordered by Empress Elizabeth, an expedition so massive it required eight years to transport all the men, equipment, and supplies across Siberia and to construct two square-riggers, the *St. Peter*, commanded again by Vitus Bering, and the *St. Paul*, commanded by a Russian named Alexei Chirikov. In June of 1741, the two ships set sail from Avatcha Bay on the Kamchatka Peninsula. After two weeks of sailing, the *St. Peter* and *St. Paul* became separated in the rain and fog.

It is believed the crew of the *St. Paul* saw what is now known as the Prince of Wales Island in extreme southern Alaska. They turned north and followed the broken shoreline with its labyrinth of channels, bays, and inlets surrounding the large and small islands of the Alexander Archipelago. Two days after the first sighting of land, they anchored at the entrance of a great bay, believed to be Sitka harbor. Chirikov ordered one of the ship's two longboats to be put over the side and sent his mate and ten men to explore the entrance. The boat was never seen again. Several days passed before Chirikov sent his boatswain and six men in the second longboat to look for the first. It, too, disappeared. The *St. Paul* remained in the general area for several days, but there were no more boats, and the drinking water was running low. Chirikov consulted with his officers, and it was decided to return to Kamchatka with all possible haste.

The *St. Paul* reached Petropavlovsk, its point of origin, in October of 1741 and the returning sailors told of the abundant wildlife they had seen – the swarms of sea otter, seals, and sea lions along the rocky coasts.

The sister ship, the *St. Peter*, had taken a northeasterly course after losing sight of the *St. Paul*. Its crew also saw land – the towering peaks of Alaska's St. Elias range.

During the return voyage to Kamchatka, the now scurvy-ridden crew had to battle fog and rain, gale-force winds, and a violent storm which blew the ship hundreds of miles into the Pacific. It wasn't until the first of November that they finally encountered a land mass, which turned out to be an island, one of the Commodore group off the Siberian coast of Kamchatka. Bering, the captain, died and was buried on the island that took his name. Other members of the crew survived, recovered their strength and built a boat from the remains of their ship, which had been wrecked when they landed. In August of 1742, forty-six of the original seventy-seven-member crew sailed into Petropavlovsk with a cargo of valuable furs obtained from the island.

Here was proof for the *promyshleniki* and the Cossacks that the land to the east was rich in furs. The sea otter that ventured so rarely onto the Siberian coastline existed elsewhere in great numbers. Undaunted by distance – after all, they had already covered some five thousand miles – they were drawn by this far-off land. The longing to see what lay beyond those waters was strong, a craving to conquer this new land and claim it, too, for the Tsar. Russia already stretched across Europe and Asia. Why not America as well?

By 1742, England had a dozen colonies along the Atlantic seaboard of North America; France had claimed the territory of the Mississippi River from its headwaters to its mouth; Spain had conquered Mexico and the California coast. Russia looked to take her share of the rich North American continent.

Prologue

Petropavlovsk-Kamchatski, Siberia
August 1742

Muffled shouts from outside roused Luka Ivanovich Kharakov from his slumber. He came out of the crude bunk reaching for the musket he'd laid beside it the night before. Nerves twitched along the jagged scar that half closed his left eye and scored his cheekbone before it disappeared into a heavy beard. Now fully awake and alert, he paused to determine the direction of attack, then caught the tenor of the commotion outside, the lack of alarm in it. Simultaneously it registered that he was inside the stockaded walls of the *ostrog* at Petropavlovsk, not in some isolated winter hut in the wilds of Siberia.

As the twitching near his eye eased, Luka felt the heavy pounding in his head take over, the result of a night spent drinking *raka*. The sounds of excited cries and barking dogs continued outside. He slipped the hide-trimmed cloth mantle over his head but didn't bother to girdle the open sides shut with his belt. He pulled a homespun hood over his shaggy hair, then went outside to investigate.

A dreary misting rain fell from the leaden clouds hanging over the August green hills surrounding Petropavlovsk. Mindless of the miserable weather, the inhabitants of the fortress were hurrying toward the harborfront located on a quiet inlet of Avatcha Bay.

Luka followed them. Ships came painfully seldom to this south-easternmost tip of the Romanov Empire of Russia, and any appearance of one was an event.

Only weeks ago, Luka had been told, Chirikov had sailed from this very port in the *Sv Pavel*, bound for Okhotsk. The Cossacks stationed at the ostrog had related to him the stories that the *Sv Pavel* crew had told them of their voyage to northern coasts of the American continent, confirming the native rumors of a *bolshaia zemlia* – a great land – beyond the dark waters, a voyage from which their sister ship the *Sv Petr* had never returned. Perhaps the wretched, often stormy weather of these seas had forced the *Sv Pavel* to turn back.

Luka hoped so. He wanted to learn more about the multitude of islands where they claimed the sea otter, which were so rarely seen on the Kamchatka coast, abounded in vast numbers.

A *promyshlenik* – fur hunter – he knew the value of skins, especially the rare sea otter. Its pelt would fetch ninety rubles – more, it was claimed – on the China frontier.

As he neared the wharf, Luka saw no ship at anchor in the bay, only a crudely built craft no more than thirty-six feet in length tied up to the dock. Screeching seagulls wheeled overhead, adding chorus to the turmoil attending the arrival of the strange vessel. Everywhere, people were embracing wild-looking men dressed in skins.

He recognized a Cossack who was hurrying back to the ostrog as one he'd drunk with the night before and stopped him. 'What is all this excitement? Who are these men?'

'The *Sv Petr!* They did not die!'

Luka stared at the ragged bunch of men, some forty in number, many of them with toothless grins and all of them with long, straggly beards, and dressed in animal skins. The ship had not been lost at sea with all hands aboard as everyone had believed, Luka realized. Some had lived to tell the tale – the tale of the great land that Luka wanted most to hear. He moved into their midst, catching snatches of conversation while he stared at their fur garments, recognizing the pelts of sea otter, fox, and seal.

'Our cables broke and the ship was thrown onto the rocks . . .'

'. . . thought we had reached Kamchatka . . .'

'No. Bering is dead. Lagunov, too. We . . .'

'It turned out to be an island . . .'

Stopping, Luka turned toward the man who had just spoken. Half of his teeth were gone and the rest were blackened from scurvy. But Luka observed the fox-skin garment the man wore, not the stench of his body.

'Where is this island?' Luka wanted to know.

'East of here. I don't know how far,' the man responded, eager to talk of the misadventure now that it was over. 'We sailed ten days ago, but out boat began leaking only three days out. We had to throw most of our lead and ammunition overboard to keep from taking more water. It's a miracle we got here at all.' Quickly he crossed himself, the gesture from right to left in the Russian

Orthodox fashion. 'We built the boat ourselves from the wreckage of the *Sv Petr*. All the ship's carpenters had died and –'

Luka Ivanovich Kharakov was a promyshlenik, not a sailor; his interest centered on the fur the man wore and where it had come from, not how the man got here. 'There were fox on this island?'

'Everywhere.' His unpleasant grimace exposed toothless gums on top. 'When we first went ashore on the island, the Arctic fox was the only animal we saw. Bold they were, too,' he declared and cursed them roundly. 'When somebody died, we didn't have a chance to get him buried before the foxes were there tearing away at his corpse. It was nearly impossible to drive them away, and we couldn't spare the powder to shoot them. All of us were weak. Only a few had the strength to hunt in the beginning.'

'What about the sea otter?' Luka indicated one of the other survivors clad in a long garment made of sea otter pelts sewn together. 'Were there many of them, too?'

'The waters around the island were filled with them.' The man smiled triumphantly, then caught Luka by the arm with taloned fingers and led him to the wharfside. 'Look.'

Bundles of furs sat on the ground, the stacks growing as more were unloaded from the hold of the boat. Amidst the bales of fox and seal skins, Luka recognized the dark, glossy pelts of the sea otter and knelt beside one of the bundles. With a knife, he cut the rawhide strings that tied them together and the skins tumbled loose.

He picked up one and ran his hand over the nearly black fur, watching the iridescent shimmer the action created. He dug his fingers into the soft, thick hair, burying them nearly an inch in depth before touching the hide. And the size of the pelt – five feet long and two feet wide – almost three times the size of a sable skin. It was a prime fur – worth its weight in gold. It was 'soft gold.' All around him were more bales, containing forty skins to a bale.

Once, two years ago, he had killed ten sea otter trapped on a massive ice floe that had ground into the Kamchatka coast. Ten pelts, and Luka had thought himself most fortunate. Now he looked on these hundreds with a reverent greed.

'. . . maybe nine hundred pelts. And that's not counting the skins of the blue fox and fur seals.'

Luka caught the last half of the man's boast. The muscles in his throat constricted with frustration and half-formed resentment.

3

He was the hunter. What were these sailors doing with a fortune in furs? Every winter he went out into the wilds to trap sable and came back with fewer and fewer, barely making a living while risking his life in the brutal Siberian cold among uncivilized tribes of hostile natives, like the Chukchi, who had given him this scar he carried on his face.

'This island, did you kill all the sea otter there before you sailed? Were there any left?' He glared at the man, who drew back from the piercing gaze of those dark, deep-set eyes and the silent menace of the jagged white scar that ran from brow to beard.

'Yes. I told you they were all around the island.' The man snatched the pelt and hurriedly retied the bundle, then moved away to find someone else interested in hearing his tale of survival.

His hands were empty, but Luka could still feel the sensation of the soft, thick pelt beneath his fingers. There were more questions he wanted to ask, but he raised no objection when the man scurried from him. Bundles of the valuable pelts were piled in front of him, and voices babbled on all sides. Yet his attention was claimed by none of these. His eye was on the distant horizon, beyond the small arm of Avatcha Bay, his gaze narrowing in an attempt to see beyond it.

His was the blood of the promyshlenik, running fast with the urge to see what was over the next mountain. But for Luka Ivanovich Kharakov, there was no mountain before him. The sea hemmed him in. Yet somewhere across that gray, storm-tossed water lay the 'great land' of endless mountains and rivers, a place of untold riches.

While he looked at that which he could not see, he was tugged by a deep longing – peculiarly Russian – an exalting kind of homesickness for a place he had yet to see. His forefathers had crossed the Siberian steppes and the Stanavoi Mountains and entered the Kamchatka Peninsula, pursuing the sable. The old hunting grounds were nearly exhausted, yet he stood on the brink of a new one. Distance was nothing to fear. Only time. He was twenty-five, his youth gone. The wealth he sought waited out there.

Screeching gulls wheeled overhead, buffeted by the strong winds that blew the mist from the sea against his face. Low clouds scudded inland. Still he stared at the spot where the dark gray sky melted into a dark gray sea.

That he was here, on this day, to see with his own eyes the evidence that there were indeed islands where the sea otter swarmed, was surely an omen. Yesterday he had nearly decided not to spend the night in Petropavlovsk, and instead to push on to the gathering place where he was to meet with the other members of this winter's hunting artel. He had only intended to stop long enough to obtain the priest's blessing for a successful hunt. He hadn't bothered to do that the year before and his sable catch had been small.

It bothered Luka Ivanovich Kharakov not at all that his sudden religious urge had superstitious origins and a moderate degree of avarice. Just as it had not bothered him to go from praying at the small church at Petropavlovsk to drinking with some of the Cossacks at the garrison.

The return of the survivors from Vitus Bering's shipwrecked crew prompted Luka to delay his departure from the village one more day and participate in the celebration. The *praznik* that was given was one of the best he'd ever attended. Yesterday, meat, vodka, and tobacco had seemed to be in scarce supply, yet they appeared in abundance at the festivity. Guzlas furnished music for dancing, while women and young girls from the native huts were plied with liquor and otherwise cajoled to partner the men.

During all the merrymaking, Luka managed to speak to various members of the ill-fated crew. All, to varying degrees, corroborated the story of the first. He learned all he could about the craggy, treeless islands that rose from the sea and arched across it like a gigantic boom, and the surrounding waters teeming with fur-bearing sea mammals.

That winter, he hunted the sable in the Siberian steppes and, on the odd clear days, observed the three mock suns that formed an arc over the real one. He had time to reflect on the stories and visualize in his mind the multitude of pelts that had been stacked on that wharf. The faraway land called to him. During his young years, he had wandered the length and breadth of Kamchatka, and now his soul ached for the land beyond the horizon. He would go there, he vowed. It was his destiny. The fur wealth that had eluded him here in Kamchatka, he would find in those islands off America.

Part One

The Aleutians

1 *September 1745*

Bellied by the wind, the square sails of softened reindeer hides pulled at the leather straps that tied them to the spars of the double-masted vessel. Little water seeped through the moss-caulked cracks of the green-timbered craft as the bow nosed first toward the sky, then dipped toward the bottom of a wave trough. Modeled after a boat designed for the river trade on the Volga, the flatboat had almost no keel, which allowed it to be easily beached yet remain remarkably stable in the water. Because of the chronic shortage of iron, its green-timbered planks were lashed – or 'sewn' – together with leather thongs, giving rise to its name *shitik* from the Russian verb *shi-it* which means 'to sew.'

In any compass direction all that could be seen from the crowded deck of the river vessel was the sullen Bering Sea heaving and rising. Luka Ivanovich Kharakov stood on the crowded deck, his feet slightly spread against the roll of the shitik, watching the flat horizon to the southeast.

He was unconcerned that the shitik had never been intended for ocean waters. Two years before, a similar vessel commanded by a Cossack sergeant from a Kamchatka garrison had set out on an expedition to the Komandorskie island group, where Bering had died. It had returned safely last summer with a rich cargo of furs, proving to any doubters the seaworthiness of the craft. Luka had not been among the skeptics. He had been refused the chance to join the company of men who sailed aboard the shitik *Kapiton*, rejected in favor of the surviving sailors from Bering's crew.

Nor did it bother him that this shitik had been constructed by men with no knowledge of shipbuilding. He had been one of them, whose experience was limited to the building of smaller boats to navigate Siberian rivers or traverse the lakes. The only one among them who could claim an acquaintance with the sea was the shitik's navigator and commander. A silversmith by trade,

9

Mikhail Nevodchikov had come to Siberia in search of furtune. At Kamchatka, it was discovered he had no passport and he was pressed into government service as a crew member aboard Bering's ship, the *Sv Petr*. Despite the man's dubious credentials, it was claimed by some that Nevodchikov discovered the near islands of America, the group Bering had called the Delusive Islands.

It was for these the shitik steered its southeasterly course. Six days before, the boat had sailed from the mouth of the Kamchatka River and bypassed the Komandorskie Islands, where the garrison sergeant had taken a second expedition. Favoring winds had steadily pushed the vessel toward their destination, the virgin hunting grounds they wouldn't have to share with another hunting party.

With timbers groaning, the shitik climbed another swell. After six days at sea, the craft's shuddering moans had become a companionable sound, not a cause for alarm. Many times during those first days, Luka had expected the watery canyons between the ocean swells to close and swallow the sailing vessel, but each time the boat had scaled the wall of a wave, then plunged sickeningly into the next deep valley and survived. At the beginning of the voyage, he had been plagued by a mild queasy feeling, but the heaving motion no longer bothered him.

The stomachs of some members of the hunting party were not so strong. The stench of seasickness mingled with the fetid odor of unwashed bodies and tainted the wind. Near him, someone groaned at the sudden lurch of the shitik into the next trough. Luka glanced indifferently at the man half sprawled on the deck and half propped against the rail. The man held his stomach with limp arms while his head lolled to the side, his eyes shut and his mouth sagging open, vomit drying on his beard and clothes.

Disinterestedly, Luka watched the Cossack Vladimir Shekhurdin move from one ailing man to another, wetting lips with a moist cloth and squeezing drops of water into parched mouths. Luka looked over his comrades on deck. The hunting party was composed of a rough breed of men, some fifty in number, promyshleniki by trade, but their backgrounds were varied. Some were criminals – thieves, tax evaders, or murderers. Others were exiles, others serfs fleeing the tyranny of their masters. And some were like himself, the sons of promyshleniki, possessed by a lust to roam. Their assorted pasts mattered little to him. His own life had its shadows, its brutality and violence.

His glance fell on the distinctive features of a Kamchadal – the thickly lidded eyes and the broad, heavy facial bones of the Mongol race. He touched a hand to the scar on his face, feeling the coldness of hatred course through him for this tribal cousin of the Chukchi who had butchered his father and permanently disfigured him. A handful of Kamchadals were included in the hunting expedition, baptized by the church and thus the equal of any Muscovite. But not to Luka – never to Luka.

Jostled from behind, Luka swung testily around, then controlled the impulse to retaliate for the accidental shoving as Yakov Petrovich Chuprov regained his balance on the heaving deck. He held the steady gaze of the man's wise eyes for an instant, then curtly nodded to him. Chuprov's reputation as a hunter was well known to him, and Luka chose not to tangle with this sandy-bearded man who might be elected to lead the hunt. Only moments ago he'd seen Chuprov talking with the navigator.

'How long before we reach the islands? Did Nevodchikov say?' Luka asked. Since passing the Komandorskie Islands, they'd seen no land, only slate-gray sea and sky with occasional glimpses of the sun splitting through the clouds.

'He thinks it will be soon.' A seagull swooped low across the shitik's bow. 'According to him, the seabirds are a sign we're near land.'

Luka noticed the increased number of birds in the air, but he recognized few of them. He was versed in land animals rather than the creatures of the sky and sea. The prospect of finally seeing the land that had haunted him these past years filled him with hard satisfaction. 'Do you believe Nevodchikov?'

'The winds have been steady and the weather fair.' The promyshlenik shrugged. 'He's been here before. I have not.'

From the starboard side of the deck, one of the seasick Kamchadal natives called for water. The tall, erect figure of the Cossack Shekhurdin made its way across the crowded deck. Luka gazed with contempt at the Cossack's proud, lean face with its neatly trimmed beard.

'Are you going to waste our water on him, Vladimir Andreivich?' Luka challenged, addressing him by two names as was the Russian custom. The first was his own, the second his father's, Vladimir son of Andrei.

'The man is thirsty,' Shekhurdin continued, undeterred.

But his way was quickly blocked by a second promyshlenik, a

big, heavily muscled man. 'You might as well heave it over the side as to give it to him. That's where it's going to end up anyway.' Belyaev's grin revealed the wide gap that separated his front teeth, giving him a deceptively stupid look, but his black eyes were small and sly. Shekhurdin attempted to go around him, but Belyaev wouldn't let him pass. 'I say he doesn't get any water.'

'I recall seeing you heave your guts over the side once or twice.' The Cossack wasn't intimidated by the promyshlenik.

'But I fetched my own water when I was thirsty.' Belyaev continued to grin, the shaggy black beard and mustache around his mouth drawing attention to the dark space between his teeth. 'If that Kamchadal can't do for himself, throw him overboard. It will just make our share of the skins that much bigger.'

Luka agreed. All the men on the expedition had been engaged on a share basis. Half the proceeds of the hunt belonged to the two merchants who had financed the voyage, and the other half would be divided among the crew, one share to each man, with the exception of the navigator, who received three, the *peredovchik* – leader – two, and one for the church. If the hunt was successful, a promyshlenik's share could amount to a small fortune, enough to buy a farm or a business – or stay drunk on vodka for a year.

'Look!' someone shouted. 'What's that black shape on the horizon?'

The confrontation on deck suddenly lost its importance as Luka swung around to scan the horizon that was sometimes above and sometimes below the plunging and rearing prow of the shitik. A man scurried up the rawhide rigging onto a spar of the square mainsail. Everyone tensely waited for some word to sound above the groaning timbers of the heaving boat.

'Do you see anything?' Luka shouldered his way to the railing near the bow.

Interminable seconds passed before an outflung arm pointed in the direction of the starboard bow. 'Land!'

Everyone crowded closer to the right side of the deck. A minute later a cheer went up at the sight of a mountainous headland thrusting out of the sea. Even the weakest of the seasick men managed to find enough strength to haul himself up to the rail and stare at the blessed vision of land.

Slowly and steadily, the simple sailcraft approached the island. Luka felt a lift of excitement, the kind that always accompanied the coming into a new territory, a keening of the senses and

12

sharpening of the wits. They were close enough to hear the breakers crashing onto the rocky shore at the island's base.

As they skirted the north side of the island, Luka studied the treeless terrain, green with thick vegetation. Even the rocks wore a hairy growth of grasses. Inland, jagged mountains stood in tortuous ridges, indicating the island's volcanic origins. They loomed forbiddingly, void of plant life, while below a lush valley beckoned, the wind rippling the tall stalks of thick rye grass into waves.

A man was sent forward to take soundings while the navigator, Nevodchikov, skirted the half-submerged rocks and avoided the hidden shoals lying off the northern shore.

They rounded the island and turned south, sailing past the easternmost promontory and the wide bay it protected on the southeastern side. There were ample sightings of sea life amid the kelp beds off the rocky coast. In his eagerness to view the numerous sea otter curiously poking their heads out of the water, Luka crowded in with the other men at the rail. It was a sight to thrill a fur hunter's heart.

A solid cloud cover hid the sun, but Luka noticed the subtle change in temperature, a slight infusion of warmth at this place where the cold waters of the Bering Sea mingled with the warmer currents of the Pacific. The mewing cry of seabirds accompanied the rippling crack of the sails in the wind and the rhythmic slap of the waves against the boat's hull. The jagged stone cliffs of the island were whitened with their droppings. He scanned the protected bay and its shore without finding any evidence of habitation, yet he distinctly remembered the navigator making mention of the presence of a savage race on these islands.

'I thought there were natives living here.' He voiced his thoughts to the man on his left, Shekhurdin.

'Maybe not on all of the islands,' the Cossack suggested. 'Bering Island wasn't inhabited. This one may not be either.'

'It's a big island – some seventy versts long, I would guess. There might be villages elsewhere.' Luka wasn't about to let his guard down. And he did not like Shekhurdin's air of authority.

The man had all the makings of a leader. He was intelligent and experienced, and despite the deceptively lean appearance Shekhurdin's height gave him, the man was strong. His courage was evident in the way he had met Belyaev's challenge. But his evenhanded treatment of the Kamchadals on board rankled Luka.

13

The soft hide sails billowed full with the wind as the bow of the flat-bottomed boat swung away from the island, changing course.

'Why are we moving away?' Belyaev's rough voice demanded. 'There's otter here. Why are we not stopping?'

'That's like you, Belyaev,' Luka mocked. 'You see something you want and grab for it without taking time to see if anything better is around.'

A few guffaws of laughter followed his observation, suppressed, however, in case the sometimes belligerent Belyaev took offense. But an ever-ready grin split his black-bearded face. 'If there is something better, I will take that, too!' he declared. 'At least the first one will not slip through my fingers while I wait to see if there is more.'

But the shitik continued on its course away from the first island in the chain to search for the next. Luka watched the island receding from his view, the first land he'd seen in days. The ocean wasn't his element, and he was as anxious as everyone else to get off this crowded boat and walk on solid ground. But not so anxious that he didn't want to explore.

'For once I agree with Belyaev,' Shekhurdin said when Luka faced the sea again, straining his eyes for a glimpse of another speck of land. 'I would have anchored in one of the bays.'

Luka looked at Shekhurdin's proud profile, the thin straight nose as narrow in its outlook as its owner. 'It's morning. We have plenty of time to scout the next island.'

'Presuming, of course, there is one. We only have Nevodchikov's word on that – a peasant, a silversmith whose only experience is sailing with that Dane Bering.' He spoke in an undertone, matter-of-factly. 'We need to replenish our supply of fresh water. I would have done so at that island while we had the chance before proceeding further. We could have gotten some fresh meat as well. We aren't that well provisioned.'

His reasoning was valid and Luka didn't quarrel with it. Arguments could always be made in favor of one position or the other. They had set out on this voyage with only a small stock of provisions – some hams, a small quantity of rancid butter, a ration of rye and wheat flour so there would be bread on religious holidays, dried salmon, and most importantly, an ample supply of starter for sourdough bread to prevent scurvy. They expected to hunt and fish for the rest of their food.

14

'I, for one, want to see more of these islands,' Luka stated. A good hunter chooses the best hunting grounds, not the first one where he finds his game.

Shekhurdin lingered only a few minutes longer, then pushed away from his position at the deck rail and wandered amid other members of the expedition. The shitik continued on its south-southeasterly course across the lead-colored sea while gulls wheeled overhead and diving cormorants fished the waters.

It wasn't long before Luka heard vague grumblings of discontent among the promyshleniki. The island was no longer in sight and a second was yet to be spotted. He heard mention of the dwindling water supply and guessed the source of dissension.

Around midday, the second island was sighted. As the craft approached it, the attention of the crew was divided between it and their captain. Luka felt the tension in the air – the men waiting to see what the decision would be this time.

The second island appeared smaller than the first, but the boat's approach to it was the same, sailing parallel to the ragged coastline. As they neared the entrance to a horseshoe-shaped cove, the sides marked with jagged fingers of rocks thrust out of the water and the center arc a curving beach of white sand, Luka saw Chuprov speak briefly to the navigator. Seconds later, the order was given to lower one of the square mainsails.

When the shitik swung toward the green cliffs beyond the white beach, the tension of the crew eased perceptibly, with smiles and murmurs of satisfaction. A man was ordered to the bow to take soundings and keep a lookout for submerged rocks.

'We'll anchor here for the night.' Nevodchikov lifted his voice to make the announcement to the entire company.

'Will we be going ashore?' one of the men shouted.

'Not until morning. Then Chuprov will take a party ashore to look for water. We'll use the daylight hours to explore the area and select safe anchorages for the night until we find the best location for wintering.'

Luka saw Shekhurdin stiffen and his face grow cold with anger that he had not been chosen to lead the shore detail. Luka approved of both the decision and the choice of leaders; he respected Chuprov's experience and judgment more than he did the Cossack's.

After the shitik was maneuvered into the cove, the sails were furled and the wooden anchor weighted with stones was thrown

15

over the side. The inviting stretch of beach gave no sign of native habitation. The afternoon hours were not wasted in idleness or land watching. In anticipation of the next morning's shore party, the dinghy was checked, muskets were broken out and cleaned, and the empty water casks were set out in readiness. Meanwhile, the boat rocked at anchor beneath clotting clouds, the waves slapping at its sides as the surf rolled toward the beach and crashed on the rocky borders of the bay.

With the coming of first light, men stirred on deck. Luka joined the short line of men waiting for their morning ration of water, eager to rid his mouth of the cottony taste of sleep. There was much yawning and stretching and scratching of beards, but little talking to interrupt the sound of the wind and waves.

When it was Luka's turn at the water cask, he dipped the cup in to fill it, then lifted it to his mouth. After the first swallow of the stale water, he paused and glanced idly toward shore, where he'd soon be landing with the morning party enlisted yesterday by Chuprov. The beach was no longer deserted.

'Where's Chuprov?' He snapped the question while his attention remained riveted to the beach.

'Why?' someone growled.

'Get him. We have visitors.' Luka gestured with the cup toward the large gathering of natives on the beach.

Forgetting the dryness of his mouth, he shoved the half-full cup into the hand of the next man waiting in line and moved to the railing. The rest of the startled company stared, too stunned to move for several seconds. Somebody shouted to alert the promyshleniki as others crowded around the rail by Luka.

'How many's there?' one asked.

'Looks like nearly a hundred,' another guessed.

The native wore strangely styled coats and odd-shaped hats on their heads. At this distance, it was difficult to judge, but the coats appeared to be made of feathers and hung to their ankles. Their feet were bare. Their hats were shaped like asymmetrical cones with the long side projecting in front to shade their eyes.

Upon seeing all the men on the shitik's deck, the natives began shouting in some unintelligible language and moving about, waving spears and bows and arrows over their heads. About the same time, Luka caught the sound of beating drums. It ran up his back, bristling the hairs on his neck.

'Where did they come from?' the man beside him wondered aloud.

No one ventured a guess. Chuprov came on deck, and the men moved aside to let him through to the rail. Using a spyglass, he studied the large band of natives dancing on the beach and stabbing the air with their spears.

Belyaev shouldered in next to Luka. 'I think they will attack. We should get ready for them.'

Chuprov lowered the spyglass to study the whole of the scene. 'Pass out the muskets and powder,' he ordered without turning.

Belyaev smiled and moved away from the rail to carry out the command. Belyaev liked the things that fired the flesh – women, vodka, and fighting. Luka shared his bloodlust, but his own was rooted in a deep, abiding hatred.

The place at the rail was quickly taken by Shekhurdin. 'According to Nevodchikov, these natives are supposed to be friendly. Mikhail Alexandrovich,' he called to the navigator standing at the back of the promyshleniki. 'Did you not say the natives on these islands helped you on your return voyage?'

Luka half turned to catch the navigator's answer, although Chuprov expressed no such interest. 'Yes,' Nevodchikov confirmed. 'We had run out of fresh water. We managed to communicate our plight to some natives in a boat, and they brought us two containers – made from seal bladders.'

Facing the beach again, Shekhurdin studied the dancing gyrations of the colorful costumed natives. 'It appears to me they want us to come ashore. See the way they beckon. They are not threatening us in any way.' He angled his head toward Chuprov, something challenging in its tilt. 'If a party went ashore with the empty casks, they might direct us to fresh water.'

'They are armed and outnumber us.' Luka rejected the suggestion.

'Cossacks have always been outnumbered by their foes, but it never stopped them from marching across Siberia and claiming it for the Tsar. Our weaponry is vastly superior to theirs. Muskets always win over spears.' Every promyshlenik on board had fought with hostile natives at some time in his life, and the odds had never been in his favor. But as far as Luka was concerned, it was one thing to be caught in that situation and another to seek it.

'We will wait,' Chuprov replied impassively. 'There will be plenty of time to fight, if it's necessary.'

17

The beating of the native drums continued to sound, their pounding rhythms accompanying the wild dancing that followed no apparent pattern. It appeared spontaneous and contagious; one exuberant native would start dancing and others would join him. When they became exhausted, a few more would begin. Always there was singing, but that, too, was a confusion of voices. The natives seemed to be whipping themselves into some sort of frenzy.

'Can anyone understand what they are saying?' Luka asked Chuprov.

'It isn't Kamchadal. What about Koriak?' he suggested, referring to another native tribe in Siberia.

'No, I can understand Koriak – and Chukchi, too,' someone in the group answered.

'Maybe they're Aleutorski.' A second mentioned a race of Siberian natives who lived on the coast and aggressively resisted all Russian attempts to make them pay tribute.

The name sent a rumble of apprehension stirring through the whole company. They eagerly turned to accept the muskets, lead, and powder Belyaev distributed among them. As Luka began to load and prime his firelock musket, Chuprov left the rail and headed for the boat's hold. He returned shortly carrying a few packets from the small cargo of trade goods on board, which mainly consisted of cheap glass beads, cloth, tin and copper utensils, knives of poor quality, and needles. Chuprov's packets contained the latter two.

'What are you going to do with them?' Luka questioned.

'Give them as presents, and maybe dissuade them from any hostile intention.' A smile curved Chuprov's mouth but never quite reached his eyes.

'A taste of this lead will go farther in changing their minds.' Belyaev lifted his musket slightly, his thick fingers tightly embracing its barrel.

'You are more bloodthirsty than those savages, Nikolai Dimitrovich,' the Cossack Shekhurdin accused contemptuously. 'They may have come here to trade. What if they have otter skins?'

The argument didn't sway Belyaev. He grinned wickedly; if the natives were killed, Belyaev believed, he would still have their sea otter pelts – if they had any – for nothing. Such cruelty was neither shocking nor repellent to Luka. He had lived in the Siberian wilds long enough to have learned that survival among hostile inhabitants often depended upon intimidation through fear. Luka regarded it as a necessity. Besides, he didn't trust any native. They were a treacherous breed, all of them, and the Aleutorski – or Aleuts, as they were often called – more than others. He traded with them when he had to, but he never turned his back to one of them.

At the railing, Chuprov hailed the natives on the beach and waved the packets over his head to attract their attention. His action appeared to excite them. As they hopped wildly about and beckoned him to come ashore, the drumming grew louder. Ignoring their invitation, Chuprov heaved the packets toward the beach. When the waves washed them onto the sand, several barefooted natives scrambled to retrieve them. The rest of the party massed around them on the beach, creating a mass of strangely designed, highly decorated hats. The packets' contents were displayed, to the wonderment of the group, and the items passed around to be examined and tested by various individuals. It wasn't long before the natives reciprocated and threw freshly killed birds to the shitik.

'They want to trade.' Shekhurdin was quick to assure his fellow Russians that he had accurately guessed their friendly intentions all along.

There was more beckoning for them to come ashore. Cradling the musket in his arms, Luka glanced sidelong at Chuprov. The promyshlenik continued to view the natives' wild antics with skepticism.

'We do need water,' Chuprov said quietly.

'Yes.'

Following Luka's grim acknowledgement, Chuprov turned from the rail. 'Hoist the dinghy over the side.'

Luka was among the five men selected to accompany Chuprov to shore. Armed with muskets, they climbed into the wooden rowboat, taking with them one water cask to be filled, and waited for Chuprov to join them. When Chuprov climbed into the boat, he had with him more articles of trade – tobacco and pipes. They set out for the beach, with Luka and another man at the oars.

Several yards from shore, they reached shallow water and shipped the oars, letting the crest of a wave carry them closer. Grabbing his musket, Luka swung over the side and waded in the thigh-deep water to haul the boat onto the sand. Several of the natives rushed forward, and his muscles tensed, but they came to help pull the boat onto the beach.

19

He had a good look at their weapons, which consisted of primitive stone-tipped spears and arrows. He moved quickly to Chuprov's side when the promyshlenik stepped onto the sand. Individually, they could be overpowered, outnumbered as they were by these Aleut natives, but as a group they presented a formidable opponent.

The air was cool, but Luka could feel the sweat dampening his skin as the natives crowded around them talking excitedly in their strange tongue. He licked his dry lips and adjusted his grip on the musket, keeping a finger close to the trigger. Blood pounded in his ears while he kept his glance moving.

The natives' long coats were made of bird skins – mostly cormorants, puffins, and murres, the feathers worn on the outside – and trimmed with the throat fur of sea lion. Their strange hats were made from thin strips of wood bent into shape, then glued together. They were brightly painted with swirling geometric designs. Some were adorned with feathers or carved ivory figures. But Luka was more interested in the faces beneath the projecting hats. They shared the Mongol features of many of the Siberian tribes, including the Aleutorski – the thick eyefolds, broad facial structure, and slightly flattened noses. Their hair was black and straight, and their eyes dark brown. Many of them had thin moustaches and spiky beards, but none had the thick, full beard growth of the Russians.

The eager way they crowded around Luka and his small party was almost childlike. The natives were curious about everything, pointing to his garments, the knife he carried, and his boots, then jabbering unintelligibly. Standing shoulder to shoulder with his fellow promyshleniki, he managed to keep the natives at bay, alert for any change in their behavior.

Out of the corner of his eye, he noticed Chuprov offer the pipes and tobacco to the natives. They examined them curiously, obviously having no notion as to the use of either. One of the natives gave Chuprov a stick with the head of a seal carved in bone, then gestured toward a musket, indicating he wanted it.

'No.' Chuprov was cold in his refusal.

Luka watched the smiles disappear from the faces of the Aleuts and felt the atmosphere change. Anger darkened their expressions and in his peripheral vision he saw several natives converge on the beached dinghy.

'The boat!' He yelled the warning to the others. They fell back around it, forming a protective arc to guard their only means of transportation back to the shitik. Immediately the natives began thrusting their spears at the boat's wooden sides. The rest of the natives pointed the sharpened stone tips of their weapons at the beleaguered promyshleniki.

Without being told, Luka knew they were on their own. The men aboard the shitik could give them no help. The craft was anchored out of musket range, and they had the shitik's sole dinghy in their possession. If they were to get back to the shitik, it was plain they would have to fight their way. He could hear the clunk of the spears being deflected by the boat's wooden sides and wondered how long it would withstand the onslaught.

'Fire!' Chuprov shouted.

There was no need to choose a target. There were too many, too close. Instantly Luka's finger tightened on the trigger, and the green cliffs around the bay echoed the thunder of musketfire. Blood gushed from the hand of a native near Luka, staining the white sand. Frightened by the explosive discharge of the guns, most of the natives fell back. While three of the promyshleniki hurriedly reloaded their weapons. Luka helped the other two drag the boat into the water.

As soon as it was afloat, he shouted to the others. When the natives saw they were getting away, they attacked, charging the men running through the surf to the boat. The muskets were discharged again, this time their thunderous report causing only a brief hesitation. There wasn't time to reload again and the men scrambled hastily into the dinghy amidst a hail of flying spears. Luka hauled on the oar, propelling the boat through the incoming waves toward the shitik. Miraculously they reached it almost unscathed, suffering only a few minor cuts.

Once on board the sailing craft, the order was given to hoist the anchor and raise the sails. After they were out to sea, Luka stood on deck, his feet braced against the roll of the craft, and his face damp from the salt spray. He watched the low, scudding clouds, waiting for his second look at that first island, their new destination.

That night they anchored in one of the bays at the first island they'd sighted. The hostile encounter with the natives instilled a degree of caution, and a watch was posted.

2

The next morning, Chuprov went ashore with an armed party. They found tracks, confirming the presence of natives on the island, but none were encountered. Nor was any source of fresh water found in the immediate vicinity of the bay. The shitik sailed again, hugging the coast as closely as the jagged reefs and half-submerged rocks allowed, while they searched for another place to land.

By nightfall there was considerable grumbling among the promyshleniki. The supply of fresh water was down to one last keg. As men will do, they began to talk about their missed chances, the things that should have been done differently. If they had stopped at the first island initially . . . If they had captured a native and taken him hostage . . . *If.* Shekhurdin's name was mentioned as frequently as Chuprov's.

Shortly after dawn the following day, Luka was assigned to a landing party in case his skill at sign communication would be needed. This time the party was headed by Shekhurdin.

The winds were strong, sweeping down the craggy mountains in powerful gusts, whipping over Luka's bearded face and sometimes stealing his breath. There were no trees; the wind never gave them a chance to take root. Occasionally he saw a stunted shrub growing low to the ground, its branches spread close to the rocks to offer little resistance to sweeping wind.

Walking was laborious. In the rough terrain, sharp volcanic rocks jabbed at the soles of boots or scraped skin when one stumbled and fell. The inland valleys were rank with tall weeds, coarse grasses, and ferns. The thick growth concealed the spongy tundra beneath it, a quicksand of matted compost with a thin crust of volcanic ash. It sucked at boots, making each step an effort. All the while, the small scouting party stayed as close to the coastline as the terrain permitted, to keep the slow-moving

22

shitik in sight and signal for help if they needed it.

Late in the afternoon, after climbing and clawing his way to the crest of one of the serrated ridges that extended from the inland mountains like giant bony talons, Luka paused to catch his breath. He was winded and panting from exertion, his muscles out of condition after so many days aboard the shitik. He found a rocky place to sit on the lee side of the ridge. The rest of the scouting detail scrambled tiredly over the top and paused in staggered positions to rest with him, sheltered by the bony spine from the incessant wind.

Below him lay a wave-capped bay and a valley stretching back from its beach. As Luka scanned the area, he spotted the white torrent of water tumbling down from a tall green cliff, then located the stream that formed at its base and meandered half-hidden through the valley's tall grasses before it emptied into the bay.

'Look. There's water,' he informed Shekhurdin.

The Cossack's slumped shoulders straightened. 'Let's go,' he ordered crisply, finding renewed strength now that his mission ashore had located its objective.

Luka exhaled a heavy breath and picked up the musket he'd laid beside him. He forced his cramping legs to support him again, then adjusted the ropes that lashed the wooden barrel to his back and cut into his shoulders. He started down the steep ridge after Shekhurdin. Wet grass made the footing slippery as they worked their way down.

On the flat, they struck out across the high grass valley. With each step, the boggy ground undulated around them, the grass-covered earth rolling in waves like the sea. Luka scanned the area for any signs of life, the hunter in him alert for the presence of fox in the valley or sea otter in the rocky bay. Twice they'd come across tracks left by natives, but that had been early in the morning.

Along the foot of a promontory jutting out to form a side of the bay, something caught his eye. He slowed his steps and caught a movement amid some humps of earth. Stopping, Luka focused on it, attempting to distinguish whether it was man or animal.

'An Aleutorski.' Unknown to Luka, Shekhurdin had stopped when he did, observing his absorption in some distant object. The rest of the weary party had paused gladly to look. 'Do you see more?'

'We are too far away.' Luka shook his head. The hillocks made it difficult to see.

'I don't think he's seen us yet.' The Cossack's eyes gleamed with the chance that was before him. 'I want him captured and taken back to the shitik.'

It was common practice among the Cossacks to take hostages to insure their safety amid native tribes. Preferably they took the children of chiefs or important members of the tribe. But Shekhurdin was more than willing to take whatever was available.

Crouching low, they slogged through the mire toward the grassy mounds where the native had been spotted. He had disappeared from view behind one of the low hills.

When they were within a hundred yards of the first hillock, a figure emerged from the top of it. Luka froze to keep from attracting attention. The tall figure was a woman dressed in some sort of fur garment. Her head was bare, and he could see the black sheen of her hair gathered at the back of her head in a bun. For an instant, she appeared poised like a statue, then Luka realized she was looking directly at him. A second later, she called the alarm and ran down the mound.

Shekhurdin rushed forward, motioning with a sweep of his hand for the others to follow. Luka was a step slow in responding. The spongy tundra made speed difficult. By the time they reached the grassy knolls, they could see the small band of natives, mostly women and children, running along a cliff and heading inland toward rocky hiding places in the mountains.

'It's no use.' Luka stopped, breathing hard. 'We will never catch up with them before nightfall.'

Grudgingly, Shekhurdin agreed and called off the chase. 'How many men were in the band?'

'Five is all I saw,' one of the promyshleniki panted.

'This is obviously their village.' The Cossack glanced at the baskets left lying on the ground and the stands for drying fish. 'They must live in underground *barabaras* like the Kamchadals.'

Luka eyed the top of the grassy mound where he'd seen the woman emerge. 'Maybe some are hiding inside.' Hefting his musket to a ready position, he walked up the rounded earth dome.

As he approached the hatchway entrance on top, he moved with caution. Kneeling beside the only entrance to the native hut, he peered into the shadows below. Nothing moved. There was no sound except the wind rushing through the grasses and the crash of the surf on the shore. A notched log served as a ladder to reach the floor of the hut. Luka descended it warily, half blinded by the smoke from a whale-oil lamp that sent flickering light into the shadowy reaches below him and emitted considerable heat.

When he set foot on the tamped-earth floor, the dried grass strewn over the floor rustled beneath his feet. He backed away from the ladder, then pivoted slowly, looking in all the dark corners. The barabara was large, measuring some forty feet in length and twenty feet wide. Whalebones served as rafters to support the sod roof, and vertical posts hewn from driftwood formed the wall supports, with longer ones used to hold the cross beams.

Woven grass mats hung from the timbers, dividing the hut into compartments. Luka moved carefully toward them, pushing one after another open with the muzzle of his musket. There was no one hiding inside.

Partially relaxing his guard, he studied the items left behind. A burning moss wick floated in a pool of whale oil contained by the basinlike stone lamp. It sat on its own stand, providing heat for cooking and warming the interior. He found a child's cradle, cooking utensils, wooden dishes and stone pots, many implements made from bones, but no pottery. There were many baskets of sizes varying from very tiny, which contained needles made out of bone, to very large. All were made from grass and woven so tightly they were like cloth. Most were fitted with lids woven from the same material. Luka picked up one that was half finished, the thin strands of grass sticking out like fringe, then he tossed the unfinished basket aside. Immediately he began scavenging, turning over baskets in search of food.

'Luka Ivanovich.' Shekhurdin called to him from the hatch opening in the roof. 'Did you find anything?'

'No.' He moved to the crude ladder. Then he spied a large basket sitting in the shadows that he'd overlooked. When he lifted the lid, he discovered a quantity of seal blubber inside. Carrying the basket, he climbed the notched log to the top. Emerging from the hole, he shoved the basket onto the sod roof. 'This is all there was,' he told Shekhurdin.

'We will camp here tonight,' Shekhurdin declared. He took no more than passing interest in the contents of the basket. 'In the morning, we will signal the shitik to send the boat ashore.'

During the remaining light of the cloud-covered afternoon, they filled the water casks at the stream and carried them to the village site, then combed the beach for driftwood. When dusk came, a fire blazed in the cooking pit on the leeward side of the barabara. They hunkered close to its warmth and chewed on the blubber.

Taking the first watch, Luka sat with his arms folded around the musket and studied the darkened landscape from his vantage point halfway up the mound. Below him, the firelight flickered, and he listened to the first snores of sleeping men. The sea glistened, ridged with whitecaps, and the wind ran through the grasses, the sound accompanying the rush of the waves. Occasionally he heard the flapping wings of some night bird or the strange laughing calls of the storm petrel.

Overhead, the clouds parted to give him a glimpse of the brilliant dusting of stars in the sky. He sat in silence – his mind turned inward to those private thoughts that come to a man alone. At twenty-eight those thoughts had molded him and made an inner world filled with visions and dreams of tomorrow. His mind wandered, recalling disconnected things – the sing of the wind in the shitik's sails, the sizzle of a snowflake on hot ash, the warmth of the long summer sun – and the sound of that native woman's voice lifted in alarm.

He shifted position, briefly irritated by the thought, then pondered its cause. He felt the loneliness surrounding him and guessed that it was natural for the thoughts of a man alone to turn to a woman. He saw her again in his mind and wondered why that image remained with him.

He'd slept with native women before, giving release to the hot urges inside him and some of the hatred, too. He knew no other kind of women, except his mother, who was a dim memory of someone soft and warm. Soft. There was nothing soft in his life now except for furs – the deep, shining darkness of sea otter pelts. That was the softness he sought now.

In the morning, they spotted the shitik, moving under half sail near the mouth of the bay, and signaled for the boat. They waited on the beach with the filled water casks as the dinghy was rowed to shore and nosed aground on the sand. The barrels were quickly loaded and Shekhurdin climbed aboard. Luka and two others

26

shoved the boat off the sand, then waded ashore to wait for the boat to return with additional men. Shekhurdin intended to capture the natives they'd seen.

A misting rain fell, driven by the wind. Luka checked the powder in his musket pan to make sure it was still dry and sat with the others on the sand to watch and wait. There was nowhere to seek shelter from the miserable weather on this exposed stretch of beach – no shielding trees anywhere on the island, nor any rocky windbreak – so they endured in silence. In the bay, Luka spotted a sea otter floating on its back and feasting leisurely on a shellfish held between its paws. He smiled the smile of a cat that watches the mouse at play, knowing how short-lived its freedom will be.

Within an hour, the dinghy loaded with promyshleniki headed back toward the beach. Luka scanned the boat's occupants and located Shekhurdin. The landing brought an end to the idle wait. After the scouting party, now doubled in size, had assembled on the beach, the rowboat set out once more for its mother craft. Shekhurdin led his armed force inland, striking out in the direction the fleeing natives had taken.

Yesterday's trek had prepared Luka for the rigors of the morning walk, but the newcomers from the shitik had to struggle on their sea legs over the rough terrain.

Shortly after midday, they sighted a band of natives on a bluff along the seacoast. There appeared to be as many as fifteen, but it was difficult to determine whether this was the same band they had seen the day before. Again Shekhurdin ordered the men forward, confident of trapping the natives on the bluff and taking captives.

'No one fires unless I give the order,' the Cossack instructed. 'We want hostages, not bodies.'

The wind covered the sound of their approach, and the attention of the natives was directed seaward, apparently absorbed by some object, possibly the shitik on its explorations along the coast. They were almost on them before a warning was shouted. Instantly, the adult males grabbed their weapons and formed a rear guard to cover the retreat of the women and children.

As Luka rushed forward in the attack, he saw a native woman scoop a boy child into her arms and flee before him. A second later, he was confronted by a native brandishing a spear. Gripping the long barrel of his musket like a battle staff, he knocked the oncoming spear aside, then immediately slammed the curved shoulder butt into the man's stomach. As the native doubled over, he laid the barrel alongside his head and knocked him to the ground. Instinctively, the native rolled away from him and managed to stagger to his feet, swaying drunkenly while looking for his weapon.

Luka took a step toward him, intent on finishing his opponent and smashing the hated features. At the last second he saw the spearhead coming at him from the side and dodged its sharp point, then turned and grappled with its owner. The rush of battle was in his veins, a good, hot feeling that made all his senses come alive. The man's upper body strength was too much for Luka, and he gave way, seeking a better leverage by tumbling backwards to the ground and spilling the man over his head. Scrambling to his feet, he saw the native spring to his and immediately run after the women and children. Luka started to give chase.

'Let him go!' The shouted order came from Shekhurdin. 'We have our hostage.'

While his lungs labored for breath, Luka turned and saw a young male, a youth not much more than fifteen, struggling wildly in the hold of two promyshleniki.

The skirmish over, the promyshleniki regrouped around the hostage. Luka took a step to join them as the youth's arm was twisted behind his back and he grimaced silently in pain. A sudden cry from somewhere to his left startled Luka. He swung toward the sound, leveling the barrel of his musket.

An old woman stood beside a tumble of boulders where she must have hidden during the attack. She held her shoulder as if it hurt. Advanced years had bent her once tall frame and turned her hair the color of the clouds, but her tanned face was relatively unlined except for the crevices fanning away from her eyes. Luka stared at the string of dots tattooed across her cheeks and the parallel lines running down the center of her chin. Two button-sized pieces of bone projected from the skin below the corners of her mouth. Lastly, his glance fell on the long coat made from the pelts of sea otter.

'Where did that old woman come from?' Shekhurdin's demand put everyone on guard, her sudden appearance making them wonder if more natives were hidden nearby, perhaps waiting to leap on them and catch them unaware.

'I turned around and there she was,' Luka said. 'She must have been hiding in those rocks.'

Shekhurdin motioned for two hunters to check the area and see if there were any more. Meanwhile the cordon of guards around the hostage closed ranks. The old woman, instead of running from them, hurried toward them. Luka frowned at her actions. The youth yelled something, his tone seeming to warn her away. The nearest promyshlenik silenced him with a restrained clip of his musket butt alongside the head. The boy fell to the ground, dazed by the blow. Again, the old woman cried out and pressed a hand to her head as if she had felt the blow, then rushed toward the boy. Shekhurdin stopped her before she reached him and shoved her backwards.

'Go!' He waved his hand, directing her to follow the other members of her fleeing band. She simply stared at him, taking no advantage of the opportunity he gave her to escape. 'Go! Go with the others!' Impatience roughened his voice and made wild the swing of his arm. The old woman looked past him at the boy, then said something to Shekhurdin in that strange tongue and gestured toward the youth. 'Stand him up and let her see that he isn't hurt,' he commanded the men guarding the hostage. They hauled him to his feet and let him stand on his own. 'You see,' Shekhurdin said to the old woman, accompanying his words with hand gestures in an attempt to make her understand him. 'He is unharmed. Go tell your people that.'

She stood silently, apparently comprehending nothing. Taking her by the shoulders, Shekhurdin turned her around and pushed her in the direction the natives had gone. The impetus carried her a few steps forward, but she stopped and turned back. Exasperated by her stupidity, the Cossack swung away from her and dismissed her with a wave of his hand.

'Everyone move out,' he ordered.

Before falling in line with the other promyshleniki, Luka took one last wary look at the old woman. He was inclined to believe she was being obstinate rather than stupid, although he didn't know why he had that impression. Somehow he wasn't surprised when she started following them.

'Maybe she is his mother,' someone suggested.

'She's too old,' another insisted.

Several times they tried to drive her off, but on each occasion, she retreated a few steps and stopped, then started following when they resumed their march. Finally they simply ignored her, all except Luka. It made him uneasy to have a native behind him – even an old woman. She was still tagging along after them when they arrived at a stretch of coast where a boat could land. While they waited for the shitik to appear, she remained a little apart from them, always – it seemed to Luka – watching the youth. He guessed that she wanted to learn where they were taking him.

When the shitik hove into view, Shekhurdin signaled for the boat. Luka was not included in the first boatload of promyshleniki to return to the vessel with the hostage, and he stood to one side while the young male was forced into the boat. When the old woman saw him getting into the wooden dinghy, she ran toward it.

'Get away, you old fool!' Shekhurdin roughly pushed her backwards, and she stumbled onto the sand. Glaring at her, the Cossack took his position at the prow of the boat to accompany his hostage and gestured to the men remaining ashore to shove them off.

The woman scrambled to her feet, but Luka caught her before she could run into the water after the dinghy. She jabbered something to him and pointed at the bare-masted shitik anchored offshore. He shook his head and firmly set her away from him, admonishing her to stay with his upraised hand. He noticed the determined set of her mouth, but she made no further attempt to go after the boat. He watched her for a minute, then satisfied it wasn't some ploy, left her and wandered over to stand with the six other promyshleniki waiting for the dinghy's return trip. While they discussed the excellent hunting prospects on the island, he kept an eye on the old woman.

As the dinghy approached the beach again, Luka walked to the water's edge to meet it. Its nose had barely entered shallow water when the old woman darted past him and scrambled into the boat before anyone could stop her. She plunked herself down on one of the seats and folded her arms in front of her, rigidly asserting her refusal to budge.

Luka surveyed her grimly. 'If you are that determined to go aboard the shitik, old woman, we will take you.' He motioned for the other promyshleniki to let her be.

With the help of another man, Luka pushed the boat into the water, then climbed in. There was space on the seat beside the old woman and he settled himself onto it. He glanced at her, puzzled by the lack of fear she showed. But she kept her eyes to the front, looking to neither side and centering all her attention on the shitik where the youth had been taken. Luka assessed the glossy dark garment of sea otter skins she wore. The fur showed wear in places, but the pelts were prime.

As soon as the dinghy was tied up to the shitik, Luka climbed aboard and waited by the rail to haul the old woman aboard. When Shekhurdin saw her, he exploded. 'What is she doing here? Why didn't you leave her on the island?'

'She insisted in coming,' Luka replied. 'And I thought' – Luka went on, pushing the old woman forward so the others could see her – 'the men might like to have a look at her coat, made from the pelts of sea otter.'

Belyaev was the first to step up and closely study the quality of the furs. Then he lifted the old woman's chin so he could see her face. 'Ugly old hag.' He grinned. 'Wonder if she has any teeth left?' He stuck a thumb and finger into her mouth to pry it open and she bit down – hard, judging by the way Belyaev yelped and pulled the injured digit away. 'Why, you old witch –' He raised an arm to backhand her, but Chuprov checked the swing with a steel grip of his wrist.

'Neither of these hostages is to be abused.' The command was issued to everyone. 'We will gain nothing if the natives learn we have mistreated the hostages.'

With an effort, Belyaev controlled his temper and slowly brought his arm down. He sneered at the woman, then turned away, changing the sneer into a jeering smile directed at Luka. 'The next time you bring back spirited female hostages, Luka Ivanovich, make sure they are young ones. An old witch like this one could give me no pleasure.'

'A woman is a woman. The nights are dark. You couldn't see her face.' Then Luka smiled. 'Or maybe you fear what she might bite next?'

A dull red crept under Belyaev's skin at the hooting laughter the remark drew. He glared at Luka, then swung away, making a contemptuous sound in his throat. The old woman took advantage of the distraction and quickly crossed the deck to the boy.

3

Weaver Woman, as she was called by her people, quickly looked Little Spear over to see if he was seriously hurt. There was a knot on his temple the size of a gull's egg, but his eyes were clear. There showed in them a small gladness that she was here with him to share this ordeal.

But that was as it should be. They were *anaaqisagh* to each other. That is, dependent upon each other. It was a custom of their people that when a child is born an older person is appointed anaaqisagh to him. From the time Little Spear was small, Weaver Woman had made certain he had food, clothing, and instruction. Everything was shared between them. When he was in pain, she cried for him.

Weaver Woman had lived for sixty summers, and Little Spear for only sixteen, but the link solidly bound them in inter-dependence. Now her bones were getting stiff with age, her fingers gnarled with pain. Still she managed to force her aching hands to weave the grasses into the fine baskets that were the trademarks of her skill. Soon, not many summers away, it would be Little Spear who would help her out of this world as she had helped him into it, caring for her as she had cared for him.

That was the way. It was what had brought her to this strange boat made of wood among this odd-looking race of men. All that happened to Little Spear must happen to her. She would have failed in her duty to him if she had not done this.

Her legs were tired, so she sat down on the rough planks of wood. Little Spear joined her. The habits of observation had taught each of them when to speak to a man and when to stay out of his way. All the signs told them the latter for this band of men, signs easily read by anyone trained to watch for them – the look of their faces, the pulsing veins in the temples, the thinning of the lips. So they sat silently.

Weaver Woman noticed the slash in the skin side of Little Spear's parka where it had been cut in the fight. The feathered side was against his body, as it should be, since the weather was warm and this was not a social occasion. She wished she had her needles to mend the tear for him, but they were in the hut.

Covertly she studied the men milling about the boat. The sky was full of storm signs. Weaver Woman wondered why these men did not see that. Her glance lingered in dislike on the big one with all the black whiskers on his face, the one who had stuck his fingers in her mouth. He had the cold, cruel eyes of the white-headed eagle, an evil darkness in the centers. She didn't trust him.

The one who had stopped him from striking her, the one with hair the color of a seal pup, that one must be the chief, Weaver Woman concluded. She hadn't made up her mind about him yet. He was the one the husband of her daughter had described after he had paddled over from Agattu Island yesterday to warn them about the strange raiders with the thunder sticks. His village had danced a welcome for them, but when this man had brought his warriors onto the beach, he had accepted a beautiful carved ivory stick, very valuable, then refused to give his iron stick in return. That was very bad. According to her daughter's husband, he shouted to the sticks and they made a loud noise – louder than thunder. And a cousin who had been too close received a hole in his hand. Weaver Woman didn't think the light-haired man respected the ways of the people.

Half fearfully, she wondered what was to become of them. They would probably be taken in this boat to the village of these men and made their slaves. Little Spear was young and strong, but she was old and not much use any more. Maybe they wouldn't keep her. As the thought crossed her mind, she looked at the man with the scar eye. The jagged mark across his face gave him a mean look. She had seen the wish to kill in his eyes, yet he hadn't thrown her off the boat. He'd made the other men let her come.

The wind picked up in strength, and Weaver Woman hunched her shoulders and lowered her chin so the stand-up collar of her parka could afford her some protection from the gale. The storm rolled toward the strange boat, appearing like a solid wall of black. Only now did these oddly dressed men notice it.

She listened to their shouts, catching the desperation in their voices without understanding the words, and watched them scurry about the boat. She wondered if they were from *alyeska*, the mainland. They obviously were not from these islands or they would know how quickly storms could strike and would watch for the signs before the wind lashed the sea into a fury.

Waves tossed the boat about wildly. The wood made groaning sounds, as if it was in great agony. Someone yelled and she saw the little wooden boat floating away, its rope trailing in the water. The rain came down in sheets, drenching everything and everyone. Some men grabbed her and Little Spear and made them go down into the belly of the boat.

As the storm raged, the shitik wallowed helplessly in the heavy seas, the gale-force winds driving it away from the island chain. Only the navigator, his mate, and occasionally Chuprov remained on deck, trying to keep some control of the shitik. Everyone else, including the two hostages, took refuge below.

The green timbers of the shitik's hull creaked and shuddered constantly. Someone manned the pump at all times, struggling to keep the vessel from taking on more water than she could hold. The close confines below deck reeked with the smell of dried fish and unwashed bodies. Vomit created a stench that was almost unbearable. Yet no one dared venture on deck for fear of being washed overboard by the tempestuous waves.

As the day wore on with no abatement of the storm, nerves and tempers threatened to break. The feeling of utter helplessness worked on Luka. He grew angry with this hell that refused to end. He couldn't believe that he'd come this far only to be denied the riches he sought. The idleness nearly drove him mad. He couldn't stand to sit there in the dark, stinking hold and listen to the shuddering groans of the vessel, wondering how much more punishment it would take, wondering when he'd hear the crack of timber and feel the rush of sea water closing around him.

Getting to his feet, he grabbed the support of a cross beam to balance himself against the wild pitching of the shitik. As he made his way over to the keg of dried salmon, he stumbled over a body in the shadows. A booted foot kicked at his leg in retaliation. Luka kicked back and went on.

'Anybody want some food?' He lifted off the cover and scooped out a handful of dried chunks. Someone answered affirmatively from the near corner, and Luka tossed a piece in his direction. Beside him a man moaned. 'Want one?' He offered a chunk to the half-supine man.

The man's eyes opened and focused on the fishy object, then he gave another groan. Convulsively his stomach heaved, disgorging its meager contents. Vomit bubbled from his mouth, slowly dribbling out of a corner to roll into his beard.

Derisively Luka snorted and moved on. He paused in front of Shekhurdin, who managed to appear less disheveled than the rest of the company. He met the Cossack's empty, hollow-eyed stare. 'Better eat if you've got the stomach for it,' Luka advised.

Shekhurdin reached out and took a chunk of salmon, then carried it to his mouth. He tore off a dry stringy bite with his teeth and chewed on it. 'Give the hostages some.'

All his instincts rebelled against sharing their meager food supply with savages, but he suppressed them, aware of the practical value of looking after hostages well. Irritably he nodded a reply to Shekhurdin's directive.

He located the pair huddled in a corner and maneuvered around slumped bodies – some sick and some simply dispirited – to the hostages. Bracing a hand against the bulkhead, he offered the hunks of dried salmon to them. The boy turned his sickly pale face away from the sight of it, obviously fighting nausea. Luka tossed a chunk onto his lap. When he started to give one to the old woman, he was roughly shoved from the side and the lurch of the shitik sent him sprawling. He struck his head on something when he fell, and he rolled onto his side, trying to stop the spinning blaze behind his eyes.

'The woman is old.' Belyaev's bulk towered over him. 'She's going to die anyway, so why feed her?'

'You fool, Belyaev,' Luka jeered as the shitik yawed badly and a rush of sea water spilled down the hatchway. 'We're probably all going to die.'

Metal flashed as Belyaev pulled his knife from its belt sheath. 'Then let's kill them now. If we're going to die, let's make sure they're dead first.'

Luka saw the madness of a trapped animal in Belyaev's face, the wild violence that came with the fear of approaching death. Although he believed this wasn't the time to kill the hostages, he had no intention of risking his life against Belyaev to protect them. The natives weren't irreplaceable; more hostages could be taken. He lay unmoving as Belyaev swung toward the pair.

Shekhurdin stepped out of the shadows and placed himself between Belyaev and the hostages. 'I took them prisoner. I will say when they die, Belyaev, not you.'

'Out of my way, Cossack.' Belyaev reached out to shove him aside.

With unexpected swiftness, Shekhurdin launched himself at Belyaev, grabbing for the knife arm. Both came crashing down. Luka heard the clatter of the knife skittering across the planks and realized Belyaev was disarmed. The bodies thrashed together on the floor in the semi-darkness.

The close confines of the hold gave the advantage to the heavier, more muscled Belyaev and deprived Shekhurdin of space to use his superior swiftness. Within minutes, Belyaev overpowered him and emerged astraddle the Cossack with his stubby hands at his throat. Luka saw the killing lust that contorted Belyaev's face as he throttled the man's windpipe and stretched out of reach of the fingers trying to claw out his eyes.

Seeing the strength leave Shekhurdin's arms, Luka scrambled to his feet. The killing of a fellow promyshlenik was murder. He could not sit idly by and watch. He locked an arm around Belyaev's neck from behind and bent him backwards, straining to break the stranglehold. At last Belyaev clawed at his arm, his hands free from the Cossack's throat. Stepping aside, Luka used his leverage to hurl Belyaev backwards to the floor. When he started to get up, Luka kicked him back down.

'The Cossack has friends who would see you dead,' he warned, then knelt beside the victim. His fingers felt the weak beating of Shekhurdin's pulse beneath the brown beard. 'You're lucky, Belyaev. He's alive.'

He straightened to his feet as Shekhurdin stirred, reaching to clutch his throat. Moving away, he went to retrieve the knife, hearing the revived man's coughing gasps for air. When he returned with Belyaev's knife, Shekhurdin was sitting up, his shoulders hunched with the effort to breathe.

Bypassing him, Luka walked over to Belyaev and gave him the knife, hilt-end first. 'Sheathe it.'

Resentment glittered in Belyaev's eyes, but he jammed the knife into its leather case.

'You'll pay for this, Belyaev,' Shekhurdin threatened hoarsely.

'I'm trembling in my boots,' he mocked, but he threw a

malevolent glance at Luka and muttered savagely, 'You should have let me kill him.'

Turning, Luka saw the bitter black points of hatred in Shekhurdin's eyes. He watched him crawl back to his space along the bulkhead, a loser in battle, and guessed that the Cossack would have preferred death to the ignominy of defeat. The promyshleniki would never elect him peredovchik now. The opportunity to bring himself to the attention of the powers in Siberia as the hunt leader was gone.

In the darkness, someone murmured prayers, but the repetitive chant had no meaning to Luka. He remembered the ikons in the church at Petropavlovsk and the black-robed priests. God lived in the church, but Luka didn't believe He was anywhere near this hellhole of a boat. They were alone. If this storm didn't end soon, they'd all probably go mad and kill each other. Even he wasn't sure he could face another day of this.

In the night, the storm spent its fury and Luka awakened to rain, just rain. He went up on deck and let it wash the stench of the hold from him – a stench that also included the smell of madness.

The sails were unfurled and the navigator set a course for where he believed the island to be.

Chuprov paused beside him. 'We have no choice. If we find the island, we'll have to seek a wintering place where we can beach the shitik. We've lost our anchor and our dinghy.' He smiled crookedly. 'We'll get there, with *bozhe pomoshtch* – God's help.'

Luka glanced toward the two Aleuts on deck. At that moment, the old woman turned, a smile wreathing her face. Her pointing finger directed them to look off the port side. 'Attu,' she said. Far away, on the distant horizon, Luka could see the mountainous headland of the island.

It took them half a day's sail to reach it. In their previous exploration of the island that the native woman called Attu, they had seen a likely bay where they could winter. They searched it out and waited for high tide, then sailed into it and beached the flat-bottomed craft on the sand.

At sea, the navigator, Nevodchikov, had been the final authority. Now that they were on land, the promyshleniki elected their own leader. Yakov Petrovich Chuprov was chosen.

That night Chuprov offered prayers to the patron saint of their expedition, then ordered bread to be made from their rationed supply of flour and precious sourdough starter, and wisely passed the jugs of kvass around, a brew made from fermented grain. With their stomachs full and the rosy glow of liquor in their eyes, life looked good once more and they could drink to the sea they would not have to sail again until next year, when they would return with a cargo hold bulging with sea otter pelts. So they drank, and sang, and danced Cossack-style, legs and feet flying, bodies whirling.

Come morning, Chuprov had Luka accompany him as he led the old woman a distance away from the beached boat. Through Luka, he presented her with a kerchief, metal needles, and a thimble, which Luka had to show her how to use. Then, using sign language, Luka communicated Chuprov's request to her.

'You are to return to your village.' He tapped her shoulder, then walked his fingers through the air toward the mountains. 'Tell your people' – he gestured to his mouth – 'that our leader wishes to see them. He wants to trade with them.'

Luka doubted that the woman understood, despite the affirmative nodding of her head. He made it as clear as he could that the boy would remain with him for the time being, letting her think he might release him when she came back with her people. Not knowing how far her village might be from the bay, he gave her a small amount of the seal blubber they'd taken from the hut and a container of water, and watched her walk with quick steps toward the ragged cliffs.

'Do you think she'll come back?' Chuprov asked.

'We've got the boy. Someone will come for him,' Luka stated. 'It's just a matter of whether or not they come with spears.'

From his perch on the hillside, Many Whiskers scanned the area around his village, his gaze making long sweeps of the sky, sea, and land. He watched for many things – the boat of raiders, driftwood, whales or sea lions swimming close to the island, flocks of ducks, and the comings and goings of his village.

While his eyes worked, his thoughts wandered. There were many things to ponder. It wasn't a happy time in his village. He had only to look at the women weaving death mats in which to wrap the bodies of his son, Small Hand, and his cousin, Moon Face. Both had died from the wounds they received during the fight with the raiders when Little Spear and Weaver Woman were captured. He had followed the strange men and watched them take his mother and cousin onto their large boat made of wood. The loss was great for him to bear, both his mother and his son taken from him – the past and the future.

There were many stories in his tribe of strange boats wrecking on their shores with men of another race aboard. Their boats were made of wood and held together with pieces of a hard substance – harder than rock. Many Whiskers knew such things to be true. His brother Strong Man had traded many skins for one palm-sized piece of this harder-than-stone substance. Through his massive strength and much pounding, Strong Man had shaped it into a sharp spearhead for his harpoon. Many Whiskers had seen it – touched it. And the raiders who had killed his son and taken his mother, Weaver Woman, had long hollow sticks of it. He had seen them, too, in the fight, although he hadn't heard them roar like thunder the way his sister's husband from Agattu claimed they did.

He had lived thirty-eight summers. The hair above his lip had grown thicker and wreathed the curve of his jaw and chin. But he was not a wise man. The Creator did not guide his thoughts the way He did Strong Man's, and bring him understanding. Many Whiskers didn't know what any of this meant. Death, like birth, was a way of life. But these strange raiders with their thunder-sticks harder than stone, they troubled him.

The air stirred softly around him. It was a rare calm day, proving indeed the wind was not a river. Maybe the wind would not again blow the raiders to the island in his lifetime. Perhaps this incident would become another tale for Storyteller to relate in the evenings.

He spotted an object entering the bay. Many Whiskers quickly identified its shape as that of a kayak, paddled by a single occupant. Strong Man, he knew, had left the village to go fishing. He waited to see whether it was him returning or someone from another village coming to visit. As the kayak approached the village beach, riding a wave, he recognized his brother, Strong Man, and saw the catch of halibut lashed on the deck of the kayak.

When Many Whiskers turned to look at the village, he noticed an old woman laboriously making her way down the trail that climbed the green cliffs behind the village. It looked like Weaver Woman. He rubbed his eyes and looked again. It was she.

Shouting, he ran down the hill into the village to tell the others.

The instant Winter Swan heard the alerting shout, she thought the raiders had returned. She hurried to her feet, dropping the half-finished parka on her lap and scattering the skins of the tufted puffin yet to be sewn together. Her young son, Walks Straight, was sitting on the ground only a few yards away, throwing darts at a whale-shaped target hanging from a stick. Winter Swan ran over and swept him into her arms to flee, her heart pounding with fear. But she didn't know which way to go – which way the raiders were coming. Pausing, she looked to her husband's brother, Many Whiskers, for direction as he entered the village he'd thrown into a turmoil with his cry. But there was no alarm in his expression, only a wondrous look.

'Weaver Woman! She comes!' he told them and pointed toward the cliffs.

Weaver Woman. For a moment, Winter Swan thought some craziness had touched him and wondered if he had been struck on the head during the fight with the raiders. She clutched her son more tightly, mindless of the size and weight of his body five summers old. The figure coming toward them did belong to Weaver Woman. Staring, Winter Swan lowered her son to the ground, then moved in a daze with the others to welcome the old woman back to the village. The customary silence, the avoidance of unnecessary conversation, the sometimes going through an entire day without speaking was shattered by a barrage of questions from all sides.

'How did you get away from the raiders?'

'I saw them take you and Little Spear to their big boat before the storm came and took it away.' Many Whiskers gazed at the woman with shining eyes.

'We thought we would never see you again.' Often in these last days, Winter Swan had looked with sorrow at the unfinished basket that Weaver Woman had been working on before she was captured, believing she would never again see those gnarled but highly skilled hands raddling the grasses into tightly woven patterns.

'Where are the raiders?'

'What of Little Spear?'

'He is with them.' The gray-haired woman regained her breath and everyone fell silent to listen to her tale. 'They let me go after the storm. The sea was very angry and tossed their boat all over, making it cry and shake with pain. Many times I thought the sea would swallow it.'

Several of the men nodded in understanding, recalling similar experiences in their kayaks. 'Where is the boat now?' one asked.

'They have taken it out of the water and dragged it onto the beach.' Weaver Woman identified the bay where the strangers had landed. 'I think they want to stay on the island and hunt. Their headman gave me these things when he let me go.' She showed them the marvelous material with threads so tiny and so closely woven that she, with all her skill, could never duplicate. 'And look at these needles, made from small slivers of harder-than-stone. And this.' She held up the thimble for her finger and showed them its use.

'Little Spear?'

'He lives,' she assured the boy's mother. 'The headman kept him. I don't know why. I think he wants you to come get him.' Her glance encompassed everyone gathered around her. 'He wants all of you to come.'

An uneasiness spread through them at the invitation. Many Whiskers explained to his mother that Moon Face and Small Hand had been badly injured in the fight with the raiders and had died from their wounds.

'What do they want of us?' Stone Lamp, the headman of their village and father of Little Spear, questioned the invitation.

'Maybe it is a trick to capture all of us and take us to their village across the waters and make slaves of us,' Quick Eyes suggested and turned to face the shoreline. 'Let us ask Strong Man what he thinks.'

With relief, Winter Swan saw her husband striding toward them carrying three large halibut as if they weighed no more than a basket of duck feathers. A wooden visor encircled his head and shaded his narrow eyes. His hair was straight and black, and a thin spiky mustache shaded his upper lip. She immediately felt calmed by his presence and proud that he was her husband. His thickly muscled neck merely hinted at the massive brawn hidden beneath the waterproof parka made from the intestinal linings of the sea lion. But Winter Swan knew it was the spiritual power he had gained through his strength that prompted the village elders to seek his counsel.

Strong Man listened attentively while Weaver Woman told him her story and showed him the gifts the raiders had given her, then ended the account with the invitation. Despite the fact that Weaver Woman had been well treated and Little Spear unharmed, and the gifts were truly wondrous, Winter Swan didn't trust the strange-looking men. But, like the others, she waited for Strong Man's opinion.

After considering the matter carefully, he announced, 'We should talk to them. If they have come to hunt on Attu, there should be peace between us.' Of necessity they were a peace-loving people. Obtaining sustenance from the sea required a hunter's full energies. If the village was to be fed, little time could be spared for warfare.

'What about the killings of Small Hand and Moon Face?'

'If we killed two of the strangers in punishment, would that restore peace?' Strong Man's question made them realize it would not. Perhaps the killings had appeased their anger and the offenses would not be repeated. Either way, they realized there was nothing to be gained by maintaining hostilities.

4

All of the more than thirty village inhabitants, including the children, rode in the village's large open skin-boat to the bay where the strangers waited. Weaver Woman, like everyone else, wore all her finery except for the necklace of amber stones, which she had given Winter Swan to wear. The wife of her son was young and had not so many ornaments as Weaver Woman possessed. But neither had she when Kills-Many-Whales had brought her to the village to live in his family's home and give him children. Her husband had died many years ago, killed by the very creature he was so famed for hunting. The amber necklace had been a present from him the summer he died.

She glanced at the necklace of hard yellow stone lying against the dark fur of Winter Swan's coat, then at the young woman. Earrings of bone carved in a flower shape adorned her ears, their white contrasting sharply with her jet black hair. The labrets below her mouth corners were thin bone discs that artfully drew attention to the soft, full curve of her lips. Her lightly tanned skin was as smooth as the surface of the water in a stone pot, with a soft undershading of pink in her cheeks. There was a quiet strength in her features, an inner shining. Weaver Woman thought highly of the wife of her son Strong Man. In some ways, she felt they were 'like each other' and thus bound.

A small boy, five summers old, blocked her view of Winter Swan as he climbed up to stand on the seat so he could see over the high sides of the skin-boat. Thick, straight hair covered his head in a shining black cap. He carried himself so tall and straight that he appeared like a little man. The sight of him eased the ache in her bones. Here was the continuation of her flesh, young and vital, not old and tired.

'Are we almost there?' Weaver Woman's grandson, Walks Straight, asked his mother with adultlike seriousness.

'Soon,' Winter Swan assured him.

Two seats ahead, a young woman turned to look at Weaver Woman. Curiosity glittered in her dark eyes, framed in a face that was warmly alluring. 'If these strange men are not raiders, why did they not bring their women?' Summer-Face Woman questioned boldly.

'Because they have come to hunt. The sea animals would smell the women and run away.' Weaver Woman had no patience with her or her question. She felt sorry for her grandson, Cliff-Walker, for choosing this woman whose eyes were always looking elsewhere. After reflecting on her answer, Weaver Woman turned to her eldest son, Quick Eyes. 'I think these men will ask permission to hunt in our territory.'

He made a sound in his throat, acknowledging he'd heard her words, but said nothing. It was up to the headman of their village to decide whether to allow this. His far-seeing gaze swept the entrance to the bay, seeking the channel clear of hidden rocks. Like all the other men, he was dressed in his elaborately trimmed bird-skin parka with the feather side out. A long spray of sea lion whiskers festooned the peak of his wooden hat painted in a swirling design of colors. It was important to impress these visitors and establish good relations with them. They were a peace-loving people, willing to blame misunderstanding for recent events. If the sea that sustained them with its bounty took a life, they did not seek to avenge it. A harmony must be found.

As the large native boat – made from the sewn-together skins of the sea lion stretched across a framework of driftwood ribbing – entered the bay, the occupants saw the huge wooden boat sitting on the sand like a beached whale. When the vessel had first been sighted off the island, they had thought it to be some new kind of monstrous whale. Later, when it had come near the coast, the scanners had reported that it was some sort of boat belonging to a strange people.

The hairy-faced ones were standing on shore watching them arrive – silently. 'Why do they not dance a welcome?' Quick Eyes questioned Weaver Woman.

'That is not their custom.'

'They are visitors,' said Stone Lamp, the headman of their village. 'We must make them welcome.'

'They carry their thundersticks,' one of the men observed.

'I think they are not so powerful that Strong Man could not

44

break them,' Summer-Face Woman asserted as she bestowed an admiring look on Winter Swan's husband.

The parka of puffin skins concealed Strong Man's arms and torso, the mighty muscles that had earned him his name. From the time he was a small boy, he had undergone special training to achieve his physical prowess. Few subjected themselves to the severe regimen, and fewer still completed it. Everyone knew that to possess such great power would mean a premature death, and life was precious.

However, those worthy of the title Strong Man achieved a strength of spirit and great wisdom as well. So Strong Man's head did not turn to bathe in the warmth of Summer-Face Woman's look. It was something that didn't last – like the brief heat of the sun before the clouds closed around it again – or the days of warmth that gave birth to wildflowers before the season fled from the long, stormy months of cold and rain. Weaver Woman was pleased that her son knew this.

When the native boat was sighted entering the natural harbor of the bay, all the promyshleniki were alerted, and muskets distributed among them. A half dozen men accompanied Chuprov to the water's edge to confront the boat's occupants while the rest remained behind guarding the beached shitik. Three days had passed since they had released the old woman. Even though they had the native youth as hostage, their previous encounters with the island natives made them all wary; and Luka was doubly vigilant and distrustful, a tiny muscle jerking convulsively in his cheek where the scar ran.

'Are they carrying weapons?' The spyglass enabled Chuprov to see what Luka's naked eye could not distinguish at this distance.

'No. They have women and children with them.' Chuprov lowered the spyglass with a satisfied look. 'They would never expose them to danger. I think we can relax.'

Luka reached the same conclusion, and shifted his position on the sand, his taut muscles loosening. When the large skin-boat came close to shore, Chuprov detailed two men to help the natives land.

'Their boat looks similar to the *baidars* the natives build in Siberia,' Chuprov remarked. 'A baidar such as that could be very useful to us since we lost our dinghy in the storm. I wonder what they would take in trade for it.'

45

The need for a boat had been on Luka's mind. The sea otter lived in the offshore waters, rarely venturing out of its natural element onto land. To successfully hunt them, a boat was necessary. The only source of wood on the island was the driftwood the sea occasionally washed ashore. The baidar offered a solution to the problem. Luka studied the natives climbing out of the skin-boat. Of the adult males on board, only seven were of fighting age; the others were too young or too old to pose much of a threat. If the natives proved resistant to trading, they could be easily overpowered and the boat seized. Luka considered their need sufficient justification for the action. If the boat was not theirs today, it would be tomorrow.

He spotted the gray-haired woman among the band of colorfully dressed natives getting out of the baidar. 'The old woman is with them.'

'Good,' Chuprov murmured, and quickly spotted her among the other members of her village assembling on the beach. When he heard the first thump of a tambourine-shaped bladder drum, he raised his eyebrows in an expression of forced patience. 'I have the feeling we are going to be treated to another demonstration of native dancing.'

As the primitive performance began, the promyshleniki guarding the shitik drifted forward to watch, drawn by the presence of the children. These sometimes barbaric, sometimes cruel Russian hunters had an inherent affection for children. Even Luka, whose prejudice ran deep, found the antics of these black-haired, black-eyed children appealing as they tried to copy the dance of their elders.

When the last echo of the drums and singing was swallowed by the green cliffs, the old woman brought the leader of her village over to greet Chuprov. The man was tall, typically broad of feature, with leather-smooth skin. The scattered strands of gray in his hair were the only indications of his age.

Chuprov ordered presents of handkerchiefs, needles, and thimbles to be distributed to the natives. After the commotion died down, he signaled Luka to translate his words to the native leader through sign. 'Tell him that we come from a land far across the waters, many days to the west. Our ruler is a great and powerful woman who is very wise and very generous to those who would be her friends.'

The native's reaction at learning the Russians followed a

female leader satisfied Luka that his sign language was being understood. 'I think he finds it strange that men would let a woman lead them,' he said to Chuprov.

'Stress again how powerful she is, the vastness of the land she rules, and the multitudes of tribes and peoples she commands,' Chuprov instructed and waited until Luka had conveyed his message. 'Tell the chief that, like the women of his village, our Tsaritsa prizes the fur of the sea otter above all others. Tell him that we have seen the abundance of sea otter in the waters around this island and that we have come to hunt them.'

Watching the native's hands and interpreting their motions, Luka translated their meaning. 'He says it is true, the sea otter –' Luka hesitated uncertainly. 'I believe he referred to the sea otter as his brother – his brother the sea otter lives in the island waters in large numbers. And the chief gives us permission to hunt them in his village's territory.'

'Tell him that if his hunters bring us the skins of the sea otter we will trade for them.' Chuprov indicated the array of goods displayed on a blanket behind them. The assortment ranged from necklaces of cheap beads to copper and tin utensils and some knives of poor quality.

The Aleut leader looked over the goods with interest, then signed his reply. 'He says he will tell his hunters of your offer. But that it is much work to kill a sea otter. It takes many hunters. The men in his village may bring us some skins to trade, but he says the meat of the sea otter doesn't taste good and his hunters must hunt for food to fill the stomachs of their families.'

'Tell him I understand.' Chuprov paused and glanced at Luka, a sly gleam appearing in his eyes. 'And tell him that our Tsaritsa expects to receive a tribute from his village – a gift of ten sea otter pelts per hunter. When our boat leaves next summer, we will take his gifts to her.'

Luka conveyed the message to the Aleut leader, fully aware that the law exacting tribute from the natives did not extend to this new land. If the tribute was collected, he suspected Chuprov would make a gesture of turning some of the pelts over to the government's agent in Siberia, but the rest would be included in the season's catch, and each man's share would be worth that much more.

There was no reaction from the chief to the attempt to elicit furs without paying for them. Instead, he changed the subject.

'He wants to know about the boy,' Luka said.

'Belyaev, bring him here,' Chuprov ordered. An air of expectancy settled over the natives as they watched the black-bearded hunter walk to the large wooden craft that sat on the sand well above tideline. When Belyaev came back with the youth walking freely at his side, a murmur ran through their ranks and the tension eased from their faces. Chuprov escorted the boy the last few yards to the chief. 'Tell him that we have not harmed his young hunter and that we have kept his belly full.'

'He says he is glad to see his son.' Luka stressed the last. By a stroke of luck, they had a valuable hostage.

Chuprov smiled faintly. 'Explain to the chief that we'd like to keep his son – that he is an intelligent boy.' Then he paused. 'You know what to say, Luka Ivanovich. Convince him that we want his son to learn our language. Anything to keep him in our hands.'

Surprisingly, the native leader agreed to the proposal without argument. The atmosphere on the beach became friendly. Chuprov invited the villagers to take a closer look at the trade goods on display, then drew the chief aside.

'Tell the chief that we'd be happy to take that worthless skin-boat off his hands,' Chuprov instructed Luka. 'Ask him what he would like in trade for it.'

'The chief says the baidar is the only one his people have. If they traded it, his people wouldn't have any way to return to their village.' Luka carefully watched the nimble movements of the man's hands. 'He says it is a long walk to his village and it's dangerous to cut through the inland mountains. The ground often trembles and big rocks fall.'

'Ask him to think about it,' Chuprov persisted. 'Tell him his people can build themselves a better boat.'

'He promises he'll consider it.'

Chuprov motioned toward the trade goods. 'Have him look over our wares and consider what he might like in trade.'

Accepting the suggestion, the chief joined his villagers and surveyed the merchandise on display. Some of the promyshleniki mingled with the natives, but Luka remained on the sidelines watching. Soon the villagers were taking the presents Chuprov had given them and were piling into the baidar to leave.

'What about the boat?' Luka stared at the native vessel.

There's much work to be done before we can begin hunting.

We have plenty of time,' Chuprov stated, smiling faintly. 'The chief appears to be cooperative. I think we can persuade him to part with it.'

During the next two weeks, the promyshleniki established their base camp on the bay and concentrated on laying in a supply of food. The waters provided a bounty of fish, and the skies overhead supplied a multitude of seafowl. To the delight of the promyshleniki, a variety of sweet grass grew in the valley, assuring them of a winter's supply of liquor. The sun seldom made an appearance, but the thick fog and wind usually did. Yet the mild climate of the island seemed almost balmy compared to the brutally cold weather of Siberia.

The third week Chuprov divided the promyshleniki into five groups. The largest one would remain at the base camp under his personal leadership to hunt, superintend the distribution of supplies, and guard their hostage, the son of the tribal leader. The other four would go to different points on the island to make contact with other villages and establish outlying camps from which to hunt.

In addition, he appointed the four men who would be in charge of each hunting party. As Chuprov was about to name the promyshlenik to lead the group Luka was in, Luka noticed the way the Cossack Shekhurdin squared his shoulders and stood a little straighter. There was little doubt that he expected to head the party. When Nikolai Dimitrovich Belyaev's name was called instead, Shekhurdin stiffened and clenched his hands into fists at his sides. Luka smiled faintly, knowing how much the Cossack hated Belyaev, and how doubly galling it was for Shekhurdin to lose out to him.

'Those of you I have just named to be leaders of your group' – Chuprov began the instructions – 'I want you to keep a close eye on your men. Keep them honest. Make certain they hide nothing away for their own use. Watch closely so that they don't eat secretly. And you, promyshleniki, watch your leaders, and make certain they obey our rules. All infractions are to be reported to me when you return.'

The meeting was concluded with a prayer for a successful hunt, then the promyshleniki dispersed. Those who were leaving went to gather together their gear and supplies to make their trek over the island and establish outcamps.

49

Later in the morning the four groups of hunters set out, each to its own quadrant of the island. Luka's band struck out for the southeast side, an area with which he was already familiar. His pack was heavy and cumbersome. Everything they needed had to be carried on their backs. In addition to his personal belongings, each man's load contained a few days' food supply, including a bag of flour for the making of bread on Holy Days, fox traps, harpoons and nets for the taking of sea otter. They went armed with muskets, swords, lances, and pistols. Belyaev had charge of the vital sourdough starter.

About midafternoon, Belyaev called a halt, ordering a short rest stop. Luka shrugged out of his heavy pack and lowered it to the ground, the muscles in his shoulders and back aching from the strain of carrying its weight. He sat down beside it, stretching and flexing to ease the stiffness. As he glanced over their back trail, he recognized the cliff where they'd captured the boy. Since their approach to it had been from a different direction, he hadn't been certain it was the same one until now.

'Somewhere around here is where you captured the chief's son, isn't it?' At the sound of the question, Luka turned back and encountered Belyaev.

'That cliff.' Luka indicated the location with a jerk of his head.

'How far is the village from here?'

'Two – maybe three hours' walk.' He scanned the coastline ahead of them, trying to identify landmarks. 'See that point of land. It's on the other side along the shores of a bay.'

Belyaev studied the clouded sky, trying to estimate the number of daylight hours left. 'We should reach it before the light goes,' he concluded, then grinned at Luka. 'It will be a good place to make camp tonight – and maybe have somebody else do our cooking.'

'The village has a baidar, too,' Luka reminded him. 'We're going to need one.'

'Yes.' His grin widened.

Rising, Belyaev gave the order to move out. With their packs shouldered once more, the band set out again. Belyaev picked up the pace of their march, intent on reaching their destination before the light faded.

When they topped the cliff behind the village, Luka paused to look over the setting and gauge the native strength. He counted fifteen men scattered over the site, some sitting and staring seaward, others engaged in various tasks. Two were on the beach, where a half dozen one- and two-hatch kayaks – known in Siberia as 'bidarkas' – rested on the sand. A screaming, soaring flock of seagulls fought over the discarded fish entrails where a group of women were cleaning some fish. The wind carried a shouted warning from the village. A second later, Luka spotted the man hurrying off the earthen mound that roofed the native dwelling to alert the villagers to the approach of the Russians.

With trepidation, Winter Swan watched the band of strangers make their way down the cliff path toward the village. Instinctively she gripped the carved bone handle of the fan-shaped knife more tightly, forgetting the cleaned halibut she was slicing into chunks. Strong Man came up behind her, his bare calloused feet making little sound on the sand. She turned to look at him, but his attention was centered on the approaching visitors.

'Why have they come?' she wondered.

'To visit. Maybe to trade.' He seemed unconcerned.

Her instincts were not so trusting. Winter Swan watched her husband walk away to join the headman and greet the new arrivals.

Beside her, Summer-Face Woman went to work on the gutted halibut with renewed vigor, deftly cutting strips of the white flesh from the bone. 'We must prepare these fish so we may feed our visitors,' she said, then cast a quick, excited smile in Winter Swan's direction. 'There will be much singing and dancing tonight.'

'Yes.' Winter Swan forced her attention back to the fish, but without the enthusiasm for the chore that Summer-Face Woman exhibited.

'Maybe one of the strangers will offer presents to sleep with me tonight.' As Summer-Face Woman considered the possibility, her dark eyes glittered.

Winter Swan knew she would not accept if an offer was made to her, although it was her right to do so if she wished. A man did not own his wife's body. She was free to lay with another man if she chose. But Winter Swan had never found the pleasure in another man's arms that she had with Strong Man. And she certainly shared none of Summer-Face Woman's curiosity for what it might be like to couple with one of the strangers.

51

Out of the corner of her eye, she saw the men from another land enter her village. All the men were there to welcome them except for Many Whiskers and three others who were away hunting. As soon as the fish was cut up, Winter Swan assisted the other women in their hurried preparations to accommodate their unexpected guests in the communal dwelling.

While the meal was being readied, Winter Swan and Weaver Woman pushed aside the covering of dried grass to clear an area of the packed earth floor for the dancing that would come later. As they finished, the headman descended the notched log ladder from the hatch opening in the roof, escorting his visitors into his familial home. Winter Swan was immediately conscious of the tension in the air and the suspicious way the men looked around. The strangers gripped their thundersticks as if ready to use them. Their behavior made her uneasy, and she glided quickly out of their way.

The barabara was soon crowded with villagers and guests. The tension seemed to lessen when the women served the meal of raw fish seasoned with berry paste. Using hand signs, Strong Man and his male relatives established a halting communication with the strangers, but there were many gaps in the primitive conversation.

The earthen walls of the half-buried barabara held in the warmth given off by the stone lamps and the body heat from so many people gathered inside. Seeking relief, Winter Swan followed the lead of other members of her village, both male and female, and removed her long parka of otter skins so the air could touch her bare skin. Seldom did her people wear clothes inside the barabara except on the coldest of winter days, and sometimes on exceptionally warm summer days they went about their work outside without any covering.

As she moved among the strangers picking up the empty serving bowls, she was conscious of the way they stared at her. Little by little, Winter Swan had become accustomed to the strangeness of these men, their round eyes and thickly whiskered faces, but their peculiar clothing she continued to regard as very confining and wondered how the air ever touched their skin. She suspected they must be very warm in their close-fitting garments. Sweat trickled down the brows of some, but none made any attempt to remove their clothes.

With the feasting over, it was time for the dancing to begin.

Winter Swan watched with pride as Strong Man took off his bird-skin parka and stowed it inside their private cubicle in the barabara. His naked body bulged with massive muscles, his arms and legs like sinewy trunks, and his broad chest and shoulders like an ocean-smoothed rock. The long torsos of all the men in her village were notable in their high muscle relief and little fat. Yet, next to Strong Man, they resembled female fur seals next to a beachmaster bull. Winter Swan heard the strangers murmuring in their alien tongue and knew they were impressed with the might of her husband.

When Luka first noticed the natives removing their parkas and saw they wore nothing underneath, his interest was aroused by the paleness of their skin. Unlike their ruddy faces and hands, which were exposed to the elements, their bodies were a creamy shade of ivory. He stared at the bare-breasted women walking among them, then he saw the muscled brute of a man.

'Would you look at that one?' he murmured to Belyaev seated beside him. Reluctantly the Russian hunter dragged his attention away from the naked women in their midst. 'He looks like trouble to me.'

'I would not want to get crosswise of him,' Belyaev agreed thoughtfully. 'I would wager he could strangle a man's neck with each hand and wrap his legs around a third and choke him to death, too.'

'We need to watch him.'

Belyaev grunted an acknowledgement. 'Have you noticed the women? They aren't bad to look at even with those ivory buttons poking out of the skin by their lips. I feared they were all going to look like that old hag you brought to the shitik. I wonder if we could persuade any of them to warm our beds tonight.'

'With the likes of him around, I wouldn't try to find out if I were you,' Luka advised dryly. 'That is, unless you keep your musket primed and handy.'

'Have you ever kept a native woman before, Luka Ivanovich?'

'No.' It would have meant turning his back to one of alien race, trusting one to an extent, and that was something he'd never been able to bring himself to do. He'd always limited his contact with native women to the duration of sexual intercourse, then kicked them out of his bed.

'I had one once. A lot can be said for having a woman around when you want one.' Belyaev smiled crookedly. 'She's good for more than warming your bed. She cooks and sews and tends you. Eventually they all start making demands, but then you send them back to their village and get a new one.'

'Yes.' Luka watched the four naked men assemble near the area where the dirt floor had been cleared of the loose grass covering. They were joined by other natives with bladder-skin drums.

He didn't like being trapped in this barabara with all these natives. It didn't allow for any fighting room. If the natives did attack, they'd play hell getting out of here. And the fighting would be hand to hand; their muskets wouldn't do them much good. All this food, dancing, and show of hospitality could be an act of treachery designed to lull the promyshleniki into letting down their guard, then the natives would fall on them.

'I have been thinking.' Belyaev watched a native woman walk by, noting the sway of her hips. 'This would be a good site for our winter quarters. The cliffs shelter the valley from the wind, the stream provides us with fresh water, and the bay contains fish. There are plenty of sea otter in the area. If we build our camp by the village, we will have access to the native boats – and their women.'

'And it will make it easy for them to murder us in our sleep,' Luka added.

'I have been thinking about that, too.' He grinned widely, the action as always drawing attention to the prominent gap between his front teeth. 'And I haven't been able to figure out what use these natives are to us. They don't pay tribute. They have no wish to hunt sea otter. And they don't want to trade us their boats. They act friendly, but so did those natives on the other island. And you had to fight your way off that beach. It occurs to me we could eliminate some problems if we did away with some of the obstacles around here.'

Luka glanced around the room, considering the present odds again. He had no more compunction about killing a native than he did about squashing a beetle. Ultimately it might come down to killing or being killed.

'Not here. Not now,' Belyaev said. But he had made it clear to Luka that if the promyshleniki could not get what they wanted, they would take it.

Hands beat a primal rhythm on the bladder drums while the

naked dancers leaped onto the packed earthen floor. Luka stared at the brawny native, all sinew and glistening flesh. He represented the strength of the tribe, their symbol of power – and the greatest threat to the promyshleniki.

5

While Winter Swan prepared the day's first meal, Strong Man went through their son's morning ritual of exercises, making a game of them. She listened to the wordless sounds Strong Man made as he gently pulled Walks Straight's arm directly over his shoulder and back behind his head, making the joint supple. Usually it was her son's uncle, Many Whiskers, who played with him, but he was still away from the village hunting.

She glanced over to watch her husband massaging their son's knees. Walks Straight sat on a box with his legs straight and his feet resting on another box while Strong Man pressed lightly downward on his knees. Bending his foot forward and backward as far as it would go, Walks Straight stretched the hamstring muscles along the back of his leg. In another five summers, Walks Straight would be able to sit comfortably in a kayak with his legs outstretched and not suffer from cramping. This conditioning would serve him well in the future, but at the moment, Winter Swan simply enjoyed watching the two of them together.

All too soon the food was ready and she had to interrupt their play. As the two of them came to eat, Walks Straight marched beside his father. It always amused her to see how proudly he carried himself, but she never let it show.

The incomprehensible tongue of the strangers drifted into the barabara through the opening in the roof. 'Will they be leaving today?' she asked her husband.

'No. They are going to stay here.'

'How long?'

'Until next summer, when they will leave for their land across the waters.'

Frowning, she glanced about their family dwelling, remembering how crowded it had been last night. 'But they cannot stay here. There is not enough room.'

56

But it was more than the lack of room that worried her. The way some of them had looked at her made her uncomfortable in their presence. She had never had this feeling when men from other villages had looked at her, showing their desire to lie with her. It was a sensation she couldn't explain, but she knew she didn't like it.

'They will build their own.'

But it wasn't enough that they would sleep somewhere else. She wanted them to leave the village and never come back. She kept remembering the deaths of Small Hand and Moon Face. Her people on Agattu would not have been so willing to forget them as Strong Man's family was. They had attacked these strangers and driven them away from the island.

'Why do you trust these strangers?' She was troubled by his calm acceptance of the situation. 'I cannot. When they look at me, the thing that is in their eyes is not good.'

'It is only that their faces are different from ours.'

'And their ways are different,' Winter Swan argued. 'Have you forgotten they killed Small Hand and Moon Face? They were hostile to the people from my village on Agattu. I think they are bad. We should not let them stay. We should make them leave the island . . . and fight them as my people did if they refuse. Speak to the headman and warn him of the danger of letting these strangers live among us. He will listen to you.'

'But they have come in peace to hunt our brother the sea otter. How can we make war on them?' Strong Man frowned. 'That would be wrong.'

'They will bring suffering to our village. It is a thing I feel,' she persisted.

'As long as they live in peace with us, we will live in peace with them. The suffering will come if we make war on them.'

Winter Swan watched her husband while he ate, wanting desperately to believe in his wisdom.

Luka watched the Aleut emerge from the roof hatch of the barabara. The ocher-stained bird-skin parka hung to his ankles and concealed his powerful physique, making him appear no different from any other native man, but Luka knew better. A glimpse of that thick neck was all he needed to identify him. Last night he had witnessed the native's suppleness and agility in the dance. He observed it again as the man walked down the mound to the village common, the little boy at his side copying his movements.

By his count that put the number of native men, young and old, at fifteen. He glanced at Belyaev, wondering at the promyshlenik's true intentions after the things he'd said last night. At the moment, his attentions were focused on a native woman. Luka watched Belyaev saunter over to her. She looked at him with interest gleaming in her dark eyes. Luka had learned long ago that sex was an indiscriminate instinct.

'I like your parka.' Belyaev smiled and pretended to admire the garment. He felt the thick otter fur along the point of her shoulder. She moved slightly but didn't attempt to escape his touch. Encouraged, Belyaev grew bolder. 'The fur is soft. It makes me wonder if your skin is as soft underneath this parka.' He stroked the front of the garment and stopped his hand when it was over her breast, leaving it there. 'I would wager it is.' His suggestive action and tone seemed to unnerve her. She backed away from him and turned as if to flee. Belyaev grabbed her arm. 'Don't run away. We were just getting acquainted.'

She struggled, trying to pull free of his grip, alarm now showing in her expression. One of the natives stepped forward and spoke sharply to Belyaev in his Aleut tongue. A translation of his warning to let the woman go was unnecessary; his challenging posture made it clear. Luka watched them tensely, waiting to see if a fight would erupt.

'She belongs to you, does she?' Belyaev smiled coldly at the native and released the woman. 'I was just admiring her parka,' he explained through sign and stared at the native until he backed away. As soon as he did, Belyaev called him back. 'Maybe your wife would be interested in trading that fur parka of hers for a few trinkets.' He motioned for the man to follow him as he walked over to his pack lying on the ground.

When he opened the pack and dumped the contents from a small pouch onto the trampled grass, more natives milled around to see. He started to hold up a string of red beads, but one of the natives spied another object in the pile of goods and grabbed it out, jabbering excitedly. Curious, Luka stepped closer. It looked like a rusty iron bolt, yet all the natives were eager to examine it.

Luka frowned. No other trade article had created such a stir among the natives. They turned excitedly to show it to the Samson of their tribe, and watched while he inspected it. His affirmative nod started them all jabbering again. Belyaev demanded the return of the iron bolt. Reluctantly it was given to him. Then he was immediately besieged with offers to trade, but he repeatedly shook his head and returned all the articles to his pack.

'Why doesn't he trade that worthless piece of iron for the bidarka?' Shekhurdin frowned with disapproval. Luka wondered the same thing.

'He has a reason.' Although Luka couldn't guess what it was.

'And what is his reason for wasting the morning? We should be erecting our winter camp and gathering a store of food. He has sent out no men to explore and locate the good hunting areas. He's kept them all here – idle. Some leader we have,' the Cossack declared scornfully.

'Maybe he expects trouble.'

'Not from these natives. Chuprov has the chief's son as hostage. And the chief has already offered to have his people help in the construction of our quarters. We have nothing to fear from them.'

Luka didn't put much stock in that opinion. Turning from his pack, Belyaev rose and slipped a hand inside his shirt, then walked toward them. Luka frowned. If he hadn't seen Belyaev put the iron bolt in his pack, he would have sworn he had just slipped it inside his shirt.

'I have a feeling they would trade their mother for that piece of iron.' Belyaev smiled.

'Why not find out?' Shekhurdin challenged.

'You have little experience at trading, have you?' His expression showed contempt for the Cossack. 'It isn't something you rush with these natives. The longer you wait, the more they want what you have and the higher the price goes.'

'Are we traders or hunters?' Shekhurdin retorted.

'I don't know what you are, Cossack,' Belyaev jeered. 'I only know you are lucky to be alive. If you want to stay that way, get out of my sight.'

The Cossack's face became mottled with an impotent rage. After an instant's hesitation, Shekhurdin pivoted sharply on his heel and stalked away. Having been bested by him in a fight before, the Cossack didn't seek to pit himself against Belyaev again in combat. But Luka knew he would seek another means to defeat him if he could.

'Hey! Get away from my pack!' At Belyaev's sudden shout,

Luka instantly swung back to face the natives. One stood closer to the pack than the others. Belyaev strode back to his bundle and immediately searched through its contents. 'It's gone,' he accused, coming to his feet to confront the native who had first picked up the iron bolt. 'You stole it, you thieving savage? Where is it?' He grabbed the Aleut's wrist and forced his hand open, but the palm was empty. So was the other one. 'Where have you hidden it? Which one of these accomplices did you give it to?'

Belyaev dug his fingers into the parka's standing collar and tightened its circle to press his fist against the man's throat. Alarmed, the native struggled against his grip while his comrades looked on uncertainly. Belyaev gave him a shove backwards into the others.

'He stole the iron,' Belyaev announced to his promyshleniki. 'If we let him get by with it, they will steal everything we have. We must make an example of him.' He turned to the hunter immediately to his left. 'Shoot him.'

It was virtually point-blank range. As the hunter cradled the wooden butt close to his shoulder, Luka braced himself for the explosive report, his battle senses sharpening. The musket boomed, belching fire and powder smoke. A woman screamed, and the impact of the lead ball knocked the native to the ground, mortally wounded. Somewhere a child started crying.

Instead of falling back in terror, the strong man of the village leaped forward – too quickly for Luka to react. He grabbed the fired musket from the promyshlenik's hands and bent the long barrel into the shape of a horseshoe. The display of strength initially stunned everyone into immobility. Then the disarmed hunter pulled his knife and attacked the powerful Aleut.

'No!' Luka shouted the warning, recognizing a knife blade would never stop this native.

But the promyshlenik didn't hear him or didn't heed him. The Aleut seized his knife arm and snapped it like a twig, then closed his fingers around the man's throat. The other natives, seeing his successful opposition, rushed to attack.

'Kill them! Kill them all!' The bellowed order galvanized the Russians into action.

Luka moved quickly into position for a clear shot at the muscular Aleut and fired. He saw the body go rigid with death shock as a small round hole appeared in the man's temple. There wasn't time to watch him crumple to the ground or to reload. Out of the corner of his eye, Luka detected a movement and swung to meet the thrust of a knife.

Arching out of reach of the stabbing blade, he grabbed the man's wrist and twisted it to drive the knife into the man's own stomach, then used a ripping motion to finish the kill. A red fountain of blood spewed from the man's mouth, spraying Luka. The staccato-like roar of musketfire, the screams and shouts, the uncertain bawling of confused and frightened children all clamored in the distance. For Luka, nothing was as loud as the rush of blood in his own ears and the pounding of his heart. They blurred all the other noises of battle.

The killing had begun. There was no stopping it now.

Winter Swan left the barabara shortly after Strong Man. Seeking to avoid the strangers who made her so uncomfortable, she didn't join the women of her village. Instead she took a basket and went to the grassy meadow behind the village to pick berries.

She hadn't wandered very far when she heard a booming roar followed by a woman's shriek. Startled, Winter Swan dropped the basket. The thunderstick – it had to be. She could see the commotion in the village, people running in all directions like puffins. The sobbing cry of a bewildered child reached her. Fearing for her son, Walks Straight, she ran toward the village.

In the center of all the turmoil, she saw Strong Man, his hands around the throat of one of the strangers and his face cold with rage. A second later she located Walks Straight solemnly watching his father. Sobbing with relief, she swept him into her arms and hunched her shoulders protectively around him, flinching at the deafening noise from more of the thundersticks. She started to run from the village and remove her son from all this danger.

Walks Straight cried out. Winter Swan turned to look as Strong Man slowly sank to the ground, his features frozen in a death mask. Blood trickled from a hole in his temple. She gasped in horror, then saw more bloodied bodies lying on the ground, none of them strangers. The resistance of the Attuans was broken. The remaining men started to flee, but the raiders pursued them. She saw three of them catch Stone Lamp, the aging headman of the village, and fall on him with their knives.

Struck with terror, she feared they would all be killed. Her one thought was to run to the cliff trail and hide in the mountains. But when she started toward it, Weaver Woman stopped her.

'No. There is no escape that way.' Tears streamed down the cheeks of the old woman, but her eyes held no panic. 'They chase everyone down and hack them to death.'

'Walks Straight.' She cupped her hand over the back of his head, pressing him tightly against her. 'I must hide him from them.'

'Come.' Weaver Woman hurried up the earth slope of the barabara to the roof entrance, then pushed Winter Swan onto the log ladder to descend first. Her old legs were not as agile as Winter Swan's and she was slower climbing down the notched steps. 'Hide him in the wall hole.' She gestured impatiently in the direction of a cubicle.

'Yes.' At last Winter Swan understood.

She ran to the private cubicle along the wall, partitioned with grass matting, and lifted aside the long woven mat. Behind it, a compartment had been dug into the earthen sides of the dwelling to create a small storage area. She hugged Walks Straight very tightly for an instant, wondering if she would ever hold his small body again, then set him in the hidden compartment. There was little room for him. He had to sit with his knees drawn up and his head brushing the earthen top.

'Listen very carefully to me.' Her voice wavered. There was fear and bewilderment in his eyes. Winter Swan struggled to achieve a measure of calm. 'You must stay here and hide. Make no sound. No matter what happens – no matter what you hear, stay where you are . .,. until . . . all those strangers have gone away.'

'Where will you be?'

'Do not worry about me.' Weaver Woman smiled to keep from crying. 'Stay here.' The shouts and shrieks of terror from outside was lessening. Soon the strangers would be coming to see if anyone was inside.

Wrenching her gaze from her son's face, Winter Swan forced her hand to lower the matting and conceal him from her sight – and that of the strangers. Weaver Woman helped her smooth the woven grass covering so it hung straight. Then quickly they moved away from it to the center of the barabara.

A face appeared in the roof opening – a full-whiskered face with round eyes. Winter Swan recoiled, but there was no place to run. Weaver Woman stood quite calmly. Instinctively she moved closer to her. The man turned his head and shouted something, then started down the ladder carrying his thunderstick. Almost immediately another stranger crouched beside the hatch.

The first man climbed halfway down the ladder, then jumped to the floor. He moved warily about the barabara, searching the cubicles and constantly glancing back at them. Winter Swan held her breath, afraid he would find her son's hiding place. Her throat muscles strained with a silent cry for him to be still. Finally the man approached them and motioned them to ascend the ladder. Winter Swan let the old woman go first, wanting to stay behind near her son as long as she could. She felt the hard prod of the thunderstick push against her back, but dared not cry out for fear Walks Straight would forget and come running out to see what was wrong.

From atop the dwelling, she could view the carnage, the scattered bodies of the men twisted in their death throes, the women going from one to the other weeping, and the children wandering about, tears streaking their bewildered faces. All the men were dead, every one. The strangers had spared only the women and children. Winter Swan supposed they intended to carry them off to their village across the water and make slaves of them.

Of their own volition it seemed, her feet carried her down the earthen mound to Strong Man's body. The strangers made no attempt to stop her. She knelt beside him, staring into his lifeless eyes. Crying softly, she reached out and gently pressed his eyelids down to shut them.

Her shoulders bowed under the weight of the guilt she felt. She had wanted the strangers off the island. She had wanted the men of the village to fight and expel these intruders. They had tried, and now they were all dead – including Strong Man, her invincible husband. She traced his broad cheek with her fingers, his skin still warm yet lifeless to her touch.

Surveying the scene, Luka counted fifteen dead the entire adult male population of the village. He looked at his fellow promyshleniki, noting lingering wild-eyed looks on their faces. Their casualties were light, a few cuts and Khmetevski's broken arm. Turning, he inhaled deeply to settle his jangled nerves and smelled the stench of blood, powder smoke, and the sweat of battle on his clothes. He felt neither satisfaction nor regret over the extermination of the natives. The killing was simply over; a potential threat had been eliminated. He went to report to Belyaev.

63

'They are all dead,' he confirmed. 'What do you want done with the bodies?'

'Let the women take care of them in their own fashion. It will keep them occupied.' He smiled coldly.

Luka nodded a response, then happened to glance at the woman kneeling beside the body of the powerful man he'd killed. He saw her close the man's eyes. The wetness of tears that highlighted her cheekbones made him feel vaguely uncomfortable. The sensation didn't last as Shekhurdin came striding into his field of vision, his shirtfront splattered with blood. He appeared sickened by what he saw and trembled with rage when he confronted Belyaev.

'You are no hunter, Belyaev. You are a bloodthirsty murderer who enjoys killing for the sake of killing!'

'You look pale, Cossack.'

'You massacred these people for a worthless piece of iron.' His teeth were clenched so tightly together he had to force the words through them. 'Where is it now, Belyaev? Where is this chunk of metal that you ordered all these men murdered for?'

Belyaev reached inside his shirt and pulled out the iron bolt. 'I have it.'

'And I wager you had it all the time,' Shekhurdin accused thickly. 'You wanted an excuse to kill them. That was what you wanted, was it not?'

'Yes. Now I have boats that cost us nothing, a winter shelter already built – and women to cook, sew, and warm our beds.'

'It was the women. All this was so you could have a woman. That is why you did not have them killed.' His lip curled in disgust.

'Come, Shekhurdin, are you saying you don't want the company of one of these women?' Belyaev taunted. 'Or maybe you are not man enough?'

'You have no brain. You think with your cock! Do you not realize what you have done here? The hostage Chuprov holds is useless to us now.'

'Chuprov can get himself another.' He shrugged his unconcern.

'You fool! Why should the natives trust us after this?'

'What do I care whether they trust me? Let them fear me,' Belyaev declared.

'You will answer for this unprovoked massacre, Belyaev,'

Shekhurdin threatened. 'I intend to make a full report of your actions.'

'Go ahead.' A taunting smile continued to lurk in his expression. 'Who will care about the death of fifteen savages? God is high in His heaven and the Tsaritsa is far far away. Tell Chuprov. It will change nothing.'

'I will tell him. And if he does not have you flogged, I will tell the government agent in Bolsheretsk.'

'You make me tremble with your threats, Cossack,' Belyaev said, then threw his head back and laughed heartily. 'Go. Go and report my crimes to Chuprov.'

'I will. Then I will watch the whip take the skin from your back,' Shekhurdin promised and started to leave.

'Take two men with you, Cossack,' Belyaev called after him. 'To carry the powder and ammunition Chuprov will send back.'

6

Fog shrouded the massacre site. Wispy threads of it trailed into the semi-subterranean dwelling from its dirt-roofed entrance, attempting an invasion, but the wavering flames from stone lamps held it at bay, sending up curls of dark smoke from the burning moss wicks that floated on pools of seal oil. The boisterous promyshleniki sat on the floor in the light, heartily consuming the food prepared for them by the Aleut women who cringed in the shadows.

Belyaev shouted for water, then watched with dark eyes gleaming as a young woman hastened forward at his bidding, bringing him a water container made from the heart sac of a sea lion. He took it from her and poured some water into his mouth, then spat out most of it.

'A man needs something stronger,' he declared to his men. 'Tomorrow we will send the women to gather sweet grass for us. Then we can distill our own spirits. A man needs his daily draft to keep the chill from his bones.'

The Russian hunters echoed his sentiment. Belyaev thrust the container in the direction of the native woman. When she took it from him, he looked up at her, his interest aroused by the play of the lamplight on her face, highlighting its bone structure. He closed his hand around her ankle, forestalling her retreat.

'Enough food.' He set aside the wooden dish, with a leer. 'It's time we sampled the rest of our spoils.'

His hand glided up her leg, lifting the ankle-long fur parka to reveal a muscled calf. She pulled away from him and backed toward the huddle of silent women in the shadows. Belyaev got to his feet and unhurriedly pursued her, circling to block her from the other women. He stalked her in a cat-and-mouse game, pouncing and retreating, letting her think she could slip by him, then jumping to block the opening, laughing all the while.

Luka watched the sporting play while he scraped his bowl clean with his fingers, then licked off the fish flakes that clung to them. Finished, he wiped his mouth with the back of his hand, dragging it across his beard as the Aleut woman feinted in one direction, then bolted in the other.

'Catch her, Nikolai Dimitrovich!' The men laughed at her near escape from their leader.

But Belyaev grabbed her before she reached the women and hauled her against his body. When she tried to struggle loose, he cuffed her alongside the head. Her resistance crumpled instantly. He snagged his fingers in the black bun of her hair and forced her head back, making her look at him.

'You had eyes for me this morning,' he reminded her, grinning. 'Now you have me.' Turning, he surveyed the others. 'What are you waiting for? Here, Luka Ivanovich.' Still holding the first captive, he grabbed the arm of the nearest woman and slung her forward. 'Take this one.'

She stumbled and fell, sprawling onto the grass-strewn floor beside Luka. She made no attempt to rise, nor did she lift her head to look at him, her attitude one of submission. He looked at the jetblack sheen of her hair and the flash of white bone stuck through her earlobe. He felt little lust, but he knew what the rest expected of him.

Rising to his feet, he seized the arm she used to brace herself off the floor and pulled her along with him. She kept her head down, her face averted, but he had no desire to look upon it. Luka paused, glancing at the partitioned cubicles that lined the sides of the barabara, and chose the nearest one. When he moved toward it, hauling her with him, the woman offered her first resistance. A yank from him ended her opposition, and she went inside ahead of him.

Luka lowered the inner wall matting to obtain privacy, not wishing to perform for the entertainment of his comrades. Turning, he saw her crouched on the sleeping mat well away from the solid wall of the native dugout. Now she watched him. Despite the shadowed dimness, he recognized the woman as the one he'd seen kneeling beside the body of the village strong man – the man he'd killed.

His hesitation was brief. He signaled her to remove the sea otter parka, wanting only to get this over. She was slow to respond to the command, exhibiting an unwillingness as she gathered up the sides of the parka and pulled it over her head. The sight of her pale skin, glistening like polished ivory in the darkness, briefly entranced him. His hands hesitated on the fastening of his trousers while his glance shifted from the rosy-brown points of her nipples to the curling black hairs of her pubes, both standing out vividly against her pale skin. He loosened his trousers and let them drop around his knees. She lay on the sleeping mat, with her head turned and her eyes closed, her body steeled to accept him.

Her body was that of a woman, but the labrets and tattoos on her face belonged to a native. Luka mounted her without pre-liminaries, forcing his engorged muscle into her dry vagina, then driving it into her again and again while she lay unmoving, her lips pressed tightly shut. Long weeks of sexual abstention hastened his ejaculation.

With the fading of the last climaxing shudder, he let his weight sag onto her while he regathered his strength. Vaguely he was conscious of sweat trickling under his shirt collar, the pounding of his heart, and the labored roughness of his breathing. But the sexual gratification brought an ensuing emptiness of pleasure. He levered himself off her and straightened to pull up his trou-sers, aware that she still had not moved, although he didn't look at her.

Abruptly he left the cubicle to return to the communal area, refastening his pants as he went. Luka stopped and lit his pipe, ignoring the debauchery going on and the occasional burst of ribald laughter and obscenity that accompanied it.

Huddled against the smelly earthen walls of his hiding place, Walks Straight was frightened by the sounds he heard without. Only moments ago there had been noises in his parents' cubicle – the grunting breath of a man and the rhythmic rustle of bodies coupling together. But he hadn't heard the soft mewling sounds his mother usually made when she entwined her body with her father's. The man had left, but he was certain his mother was still there.

He was frightened and hungry. He knew she had told him to stay in this place, but it was black in here and he didn't want to be by himself any more. Quietly, carefully, Walks Straight pushed at the woven matting until he could see into the cubicle. After the inky darkness of his hiding place, the light filtering through the side slits of the woven grass partitions seemed bright. His mother lay naked on the sleeping mat, staring vacantly at the grass-thatched ceiling. She was so still – the way his father had been after he fell.

Alarmed, Walks Straight forgot all caution and slipped out of the hollowed earthen compartment. At the rustle of the grass matting, Winter Swan's heard jerked toward him. He stopped guiltily, knowing he should have remained in that dark, stuffy hole. As she hurriedly sat up, she cast a frightened look over her shoulder, then reached for him. She started to push him back to the hiding place, then hesitated and pulled him into her arms, hugging him tightly.

Something was gravely wrong, but he didn't know what it was. She clung to him and he was conscious of the firm roundness of the breasts pressing against his skin. There was no reassurance, no comfort in her arms, and he became a little more frightened.

The grass curtain separating the cubicle from the large inner room of the barabara was suddenly lifted. Walks Straight blinked, unaccustomed to so much light. The looming figure of a man – one of the strangers – blocked some of it. As his mother clutched him more tightly and moved as if to shield him, Walks Straight stared at the man's face and the ragged white scar that half closed one eye.

The man's hand moved and his mother cried out softly, but his arm went past them to lift the half-twisted wall matting and expose the former hiding place. Walks Straight saw the man look at him again, then he turned and left the cubicle. It was several long minutes before the tenseness went out of his mother's body and she stopped holding him so tightly.

Sunlight splashed through a break in the clouds and the waves reflected its glitter. Two Russian fur hunters stood thigh-deep in the waters of the bay and held the bidarka steady while Luka climbed into the long and sleek Aleut version of the kayak. Settling into the single-hatch opening, he stretched out his legs, feeling the pull on the muscles in the back. Someone handed him the double-bladed paddle. He nodded to his two assistants that he was ready.

The village had only one baidar. It wasn't practical for all ten promyshleniki to hunt sea otter in the same large skin-boat. The dozen bidarkas on the beach offered alternative transportation for the hunters and the opportunity to hunt in different areas. But the bidarkas were such small, light craft that the hunters were concerned how they would handle the heavy-running seas. Luka decided to check one out in the protected waters of the bay.

With a push, the promyshleniki launched the bidarka into the waves. Luka dipped a blade into the water. Almost immediately, the skin boat capsized and Luka found himself submerged upside down in the murky-green water, its surface glittering with sunlight. He flailed wildly with the paddle, trying to right himself and the boat, but nothing he did seemed to work. His lungs started burning, his body straining for oxygen. He dug one end of the paddle into the ocean's bottom and tried to push himself up, but he only succeeded in stirring up the silt on the bottom, clouding the water already churning with his bubbles.

Suddenly the bidarka started to right itself – or so it seemed, until a pair of hands grabbed him and pushed him up with the boat. Coughing and choking on the water he'd accidentally swallowed, he managed to focus his gaze on the two men who saved him and were now pushing the bidarka into shallower water.

'I damned near drowned,' he said between gulps of air.

'Are you not man enough to handle that little boat, Luka Ivanovich?' Belyaev taunted from shore.

Luka glared at him and told his two rescuers, 'I'll try it again as soon as I catch my breath.'

The second time, he wasn't so quick with the oar, waiting to get a feel of the craft's balance. The first few were tentative dips of the blade, but when he dug the oar into the water, his center of gravity shifted, overbalancing the bidarka, and it capsized again. Again the promyshleniki had to come to his rescue. On his third try, he went farther – into deep water – and turned over. This time he managed to right himself, but not before swallowing a large quantity of water and feeling the cold terror of a watery grave surround him.

As he sat slumped in the snug hatch, coughing up water and vomit, afraid to move lest the bidarka flip over again, the outgoing tide threatened to carry him into the open sea. Luka heard laughter coming from the shore and looked up to see a ten-year-old Aleut boy paddling out in a bidarka. Skillfully, the boy maneuvered his slender boat alongside Luka's and lashed them together. Although there wasn't a glimmer of a smile on the boy's face, Luka could have sworn the child was laughing at him. In a sullen silence, he suffered through the ignominy of being rowed to shore by a child.

When the long pointed bow touched the sandy bottom of shallow water, Luka wasted no time climbing out and wading to shore. He ignored the ribbing from his comrades. At the moment, he felt nothing could induce him to venture out again in that deathtrap.

From the tideflats where she gathered sea urchins and clams, Winter Swan had witnessed the debacle. She had strained with the effort to will the sea to fill the man's lungs with its saltwater. But the man to whom she had become a slave walked on the beach, safe. Her hope died. Nothing could free her – or the rest of her village. The thundersticks gave the strangers too much power. She had learned the bitter lesson that her people could not fight and win.

Something caught her eye near the mouth of the bay. The clouds came together, shutting out the sunlight. Without its glare in her eyes, she could see two bidarkas heading for the beach. She had feared this day when Strong Man's brother, Many Whiskers, returned with the remaining hunters from the village. The strangers had killed all the other men. They would kill them, too. Winter Swan shouted to warn them, but the wind carried her cry to the strangers. They saw the bidarkas and picked up their thundersticks. Winter Swan watched helplessly as Many Whiskers and the others approached the shore, unaware of the danger.

Luka studied the way the natives in the bidarkas positioned their craft to ride the wave, backpaddling slightly to keep from shooting the crest. He experienced a reluctant admiration for their skill, appreciating the difficulties involved. When he saw the carcasses of sea lion and otter lashed to the decks, their ability rose another notch in his estimation. The gleaming fur was one thing that could get him back into a bidarka.

'Shall we kill them?' someone asked Belyaev.

'No,' Luka said. 'Let them teach us how to handle their boats.'

Belyaev opened his mouth to contradict him, then considered the suggestion and slowly nodded his agreement. 'You are right. They can be useful to us in many ways. After all, what can four hunters do against all of us? We do have their women and children. They will do what we tell them.'

When the Aleut hunters came ashore expecting the same

friendly relations they'd shared previously with the strangers, they were taken by surprise, stripped of their weapons, and made prisoners by the promyshleniki. They herded the natives to the village, their arrival coinciding with the return of Shekhurdin and the other two hunters from the artel's headquarters.

'Well?' Belyaev challenged the stern-lipped Cossack when he reported to him. 'What did Chuprov say?'

'Nothing,' Shekhurdin replied, baring his teeth.

'He sent more powder and lead,' another of the returning party said, smiling faintly at the Cossack.

'What did I tell you?' Belyaev gloated.

Winter Swan didn't have an opportunity to speak to Many Whiskers until evening when she brought him his food. By then, he'd already learned about the deaths of the others. There was grief in his eyes when he looked at her, grief and despair.

'What should we do?' he wondered bewilderedly. 'I ask myself what Strong Man would do. Would he escape and go to the other villages on the island and gather their hunters to make war on these strangers? Is that what we should do?'

'No.' She had wanted fighting before. Now she saw the futility of it. 'They would defeat us with their thundersticks. They would kill us all. See.' She showed him the partially flattened ball of lead. 'This is what kills. I dug this out of the hole in Strong Man's skull. I think it was thrown by the thunderstick. I have seen them put these into the hollow end.'

'My heart rages against them,' Many Whiskers declared.

'As does mine. But Strong Man was wise to counsel peace.' Winter Swan struggled to think as her husband had and to abide by his beliefs. Hers had brought anguish to the whole village and the pain of enslavement. 'You did not resist them. And they did not kill you. If the others had not fought, the strangers may not have killed them. Strong Man would be alive if I had not urged him to use his strength against them. I must bear the weight of that.'

Luka saw the two of them huddled together plotting some conspiracy, and he crossed over to them. He grabbed the arm of the woman he'd made his concubine and shoved her to the other side of the room. 'You are wrong if you think to murder me in my sleep, woman!' His voice rumbled with the threat. She kept her head bowed in submission.

7

The incident singled out the unusually thick-whiskered native for Luka's notice. He chose the Aleut to teach him the mastery of the bidarka. If any treachery was planned, he wanted the native in his sight. Yet the man seemed placid by nature. No matter how much Luka goaded him, the hunter never displayed anger, and never once did he lose patience with Luka's ineptitude in a bidarka.

By a month's end, Luka had successfully negotiated the length and breadth of the bay and ventured into the open sea. In addition, he had picked up a modicum of Aleut, and the native had learned a smattering of Russian words. They communicated with each other in a convoluted combination of sign language, Russian, and Aleut.

During that length of time, the promyshleniki had familiarized themselves with their particular section of the island and stockpiled a supply of food. The latter was something the Aleuts weren't accustomed to doing. The sea was their farm, which they harvested as they needed, and their lean times rarely lasted long. They had known hunger but never starvation. The biggest chore for the Russians was convincing the native women they preferred their food cooked instead of raw.

Eager to collect the fur bounty of the ocean, Luka set out with huge expectations only to have them coming crashing down. First he discovered the limitations of hunting in the large, open skin-boat. While the baidar was capable of holding a party of hunters, its size made it difficult to approach the sea otter, and unwieldy in pursuit. Rarely were they able to get close enough to throw a harpoon. They tried shooting the otter with muskets only to learn that a dead sea mammal sinks almost immediately. Luka watched too many of the prize animals slip out of sight in the dark waters.

The long, sleek bidarka was best suited for hunting his quarry. Again, Luka enlisted the services of the Aleut whose name, he had learned, was Many Whiskers. This time he wanted him as a guide. At first they went hunting in a two-man bidarka, with Luka occupying the rear seat so he could keep an eye on the native.

Luka had always prided himself on his skill as a hunter. But there was a vast difference between hunting on land and hunting at sea. Land is solid. A man can walk on it. If he gets tired, he can lie down and rest. An animal leaves its spoor on it. When it storms, a man can take shelter and wait till it's over.

But the sea, the sea was constantly moving, flexing its muscles, heaving and falling and rising in mighty waves. Rarely was its surface calm, especially in the winter when the winds blew with gale force, lashing the sea into a froth of spindrift and driving snow and ice sideways. The sea was dangerous as well because it lulled one's senses, and the unwary one was always at risk of being engulfed. Luka was ever conscious that a plunge into its icy waters meant death within minutes.

And there were no landmarks on the open ocean. Countless times Luka became totally disoriented, with no idea in which direction the island lay. At first, he thought Many Whiskers had deliberately gotten him lost, that it was all part of some trick to kill him. But the Aleut was never lost, and always brought him back to the island safely. When he questioned the native, he was told he 'remembered' the way – the direction he'd taken, for how long, when he'd turned, which way – then compensating for wind change, he reversed the steps.

Hunting a sea otter was first a matter of sighting it, then getting close enough to spear it. Neither was a simple task. The first involved constantly scanning the undulating waters, and the second sometimes involved hours of patient stalking. According to Many Whiskers, it was best if there were a half dozen bidarkas so the mammal could be surrounded each time it surfaced from a dive. That way it would tire more quickly.

Also Luka discovered that the Aleut's weaponry was superior to his own. The native's harpoon launched from a throwing board had a greater range than his javelin-style harpoon. But his bitterest discovery was his inability to handle a single-hatch bidarka and hunt at the same time. He was only successful when he hunted in tandem with the Aleut.

*

Outside the barabara, a February blizzard howled, but it was snug and warm inside the native dwelling. A half dozen promyshleniki sat on the grass-covered floor playing cards, a mixture of grumbles and triumphant chortles coming from their midst. Other hunters idled around the perimeter watching the game or playing with Aleut children, while a few stood beside a copper caldron and its supply of raka, a strong liquor distilled from steeped sweet grass whose natural fermentation process had been hastened by the addition of some precious sourdough starter.

Sitting off by himself sucking on a dead pipe, Luka absently studied the musket barrel sticking out of the caldron's crude wooden cover. It was a mark of the peace and security they enjoyed in the village that one of their weapons could be broken down and used for the drawing off of spirits. They had nothing to fear from the natives. His glance strayed to Many Whiskers, who was busy carving some design on a new harpoon head. The Aleut had a weapon in his hand, yet Luka had no impulse to reach for his own. There had been too many opportunities over these past months for Many Whiskers to kill him and throw his body into the sea, if that had been his desire. Luka didn't understand these natives who seemed to have no passion for hating. They had killed their people and taken their women, yet the Aleuts displayed no malice.

He rubbed the scar on his cheek and stared at the growing stack of bundled otter pelts stored along a wall of the barabara. He'd brought back his share this winter, equal to any other promyshlenik, but the overwhelming percentage came from the four Aleuts forced into hunting with them. Frustrated, he bit down hard on the pipestem.

The rustle of dried grass alerted him to the approach of another as the Cossack Shekhurdin wandered over, a cup in his hand. Luka glanced up briefly, then took the pipe from his mouth and knocked the bowl against a wooden support, scattering cold ashes.

'Why aren't you over there drinking and gambling away a part of your share of the season's catch, Luka Ivanovich?' Shekhurdin crouched down, sitting on his heels. 'Or are you too busy counting up your share?' He indicated the bundles of glossy pelts that so absorbed Luka's interest.

'Perhaps.' Luka chose to ignore the Cossack's baiting tone.

'You came only for furs, you and the others. You must be feeling very satisfied.' He lifted the cup and slogged down another swallow of the home-brewed liquor.

The Cossack's comment aggravated the frustration Luka already felt, because he wasn't satisfied. 'The Aleuts call the sea otter their brother. They, too, are at home on this wild sea. They eat the things that live in its waters, make their clothes, weapons, and boats from its creatures. They live off the sea, not the island. Sometimes I think they only crawl onto it to rest. They know the sea and its creatures, the way I know the land.'

'I never expected to hear you singing the praises of a bunch of native sea hunters when you are sitting here looking at a fortune in furs,' Shekhurdin mocked.

'There is wealth there, but I keep wondering how many more pelts we could have had if those Aleuts were still alive. With fifteen more to hunt for us, we would have had to build another hut just for the skins.' Luka looked back on the massacre with bitter regret. The means to a fortune bigger than he had ever dreamed had been destroyed that day. Knowing what he'd lost, he could never be content with what he had.

'Yes. That is true,' the Cossack murmured, almost to himself.

Luka pushed to his feet and left the Cossack to his mental calculations of the lost profits. Unwilling to join the noisy group of promyshleniki around the card game, Luka paused beside the notched log ladder. He felt the draft of cold air from the hatchway. It swirled the thin trail of dark smoke from the stone lamps' flames. He wondered how long the storm would last. He was anxious to resume the hunt and make up for the lost pelts.

A pair of small boys scuffled on the floor, wrestling over a dart. Luka recognized the younger of the two as his concubine's son, Walks Straight. He watched the future sea hunters while other promyshleniki urged them on. With two so young, the fight didn't last long. Walks Straight emerged from the tussle proudly holding the dart, his small shoulders squared and his head erect.

Belyaev walked up behind the boy and snatched the dart from his hand, then dangled it just out of reach. Laughing uproariously, he teased the boy with it, making him jump, then pulling it back. The youngster quickly realized the futility of his efforts and launched himself at Belyaev, pummeling his legs. Belyaev reacted in mock fear to the puny assault.

Luka found it amusing as well, until the boy's mother intervened and dragged him away, scolding him for attacking his tormentor. The boy appeared downcast and a little sullen. When Belyaev offered the object to him, Walks Straight refused it and walked stiffly to another side of the room. Belyaev gave it to the woman instead. She glanced at the boy but didn't take it to him.

Her name was Winter Swan, Luka had learned. As Many Whiskers had explained it to him, she was called after the swan that came to the islands only in the early winter. Luka had recognized the graceful bird when it stopped on its annual visit – the whooping swan from his native Russia. And there was about his woman a grace and disciplined energy, an innate dignity despite the often-bowed head. He watched as she resumed sewing the bird-skin parka she was making for him.

That night as he lay beside her in the darkness, making no demands of her, Luka considered how accustomed he had become to her strange methods of adornment. The labrets and tattoos no longer repelled him. They were no more disfiguring than the scar on his face. She cooked, sewed, cleaned his pelts, and obeyed. For a native woman, she was good.

He thought of her body, the color and texture of ivory yet warm and alive. He shifted onto his side to look at her, unable to tell if she was sleeping. The desire that hadn't been there before now heated him. Although touching was seldom part of the act, he slid his hand under the skin robe and onto her stomach to convey his want. When he felt the swelling of an area that had always been flat, Luka hesitated, then explored the distended area with his fingers. She started to shift into a position that would allow him to mount her, but he checked the movement with the pressure of his hand.

'Are you with child?' He frowned, then saw she didn't understand. Her newly acquired and limited Russian vocabulary didn't include that phrase. 'Child,' Luka repeated and indicated her stomach.

'Yes.' She nodded once.

He felt a small movement beneath his hand as if the infant in the womb were confirming its presence. Removing his hand from her stomach, Luka rolled onto his back. He had not considered the possibility that she might have his child. Some hunter the boy would make, he thought idly. This new land could provide great riches for a hunter. But that brought back the recollection of the fortune he might have had. He stirred in agitation, silently cursing the scant daylight of winter and the fierce storms that hampered his hunting. At least here the ocean did not freeze as it did in northern Siberia, and the waters were occupied year-round by the sea otter.

Each day the sun stayed longer in the sky, with its light only rarely breaking through the ever-hovering clouds and fog to shine on the island of Attu. The ice-choked Bering Sea that had battered the rocky coasts all winter grudgingly allowed the warm Pacific currents to dominate the island. The treeless landscape acquired a lush growth of green foliage as rye grass, heather, and *putske* – wild celery – vied with vast fields of lupine, marsh marigolds, and a host of other wild-flowers.

The promyshleniki hunted at a fevered pace, conscious of time running out. Soon, too soon, they would have to make their return voyage, yet there were more sea otter, seals, and sea lion to be taken. Greed pushed them; the more pelts, the bigger their share would be. Every hour the weather permitted, they were out in their boats armed with harpoons and clubs.

For the native women, the time was equally busy. In addition to the cleaning of the skins the hunters brought back to the village, there were berries to pick and grass to dry for the making of baskets and matting. This was the season when the streams were filled with spawning salmon. The catching of these was the work of women, children, and the elderly. Rack after rack of drying salmon lined the village. They did all this, plus the cooking and sewing that went on all the time.

Returning from a successful hunt, Luka helped his Aleut part-ner, Many Whiskers, haul the two-man bidarka onto the beach, careful to avoid any sharp rocks that might puncture the skin sides of sea lion hide. His legs were cramped and stiff from long hours of kneeling in the boat. He simply could not sit in the bidarka with his legs outstretched the way the Aleuts did. The strain on his muscles was too much.

They unloaded the bloodied furs they'd stowed inside the Aleut kayak, having previously gone ashore to skin their kill so they could keep their load light and hunt longer. Together they carried the pelts to the village. Luka glanced at the sky, trying to gauge the hours of daylight left and debating with himself whether or not to go back out after they'd eaten. It seemed to require too much effort to make a decision, so he postponed it, hoping some hot food would replenish his energy.

Off to his right, he noticed three promyshleniki wearily tramping over the faint trail to the sweat bath the hunting party had constructed. Maybe later, he told himself, postponing that decision, too, and slogged on to the village. He spotted Winter Swan on her knees, bending over a seal skin, scraping bits of flesh from the hide. Pausing, she straightened and pressed a hand to the small of her back, arching her spine. Her stomach protruded roundly, making it appear as if she carried a large ball inside the parka. When she returned to her task, there was little space between her belly and the ground.

Luka guessed that her time would come soon, but he thought nothing of the long hours she worked. She never complained. And native women were strong. They were used to such things, so he expected nothing else of her. He walked over and dropped the fresh skins beside her.

'I am hungry. Fix me something to eat,' he ordered, then moved off a ways to escape the smell of the putrefied seal flesh. He sank to the ground in fatigue and watched her ungainly attempt to hurry to do his bidding.

'Men come.' Many Whiskers pointed to the cliff trail.

Lifting his head, Luka stared at the figures in Russian dress. As they approached the village, he was able to make out the sandy color of one man's beard. Chuprov. Overcoming his lassitude, he stood to greet the artel's leader.

'Tell the other hunters in camp,' he instructed the Aleut.

By the time Chuprov arrived at the village, the rest of the promyshleniki were on hand to welcome him. Cups were filled with the latest brew of raka and passed around to all. Belyaev waited until the travelers had quenched their thirst and rested a few minutes before addressing the purpose of the visit.

'What brings you to our camp, Yakov Petrovich?'

'Nevodchikov says we must sail for home within two weeks,' Chuprov stated. 'We need that much time to transport all the furs to the base camp and ready the shitik for the voyage.'

'No.' Luka involuntarily protested, and once he had objected to the decision, he was obliged to defend it. 'The hunting is good. The weather is good. Why should we go now? Why not wait a few more weeks?'

'Nevodchikov claims the winds favor the trip at this time of year. The voyage will be an easy one.'

'What does it matter whether the winds favor us?' Luka put his argument to the entire group. 'Would you care if the seas are rough or the voyage lasted a few more days, as long as the shitik's hold bulged with furs? Did we come all this way only to go back with less than we could have taken if we had stayed a few weeks longer? Think of how many more otter and seal we could kill in two weeks. Easily fifty, maybe a hundred. That's nine thousand rubles in the China trade. I say that is worth staying for.'

'I agree!'

'Yes!'

'Stay!'

'Luka Ivanovich is right!'

A chorus of voices shouted agreement. Luka smiled firmly in satisfaction. He knew if Chuprov insisted on sailing so soon, the promyshleniki would vote him out of leadership.

'What do the other camps say?' Luka challenged.

'They are reluctant to leave now,' Chuprov admitted. Again a rumble of agreement came from the Russian hunters.

'You are the peredovchik,' Belyaev stated. 'You still give the orders. You tell the navigator when we will sail for home.'

Chuprov surveyed the band of hunters, then gave way to the majority opinion. 'We will sail in mid-August. No later.'

The loud and steady hum of bumblebees came from the thick stand of monkshood. The deep blue flowers swayed in the wind, rivaling the rare blue sky. Winter Swan ignored the highly poisonous plant in her search for edible roots, but she wasn't so successful at ignoring the nagging pains in her back. When she stooped down to pick up her basket, the first sharp contraction stabbed her. It passed quickly, but she knew it was her time. She called to Weaver Woman, who hurried to her side. Immediately they started back to the village, walking slowly.

The contractions were strong and evenly spaced when she reached the village. Little Flower, the widow of Stone Lamp, the midwife of the village, was summoned while the other women helped her into the barabara. No mother or baby had ever died when Little Flower was present at the birthings. Even when the baby came the wrong way, she knew what to do. Once she had cut a woman open, taken the baby out, sewn her together again, and both had lived. Winter Swan had no fears with Little Flower to assist her, not even when the pains became so bad she thought they would tear her apart.

'The head comes,' Little Flower assured a squatting Winter Swan.

Then she, too, could feel the life bursting from her. A smile of joy and relief broke from her when a moment later she heard its cry. She saw Little Flower pass the red and wrinkled infant to Weaver Woman to clean.

'It's a girl,' she told Winter Swan. 'Strong like her mother.'

When the baby was placed in her arms a short time later, she lovingly inspected the tiny infant for herself. Black hair as thick and soft as duck down covered her head. The redness and the wrinkles she knew would soon go away. She gazed in wonder at the small mouth and nose, and the little fingers each with a perfectly formed nail. The eyes, however, were round – like those of the man called Luka. But Winter Swan didn't mind. She was lucky to have such a good master, she reminded herself. He treated her well, and had never struck her in anger as some of the other men had their women. If sometimes her heart cried for happier days, she looked to her own error in speaking against peace.

But with this baby in her arms, she felt happy again. She was glad it was a girl, even though she knew the village needed hunters. A girl child could help with her work and understand certain things that a boy never would. A daughter was very special.

The baby squirmed, and her little mouth opened like a hungry nestling's. Winter Swan guided it to her nipple. She smoothed the black fluff atop her daughter's head with a stroking finger while the baby suckled.

Later after the baby was asleep, Weaver Woman brought Walks Straight to see his new little sister. He peered uncertainly at the baby in the wooden cradle Many Whiskers had made for it. A little fist waved in the air. When he touched it, the little fingers curled around his forefinger. His smile of surprise was filled with wonder. Winter Swan gazed proudly at her two beautiful children.

The clouds were pink-etched with twilight when Luka returned from his hunting. He looked around for Winter Swan with faint irritation, wanting some food and a cup of raka – and maybe the aching muscles in his back rubbed. Her hands were adept at easing their soreness.

'Winter Swan have baby,' Many Whiskers said.

The words didn't register for an instant. Then Luka stared dumbstruck at the Aleut's smiling eyes. His child was born. He tried to think what that meant. But he was suddenly engulfed by the promyshleniki in camp, their hearty voices bombarding with congratulations that were sometimes ribald and sometimes mocking. They pounded him on the back, then laughingly pushed him toward the barabara. At first Luka felt a little foolish, but as he climbed the mounded roof, there was a faint spring to his stride. He was only vaguely conscious of the men following him to have their look at the newborn infant only a few hours old.

Halfway down the ladder, he saw Winter Swan sitting beside the cradle, her legs curled under the parka, only a single bare foot showing. Her head was bent toward the yet unseen infant, the glow from the stone lamp shining on her hair. The sight triggered an image in his mind – the ikon of the Virgin in church. She looked up and the illusion vanished at the reality of the labrets below her lip corners.

Moving quickly, Luka crossed to the cradle and knelt down to look upon his son for the first time. The little mite looked so small lying there making faces in his sleep. He didn't look at all as Luka had expected. As a matter of fact, he was rather ugly. Tentatively, Luka brushed his fingertips over the mass of hair covering his head, black as midnight and soft as eiderdown. The baby's forehead puckered in a frown.

'How does it feel to be a papa, Luka Ivanovich?' Belyaev's lips split in a grin that showed the gaping space between his front teeth.

Luka straightened to tower above the cradle. 'He will make a fine hunter someday.' He spoke gruffly so he wouldn't appear soft, then stepped back so his comrades could view his son.

'No hunter,' Winter Swan said and lifted aside the covering to expose the baby's smooth pubes. 'Girl.'

Sharp disappointment followed the initial shock of the discovery. He had never considered the child would be other than a son. The mocking laughter from the promyshleniki added to his chagrin. What good was a girl, he thought in disgust.

'What are you going to name your daughter?' a taunting Belyaev wanted to know. When Luka flashed him an irritated look, the man grinned. 'Come now, Luka Ivanovich. The babe must have a name.'

He hesitated, but if he didn't call her something, the men would never let him hear the end of it. 'Tasha.' It was a common enough name. 'Tasha Lukyevna,' he said, giving the girl child the status of his daughter.

'Tasha.' Winter Swan tried out the sound of the name, then gazed at her daughter and gently tucked the soft cover around her. 'Tasha,' she murmured.

8

Continued good weather and good hunting prompted a second postponement of the shitik's departure from the island of Attu. Not until the end of August did the promyshleniki begin loading their catch of furs into the large baidar to be transported to the base camp.

All week, Winter Swan had listened to their talk of leaving, and then she watched them tote the bundles of fur pelts to the baidar. She stood amid the noise and confusion in the barabara, clutching her daughter, Tasha, in her arms and holding her son's hand to keep him at her side. All around her, the men rummaged through the cubicles, gathering their belongings and rolling them into bundles.

She watched as Luka tied his bundle, and she waited uncertainly for some directive from him. She was his slave. Surely he was going to take her to his village across the waters. But he hadn't told her to pack. Winter Swan was suddenly afraid that he'd put her on the baidar without any of her property. She couldn't bear the thought of leaving everything behind. Acting quickly, she laid Tasha in her cradle and began collecting essential items – her tiny basket of needles, her crescent-shaped knives for cleaning and skinning, a root digger, and a few other articles.

When she reached past Luka for her best parka and pouch of valuables, he grabbed her arm. 'What are you doing?'

'We go to your village,' she said, then saw his frown of surprise. 'You take us?'

'No.' He bent his head, avoiding her gaze, while he quickly finished tying his bundle. 'You will stay here. There isn't room for you.'

She sat back on her heels, bewildered.

Later she stood on the beach with the other women and children and watched Many Whiskers and the other three Aleuts, the only adult males left in the village, push the heavily laden baidar into deeper water. The wind whipped the misting rain against her face, obscuring her view of the boatload of men.

When the baidar headed out to sea, Winter Swan realized the village was free. Their masters were leaving. But the exultant lift of her spirits didn't last, dashed by a sense of abandonment. They were free, but how would they live with only four men to hunt and provide sustenance for the entire village? She clutched the baby closer to her breast.

By the time the promyshleniki gathered at the base camp, repaired the winter damage to the shitik, recaulked its seams, collected provisions for the return voyage, launched the vessel, and loaded their valuable cargo of furs, two weeks had passed. In the middle of September, they hauled the new wooden anchor from the water, unfurled the reindeer-hide sails from the spars of the shitik's twin masts, and sailed for Russia. Their young orphaned hostage accompanied them, now the ward of the navigator Nevodchikov, who had become very attached to the native boy over the past year.

Heavy gray clouds hid the volcanic peaks of the island, and angry waves lashed its rocky coast. Luka stood near the stern of the flat-bottomed vessel and watched the island grow smaller and smaller. With his feet spread for balance, he swayed with the roll of the shitik as it bucked the ocean swells.

Belyaev made his way across the heaving deck to the stern. 'How much do you think our cargo is worth, Luka Ivanovich?' The sum was a constant source of speculation among the company.

'I say a hundred thousand rubles.' He doubted that the price of a pelt had changed very much during the year they'd been gone.

'What are you going to do with your share?' Everyone was making plans for the ways they were going to spend their fortune, ranging from the practical to the wasteful. It was a way to pass the time. Most of them, Luka suspected, would end up drinking and gambling it away. There were few luxuries for a man to spend his money on in the dreary, isolated towns of Siberia. The man who achieved riches usually left. Those who stayed rarely kept theirs.

'I am not going to lose it playing cards in some tavern,' Luka stated.

Belyaev laughed. They all said that. 'Then what will you do?'

As he stared at the island, Luka noticed a sea otter watching the shitik from a safe distance, its head bobbing above the water like a cork. 'Maybe I'll come back,' he said. 'Maybe I will use my share to build a vessel of my own and finance another expedition to these islands.' The profit from such a venture would be staggering, he realized. So many sea otter lived in these waters he could come again and again.

'It was good on the island – plenty of fur animals and the women were not bad either, eh?' Belyaev grinned and heartily slapped Luka on the back.

His mouth crooked in response as Luka thought of the tall and stately Winter Swan. Again he regretted that the infant had not been a boy.

Everyone had known from the beginning of the voyage that their delayed departure meant they would encounter adverse conditions. The second day out, the seas became rough and the weather turned bad, rain and wind thrashing the boat. And the conditions never improved for long.

By the fourth week, their water supply was reduced to the rain they could catch, and the food was nearly gone. Gums began to bleed and breaths turned foul as men grew weak from scurvy. The men began to fear that they had left too late.

The shitik battled the waves and the contrary winds for two more weeks, taking a beating while the men struggled to keep her afloat, mending her torn sails, shoring her masts, repairing her cracks and praying their luck had not run out. No one labored any harder than Luka.

Lurching with the boat's violent motion, he made his way to the two hunters manning the pump and tapped the shoulder of the nearest to take his turn at the pump. Although the men were relieved frequently, they were barely able to stay ahead of the steady seepage.

A muffled shout came from above deck. A moment later a man yelled down the hatchway, his voice rising on a hysterical note of joy. 'Land! Land!'

Until that instant, Luka had not realized how close he had been to giving up hope. Now it soared through him, giving him the strength of ten men and making him forget the pain of his bleeding mouth. He abandoned his post and the pump and scrambled up the hatchway to see the sight for himself.

A wave inundated the shitik's deck, nearly washing Luka overboard as he emerged topside. He gripped the railing, water running down his body and dripping from his hair and beard. A corner of a sail flapped loosely, the leather thong that once secured it flailing the air. Blinking away the stinging saltwater, Luka peered at the horizon. At first he saw nothing except a black bank of clouds. The shitik shuddered ominously as the next wave crashed onto her decks, drenching him again. That was land, not clouds, he realized.

'Kamchatka! That must be Kamchatka! We're going to make it!' he shouted exuberantly and threw back his head to cackle wildly, mindless of the next engulfing wave.

The forward sail broke its line and whipped out from its spar, flopping uselessly like a broken wing. There was a mad scramble to secure the sail before the wind tore it off completely. Luka came to his senses and joined the struggle to capture the heavy wet hide and tie it down. They had yet to make land, although the storm was driving the weltering shitik toward it.

With its square-rigged sails, the shitik was not highly maneuverable in good weather; in a storm, it was all but unmanageable. As the boat neared the coastline, Luka could hear the thundering crash of the breakers. Now and then he could see the plumelike spray of foam where jagged rocks offshore prematurely broke a wave's force and turned it back on itself. The flat-bottomed boat strained to hold a course off the coast, but it was no match for the power of the sea. It was driven closer and closer to shore.

Luka saw the pointed tip of the shiny black rock looming ahead of the bow and shouted a warning to the navigator. The shitik groaned as she tried to answer the rudder's command, her bow veering slightly away from the rock, but not enough. A second later came a deadly scrape, followed by the grinding splintering of wood. Then the shitik shuddered violently, jolting to a stop as timbers cracked open. The impact threw Luka to his knees.

'Get the boat over the side! She's going to break up!' someone shouted.

There was a mad scramble to abandon the vessel as sea water poured into the rip in her belly. Luka fought his way through the tide of men. When Shekhurdin attempted to shove past him to reach the boat, Luka grabbed him. 'The furs. We have to save the furs!'

'You save the furs, Kharakov,' the Cossack snarled. 'I choose to save myself.'

Letting him pass, Luka looked at the panicked mass scurrying for the rail. 'Belyaev!' he shouted to the black-bearded promyshlenik. 'The furs! We must get them into the boat!'

The stocky hunter hesitated by the rail, then moved away from it to join Luka. 'Quickly. We must move quickly,' he urged.

They broke open the cargo hatch. Luka swung into the flooding hold and began tossing the bundled pelts through the hatch hole to Belyaev. They worked feverishly, conscious of each shuddering groan of the dying shitik. Each bundle that landed on deck, Belyaev grabbed and tossed to the boat lying alongside while men scrambled over the rail or jumped into the churning waters to swim for the shore thirty yards away. Waves continuously hammered the snagged shitik against the black rock.

In the hold, Luka waded through the cold saltwater and hefted another bundle of pelts from a stack, then moved back toward the hatch. He heard the loud, ominous crack of the timbers and felt the boat shift under his feet as he heaved the furs through the opening.

Belyaev appeared at the hatch. 'No more! Come now!' He urgently motioned for Luka to leave the rest of the furs. 'The boat is casting off. They won't wait.' Belyaev disappeared from view.

Luka took a step to follow, then hesitated and turned back for one more bundle of furs. A powerful wave struck the shitik, snapping it in two like a branch broken over a man's knee.

Belyaev jumped from the rail, diving into the water. He surfaced quickly and swam for the longboat. Someone threw a line to him. He grabbed it, wrapping it around his arm, then held on as they pulled him to the boat.

After they had hauled him on board, a promyshlenik asked, 'Where is Kharakov?'

'There.' Panting, Belyaev pointed to where the shitik had been, but nothing remained, only some floating bits of wreckage torn loose from the vessel before it went under.

9

For five summers, no more strange boats came to the island of Attu, and the Aleuts lived as they always had, while their brother the sea otter frolicked in the waters, rarely molested. Sometimes on a long winter evening, a storyteller would recount the time when the bearded men stayed on their island. And in nearly every barabara there was a round-eyed child as evidence of their visit.

Then another boat came to Attu, filled with men who spoke the same tongue as the first visitors. Cossacks, they called themselves. They told the Aleut hunters they had to pay tribute to their great and powerful woman ruler across the waters, and the tribute was to be in the form of so many sea otter pelts. They also promised to trade pieces of iron for otter skins. But when the Aleuts went hunting, the Cossacks made free with their women.

Soon more boats came. One would leave and another arrive to take its place. Some treated the Aleuts fairly, others did not, but any opposition was quickly and brutally suppressed.

Ten summers after the first boat came, one which looked like all the others landed on the island. But the man who commanded it was different. His name was Andrei Nikolaivich Tolstykh. He had eyes the color of the sky when the clouds didn't cover it. He didn't wear the usual rough garb of the Cossacks; his clothes were a different style and made from a finer cloth. On his finger was a ring with the design of a two-headed bird.

But it was more than his appearance that made this Cossack, Andrei Nikolaivich Tolstykh, different from the others who had landed at the place now called Massacre Bay. He treated the Aleuts fairly and punished any of his men who tried to cheat them. He paid for the services of those natives who hunted for him, and traded iron for otter skins. Among the children who were placed in his care were Walks Straight and his half sister, Tasha. They were treated kindly and taught to speak the Cossack tongue. Leaders had promised others before them that they would teach them their language, yet rarely had anyone learned more than a smattering of words.

From Andrei Nikolaivich Tolstykh, the Aleuts of Massacre Bay learned that the great woman ruler of his country had been greatly displeased when she heard about the murders committed by the first Cossacks to land on Attu, and that the guilty ones had been punished for their crimes against the Aleuts. He instructed the Aleuts to come to him if any of his men abused them or treated them unfairly, and he would see that they were punished.

The Aleuts did much hunting for him because of this. And there was peace on the island. They were sad when his boat left the following summer, loaded with more than five thousand sea otter pelts. Tasha was sorry to see him leave, too, but the Cossacks always left. Many said they'd come back, but few did.

As always, more Cossacks arrived to take the place of those who left. So it went.

For as long as Tasha could remember, there had been Cossacks on the island, although her mother had told her of the days when it was not so. She'd heard the story of Strong Man's death many times, the man who was the father of her half brother, Walks Straight. Somehow she thought the Cossacks who had killed Strong Man must have been very different from many of the ones she knew. She admitted that some cheated the Aleut hunters and some beat the women, but they had always been kind to her and fascinated by her round black eyes that slanted ever so slightly. She remembered them playing and laughing with her; letting her chase them or pretend to serve them food. And her memory was colored by the man Andrei.

They said she was Creole – half Cossack and half Aleut. Now, at fifteen summers, she was tall like her mother, and she had her mother's strong cheekbones and smooth skin. But her face was more slender and her features not so broad. Near the corners of her lips, there were two faint scars where labrets had been inserted when she was a child. Long, long ago a Cossack had insisted that her mother, Winter Swan, remove them and let the skin grow shut.

Tasha entered the village carrying a basket of sea urchins she'd gathered on the tideflats. A group of Cossacks lounged outside a barabara they'd built, with an opening in the side instead of the top. They saw her coming and turned to watch.

'What do you have in your basket, Tasha?' one of them called.

'Sea urchins. Young, tender ones, too,' she answered.

'Is that the way you like them, Fedor Petrovich? Young and tender?' Another laughed and poked the Cossack who stared at her so intently. The one called Fedor lashed out with a swing of his arm.

Tasha walked on to her own barabara. She was aware of the interest Fedor showed in her. So far he hadn't offered any presents for her, but she expected he would soon. She was of the age to take a husband.

'Why do you speak to those Cossacks?' The sudden demand from her half brother, Walks Straight, took her by surprise. She hadn't noticed him sprawled on the lee slope of the barabara.

'They asked me a question and I answered it,' she replied.

Walks Straight rolled to his feet in a quick fluid movement. The proud, erect carriage that had marked him as a youngster characterized him as a full-grown man of twenty-one summers. Beneath the bird-skin parka, his chest and shoulder muscles were highly developed, the result of a hunter's long hours paddling his bidarka at sea. Straight black hair, shiny as a raven's wing, hung to the standing collar of his parka and framed his tanned flat-boned face. He had the keen eyes of a hunter, too, observant of every detail, including the greedy way the Cossacks looked at his sister. It was one more reason to resent them. They were always taking from the Aleut. Filled with a young man's pride, he was offended by their actions and could not understand why his people accepted it so meekly.

'You talk to them too much, Tasha.' He followed as she walked past the salmon-drying racks.

'They are my friends.' She stopped near their mother and the old white-haired Weaver Woman. The two women were busy smoothing the inner skins of cormorants with an abrader, taking care not to damage the feathers on the other side. The skins were for a new parka, and the garment would belong to a Cossack. The knowledge further irritated Walks Straight.

'They are not our friends. Look how our mother labors for them.' He was conscious of his mother's glance, but he avoided the admonishing look.

'They pay her for it.' Tasha sat down on the ground near the working pair to begin cleaning the sea urchins to remove the tender meat inside.

'Maybe they will. They told me they would give me a piece of iron for ten sea otter pelts. All week I have hunted. But when I bring them the ten skins today, they refused to give me the iron. They say they wanted twelve.' His jaws clenched as he recalled the incident. 'They took my ten pelts, then told me I must bring twelve more to have the iron. When I tried to say I must only bring them two more, they laughed at me. They said I must have twelve all at once. They have my skins and the iron. They cheated me and I could do nothing.'

'Not all Cossacks are like that,' Tasha asserted. 'Remember Andrei Tolstykh. He was honest.'

'He collected tribute,' Walks Straight retorted. 'Why should we give pelts to some woman ruler who lives far away across the waters? They say if we do, she will protect us, I say it is another trick to cheat us out of our furs.'

'It is the way they live,' his mother, Winter Swan, inserted quietly, attempting to calm him. 'We must respect that.'

Walks Straight swung on her, then paused to stare for an instant at the strands of gray in her hair. It pained him sometimes that she could not understand his resentment of the Cossacks. Yet always in his mind the words of the storyteller sang, recalling his father's great strength and the day of the great battle when Strong Man had bent the Cossack's iron thunderstick with the power of his bare hands. His father had died resisting the Cossacks. Walks Straight was proud of that. Yet his mother thought of that time only with sorrow. He did not wish to hurt her more with his anger at the Cossacks, but he must say what he believed if he was to honor his father's memory.

For her sake, he tempered his words. 'Can we respect their ways and still respect ourselves? Our people lived on this island long before they came. We should make them leave.'

'We have always made visitors welcome,' she reminded him.

'Even visitors who steal from us?' Walks Straight challenged. 'Dancing Boy took a necklace of beads and they whipped him until his back was raw. Why do we allow them to take what is ours?'

'It does no good to punish someone for a wrong.' She shook her head firmly. 'It does not restore peace.'

'I know it isn't the way of our people to punish a man for a single wrong act. But if he continues to repeat the offense, then something is done to stop him.' He observed his mother faintly lowering her head, a silent admission that he was right. 'We should punish the Cossacks for their wrongs.'

Winter Swan paused in her labors, holding the pumice abrader in her hand. 'The Cossacks are too many. They are too strong. We have no weapon to match the thunderstick they call a musket. We must maintain peace.'

'If we had their muskets, we could fight them. I know how to make it shoot the round balls. I have watched them many times and have seen how much black powder they use to make the musket go off.'

'They will never let you have one,' Tasha declared. 'No matter how many sea otter pelts you offered, they would not trade one of their muskets for them. I have seen others try.'

Walks Straight knew this was so. 'Someday I will have one.'

'Do nothing foolish, my son.' Winter Swan looked at him worriedly.

It was useless to argue, he realized. A woman did not feel the things in her heart that he did. 'No,' he said at last.

His hunter's eye was drawn to the sea. A pair of sails broke the flatness of the horizon. Walks Straight stiffened, resenting the presence of yet another Cossack boat in his waters. He watched the ship turn into the bay.

'More come. When will they stop?' he wondered.

Others in the village observed the shitik sailing into the bay. Curiosity and the custom of greeting visitors to the island drew Cossack and Aleut alike to the beach. The cormorant skins and sea urchins were set aside for the time being as Tasha hurried ahead while Walks Straight hung back with his mother and the old, slow-moving Weaver Woman.

Tasha watched the sails come down and saw the splash of an anchor being dropped into the water. Soon a yawl was lowered into the water and several Cossacks climbed into it and rowed toward shore. The man seated at the prow looked vaguely familiar to Tasha. She stared intently at him as the boat drew nearer to the beach. There was something about his angular features and the beardless, slanted jaw-line that jogged her memory, but the silver wings in his brown hair were distinctive, and she couldn't recall having seen a man with hair like that before.

When the boat nosed into shallow water, two Cossacks hopped out to haul it onto the sand with the aid of two Aleuts. People kept getting in her way, making it difficult for Tasha to have a clear look at the man. He stood up, briefly towering over the heads of others, and Tasha noticed his eyes – blue like the sky.

'Look!' she cried and moved quickly through the crowd to her mother's side. 'Look who it is! Andrei Tolstykh. He comes back!'

Barely able to contain her excitement, she hurried forward and worked through the crowd until she reached the inner circle of on-lookers. Except for the silver-gray of a gull's wings in his hair, Andrei Tolstykh had changed little in the five summers since she'd last seen him. His build was tall and lean, not nearly as muscled as an Aleut's. He dressed differently. Instead of the mantles, hooded hats, and trousers of the other Cossack hunters, he wore a black square-tailed coat that buttoned at the waist and tight-fitting knee breeches that showed the muscles in his legs. There was a quiet vigor about him, and a calmness – as now when he stepped forward to greet the villagers.

'Where is your chief?' he inquired in Aleut.

'He died two summers ago,' Many Whiskers replied. 'I am Many Whiskers, the headman of the village now.'

Tolstykh switched to the Cossack tongue. 'He was a good friend to me. I regret to hear that he is no longer with us. Five years ago he gave me permission to hunt on Attu. We knew peace together.'

'I remember you, Andrei Tolstykh.' Many Whiskers nodded his head. 'You lived in peace with us and traded fairly for our skins.'

'I have come again to your island to seek permission to hunt so that we may live together once again in peace and fellowship.'

Many Whiskers slowly shook his head. 'I cannot give you permission to hunt. Already there are three boats of Cossacks on Attu. We have room for no more. You must go to another island.'

Tasha reacted with dismay to the pronouncement. She knew that Walks Straight had often complained how much more difficult it had become to find and kill the dwindling number of sea otter. More hunters would mean there would be even more competition. Yet knowing it didn't lessen her disappointment that Many Whiskers was sending away the Cossack who had once been so kind to her.

Although Andrei Tolstykh appealed the decision, Many Whiskers remained adamant. 'Would you permit us to anchor in your bay for several days?' Andrei then asked. 'My men are tired after our long sea voyage and are in need of rest. Our supply of food and fresh water is low. If we are to continue to another island, we will need to replenish them.'

'You may stay, and you may gather food. But you are not permitted to hunt,' Many Whiskers stressed.

'Please accept these gifts I have brought for you as a token of my good will.' Andrei signaled to his men to bring the presents forward.

In addition to the large cast-iron kettle and boots of goatskin for Many Whiskers, there were enough cloth for each Aleut to have two shirts, fifteen pounds of rye flour, needles, four heavy jackets, warm mittens for winter and light gloves for summer, and a sash for every man in the village.

Such generosity from the Cossacks was uncommon. When a request was refused, the gifts were usually taken back. Many Whiskers was moved by the gesture. Tasha wished he could send one of the other vessels away and allow Andrei Tolstykh to stay, but permission had already been granted to the others and couldn't be rescinded.

'I regret that I don't speak your Aleut language very well. Unfortunately none of my men do either. Since we will be journeying to a new island where the natives will not know our language either, I will need Aleut interpreters. Perhaps you could allow two or three of your villagers to accompany us and translate our words to your neighbors.'

'I will consider your request,' Many Whiskers replied cautiously.

'We want the natives to know we come in peace – to trade and hunt with them. Interpreters would assist us greatly.' Andrei Tolstykh inclined his head. 'I will await your answer. In the meantime I will return to my vessel and send some of my men back for water.'

'I invite you to come to my barabara so we may celebrate the return of Andrei Tolstykh.' The extension of hospitality was the obligation of the village headman. 'I will have my women prepare food. There will be dancing and singing.'

'I am honored.' He bowed slightly at the waist.

As Many Whiskers turned to escort Andrei Tolstykh to the communal family dwelling, Winter Swan spoke near Tasha's shoulder. 'Come. We have much to do.'

'I wish to speak with him,' she replied earnestly.

Tasha was gone before her mother could object. She hurried quickly to place herself in Tolstykh's path. She waited for him to notice her. When he did, Tasha bobbed a curtsy the way she'd been taught.

'Welcome to Attu, Andrei Tolstykh.'

Stunned by this strikingly beautiful and unusual native woman, Andrei Nikolaivich Tolstykh stopped to stare. Seeing those round black eyes and that slender face, he concluded she must be a Creole. It was a full second before he realized she had addressed him in Russian. He looked again at the native parka of sealskin fur trimmed with otter, her bare feet, and the jet-black hair pulled into a bun native-style. She was definitely a half-breed, obviously taking the best from both races, Andrei decided.

'Do you not remember me?' she said anxiously. Frowning, he stared at her face again. 'I am Tasha.' She reached inside the collar of her parka and lifted out a necklace with a silver cross of the Orthodox design. 'You gave this to me.'

'Tasha,' he repeated incredulously. This stunning creature was the scrawny, big-eyed girl who had been one of his hostages five years ago. 'You have grown so much I didn't recognize you. You are a lovely woman.'

He marveled at the transformation. Her looks had always been unusual and vaguely arresting, with her incomparable skin and deep black hair and eyes. Andrei noticed how expressive her eyes were, presently betraying an eagerness that her face didn't show.

'I am pleased you remember me.'

'How could anyone forget you, Tasha?' The longer he looked at her, the more he asked himself that question. There was something exotic about her almond-shaped eyes and the high cheek-bones. No man could look at her without being aroused by that blend of the savage and the civilized. He was past forty, but he was not so old that he didn't feel a stirring of lust. 'How old are you now, Tasha? Fifteen?'

'Yes.'

'You must have a husband.'

'No. There are few Aleut men on the island I can marry. And the men from neighboring islands seldom come here to visit since the Cossacks are here all the time.'

'You will find yourself a husband,' Andrei stated confidently.

She started to back away. 'I must go now. There are many preparations to make for the celebration.'

He watched her glide swiftly toward the village, then reluctantly turned to rejoin the village chief. He had counted on the previous good will he'd established with the islanders on Attu to facilitate this stay. Now he had to journey into new territory. He knew how valuable it was to have the cooperation of the natives. Somehow he had to persuade this chief to give him Aleut interpreters for hostages, to help insure his safety and the success of his expedition.

The day after the celebration, Tasha sat on the lee side of the barabara, sheltered from the wind, and worked at the tiny basket she was weaving, a basket so small it would fit into the palm of her hand. Although Weaver Woman's aged fingers had lost their dexterity for such fine work, she directed Tasha's hands.

Long blades of rye grass lay in a shallow basket. Each had been carefully dried to achieve the desired shade, the amount of time exposed to the sun varying, depending on the darkness or lightness sought. Tasha selected one from the loose pile. With fingernails grown long especially for that purpose, she carefully split the grass blade lengthwise into a narrow strand, almost as fine as a thread. As she dampened the grass to make it pliable, she glanced at her mother, who was busy sewing the cormorant skins together to make a parka.

'I like Andrei Tolstykh. He is a good man,' she said.

'You are a foolish woman!' The explosive denunciation came from Walks Straight. He rose to his feet, abandoning his scanning post on the curving slope of the barabara.

Tasha started to justify her statement, then looked at her Aleut brother. He was still nursing the wounds to his pride from his last encounter with the Cossacks. His mind was set against them. It was hopeless to argue, but she had her own opinions. Returning her attention to the basket, she announced firmly, 'I wish that Many Whiskers had given Andrei Tolstykh permission to hunt.'

'I wish he would send all the boats away, make all the Cossacks leave,' her brother retorted and strode toward the beach.

His attitude troubled Tasha and prompted her to question her own, but it was difficult to hate as Walks Straight did when she hadn't suffered any such injury. She knew the Cossacks had wronged her brother and others, yet, when she thought of Andrei Tolstykh, she knew he would not commit such an injustice.

'Your legs are young, Tasha,' Weaver Woman said in a voice

raspy with age. 'Fetch my pumice abrader. This skin is still rough.'

With knobby fingers, she felt of the inner skin of the cormorant, but her hand paused in its investigation as she watched the young girl lay the unfinished basket aside, the long vertical strands of the cream-colored grass dangling like a heavy fringe. Her attention remained on Tasha until she was well away from their worksite, then she shifted it to Winter Swan. Her hands ached. Every day she had to stick the needles in the special points on her body to take away the pain.

'I am an old woman. My eyes have seen many things,' Weaver Woman declared. 'When I look at your son and your daughter, I see trouble coming . . . much trouble.'

Winter Swan hesitated before pushing the threaded needle through the cormorant skin. 'Why do you say that?'

'There is anger in your son's heart toward the Cossack.'

'Walks Straight will not act foolishly. He knows they are too many and too strong.'

'He is a young man. He does not like to be made to look foolish and stupid.' Weaver Woman slowly shook her head. 'He will challenge the Cossacks.'

Winter Swan resisted the idea with an answering shake of her head. 'He knows they will kill him.'

'Young men do not think of dying. It is only the old who know that death is always close.' She watched Winter Swan's face; it told her she wished to speak of this no more – and that her talk had aroused worried thoughts. Respecting her wish, Weaver Woman pursued another course. 'You have eyes, Winter Swan. You have seen the way the Cossacks look at your daughter. It is different from the way they look at the rest of their women. It is the roundness of her eyes, I think. They have not lain with her yet. But soon they will take her to their barabara and make her live with them.'

'The Cossacks always take women.' It was only because she had grown old that none wanted her now. She knew the pain of the experience and did not want it for her daughter. It hurt her to think of it. 'There is nothing we can do.'

'The Blue-Eyed One has been fair to the Aleut. He does not cheat us. He does not take baidars or let his men have us make parkas without paying for them. He has treated well the Aleuts who have stayed with him to learn the Cossack language.'

'That is true.' Winter Swan resumed her stitching of the skins.

'I heard him ask Many Whiskers to send Aleuts with him on his boat to speak for him at the other islands. It would be best if Tasha and Walks Straight went with him. Both can speak the Cossack tongue.'

'Both?' Winter Swan could not hide the shock and dismay she felt at the suggestion. She wanted her children at her side, even though they were grown. Someday Tasha would go with her husband to the village of his family, but that was not yet. 'No.'

'It is best,' Weaver Woman insisted. 'If Walks Straight is treated fairly, his anger will not be so great. If he is to find a wife, he will need to visit the villages of other islands.'

The logic defeated Winter Swan. 'It may be well for Walks Straight, but Tasha need not go.'

'Search your heart. Ask yourself which is best. If Strong Man lived, what would he counsel?'

'It is not my decision to make.' Winter Swan took refuge in that. 'Many Whiskers must decide whether to send any from our village with the Blue-Eyed One, and who shall go.'

'He is now your husband. You can speak to him about this. We have made many sacrifices for the sake of peace. This time you may choose which sacrifice to make.' Weaver Woman examined the cormorant skin again, then returned it to the pile to be used in the parka. 'This is smooth enough for a Cossack.' Fighting her age-stiffened joints, she pushed to her feet. 'My body says it is tired and needs rest.'

With laboring steps, she shuffled up the barabara's mound to the roof entrance, passing Tasha on the way. Soon she would no longer be able to negotiate the notched log on her own; instead, she would have to ride on the back of her son Many Whiskers. Once the task of carrying her would have fallen to her anaaqisagh, Little Spear, but long ago he had left with the first Cossacks, never to return to Attu. Nearly every time a Cossack boat left these waters, one, two, or three Attuans were on board, mostly children born to the women with whom the Cossacks had lain during their stay on the island. Weaver Woman knew her daughter-in-law had been fortunate to have her children beside her these many summers. Now it was time to let them go.

More than a week had passed since Andrei Nikolaivich Tolstykh had anchored his vessel, the *Andreian i Natalia*, in the bay. Much

99

of the time he spent studying the chart of these islands drawn by Admiral Nagaiev from the journals of Bering and Chirikov. A merchant by trade, Andrei had a strong gambling streak in him. The profits to be made from ventures to these islands were so great they more than compensated for the risks involved crossing the stormy sea. Yet he'd made his fortune three times over and still he came – a gambler needing to beat the odds one more time.

In retrospect, Andrei was almost glad the chief had denied him permission to hunt on Attu. These last few days he'd spoken with several Cossacks on the island and some of the natives. Although the sea otter continued to populate the waters off Attu, their numbers had dwindled and they had become more wary, diving at the first glimpse of a boat. The longer he looked at the charts of the island chain, the stronger grew his desire for the unknown. Initially, he had been forced to look eastward. Now he did so with eagerness, gleaning every bit of information he could from the natives about the islands to the east. These Aleuts were inveterate sea travelers, paddling long distances in their bidarkas to visit or trade with other island villages in the more than thousand-mile-long archipelago. Unless a native personally had been to a place, he professed no knowledge of it, never relating hearsay – a trait that proved very frustrating for Andrei.

Aware that his departure from Attu could not be delayed much longer, Andrei went ashore to seek out Many Whiskers and speak to him again on the matter of interpreters. The relationship that existed among the islanders made hostages imperative. They might be his one hope if he encountered hostile natives to the east, as well as being useful as interpreters.

As he approached the chief's barabara, Andrei noticed the girl walking through the sun-splashed meadow purpled with blossoming lupine. Her head was held high, her face upturned to the rare sun. Andrei halted to stare at the Creole woman child. Carefree, she swung a basket at her side, its rhythmic motion matching her long, easy strides.

The colorful silk scarf he had intended to give her as a present was tucked inside his jacket. He'd been carrying it with him for several days now, planning to give it to her each time he came ashore, but the more pressing matters of his expedition had always sidetracked him. Now he found himself wondering how he could have let her slip his mind.

He motioned for the two promyshleniki accompanying him to

remain where they were and walked alone to meet her. He watched her expression light up when she saw him – and the eagerness in her eyes that seemed almost bold. It flattered him that she should show a liking for his company. Briefly he regretted that she was a woman. A man would have more influence on the chief should Andrei gain his trust and persuade him to speak on his behalf. But her presence quickly dominated his thoughts.

'Good morning, Tasha.' He gazed at those round, slanted eyes, black as onyx.

'Good morning, Commander Tolstykh.' She made another small curtsy. She did it so naturally that it didn't appear out of character despite her native garb.

His glance shifted to the basket in her hand. 'I see you have been picking berries.'

'They are very plentiful this summer. Would you like some?'

'No. Thank you.' He remembered the scarf and reached inside his jacket. 'I have something for you, though.' The scarf was made of China silk in a vivid crimson. As he handed her the square of folded material, the slick silk worked free of its fold and slithered out of his grasp. Tasha caught the strip of cloth. A look of wonder stole over her face.

'It is beautiful.' She set her basket on the ground to feel the material with both hands. 'What is this cloth that is smooth as a feather?'

'It's called silk. It comes from China.' Andrei knew the value of the China trade. The only commodity Russia had that interested China was the fur of the sea otter, and their demand for it exceeded Russia's ability to supply it, making the pelts so much more valuable. And the Chinese didn't care whether the pelt was prime, as they had perfected some technique to dye it and retain its natural look. One of their treated furs looked no different from the very best quality pelt. A single pelt on the China frontier brought as much as three hundred gold rubles. Silk, to Andrei, represented China, and China trade meant sea otter pelts worth more than their weight in gold.

'Silk,' she murmured and touched it to her cheek. The vivid red against the black of her hair and the ivory of her skin made a striking picture.

'Here.' Andrei took the scarf from her hands and draped it over her head, then crossed the trailing ends to cover her shoulders. The transformation was remarkable. He seemed to be

101

looking at the bust of a Russian woman with a tantalizingly foreign allure. He was slow to let go of the scarf and bring his hands to his side again.

'This is how it is worn?' she asked.

'Yes.' Andrei continued to stare, stirred by her.

'Are you going to the village?'

'Yes. I need to speak with your chief.'

'I will walk with you.' She removed the scarf and attempted to fold the slippery material into a small square. After several tries, she succeeded, then picked up her basket of ripe berries.

As they started toward the barabara, Andrei observed Many Whiskers waiting to greet him. He guessed the chief had been told that he had come ashore to see him. It was vital that he convince the Aleut to let him take some of his people with him. Conscious of the pad of bare feet walking beside him, Andrei turned his head slightly to look at the girl. Even though his thoughts were on the meeting to come, her profile made its impact on his senses. There was a moment when he knew a man could lose himself in her, then his thoughts took a different turn. Earlier he had dismissed her usefulness. Now Andrei reconsidered.

'Tasha, I have to talk to your chief on an important matter. I want to be certain my words are clear to him. Will you speak for me?' Andrei smiled.

'I would be happy to translate for you,' she agreed. Her dark eyes studied him keenly. 'You wish to speak to Many Whiskers about having someone from our village accompany you to the other islands and translate for you.'

'You know about my request?' Andrei was faintly surprised.

'I have heard Many Whiskers seek the counsel of my mother and others about this.'

He frowned curiously. 'Why would he consult your mother?'

'Before she became Many Whiskers' second wife, my mother, Winter Swan, was the wife to Strong Man, the brother of Many Whiskers. He had great physical and spiritual powers. I think Many Whiskers wished to know from my mother how Strong Man would have felt on this matter. He had great respect for Strong Man's wisdom of such things.'

'What did your mother tell him?' Andrei had not known she was a member of the chief's family, but he had no qualms about soliciting information from her.

'I do not know.'

'What do you think she said?' He saw her reluctance to speculate on something she did not know and pressed for an answer. 'It is important, Tasha, or I wouldn't ask. I must have the chief's help in this so that I can hunt and trade with other islanders in peace and friendship.'

She hesitated a moment. 'The storytellers say Strong Man believed we should live in peace with the Cossacks.'

'He was a wise man.' A feeling of satisfaction took the edge off his tension. The winds seemed to be blowing his way. He smiled warmly at Tasha, realizing that she could be valuable in his meeting with the chief.

His men fell in behind them as they approached the chief. After greeting the mustached Aleut, Andrei explained the reason for Tasha's presence at his side, concerned that Many Whiskers might object to the inclusion of a woman in their talks, but the chief nodded his approval.

'Soon my vessel will be sailing from your bay to the islands in the east. You are an important chief on Attu. Your name is spoken with respect on other islands.' Andrei had no idea whether that was true or not, but a little flattery never hurt. He waited until Tasha had finished her translation, then continued. 'I wish to carry your greetings when I visit the villages to the east, so they will know we lived together in peace and traded fairly with one another.'

Andrei knew the chief understood much of what he said in Russian, but he listened patiently to Tasha's translation of it. His command of Aleut was limited, but Andrei detected a few words of embellishment that Tasha added and realized he had an ally.

'The name of Andrei Nikolaivich Tolstykh is also known in the islands as one who does not cheat the Aleuts.' Tasha provided a Russian translation of the chief's response, much of which he had understood. 'That cannot be said of many of the Cossacks who come to hunt and trade on our island.'

Andrei had previously encountered the ill will created by other Russians out of greed. 'It is important for the Aleuts on the islands I visit, to know that I come in peace and friendship. If Many Whiskers will consent to sending interpreters from his village with me, they can not only translate my words for me, but they can also speak from their own knowledge of my fairness in trading and my desire for peace with the Aleuts.'

'I have come to a decision on this.' Tasha translated Many

Whiskers' response, then paused to await the rest of it. Andrei schooled himself not to react, no matter which way it went. 'He has chosen my brother, Walks Straight, to accompany you.' He was both relieved and disappointed by the decision. One was better than none, yet he preferred to have a minimum of two Aleuts with him. 'He regrets that he cannot spare more hunters to go with you.'

'Tell him I understand.'

'Many Whiskers says that my brother is a good hunter and can help you find the islands where the sea otter are plentiful. And my brother understands the words of your tongue much better than Many Whiskers does.' She ceased a verbatim translation of the explanation. 'It is also known that he does not like Cossacks. For him to speak in favor of you will carry much weight.'

Unconsciously, Andrei nodded approval, admiring the shrewd reasoning behind the choice. As the chief continued to speak, Andrei missed what he said and had to wait for Tasha to relay it to him.

'Many Whiskers says also that you will need a woman to cook and sew for you, and the women in the eastern islands do not know how to prepare the food the way the Cossacks like it.' She suddenly appeared stunned. Instead of concentrating on the chief as she had been doing, she turned to him, her dark eyes wide with surprise. 'He says he knows your Cossack wife did not come with you . . . that she stayed in your land across the waters. Since you will have need of one . . . he offers me as your second wife. As a token of his friendship. He asks no gifts in return.'

Equally stunned, Andrei stared at Tasha. The chief had to know that he was not averse to the company of a native woman in his bed. During his previous visit to the island, he had obtained one for a few presents to her family. By Aleut custom, she had been his wife. They had no marriage ceremony as such. The contract was sealed by the presenting of gifts to the woman's parents. Andrei also knew that to refuse the chief's generosity in this case would be tantamount to an insult. He was thankful that the chief continued to speak, allowing him more time to think.

'He says that I make fine parkas and know how to cook food the Cossack way. He says also that I can be of use to you in speaking your words to the villagers in the eastern islands. He knows that you will treat me well and be a good husband.' She blushed slightly. 'He also says you will find the women of Attu are much more pleasing to the eye than the women on other islands.'

Pleasing to the eye seemed an understatement to Andrei as he gazed at Tasha. With difficulty, he refocused his attention on the chief, trying not to think of the long months – and long nights – ahead.

'Tell your chief that I am overwhelmed by his generosity – and very pleased. He does me great honor and I accept his wise decision. Please inform him that I wish to sail with tomorrow's tide.'

10

Overhead, mewling seabirds wheeled, their ivory wings flashing white against a backdrop of gray clouds. Leaping and diving, a porpoise swam alongside the vessel's bow as though escorting it out of the bay. A steady wind bellied the sails. Tasha turned her face into the wind and gazed at the wide stretch of sand, the bidarkas lined up on the shore. From this distance, the outline of her village was barely discernible and then only because she knew where to look.

Her heart ached to be leaving all that was familiar to her – the island, her home, and family – her mother and old Weaver Woman most of all. But her regret wasn't equal to the excitement she felt. Hunters frequently traveled to other islands to trade or visit, but women seldom went unless the whole family, sometimes the whole village, made the journey. Tasha hadn't been off the island since she was a little girl. Then it had been a trip to nearby Agattu to visit her mother's family. Now, she was on her way to some unknown destination. Andrei Tolstykh, her new husband, had indicated to Many Whiskers that it might be as many as two summers before he returned to Attu.

Turning, she asked her brother, 'Where will we go?'

'I have told the Cossack about Adak and the small islands clustered around it where the sea otter live in large numbers.' The reluctance with which he had imparted the information was evident in the flat tone of his voice. Walks Straight did not share Tasha's enthusiasm for this adventure.

'The hunting will be good there.'

'If the villages give him permission to hunt in their territory,' added Walks Straight.

'They will. He will give them gifts in exchange, and we will tell them that he seeks to trade with them and live in peace.' She saw the skepticism in his look. 'You know this is true. He is not like the others.'

'No,' he conceded grudgingly. 'But he is a Cossack. Don't trust him too much.'

Lately when he looked at his sister, vague memories stirred of another time when the Scar-Eyed One had made his mother cry. Now Tolstykh was her husband. He didn't want his sister hurt, yet he felt powerless to prevent it. And he hated the Cossacks for making him feel this way. He had agreed to accompany the smooth-faced commander partly to honor the wishes of Many Whiskers and his mother, but mainly he hoped that by leading the Cossacks to new hunting grounds, they would all eventually leave his home island.

Walks Straight could tell by the look in Tasha's big dark eyes that she paid little heed to his warning. She never looked beyond the sky color of the Cossack's eyes to see the selfish greed. Before the Cossacks came, the Aleuts never killed just to take an animal's skin. Now they killed the otter, took its fur, and threw its body to the sharks. It was not their way, and the Cossacks were to blame.

But his sister was a woman. She couldn't understand that the life of a hunter was tied to that of his prey. Still he tried. 'To the Cossack, an Aleut is like the sea otter. When they have taken what they want from him, they will throw the rest away.'

The waves crested to six feet in the heavy-running sea. When the vessel breasted the first of them and it broke across the bow, Tasha felt a rush of exhilaration. The journey had begun. She stood at the rail watching the roll of the sea and listening to the straining groans of the boat's timbers as it slammed into another wave.

Within an hour, her head was pounding dully. The constant pitching of the vessel made the horizon go up and down with sickening regularity. The undulating motion made her stomach churn. She started feeling hot, and perspiration coated her skin. Moving closer to the bow, she let the sea spray cool her face, but it didn't ease the rising pressure in her stomach. Her knees felt strangely weak.

It slowly came to her that she was getting seasick. The symptoms she had were the ones Weaver Woman had described when she told about two Aleut hunters on Attu who suffered from this malady. Tasha struggled to control her growing queasiness and tried to fix her gaze on some object that didn't move, but her senses constantly told her of the heaving motion of the deck.

They didn't alert her, however, to the sound of approaching footsteps.

Once they were clear of the offshore reefs and well out to sea, Andrei ordered his mate to set an easterly course and relaxed his vigilance. He knew the dangers of this ocean, the quick onset of its fogs, high winds, and storms; and he took his time of ease whenever it came. As he left the mate at the helm, Andrei noticed Tasha standing at the bow, poised like a figurehead, her face lifted to the spray. The sight awakened fires in him that had long lain dormant. He walked to the bow.

'The winds favor us.' At the sound of his voice, she swung around. Andrei had a brief glimpse of the pallor of her face and the hugeness of her eyes.

A second later, she turned back and reached for the rail, to lean over the side. Thinking that she intended to throw herself overboard, Andrei grabbed for her. As his hands caught her shoulders, he felt the convulsive heave of her body and heard the retching sound she made. The vomiting spasms came one after the other until she finally sagged against the rail, too weak to support herself.

His hands continued to steady her against the pitching and rolling of the vessel. Reaching inside his heavy coat, he took out his kerchief and wiped the spittle from the corners of her mouth and chin. She was drenched with sweat, but her skin felt clammy to the touch. She murmured some sound of gratitude, the words unintelligible.

A pair of callus-toughened feet entered his side vision, sticking out from the length of an inverted bird-skin parka, the red-ocher-dyed skin to the outside. Andrei looked up at Walks Straight and met the accusing glare of his eyes.

'She is seasick,' he announced.

The Aleut's glance swept Tasha's pale face as if to confirm it, then he grunted something and walked off, apparently indifferent to her illness. But her weakened state aroused Andrei's protective male instincts.

He motioned to one of the promyshleniki on deck to come help him, then said to Tasha, 'We will take you below where you can lie down.' Her head moved, but he wasn't sure it was an acknowledgment.

The continuous rise and fall of the vessel made it difficult to keep their balance as Andrei and the promyshlenik lifted Tasha to her feet. She made a feeble attempt to help them, but the effort was almost more of a hindrance. She moaned softly as they worked their way across the lurching deck to the hatchway, her slack body leaning into Andrei.

The hatchway wasn't wide enough for three. Andrei nodded a dismissal to the Russian hunter. 'I will take her from here.' He half scooped her limp body into his arms and carried her down the steps.

Pausing outside his cabin, he kicked the door open and maneuvered them inside his quarters. Her head lolled against his jaw, the texture of her hair silken against his skin. He glanced down at her as she moaned again, then carried her to his bunk and set her down.

Andrei knew that he'd been wanting her in his bed, but this wasn't the circumstance he'd had in mind. Sweat beaded on her forehead and above her lips as she sat on the side of the bunk barely able to hold herself upright. Andrei glanced at the long fur parka she wore, remarkably unstained by vomit.

'Let's take this off,' he muttered, mainly to himself, since he doubted she was in any condition to understand him.

After some difficulty, he managed to get it over her hips. After that it was easy to pull it over her head. Briefly he was treated to the sight of her nude body, the young upward thrust of her breasts. She swayed without his support, and he reached out to steady her, feeling the firmness of her flesh, a sensation he hadn't enjoyed in some time. His wife's body had long been flaccid, and there were few whores in Siberia who were not fat or infected or starving bags of bones. Siberia was a place where young women quickly became old. A rich man like himself had his choice, but the pickings were slim.

A groan came from Tasha's throat. She looked at him, her eyes appearing as round as saucers. Suddenly she clamped a hand over her mouth. Reacting swiftly, Andrei grabbed the chamber pot and lifted its lid in time to catch the spewed vomit.

When she had finished, he laid her down on the bunk and reluctantly covered her naked body with a blanket. He moved away to moisten a cloth with water from the container in his cabin, then came back to the bunk to wipe her damp face. She lay motionless with her eyes closed, the fringe of black lashes making long shadows on her pale skin. Andrei noticed she was lying on the knot of her hair and gently reached beneath her head to

109

loosen the confining bun. He fanned it away from her face, letting the smooth strands slide through his fingers.

'I feel so sick,' she murmured weakly.

'I know you do.' Andrei folded the damp cloth and laid it across her brow.

Rising, he looked at her a moment, then walked over to the table where his charts of the island chain were spread out. He studied them again, searching to see if there was another cluster of islands besides the one he'd found that matched the description Walks Straight had given him.

Several more times she threw up, until there was nothing left in her stomach except bile. Eventually exhaustion claimed her and she fell asleep. Andrei remained in the cabin a while longer, then went topside to check on their course. He stayed on deck only a short time, drawn back to his quarters by the thought of Tasha lying in his bunk.

Come evening, she was racked by dry heaves. Andrei had some broth prepared for her and fed her a spoonful every few minutes. Some of it eventually came up. It wasn't compassion or pity that kept him in the cabin. Andrei guessed it was the opportunity to indulge in his growing fascination for this Creole – to stare for as long as he liked at the curve of her cheekbone or the nipple of an exposed breast, and to imagine whatever he chose.

A knock sounded on his cabin door. 'Yes, what is it?' Andrei demanded.

'It's fog, sir, thick as curdled cream.'

'I'll be right there.'

Andrei waited for the footsteps to retreat, then walked over to the bunk and tucked the blanket around Tasha once more. She moaned softly in her sleep. He stroked her cheek with his finger, her skin so smooth and cool to his touch. She stirred. Reluctantly he turned and left the cabin.

On the deck, a dense fog swathed the vessel, obscuring the outline of the bow and hiding the top of the masts. Visibility was reduced to a few yards. An eerie stillness heightened every sound. The clump of his boots rang hollowly on the slick deck as Andrei moved to the helm. Wisps of mist swirled around him, disturbed by his passing, while water dripped from the sails. Only the motion of the deck and the slap of the waves against the wooden hull confirmed they were still at sea and not drifting on some ghostly cloud.

110

The compass indicated the vessel was maintaining its easterly heading, but it was impossible to see what was ahead of them. According to his charts, all islands were supposed to be to the south of their present course, but the map details were sketchy at best. Andrei did not need to warn any of the men to be alert for the crash of breakers or the presence of kelp beds that would mean they were near land. The blinding fog made them all vigilant.

It was well into the early hours of the morning before Andrei returned to his cabin, satisfied his vessel was in no immediate danger. Tasha lay draped along the side of the bunk, uncovered from the waist up. The sight of her body aroused a surge of energy that overcame his tiredness. But however great the temptation to crawl into the bunk with her, the smell of vomit was a sufficient deterrent.

Finding her nudity too much of a temptation to resist, Andrei took one of his cotton shirts from his sea chest and slipped it on her. Her lashes fluttered open once when he lifted her and pushed an arm through a sleeve. After fastening some of the buttons, he let his hand cup the jutting roundness of a breast, feeling the way it filled his palm. She moaned, turning her head to the side. Grimly he recognized that the low sound came from her sickness, not from pleasure.

He pushed to his feet and gathered up the extra blanket on the bunk, then walked to the lamp swaying from a cross beam. He turned down the wick, allowing only a small flame to throw off a dim glow. The lurking shadows immediately closed in. Wrapped in the blanket, he sprawled in the chair, letting the dipping swing of the boat rock him. Sleep was a long time coming as he stared at the female in his bunk – his native bride.

For an entire week, Andrei spent the bulk of his time in the cabin, where Tasha alternated between bouts of violent seasickness and a nauseated stupor. She had lucid times when she objected to being spoon-fed the broth or gruel he'd had prepared for her and tried to do it herself, but she hadn't the strength. Twice he bathed her, the motion of his hand invariably becoming a caress.

Several times her Aleut half brother entered the cabin unannounced to see how she was. Andrei always detected an element of distrust in the young man's eyes, but the Aleut never said anything, simply lingered a few minutes and then left. There was no doubt in Andrei's mind that Walks Straight didn't like Russians. Even without the chief's saying so, he would have known it. The native hunter had held himself aloof from the whole company during the voyage thus far. Sometimes Andrei wondered how much he could trust him, but it was plain that the Aleut thought a great deal of his half sister. As long as Andrei had her, he had a hold over him.

While the water heated in the brass samovar, Andrei added the loose leaves of China tea to the small pot. Holding the teapot under the spigot at the urn's base, he turned the handle. Nearly boiling water plunged over the tea leaves in the bottom of the pot, releasing their piquant aroma. It was a welcome smell in a cabin that reeked of sickness. Andrei let the tea steep for a few minutes, then poured it into two glasses in metal holders. He carried one to the bunk where Tasha sat propped against the bulkhead and gave it to her. The cuffs of his cotton shirt were rolled back to free her hands. They slipped further down her forearms as she lifted the glass to her lips with both hands. She took a small sip, then weakly lowered the glass to rest it on her lap.

'I think I'm feeling better,' she said, but her voice lacked strength.

He smiled absently, aware that she had been keeping down more fluids these last two days. 'Would you like to go up on deck after you finish your tea and get some fresh air?'

'Yes, I would.'

He carried her topside, swaddled in a blanket, and settled her on a keg in a sheltered corner of the deck where the wind couldn't reach her. His attitude toward her was neither gentle nor solicitous; rather it was possessive, leaving the men in little doubt that their commander had claimed her for himself alone.

Breathing in deeply, Tasha filled her lungs with the sweet, fresh air. The motion of the shitik didn't seem to bother her nearly as much. She hoped fervently that she had finally become accustomed to it. She never wanted to be that sick again. It shamed her to think how much trouble she had been to Andrei, yet she was warmed, too, by the memory of the countless times she'd opened her eyes and found him there watching over her.

Her eyes sought him out among the hunters on deck. She decided she liked his craggy profile as much as she liked his eyes. There was strength and determination in it, along with a canny intelligence. Beneath the blanket, she touched the shirt of his she wore. She had gotten used to the feel of its material against her skin and the protection it offered from the scratchy blanket. He had been good to her. Even Walks Straight had to acknowledge that. She saw her brother standing alone at the rail, scanning the sea. She realized he would never make friends with the Cossacks, not even with her new husband.

The outing quickly tired her. The least effort seemed to exhaust her. It frightened her to realize how weak she had become, when she'd always been so strong. She sagged against the hatchway's bulk-head and shut her eyes to rest a moment. A hand touched her shoulder. Tasha looked up to find Andrei bending over her.

'Do you feel all right?'

'I am tired,' she admitted.

He said no more and picked her up, carried her back to his cabin below deck and set her down on the bunk. Tasha rolled onto her side and fell asleep almost as soon as the door swung shut behind him.

The following afternoon, Tasha lay in the bunk. Her stomach felt comfortably full from the small bowl of soup she'd eaten. Andrei had assured her that food and rest were what she needed to get her strength back. Yet now that she was feeling better, the idleness made her restless.

She heard a sudden commotion on deck – muffled shouts and the clumping of boots. She strained to catch the cause of the excitement but she could only understand snatches of words. The cabin door swung open and her brother stepped soundlessly into the room.

'What is happening? Have they seen a whale?' Nothing else in her village would have created such a stir.

'They have sighted the islands. The tall, pronged peak of Adak stands clear of the clouds. The boat heads for it now.'

'Then we have arrived,' Tasha said.

'Soon they will see how good the hunting is here and they will know I did not lie.'

She looked at her brother. 'Did they think you had?'

'I heard some of them wonder if I was guiding them into the middle of the sea. One of them cut a hole in my bidarka so I could not escape in it,' he answered bitterly.

'Is it a big hole?' Without his bidarka, a hunter was powerless.

'It crosses almost two skins.'

'I will patch it for you,' Tasha promised, then asked, 'Does Andrei know of this?'

'It would do no good. The Cossacks claim something fell on it, but I know the way a hide looks when a knife cuts it.' His resentment went deep, and this incident was like sea water on an open wound. Tasha understood, too, that Walks Straight was saying this to warn her. 'You are feeling better?' he asked at last.

'Yes.' She nodded.

'Good.' His gaze lingered on her another minute, then he turned and walked out of the cabin.

Alone again, Tasha listened to the waning flurry of activity on the deck overhead. With the island in sight, Andrei would soon have need of her to speak to the villagers for him. She swung her legs over the side of the bunk and stood up to test her strength. She wobbled uncertainly for an instant, but they held her. Walking slowly, Tasha crossed the cabin to the table and stopped there to lean against it, fighting the light-headed feeling. She heard footsteps approaching the cabin and recognized them as Andrei's. The door swung open as she turned toward it, keeping a hand braced on the table for balance.

'Tasha –' The sight of the empty bunk stopped him in midstride. With a jerk of his head, he looked around and saw her standing by the table. The lines of his forehead gathered into a frown. 'Tasha, what are you doing up?'

'I had to see if I could walk by myself. I wouldn't be much help to you lying down.'

The tails of his shirt hung down to her thighs, leaving a long expanse of bare leg exposed to his view. Andrei noticed the barely perceptible buckling of her knees and realized she was less steady than she appeared. He moved quickly to her and girdled her waist with his hands, catching up the loose material of his shirt. Her hands immediately grasped for the support of his upper arms as she swayed into him.

'From now on, Tasha, let me decide how best you can help me.' Until this minute, Andrei hadn't realized how tall she was. She stood eye-level to his chin. When he tipped his head down, it brought her face closer still. He was conscious of the bareness of her skin beneath his shirt and the firm feel of her flesh.

Too many times these last days he'd held her naked limp body and wished for her to be alive in his arms. Too many times his hands had caressed her and received no response. Now her hands

114

were clutching him, never mind that it was out of weakness. His gaze shifted to the full curve of her lips, parted slightly.

The burning look in his eyes was one Tasha had seen before when a man desired to lie with a woman. It heated her skin and made her feel warm all over. The band of his arm circled her back and pulled her against him. She was instantly conscious of his thighs and torso.

She knew about this touching of the mouths the Cossacks called kissing. Curiosity held her motionless when he lowered his head and covered her lips with his mouth. At first she found the pressure unpleasant, then she discovered that if she didn't hold her mouth so still, the sensation wasn't so bad. She was just beginning to enjoy it a little when he abruptly pulled away, holding her at arm's length. The sudden movement made her head swim dizzily.

'I'll be damned if I am going to make love to a woman who is too weak to do anything more than lie there,' he muttered thickly and ushered her over to the bunk. 'Stay there until you are stronger.'

'Moving makes you stronger, not lying down,' Tasha said, but she was conscious of the shakiness of her limbs.

'You have done enough moving for a while,' he ordered, then paused. 'Why are you looking at me that way?'

Tasha could only blame her recent illness for making her think so slowly, but it finally registered that he had desired to lie with her. Many Whiskers had given her to him, but Andrei wanted her. She looked at him now with new interest, regarding him as a potential lover. Despite his many summers of life, he looked vigorous and healthy.

'You do not regret that Many Whiskers gave me to you. You wanted me,' she said.

'That is a small way of putting it, Tasha.' She heard him sigh.

'I have heard that Cossacks are rough with women.'

He studied her long and hard before he answered. 'Sometimes a man's needs are great and he forgets his own strength. Stay in that bed and rest before I forget mine.' He swung around and left the cabin. Tasha smiled, secretly pleased by her discovery.

11

The volcanic islands were strung together in a thick cluster, creating a multitude of bays, passes, and reefs. Andrei let his gaze wander over the towering cone-shaped mountains that dominated the view, then studied the complex coastlines of the treeless islands – sheer cliffs, rocky shores, and beaches of sand and shingle. But it was the reef systems and island straits that interested him the most. Seaweed and kelp beds grew along the reefs, providing food for the sea urchins, abalone, and shellfish upon which the sea otter dined. And the passes between the islands were channels for migrating mammals like the fur seals and whales. The feeding grounds were rich, and the multitude of sea otter already sighted proved that the hunting would be equally rich.

'This area is an excellent choice.' Andrei straightened from the rail and glanced at the Aleut standing beside him.

'It is as I said it would be.'

'Yes.' But Andrei wondered at his motives. Somehow he doubted that the Aleut had directed them to this island group out of any desire to be helpful and cooperative.

Whatever his reason, they were here. Andrei again turned his attention to the rocky coast. With his first glimpse of the tightly clustered islands, a strategy began to take shape in his mind. To fully exploit the fur potential of the area, he would need to split his promyshleniki into small parties and spread them throughout the islands. With only three or four in a group, his men would be highly vulnerable to any hostilities from the natives. It was imperative that he establish friendly relations with these islanders.

As the shitik continued to sail close to the main island, they inspected its many bays and coves in search of a wintering site. On the western side of the island, two small whales were sighted, beached on the shore. The meat and fat from the mammals represented a supply of food for his crew. Andrei ordered a landing party to go ashore and retrieve it, instructing the Aleut to accompany them. Taking no unnecessary risks, he had muskets broken out. After he had passed out six, the number of promyshleniki assigned to the party, a seventh pair of hands reached to take the next. Andrei glanced up in surprise and encountered the steady gaze of Tasha's half brother.

Andrei shifted his grip on the musket and cradled the barrel in the crook of his arm. 'No.'

'I should have a musket. I go ashore with the others,' Walks Straight asserted.

'No.' It was an unwritten law on the Russian frontier, which now extended to these islands not yet a recognized portion of the Romanov Empire – no muskets or swords were ever given to natives. Only fools armed the primitive people whose land they came to occupy. It was too likely those same weapons would be used against them. 'You have no need for one.' Moving away, he ordered the boat to be lowered over the side.

As soon as the promyshleniki had butchered the carcasses and loaded the whale meat and fat onto the shitik, they continued their search for a likely place to winter on the island. They encountered an islander in a bidarka, a man known to Walks Straight, who had visited his village a few years ago. They presented him with some of the whale meat. He directed them to a sheltered bay that had a freshwater stream and promised to bring his people to visit them. Everything went smoothly – more smoothly than Andrei had dared hope.

The island blazed with the final days of summer; scarlet fireweed, purple lupine, and orange buttercups waved in the wildflower-lavished meadows and marshes. Thick clouds rolled across the sky, chased by a high strong wind, but on the beach where Tasha walked there was only a slight breeze to stir her hair, once more pulled back into a bun. This was her first trip ashore since they'd anchored in the bay two days ago.

'The ground feels strange to walk on,' she said to Andrei. 'It doesn't rock like the boat.'

'Your legs will get used to it.'

Tasha paused to look around her and assess the location that had been chosen. Low tide exposed a reef where octopus could be

117

snared from their caves and seaweed and urchins collected. The tidal flats and pools were a source of shellfish and ducks. The protected bay permitted fishing even when storms lashed the seas. Cormorant and puffins nested on the nearby cliffs, offering a ready source of eggs and skins for parkas. It was possible the salmon might visit the stream. And it wasn't far to walk to the meadows where there were edible plants and grasses for baskets.

'This is a good place.' Its only flaw appeared to be the scarcity of driftwood on the beach, indicating the currents didn't carry it into this bay.

'It will do.' A discussion over his winter camp was not a topic that interested him, especially when his mind was on her.

She stood with her back to him, the fur parka hiding the supple young body he was so familiar with – although not as familiar as he wanted to be. Andrei stepped closer to her and laid his hands on her shoulders, unconsciously kneading their rounded points cushioned by the dun-colored fur. She moved slightly in surprise at his touch, but the pressure of his hands didn't allow her to turn. Her freshly washed hair gleamed with the black brilliance of a raven. He bent closer, nearly touching the black shimmer with his lips.

'I want to sleep in my bunk tonight. I want to lie with my wife.' He heard the thickness in his voice, aroused by the mere anticipation of bedding her. When he sensed her hesitation, he had a fair idea of what drove men to rape. Roughly he turned her to face him, but the lively, bold light dancing in her eyes made him suck in his breath.

'I would be happy to lie with you, my husband,' she announced in flawless Russian.

At that moment, Andrei was half convinced she was some sort of enchantress. From the start he had been fascinated by that melding of Aleut hair and skin with Russian features and intrigued by her large dark eyes that slanted upward at the outer corners.

'Andrei,' he said. 'Andrei Nikolaivich.'

'I would be happy to lie with you, Andrei Nikolaivich.' Her gaze never left his face. He almost believed that she looked forward to it as much as he did. Most women he'd known had lacked passion, however practiced their skill, but he found himself wondering about Tasha and the primitive blood that mingled with the Russian in her veins.

That night, with the lamp turned down to a soft glow, he caressed her milk-white body. She was neither limp nor indifferent under his hands, but alive and sensitive. It was not a desire to arouse that prompted him to prolong his mounting of her, but a selfish enjoyment of the little sounds she made in her throat and the suggestive way she moved against his hands. He had spent too many sleepless nights in that chair staring at her motionless form in the bunk and imagining this moment to hurry it.

Too aroused to hold back any longer, he plunged himself into her. When he breached her virginal membrane, a sense of power surged through him. He plundered the riches of the soft body that no man had claimed before him, and reveled in its treasure. His climax came with shuddering force.

Hot and sweating, he rolled off her, his heart pounding wildly in his chest. As he lay there struggling for breath, Andrei tried to recall the last time his pleasure had been so great. Turning his head, he gazed at Tasha as she ran a hand over her stomach as if trying to ascertain the changes in her body. She had made him feel like a virile two-year-old stud instead of an aging stallion. Something told him that now that he'd had her, he'd never want to let her go.

In the following months, the base camp was established on Adak Island, and Andrei journeyed to some of the neighboring villages in the island group, always accompanied by Tasha. Everywhere he got a friendly reception from the natives. Immediately he dispatched small parties of promyshleniki throughout the islands to set up out-lying camps. Nearly all the natives they had encountered thus far had stated their desire to become faithful subjects of Her Imperial Majesty and pay otter skins in tribute.

Everything was exceeding his expectations – including Tasha. Andrei found himself becoming completely enamored of her. In bed, no act was unnatural to her. She was totally uninhibited, free to show her newly discovered passion. But surprisingly, he found himself equally stimulated by the quickness of her mind and her eagerness to learn anything and everything. Everything he took for granted was new to her. As he started seeing these things through her eyes, he experienced the wonder of them all over again. She was an elixir of youth to him, and sometimes Andrei felt almost drunk. Suddenly he didn't mind the long winter nights in this part of the world and even regretted the lengthening hours of daylight that came with spring, despite the increased hunting time it allowed his men.

Returning from an inspection trip to an outlying station, Andrei sailed the baidar into the protected bay and headed for the stretch of sand where the *Andreian i Natalia* was beached. A long, slender Aleut kayak lay on the shore not far from his vessel. As the baidar approached the beach, Andrei noticed two native hunters standing with three promyshleniki assigned to his headquarters. When they saw his skin-boat, they walked to the water's edge to await his arrival. The two Aleuts stood back as the promyshleniki waded a few steps into the surf and hauled the baidar onto the sand. Andrei stepped out of the boat and glanced at the two natives, recognizing neither of them.

'What do they want?' He collected his musket and gear and slung the latter over his shoulder.

'I think they have come to trade,' the promyshlenik Popov answered. 'They brought some pelts, but I don't understand enough of what they are saying to know what they want.'

'Where's Tasha?' Andrei frowned. Since this had been a one-day trip, he hadn't taken her with him.

'She left around midday. I think she was going to the hot springs.' The promyshleniki knew well enough not to follow her. Andrei's orders regarding the natives were strict – and those regarding Tasha even stricter.

'Has Walks Straight come back?' Well over a week ago, Tasha's half brother had asked permission to do some hunting on his own.

'No.'

'Very well. I will try to find out what they want.'

After a somewhat stilted conversation with the Aleuts, amplified by hand signs, Andrei was able to ascertain the pelts were payment of their tribute. Part of the initial confusion had been caused by their insistence on being given something in return. Finally he figured out they wanted a receipt. Without proof it had already been paid, another Cossack could demand payment of their annual tribute.

As soon as he'd given them the receipt, they carried their bidarka into the water and climbed into the separate hatches, securing the waterproof hatch cover made of mammal gut around them to prevent seepage. Andrei watched them paddle deftly through the surf, then looked in the direction of the tidal pools

120

warmed by hot springs a short distance up the coast. After a second's hesitation, he set out for them.

Although it was April, only a hint of spring's greening touched the drab landscape of the island. The blunted cone tops of the volcanoes were hooded with snow, which the wind stirred up and blew into wispy streamers trailing down the slopes. As Andrei walked along the coast, he studied the island straits. In another month the fur seals would be coming through these passes on their annual spring migration north. In the fall they returned, heading south with their young. No one knew where they went, although according to Aleut legend they massed by the hundreds of thousands on an island to the north.

The face of the ragged coastline changed, broken by the wide river of rock that swept seaward. Long ago it had been molten lava from the island's volcano. Then the sea had cooled it, hardened it into a stone river, its waves and ripples permanently solidified and smoothed by the breaking surf. Its low places became tidal pools, collecting the sea water and mixing it with hot springs that originated somewhere near the volcano's core. The waters in the tidal pools were sufficiently warmer than the air to give off a misty vapor.

As Andrei climbed onto the old lava flow, the glare of sunlight off the water nearly blinded him. He stopped to shield his eyes with his hand and looked for the wisps of steam that marked the sunken pools. Instead he saw a naked statue of a woman, carved of ivory, facing the sun with arms upraised as if to embrace it. It was a full second before he realized it was Tasha. Backlighted by the sun, she didn't look real.

He scrambled over the smooth rocks, the sound of his footsteps muffled by the crash of the breakers. 'Tasha, what are you doing?' he demanded when he reached her. Then he noticed the raised flesh of her skin. He grabbed up the fur parka she'd dropped on the rocks and wrapped it around her. 'I have seen you walk through snow in your bare feet so you wouldn't wear out your boots, but this is ridiculous. That wind is cold. What in the name of St. Nikolai were you thinking?' He pulled the ends across in front of her, binding her tightly inside, but effectively covering only her torso.

'When a woman is with child, she should show her body to the sun,' Tasha replied calmly. Stunned, he loosened his grip on her parka and she slipped out of it and walked to the rock edge of a

121

tidal pool. 'The water is warm. Come enjoy it with me.'

'Are you saying . . . that you are going to have a baby?' Andrei followed her, hardly believing what he'd heard.

'Yes.' She lowered herself into the misty rock pool until the water was up to her neck. He started to follow her in. 'Andrei Nikolaivich, you will get your clothes wet. Take them off.' Hurriedly he stripped and slid into the warm water.

Moving to her, he said again, 'You are going to have a baby?' When she nodded, her eyes smiling, he ran his hand over her stomach, but it still felt as flat as it always had. 'Are you certain?'

'The baby is small yet. It will come at summer's end.' Her gaze searched his face. 'Are you happy?'

'Happy.' He'd given up hope of having a child of his own, since his son had died in infancy and his wife, Natalia, had never conceived again. To learn that Tasha – the woman who had given him such joy – should also give him a child, it was more than a man could ask. 'You will never know how happy I am at this moment.' He folded her gently in his arms, then kissed her long and hard while the warm water lapped around them.

Afterwards, she slowly rubbed her forehead against his lips. 'I am happy, too.'

Andrei pulled his head back to look at her. 'He will be a beautiful baby.' He felt very potent and very proud. Tasha had done that for him.

'It might be a girl,' Tasha warned him.

'Girl. Boy. It doesn't matter. *It* will be a beautiful baby with you for its mother.'

'And you for its father.' She gazed at the rugged tanned face she'd come to adore. With wet fingers she brushed the wide silvered streak of hair at his temple. 'It is the custom to live in the husband's village,' she said; but he missed the way she looked at their island surroundings. 'Tell me again about your village – this town called Irkutsk where you live.'

'Would you like to see it yourself?' For a long time, Andrei had been wondering how he could possibly leave her. The more he thought about it, the more he realized there wasn't any reason why he couldn't take her back with him. This expedition was going to net him another five hundred thousand rubles or more. He could afford to set her up in a house, keep her as his mistress, especially now that she was carrying his child. There was no reason for Natalia ever to know. Wives turned a blind eye to such arrangements anyway.

She listened enthralled as he described the dwellings with walls of stone and things called windows made of glass that let you see outside, the paths that were covered with planks of wood for people to walk on or ride some four-legged animal called a horse, and the special building where people told stories by pretending to be the people in the stories. She marveled at the description of his dwelling divided into rooms with one for sitting, one for eating, one for cooking, and one for sleeping.

'It sounds so strange this place where you live.'

'Maybe we will visit St. Petersburg. We can ride there in a troika –'

'Troika? What is that?'

Andrei laughed, and described the vehicle drawn by three horses abreast. At the moment, he could think of nothing more enjoyable than seeing Russia through her eyes.

It all sounded fascinating to Tasha, if a little bit frightening. Yet she knew that as long as she was with Andrei, everything would be all right. So many good things had happened to her since she'd been with him, like the baby growing inside her.

'When will we go?' She moved her arms in the water to keep the warmth flowing around her.

'Not this summer. The hunting is too good. And I wouldn't want to risk anything happening to you on the voyage. The seas can get very rough. We will wait until next summer.'

'Walks Straight will be surprised when he learns he is to be an uncle.' Tasha could hardly wait to tell her brother that she would be going to live in a Cossack village, even though she knew he wouldn't be happy about it.

'He is still away hunting,' Andrei said.

She looked sharply at him, detecting something in his tone. Where her brother was concerned, she always felt a little defensive. 'You think he has left and won't come back. He will. He agreed to come with you so you could speak to the villagers through him. He will not leave until you do. Sometimes he goes far to hunt. He was tired of the Cossacks. He says they are not good hunters.'

'Not as good as the Aleuts,' Andrei admitted. 'Walks Straight has been gone a long time. I was concerned something might have happened to him.'

'He will be back soon.' Clouds covered the sun. Suddenly the water didn't seem as warm. 'We should leave. Our skin will be shriveled like a clam.' Tasha glided through the water to the side of the rock pool and pulled herself up on its smooth ledge. The wind blew over her skin and made her shiver as she reached for her parka.

Another week passed before Walks Straight returned. Two dozen otter pelts, all nearly six feet long, were unloaded from his two-hatch bidarka, but there was no happiness in him despite his considerable success. When Andrei attempted to welcome him back to camp, Walks Straight faced him proudly and defiantly and insisted on trading his pelts immediately.

The bargaining didn't last long, and it seemed to Tasha that Andrei had been very generous to her brother. In exchange for the two dozen pelts, Walks Straight received a hatchet, glass beads, and some tobacco, yet he still didn't appear satisfied.

While Andrei accompanied his men to the wood building where the furs were stored, Tasha brought her brother some food. She sat on the ground across from him and watched him eat, waiting for the usual facial indications that invited talk. It was this carefully observed rule of behavior in Aleut society not to intrude on another's thoughts that enabled thirty or forty people to live communally in a single dwelling and still retain some privacy and peace. Tasha had found the Cossacks were not so considerate. Walks Straight was half finished with his meal before he acknowledged her presence with a look signaling his willingness to communicate.

She wanted to tell him her news, but she held back, sensing it wasn't the time. Instead she chose to question him and let him speak what was on his mind. 'You had good hunting. Did you go far?'

He nodded, shoveling the raw fish into his mouth with his short, thick fingers. After a few chews, he swallowed the food. 'I went to the Umnak and the Unalaska islands. The Cossacks are there, too – three boats of them.' He looked at the chunks of fish in the carved wooden bowl as if they had lost their flavor, then set it aside. 'They cheat the Aleuts. They steal their pelts, their baidars and bidarkas and other things they want. They force the men of the village to hunt for them, and while they are away the Cossacks carry the women off and make them lie with them and beat them if they refuse.'

'These things are wrong. The Cossacks will be punished when their leaders learn of this in Russia,' she said. Andrei had told her that his rulers insisted the natives be treated fairly and punished those who committed wrongful acts against them.

'When will that be?' Walks Straight scoffed at such ineffectual justice. 'It does no good to our people now.'

'No.' Tasha bowed her head under the weight of his logic.

'We must stop them.'

Looking up, she met his dark gaze filled with resolve. Instantly she felt uneasy. 'How can we do this?' Her eyes skimmed the short-cropped black hair covering his forehead and the thin black mustache growing below his wide nose. Both narrowed her focus to his heavy-lidded eyes set above long cheekbones.

'Some of the headmen on Umnak and Unalaska are saying that all villages must unite and rise up against the Cossacks and put them all to death.'

'Not all the Cossacks.'

'We have tried to live in peace with the Cossacks since they came to our islands. But they have committed wrongs against us from the beginning when they killed my father and all the men in the village,' Walks Straight reminded her. 'We didn't punish them for their wrongs, so they continued to do them. The village elders on Umnak and Unalaska have counseled and agreed that the Cossacks must be put to death or they will go on doing wrong. If we are to know peace, we must rid our islands of the Cossacks.'

'If the village elders have decided this, it must be the only solution, but surely they did not mean *all* the Cossacks. Andrei Nikolaivich lives in peace with the Aleuts. His men, too. They have done no wrong.'

'The elders say the tribute is unfair. The Cossacks are strong and their weapons are powerful. But our numbers are greater than theirs. The men in all the villages on all the islands must unite. We must attack them as one, suddenly, with no warning. That way we can beat them.' Although he spoke quietly, his voice rang with his commitment to the cause. 'I have promised Kills Many Ducks I will speak to the villagers here so that all will fight the Cossacks.'

'You would not kill Andrei Nikolaivich,' she protested. 'His child grows in my belly. He is a good, fair man. Why would you make war on him?'

'He would make war on us when he learns Cossacks are being

killed.' Walks Straight stood up to tower above her. 'You are thinking selfish thoughts, Tasha. Many of our people are suffering under the cruel hand of the Cossacks. They know no peace. And they will not as long as a single Cossack lives.'

As her brother went to his bidarka to gather his gear, Tasha realized it was true what he said about her. She thought only of her own happiness with Andrei Nikolaivich. She hadn't experienced the oppression her people suffered. She was torn by the love she felt for a Cossack and her loyalty to her own kind.

The lamp wick was turned up to throw more light on the chessboard sitting in the middle of the table. Tasha stared at the regular pattern of light and dark squares, but she saw few of the remaining pieces that occupied them, white and black blurring together with the squares. She barely noticed when Andrei captured her black knight, recognizing only that it was her turn.

She stared at her chessmen and attempted to plot out their moves, but she couldn't concentrate. Finally she picked up a pawn and advanced it a square. She leaned her elbows on the table to await Andrei's next move on the board. It came quickly.

'Checkmate,' he announced, and Tasha had to look at the board again before she saw his bishop had her king in check and no counter move could save him. 'That is the first time I have won a game from you in a long time. Are you feeling well?'

'Yes.' She watched him begin to rearrange the pieces to their respective sides of the board.

'Do you want revenge?'

His question struck too close to her own thoughts. 'Would you want revenge if you were beaten?'

'Naturally. I would want a chance to get even.'

'My people never have a chance to get even when they are beaten by the Cossacks.'

Andrei stopped what he was doing and frowned at her. 'What brought this on?'

Tasha couldn't implicate her brother. 'It is true. On Attu, the Cossacks cheat the hunters out of their furs, or make them pay tribute more than once. There is nothing my people can do about it. You don't do this . . . but still it happens to others.'

'It's wrong. When such occurrences are reported to the Tsaritsa's agent, the guilty are punished for them.'

'Who reports these things?'

'Other Cossacks, like myself, who disapprove of such things. Not every misdeed reaches the ears of the governor general, but most do.' He watched her closely with narrowed eyes. 'Why? Has something happened?'

'I was thinking of home and how it is there for my family.' Which was a half-truth, but she couldn't tell him about the wrongdoings on Umnak and Unalaska without betraying her brother. 'But you would turn against another Cossack if he mistreated an Aleut?'

'Yes. If it was one of my own men, I would see that he was punished. Otherwise, I would report him to the proper authorities when I returned to Siberia.'

'There is nothing you can do in the meantime.'

'It is not my place to control the actions of men other than my own. I am not the law.' His voice was becoming curt and impatient.

'What if a Cossack committed a wrong against an Aleut and the Aleut sought revenge for that wrong? If he attacked the Cossack, what would you do?'

'I would have to stop him.'

'Even if you knew the Aleut was right?'

'How could there be peace in the islands if such a thing was allowed to happen? It would only create more trouble.' He pushed out of his chair. 'This conversation is pointless. There is nothing to be gained by discussing it further. You don't understand the situation, Tasha, or you would not ask such foolish questions.' He grabbed up his pipe and tobacco and left the cabin.

She stared at the pieces on the chessboard, separated by color and lined up facing each other. She saw, too, the fallacy of Andrei's argument. The Cossack could commit wrong without fear of reprisals from other Cossacks, but an Aleut could not. He would stand by while a Cossack did injury to an Aleut, but would not if it was the other way around. He was not as fair as she had believed him to be. With a heavy heart, Tasha realized that Walks Straight was right. If the Aleuts made war on the Cossacks, he would fight them. There was such pain in this knowledge because she loved him so.

As spring progressed into summer and her belly began to swell with the baby growing in her womb, Tasha found some consolation in her brother's inability to persuade the villagers on the local islands to unite against the Cossacks. The Blue-Eyed One traded fairly with them and they saw no reason to rise up against him because of the problems other villages were having with their Cossacks.

Walks Straight went on another supposed hunting expedition, but instead journeyed to Unalaska to report his failure to villagers. When he returned, she hoped this talk of war would be over, but it wasn't so.

'They are determined to rid themselves of the Cossacks,' he told her. 'They say they will show their Aleut brothers there is no reason to fear the Cossacks. All the villages of Umnak and Unalaska are of one mind. They plan now how to do this.'

'What will you do? Will you join them?'

'I do not know.' But she could see the desire in his eyes. 'They want me to stay here. Maybe when these Aleut hunters see the Cossacks can be beaten, they will fight them, too.'

'No.' It was a faint protest, barely audible.

'Will you tell Andrei Nikolaivich of our plans?' he questioned sharply.

Silently she shook her head.

12

Bald eagles dotted the sky, their dark wings spread as they rode the island thermals, circling higher and higher. Below, wind stirred the tawny grasses gilding the meadows. The lichen- and moss-covered upper elevations sported the reds, yellows, and oranges of autumn's colorful palette. Yet the warmth of summer lingered.

Outside the Cossacks' dugout, the upper half walled with drift logs, a dozen promyshleniki gathered for the ceremony. Andrei took the week-old infant from Tasha's arms, carefully supporting its head, and awkwardly shifted the bundle into the cradle of his arm. Tasha retucked the ends of the blanket square around the squirming body and ignored the angry cries of protest. Andrei pushed the edges of the blanket away from the baby's neck and rocked him gently. His chest swelled with pride as he gazed at his newborn son, but he experienced a flash of disturbance when he noticed the raveled ends of the wool blanket. His son deserved the best.

'You should have a christening gown,' he murmured to the infant, then smiled when the wind lifted the corner flap of the blanket and revealed the full head of soft black hair. Andrei was certain no baby had ever been as beautiful as his. He glanced at the somber-faced promyshleniki, then turned to Tasha. 'They are waiting for us.'

'I have been thinking – maybe I should be baptized, too.'

His head came up slightly as he inwardly recoiled from the idea. He had never considered himself an overly religious man, and he had never considered his relationship with Tasha to be an adulterous one. After all, she was a half-breed, a heathen. But there was something more sinful about bedding a Christian.

'There is no need,' he told her. 'Baptism insures that our son will not have to pay tribute when he is grown. Tribute isn't collected from women.' Cradling the small infant in one arm, he placed a hand between Tasha's shoulder blades and guided her toward the waiting group.

This was the first opportunity for the promyshleniki to view their commander's son. When Andrei reached their party, they crowded around him, anxious for a look at the child. Comment, compliments, and congratulations filled the air for several minutes. Eventually Andrei called for quiet and, in front of his gathering of witnesses, baptized his son.

'The servant of God, Zachar Andreivich, is baptized in the name of the Father, amen, the Son, amen, and the Holy Spirit, amen.' He made the sign of the cross, his hand moving right to left in the tradition of his faith.

With the ceremony concluded, the celebration began. Cups of kvass were handed around and loud toasts were made to Zachar Andreivich. But the shouts and laughter and general revelry were considerably more noise than young Zachar Andreivich was accustomed to hearing. When his whimpers of protest weren't heeded, he unleashed a full-blown bawl.

'I will take him.' Tasha came to Andrei's rescue, and he gratefully handed her their squalling son.

She laid the baby against her shoulder, holding his head, and bounced him gently to hush his cries. Andrei watched her walk away from the boisterous group of Russian hunters. In some ways, she was more beautiful than before. If it was possible, she pleased and excited him more than she ever had. Yet lately he'd been having misgivings about his plan to take her to Russia with him.

He looked at her black hair sleeked into a bun native-style, her long sealskin parka trimmed with otter and embroidered trade beads, and her bare feet with soles hardened by calluses. Maids, dressmakers, and cobblers could change her outward appearance. But when he tried to imagine her playing whist at the governor's home or dining at a merchant's house, or attending the theater, he couldn't. His culture was completely alien to her. No matter how beautiful she was or how fashionably dressed, she wouldn't fit into the social life at Irkutsk.

It troubled him greatly, but so did the thought of leaving her behind. And there was his son. He had a duty and obligation to him. Andrei had waited too long for a child. He couldn't give him up any more than he could give up Tasha. It was a problem he wrestled with many times during the long nights of autumn and early winter.

Snowflakes swirled in the night air. A thin layer of snow covered the ground and provided clear impressions of the two sets of bare footprints leading away from the village barabaras where the muffled beat of drums originated.

Tasha walked swiftly through the light snowfall, keeping pace with her brother's long strides. Years of exposure had hardened her feet against the cold. Now she was more conscious of aching pressure in her breasts, full with milk. She hurried through the frigid air.

The communal feast held by the village to give thanks for the bounty of the sea had given her a contentment of spirit. The ceremonial foods and ritual dances had satisfied her need to feel close again to the ways of her people. She was glad Walks Straight had persuaded her to leave little Zachar in Andrei's care and go to the annual feast with him. She only wished she had taken the baby along so she could have stayed longer, but Andrei had stubbornly refused to allow her to expose their son to the snow and cold even for the short trek between the barabara and their dwelling.

'Little Zachar must be very hungry by now. I should have left sooner, but I didn't want to miss the masked dancers.' Each word was accompanied by a puffy cloud that the wind whisked away.

'It is wise to thank the Creator for the bounty of His sea or He may withhold it in seasons to come. And it will be good for Zachar to have the hunger of an empty belly for a short time,' her brother insisted.

'Yes, but Andrei Nikolaivich does not like for him to cry. The least little sound Zachar makes, he picks him up. I have never seen a father carry on so about a child.' But she said it proudly.

Andrei spent countless hours with their son. And since the birth of their child, his passion for her seemed to have become greater and his lovemaking more ardent. Everything was going so well. Even the murmurings of war had ceased. At least Walks Straight hadn't spoken of it again.

As they reached the door to the small hut, partially hollowed out of the side of a hill, Tasha turned to her brother. 'Will you come in and see little Zachar? He grows so much.'

But he shook his head and faded into the night, his bird-skin parka quickly blending with whirling snow and blackness. She opened the door and stepped inside the hut, immediately feeling the warmth of the interior. She shut the door quickly to keep in the heat of the lamp and turned, hearing the beginnings of a whimper. Andrei paced the room, jiggling his cranky son against his shoulder. As Tasha moved into the room, she noticed little Zachar sucking on his fist.

'He is hungry,' Andrei said.

'I know.' She pulled off her parka and laid it on the wide cot.

Wet circles of milk stained the front of her shirt. She unfastened the buttons as she sat down on the cot. Andrei brought their hungry son to her and placed him in her lap. His mouth sought her nipple almost before she had him positioned in her arms. He suckled noisily when he found it, his long-lashed blue eyes looking up at her.

Sitting in his chair, Andrei watched them. If they were in Russia, his son would have a wet nurse. He leaned forward, resting his elbows on his knees and clasping his hands together. He dipped his head slightly to block the sight of Tasha's hair glistening with droplets of melted snow.

His son was precious to him, more precious than he had dreamed. Andrei wanted things for him – things he could give him, and would give to him – even though it meant he would have to leave Tasha behind. It simply wouldn't work to take her with him.

'What troubles you, Andrei Nikolaivich?'

He lifted his head but couldn't quite meet her inquiring gaze. 'I was thinking of home.'

She made an understanding sound. 'It is almost time for your celebration.'

'Christmas.' He finally guessed what she meant.

'Tell me about your town, Irkutsk, again so it will be familiar to me.'

Andrei hesitated. The opening was there, yet he was reluctant to take it even though he knew he must. 'I have reconsidered. You would not like it, Tasha,' he said finally, then hurried on before she could question him. 'Siberia isn't like the islands. It is gray and drab.' He didn't mention the copper-domed churches glinting red in the sun. Red was the color of happiness in Russia. 'Our homes, our food, our way of life are different from what you know. It would be very strange to you. I see that now. You would have no family there, no friends. It is cold there, Tasha. Very cold.'

'That would not bother me.' Her eyes were wide, her expression revealing her attempt to understand.

'What would you do there, Tasha? There is no grass to weave baskets, no skins to clean, no bird skins to make into parkas, no salmon to catch in the streams, no sea urchins to collect on the reefs – nothing. There would only be rooms – rooms to sit in, sleep in, eat in, cook in. That is all. You would be very unhappy. And I care about you too much to see you unhappy.'

'What about the dances and the building where people tell stories?'

'That takes up only a little time of the day. Soon you would tire of that, too.' Andrei knew he was right. Even if she could learn to accept those things, there was still the problem of his son – and his wife, Natalia. Natalia might have turned a blind eye to Tasha alone, but it would hurt her deeply to have Tasha and Zachar there, the son she had so longed to give him born to another woman. And he could never hide his pride in the child. He knew also that Natalia would gladly raise his son. Tasha alone she could accept; Zachar alone she could accept, but not the two of them together.

'It is different for our son,' he continued quickly. 'He can learn the ways of my people. I want him to have an education – to learn to read and write – make marks on the paper – and study wise things. I can do this for him.'

Her arms protectively circled the baby nursing at her breast. 'You would take Zachar from me.'

'Only for a short time, Tasha,' he assured her earnestly. 'Other Aleut children have gone to Russia to learn our language and our ways and to study our knowledge. They have come back.' He also knew Aleuts had been taken to Russia, claimed as godsons, and later adopted. Zachar would not have to be his bastard child. He could eventually be regarded as his legitimate heir. 'Zachar will come back, too. So will I. Tasha, I have to take this cargo of furs to Russia this summer. I am a merchant, a trader. This is what I do – the same as Walks Straight is a hunter. I will return for more furs, and Zachar will be with me.' At least until he reached the age to be in school. 'We will be together again as we are now – here on the islands where you are happy. Do you understand?'

133

Tasha stared at him with her dark, suddenly expressionless eyes for a long time. Then she said, 'I understand.'

Andrei straightened in his chair, relieved. He wasn't certain what he had expected her reaction to be – rage maybe. But her sharp native intelligence had listened to reason.

He smiled. 'It is not something we have to worry about now. It will be a long time until summer comes.'

'A long time,' she murmured and stroked the soft black hair on their son's head.

As the sun neared its winter solstice, the daylight hours shortened. Activity in the camp and the nearby village was at its peak during that time. Few paid any attention to Tasha as she hurried along the muddy path through the snow. The winter landscape was a mixture of stark white snow and black rocks, surrounded by gray clouds and gray-green water. A flock of auklets darkened the sky like a thick trail of smoke heading out to sea. But Tasha's gaze was focused on her brother. He was crouched beside his bidarka, checking a section of its hide cover. He stood up when he saw her coming.

For two days she had waited for the opportunity to speak to him alone. She wasted no time coming to the point. 'I have to leave. Zachar and I have to leave the island,' she quickly corrected herself. 'Will you take us from here?'

'Why?' Her brother glanced sharply in the direction of the hut. 'Has he harmed you?'

'No. He plans to take my son.' Agitation stirred her, and the pain of betrayal by someone she thought she could trust. 'Next summer he wants to take Zachar with him when he goes to his village. I am not to go with them. He says I should stay here and he will come back.' She didn't believe him. Of all the things he'd said to her the other night, one thing had been clear. 'He would steal my child.'

'Cossacks can never be trusted.' Walks Straight glowered at the party of promyshleniki setting out to check their trap lines.

'I must take Zachar and leave the island while Andrei Nikolaivich sleeps. I cannot wait.'

'Where will you go?'

Tasha shook her head, having no answer. 'I cannot go home to Attu. He would find us there.'

'My friends in Unalaska would welcome us to their village. He would not know to look for you there. We would be safe.' His face smoothed with decision. 'We must leave tonight.'

'I have gathered my things and hidden them. As soon as he sleeps, I will take them from their hiding place and slip away with my son.'

'I will take the Cossacks' baidar and meet you where the waters run under the shelf rock.' With their plans made, Tasha returned to the hut and her sleeping child to await the coming of night.

The night was filled with the quiet murmurings of the sea as the baidar sailed through its waters. The swaddled baby in Tasha's arms made a few protesting noises, but there was no one to hear except her brother. The island of Adak was well behind them. Only Zachar's cradle remained at the hut. Everything else they owned was in the large skin-boat, including her brother's bidarka and all his hunting equipment. Walks Straight would build Zachar another cradle when they reached Unalaska.

The undulating waters glistened with a silvery sheen. Overhead, broken clouds revealed the stars in the night sky and the singing lights that dipped and swayed in changing white-green waves.

13

On Unalaska Island, final preparations were under way to engage the Cossacks in battle. The villagers were observing the rituals and appealing to the Creator's protective presence. The strategies were set. It was to be a coordinated effort among the villages on the islands of Four Mountains, Umnak, Unalaska, and the surrounding smaller islands. The enemy strength in the area was estimated at less than two hundred Cossacks, while the Aleuts numbered more than three thousand warriors.

All summer and fall they had pretended friendliness to the Cossacks so they would be encouraged to divide into smaller hunting groups as was their practice when they didn't feel threatened. The Aleuts had carefully observed the routines of the Cossacks and used their patterns to plot ambushes.

Listening to their final plans, Tasha realized that the formidable Cossacks could be overpowered and killed. The bitterness in her heart made her glad. They should be punished for the wrongs they had done and the suffering they had caused, suffering with which she now empathized.

The village where Tasha and her brother had taken refuge with her son was on an island in the large bay carved into the northern end of Unalaska. It was a small village, composed of twenty hunters living communally in a single barabara. A short distance from the dwelling, a party of eleven Cossacks had built a winter hut from driftwood. They came from a boat anchored in the bay which could be seen from the island when the fog didn't hide it.

After Zachar finished nursing, Tasha laid him in his new cradle. Walks Straight entered the barabara accompanied by two other hunters. Triumphantly he displayed the knives he'd obtained in trade from the Cossacks, then passed them out to the other hunters.

'Tomorrow the Cossacks will know why we wanted so many knives,' he announced, and the Aleuts smiled and nodded their understanding. Walks Straight strode over to the cubicle where Tasha sat. The eagerness for battle was in his eyes as he squatted beside her. 'It begins in the morning. Before the sun comes up, you will take little Zachar and hide in the hills with the others. The old ones have agreed to stay so the Cossacks will not become suspicious.'

'I will stay, too.' Tasha knew the plan. Every morning half of the Cossacks left the hut to check their foxtraps on the island. One of the villagers would lure them into an ambush. The Cossacks remaining at the hut always came to the barabara. The rest of the hunters would attack them once they were inside. 'Little Shell will look after Zachar for me.'

Her offer pleased him. At last they stood on the same side. 'You will remain outdoors in the morning. When the attack begins, you will join the other women in the hills.'

'I will.'

After its flame was extinguished, the stone lamp was moved to the far end of the barabara so it would not be upset in the coming fight and its oil spilled. The daylight streaming through the roof hatch left much of the barabara in shadows. Two of the Aleut hunters stood within its spray of light, their clubs and knives hidden in the folds of their parkas. Walks Straight waited in the shadows with the others, positioned close to the notched log down which the Cossacks would soon descend. His nerves were tense, all his senses straining, the blood thumping loudly in the vein along his neck. He tightened his grip on the hunting club.

A short time ago, Looks Like Copper, the sentry posted on the barabara's roof, had signaled to let them know that one group of Cossacks had left the hut to check their foxtraps. If the pattern stayed true, soon the other Cossacks would be making their regular visit to the barabara.

Suddenly greetings were called in the Cossack tongue. Footsteps approached the opening in the roof. Walks Straight watched as Looks Like Copper came down the notched log first. Very low, the Aleut murmured the warning, 'Three come. One carries a hatchet.'

Walks Straight sank deeper into the shadows, turning his body slightly so that it wouldn't appear his interest was centered on the

Cossacks climbing down the ladder one after the other, the log groaning under their weight. The big-nosed one carrying the hatchet came last. As he neared the bottom, the first two Cossacks appeared to sense something was wrong.

'Agghh!' Walks Straight yelled the signal to attack and, with a mighty swing of his club, struck the closest Cossack between the shoulders, driving him to the earthen floor.

Immediately Walks Straight leaped onto the body and repeatedly plunged his knife into the Cossack's back, while all around him clubs and knives were striking amidst shouts in Aleut and Cossack. A second Cossack went down and two Aleuts fell on him with their knives.

As Walks Straight abandoned the body of his slain victim, the big-nosed Cossack, badly wounded, began swinging his hatchet like a madman, slashing it back and forth, driving the Aleuts back while he retreated to the ladder. Walks Straight attempted to block his escape from the barabara, but the bloodied hatchet blade arced toward him. He jumped back and felt the scoring burn as the blade sliced through his parka and cut the fleshy part of his chest. Ignoring the pain, he went after the Cossack on the ladder, but the threat of the constantly swung hatchet prevented him from snaring the man's boots and dragging him down.

All but two of the Aleuts followed Walks Straight up the notched log after the fleeing Cossack. Those two had suffered severe wounds inflicted by the hatchet-swinging man. As Walks Straight emerged from the hatch opening, the big-nosed man broke into a staggering run down the mound and yelled a warning to the Cossacks still in the hut. One Cossack hurried out of the bushes some distance from the hut, fastening his trousers. Walks Straight saw that he had little chance of keeping the hatchet-armed man from reaching his dwelling, but the other Cossack had no weapon. He ran quickly to intercept him.

They surrounded him a few yards from the hut. Walks Straight saw the panic in the man's eyes as he came at him with his knife. The Cossack grabbed his knife arm and Walks Straight strained to over-power him, feeling the blood trickling from the slash across his chest. Some of the Aleuts had grabbed spears before leaving the barabara. One stabbed the Cossack. His mouth opened with shock and horror as his grip loosened. Walks Straight quickly drove his knife blade into him. The Cossack went to his knees while the rest continued to stab him with their spears.

Almost simultaneously it seemed, deafening explosions rent the air and two Aleuts were spun around by some invisible force. The Cossacks' muskets. The man on the ground still moved. Aware that the Cossacks needed time to reload their weapons, the warriors stayed to finish their victim.

A Cossack broke from the hut and came slashing into their midst with a big knife. It ripped into Walks Straight's side, cutting the flesh but missing the organs. He staggered backwards, clutching the deep gash to stop the pumping of blood from it. Another Aleut fell under the man's knife. The Cossack scooped up his fallen comrade and began retreating toward the hut as another volley of musketfire thundered through the air.

With their own strength severely depleted by wounds, the Aleuts retreated out of musket range. Walks Straight paused for breath, the smell of blood and battle sweat strong in his nose. He was conscious of the draining weakness, the trembling of his muscles with fatigue.

'We have them trapped.' Walks Straight sat down, breathing heavily. 'Their muskets can keep us from getting in, but soon they must come out for food and water. We will be ready.'

'Only four live, and two are badly wounded,' Looks Like Copper stated. 'We have heard nothing from the others. Do you think they were successful in killing the Cossacks?'

'We will soon know.' One or the other would be coming back to the village. Walks Straight pushed to his feet, holding his wound, the sticky blood blackening his parka. 'Come. We must let out the power in the bodies of the ones we have killed and take our wounded to the summer camp where the women wait.'

Three of the Aleut warriors remained near the hut in case the Cossacks attempted to flee to their baidar. The rest returned to the barabara. While some helped their two wounded fighters up the ladder, Walks Straight and the others took out their knives and started cutting the arms and legs off the bodies of the slain Cossacks. Once the extremities were separated from the bodies, they were cut apart again at the joints. Finally they gathered up the parts, carried them out of the barabara, and threw them in the sea, thus insuring themselves against a fatal encounter.

Like the other injured, Walks Straight washed his wounds in the sea and bound up the gash in his side, but he didn't accompany the five other wounded hunters when they set out for the summer camp, the ones able to walk helping those who couldn't.

He stayed with the other Aleuts to maintain their siege on the Cossacks' hut.

Shortly the ambush party returned to the village. Walks Straight looked with envy at the two pistols and muskets they had captured after annihilating the enemy.

'Show the Cossacks in the hut the weapons and clothes you have taken from their comrades so they will know they are alone on the island,' Walks Straight instructed, and two of the warriors stepped out in full view of the hut and waved their plunder for the men inside to see.

At the first sounds of a struggle inside the barabara, Tasha had abandoned her supposed search for driftwood and motioned for the two old women of the village to come with her. Together they had made their way across the hills of the narrow island to the summer camp located near a stream where salmon came during the spawning season. There they had joined the rest of the villagers – women, children, and men too old to fight – and waited for word of the outcome of the attacks.

Zachar slept in the cradle alongside Tasha while she filled the worry time by sewing a small rainproof parka for him. She kept remembering the rumble of musket shots vibrating through the island hills. The sounds around her now were the rush of the wind, the mixed cry of the seabirds, and the voice of an old man recounting his days of valor to some young child.

Pausing in her sewing, she scanned the horizon in the direction of the village, a horizon dominated by the snow-covered volcano on Unalaska Island towering into the clouds. She sighed and resumed her stitching. Little Zachar stirred. For an instant she saw something of Andrei's features in her son's face and she felt a sharp stab of pain that quickly fled.

Someone called out in distress. Looking up, Tasha saw a group of hobbling, staggering warriors approaching the camp. There were nine in all, most of them half carrying or half supporting each other. Quickly she laid her sewing aside and joined the other women rushing to help the wounded, bloodied men. Her gaze searched the faces for her brother. Her relief was mixed when she saw he wasn't among them. The expression on the faces of the injured gave her hope; there was the light of victory in their eyes.

But this wasn't the time to be asking questions. Tasha set about tending the wounds of the battle's victims. Like the other

140

Aleut women, her skill in treating wounds came from a variety of sources. The almost daily butchering of sea otter whose anatomy compared to a human's gave her a knowledge of the body's bones, muscles, and organs. The dexterity of her fingers came from weaving fine grasses, and the deftness of her suturing came from constantly sewing garments and skin covers for baidars and bidarkas. From her elders, she had learned the means of blocking pain by sticking needles into certain sites on the body.

While she worked, she learned that some of the casualties came from the attack on the Cossacks in the village and that four had been hurt in the ambush of the ones checking traps. One man was also able to tell her that Walks Straight survived and stayed to watch the four Cossacks trapped in their hut.

Little Zachar awakened and cried to nurse, but his need wasn't as great as these men's, so she let him cry. Carefully she cut open a man's belly where the musket ball had made a round hole. As she probed for the lead ball, she saw the juices from the man's stomach and knew the organ had been pierced. She knew the man would surely die, yet she went ahead and retrieved the musket ball, sewed shut the hole in his stomach, then sutured the wound closed. She moved away from him, briefly consoled that the needle would block much of his death pain.

Now her breasts ached with the milk they held, and Tasha went to her wailing son and relieved the discomforts of both of them. Her body rocked gently while he nursed.

As long as the threat of fighting remained, the young, the old, the women, and the wounded stayed at the summer camp, while the warriors continued their siege of the Cossacks' dwelling.

After four days, word came that it was safe to return. The four Cossacks had slipped away from the island during the night, reaching their baidar under the cover of darkness and leaving the bay.

'We made no attempt to stop them,' Walks Straight admitted to Tasha. 'We dared not charge their muskets in the darkness. There were not enough of us.'

'They escaped. Now they will warn others.' She knew surprise was the Aleut's best weapon.

'There is no one to warn.' Satisfaction curved the line of his mouth. 'The Cossacks living in the camp on the next island have all been killed. And their boat anchored in the bay is no more, and

141

the men who were on it are dead. There is nowhere for them to hide. We have sent word to the other villages to watch for the four Cossacks.'

'What of the other Cossacks and the other four boats?' Her fear was that if any Cossacks should escape, they would carry the word of the uprising to their comrades on other islands. She worried that Andrei would come to Unalaska. If he found her here after she'd run away from him, he would surely take Zachar from her.

'Some have already been attacked. The rest will be soon.' He hesitated before continuing. 'I am going to Makushin village on Unalaska, where they gather warriors to attack the Cossack dwelling on the shore of the bay.'

She saw that he intended for her to remain here. But these Aleuts, while they had been kind to her, were strangers. Walks Straight was her brother. She could rely on him in time of need.

'We will go with you, Zachar and I.'

'There will be danger,' he warned.

'As long as there are Cossacks on the islands, there will be danger. If any get away, there will be more danger.' It was strange to hear those words coming from her mouth.

Once she had wished all Cossacks could be as fair and good as Andrei Nikolaivich Tolystykh. But it was not fair and good to steal a woman's child. Walks Straight had warned her that Andrei would take what he wanted and leave her to cry. Tasha wished she had listened to him then. Now the hurt she felt made her cold inside and she wanted to lash out. But her heart longed for the thing she had lost.

'We will leave with the morning sun,' Walks Straight said.

A war party of seventy Aleuts gathered to advance on the dwelling where their scouts had told them fifteen Cossacks lived. In the bay, the Cossack boat rode at anchor. All of the warriors carried bundles of sea otter skins so the Cossacks would think they came to trade. But the headman of the Cossacks acted suspicious of them.

'He said if we came to trade, then ten could approach his dwelling at one time, no more,' Walks Straight told Tasha as they sat close together in the crowded barabara that evening. He was frustrated and angry. 'Ten – against fifteen Cossacks with muskets and pistols and sabers. We could do nothing. There was no

142

chance to surprise them, no chance to fall on them with our superior numbers. We had to trade and leave.'

'What will you do now?' She watched him straighten his back, then wince with pain from the wound in his side, but he had refused to let her look at it.

'A hunter who stayed to watch the dwelling returned to the village a short time ago and reported that three men who hunt with the Cossacks but are not Cossacks came to the dwelling.' Tasha suspected her brother referred to the people Andrei called Kamchadals, who were a tribe like the Aleuts but lived in Russia. 'He said they showed great fear and he believed maybe they escaped from one of the boats we destroyed.'

'They have warned the Cossacks. You will have no chance to surprise them,' Tasha said. 'They will be ready for you.'

'Word has been sent to other villages. We will need more warriors if we are to beat them,' he admitted.

It required two days for the Aleuts to assemble a larger force and make their attack on the Cossack village. Armed with spears and bows and arrows, they launched their assault, but the musketfire from the hut repelled them. Again they were forced to lay siege to the camp, occasionally exchanging arrows and lead balls with the Cossacks and carrying their wounded to the rear. Again the Cossacks slipped away and reached the safety of their shitik in the bay, but they didn't set sail.

Returning to the barabara of the village that had taken them in, Walks Straight knew the taste of disappointment. He walked past his sister without speaking and sat down on the sleeping mat where his sprightly nephew lay on his stomach, arms and legs waving. He listened to the baby's happy gurgles and watched him push up on his little hands to test the strength of his small arms. Walks Straight caught one of the hands and squeezed the four fingers until the joints turned pale. It was an exercise to be done regularly if the child was to have warm hands as an adult. Walks Straight squeezed the fingers of the other hand, conscious that Tasha watched and waited for him to speak.

'Most of the warriors have returned to their villages,' he told her. 'Their families are hungry and they must hunt for food.'

'The Cossacks only have to worry about themselves. They have no families to feed.' Tasha acknowledged the burden of women and children in times of war.

143

'They also say that while the Cossacks are on their boat it is too dangerous to attack them from the water. They can kill too many of us with their muskets before we can reach their boat.'

Tasha nodded. 'Why have the Cossacks not sailed from here? Why do they stay?'

Walks Straight shook his head, then reconsidered the question. 'Maybe they believe others of their party live. Maybe they think we have not killed the rest, so they wait for them to come.'

Through the rest of the winter and into early spring the shitik remained in the harbor anchored near shore. The Aleuts kept a constant watch on the boat, firing arrows at any Cossack foolish enough to expose himself for long. At the time when the adult male fur seals swim through the island passes heading to their unknown rookery to the north, the Cossacks raised the boat's sails and left the bay. Walks Straight watched it go and derived some satisfaction from the storm signs in the sky. The following day a gale struck Unalaska, its fierce wind whipping up the sea and driving the rain sideways against the island.

Word later came from Umnak Island that the boat had wrecked on their shore, and local warriors had attacked the survivors, killing five and inflicting wounds on all the rest before they were finally driven off. The Cossacks hadn't been able to prevent the warriors from looting the wreck of their boat. Now their plunder was available for trade. From them Walks Straight obtained a musket and a small amount of powder and lead balls in exchange for the baidar in which he and Tasha had fled from Adak. Countless evenings during the summer Tasha watched him cleaning his prized possession, as he'd seen the Cossacks do.

Throughout the summer, reports of isolated skirmishes between the Aleuts and the handful of Cossack survivors holed up on Umnak Island reached their village. But a sense of peace pervaded the islands as they resumed their old way of life, rid of the Cossack oppression.

When the berries were ripe and the whales were coming into the bays, more than once Tasha looked at her small son and remembered this was the time when the Cossacks usually left to return to their land across the sea.

The sails of a Cossack boat were sighted off Unalaska Island. Apprehensive that the boat might belong to Andrei, Tasha urged her brother to learn who these Cossacks were and where they landed. Walks Straight went with the small scouting party sent to observe the strength of the Cossacks.

Many of the Cossacks' firearms were in Aleut hands; but the hundred or so muskets and pistols were widely scattered among the warriors on the various islands in the group, and their supply of ammunition was low. Even though they possessed some Cossack weapons, the Aleuts weren't able to mount an offensive against a large body of them. They realized they would have to allow the Cossacks to land on their island if that was their intention.

The scouting party located the Cossack vessel at anchor in one of the bays. 'Look.' Killer Whale directed their attention to some men moving around on deck. 'There is Solovey.'

'Who is Solovey?' Walks Straight questioned.

'A Cossack who brought his men to our island once before to hunt and collect tribute.'

After studying the vessel and its men a while longer, Walks Straight announced, 'We should talk to them.'

They went down to the beach and waved to the Cossacks on board to come ashore. Soon men were dispatched to the beach in a wooden boat. Killer Whale pointed out Solovey to Walks Straight. The tall, bulky dark-bearded man with the big hooked nose sat in the front of the boat. His eyes appeared hard and wise. When he stepped onto the sand, the Cossack Solovey greeted Killer Whale first, then gave them all gifts of tobacco.

'You are brave to come to this island, Solovey.' When Walks Straight spoke to him in the Cossacks' tongue, the man turned sharply to face him.

'Brave?' One thick brush eyebrow was arched higher than the other. 'Why do you say that?'

'Have you seen any Cossack boats?'

'No.'

'You will find none here,' Walks Straight informed him. 'We have destroyed all the Cossack boats on Unalaska, Umnak, and the Islands of Four Mountains.' He observed the blood drain from Solovey's face, then rush back to redden it.

'How have you destroyed them?' he demanded.

'Some were cast onto the shore and broken on the rocks. Others we burned.'

'Where are the men from these ships?'

'We killed them.'

Solóvey stared at him in disbelief. 'How did you kill them?'

Walks Straight detailed the accounts of the ambushes, telling the Cossack how the Aleuts lured his comrades into the hills, then fell on them with their knives, slicing their hamstrings so they couldn't run, then killing them. He described the ruses used, bringing pelts to trade with strips of leather tied tightly around them so the Cossacks would have to use their knives or swords to cut them and how the warriors used that moment to slit a Cossack's throat.

Although Solovey's face became more red with anger and he trembled, he continued to look at Walks Straight with doubt in his eyes. 'Where are the bodies of the ones you claim you killed?'

Pointing to the sea, Walks Straight said, 'We cut their arms and legs into pieces and threw them in the waters so there would be no more danger from them.'

Solovey swore so rapidly in the Cossack tongue that Walks Straight couldn't understand him. Immediately, Solovey questioned the other Aleuts to verify that what Walks Straight had said was true. When they confirmed it, Walks Straight observed the man's sudden wariness. A pistol was tucked inside his belt and the Cossacks around him were all armed with muskets, while Walks Straight and the Aleuts carried only knives. They numbered four and the Cossacks were seven. Yet Solovey looked at them like an otter assessing the closeness of danger, then he swung his glance to the rolling hills beyond the beach as if expecting to find more Aleuts hiding.

This was the reaction Walks Straight had sought. He wanted these Cossacks to have fear in their hearts. That's why he had told Solovey about the killings of the Cossacks in detail. After learning what had happened to their comrades, they would be afraid of the Aleuts – and afraid to stay on the island. There was no need to fight the Cossacks if they could frighten them away instead.

When they set out in the yawl again and rowed toward the anchored *Sv Petr i Sv Pavel*, Ivan Solovey noticed more than one of his men glancing apprehensively back at the Aleuts on the beach. Their uneasiness only added to the rage that seethed inside him.

'Do you think what they said was true, Solovey?' one of the promyshleniki questioned.

'They are boasting,' Solovey asserted sternly, determined that fear and panic would not sweep through his company. 'Perhaps they killed two or three Russians. But to wipe out the companies of five ships? Impossible!'

'Why would they claim they had?'

Solovey wondered himself what purpose it served for the Aleuts to confess to such heinous acts. 'They are savages. You cannot believe their lies.'

'But what if it is true?'

'We will find out if it is,' Solovey stated.

When they reached his vessel, the story of the slaughter of Russians was instantly related to the other promyshleniki on board. Solovey tolerated the ensuing chaos of clamoring voices demanding answers and raising questions for only a short time.

'Silence!' he bellowed above the uproar and moved to stand in the center of the deck where all could see him. Gradually the din faded to an occasional mumble while he stared at each man in turn. His gaze stopped at the Cossack Korenev, who was assigned to the vessel as the government's tribute collector. 'Tomorrow, Korenev, you will take twenty men, all armed with muskets and pistols, and make a reconnaissance along the coast. See if you can find any evidence to support these wild claims of the Aleuts.'

The action established a degree of order and discipline among his company again. But like the promyshleniki, Solovey waited anxiously for the Cossack to return with his report. It was hard to believe that two hundred well-armed Russians could be slaughtered by a bunch of savages armed only with bows, arrows, and spears.

Everyone gathered on deck when the boat carrying Korenev and his men approached the vessel. Solovey met him as he climbed on board.

'What did you learn?'

'We came across only three native dwellings. All of them were vacant. I think the Aleuts took to the mountains when they saw us coming,' he answered.

Cowards, Solovey thought to himself. 'Did you find anything that gave credence to their story?' he demanded.

The Cossack squared his shoulders. 'We did recover some Russian clothing, two pistols, and a sword from the barabaras. I would have to say that some Russians had been killed by these savages in order for such items to fall into the hands of the Aleut.'

14

No one dared approach Andrei Tolstykh as he stood on the vessel's aft deck. All avoided those ice-blue eyes that could look a hole right through a man and make his skin shiver. None of the promyshleniki spoke of the change in him since the Creole girl had run off with his newborn son less than a year ago – and certainly not within his hearing. While he remained clean-shaven and dressed with his customary care, Tolstykh was gaunt of cheek now, his eye sockets hollowed and dark and his lips pressed thin. His breath reeked with the smell of kvass, yet the potent brew never seemed to have an effect on him.

The few promyshleniki who were at the base camp that winter morning when Tolstykh discovered the girl was gone remembered the frenzied search of the island he'd conducted. The villagers had been rousted from their barabaras and their dwellings nearly torn apart when he failed to find her or his son among them. Many times they had described to their fellow hunters who'd been at the outlying stations the look on Tolstykh's face when he was informed a baidar was missing and the girl's Aleut brother was nowhere to be found in camp, how motionless he had become, how everyone had instinctively moved back a step, sensing his fury and wanting to be out of his path. But there were no words to describe the wrenching experience of watching a man about to go mad and the uneasiness that followed when he didn't.

In the past months, Tolstykh had relentlessly scoured the island group where the promyshleniki hunted, going to every village and questioning all the natives, demanding otter skins or answers. The vessel's cargo hold was filled with the former. One answer had sent their vessel on this easterly course instead of westward and home to Russia. A native had claimed the girl's brother had twice visited a village on Unalaska Island.

Oblivious to the wind-driven raindrops that pelted his face, Andrei scanned the rain-blurred coastline of the large island marked by a multitude of fingered inlets and sweeping bays. Five Russian vessels were reportedly operating in this region, yet he'd seen none, and no structures on shore indicated the locations of outlying camps. The primal instinct that had directed him to this island grew stronger as they sailed past the entrance of a double-tine-shaped bay and rounded a shoulder of land. His son was somewhere on that island, and Andrei didn't attempt to explain the certainty he felt, even to himself. If he had to tear the island apart rock by rock, he'd find Zachar.

Beyond the promontory of land, a wide bay sunk its watery talons into the neck and shoulder of the island. Obeying the inner voice that spoke to him, Andrei ordered the vessel into the natural harbor, fully aware that they had bypassed several bays that could have provided an equally safe anchorage.

Another shitik sat at anchor in the calmer waters, its sails furled and its masts bare. At the sight of another vessel, the men stirred on deck. After three years they were tired of their own company, eager for the glimpse of a new face, maybe a familiar one, and anxious for any word from home. But Andrei's interest was centered solely on the information he might be able to obtain that would lead him to his son.

With blankets hooding them against the rain, the sentries on the shitik's deck eagerly hailed the *Andreian i Natalia* when it hove alongside their vessel and dropped anchor. Andrei didn't answer their call; instead he studied the armed hunters and the makeshift defenses on deck. The Cossack Maxim Lazarev answered the hail. The sentries appeared disappointed to learn they were recently from Adak. They were under the command of Ivan Solovey, who was ashore with the main contingent of hunters, they said in response to Andrei's subsequent demand to speak to their leader.

Impatient to speak with the man and get on with his search, Andrei ordered the yawl to be lowered over the side. 'Go well armed,' one of the sentries advised. 'There has been trouble.'

Two more sentries met the boat when it landed on the island, and escorted Andrei and his small party to the fortified camp. He sensed the edginess in camp, an edginess that became apparent when he entered the winter hut and the men inside visibly started at the opening of the door. Andrei recognized Ivan Solovey, although he knew the man mainly by his reputation at Okhotsk for gambling, drinking, and whoring away three years' worth of fur profit in one. *Soloviev* was the Russian word for nightingale. There was nothing about this coarse, darkly bearded man that resembled the sweet-singing bird. It was said his men gave him the nickname Oushasnui Solovey, Terrible Nightingale.

'I am Andrei Nikolaivich Tolstykh, commanding the *Andreian i Natalia*.' Andrei made a small nod of his head that suggested a courtly bow. He was well aware his name was known to Solovey – and all who sailed from Okhotsk.

'Ivan Petrovich Solovey, commanding the *Sv Petr i Sv Pavel*. Welcome to Unalaska, Andrei Nikolaivich.' In a hearty, comradely fashion, he used both hands to clasp Andrei's right hand and arm. 'We had begun to think there were no other Russian vessels in the area.'

'I had heard there were five operating in this island group.'

Solovey suddenly appeared to become conscious of other ears in the room listening to their conversation. When he spoke again, his voice fairly boomed with good cheer. 'What kind of host am I, letting you stand there all wet and cold?' He took Andrei's cloak and tossed it to one of his men. 'Come with me,' he told Andrei. 'I have something that will warm your blood again.'

After signaling his men to remain behind, Andrei followed Solovey to the private room in the rear of the hut. There were no chairs to sit on, only a rope-strung cot and some wooden barrels. A samovar sat on one of them. Solovey closed the crude planked door, then walked over to the cot and removed a bottle of cheap brandy tucked inside the blanket.

'Have a seat.' Solovey gestured toward the barrels.

Andrei continued to stand. 'I am sailing under the special protection of an imperial ukase granted by the Empress Elizabeth Petrovna –'

'Then you have been gone a considerable time, Andrei Nikolaivich.' Solovey poured equal portions of brandy into a pair of mugs, then laced the cheap liquor with hot water from the samovar. Turning, he offered one of the mugs to Andrei. 'She died. Her nephew Peter succeeded her to the throne for a short time – a very short time. Now it is his wife, Catherine the Second, who rules Russia. It is said she intrigued to have him assassinated.' He lifted his mug in a mock salute. 'It is a fool who trusts a woman.'

'Indeed,' Andrei murmured, staring at his cup, then lifting it to drink. It sickened him to think how besotted he had been with Tasha, how trusting. 'Two hostages escaped from my protection. I have reason to suspect they fled here to Unalaska. I would appreciate any assistance you can provide to aid my search of the villages on this island.'

'I think you do not understand the situation here.' Solovey's expression became hard and thoughtful. 'I am not certain that I do.'

'One of your men mentioned there had been trouble.'

'It may be more serious than that.' Solovey glanced at the door, then lowered his voice. 'The natives on the island have been bragging that they killed all the Russians who were here. The five vessels you spoke of? We have found none.'

'Perhaps they sailed for home,' Andrei suggested.

'Perhaps. And perhaps they were massacred, their bodies cut into pieces and thrown into the sea as the Aleuts claim – and the shitiks burned or sunk. I do know the natives have muskets and Russian clothing in their possession. And I do know we have been warned to leave – or suffer the same fate as our comrades.' Solovey drained the liquor from his mug and walked back to the bottle sitting by the samovar to refill it. 'I doubted it in the beginning. But I have heard the same stories from more than one Aleut – some that I knew from previous voyages. With minor variations, they are all the same.' The hand holding the tin cup trembled. 'They all related in great detail the way they slit the hamstrings of the Russians so they couldn't run, then hacked them to pieces.'

'If what you suggest is true, several villages would have had to band together.' Andrei frowned.

'Yes.' Solovey looked him steadily in the eye. 'Now they play with our minds, spread fear among my men. They promise to wait until winter when I divide my force into hunting parties, then they will ambush each one and kill us all – as they did the others. But they will not find us so easy to kill. So now it is my turn to ask you to aid me in avenging the deaths of our countrymen. We cannot allow their murders to go unpunished.'

The statement reminded Andrei of what he'd told Tasha the previous year – that a native must be punished for any crime against a Russian regardless of the provocation. He believed it now more strongly.

151

'It matters not whether there has actually been a massive uprising by the Aleuts,' Andrei stated. 'Whether it is true or they are talking merely to build up courage for the deed, their voices must be silenced. We must crush this seed of rebellion before it spreads to other islands.'

'That is my thinking as well, Andrei Nikolaivich.' Solovey grinned as he picked up the brandy bottle and sloshed more of its contents into Andrei's mug. 'It is not enough for them to bow their heads to us. I want my foot on their neck.'

'Have you been able to determine the strength of the various villages on the island?'

'My priority has been to establish myself firmly on the island and instill order and discipline among my men.'

'Since the natives have shown such a willingness to talk, we must question them on the things we need to know.' If, as he suspected, Tasha and her brother had fled to this island with his child, their presence would be known by the Unalaskans. It would simplify his search and lessen the risk to his son if he knew where they were hiding.

By the time Andrei left to return to his vessel, the bottle of brandy was empty and the tales of the alleged massacre of more than two hundred Russians were on the lips of his men, as told to them by Solovey's promyshleniki. Hearing the atrocities committed by the Aleuts made Andrei all the more determined to find his son and remove him from these savages.

After it became apparent to the Aleuts on Unalaska that Solovey had no intention of leaving the island, plans were formulated by the village elders and the war leaders to launch an attack against the Cossack encampment. Its location on an open stretch of land near the beach provided its defenders with a clear field of fire. There was no ground cover, no way to approach it without being seen, which meant they would be exposed to the superior firepower of the Cossacks. Unless, Walks Straight suggested, they waited for the thick fog that so frequently blanketed the island to launch their attack. It was agreed.

But the arrival of the second Cossack vessel created a concern among the leaders. They had learned they could defeat the Cossack with a combination of surprise and superior force. Now they were unsure of the number they would be facing in an attack. The sheeting rain had made it impossible to determine if the Cossacks on board had landed. Twice, men had been seen in a small boat near the beach.

Because of Walks Straight's ability to speak and understand the Cossack tongue, he was chosen, along with Killer Whale, to visit the enemy encampment on a pretext of trade to assess their strength. Walks Straight carried the bundle of a half dozen sea otter pelts under his arm and, together with Killer Whale, set out from the temporary camp where the warriors had massed preparatory to the attack on the Cossacks. As was always the case, the women and children, including Tasha and her son, had been sent to a fortified village elsewhere on the island.

As they approached the camp, still out of musket range, Walks Straight heard the shout of the Cossack guard alerting the others to their presence. Several times in the past they'd made excuses to meet with the Cossacks, so this occasion would not seem unusual to them, Walks Straight knew. Continuing forward at the same pace, he observed the quickened activity in the camp and the sharpness with which the Cossacks scanned the other sides.

'We have come to trade!' Walks Straight called in their language and held up the bundle of pelts for the guard to see.

Motioning with his musket barrel, the Cossack gestured for them to come ahead. He waited until they were several steps past him, then fell in behind them while another man took his place. Walks Straight saw no unfamiliar faces among the men stationed outside as he and Killer Whale approached the hut. Solovey stood by the door, waiting for them.

Walks Straight halted a man's length from him. 'We have come to trade,' he repeated.

Solovey's glance briefly dropped to the otter skins he carried, then lifted to the pair of them. 'We will go inside out of this wind.' He pushed the door open and walked into the hut ahead of them.

All previous meetings had been held outside. Never before had they been allowed within the structure. Walks Straight moved quickly to take this opportunity to count the Cossacks inside and gauge the stoutness of the dwelling.

Conscious of so many eyes watching him with distrust, Walks Straight glanced swiftly around the long, dimly lit room, scanning the bearded faces turned toward him for that of a stranger. There was no unfamiliar face among the more than three score men in the room. The door was swung shut behind him, closing out the gray light of the rainy day. Walks Straight half turned, feeling trapped, then forced his muscles to relax as Solovey approached him.

'Show me what you have.' Solovey nodded at the skins tied in a bundle. When Walks Straight started to offer it to him, the Cossack shook his head. 'You untie it.' Walks Straight knew Solovey was remembering the stories told him about the cutting of a Cossack's throat while he was busy untying bundled furs. It gave him satisfaction to know Solovey felt this need for caution when he and Killer Whale were the only Aleuts in the camp.

After unfastening the leather string, Walks Straight laid the pelts on a nearby barrel and stepped back so Solovey could examine the skins. The dank room smelled strongly of tobacco and the peculiar odor of Cossack bodies. Muddy water dripped from the sod-thatched roof of the structure. Walks Straight listened to the whistling wind, using the sound it made to help him locate the board-covered slots along the shadowed walls through which muskets could be fired.

'These pelts are worth very little. Look at the scars,' Solovey stated.

Although he knew the skins were of inferior quality, Walks Straight argued with Solovey over their value so Killer Whale could have more time to study their enemy. 'You should give me what I ask, Solovey. These pelts may be the only fur you will see. You are afraid to send your hunters after the sea otter.' He watched the Cossack redden at his taunt.

'You ask too much for them.'

'Where are the Cossacks from the other boat in the bay?' Walks Straight stacked the skins in a pile and wrapped the rawhide string around them. 'Maybe they will be more willing to trade for them.'

'Go out to their boat and ask them.'

'Are none of them here?' Walks Straight studied the men in the room, this time making no attempt to conceal his interest. All of them he'd seen before or recognized from descriptions.

'No. Our quarters are barely large enough for ourselves.' Solovey tilted his head at an inquiring angle. 'How many live together in your barabara?'

'Forty-two.' He picked up the furs and tucked them under his arm.

'Counting women and children?'

'Yes.' He heard voices coming from outside the hut and the sound of footsteps slogging through the mud approaching the door. Briefly, the daylight made a black silhouette of the man who entered, then he stepped through the opening and pushed the door shut. Suddenly Walks Straight saw the distinctive wings of white hair at the man's temples and stiffened in shock. The blue eyes that stared back at him unmistakably belonged to Tolstykh. For so long Tasha had feared he would come here searching for them, but Walks Straight had never believed Tolstykh would look for them here.

The blood started to pound in his head. He had to get away and warn Tasha. Quickly he shifted his grip on the furs, then hurled the bundle at Tolstykh's head, and bolted for the door. 'Stop him!' Tolstykh shouted. Walks Straight managed to pull the door open just as someone grabbed him from behind. While he struggled to break loose, Killer Whale darted past him to freedom.

More arms closed around him, and Walks Straight strained under the weight of so many more hanging on him. Desperately he fought against them, even after he knew there was no hope of escaping. Finally he stopped struggling.

'Bind his hands.' Andrei looked on from the side, satisfied now that Tasha's brother was well and truly caught. The search was almost over. He could nearly taste the moment of victory when he would reclaim his son. Andrei waited until the savage's wrists were tied tightly behind his back, then issued an order to the promyshleniki surrounding the native: 'Step away from him.'

After a momentary hesitation, they shifted to flank their prisoner. Andrei moved forward to confront him. 'Where are they?' His demand was met with silent defiance. 'You will tell me,' Andrei vowed.

A mud-splattered promyshlenik appeared at the doorway. 'The other one got away,' he reported to Solovey. 'He's wounded. Should we go after him?'

'No,' Solovey said, looking at their prisoner. 'This one will tell us all we need to know.'

'Put him in the boat,' Andrei ordered. 'I'm taking him out to the *Andreian*.' Anticipating a protest from Solovey, he faced him. 'This Aleut is my hostage. You are welcome to be present while I question him.'

For a moment, Solovey appeared to be on the verge of challenging him, then he thought better of it. Tolstykh was a wealthy merchant, wielding considerable power and influence in Siberia and sailing under an imperial ukase. Solovey grudgingly yielded.

Heavily guarded, the tall Aleut was led by a rope around his neck to the beached yawl from the *Andreian i Natalia*. Few words were spoken as the boat was launched and they set out across the sullen waters of the bay to the vessel anchored near the *Sv Petr i Sv Pavel*. There were few sounds beyond the occasional screech of a seabird and the rubbing of the oars in their fulcrums.

From his aft seat in the yawl, Andrei stared at the black head of Tasha's Aleut brother sitting so erectly in front of him. His shoulders were pulled back by the rope binding his hands and wrists together behind his back, emphasizing the straightness of his posture. The pride and dignity in his bearing galled Andrei.

In all his dealings with the Aleuts, he'd been fair. Every time he recalled how concerned he had been about Tasha's feelings, he became angry and bitter. What an old fool he'd been to think she cared for him. For too long he had forgotten that she was half savage. It was plain that she resented him, as all the Aleuts resented the Russians. Her brother had never masked his feelings. His very presence on Unalaska proved to Andrei that he was involved in fomenting this uprising by the natives.

Even if it weren't for his son living somewhere on this island, Andrei would have remained at Unalaska to quell this revolt before it spread along the chain. No Russian, promyshlenik or merchant, considered abandoning any part of the archipelago to the control of the native population. Too many fortunes could be made in these waters to let ignorant savages stand in their way. They had conquered two continents and a half dozen races and had learned to silence local protests with the sword.

Once they were aboard the vessel, the interrogation began. Andrei concentrated his questioning on the size and strength of the resistance, the location of villages, their number of warriors, and the quantity of Russian firepower that had fallen into Aleut hands. The whereabouts of his son he saved for later.

Not a single question was answered. A part of Andrei was glad Walks Straight had refused to talk – the part of him that was going to enjoy loosening Tasha's brother's tongue. He studied those flat black eyes for a moment, then smiled.

'You will tell me what I want to know. You will tell me *everything* I want to know,' Andrei murmured, then swung his attention to the flanking guards. 'Strip him and tie him to the mast, then bring the knout.'

The knout was a deadly whip. Its dried and hardened thongs of rawhide were interwoven with sharp wires, hooked to tear the flesh of its victim. In Russia, it was an instrument of corporal punishment. Few survived a sentence of a hundred and twenty lashes.

The promyshleniki tied their naked prisoner to the forward mast, stretching his arms high above his head. His long, pale torso and wide, thickly muscled shoulders provided an unmarred surface to test the cruel efficiency of the Russian whip.

'Gag him,' Andrei instructed. 'Sound carries a considerable distance over water. There is no need for his friends to hear his screams.'

When the kerchief was in place, Andrei signaled his Cossack officer to begin the flogging. At the first lash of the whip, the Aleut's body jerked convulsively. The hardened thongs left criss-crossing streaks of red on the broad back. Blood ran from the furrows gouged in the skin. Again the Cossack brought the whip down hard, its many tails splaying across the shoulder muscles, its sharp hooks ripping open more flesh. Walks Straight writhed under it.

By the time a half dozen lashes were administered, his back was coated with blood. Andrei watched the way Tasha's brother cringed close to the mast when he heard the faint whooshing sound of the knout slicing through the air before it struck him. His arm muscles bunched, his wrists strained against the knotted ropes that bound him in place. Then the flesh-shredding thongs landed, splattering blood and bits of skin. The kerchief gag choked off the scream, turning it into an inhuman groan.

Andrei's attention was centered on that back, mesmerized by the rise and fall of the whip upon it. He watched the brutal knout come down again and again, the rawhide strips darkened with blood.

Then the body ceased to convulse in pain. Walks Straight slumped against the mast, his head lolling to the side, knees bent, the knotted ropes around his wrists holding his full weight while blood trickled down his arms where the ropes had rubbed his skin raw.

In sudden panic, Andrei realized Walks Straight was unconscious. He couldn't remember how many strokes of the lash had been administered. A dozen? Twice that? He'd lost count. Swiftly he moved to grab the arm of the Cossack before he could bring the bloodied knout down again.

'If you have killed him, yours will be the next blood the knout tastes.' Andrei trembled with anger. The Cossack nervously retreated a step, the excited flush draining from his face.

'He lives,' Solovey announced after checking out the flogged native and then removing the dirty kerchief that gagged him.

'Water will revive him,' Andrei stated, masking his relief. He glared at the Cossack. 'Fetch a pail.'

'Of sea water,' Solovey inserted, smiling with animal cunning.

Glancing at the raw, red flesh the whip had exposed, Andrei nodded slowly. 'Yes, fill the pail with sea water.'

After the Cossack lowered the wooden bucket over the vessel's side and filled it with the cold brine of the bay, he carried it over to the motionless body and heaved the contents onto the masticated flesh. A deep-throated groan of agony rent the air as the Aleut arched rigidly.

'Cut him down,' Andrei ordered.

Two promyshleniki from Solovey's camp sliced the ropes that bound him to the mast. Another moan came from him as he sagged to his knees. Gripping his arms, the Russian hunters hauled him to his feet and dragged him around to face their leader, who had come to stand beside Andrei. But Walks Straight was only half conscious, his head hanging low, his chin nearly touching his chest.

Andrei grabbed a handful of black hair and pulled his head up so he could see the Aleut's face. He gazed indifferently at the tears streaming from glazed eyes. 'How many warriors are on this island?'

'Four' – he rasped hoarsely – 'maybe five . . . hundred.'

'Where?' Andrei demanded.

'Most . . . scattered . . . villages.' Each word seemed to require great effort.

'Where's the greatest concentration of warriors?' Andrei persisted, but Tasha's brother looked at him dully and closed his mouth in a mute show of resistance, moving his head slowly in denial. 'Pour some more saltwater on his back,' he told the

Cossack officer as he let go of that black hair to step back. 'But do it slowly.'

As the sea brine trickled onto his mangled back, a strangled cry of pain erupted from deep inside the Aleut's throat. He arched convulsively. Andrei watched him writhe and twist as the torture was drawn out. He smiled faintly in satisfaction when he heard the murmured plea, 'No, no,' mixed in with the long moan. With a wave of his hand, he signaled the Cossack to cease pouring.

'Where's the greatest concentration of warriors?' Andrei repeated his question while faint tremors quivered through the Aleut. This time when he met Andrei's gaze, his eyes held fear.

'Not far . . . temporary camp . . .' His breathing was rough and shallow, racked with the pain consuming him. 'Two hundred . . . two hundred fifty warriors.'

'So close,' Solovey murmured.

'Why are there so many in one place?' Andrei demanded.

Broken by the unendurable pain, and the threat of more, he eventually told them everything – the reason for coming to the camp, the plan to attack it under the cover of fog, the number of firearms in the Aleuts' possession – no detail was withheld.

As soon as it was determined there was no more to be learned, Solovey set out for camp with his men to prepare for the coming attack. Andrei promised to support him with a contingent of men from his vessel, but the reinforcements wouldn't be transported ashore until the fog came in, so the Aleuts wouldn't be aware of the camp's increased strength.

When the boat carrying Solovey and his men pulled away from the *Andreian i Natalia*, Andrei turned to the semi-conscious form sprawled on the deck. Hardly an inch of flesh on the man's back remained intact. Unmoved by the gore before him, Andrei crouched down beside him and grasped the black hair to lift the man's head.

'Where is Tasha? Where is my son?'

Her brother babbled an unintelligible answer in his native tongue. Andrei roughly tightened his grip, yanking the head back a little farther. 'In Russian,' he ordered.

Although the response was barely coherent, Andrei understood enough. His fingers released their grip on the black hair, letting the head fall back to the deck. Straightening, Andrei faced northward. The misting rain reduced the visibility, hiding the other side of the bay. His son was there in a large village where the women and children had been sent. Soon he would hold him in his arms again. The certainty of it flowed through him like an invigorating tonic.

'What do you want done with the prisoner?' the Cossack asked in a hesitant voice.

'Tie him up.' Andrei walked away.

15

The thick gray-white fog seemed to muffle all sound. A horde of wraithlike figures moved stealthily forward in the eerie stillness, closing silently around the crudely built hut. A few of the natives wore vests of armor made out of vertical rods of wood lashed together with sinew, the garment signifying their status as village headmen. The war party crept to within thirty feet of the structure, apparently undetected. Suddenly, without warning, the Russians inside opened fire. At point-blank range, the result was devastating. The Aleuts attempted to charge the hut but the barrage of musketfire drove them back. Giving up the battle, they fled the scene, leaving a hundred of their dead behind.

Aboard the *Andreian i Natalia*, Walks Straight was briefly roused from his pain-filled stupor by the thundering report of the muskets. He heard the death cries of his warrior comrades and felt the crushing guilt of his betrayal. A tear ran down his cheek as he lay open-eyed, staring vacantly into the swirling fog. It was the pain, that's why he'd done it. They had to understand what it was like to be locked in the throes of a killing agony and not die. He shut his eyes, but there was no release from the suffering that tortured his body and his mind.

When the fog finally thinned, eliminating the possibility that the natives might try another sneak attack, the Russians ventured out of the hut. The wounded they found among the battlefield dead were mercilessly dispatched, and the bodies heaped in a common grave. After locating the abandoned encampment of the war party, they destroyed the temporary dwellings and several baidars.

Frustrated, Solovey looked over the demolished camp. 'Those bloodthirsty natives have probably scattered to all points of the island by now.'

'I think not,' Andrei said and motioned for the two

promyshleniki guarding his prisoner to bring him forward. Weakened from the loss of blood and immobilized by the excruciating pain from his back, he had to be bodily dragged over. 'Where would the warriors have gone when they left here?' There was a barely perceptible shake of the head, denying any knowledge. 'Would they have gone to the village where the women and children are?' Andrei demanded confidently and noted with satisfaction the small nod of agreement.

'I wondered why you kept the bastard alive.' Solovey smiled in approval. 'This village, how far is it from here?'

'An hour's march.' Andrei knew he needed to say no more than that. By nature, Solovey was cruel and given to excess. Avenging the massacre of his fellow countrymen provided the Russian with a ready excuse to indulge in his brutal passions.

Solovey called his men together and informed them of their new objective. 'Before the day is over, these savages will learn how costly it is to spill Russian blood.'

The lookout's warning came too late to evacuate the women, children, and wounded from the village. Everyone took refuge inside the earthen-walled barabara. The dwelling had been built for defense, with interior posts supporting an upper wooden walkway from which warriors could shoot their arrows through apertures in the roof. The men scrambled up notched logs to take their defensive positions and await the assault of the Cossacks.

With her son, Tasha joined the mothers, who gathered all the young ones at one end of the barabara, thus freeing other women to look after the wounded and infirm. All around her, children whimpered and cried, confused and frightened by the panic they sensed in the adults. Tasha felt it, too, and held an infant child more tightly in her arms, at the same time trying to keep Zachar beside her. A young girl, ten summers old, finally picked him up and hugged him close to her slim body, drawing comfort from him as much as she comforted.

A musket boomed, scaring screams from children, but it was just the beginning. The singing of bowstrings couldn't match the roar of the Russian weapons, and the shower of arrows was answered by a hail of bullets flying through the defensive openings. Amidst the noise of battle and sobbing children came the cries of the wounded as the impact of bullets sent them spinning off their perches onto the crowded floor of the barabara. One

162

landed in front of Tasha, half of his face blown away. She stared in horror at the bloodied cavity where a cheekbone and eye had once been.

The futility of their fighting quickly became apparent to the surviving warriors, and they abandoned their defensive positions, hauling down the notched logs behind them. They sat down among the others to wait, shielded by the dirt walls of the semi-subterranean dwelling, while lead balls continued to thwack into the ceiling rafters.

The musket barrage tapered off, then stopped. In the ensuing silence, the beat of Tasha's heart sounded in her ears. Tensely, she strained to hear some sound above the soft whimpers of the children and the low moans of the wounded. She huddled more closely against the woven-grass matting that covered the earthen wall, protectively cradling the infant in her arms. She glanced at her son, assuring herself that he was faring well in the young girl's care.

As the silence lengthened, with no sound coming from outside, her attention strayed to the roof of the dwelling. The hatch was the only way out and the only way the Cossacks could get in. She watched for any telltale sifting of dust from the sod roof that would warn of their approach. Nothing. Her anxiety grew with the strain of waiting. She didn't believe, as some were murmuring, that the Cossacks might have left.

The soft scratching sound, not unlike that of an animal digging in the earth, was so faint that Tasha didn't notice it at first. When it finally penetrated her consciousness, she stiffened away from the wall in alarm, then looked back at it, trying to determine the direction of the sound. As she was about to warn the others that the Cossacks were digging a hole in the side, the scratching stopped. Tasha waited, but it didn't resume. Tasha loosened her hold on the baby and once again turned her back to the wall.

A tremendous force pushed her from behind, propelling her forward. Instinctively she half turned to let her shoulder absorb the impact of the fall and protect the baby. She never heard the explosion that blew in the wall and only knew the shock of motion followed by an enveloping blackness.

When she came to, frantic wails made the first impression on her senses, followed by cries of terror and panic from the villagers. Tasha was conscious of a heavy weight pinning her legs as she shifted position to check the baby. A thin layer of dirt covered much of its face, getting into its eyes and mouth. Tasha wiped as much of it away as she could while she realized that somehow the wall had caved in. It was the weight of its dirt that trapped her legs.

Cossacks streamed through the breach in the wall, intent on the warriors and ignoring the women and children. Twisting and clawing, she managed to pull her legs free of the dirt and crawl through the debris to a dark corner, hugging the baby to her breast with one arm. Panic reigned as people ran in all directions trying to escape the swarming Cossacks. Tasha struggled to avoid catching the terror in the air while she looked at the confusing mass, trying to locate her son. She was still dazed from the concussion of the blast, her head ringing.

She saw the body lying motionless beneath a cross beam that had collapsed during the cave-in. It was the young girl who'd been holding Zachar. Tasha went cold with fear. Hurriedly she laid the baby on the floor and pulled a torn section of woven matting over the infant to conceal it, then scrambled over the dirt and debris to the girl's body, fearing that her son might have been crushed beneath the beam as well.

She rolled the timber off the inert girl. Zachar wasn't beneath her. She looked wildly about and saw a pair of chubby legs sticking out from a nearby pile of dirt. 'Zachar,' Tasha cried and attacked the pile, frantically clawing and digging at the smothering dirt.

Intent on rescuing her son, Tasha was mindless to all movement around her. Suddenly, she was violently shoved aside. She tried to scramble back to the pile, but Andrei had taken her place. For an instant, she stared at him in frozen panic. He had come for his son, as she had always known he would. He would take Zachar from her.

Wildly she threw herself on him, hitting and pulling, trying to drag him away from her son, but he paid no more attention to her than a nest-robbing raven pays to the panicked flutterings of a mother wren. A part of her was conscious of his hands tunneling alongside the child's body. The dirt fell away as he lifted the little boy. Tasha abandoned her assault at the sight of the child's blue lips and discolored face, unmistakable evidence of suffocation. But the boy wasn't Zachar, and a tremor of relief shuddered through her.

'No,' Andrei moaned rawly.

Seeing the tortured look of grief in his expression, Tasha

164

reached to take the dead child from him and tell him it wasn't their son. He saw the movement of her hands and turned on her. She glimpsed the madness in his eyes. He swung his arm wildly, the back of his hand striking her squarely on the cheek. Pain exploded in her face as the force of the blow knocked her to the dirt floor. Stunned, she lay there tasting the blood in her mouth while black waves swam before her eyes.

A pair of boots walked by her. Through the swirling mist of her vision, Tasha saw Andrei gently lay the dead child on a grass mat, then stumble blindly through the gaping hole in the earthen side of the barabara. He believed their son was dead. Now she had to find Zachar and get away, Tasha thought.

One whole side of her face continued to throb painfully as she pushed to her feet and staggered back to resume her search for Zachar.

A bearded Cossack loomed before her, a bloodied sword in his hand. Tasha recoiled from the killing lust she saw in his eys. But he grabbed her by the shoulder and roughly shoved her, pushing her into the flow of frightened villagers being herded outside. She was trapped like all the others.

As she emerged from the barabara, a Cossack motioned her toward a group of women and children huddled together. Tasha hurried to join them, casting fearful glances about for Andrei, but he was nowhere to be seen. She looked anxiously back at the barabara, wondering what had happened to Zachar, and noticed that the men were being grouped separately from the women and children. Tasha remembered the story of the massacre on Attu when Strong Man was killed, and felt a sickening knot of fear in her stomach.

Just then an old woman came out of the dwelling carrying Zachar in her arms. The joy she felt that her son was alive and well almost compelled Tasha to rush out to reclaim him, but she was afraid Andrei might be somewhere nearby watching. It was better that he believed Zachar was dead. No longer did she feel any of the compassion that had so briefly influenced her. After the old woman joined the group, Tasha moved to stand behind her.

From inside the barabara came a choked cry. 'They are killing our wounded,' a woman wailed.

Soon the man the islanders called Solovey led his handful of Cossack murderers out of the dwelling. Tasha recognized him from the description Walks Straight had given of his hooked nose and gleaming black eyes. The Cossack leader ignored the women, walking instead to the cordon of men guarding the warriors.

One by one, Solovey ordered warriors dragged from the group and killed. Some were put to the sword and others shot. The Cossacks seemed to find pleasure in the killing. Tasha was riveted by the horror of the scene, unable to look away even when her sanity cried for a respite. Her spine tingled from the wails and grief-stricken screams of the women when a son or loved one was selected to die. The brisk wind blew the smell of death to her, and she tried to keep from breathing in the odor. She was glad Walks Straight had not returned from battle and wouldn't have to know the terror of waiting to die.

'This is taking too long and there is no sport in it,' Solovey declared to his men. 'We are wasting precious powder and lead on these scum of the islands.'

'Shall we put them all to the sword?'

'No.' The Cossack leader grinned. 'I have a better idea. Who will wager to see how many men a single musket ball will kill? I have twenty rubles that say it will be ten.'

Tasha wished fervently that she didn't understand their language, that she didn't know what they were saying when the Cossacks shouted their wagers. A dozen warriors were dragged from the steadily dwindling group of males and tied closely together, one behind the other to form a single line. She began to notice how distracted the Cossacks were by the proceedings as they moved closer for a better view, leaving the rear area of her group unguarded. Tasha feared what would happen when the Cossacks turned their attention to the women and children. There might not be another chance to escape. Hurriedly, she claimed Zachar from the old woman and began inching her way to the back of the group. Five steps separated her from the nearest woman, yet none of the Cossacks noticed.

The instant she heard the firing of the musket, Tasha turned and ran, with Zachar bouncing on one hip. She raced for the small ridge, knowing if she could make it over the top without being seen, her escape would be successful. Voices were raised behind her, but none called attention to her flight. When she crested the grassy rise, she heard a Cossack shout that nine were dead.

166

She stumbled down the slope and sank to her knees. She was out of breath and panting, her arms aching from the weight of her son. She looked toward the inland mountains where there were caves in which she could hide. She didn't dare linger so close to the Cossacks. Rest could come later when she was safely away.

Tasha sought refuge from the cold wind in a cave containing the mummified remains of an Aleut woman. All the dead woman's possessions lay about the cave, the wooden dishes, knives, baskets, and other utensils perfectly preserved. The mummified body itself, bundled in sea lion skins and wrapped with braided sinew, rested in its wood-framed cradle atop a platform. The mummification of the dead was a custom practiced by the Aleuts of the eastern island groups, but Tasha's people on Attu and the near islands didn't believe in mummies. She entered the cave without concern.

It was snug and warm inside, and she was exhausted from the climb. The muscles in her arms trembled with weariness as she set Zachar on the stone floor. He crawled directly over to investigate the baskets sitting out below the platform. For the time being, Tasha left him to explore the cave, and she walked over to the platform. As she lifted the mummy bundle, its body wrapped in a tightly flexed position, she handled it respectfully and carefully sat it upright on the platform of hewn planks, so she could borrow its cradle for her son.

After Zachar was ensconced in its leather basin, Tasha sat down to rest. But each time she closed her eyes, macabre visions danced before them.

She was alone, far from her island home, without the security of a family member for the first time in her life, and unsure whether any of her new friends at the village were still alive or not. She looked at her son, frightened suddenly by the responsibility that was solely hers now.

That night she nursed her son while her own stomach made hungry growls. She knew she wouldn't be able to keep that up for long. As she borrowed the grass mat from the mummy's platform to cover her and Zachar while they slept, Tasha regretted that these Unalaskans didn't provide a supply of food for their dead.

Obtaining food took primary importance the next day. Tasha couldn't risk returning to the village as long as there was a chance Andrei was still there. Not far from the cave, the ocean offered an abundant supply of food. With Zachar in the cradle strapped to her back, she set out for the shore.

When she reached the coast, the tide was at its ebb. She paused behind a jumble of boulders that guarded a short stretch of exposed sand and scanned the area before she ventured out. A circle of rocks hemmed in a portion of the beach. Tasha left Zachar there while she went to gather their food. She dug for clams and harvested some kelp from the shallow waters, using a knife borrowed from the cave and stowing her food in a borrowed basket.

A flock of sanderlings that had been sharing the beach with her suddenly took flight. The rush of wings signaled alarm, and Tasha turned. An old man came staggering and weaving across the sand, his hair white as the head of an eagle. He was naked, his hands tied in front of him, his elbows and knees bloodied from frequent falls.

Alarmed that he might be pursued by Cossacks, Tasha broke into a run toward the circle of rocks where she'd left Zachar. The old man stumbled and fell, tried valiantly once to get up, then slumped motionless. Tasha hesitated uncertainly, listening for the sounds of pursuit. All she could hear was the ocean.

Warily she walked over to the old man. His back was one large crusty scab of dried blood with greenish pus oozing from the cracks. The sight made her empty stomach churn nauseously. She swallowed down the bile that tried to rise in her throat and tentatively touched an arm partially trapped beneath the man's body. His skin felt fiery hot. He moaned, lying face-down in the sand. When he turned his head to the side, Tasha saw his face.

'Walks Straight.' She stared in disbelief, then ran her fingers through the white hair on his head. It was real. Nothing came off on her hand. This was her brother, although she couldn't understand how this could happen. When the initial shock faded, she struggled to get her hands under his chest and push him upright.

After she got him on his knees, he seemed to notice her, but there was no recognition in his watery, red-rimmed eyes. 'Help me,' he pleaded hoarsely.

'I will,' she promised, crying softly.

Somehow she managed to get him up the mountain to the cave. Then she began the task of cleaning his inflamed back. Mercifully, her brother passed out when she started peeling away the scabs. In all the bloody aftermath of battle, she'd never seen a wound like his. She vomited at the sight of the raw, festering flesh, then cried helplessly before finally regaining control of her emotions. The village shaman had been murdered by the Cossacks. There was no one else to whom she could go for help. She had to treat him herself.

Endlessly she bathed his back and applied poultices made from herbs she gathered. She searched for food, fed Zachar and Walks Straight, and fetched the water. Countless nights she cried from exhaustion and fear while she sat through her brother's bouts of delirium.

One night he was fairly coherent in his wild ramblings. Tasha wiped the sweat from his face with a damp kerchief and absently listened to him begging for the pain to stop, a plea she'd become inured to. Then she thought she heard him speak Andrei's name.

'What happened? Who did this?' She asked the questions that had gone unanswered since the day she found him, doubting that he heard her, or understood if he did.

'Tolstykh. He hit me.' Pain contorted his features. 'The leather . . . there were teeth in it . . . I did not want to tell.' He sobbed like a little boy.

'Tell what?' Tasha frowned.

'Can you hear them?' He opened his eyes wide in fear. 'I did not want them to die. He made me tell.'

Gradually it all came out, although Tasha had to piece much of it together. She was sobered by his confession of betrayal, not only of the warriors but also of her. Yet, over the past days, she had grown to appreciate how great his pain was. She could understand and forgive.

'I have shamed Strong Man,' Walks Straight cried brokenly. 'He died bravely, defending his people. I . . . I was too weak.' He shuddered and mumbled something else. Tasha ached with pity for him, and saved some for herself.

His body healed slowly. Even after he recognized her, Walks Straight seldom talked. He couldn't bring himself to speak of his shame to her, and Tasha couldn't bring herself to tell him she already knew. Neither mentioned the recent events. Still painfully sore, he spent most of his time lying on his stomach, staring at the ground. Not even Zachar's antics aroused his interest.

For Tasha, his gradual recovery eased the burden of caring for his every need and gave her more time to try to find food. Now she was able to leave Zachar with him so she could venture farther afield in her search. Even then she never seemed to bring back enough to satisfy all the hunger in the cave.

Snow was blowing, making the mountain trail slippery as she made her way down to the meadow nearby to search for the underground caches of rodents and steal their winter store of edible roots. A woman from the village was already there, although Tasha almost didn't recognize the bony, gaunt-cheeked face as belonging to someone she knew. She approached her hesitantly.

'Have the Cossacks gone?' Tasha asked.

The woman nodded. 'Solovey lives at his winter camp. The other boat went away.'

Relief shuddered through Tasha. Andrei was gone and she no longer had to fear losing her son. It was safe to go back. The prospect of sleeping in a warm barabara and tasting a meal of fresh fish or seal blubber almost made her light-headed.

As if hearing her thoughts, the woman said, 'There is much hunger in the village.'

'Are there no hunters left?'

'Some still live. The Cossacks killed two hundred.' The woman's expression was marked by a quiet desperation. 'Now all of us are dying slowly. Before they left the village, the Cossacks destroyed everything – the bidarkas, the throwing boards, spears, bows and arrows. The men have no way to hunt.'

The news left Tasha shaken. The villagers derived more than sustenance from the sea mammals the hunters killed. They made their kayaks from the skins, their weapons from the bones and ivory. Without the means to hunt, the men could not replace what they'd lost. They were trapped on the land, with so much of the sea's bounty beyond their reach. Tasha realized her small family would be no better off if they returned to the village.

Later she told Walks Straight about her meeting with the woman, but omitted any mention of the destruction of the village's means of survival. He would only blame himself more for leading the Cossacks to the site. Instead she stressed Andrei's departure from the island and the Cossack's absence in the village.

'It is safe now,' she told him. 'We no longer have to hide in this cave.'

But her brother sat unmoving, his shoulders hunched, his

head bowed. 'You take Zachar and go back to the village.'

The whiteness of his hair stood out sharply against the darkness of the cave's backdrop. It was the most obvious change in him, but Tasha had noticed too many others. There was little about the man before her that reminded her of her brother. His shoulders seemed permanently bowed, his posture slumped. Rarely did he hold his head up. There was no more defiance in him. His spirit was crushed, his pride broken. Sometimes Tasha had the feeling that she had patched together the outer shell of him but the thing inside that made him a man was missing. He was like that mummy on the shelf with all the skin and bones intact but the vital organs removed. She didn't need to be told that he wished he was dead. Given a choice, her brother would make this cave his tomb. She couldn't let him do it.

'I have no wish to go back to the village. Too many bad things happened there.' Now that she'd had more time to think about it, Tasha knew that for her brother's sake, it was best they didn't return there. 'We will go to the village on the north of the island where we first stayed, as soon as you are strong enough to walk that far.' She set a wooden dish in front of him containing a portion of the roots she had collected and scraped clean. He stared at the contents with disinterest and made no move to eat them.

'Go and leave me,' he said.

Tasha tried not to show how much his reply distressed her, and instead chided him. 'What would you eat? How would you live?'

'Maybe it is better if I die.'

Although she had guessed that was his wish, hearing him say it snapped something inside. 'No!' she protested. All those days and nights she had spent looking after him, all that she had endured would be for nothing. She deserved something in return. 'I need you. *He* needs you!' The sweeping gesture of her hand indicated her son. 'Who will take care of us? Who will teach Zachar how to hunt? It is fine for you to die and have no more pain or hunger, but what will happen to us? You are his uncle!' Abruptly she turned away from him, trembling with the fear that had given rise to her anger.

For a long time the only sound in the cave was Zachar's babbling, but it prompted Tasha to pick up a root and start chewing on it, even though it seemed tasteless. For the sake of her son, she had to eat.

'I will go with you,' Walks Straight said at last, speaking in an emotionless voice.

Tasha didn't react. She felt too drained.

During the course of the next several days, he made an effort to get back on his feet and be useful. Tasha could see he was just going through the motions of resuming life, but she was past caring about his lack of will. She went to the village and reclaimed the few personal belongings she'd left there and obtained an old parka for her brother.

The northern village welcomed them back. Once again they could sleep in a warm barabara with their bellies full. Over the long winter, Tasha watched her son grow chubby again and her brother regain more of his strength. He started hunting again, always alone, and kept to himself, never mingling with the men with whom he had plotted the revolt against the Cossacks. He played with Zachar, making a game of the exercises that developed the muscles he would need as a hunter, yet Tasha never saw her brother smile. Nor did he take part in any of the singing, dancing, or storytelling.

Everyone on the island knew about what the Cossacks had done. Those survivors with relatives in the other villages had been taken in by their families. Tasha was certain her brother must have heard about the extreme suffering there, but he never spoke of it. And whatever outrage this barbarism had engendered among the natives was smothered by fear that too loud a protest would incur the Cossacks' wrath again. A few villages had even made peace with Solovey.

The time of the long nights passed, and the sun began to linger in the sky. One day a storm forced a hunter from another village to take refuge in their camp. That night, while the wind and rain blew outside, everyone gathered around the visitor to learn the latest news from other parts of the island.

While Zachar slept in the cradle suspended from a cross beam of the sleeping partition, Tasha sat close to the light of the stone lamp and sewed together the intestinal skins of the sea lion to make a waterproof parka for her brother. Walks Straight sat beside her whittling a piece of bone into a properly sized shank for a fish hook.

Someone asked the hunter about the conditions at the devastated village. 'They have little food. Many have grown weak and died.' Tasha glanced apprehensively at her brother, but he gave no sign he had heard the question or the answer. 'The Cossacks have suffered this winter, too. Their teeth fall out and their mouths bleed. Eleven have died. Many are weak. Some cannot even stand.'

'Now would be the time to attack them.' It was a tentatively issued statement, a half-hopeful suggestion waiting to be seconded.

Walks Straight halted his whittling. As hesitant murmurs swept the room, testing the phrases of revolt, he rose to his feet and slunk into his sleeping cubicle, unnoticed by everyone but Tasha. He unfastened the rolled matting and let it fall to shut himself off from the communal area.

Tasha looked around to be sure no one was watching, then followed after him. When she lifted aside the woven curtain, she saw him lying on his side facing the wall. She knelt beside him.

'What is it? What's wrong?'

The silence lasted so long Tasha didn't think he intended to answer her. 'We will never be free of the Cossacks,' he said finally.

'Why? Our warriors were victorious against them before. Five vessels were destroyed and the Cossacks aboard them killed. Why can it not be done again?' she argued, trying to instill some resistance in him. 'They won a single battle. Does that mean we should give up the struggle?'

'They are too strong for us.'

'Because they have muskets?'

'Because they have the power of fear,' he replied flatly. Tasha drew back, realizing he was right. Fear was their strongest weapon. Look at what it had done to him.

The island turned green and the female fur seals swam through the passes on their annual migration to a destination in the north known only to them. And six more scurvy-stricken Cossacks died in Unalaska. Some emboldened natives urged their fellow villagers to unite in another uprising and encountered considerable reluctance, especially from those who had suffered such great deprivation. But there were others who listened. Each time such talk started around Walks Straight, he walked away. He wanted to have no knowledge of their plans, possess no information that might be tortured from him.

Although there were a few isolated skirmishes with the Cossacks, the natives mounted no genuine offensive. But the growing threat of one was enough to prompt Solovey to march his Cossacks on the villages. Most of the natives fled before him without a fight, then returned to find their dwellings ransacked, their furs stolen, their bidarkas demolished, and their weapons smashed. With relatively little bloodshed, Solovey succeeded in crushing all resistance.

Tasha gazed at the brown-turning grass. A cold wind from the northwest stung her face and pushed the clouds against the mountain peak. There were no more berries to be picked, no more edible roots to be dug, no more eggs to be stolen from the cliff nests of birds. The dried salmon from the summer's runs was all gone.

Tasha looked at the skinny legs of her son, now four summers old. Food was becoming scarcer as more Aleuts were forced to seek their food from the barren land instead of the sea. Items that had previously supplemented their diet of fish and the meat of sea mammals had become their staples. Now they, too, were gone. Soon Zachar's belly would become distended.

She turned to her brother. 'You were right. The Cossacks are stronger. By the time winter is over, hundreds will die of hunger. The old and the sick will go first, then the very young.' She paused to study Zachar. 'If we are to live, we must leave the village.'

'Where can we go?' They were trapped on the island, with no means to leave it.

'To the camp of the Cossacks,' she stated. 'They have food. They have bidarkas and weapons for hunting. We will live with them.'

'They will not let us.'

'They will.' Tasha had to believe it, and she had to convince herself that she knew the way to approach them. After living with Andrei, she knew of only one thing these Cossacks respected, one thing they feared – the Creator of All Things, whom they called God.

Once she had made her decision, Tasha wasted no time carrying it out. Walks Straight seemed to have lost the capacity to feel strongly about anything and offered no objection to her plan. They had packed their personal possessions, gathered up Zachar, and set out for the Cossack camp.

As they approached the hut, five Cossacks armed with muskets came out to greet them. Tasha recognized Solovey among them and quelled the rising uneasiness that accompanied the gruesome images the sight of him evoked. She wasn't worried that he would remember her brother. The hunched, white-haired man walking beside her bore little resemblance to the man Walks Straight had been.

'What do you want?' Solovey challenged.

'We wish to be baptized,' Tasha stated. She observed the stunned look that came into his eyes, and felt her confidence grow. 'We have learned the power of your God. We wish to be baptized and allowed to live with you.'

'You speak very well.' Solovey continued to stare at her.

'My father was a Cossack. I am called Tasha. This is my son, Zachar.' She indicated the blue-eyed boy in her brother's arms. She didn't mention her son's previous baptism, since she didn't think it would hurt him to be baptized again.

'Who is this man?' Solovey pointed to Walks Straight.

'He is my brother. He will need a Cossack name when you baptize him, too.'

The ceremonial conversion was hastily arranged. All of them were given the surname of Tarakanov, after one of the Cossacks present. And Walks Straight acquired the Cossack name Pavel Ivanovich Tarakanov.

The newly converted family was allowed to build a small barabara alongside the Cossacks' hut. Tasha Lukyevena Tarakanova was enlisted to cook for them while Pavel Ivanovich agreed to hunt sea otter for them.

16 *Autumn 1778*

Although there had been sporadic resistance by some of the Aleut natives for several more years, the punitive actions taken by Solovey and others had ended the mass revolt. Nearly half the Aleuts had died, some in battle but most from starvation and disease. Again the Aleuts and the Cossacks co-existed on the islands, the Aleuts hunting the fur-bearing sea mammals, exchanging them for food and goods, and paying their tribute in furs. There were still incidents of cruelty practised by the Cossacks, but the Aleuts had learned from others of their tribe who had been taken to the Cossack land across the waters that the ones who committed these acts were eventually punished by Cossack leaders in their faraway villages. It was their only consolation.

Walks Straight, called Pavel Tarakanov by the Cossacks, had accepted that things could never be any different. It had taken the heart from him, as it had from so many others.

As an incoming wave raced onto the beach, Walks Straight finished his repair of a small tear in his hide-covered bidarka and looked across the keel of his upturned craft at his nephew, Zachar. He watched while the boy of sixteen summers continued his inspection of his own bidarka, one he'd built himself, checking its seaworthiness in preparation for his first extended sea hunt.

The first whiskers of manhood grew thinly on his face. Like the straight hair on his head, they did not possess the black color of the raven; instead they were the muddy-brown color of the tundra. His eyes were blue – quick and far-seeing, a hunter's eyes. He wore Cossack trousers beneath his bird-skin parka. Walks Straight still clung to the old way, the way of his father. But Zachar knew nothing of it. He was used to the Cossacks coming in ships, staying for a while, lying with Aleut women like his mother, fathering children like his little brother Mikhail, then eventually leaving, only to be replaced by more Cossacks on other ships.

A large skin-boat carrying several Cossacks approached the beach, attracting Walks Straight's attention. As soon as it touched the shore, the men scrambled out of it and hurriedly dragged the boat onto the sand. Walks Straight observed their great agitation as they immediately set out toward the hut of their leader, and he followed them to learn the cause of it.

Zachar was quickly at his side. 'What has excited them?'

'Maybe they have seen a whale.' A whale would provide enough food for an entire winter. Although it was late in the season, it was possible that a stray whale, perhaps even dead or wounded, was still in the vicinity.

The one called Gerasim Grigorovich Ismailov, leader of all the Cossacks on the island and master of the sailing vessel *Sv Pavel*, anchored in the bay, came out of his hut. He was a stern, commanding figure in his uniform and heavy coat, and he possessed a navigator's arrogance, looking down on anyone not of his rank.

'For what reason have you disturbed me?' he demanded of the shaggy, ill-kempt promyshleniki before him.

'The two British ships, the same ones that were seen off the island in early summer, anchored two days ago in a bay at the northern end of the island.'

Ismailov stiffened slightly at the news. The last time the two British vessels had been reported sailing in the area, he had sent a letter to their commanders, delivered by one of the Creoles, and had received no reply.

'What is their purpose? Have you learned?' Ismailov knew the British commanders had to be aware these islands were occupied by the Russians, and he also knew the British were heavily engaged in the fur trade on the North American continent with extensive operations in the Hudson Bay area.

'According to reports from natives in the area, they are making repairs on their vessels and replenishing their freshwater supply ashore. They have landed some cargo,' one promyshlenik added cautiously, uncertain whether the intentions of the British were as innocent as they appeared.

Up to this time, the fur wealth of this long chain of islands was known only to the Russians. When the Russian merchants sold their valuable pelts on the European or Chinese markets, they never disclosed where they had obtained them. The only rivalry was among themselves, so far. Therefore, it was important that Ismailov ascertain the reason British ships were in these waters. But Ismailov was not a man who looked into shadows.

'We shall have to try again to make contact with our foreign visitors,' he stated, then dismissed the promyshleniki, and went back inside his private quarters, sparsely furnished, mainly with items from his ship's cabin.

His glance skipped over the two-year-old bastard offspring of his concubine, the boy child a product of another man's seed and not his own, then it lingered briefly on his concubine. As far as Ismailov was concerned, the native woman and his private distillery were the only things that made these wretched islands bearable. At the moment, however, there were more pressing matters that claimed him.

He unfastened his heavy coat and anticipated the touch of the hands that helped him off with it. His concubine, Tasha, served him well, catering to more than his sexual needs, whether it was preparing palatable meals, properly fixing tea in the samovar, or mending his clothes. She was intelligent, almost civilized.

'Bring me my writing papers and implements,' he instructed, then walked to the wooden table and sat down in the chair. After she had set the pewter inkstand and parchment paper before him, Ismailov picked up the fine Russian quill, then paused before dipping it in the inkwell. 'I want you to fix a salmon pie, baked with rye meal.' Presenting new arrivals in town with a gift of bread and salt was an ancient Russian custom, symbolizing a wish that the newcomers would never want for life's necessities. If his notes failed to draw any response from the British captains, Ismailov hoped the accompanying gift would.

After writing notes to both of the ships' captains, he sealed them with wax and pressed his signet ring onto the warm wax to stamp it with the imprint of the double-headed eagle, the symbol of the Romanov Empire. The following day he dispatched one of his Cossack officers to deliver his messages and the gift of salmon pie to the British.

A different matter required Ismailov's attention on another part of Unalaska Island. While he was gone, his Cossack messenger returned with one of the officers from the British ship. Tasha saw the strange-speaking man several times during his short stay at the settlement. No one could understand what he said and they had to rely on hand signs to communicate. Taşha noticed how cheerful and inquisitive he was, curious about everything. His nature seemed very different from the Cossacks'.

Bad weather kept the stranger in camp a day longer and forced Walks Straight and Zachar to delay their departure on the long sea hunt they'd planned. Although Tasha knew her son was impatient to leave on his first adventure, she was relieved that her brother had postponed it. She trusted that Walks Straight would look after him, yet she worried. Zachar was proving to be a skilled hunter, but his experience was limited to the offshore waters of the island. Venturing into the open sea would be a test of all his skill and knowledge. So many things could happen. Perhaps most of all, Tasha recognized that her son would come back a man.

Then the weather improved, the stranger left to go back to his ship, accompanied by the peredovchik and two Cossacks; but Walks Straight continued to delay their leaving, insisting they wait until the bad weather had passed beyond their intended route. Tasha was grateful for the few more days' reprieve, but she didn't have time to enjoy it. When Ismailov returned from his journey and learned of the invitation extended by the British to visit their ships and exchange map information of the area, an invitation accompanied by several bottles of fine liquor, everyone including Tasha was involved in the preparations. The sloop *Sv Pavel* had to be readied for sail, the decks swabbed from bow to stern, the sails patched, additional provisions stowed aboard, and all the furnishings returned to Ismailov's cabin, not to mention all the minor tasks like hauling water to the structure on shore housing the steam bath, gathering driftwood for the fire to heat it, and cutting grass to cushion the floor. Never did Ismailov even consider making the half a day's trek overland to the bay where the British ships were anchored. He was a navigator, the master of his vessel, and he would meet with the British as such.

On the day the sloop sailed for the north side of the island, Walks Straight and Zachar also set out on their journey. Tasha stood on the beach while little Mikhail trotted after the seagulls wheeling overhead. She wished she had checked Zachar's *kamleika* one more time to make certain there was no break in the waterproof garment. Now it was too late. She watched the two kayaks grow smaller and smaller as they headed toward the mouth of the bay and the open sea beyond. Soon she could no longer distinguish her brother from her son, but she remained on the beach, watching until they were completely out of sight.

For a long time, Zachar had waited to embark on this extended voyage, confident of his skill and certain he was ready for it. After anticipating it for so long, the excitement of actually going carried him for a considerable distance in the open water. The sea stretched from horizon to horizon, an endless undulation of dark gray waters. The expanse of it seemed to grow greater and greater. Slowly a sense of aloneness began to creep through him. Looking across the trackless sea, he suddenly felt very small. He realized how little his home island was, how big the ocean was, and how easily a hunter could become lost.

He glanced quickly at the bidarka that paralleled his, needing to be reassured that he was not alone. His uncle, Walks Straight, had not fastened the drawstring hood of his kamleika over his head, and his lank white hair was clearly visible beneath the wooden visor. There was nothing in that muscular face to indicate to Zachar what his uncle was thinking or feeling. There never was.

'Did the wind change?' Zachar thought it might have, although he couldn't remember from which quarter it had been blowing previously, and such things were crucial details.

'Yes.'

Zachar wished his uncle had said more, just for the comfort of a human voice.

Some time later, Zachar noticed Walks Straight staring to the south, where the sky had darkened to an ominous black. The fast-moving storm was headed directly toward them. He knew the procedure for riding out storms in the open sea and maneuvered his bidarka alongside his uncle's so they could lash them together to create a more flexible dual-hulled craft capable of riding out a storm that might sink a single boat.

The wind whipped the sea in advance of the black squall and drove the waves higher. All at once, it seemed to Zachar, they were swallowed in darkness. The sheeting rain hammered at the waterproof hood covering his head, the string knotted tightly at his throat to keep the water from running inside. The sea tossed their twin craft in every direction, throwing them first one way then another. The roar of the storm and the sea seemed to take over Zachar, blocking out all other sound, including the pounding of his own heart. The hull of his bidarka became an extension of his body. Each time a wave slammed into it, he shuddered under the jarring force of it.

Somewhere the passage of time lost meaning. Zachar had no idea if day had turned into night or night into day. There was only the storm; everything else seemed distant and unreal – his home, his mother and little brother, gone, beyond his reach. He was trapped in the heart of it and carried . . . he knew not where.

Even after the storm abated, it continued to roar in his head. His senses were numbed. He didn't notice that the heaving pitch of the sea had become less violent or that the raindrops on his face were from a light shower. A hand gripped his arm, and the sensation slowly penetrated his consciousness. Blinking the beads of rain from his lashes, Zachar turned to look at his uncle's impassive face.

'The storm has passed.'

The words seemed to come from far away, but he heard them and gazed at the gray drizzle and the rolling sea, realizing it was true. He felt exhaustion loosening all his muscles and draining his strength.

'Where are we?' he asked, but Walks Straight simply shook his head.

Water surrounded them on all sides, and the low-hanging clouds and heavy drizzle obscured visibility. As the two bidarkas drifted on the sea, still lashed together, Zachar watched his uncle scan the sea, searching for clues in the wave action or the tidal flow or the water texture, anything that might provide direction.

'Do you hear?' Walks Straight said, and Zachar held his breath, straining to catch whatever sound his uncle had heard. At first he detected nothing, then gradually he began to distinguish over the rumble of the sea the low thunder of breakers crashing on rocks. That meant an island, somewhere close by.

Quickly they untied their bidarkas and started paddling toward the sound. The gray drizzle concealed the shore, but the noise grew steadily louder until it became a nearly deafening roar. Zachar frowned in confusion, vaguely alarmed by this strange sound that was like no surf he'd ever heard. He rested his double-bladed paddle on the deck of his bidarka.

'That cannot be breakers,' he called to his uncle, but Walks Straight paddled on. Zachar followed him uncertainly.

The drizzle became a fine mist that revealed a dark landmass looming in front of them. Gradually the noises that had blended to make one giant roar became separate sounds – the raucous shriek of shore-birds, the pounding crash of the surf, and the overpowering bawl of fur seals.

As he approached the island, Zachar stared in disbelief. The island swarmed with seals. It appeared one large, living mass of brown-silver larvae in perpetual motion, quivering and undulating. Their numbers had to be in the millions, Zachar thought. The din of their hoarse, bellowing voices was head-splitting.

Ahead of him, Walks Straight landed his kayak on a small stretch of sand that hadn't been claimed by a bull seal. Zachar headed for the same place. He could hardly take his gaze away from the hundreds of thousands of seals – the huge beachmaster bulls, the adult females, the nearly grown pups that crawled over each other in one large seething mass. As he neared the strip of sand, something bumped into the side of his skin-boat. He glanced down, fearing he'd scraped a submerged rock, and saw a full-grown sea otter floating on its back and crunching on a sea urchin, with two more tabled on its chest. The otter appeared totally oblivious of his presence. Aware how much that pelt would bring, Zachar grabbed his harpoon.

'No! No!' Walks Straight ran into the water. The shouts and the loud splashing startled the sea otter as well as Zachar. The mammal dived quickly. Zachar lowered his harpoon, glaring at his uncle as a wave carried his bidarka closer to shore.

'Why did you do that?'

'Look around you. They are everywhere,' his uncle said, then turned and waded ashore.

Belatedly Zachar looked and saw the heads of curious otter, some no more than two boat lengths away from him. They watched him, unafraid. Confused, both by his uncle's behavior and the otter's, he nosed the bidarka onto the sand and untied the drawstring that fastened the waterproof hatch covering around his waist, then crawled out of the bidarka and lifted it farther onto the sand.

'Why did you come ashore? Look at the furs we can take.' Zachar gestured at the multitude of otter swimming in the surrounding waters.

'Have you not guessed where we are?' Walks Straight said quietly, an almost pitying look in his eyes.

'No.' Zachar frowned, confused by the question.

'This is the island the storytellers say was found long ago by the son of a village headman. Like us, he was blown off course by a storm and found this island far to the north of his home. This is where all the fur seals come to have their young and raise them. This island is their breeding ground.' As Walks Straight gazed at the teeming mass of bodies, Zachar noticed the soft glow in his uncle's eyes, a faint light where he never remembered seeing any before. 'No man has ever set foot on this island since that long-ago day. We are the first in all this time.'

'How many do you think are here?' Zachar stared at the multitude, thinking of their glossy pelts.

'Millions.' Walks Straight faced the pounding surf and watched the frolicking sea otter. 'There are tens of thousands of our brothers, the sea otter.' One climbed out of the water onto a nearby rock, and he walked toward it, stopping within an arm's reach of the curious mammal as it sniffed the air to determine his scent.

Zachar watched in amazement, then moved to stand beside his uncle. Still the otter didn't flee to the safety of the ocean. 'They are as tame as the seagull I had as a child.'

'This is the way it was in my father's time. The sea otter had no fear of us. He was our brother. He swam in the waters off our islands. Then the Cossacks came,' Walks Straight finished flatly. He turned and glared at Zachar, a strangely bright gleam in his eyes. 'Look well and remember the way it was.'

Feeling uneasy, Zachar glanced around, but he was too conscious of his uncle to see much. Walks Straight wasn't acting right.

'This is the last place where the sea otter can live in peace,' his uncle said. In this short time, he'd spoken more words than Zachar ever remembered him saying all at once. 'The Cossacks have hunted the whole length of our islands. They have killed thousands, maybe millions of sea otter. They must not learn of this place.' He paused. A breath later, he shuddered violently and groaned like some dying animal in agonizing pain. 'They must not know,' he moaned and swung wildly around to stare at the seal rookery, jammed with life. 'I cannot let them know!' he cried, and the shrieking wail of his voice shivered down Zachar's spine. Helpless and frightened, he watched his uncle appear suddenly frantic and desperate, clawing at his own face. 'They will make me tell. They will make me tell,' he mumbled wildly, then added more clearly, 'No. Not again.'

Nothing he said made any sense to Zachar. He took a hesitant step toward him, but he didn't know what to say or how to help. Suddenly Walks Straight ran to his bidarka, picked it up and carried it into the surf.

'Where are you going?' For an instant, Zachar couldn't believe his uncle intended to leave without him.

'They will make me tell! I cannot let them!' Walks Straight shouted, then he scrambled into the hatch of his bidarka and struck out with his paddle, propelling the trim craft into the surf.

'Wait!' Zachar hurried to his kayak and dragged it around to launch it into the surf, but he was neither as experienced nor as adept as his uncle at handling the long craft.

By the time he crawled into the hatch and started paddling after his uncle, he was already several lengths behind. He saw his uncle cease paddling once he was well out in deep water. Zachar thought he was waiting for him. Then Walks Straight picked up his harpoon. In horror, Zachar watched him plunge its sharp point into the hide walls of his boat. Over and over again, the arm holding the spear rose and fell as Zachar drove his bidarka with long, digging strokes of the paddle, trying to reach the wallowing skin-boat before it sank out of sight with his uncle still in it. It slipped into a wave's trough and disappeared from his view.

Zachar paddled furiously toward the spot where he'd last seen them. Nothing. There was no sign of his uncle or the bidarka. Certain that he was very near the spot, he stopped paddling. Breathing hard from the exertion, he let his bidarka drift, dipping a blade into the water now and then to maintain his position.

'Walks Straight!' he shouted, not believing his call would be heard.

Then he saw the bubbles breaking the surface of the water a boat's length to his right, a small eruption but enough to indicate where his uncle had gone down. He stared at the steadily diminishing stream of bubbles, transfixed by the sight, unaware of the tears running down his face.

'Why?' he murmured, his voice breaking.

A gamboling sea otter swam close to his bidarka, gliding effortlessly through the waves, its sleek fur glistening. It circled his boat, as close to him as the first one had been. Zachar turned the impotent rage he felt over his uncle's death on the creature. Somehow the otter was to blame for Walks Straight going crazy. But as he reached for his harpoon, Zachar could hear again his uncle's voice calling out to stop him. 'No! No!'

And he couldn't do it. He couldn't kill the otter. Half blinded by tears, he turned his bidarka to point it toward the cacophonous bedlam of the giant seal rookery.

'Why?' he shouted, but there was no answer in the deafening roar.

With leaden arms, Zachar paddled back to the strip of vacant beach and hauled his bidarka high on the sand. He gathered some driftwood and built a small fire to drive the chill of death from his bones. Eventually the embers died. Still he sat beside the blackened ash. Night came and a heavy fog drifted in, so thick he couldn't see all of his bidarka. It intensified the feeling that he was utterly alone.

Somewhere to the south was home. Zachar stared in that direction, wondering if he'd ever see it again and knowing that he couldn't stay here. If he did, he'd become as crazy as Walks Straight. In the morning he'd have to leave. Having made that decision, Zachar lay down next to his bidarka and shut his eyes. But his sleep was haunted by the vision of his white-haired uncle repeatedly driving his harpoon through the hide-covered sides of his boat to sink it.

After an absence of seven days, Ismailov sailed his sloop, the *Sv Pavel*, back to its anchorage in the bay. Again Tasha was busy, this time returning his land quarters to their former order. Always garrulous, particularly when he was the subject, Ismailov was especially talkative that evening, his tongue further loosened by a bottle of liquor from the British.

During the time Tasha had been with him, she had learned that listening to him was a vital part of what Ismailov expected from her. It didn't matter whether she understood all of what he said. Once he had attempted to explain to her that a sailing master did not drink or talk with common men. He was too important, even for the Cossack officers. But it was all right to tell her things, which only confused Tasha, but she accepted that being a woman somehow made a difference.

'I had a difficult time making myself understood,' Ismailov declared and sipped at the liquor in a glass tumbler, then blotted the moisture left on his mustache. A vain man, he kept his full beard and curly hair neatly trimmed and was rarely out of uniform. 'I do not speak English and they did not know Russian. No one knew German, and that *Capitaine* Cook's French was wretched. Did I tell you what a fool's errand his King George has sent Cook on?' Tasha nodded, but Ismailov told her again anyway. 'He's searching for a northwest passage so British ships will not have to take that long route around Cape Horn to get to China. Bering and Chirikov have already proved it does not exist. Those English think they know more than a Russian about navigation and exploration.'

As he paused to take another swig of liquor, Tasha cast a furtive glance at the small sleeping area that was partitioned off with hanging mats. She could hear Mikhail jabbering behind it.

'I managed to obtain a good deal of information from Cook, but I was careful what I told him, although I must admit I enjoyed pointing out to him that he had incorrectly shown Unimak Island as being a part of the mainland peninsula,' he bragged, then stared at his glass. 'He has mapped a lot of the mainland coast to the south. Should be helpful.' Ismailov laughed suddenly. 'He let his crew trade with some natives for sea otter skins, but nobody seems to know how valuable they are. Maybe they will never find out,' he mused. 'With their American colonies in revolt, the English might forget about this futile voyage of Cook's.'

After drinking the last of the liquor from his glass, Ismailov picked up the bottle and drained the last of its contents into the tumbler. As he set the bottle down, his hand brushed the bundle of papers lying on the table. Tasha had noticed them earlier. The markings on them bore no resemblance to the writings of the Cossacks.

'Dispatches from Cook,' he said. 'I am supposed to send them to Okhotsk in the spring so they can be forwarded to the British Admiralty.'

The letters were forgotten as she became the object of his scrutiny – and his suspicion that she hadn't been listening. 'Where is Cook?' she asked.

'He is still at the north bay. As soon as the repairs on his ships are complete and the reprovisions on board, he will leave. He plans to spend the winter at some tropical islands he discovered in the Pacific. The Sandwich Isles, he called them. Then he intends to come back next spring and search again for the north-west passage – that does not exist.'

Ismailov rambled endlessly, talking long after the last of the liquor had been consumed. Finally he staggered over to his cot, and Tasha helped him out of his uniform. He barely gave her enough time to remove her own garment before he dragged her onto the blanket with him. Many Cossacks couldn't perform after drinking so much, but liquor never seemed to affect Ismailov's potency. It was a source of pride to him. Tasha submitted to his demands, but he was too drunk to notice her lack of response. Copulation was an act that held little meaning for her any more. It was merely another part of life's routine.

Sometime in the night, she was awakened by a noise. She listened, wondering if it was Mikhail, then Ismailov rolled over and started snoring loudly in her ear. Moving his entrapping arm, she slipped out of bed and wrapped one of the blankets around her. As she made her way across the darkened room to check on her young son, the door was opened. Startled, Tasha halted to stare at the black figure coming through the opening.

'Zach,' she murmured in recognition and hurried to his side. But he made no response. She touched his arm and strained to see his face in the shadows. 'I am glad you are home. But . . . why do you arrive so late?'

There was a vague shake of his head. 'I was lost,' he murmured, and Tasha detected the troubled note in his voice and sensed something was wrong. 'When I recognized a part of the island, I . . . I did not stop until I reached here.'

'Where is Walks Straight?'

As he finally looked at her, his lips moved, but no sound came from his mouth. Again he shook his head, then let it droop. 'He's dead.'

Quickly she covered her mouth with her hand to smother the cry of grief so she wouldn't awaken her sleeping son. Pain gripped her chest until her throat ached with it and even breathing hurt. She turned away, lowering her hand to grasp the edge of the blanket and draw it more tightly around her.

'How? What happened?' she whispered.

Haltingly, Zachar told her about finding the legendary island of the seals. 'He would not let me kill any of the otter. He kept saying this was what it was like before the Cossacks came. Then he . . . he went crazy and started saying strange things . . . saying that they would make him tell.'

'Oh, no,' Tasha moaned.

'Then he went out in his bidarka and took his harpoon –' A sob broke through his voice. He wiped a hand over his face, then insisted, 'I tried to reach him. I tried!' She could feel his gaze on her. 'Why? Why did he do it?'

'He was afraid.' She felt very empty and very alone. And part of her felt relieved that her brother's torment was finally over.

'Why?' Zachar still didn't understand.

For the first time, Tasha told him the truth about his birth, how she and Walks Straight had taken Zachar and fled from Adak and what a strong, proud man her brother had been. She told him about the uprising and her brother's part in it – about the coming of Solovey and Tolstykh, the way they had tortured Walks Straight and all but destroyed him.

'He feared the Cossacks would find out that he knew the location of the seal island and would torture him again for the information.' She turned to gaze into her son's eyes. 'He died to keep that secret. You must keep it, too. No one can know where you have been or what you have seen.'

'They will ask about Walks Straight.'

'Tell them he drowned. He is not the first hunter the sea has swallowed.' Tasha moved away, retracing her steps to the cot.

A sadness washed over her as she lay down once more on the cot with the snoring man, but it wasn't the kind of sadness that caused tears. It was a deep regret that it had to happen this way.

17 *Summer 1784*

The hardness of her life began to show on Tasha's face. Exposure to the relentless wind had weathered her skin, wrinkled the soft flesh under her eyes, and deepened the grooves near the corners of her mouth. After having lived for thirty-eight of the Cossack years, she no longer attracted the interest of the Cossacks who came to Unalaska. They preferred younger women – ones the age of the girl Zachar had taken to be his wife this past winter.

Tasha slipper her needle through another blue bead and glanced at her new daughter-in-law, a Creole like herself called Katya. She was barely seventeen summers old – a good age for her son of twenty-two. Yet Katya was not the mate Tasha would have chosen for Zachar, even though she was a good worker and deft with a needle. She would have picked a girl whose mind was a little quicker, one who wasn't so quiet and plain-looking. But with Zachar away so much on hunting parties, maybe it was just as well that he hadn't chosen a wife the Cossacks in the village would covet. Suppressing a sigh, Tasha returned to her beadwork.

'A ship! A ship!' Mikhail came running toward them, shouting excitedly. He stopped beside Tasha and pointed toward the bay. Although he was out of breath, words tumbled from his mouth between pants for air. 'I saw them first. Zachar let me take the bidarka out on the bay. That is when I saw them. Come.' He started back toward the beach, afraid of missing something. 'They will be sending a boat ashore soon.'

Tasha laid aside her beadwork sewing and pushed to her feet, her joints slightly stiff from prolonged sitting. Her daughter-in-law followed suit and accompanied Tasha while Mikhail ran ahead. The arrival of any ship was a cause for celebration by the island inhabitants – Cossack, Creole, and Aleut alike.

The arrival of these ships was more momentous than Tasha realized.

One was the *Trekh Sviatiteli*, the Three Saints, a vessel developed in the shipbuilding yards at Okhotsk in Siberia. It was termed a galiot, although there was little resemblance between it and the Mediterranean vessel of the same name. Broad of beam, almost as keelless as the shitik, it had a single square gaff mainsail with an auxiliary jib and a rudder two fathoms long. There were openings for sweeps, the long oars operated from below deck and used in tacking or in heavy seas. In its large hold were domestic cattle, sheep, fowl, and lumber, metal, and tools of every kind. The ship's master was Tasha's former consort, Ismailov – older, stouter, with strands of gray appearing in his hair and beard, but still vain and arrogant and fond of women and liquor.

But the most important passengers aboard the vessel were Grigori Ivanovich Shelekhov, a wealthy merchant from Irkutsk and a partner in this colonizing expedition, and his wife, the noblewoman Natalia Alexyevna Shelekhova. The couple quickly became the center of attention when they came ashore.

Grigori 'Grisha' Shelekhov was a large man in his middle years. Clean-shaven, after the European fashion of the day, he possessed a commanding presence. He moved with deliberation, yet that surface calm failed to mask his boundless ambition and restless energies. The quickness of his narrow eyes, which took in everything that went on around him, revealed these traits.

Several years before, Shelekhov had heard about the Cook exploration and the subsequent sale of a few hundred sea otter skins to the Chinese at Canton for ten thousand dollars, a sum that had ignited a near-mutiny by Cook's crew. Shelekhov was also aware that the reports written by the English captain before his death at the hands of natives on some tropical island in the Pacific had called the Russian presence in the Aleutians and the northwest insignificant.

As soon as the knowledge of the area's fur wealth had spread, there had been an immediate incursion of British and the newly independent American ships. The appeals for government intervention made by the Russian merchants engaged in the fur trade, which included Shelekhov, were ignored by Catherine the Great. She adopted the position of laissez-faire. Shelekhov was well aware that the Russian claim on the new lands in the north was weak, since they had only established temporary bases from which the promyshleniki operated. It was his shrewd and handsome wife who suggested they use the freedom Catherine had given the merchants to establish a permanent settlement.

A tall woman, bold and aggressive, yet very pious like her husband, Natalia was handsome, with features that bore a slight resemblance to those of a Tartar. She had a head for business and enjoyed power and intrigue. In the past, Shelekhov had frequently left her in charge of his offices in Irkutsk whenever he journeyed to Okhotsk. Many hinted she had made a misalliance by marrying someone beneath her class, but the two were well paired, each feeding the other's ambition. Both of them regarded this daring venture as merely the first step in a grander scheme.

Despite their considerable wealth, they had been unable to personally finance the huge cost of founding a permanent settlement and had taken partners to raise the funds. They had purchased and outfitted three vessels, the sloop *Sv Simeon*, the galiot *Trekh Sviatiteli*, and the galiot *Sv Mikhail*, from which they had become separated in a storm. The latter's fate was still unknown. Their call at the Unalaska harbor was merely to repair their vessels and reprovision them before continuing further east. Shelekhov had the livestock rafted ashore to graze on the island grasses until they were ready to sail again.

Tasha no longer had to wonder where her youngest child was since those ponderous four-legged beasts had been landed on the island. Mikhail was fascinated by them and always slipped away to watch them. He was no longer interested in learning to handle a bidarka by himself or to perfect any of his hunting skills under Zachar's tutelage.

At the edge of the grassy meadow, Tasha stopped, keeping her distance from the beasts. Vaguely she recalled Andrei once trying to explain what a horse looked like. She wondered if it resembled at all this horned animal they called a cow. She watched as it stuck out its long, thick tongue and licked its dripping nostrils. Tasha thought it very ugly. She kept a watchful eye on it while she looked around for her son.

'Mikhail!' She saw him next to one of the short, curly-haired beasts called a sheep. 'Come. You must eat.'

Reluctantly he backed away from the creature and ran to her, the wind blowing his bluntly cropped forelock away from his face. 'You should feel his hair,' he told her. 'It is thick and deep. My fingers went in all the way to there before I touched his hide,' he said, indicating the second finger joint from the tip. 'The man watching them said his hair is called wool. They spin it into threads and make their clothes from it.'

All the way back to their small barabara, Tasha was regaled with various bits of information Mikhail had observed or been told about the strange animals. The dwelling was built in the Cossack style with a door in the side. As they neared the entrance, Tasha recognized Ismailov. With him were the big smooth-faced man and the tall Cossack woman. The three approached her dwelling. Having never seen the woman up close, Tasha stopped to stare at the voluminous material that hung all the way to the ground. It made a swishing sound as she walked. A loosely hooded garment covered her head and much of her upper body, and her hands were hidden inside a round ball of fur.

Becoming conscious of the inspection from those eyes, Tasha went forward to meet them. She looked at Ismailov and bent a knee, curtsying the way she'd been taught long ago. 'Capitaine.'

He nodded to her but addressed his remarks to the couple with him. 'This is the mother of the man I was telling you about. Tasha Tarakanov. She's a Creole.'

The woman smiled as she inclined her head in Tasha's direction. 'I am Madame Shelekhova.'

'Madame.' Tasha curtsied briefly, and noticed the woman's eye-brows lift faintly.

'Is this your son as well?' There was a touch of cool reserve in the woman's voice as she indicated the boldly staring boy beside Tasha.

'Yes.'

'We have come to speak to Zachar,' Ismailov inserted. 'Is he here?'

'Yes.' Tasha glanced at her son. 'Tell your brother to come outside.'

Mikhail retreated several steps, then turned and ran to the door. He darted inside. The door had barely shut before he came bursting out again, followed more sedately by Zachar and a shyly curious Katya.

After he had introduced Zachar to the Shelekhovs, Ismailov began to explain the purpose of the visit. 'I told them that you speak Russian very well –'

Shelekhov interrupted to take over the task. 'We will be sailing east in a few days to locate a site on which we will build a permanent village, a place where families can live. We will need strong young men like yourself to help us. Men who can explain to the natives that we come to live in peace with them, to build Russian houses and churches and schools. Ismailov has recommended you to be one of our interpreters on the expedition.'

'Russian houses.' The phrase recalled another time for Tasha when Andrei had described what it was like in his home village. The houses with many rooms, each for a purpose. It seemed part of dream, one she'd almost forgotten.

'I am honored that the Capitaine has spoken so well of me,' Zachar replied, speaking fluently in the Russian tongue. 'But if I were to go with you, there would be no one to hunt food for my family. My brother is yet too young.'

'It is responsible men exactly like you that we are seeking.' Shelekhov nodded approvingly.

'May I offer a suggestion, Grigori Ivanovich?' Ismailov ventured.

'Please do.' Shelekhov invited him to continue.

'It occurs to me that Madame Shelekhova will be requiring a woman to help her. I can personally vouch for Zachar's mother. She knows how to prepare a variety of dishes that are suitable for a Russian's palate. She is tidy and clean, which cannot be said for all the native women. And she is an excellent seamstress. Perhaps Madame Shelekhova would like to inspect the beadwork on the collar of her parka. She will find none finer, I think,' Ismailov declared. 'And Tasha speaks fluent Russian, so there will be no difficulty with language.'

'Did you understand what he said?' Madame Shelekhova questioned Tasha.

'Yes,' Tasha replied, then couldn't help asking, 'Will you be building houses with many rooms in them? One to sit and one to cook and one to sleep?'

'Yes.' Shelekhov and his wife exchanged glances, both smiling faintly in satisfaction. 'Yes, we will.'

All four members of the Tarakanov family were on board the *Trekh Sviatiteli* when it followed the sloop *Sv Simeon* out of the Unalaska harbor, bound for a large island to the east that the natives called Kodiak. In addition to them, the Shelekhovs had obtained the services of ten Aleut hunters and a second interpreter for their expedition.

Tasha stood at the rail and watched the volcanic peaks on

Unalaska Island recede from her view, remembering her previous voyage on a Cossack ship that had taken her away from her home on Attu, and the sea journey she and her brother had made when they had fled with Zachar to this island. She felt little regret at leaving. Her memory of the place would always be shadowed by the pain and suffering she'd known there.

18

Located close to the mainland of 'Aleyeska,' Kodiak Island was inhabited by a native tribe called Koniaga that belonged to the Innuit culture, the Eskimo. When Shelekhov's ships anchored in a capacious bay on the island's southeast coast, the natives were hostile to his overtures of peace. Some years before they had repulsed a Russian ship from their waters, but a fortuitous eclipse of the sun, two decisive Russian victories in battle, and the taking of hostages soon subdued the natives that Shelekhov mistakenly called Aleuts.

Shelekhov named the bay where he built his permanent settlement Three Saints Bay, after his ship. Although much of the shoreline was steep and rocky, a level spit of land extended into the bay, hooking in the shape of a horseshoe. The gravel bar provided a convenient place to beach their vessels and flat ground on which to build. Protected on three sides by water, the site was ideally suited to their needs. No trees grew on this side of the island, which was more than one hundred and fifty versts long and roughly half that wide. And the grassy hills that sloped up from the bay offered a pasture for the livestock, and dirt suitable for vegetable gardens.

The promyshleniki, nearly a hundred and fifty men, quickly went to work building the settlement. A half dozen cabins with Russian-styled gables and roofs were constructed. In addition, they built a barracks, a blacksmith shop, a countinghouse, barns for the livestock, a commissary, a ropewalk, a warehouse for furs, as well as the usual bathhouse.

Within a year, the Russian settlement on Three Saints Bay was solidly established. Gardens were planted with potatoes, turnips, and a variety of vegetable seeds Shelekhov had brought from Russia. Cattle and sheep grazed on the new green grass covering the hills, not without some loss of their numbers to the huge brown bears that roamed the island.

But Shelekhov was not content. If they were to claim this new land by right of possession, and prevent the British or the Americans from taking it over, they must expand. The territory before him was vast and untouched. Only one other settlement existed along the entire west coast of the North American continent, the small Spanish presidio of San Francisco, founded nine years earlier in 1776. It was not a settlement the Shelekhovs had come to build in Kodiak but a foundation for an empire.

In early summer, Shelekhov organized a party of some fifty promyshleniki and several Aleuts and assigned Zachar to go along as an interpreter. They sailed from Three Saints Bay in four large baidars, accompanied by more than a hundred Koniaga Aleuts in their bidarkas. Their mission was to explore and make contact with natives on nearby islands and the mainland of Aleyeska and to establish a fortified outpost on Cook's Inlet.

It was late summer before they returned. All the Tarakanovs sat together in their log dwelling once more to hear Zachar's story of his journey. They gathered around the flickering light of the oil lamp, Katya cross-legged on a grass mat covering the planked floor, Tasha on the floor close to the lampstand so she could see to make the fine stitches to mend the tear in Madame Shelekhova's gown, Zachar on the chair where all could see him, and Mikhail at his feet.

'Mountains towered above us on all sides, throwing their white peaks to the sky.' Zachar described the voyage into the great arm of the sea that the Russians called Cook's Inlet. 'Everywhere white water tumbled down the sheer sides of the mountains and fell into the sea, making a sound like faraway thunder. And there were trees with trunks five times as big around as a man, growing all the way to the water's edge. I walked among them. They stand thickly together, tall – twenty times as tall as a man – all their branches meeting to shut out the sky like this roof.'

'Is it night there all the time?' Mikhail wanted to know.

'There are holes to let the light in,' Zachar assured him, then continued. 'Many birds live among the trees. I saw ravens and white-cheeked geese, and a tiny bird that beats its wings so fast you cannot see them and makes a humming sound like a bee.'

196

'What about the natives you met? What were they like?' From the Koniaga Aleuts, Tasha had heard that the natives who lived on the mainland belonged to a warrior race.

Zachar shrugged. 'Most of them did not like Aleuts. But we traded for some skins. Several villages gave us hostages. Along Prince William Sound, we met Chugach and Kenaitze. There, many families live together in longhouses made of logs. They are cousins to the Kolosh.' The Kolosh were an extremely warlike tribe that lived along the coast to the south, a fierce band whose reputation for cunning and treachery had spread to nearly all of the northwest tribes.

As Mikhail listened to his older brother describe an encounter with a cousin of the dangerous Kolosh, a chill of excitement danced over his skin. He was envious of Zachar's thrilling adventures, the new places he'd seen, and strange people he'd met. All the things he'd done this summer that he had been so anxious to tell his brother about – like going to the school and listening to Mr. Shelekhov talk or reciting the words he'd memorized about the Holy God and making the sign of the cross exactly right – suddenly they all sounded uninteresting. Mikhail sighed. His brother had done just about everything and been just about everywhere. He guessed he'd never have anything exciting to tell him.

The second winter was a hard one for the Russian company. Many of the hunters stationed at outlying camps on Kodiak suffered from scurvy, and several died, although the Koniaga Aleuts were helpful in supplying many of them with fresh provisions. There was no shortage of food in the Shelekhov house, but Shelekhov appeared troubled by the problems besetting him. Tasha attempted to explain that winter and hunger were one and the same, but he insisted that a quantity of food must be stored away in the summer for consumption in the winter.

Whatever doubts Shelekhov might have been having about his venture vanished in the early spring with the arrival at Three Saints Bay of the long lost galiot *Sv Mikhail*, sister ship of the *Trekh Sviatiteli*. Damaged by the storm that had separated them, the galiot had reached Unalaska the previous year. There the vessel had been cast on the rocks and suffered further damage that had delayed her longer.

Shortly after the arrival of the *Sv Mikhail*, the Shelekhovs began their preparations to return to Russia, a task that involved more than just packing and transporting their belongings onto the *Trekh Sviatiteli*. There had to be a transfer of authority, and Shelekhov selected the newly arrived peredovchik Samoilov to take charge, a choice that necessitated familiarizing the man with the present operations, the systems in place, the projects under way. An endless number of orders concerning future tasks to be accomplished had to be written. Tasha overheard many of the conversations the Shelekhovs had regarding that, including mention of explorations to a place called California.

'Tasha.' The summons by Madame Shelekhova came from the main room.

Before responding to it, Tasha quickly checked the water in the samovar, but it was not yet hot enough for tea. Then she went to the main room and paused a step inside to wait for Madame Shelekhova to notice her. The tall, dark-haired woman had her back to the door-way and faced her husband, who was seated at the heavy wooden table, an array of papers spread before him and a quill lying beside a silver inkstand.

'I truly believe, Grisha, that by taking these natives back with us to illustrate the progress we've made civilizing them and instructing them in the True Faith, we will have a better chance of persuading the Tsaritsa to make an exception in our case and grant us the exclusive right to trade in this new land even though she has abolished all monopolies. All she has previously heard about this land have been reports concerning the wealth of furs – and the oppression and abuse of the natives by irresponsible promyshleniki. The latter has greatly displeased her,' Madame Shelekhova stated. 'But with our natives, we can show the scope of all we are trying to achieve.'

'We also have an excellent argument in the English ships sailing in these waters. They are laying claim to islands long ago discovered by the promyshleniki. If they should take over these islands, as they show every intention of taking over the American coast, the whole of Siberia will be exposed.' Shelekhov paused as he finally noticed Tasha standing in the doorway. Quickly he assumed a congenial expression. 'Ah, Tasha, there you are. Come in.'

'The tea is not yet ready,' she said, not understanding the significance of their plans or what they hoped to achieve.

'Tea? Yes . . . well, we'll have it later then.' He dismissed it as unimportant. 'Madame Shelekhova and I wanted to discuss another matter with you.'

'As you know, we are taking a small group of natives to Russia with us.' Madame Shelekhova took up the conversation. 'We want them to see the greatness of our towns and villages, and the way we live.'

'I know this.' Tasha had heard them speak of it on previous occasions. It wasn't unusual for Aleuts to be taken to Russia. Many had gone there over the years and come back with many stories to tell.

'Your son Mikhail is a very bright boy,' Shelekhov said, and Tasha felt a tingle of alarm. 'He learns things very quickly. We would like to take him with us so he can be educated in our schools.'

'To Russia? He is too young,' Tasha protested in vague panic. 'He is only ten summ – ten years old.'

'That is the age our children go to school and learn things like reading and writing,' Madame Shelekhova explained patiently. 'There is a variety of skills he can learn – navigation, clerking, ship-building – that will be of great benefit to the settlement when he returns.'

'No. A child cannot be taken to Russia, you said. He belongs to his mother.' That was one of the first rules the Shelekhovs had issued during the establishment of their colony at Kodiak. Never again would a woman have to fear, as Tasha had, that her child would be taken from her by its Russian father. The Shelekhovs had said so.

'He isn't going there to stay, only to be educated,' Shelekhov replied. 'Madame Shelekhova and I will see that he returns.'

'It is only temporary, as Grisha said,' Madame added. 'Visiting Russia will be a wonderful experience for Mikhail. Surely you recognize that, Tasha.'

But Tasha could only see that her young son would be leaving her and returning at some unknown time. There was a faint sound behind her. She turned and discovered Mikhail standing just around the corner of the door frame.

'Mikhail. You are supposed to be hunting with Zachar,' she accused.

Guiltily he stepped into the doorway, glancing quickly at the Shelekhovs. But he made no explanation for his presence as he looked at Tasha, an eager light in his eyes. 'I want to go.'

'It is so far,' she murmured.

'I want to go there,' Mikhail insisted, then lowered his head as if sorry that he was hurting her.

Tasha straightened and again faced the Shelekhovs. 'How long will he be away?'

'Five years.' Madame Shelekhova smiled complacently. 'It will take that long for Mikhail to finish his schooling.'

On an afternoon in early summer, Tasha stood on the long sandbar that curled into Three Saints Bay and stared at the galiot sailing toward the open sea. Her gaze clung to the small figure on its deck, her heart heavy.

19 *Three Saints Bay, Kodiak Summer 1790*

When word spread through the settlement reporting the sighting of a ship approaching the bay, Tasha abandoned the otter skins she was cleaning and hurried to the sandbar's beach. Zachar's wife followed her, slowed by the cradle strapped to her back that carried their four-month-old daughter, Larissa. As a crowd gathered around her, Tasha watched anxiously for the ship to heave into view, hoping Mikhail would be on this one.

There had been few changes at the Three Saints settlement since he'd left. No new structures had been built, although a large community of Koniaga Aleuts now lived close to the settlement. The sea winds had weathered the logs of the original buildings, and the Greek Eustrate Delarov had taken command, replacing Samoilov.

At last, Tasha was able to see sails against the horizon of a rare blue sky. Slowly the ship entered the bay and maneuvered into the calm basin that was formed by the long, curving spit of land. The brass cannons on its decks gleamed in the sunlight. As the ship anchored offshore, Tasha anxiously scanned the men moving about on deck, searching for Mikhail, but she did not see him.

Old Ismailov, the official government representative at Three Saints Bay, came striding down to the beach, dressed in full uniform, the buttons straining to hold the material together across his thickening paunch. Imperiously he ordered a boat to be launched so he could be taken out to the ship.

When Tasha recognized Zachar among the men pushing the boat into the water, she hurried over to him. 'Go with Ismailov and see if Mikhail is on the ship.' She kept pace with him, talking quickly as she went. 'If he is not, ask if they know about him.' Zachar nodded. The bay water lapped at her feet, and Tasha stopped. Ismailov climbed into the boat and moved forward to the bow. There he stood as the men rowed toward the ship, still the arrogant navigator eager to be in the company of his equals despite the years of dissipation that showed on his face.

Although Tasha doubted that Ismailov would soon return to shore, she waited until he was on board, and Zachar with him, in case her son signaled that Mikhail was there. But he made no sign, and, as always, her disappointment was strong. Tasha turned and walked back to the cabin, knowing Zachar would come there when he returned.

Much later, she was scraping fetid flesh from an otter skin when she saw Zachar slowly walking toward the cabin. She straightened to sit back on her heels, unconsciously tightening her grip on the wooden handle of the ulu she used. His head was down, his shoulders drooped, and his steps seemed leaden. Tasha felt the clawing of fear in her throat. Something bad had happened. She dropped the crescent-shaped knife and scrambled to her feet, clasping her hands tightly together as she waited for him to reach her.

'What have you learned about Mikhail?' she asked.

The glance of his blue eyes touched her face, then skipped away. 'They knew nothing. They sailed from Okhotsk last year, but they are not from Shelekhov.'

Her forehead twitched with a bewildered frown. 'Then what is it? What is wrong?'

When Zachar lifted his head, she saw the deep sadness in his eyes. 'They have found them,' he said. 'A man on the ship told me that four years ago a navigator named Pribilof discovered the islands of the fur seals.'

Choked with emotion, Tasha turned away and knelt on the ground. She picked up the ulu knife and began scraping at the otter skin again. In her heart, she cried. She cried for her brother's sake and for a way of life that was lost.

The ship anchored in Three Saints Bay was the *Slava Rossie*, the Glory of Russia. She was on a scientific expedition commanded by Captain Joseph Billings, who had sailed with Cook to these waters and now explored them again in the service of the Tsaritsa. A priest of the Orthodox Church accompanied the expedition, distinctively dressed in a black cassock and a tall conical hat.

Many of the Russian hunters became very excited when they learned of the priest's presence. Several hurried to the beach to be on hand when the black-frocked man came ashore. As the priest stepped onto the sand, carrying a rich gold cross, they kneeled and made the sign of the cross. The priest offered a prayer for the souls of the promyshleniki and the heathens whose hearts had not yet heard the gospel of Christ.

During the next two days, Zachar seemed unusually quiet to Tasha. More and more he was given to brooding silences. She knew the news of Pribilof's discovery of the seal islands had been a blow to him. There would never be a return to the old ways – not for him, not for anyone.

Several times she had noticed him standing outside his cabin and staring at the tents that had been erected on the beach by the ship's company, especially the one where the man of God called the hunters and sailors to prayer. He spent a lot of time watching Katya and their daughter, a troubled expression on his face.

One morning he came striding briskly toward the cabin. He was smiling, and his eyes were bright and clear. He went directly to his wife, Katya, and took hold of her hand. His smile seemed to beam at her.

'I have spoken to the priest,' he said. 'He has agreed to properly baptize both our daughter and you . . . and to marry us.'

' "Marry"?' Katya frowned. 'What does this word mean?'

Zachar appeared to search for the right words. 'It means we take a Holy Oath before God and you promise that I will be the only man you live with all your life. And I promise that you will be the only woman . . . And that we will live together always.' He studied her anxiously. 'Do you understand?'

'Yes.' But she seemed uncertain.

Tasha knew little about this Russian thing called marriage, but she understood what her son was doing. Just as she had once realized that survival for her and her small family meant living with the Russians, Zachar had arrived at the same conclusion. He spoke their language, wore their clothes, and lived in their style of dwellings. Now he chose to embrace their beliefs in the Creator they called God.

The following day they went to the priest. Katya and Larissa were officially baptized, then Zachar and Katya were formally married.

As far as Tasha could determine, to the Russians, living together wasn't the same as being married. Two people could agree to live together, but to do so with God's blessing gave it more meaning. The Russian way of life was different in many respects. As she watched the *Slava Rossie* sail out of the harbor, she wondered at the changes she'd find in Mikhail when he finally returned.

A year passed and no supply ship came from Shelekhov to bring provisions and replacements for the men who had already served their five-year terms. It had been three years since the last supply ship had come to the Three Saints village. Despite careful rationing, there was no more tea in the warehouse, and only enough rye flour to make breads on Sundays and Holy Days. There was considerable grumbling among the men that Shelekhov had forgotten them.

Back from a morning's fishing, Zachar gave the catch to his mother to clean and dragged his bidarka beyond the tideline. As he turned it over to let its skin sides dry, he noticed a native baidar under canvas sail approaching the beach. It was unfamiliar to him, and he straightened to study its occupants, his eyes narrowing slightly. Seagulls filled the air, partially blocking his view as they fought over the entrails from the fish his mother was cleaning a short distance away. Their beating wings and screeching cries created a clamorous din.

More than a dozen Russians were in the skin-boat, but none that Zachar recognized, although he did notice that the waterproof kamleikas they were wearing had the markings of the Unalaska Aleuts. As they neared the shore, he could see their haggard faces and straggly beards. All of them were strangers to him, not hunters from outlying camps on the island.

'Who are they?'

Zachar glanced at his mother, now standing beside him, a basket of gutted fish in one arm, and shook his head. Others from the settlement had drifted to the beach. As the baidar entered shallow water, several of its occupants jumped over the side to haul it onto the sand.

'Praise the Holy Mother, we have made it,' one of them said, his voice cracking.

The declaration seemed to loosen everyone's tongue. They were from the *Trekh Sviatiteli*, the supply ship Shelekhov had sent last year. The galiot had broken up at Unalaska during a gale and much of its cargo had been lost. Two more baidars loaded with the rest of the ship's company should be arriving soon.

'Help us. We have a sick man here.'

As Zachar helped to lift the unconscious man, delirious with fever, out of the boat, someone warned, 'Careful with him. Baranov is the new manager Shelekhov sent . . . if he lives.'

Someone ran ahead to tell the village the news while Zachar and two promyshleniki carried the pneumonia-stricken man to the settlement. The Greek Delarov, currently in command, met them and ordered Baranov to be taken to his cabin. Trailing after them, Tasha followed them inside the dwelling once occupied by the Shelekhovs. If this Baranov was the new manager sent by Shelekhov, he would surely know something about her son Mikhail. He must recover.

No one objected when she helped remove the ailing man's water-proof parka and boots, *mukluks*. His fiery skin was damp with perspiration. Quickly she covered him with fur skins.

For the next several days, Tasha took care of him, listening to his racking cough and rattling breaths, sitting through his bouts of delirium and spooning broth through his cracked lips. Many in the village didn't expect him to survive, but Tasha wouldn't relent in her efforts to keep him alive.

She sat beside the cot watching the man who was the main subject of discussion in the camp. There was nothing special about Aleksandr Andreevich Baranov physically. Short of stature, he was thin and wiry, his complexion sallow. At forty-five, he was the same age as Tasha. Age had shot strands of gray through her black hair, but his flaxen hair, tinged with red, had thinned on top, leaving him with a bald crown. He didn't look like a leader of men, certainly not the muscular, rough promyshleniki.

Zachar carried the comments being made about Baranov back to the cabin. Ismailov had nothing but contempt for Shelekhov's choice. The man was a common merchant, hardly in the class of a navigator, such as Delarov was. He had no experience in the Aleutians. Worse, he'd never been to sea before this voyage and had been seasick most of the time. Others said he was too old for this rough life. Look at how he'd taken sick traveling in the open baidar, living on a diet of raw fish and sleeping in the open.

But, claimed the survivors, his energy was boundless. While wintering at Unalaska, he had explored, learned the Aleut language, handled a bidarka, and hunted sea otter. He was resourceful and intelligent.

The conflicting reports made little impression on Tasha, who listened to them in the hope of learning something about Mikhail. Baranov stirred beneath the layer of fur robes, the heavy lids of his eyes moving, lifting. Her attention sharpened on him as he opened his eyes and tried to moisten his parched lips.

'Water.' His voice was hoarse and thin.

Tasha picked up the tin mug with the water, then tunneled an arm under his shoulders to lift him slightly and held the cup to his lips, tipping it to let the water trickle into his mouth. When he had finished, she lowered him back onto the cot. Through half-closed eyes, he dully looked at his surroundings.

'Where am I?'

Tasha studied his eyes, searching for that vacant look of delirium, but this time it wasn't there. 'You are in Delarov's cabin at Three Saints village.'

'Ah.' He breathed out a satisfied sound and immediately started coughing. Tasha sat him partially up again and let him cough up the choking phlegm in his throat. When the spasm passed, it left him weak, but he gave her a grateful look as she laid him back down.

'Do you know where my son is? Shelekhov took him to Russia six years ago and he has not returned. His name is Mikhail Tarakanov. Did Shelekhov speak to you of him?'

Lacking the strength to answer, Baranov shook his head negatively and shut his eyes. Tasha sat back in her chair, her hopes dashed again. Others had returned on a previous supply ship, but where was her son? No one seemed to know.

More than a month passed before Baranov was well enough to get up and move about the settlement that was his new domain. In early autumn, the two baidars carrying the rest of his ship-wrecked company reached Kodiak. Leaving Delarov in charge for the time being, Baranov set out to explore the island, accompanied by Zachar and some Aleuts, and to acquaint himself with the natives, who called him Nanuk – the great white hunting leader.

When spring came, the beached sloop, the *Sv Mikhail*, was launched. Delarov and the promyshleniki whose enlistments were up and who were not indebted to the company for purchases from the commissary boarded the ship and sailed for Russia.

After Delarov departed, Baranov began exerting his authority and imposing strict discipline. The Russian flag bearing the double-headed eagle of the Romanov Empire was lowered each evening with the men at attention and a cannon salute. Gambling was forbidden. Drinking was allowed only during a man's off-duty hours, and then only kvass, made mainly from cranberries. Native prostitution was forbidden; a man chose a woman and stayed with her. On Sundays and Holy Days, prayers were read. But he also organized celebrations, *prazniks*, where there was singing and dancing, in which he joined.

Summer brought calmer waters that facilitated the hunting of sea otters. Baranov gathered a native hunting fleet of six hundred two-man bidarkas at Three Saints Bay, promising the Koniaga Aleuts a quantity of iron for each skin and assuring them that a Russian promyshlenik would be assigned to each artel of bidarkas.

But it was more than a hunting expedition he planned. To the south and east of Kodiak, English and American ships plied the waters of the Alexander Archipelago and Prince William Sound, taking trade from the Russians. His instructions from Shelekhov had been very clear; in addition to the fortified outpost on Cook's Inlet, more were to be established on Prince William Sound and the southeastern coast. The Tsaritsa had not given Shelekhov his monopoly, but she had granted him the exclusive rights to the lands he now occupied – or might later colonize. Baranov fully intended to use his hunting expedition to explore these areas and locate sites for new outposts.

The mass assembly of native hunters littered the sandspit upon which the settlement stood with long, sleek bidarkas. Under the half-light of a summer night, the figures lying among them appeared like dark brown shapes. Tasha stood outside the cabin and gazed at the shimmering waters of the bay. She was getting old, she decided. Sleep frequently eluded her.

There was a soft footfall behind her, and she turned to see Zachar. 'I heard you leave the cabin,' he said.

'Summers are not good for sleeping.' She looked at the dusklike sky. In the still air of the windless night, she could hear the uneasy lowing of restless cattle on the nearby hillsides. 'I think the bears are not sleepy either.'

'You were thinking of Mikhail,' Zachar said.

Tasha didn't deny it. 'I wonder if I will ever see him again.' The ache was always with her, the bereaved feeling.

'You are not alone,' Zachar said. 'You have Katya, Larissa, and me.'

'Yes.' They were her flesh and blood, too. But Mikhail was her youngest – her baby. How could she tell Zachar, who was also her son – her firstborn – that Mikhail was somehow special? She couldn't. So she smiled faintly at him, letting him think that he had consoled her. 'That is true.' Her gaze strayed to the crowded beach. 'With so many hunters, you will bring back many otter pelts this season. You will be able to buy much tobacco.' As a Creole, Zachar worked for the company on a share basis, like the rest of the promyshleniki, and had an account of his own at the commissary.

'There is little tobacco to buy. Everyone is using willow bark to make their tobacco last,' he said.

'One day I must try smoking your pipe so I can discover this pleasure you take in it,' she decided.

Zachar chuckled softly. 'I will buy you one.'

The raucous cries of a colony of storm petrels filled the night, nearly drowning out the softer calls of auklets, murrelets, and other nightbirds. 'They are noisy tonight.' She watched a flock sweep through the sky, appearing like a long trail of dark smoke.

Suddenly she felt the ground tremble beneath her feet. But this was a land where the earth often shook. She waited for the faint movement to cease and the ground to feel solid again. Instead the tremor grew stronger, rocking her unsteadily. Zachar grabbed her and pulled her down to the heaving sand before they could be knocked off their feet.

All around them they could hear the rattle and crash of things falling and the panicked cries of those wakened from their sleep by the violent quake. The log timbers of the buildings groaned from being rubbed together as their foundations shifted. Tasha hugged the vibrating gravel, her heart racing with alarm. She heard the ominous crack of wood splitting and looked anxiously at the cabin, seeing its shuddering sway.

'Katya!' Zachar started to crawl toward the door, but Tasha stopped him.

'It is too dangerous.'

At that instant, the door burst open, swinging crazily. Katya staggered through the opening, clutching her two-year-old daughter, Larissa, in her arms. A side timber of the door frame snapped. More logs creaked and splintered.

Larissa wailed uncertainly as Katya tried to run clear of the cabin, but with each step the ground shifted violently, depriving her of balance. She fell, then protectively hunched her body over Larissa to shield her. Stumbling, Zachar reached her and kneeled down beside her.

Everywhere in the village there was chaos. People stumbling and staggering across the shaking ground like drunken sots. Barrels, kegs, tipping over and rolling. Broken debris falling from roofs and gables. In the bay, the waters danced in little white peaks, churned by the quaking under the ocean floor.

Slowly the tremor lessened in intensity and the rumbling faded. It had lasted such a short time, yet it had seemed so long to Tasha. She still wasn't certain it was over. She stayed on the ground, feeling its little shudders.

Others also waited warily before tentatively pushing to their feet. Zachar helped Tasha stand up. Inside she was still shaking as she cautiously crossed the gravel, not fully trusting the solidness of the ground.

Katya was sitting up, trying to soothe the crying daughter. Larissa wasn't the only bewildered and frightened child crying in the village. She was echoed by many others.

'You are not hurt?' Katya anxiously inspected Tasha as she stood up, bouncing her still fretful daughter in her arms.

'No.'

Tasha turned to view the destruction the tremor had wrought. Nothing was exactly where it had been. Buildings sat crookedly, some canted to one side and others turned on their foundations. Loose objects, large and small, were scattered all around. People moved among them, picking their way cautiously, still a little stunned.

'Look! Look!' The shout was followed by screams.

Tasha turned to face the bay, suddenly aware of a low rumble building into a loud rushing sound. A towering dark wall that completely obliterated the horizon loomed higher and closer. Water. It was water, a giant wave traveling toward the spit of land at incredible speed.

'Run!' Zachar shouted and caught Tasha by the waist and propelled her along with him at a run. High-pitched screams of terror mingled with the growing roar. They were caught in a stampede of people. Tasha tried to make her legs go faster, but they wouldn't. She cast a frightened glance over her shoulder.

The white-foamed top of the wave was curling high above the sandbar, five or ten times as tall as any of the buildings in its path. She could feel the wave's breath coming down, smell the sea in the air, and taste its brine on her lips. There was no escape from it.

Wet droplets struck her. An instant later she was engulfed by the wave, the force of it slapped her to the sand. Vaguely she was conscious of Zachar's hand gripping her forearm to hold on to her. Then it was only the sensation of the water, smashing her into the sand. She held her breath until her lungs felt as if they were going to burst. Still the water came crashing down.

Then she felt its sucking power, pulling, dragging, trying to sweep her away. She grabbed on to Zachar's arm, holding on to it with a death grip as the outgoing force of the wave tugged and twisted her legs. The undertow's strength was too mighty. It rolled her against Zachar and ripped them both from the sand, dragging them backwards.

There was no more strength left in her, no more air and no more will to resist the dark, watery world. Then the wave broke over her head, and Tasha instinctively gasped for air. Her knee grazed the gravelly bottom of the bay. She struck out for the shore, driving with her legs and feet to combat the current.

She had lost contact with Zachar. She wanted to look for her son, but it required all her concentration and energy to keep from being pulled out to sea. She risked little glances, but there were too many heads, too many bodies in the water. Half wading and half crawling, Tasha reached the shallower water and was able to stand, her muscles trembling in exhaustion.

Breathing hard and deep, she turned toward the sea and looked for her son. A confusion of shouts and cries for help assailed her. So many people were in the water, some floundering helplessly and others staggering toward the beach. So many people were trying to help them. Complicating everything was the debris – sections of roofs, broken timbers, wooden barrels, kayaks by the hundreds, a thousand bits and pieces of other things – all tumbling and rolling in the out-going seismic wave.

'Zachar.' She saw him, on his knees, trying to crawl that last bit of distance to shore, coughing and choking.

A moment ago she didn't have the strength to take another step. Now she ran through the water to her son. Tasha took hold of Zachar's arm and tried to drag him the rest of the way to the beach, but he was too heavy. Someone splashed through the water not far from her.

'Help me,' Tasha called.

Baranov waded over to her. Hooking Zachar's arm around his neck, he half carried and half walked Zachar to the sand, then lowered him to the ground. Tasha was right behind them. Sea water gurgled from his mouth, then Zachar's stomach muscles contracted sharply, expelling vomit and more water. He started coughing – and breathing. Tasha wiped the slime from the corner of his mouth, then looked at Zachar. He sat on the sand, hunched over, still laboring for air.

'Have you seen Katya?' he asked weakly.

'No.'

Tasha looked toward the boiling sea, but all she could see was Baranov's shiny pale head against the dark ocean. He was wading in water up to his hips, trying to reach a foundering woman – Katya. Leaving Zachar, Tasha hurried into the bay. She could just make out her daughter-in-law's cries for help.

As Baranov reached Katya, she shoved her young daughter into his arms. 'Take my baby.'

Tasha saw the heavy wooden beam as the wave action lifted one end and spiraled it around. 'Katya!' She screamed the warning, but it was no use. She wasn't there any more. 'No.' Tasha refused to believe it and waded deeper into the waves.

Baranov met her and thrust Larissa into her arms, then hurried away to help others. Tasha hugged the crying child to her bosom and stared at the place where she had last seen her son's wife, mindless of the waves breaking against her legs and the undertow tugging at her feet. She watched for a long time.

Eventually, the shiverings and sobbings of her wet, cold granddaughter as she trembled from shock penetrated Tasha's grieving vigil. Slowly she looked down at the black-haired little girl and rubbed her cheek against the child's forehead, closing her eyes tightly. After a moment, she lifted her head and waded back to the sandbar, where Zachar waited.

For what was left of the night, they huddled together, with only the heat generated by their own bodies for warmth.

As dawn came, the full extent of the devastation could be seen. Not a single building was left standing intact. The impact of the wave had toppled them all, smashed them into pieces that were scattered over the landspit. Some goods and supplies were lost or damaged. Most of the bidarka fleet had been broken up or washed out to sea. Miraculously, few lives were lost. And the sloop *Sv Simeon* sat at anchor in the basin, the landspit taking the brunt of the wave and sparing the ship.

In the settlement, the property loss was tremendous for Russian and native alike. The Koniaga Aleuts were convinced the sea gods had been angered, and they moaned over their fate. Tasha made an effort to search their cabin's rubble, but her heart wasn't in it.

Larissa came crying to her, wanting her mother. 'She drowned in the sea,' Tasha answered plainly.

But death was a concept beyond a two-year-old's understanding. 'Where is she?'

'In the sea.' Where Tasha's brother, Walks Straight, had died.

'No.' Zachar disputed her answer. 'She is in heaven. We should pray for her.' He took his daughter's hand and made her kneel down next to him. He bowed his head and repeated a series of disjointed phrases he'd heard the priest say, then crossed himself and took his daughter's hand, making the sign of the cross for her.

A little while later in the morning, Baranov called everyone together and announced the village would not be rebuilt here. He was moving the settlement to the eastern side of Kodiak, where there was timber and high ground. Furthermore, he was detailing a party of men to sail immediately with Ismailov on the *Sv Simeon* to the site he'd chosen and to begin chopping down trees for lumber to build the new town. He sent the Koniaga Aleuts home, instructing them to assemble at the new village in a month's time to make their hunt. No matter what the setbacks, he was determined to find locations for new outposts as Shelekhov had ordered.

His energy and determination revitalized the camp and transformed the apathy and listlessness of his men into action and purpose. Not even old Ismailov argued with his plan. Instead he immediately set out to make his ship ready to sail. Those not detailed to go with the navigator set to work salvaging everything they could from the scene of destruction.

The new site was surrounded by forest that provided a ready supply of building materials. Its natural harbor was not as large as Three Saints Bay, but it was deeper and better protected. Baranov called his Kodiak site St. Paul and worked alongside his

212

men with an axe. Determined not to lose the summer hunting season, he was content to have the walls in place to be roofed later in the summer after they returned from the hunt. When the Koniaga Aleuts arrived at the appointed time in nearly four hundred and fifty bidarkas, Baranov left behind a small contingent of men at St. Paul and set out with the hunters.

It was a long busy summer for Tasha. With a child to raise, she didn't have time to actively grieve. Existence was always a struggle in this land.

When the first of the bidarka fleet was sighted beyond the harbor islands, Tasha collected Larissa and joined the throng of Russian hunters and other women and children who waited at the shore. Zachar rode in the rear hatch of a two-man bidarka, paddled by an Aleut in the front. There were plenty of eager hands to help land the boats. As Zachar's was pulled ashore, Tasha waited to welcome him, gladness running through her heart at the safe return of her oldest son. Larissa crowded against her legs.

As Zachar passed his musket to Tasha, she noticed the underlying paleness in his face and the vaguely pained look in his blue eyes. Her gaze sharpened with concern. He kept his left arm close to his body and didn't move it at all as he climbed out of the skin-boat.

'You are hurt,' she said.

He paused in front of her, then reached for the musket she held. 'The Kolosh attacked us several nights ago when we were camped ashore. One of their arrows went into my shoulder.' Still favoring it, Zachar crouched down to speak to his daughter.

'Come,' Tasha ordered. 'I want to look at the wound.'

Inside their new crude quarters, Tasha examined his shoulder, satisfying herself that the flesh around the arrow hole didn't look infected. Its location was high, assuring her that only flesh and muscle had been pierced and no damage had been done to his lungs. She packed it with a poultice of herbs and wrapped it in place, then helped Zachar put on his red shirt.

'What happened?'

'They attacked our camp just before dawn when the mist is thickest,' Zachar said. 'Our guards had fallen asleep. I heard their war cries and woke up. They came screaming at us out of the dark mists. They wore helmets and strange, ugly masks over their faces. They had vests made of wood and carried war shields of wood. Unless they were very close to us when we fired our muskets, the bullets would not go through the wood.' He paused and shook his head. 'The Aleuts were too frightened of the Kolosh to fight. They would have killed us all if someone hadn't managed to get the small cannon into position.'

'Were many killed?' Tasha realized how very close she had come to losing another of her family. Her brother was dead; Mikhail was gone, maybe never to come back. She had no one left other than Zachar and her granddaughter, Larissa.

'Only two Russians. Nine of the Aleuts.'

A shudder vibrated her shoulders at the thought that Zachar could so easily have been one of them. 'The Kolosh are too dangerous. Maybe now Baranov has learned to avoid their lands.'

'The sea otter lives in Kolosh waters, too. The English ships and Boston ships trade with the Kolosh. Baranov will not let this attack by the Kolosh stop him from going there again.'

Tasha sobered at his statement. The Russians had never let anything stand in their way of taking the sea otter – not distance or natives. Her brother had fought them at Unalaska. Many Russians had died, but more had come to take their place. The Kolosh wouldn't stop them either.

From outside the hut came the shouted cry, 'A ship!'

It wasn't the old and weathered *Sv Simeon* that sailed into the narrow harbor, but a trim schooner-rigged packet bearing the name *Orel*, the Eagle. Again the inhabitants of the village thronged the shoreline, Tasha, Zachar, and Larissa among them. The word raced through the crowd that the packet was a supply ship from Shelekhov. Tobacco, flour, reinforcements, mail, news of home, vodka – they were here at last.

Tasha scanned the faces of the men on deck. Her gaze lingered on a tall, lanky figure, dark of hair and eyes. Hesitantly she touched Zachar's arm, not taking her eyes from the young man on the ship. She held her breath, an impossible hope rising.

'Mikhail,' she murmured. But was it her son? Could he have changed so much? She didn't know. She wasn't certain. Her fingers tightened on Zachar's arm. It seemed to take so long for the first boat to come ashore. Finally it landed. As she watched the young man bound from it, there was no more doubt in her mind. 'Mikhail!'

Turning, he saw her. A smile lighted his face, and he broke into a trot, heading directly to her. Tasha started crying with happiness as she moved forward to embrace the son who had left her as a boy and had come back a man of sixteen. Her fingers trembled as she touched the short dark whiskers that outlined his jaw. His face swam in her tear-blurred vision, distorting the image just enough to let her see traces of boyhood softness in his features.

'You have come back.' She could hardly believe it. She had almost despaired of ever seeing him again. 'I thought there would be too many new places and things for you to see and you would stay.'

Mikhail laughed at her fears, and the laugh had the deep-throated sound of a man. 'I have much to tell you about all that I've seen.' His glance included Zachar. 'And there are many more places I will see. I have been to navigator's school and learned how to sail ships.' His arm remained about Tasha's shoulders as he shifted to greet his older brother. Then he noticed the little girl standing beside Zachar and crouched down to her level. 'Who are you?' He smiled at Larissa, who quickly hid behind Tasha's skirts.

'My daughter,' Zachar answered for her. 'Her name is Larissa.' He studied Mikhail carefully.

Briefly Tasha related the story of her daughter-in-law's drowning. Mikhail sobered, but it didn't last for long. This occasion was too full of joy for all of them to let death cast its shadow over it.

Now there was too much to tell, many gaps to fill in, many incidents to relate. So much had happened to each of them during the years they were apart. They spent most of the day filling in those missing years.

That night, Mikhail and Zachar attended the praznik Baranov gave to celebrate the arrival of the long-awaited supply ship. Fresh meat was roasted over fires that were built at the village's new square. The huge vat of fermenting kvass was filled with buckets of vodka from the ship's cargo. Everyone had a mug of it and a packet of tobacco uncut with willow bark.

Again and again, toasts were drunk to the party's guest of honor, the skipper of the *Orel*. Yakov Egoryevich Shiltz, they called the burly Englishman whose red hair and multitude of tattoos marked him as different from them. James Shields, a shipbuilder by trade and a lieutenant in the Russian Imperial Navy, always answered their salutes with his own – fracturing the Russian language in the process, much to the promyshleniki's amusement.

The tidal wave at Three Saints Bay had destroyed the few musical instruments the settlement had had, but two of the newly arrived reinforcements had brought their guzlas with them and the praznik rang with music. The promyshleniki raided the Aleut dwellings and hauled the girls to their celebration. They ladled the vodka-laced kvass into cups for their girls and whirled them about, cavorting in high-stepping abandon. They danced and sang the mournful Siberian ballads of their homeland.

Mikhail was among the first to leave the party, staggering off to the bunkhouse with his arm around an Aleut girl; and Zachar wasn't long to follow him. But it was dawn before the last man staggered into his bed.

Meanwhile Baranov read his mail and the long letter of instruction from Shelekhov. It reiterated the need to establish new colonies, especially on the southeast coast. To that end, Shelekhov had sent Shields to him. Baranov was to begin building ships to accomplish these goals.

Part Two

Southeast Alaska

20 *Sitka Sound*
Late Spring 1802

The distinctive truncated cone of Mount Edgecumbe marked the entrance to Sitka Sound, its snow-capped peak blending with the heavy clouds. The shores of the main island were forested with towering stands of cedar, spruce, and fir, a nearly impenetrable mass of ferns and bushes growing in their shade. More islands dotted its coastal waters, adding to the maze of bays, fiords, and estuaries. Bald-headed eagles spiraled slowly in the sky that they shared with flocks of seabirds.

The copper-bottomed brig the *Sea Gypsy*, out of Salem, Massachusetts, nosed her way into the sound. A year's exposure to the elements had faded her bright yellow waist to the dark green of her topsides, but the gingerbread trim on her stern and the quickwork on her bow were undamaged by the beating the brig had taken sailing around the Horn. She was small and well built, handy and fast, her size and maneuverability making her ideally suited for the intricacies of the Northwest coast. Some in the sea trade considered brigs like the *Sea Gypsy* the pirate's own vessel.

Screens of dried bullock hides brought from the California coast lined her decks to shield the crew from arrows. An opening was left at the stern, where the trading was done. In addition to the swivel guns at the bulwarks, the *Sea Gypsy* carried ten cannons, shotted with grape, a gunner's match beside each of them. Her crew were armed with muskets and pistols – with cutlasses and boarding pikes available as well. In her hold, she carried an assortment of trading goods – shiny copper trinkets, boxes of beads, bundles of clothing, and bolts of red and blue duffel cloth – but her cargo consisted mainly of rum and crates of old muskets, relics of the Revolutionary War that had been purchased cheaply from the newly formed American government.

This was the heart of Tlingit country. One of their villages sat on a short peninsula below a rugged knoll just ahead. Their great communal houses, built of massive timbers, lined the shore facing the water. Even from a distance the tall heraldic columns of the houses could be seen, grotesque animal and bird characters carved into the wood and painted in vivid colors. They seemed to reflect the savage grandeur of the country. A log cabin of the American backwoods would have looked puny and crude alongside one of these huge, solidly built structures.

From his position on the quarterdeck, Caleb Stone watched as three canoes approached his ship. Each was carved from a single cedar log. The faces of the warriors in the canoes were garishly painted in red and black. Their hair was pulled into a knot at the back of the head and powdered with down, then adorned with black and yellow feathers.

As physical specimens, Caleb was willing to concede that the Tlingit Indians were impressive. The men were tall, frequently reaching six feet in height, bronze-skinned, muscular. They were both clever and treacherous. They walked as lords in this land and they were.

As their canoes came alongside his vessel, he glanced once at his crew, but they didn't have to be told to keep a lively eye about for the approach of war canoes from a different direction, a favorite ploy of these insidious savages who preferred taking what they wanted by force rather than trading for it. Most of his crew were veterans in the Northwest fur trade.

Caleb Stone had made a half dozen voyages here himself, the first as a cabin boy at the age of twelve, then as a common deckhand in the fo'c'sle. On the last trip, he'd sailed as the first mate, taken over command when the captain died at sea, and brought the ship back to its home port of Salem, loaded with a rich cargo of Chinese goods from Canton, where he'd sold the ship's furs for a handsome sum. Now, at twenty-seven, he sailed as master of the vessel – 'coming through the hawse hole,' as the expression went.

A tall, spare-built man, he had a seaman's sunburnt cheek and skin the color of teakwood. Long sideburns emphasized his lean jaw and echoed the mahogany cast of his hair. His gray eyes were half hidden by the slight droop of his lids, but always they showed a sharp alertness.

'They're takin' the devil's own time inspectin' the cut of our jib,' the first mate, Asa Hicks, observed in a voice dry with suspicion. Caleb made no comment.

220

'Boston men!' one of the vermillion-and-black-faced warriors shouted to them, using the term they applied to all Americans because of the large number of ships trading in their waters that carried a Boston registry. By the same token, they referred to the English as King George's men. 'Come trade!' With a wave of his arm, he signaled them to enter the island-studded bay off the brig's starboard side.

Shaking his head, Caleb called to the savages, telling them they'd be back another time to trade with them. The canoes continued to keep pace with the *Sea Gypsy*, and the invitation was repeated several times, but Caleb ignored it.

During his winter stop at Hawaii for reprovisions, he had learned from the captains of homeward-bound vessels that the Russians had built a redoubt at Sitka the previous year in an effort to extend their territorial claims to this coastal region and exclude foreign vessels. Caleb intended to make the place that the Russians called Redoubt St. Michael his first port of call and to determine for himself how much of a threat the Russians were.

Roughly six miles from the entrance to the sound, the *Sea Gypsy* came upon the settlement that had been built on a stretch of exposed beach. The palisaded fortress was constructed of timbers two feet thick, hewn from the surrounding forest, its upper story extending out two feet from the lower, with watchtowers at two corners. The roofs of several other buildings were visible behind the stockade that surrounded the settlement. A Russian flag snapped crisply in the wind.

As soon as the ship was at anchor, Caleb ordered the longboat lowered over the side. A contingent of Russians awaited his arrival on the shore. He buttoned his double-breasted pea jacket and left the collar upturned against the sharp wind, then climbed over the side into the yawl. As the sailors hauled on the oars, Caleb scanned the Russian group waiting for him.

The turbanned lad Caleb recognized easily from the descriptions of captains who had met the English-speaking Bengalese servant of the Russian manager, Baranov. Baranov himself was a short, stockily built man who wore an absurd black wig tied on his head with a colored handkerchief. Caleb had been told that Baranov affected that ridiculous attempt at fashion, but Caleb had thought the stories too ludicrous to be true. He wondered now about the other tales he'd heard concerning the prodigious quantities of liquor Baranov could consume at a single sitting. He looked over the rest of the men standing with the Russian manager, taking note of only one, a blue-eyed man with dark brown hair.

Zachar observed the meeting between Baranov and the Boston captain, and listened as the Bengalese called Richard identified Captain Stone from the ship *Sea Gypsy* and relayed his request for permission to send his men ashore to replenish their fresh-water supply.

Two years ago Zachar had left his young daughter, Larissa, in the care of his mother and brother and sailed from Kodiak Island as a member of the colonizing force chosen by Baranov to establish a fortified settlement here on the southeastern coast of the mainland – in the heart of the hostile Kolosh country. Since they'd built the redoubt on the sound, many Boston and English ships had visited it. Zachar had learned many of their words from the seamen who'd come ashore, but not enough to follow a whole conversation.

As usual, Baranov granted permission and invited the Boston man inside the stockade. This Captain Stone accepted with the same wariness and curiosity that Zachar had seen others show. Zachar trailed behind the company manager as he escorted his visitor inside the stronghold.

Within the high stockade, guards walked the parapets where the cannons were mounted, their barrels aimed at the dark under-growth of the flanking forest. A cookhouse, blacksmith's shop, warehouse, cattle sheds, and the two-story barracks encompassed the central square of the settlement.

In the square, Zachar's attention was drawn to only one of the Kolosh women. She was tall, with long, shiny black hair and copper bracelets around her bare ankles. The long-skirted and sleeved garment she wore was made from softly tanned hides that were fastened together at the sides, emphasizing her rounded hips. Over the front of it, she wore an apronlike top made from the same skin.

Zachar knew that none of these Kolosh – or Tlingit as they called themselves – could be trusted, no matter how willing they were to be bedded for a price. But where the maiden called Daughter of the Raven was concerned, Zachar abandoned all sense of caution. Every time he saw her, he wanted her, regardless of the price he must pay. Today was no different.

Leaving Baranov's escort party, he angled across the square.

When she saw him approaching, she lifted her chin, certain of his interest in her. Her long, black hair was parted in the middle and fell past her shoulders. Her eyes seemed to pull his gaze into their black centers as if he were, somehow, being absorbed into them.

He halted in front of her. His tongue felt thick and his throat tight. 'You haven't come to the village in a long time, Raven.' Zachar never used her full name.

'Zachar missed Raven?' Her eyes seemed to darken with satisfaction as she smiled at him, her lips full and soft, the lower one unmarred by the disfiguring spoon-shaped labret many of the older Kolosh women wore.

'Yes,' he admitted. He'd lain with her seven short nights ago, but it seemed much longer to him. 'Tonight, will you come to my bed?'

She tipped her head to the side, studying him with a shrewd and knowing look. 'Raven wants looking glass.'

Startled by her demand, Zachar was momentarily speechless. Usually the price of her company was a string of blue beads. A mirror was considerably more expensive. Already he was in debt to the company commissary for more than he was likely to earn this season.

'Two strings of beads,' he offered hesitantly, reluctant to bargain with her.

Her look turned cold. 'No.' She pivoted to her right.

Zachar caught her arm before she could walk away from him, regretting his attempt to negotiate and realizing that he had succeeded only in offending her. 'A looking glass,' he agreed.

She regarded him haughtily. 'Zachar want Raven – a looking glass *and* beads.'

Logic warred with his desires, insisting he should reject her price and let her walk away. If he paid it now, next time she would demand more. He stared at her face, the straight nose and the natural pink of her cheeks. He nodded slowly, angered by his own weakness.

'A looking glass and beads,' he agreed, then attempted to salvage his pride. 'If Raven does not make Zachar happy tonight, no beads.'

Her lips parted in a knowing smile that mocked him for questioning her ability to satisfy him. 'Raven make Zachar happy,' she declared and walked away. He watched her go, feeling a mixture of self-contempt and anticipation.

In the ten years since the death of his wife, Katya, Zachar had never taken another woman to live with him permanently. During much of that time, his mother had taken over many of a wife's duties, making all his garments, mending his skin-boat, preparing his meals, and looking after his young daughter, Larissa, and teaching her the things a woman should know. The sexual urges, when they came to him, were easily satisfied by willing Aleut girls in some nearby village.

And until he'd met Raven, no woman had ever attracted him to the exclusion of others, not even his late wife. It was new and unsettling to him. Sometimes Zachar wished he had stayed behind in Kodiak, that Mikhail's return hadn't freed him from the responsibility of his family. Yet he knew that even before Mikhail had come back he had virtually abandoned Larissa to his mother's care. He was a rough, unschooled hunter; there was nothing he could teach his daughter. Mikhail, with all that he'd learned while in Russia, could give her more than Zachar ever could. Now that his brother was at Kodiak, he could look after their aging mother.

Zachar kept telling himself that he had no more reason to go back. His family didn't need him. But, in truth, the thought of never seeing Raven again filled him with a kind of panic.

The oil lantern swayed with the gentle rocking motion of the brig riding at anchor in the bay. The carved mahogany dining table gleamed, its surface cleared of dishes and cutlery. Only a pair of brandy glasses and bottle remained. Caleb leaned back in his chair and watched Baranov puff on the cigar being lighted by his servant and constant companion, the young Bengalese named Richard.

After his meeting with Baranov in the afternoon, Caleb had invited the Russian to dinner on board his ship. Dawson, his steward, bent in a slight bow toward Caleb's chair and extended his arm to offer Caleb his choice of cigars, trying to be as formal as the English-trained Bengalese. Caleb was amused by the rivalry that his steward obviously felt toward his Russian counterpart. He waved aside the cigar box. Stiffly, Dawson straightened and silently closed the lid on the box, then set it on the mahogany side table and assumed his position behind Caleb's chair.

As the swarthy Richard blew out the taper's flame, Baranov

held the cigar away from his mouth and spoke. Richard translated the compliments on the meal and the excellent quality of the brandy as if he were the one speaking instead of inserting some appendage like 'he said' or 'he wants you to know.' 'I am curious what kind of trade goods you are carrying, Captain,' he stated at the conclusion of the pleasantries.

Caleb had known the conversation would eventually get around to the items in his hold.

'The usual,' Caleb said, looking at Baranov as he spoke. He suspected the Russian understood English better than he pretended. 'Scarlet coating, buttons, blankets, copper, Flushing greatcoats, iron chisels.'

While Richard relayed his answer, Caleb picked up his brandy glass and swirled its contents, then lifted the glass to his mouth, meeting Baranov's sharp gaze over its rim. Caleb had deliberately omitted any mention of the muskets and rum.

'What about guns and ammunition?'

Smiling, Caleb lowered his glass and studied the amber liquor. 'I carry those, too – and New England rum,' he admitted, lifting his glance.

The stern lecture he received from Baranov hardly required a translation. 'Trading firearms and liquor to the savages is forbidden in Russian America. It is unwise to arm them with weapons that can be used against you. You must desist from this practice at once.'

'I have traveled fifteen thousand miles to trade with the Tlingits – or the Kolosh as you call them. I want otter skins and they want guns. I have the guns and they have the otter skins. If that's their price for the skins, that's what I'll pay. I'm a trader.'

'I must make it clear how strongly I protest. Weapons are not to be traded to the natives. Truly you must see it is for the safety of all who come to our coasts.'

'May I make a suggestion, Mr. Baranov?' Caleb inquired smoothly, and received an assenting nod from the bewigged Russian before Richard had relayed his question. 'Since you are claiming all of the Northwest coast as Russian territory, that means the natives are under your jurisdiction. Why don't you simply forbid them to trade with us for guns?'

There was the faintest glimmer of admiration in Baranov's eye when Richard finished his translation of Caleb's rejoinder. Both of them were fully aware that the rule couldn't be enforced, either against the American and English merchant ships or against the Tlingits. But Baranov remained adamant in his protest against the sale of firearms and liquor to the native population.

Privately, Caleb admired the tactics of the peculiar-looking Russian, first establishing a friendly intercourse, then registering his protest. As Caleb had understood from the reports he'd received from other merchant captains, the Russians traded very little with the Tlingits, refusing to offer the one commodity most demanded by the natives, and relied heavily on the Aleut hunters they had enslaved to hunt the sea otter in these waters. Baranov had confirmed that the Russians wouldn't compete in the sale of muskets, which meant the field remained wide open. And Baranov had neither the naval power nor the manpower to stop him. There were fortunes to be made in this fur trade and Caleb intended to have one of them. With his sizable share, as the ship's master and supercargo, of this voyage's profits, he planned to buy his own ship. On his next voyage, he'd make even more.

As Caleb reached for the brandy bottle, Dawson sprang quickly to snatch it up and refill both glasses, darting a snooty look at the Bengalese servant. Now that Baranov had stated his position regarding the guns, he let the matter drop and displayed the interest of a man long isolated from the outside world for news of it.

Caleb relaxed and told Baranov what he knew about the Napoleonic wars in Europe that had reduced the number of English ships engaged in the Northwest and China trade that year. Baranov wanted to know about King Kamehameha I of the Hawaiian Islands and about the small Spanish presidio of San Francisco, two thousand miles away, the closest settlement to the Russian redoubt. Caleb couldn't tell him much about the latter, since the Spanish continued to keep their California port closed to foreign vessels, but he talked about the Hawaiian monarch. And, yes, the last he'd heard, Tsar Paul was still in power, having succeeded his mother, Catherine the Great, to the Russian throne.

The two men talked and drank, trading tales and information. The stories Caleb had heard about the amount of liquor Baranov could hold were all true. When the puckish little Russian finally left for shore, his black wig was askew, but he was walking more or less unaided by his servant. Dawson, on the other hand, had to haul Caleb to his bunk.

*

At the edge of the forest, Raven paused, still hidden in its dark shadows. She could see Zachar standing by the stockade gate waiting for her. She counted the number of sentries in the blockhouses. Always the same. The laughter of the Russian chief called Nanuk boomed from the Boston ship. She was certain there were muskets and powder, maybe even some of the new guns with cartridges on board the ship.

Other clans along the coast were angry with her Sitka *kwan* for letting the Russians build their village on the island in exchange for some beads, brass, and bottles. They urged her Sitka kwan to drive them out. Already her clan had acquired many guns, but they needed more. And the Russians always were on guard, even though her people had pretended to live in peace. Raven suspected this Nanuk was very clever.

Someone shouted to Zachar. Many of the words escaped her understanding, but she recognized the chiding tone and guessed he was being teased. She stepped out of the forest thicket and approached the gate, moving with deliberate slowness, conscious of his eyes watching her. She knew it would make him impatient for her. As she drew near enough to see his face in the spring twilight, she saw the hungering ache in his look that spoke of his great need for her. She was pleased by the power she had over him. Remembering how much he'd been willing to pay for her made her smile.

The high log walls that surrounded the Russian village cast a long shadow. Raven walked to the square of twilight that shone through the gate's opening and stopped when she was fully in its light, allowing Zachar to stare at her.

'I come as Zachar wanted,' she said at last.

The night air was cool and damp, but she could see the beads of sweat glistening on his upper lip below the thin black mustache. As he took her arm, Raven felt the faint tremor that shook his hand. Briskly, he guided her inside the walls directly to the tall barracks. All the while she was looking about to note the activity in the village.

Inside the barracks, he led her past the rooms occupied by Russians who had brought their squat, fish-eating Aleut wives with them. Zachar entered the small room that belonged to him and pulled her inside. He drew her into his arms and pressed his hot, damp lips on her mouth.

Raven brought her hands up and firmly pushed him back. 'My looking glass and beads.'

He looked at her half angrily, then moved away, walking to a corner of the room. When he came back to her, he carried the smooth glass that showed her reflection and two necklaces of blue beads. Raven took them from his hands, examined them briefly, then laid them on the floor by the wall. She untied her apron and laid it atop her new possessions, then removed her buckskin dress and turned to face Zachar, the copper bracelets jangling around her bare ankles.

'Now Raven will make Zachar happy,' she murmured huskily and walked very close to him as she moved to the cot.

A steady light rain fell from low gray clouds, pattering softly on the quarterdeck around Caleb. He stood hunched in his sou'wester, his head throbbing. He peered upward, without tilting his head, to check that the sails were loosed, then looked away from the sailor coming down the rigging with the sureness of a cat. This was one morning when he didn't miss the physical demands of a deckhand's job or the camaraderie of shipmates.

'Sails loosed, Cap'n.' Asa Hicks's deep, rumbling voice seemed to vibrate right through him.

Caleb scowled. 'Man the windlass.'

'Man the windlass!' Hicks boomed the order, and Caleb was barely able to suppress a shudder of pain. He swore that his first mate knew he had a hangover and was deliberately aggravating his condition. Hell, he'd done the same when he was mate – and delighted in the doing of it, too.

Water trickled down his neck. Caleb pulled the neckline of his sou'wester more tightly together and hunched his shoulders higher, trying to shield his ears.

'Yo heave ho!' Hicks bawled to men manning the windlass, preparing to haul up the anchor. 'Heave and pawl!'

At sea it was claimed a song was as good as ten men. Caleb flinched at the loud and hearty rendition of 'Cheerily, Men!' the crew sang as they put their backs into the handspike to turn the windlass. The clatter of the anchor chain added to the racket.

Roughly twenty minutes later, after catting the anchor, making sail, and bracing yards, the *Sea Gypsy* was under way. Caleb looked back at the Russian fort of St. Michael, half shrouded by the low-hanging clouds and the gray drizzle. The Russians could have this miserable country, for all he cared. He was only interested in its furs.

The wind was light and fair. The brig glided down the channel, carrying royals and skysails at the fore and main as well as her studding sails. Caleb watched the dark shore, the towering firs and cedars and the impenetrable undergrowth that grew almost to the water's edge.

Ahead lay the open waters of the sound, and off the port bow stood the bluff that commanded a view of the whole area. The long row of totemic-fronted houses marked the site of a village, the vividly colored columns darkened by the rain. The wood smoke rising from their massive houses was spread through the drizzle as a haze.

Hangover or no, it was time to start trading. Caleb ordered the light sails clewed up and the main topsail backed. The *Sea Gypsy* came to anchor well off the village's shore, with slip ropes attached to her cables, ready to slip anchor and make for the sea at a moment's warning of trouble.

The crew scrambled about to make the brig both a trade vessel and a bastion of defense, double-checking the lines that secured the bull-hide shields in place and closing off the forward part of the ship with a screen of sails. The cannons were moved into position forward on the deck, and their muzzles trained to rake the afterdeck. A pair of blunderbusses on swivels sat on the taffrail. Trade goods were spread on the quarterdeck in a display of wares.

There was a stir of activity along the shore. 'Look brightly, lads!' Hicks warned the crew.

'Two men aloft,' Caleb told his mate. All orders to the crew were relayed through him.

'Aye, sir,' Hicks said and sent two armed sailors up the mainmast.

Three canoes of Indians approached the brig. Caleb noticed there were two Tlingit women with the warriors. In his experience he'd discovered whenever a native woman was present during the trading, no sale was final unless she gave her approval. Invariably they drove hard bargains.

When the canoes were alongside the brig, Caleb requested that only one of the warriors come on board so he could explain the rules before the trading began. A tall, muscular warrior climbed onto the ship, his face plucked free of whiskers and painted black. A brown woolen blanket was draped across his shoulders in a manner that kept his arms free. He faced Caleb with the arrogant disdain of one dealing with an inferior.

Caleb drew the Tlingit's attention to the ship's armament, its blunderbusses and cannons loaded with grapeshot cartridges, and the two armed sailors in their lofty perch with a clear view of the quarterdeck, then indicated that there were many more men behind the canvas screen. Finally, he told the warrior that only three of his people would be allowed on board at one time and warned that if any of those three ventured further than ten steps from the rail, they would be shot, and such an act wasn't to be regarded as breaking the peace.

The warrior nodded his understanding and went back to his canoe to inform the others of the Boston man's rules. Shortly afterwards, the warrior returned, accompanied by another warrior and a squaw. The Tlingit woman was older, although her grease-rubbed hair showed no grey. The warriors treated her with deference, but Caleb had to stifle the repugnance he felt at the sight of her jutting lower lip. A spoon-shaped wooden disc, roughly the size of a snuffbox, was inserted in the slitted skin and extended her lip. The weight of it pulled her lip down, exposing her teeth and gums. In Caleb's opinion, 'Spoonbill' – as he privately dubbed her – was a revolting sight that did little to ease his hangover.

The warriors presented their fur pelts for his inspection, an assortment of full otter skins and pieces cut from a pelt. Caleb examined them, gauging their worth, while the Tlingits looked over his merchandise. Finally the bargaining began.

Trading with the Tlingits was a long and sometimes futile process, Caleb had found. They argued endlessly over the price for their furs, working on a trader's patience and shrewdly using the presence of other trading vessels in the area to drive up the price. If they weren't offered what they wanted for their furs, they simply gathered up the pelts and left, no matter how many hours had been wasted haggling.

But Caleb had also learned that the Tlingits were a highly materialistic society. A man's status in his village was determined by the number of his possessions. Like the white man's world, there were the rich and the poor, with some in the middle. Therefore, as a trader, Caleb could count on their avarice.

As the negotiations continued, he felt definite progress was being made. Then 'Spoonbill,' the squaw, said something to the two warriors. Silence descended. Caleb didn't like it.

'Boston man pay one gun and four pounds of powder for one

otter skin.' The black-faced warrior repeated Caleb's last offer, then motioned toward something behind Caleb. 'Big gun is how many guns?'

Frowning, Caleb glanced over his shoulder and realized the 'big gun' referred to a cannon. Why on earth would these devils want a cannon? he wondered. Then he carefully avoided coming up with an answer. Slowly he turned back and shrugged his shoulders. 'Many guns. Many more than you have furs,' he said.

The black-faced warrior stiffened indignantly. 'How many?'

Caleb paused deliberately. 'Forty otter skins. Full skins, no pieces, and the fur must be thick and soft.' If otter pelts had held their price in Canton, China, that meant better than three thousand dollars for one small cannon. Definitely a bargain.

'Boston man wait. We come back with furs,' the Tlingit announced.

The trading party left the ship and returned to the village in their canoes. Caleb blew on his hands to warm them and turned to his first mate. 'Tell the cook to pour some coffee.'

'Aye, sir.'

Hicks came back a few minutes later, carrying a steaming mug. 'You really gonna let those sons a' Satan have one of our cannons, Cap'n?'

'Aye.' Caleb clasped both hands around the hot cup. Cannon or musket, he didn't see the distinction. It was no more his concern what the Tlingits did with the cannon than it was what they did with the muskets. Anyway, he doubted that the Indians knew how to load it or fire it, let alone aim it at something.

A short while later, the Tlingits returned to the ship, bringing with them a bundle of pelts of considerably higher quality than the ones they had originally offered. Satisfied, Caleb concluded the trade, and the small cannon was hoisted over the side and lowered into one of their canoes.

The drizzle had tapered off to a wet mist that blurred the wooded shores. Caleb watched from the quarterdeck as the cannon-laden canoe landed. The jubilant shouts and singing from the villagers echoed across the sound.

21

A few sunlit clouds drifted lazily across a blue sky; the bay waters reflected and deepened the blue of the sky to indigo. The islands along the sound were the lush green of summer. Near the shingle beach, Zachar paused in his labors and wiped the sweat from his brow as he looked at the unfinished keel of the sloop.

The surrounding quiet seemed to intensify. Zachar glanced toward the weathered logs of the tall fort and saw little movement. It appeared almost deserted now that nearly all of the two hundred Aleuts had left to begin the summer hunt for otter.

Hot and thirsty, he crossed the hard-packed ground to the water pail and ladled out a drink. He drank half of it, then poured the rest of it on the back of his neck, letting it run inside his muslin shirt and cool his flesh. Vaguely refreshed, he returnd the ladle to the pail, hooking it over the wooden side, and flexed the tired muscles in his back and shoulders.

Then he saw her; she made no sound save the soft jingle of the copper bracelets around her ankles as she came along the beach toward him. Everything inside him seemed to become still for an instant, then all his senses started clamoring at once. He could even feel the pumping of his heart.

As Raven stopped in front of him, she kept her chin level and merely directed her gaze upwards to his face. 'Zachar is busy?'

'No. I was taking a rest.' He glanced at the fort, but there was no one to see him idling. A surge of energy swept through him, chasing away his fatigue. 'I have been wanting to see you.' Although he'd seen her frequently these last weeks, he never saw her often enough.

Smiling, she glanced at the crotch of his trousers. 'Zachar is like a young warrior. Always eager.'

He laughed; that was exactly the way he felt when he was around her. Familiarly, he placed his arm around her shoulders.

'Come. We will sit in the shade,' he said, guiding her to the shadows cast by the sloop's keel.

As they sat down, Raven shifted sideways to face him and rested a shoulder against the planked sides of the keel, but she sat very close to him, close enough for Zachar to feel the light pressure of a rounded breast against his arm. His breathing roughened as he remembered the impressions her naked body made against his, its supple movements and fiery heat, its thrilling demands.

'Zachar's village is quiet. Have all the fish eaters gone to hunt otter?'

'Yes.' He stroked her upper arm, its firmly muscled flesh bared by the broad sleeve of her buckskin garment that fell only a little below her shoulder.

'Will Zachar go hunt?'

'Would you miss me if I left?'

'Yes. Zachar gives me many pretty things.' The bead necklaces, the copper bracelets, and the silver rings in her ears were all presents from him.

Gifts. That was all he meant to her. Zachar knew it and hadn't really expected her to say anything else. Yet it hurt to hear it. His hand automatically ceased caressing her.

'Will Zachar leave?' Raven studied him closely.

Her intent gaze awakened him to the fact that he'd been staring at her. 'No.' He smiled wanly. 'I am not going hunting this summer. I will stay here at the settlement with the others.' He rested his head against the unfinished keel and draped his arms across his upraised knees, then stared indifferently at the slow-moving clouds.

'Zachar looks sad. Has Raven made you unhappy?' She leaned closer and lightly rubbed her hand over the bulge in his crotch. His stiffened penis gave a little leap against her hand.

Zachar grabbed her hand and covered it with his to press down on his aching genitals. He turned his face to her, his look full of want. 'If you want to make me happy, Raven, come live with me. I want you to be my woman.' Now that he'd spoken the half-formed thoughts that had been whirling in his mind for so long, Zachar knew it was what he wanted. 'What is the custom of your people? Do I take gifts to your parents?'

She pulled her hand free of his and drew back slightly. 'Nanuk would be angry when he comes back in his ship.'

'Baranov – Nanuk won't return for a long time, not until next summer. He has gone to Kodiak. And he wouldn't care if you were my woman.'

Raven knew her father and the other clan chiefs would be interested to learn Nanuk would not return soon. He was brave and fearless. They had no wish to face him in battle.

Not once did she seriously consider Zachar's offer. If she became his woman, he would no longer give her presents. It would be her duty to mate with him. By living with him, she would lose status in her tribe. She had nothing to gain by accepting.

But more importantly, Raven knew the plans of her people. Before summer's end, the village of the Russians would be destroyed. Other clans were banding with her kwan to attack it, and a sufficient quantity of guns and powder, obtained in trade from the Boston men, was hidden in their houses. They waited only for the moment to strike when the Russians were unaware. She and the other Tlingit women who were allowed by the Russians to freely enter the fort to mate with them reported all they saw and heard to that end.

She looked at this stupid Creole who gazed at her with hungry eyes, and she felt amused contempt. Soon he would be dead, and his head would be on the end of a pole stuck in the ground.

'Raven cannot be Zachar's woman,' she informed him coolly. 'Raven will come visit Zachar like before times.'

He nodded slowly and averted his gaze, but she observed the grimness around his mouth, a sign of some hot emotion held in check. Lithely she stood up.

'Zachar does not want to be with Raven. Raven not stay.' She heard the scrape of his boots on the packed earth as he scrambled to his feet.

'Don't go.' His fingers closed around her arm to stop her.

She looked at him insolently. 'Raven not like the way Zachar is this day. Raven come back when Zachar happy.'

There was a moment when she thought he was going to argue, then the fight went out of him. 'We are going to have a feast in two days to celebrate a Holy Day.' He released his hold on her arm. 'No one will work that day. We will have a praznik and there will be singing and dancing. Will you come, Raven?'

She smiled slowly at his statement. 'This will be in two days,' she repeated.

'Yes.'

'It is a happy time,' she said, and he nodded. 'Raven maybe come then.'

As she walked away from him, Raven forced herself to maintain a sedate pace. The minute she reached the concealment of the forest, she quickened her steps to hurry back to her clan's summer camp and report what she'd learned, certain her news would fill the camp with excitement. What better time to attack the Russian village than the day of their feast.

Idly, Zachar let the empty pail slap against his leg as he crossed the square, heading for the open gate and the cowsheds beyond by the creek. The doors and windows to the barracks stood open, their barricades raised. From inside came the high-pitched giggles of some Aleut women happily preparing for the day's celebration. Zachar could see some of the baby cradles hanging along the wall in the sunny room. Over by the cookhouse, a half dozen promyshleniki leaned on their muskets, talking and laughing in loud voices.

As he approached the gate, Zachar waved to the guard on the second-story parapet. An injury temporarily kept the Russian from any arduous task and earned him easy sentry duty. He lifted a hand in response to Zachar's wave, smoke curling from the pipe in his hand. His musket lay across his legs. As he walked out of the stockade, Zachar had a fleeting glimpse of a baidar with three promyshleniki on board before it disappeared behind one of the small islands in the channel. The three were half of a hunting party sent to bring back fresh seal meat and wild geese for the feast.

Zachar nodded a greeting to another of his comrades, who waded in the shallow water of the cove to stake out fishnets, and continued on to the sheds. There was an indolence about the sun-drenched day that reflected his relaxed, happy mood and that of those around him. Everyone was enjoying a well-earned day of rest. He passed an Aleut woman busy picking berries. Ahead of him, a young, black and white calf frolicked in the cattleyard, then scampered to its mother's side at Zachar's approach. The hammering of a woodpecker somewhere in the deep woods suddenly stopped.

The spotted cattle took little notice of him as he paused beside the split-timber rails that enclosed the yard. Distantly, he heard a shout, followed immediately by the banging of the settlement's iron ring, sounding an alarm. Turning, Zachar dropped the empty bucket and ran toward the fort. The crack of musketfire broke the quiet.

Zachar skidded to a halt at the sight of the Kolosh swarming around the stockaded barracks, hideous in their grotesquely carved beast masks with gleaming eyes and hooked beaks and long fangs. Already they were climbing over the parapets and jamming their muskets into the window openings before the barricades could be dropped. More Kolosh streamed from the woods carrying firebrands of burning pitch that they hurled onto the second-story roof. As Zachar took a step toward the beach and the skin-boats on the shore, war canoes with more demon-masked Kolosh bore down on the clearing.

Unarmed, with no chance of reaching the now barricaded fort or escaping by water, Zachar turned and raced back toward the cowsheds. Animal-like war cries rent the air, interspersed with the shouts and screams that came from inside the stockade. Sporadic musketfire signaled valiant resistance.

The Aleut woman emerged from the berry thicket with a small child clutched in her arms, her expression filled with terror and confusion. 'Kolosh!' Zachar shouted. 'Run! Hide in the woods!'

She screamed at something behind him, then darted back into the thicket. Zachar glanced over his shoulder and saw four Kolosh brandishing spears in pursuit of him. Avoiding the bushes where the woman had gone, he sprinted for the deep tangle of the forest's edge, straining every muscle in an effort to reach it ahead of the feet pounding the ground behind him. His heart felt as if it was going to burst.

He dived into the dense undergrowth, scrambling and clawing his way through the thorny bushes and thick ferns on his hands and knees. His pursuers came crashing into the brush after him. Zachar frantically looked for a hiding place, then spied the gnarled and twisted roots of a long-ago-fallen spruce. He crawled quickly to the dark hallow at the base of the log's massive trunk, slightly elevated from the forest floor by the widely spread roots. He flattened himself to the ground to wiggle into it.

When he was safely inside it, he lay motionless and swallowed to control his loud, labored breathing. He could hear the rattle of the brush as the Kolosh searched for him. They were close, very close. He held his breath, then heard the reverberating boom of a cannon from the fort.

The rustling noises grew fainter and finally faded altogether. Still Zachar waited a little longer before emerging from the dank hollow. Several times he'd heard the cannon go off. Moving silently, he worked his way through the woods to the edge of the forest close to the settlement and cautiously peered out to see if the attack had been repulsed.

Dark smoke rolled from all the buildings, yellow tongues of flame leaping and dancing from the roofs. As Zachar watched, three promyshleniki jumped from the burning second story. One, the injured sentry, was impaled on a Kolosh spear. The second was quickly cornered, and a spear ripped out his throat. The last promyshlenik landed free and ran for the forest, pursued by the Kolosh, but he stumbled and fell. They pounced on him before he could rise and severed his head.

A score of screaming Aleut women with their babies fled the burning barracks and ran directly into the arms of the Kolosh. The babies were taken from them, and swung by their heels to bash in their skulls on the hard ground, then their bodies were thrown into the water. A Kolosh warrior shouted and pointed to the woods where Zachar was hiding. He'd been seen.

Quickly, Zachar slipped back into the forest and eluded his pursuers again. By accident, he found the Aleut woman and child that he'd sent into the woods to hide. Fleeing together, they went deeper into the forest, climbing the mountain that rose behind the redoubt.

After leaving Sitka Sound, the *Sea Gypsy* had sailed into the maze of islands lying north of the sound, anchoring in the waters offshore of villages, trading, then sailing on. The brig's circuitous route eventually brought her back to the sound.

Caleb decided to call at the Redoubt St. Michael, replenish the freshwater supply, and learn what rival ships were operating in the area. As captain, he never fraternized with his officers or crew. In truth, Caleb was tired of his own company and looked forward to another evening drinking with that cagey Russian rapscallion Baranov.

The prospect put him in a good humor. There was a half smile on his face as he gazed off the starboard bow, waiting for the initial glimpse of the Russian colors waving from the fort's flagpole. The sun was warm on his back, and the wind steady.

'Cap'n, we're bein' hailed from shore.' The first mate, Hicks, handed him the spyglass. 'Three degrees off the starboard bow, there by the mouth of that little river. It looks like a white man.'

Caleb lifted the spyglass and located the figure waving at his ship. The man's clothes were in rags, but he appeared to be white, not an Indian dressed in white man's clothes. Probably a deserter from some ship, Caleb guessed, and lowered the glass.

'Lie to and lower a boat, but make certain the men go well armed. It might be a trap.'

'Aye, sir.' Hicks began barking orders to the crew.

The yawl was sent out and returned a short while later with the man aboard. As it came alongside the brig, a seaman shouted up, 'It's one a' them Rooskies.'

The man was somewhere in his late thirties, early forties, Caleb judged, tall and more leanly built than most of the Russians he'd seen. His hair was dark, but his eyes were blue. His shirt and trousers were nearly in shreds, and his flesh bore scratches, both old and new, that indicated he'd been living in the woods for several days. The ship's cook, Old Swede, brought him a mug of coffee and a piece of hardtack. The man tore hungrily into the biscuit, making it clear he'd been a while without food.

'He was jabbering something about a woman,' one of the crew ventured.

'Woman,' the Russian repeated and gazed earnestly at Caleb. 'Woman, yes.' He pointed to the shore, then made a cradle of his arms and rocked them to indicate a baby.

'It seems we have a woman and a baby hiding out there somewhere, Hicks,' Caleb said. 'Send the boat out again and see if the men can't find them.' Then he turned back to the Russian. 'Are you from Redoubt St. Michael?' The Russian frowned his lack of understanding. 'What the hell do they call it?' Caleb muttered to himself. 'Mikhailovsk?'

'Kolosh,' the man said grimly, then through a series of signs and pantomimes gave Caleb to understand the fort had been attacked by the Tlingits several days ago. The man had been hiding in the woods ever since. He wasn't sure if anyone else had survived.

The men in the yawl located an Aleut woman and small child hiding in the rocks along the shore and brought them back to the ship. The woman was frightened and half starved. Caleb sent all three to the cookhouse for a meal and ordered Hicks to proceed on their course to the Russian fort.

All that remained at the site was a blackened rubble. Caleb had been given to understand by the survivor that Baranov had left more than a month before to return to his headquarters at Kodiak. A force of roughly thirty Russians had remained at the fort. With them had been twenty of their Aleut squaws. Caleb ordered the *Sea Gypsy* anchored offshore.

'Sail ho!' shouted one of the *Gypsy*'s crew, high in the rigging.

A twenty-gun vessel flying British colors hove into view. Caleb read the name painted on the ship's bow, the *Unicorn*, and recognized her as a veteran Nor'wester, commanded by the notorious Captain Henry Barber, who had a reputation of being one of the most brutal and dishonest traders on the whole Northwest coast. Many claimed it was his indiscriminate acts, occasionally robbing and sometimes killing the Tlingits who came to his ship to trade, that were responsible for the hostile attitude of the Tlingits.

From his quarterdeck, Caleb could hear the British captain's profanity as he raged at the sight of the burned-out fort, roundly cursing the "murdering bastards" who had committed the deed.

That afternoon, Caleb gathered a heavily armed landing party and went ashore. The survivor, who had identified himself as Zachar Tarakanov, accompanied him, his tattered clothes replaced by hip-hugging trousers and a voluminous checked shirt from the ship's store.

A grisly scene awaited them. Along the beach lay the bloated bodies of infants washed ashore by the tide. Beyond, Russian heads, impaled on sticks, sat drying in the sun, dark beards matted with dried blood, mouths gaping, white teeth grinning, eyes staring. Big black scavenging ravens hopped about the naked decapitated bodies that lay rotting on the ground. Efforts to chase the birds away from the decomposing corpses met with little success. The ravens flapped their wide wings in irritation, uttering their harsh calls, then hopped a few yards away to another body. The stench was sickening.

The heavily palisaded fort was nothing but charred ash. All that remained was the half-melted barrel of a cannon. Knowing the greed of the Tlingits, Caleb suspected they had thoroughly looted the storehouses before the flames had devoured the buildings. He ordered the crew to bury the bodies where they lay.

Zachar stared at the ravens, so shiny and black in the sunlight. The raven was a deity of the Kolosh, regarded as the Creator. A hundred times during the eight days he'd spent hiding from the

Kolosh, he'd raged at the timing of the attack. Everyone had been off guard, distracted by the prospect of a praznik.

But he had told Raven. Zachar turned away from the carnage, unable to look at his dead comrades. He had betrayed them, as she had betrayed him. Anger vibrated through him, anger and hurt. He walked back to the beach and sat in the boat with his back to the massacre site, his hands clenched into fists.

A third ship arrived at the scene, the *Alert* out of Boston, commanded by Captain John Ebbets. When he learned of the disaster, he called for a meeting with Captain Barber of the *Unicorn* and Caleb from the *Sea Gypsy*.

That evening the three captains sat around Ebbets' table in his quarters on the *Alert* and discussed the situation. As Caleb listened to the vengeful rhetoric being espoused by his English and American counterparts, he wished heartily for a drink. Unfortunately, Ebbets didn't imbibe the devil's spirits. A particularly acidic brew of black coffee was the only refreshment provided. Caleb was no more interested in it than he was in the direction this conversation was taking.

'I say we must stand together in this,' Ebbets declared, and waved a hand at Caleb. 'Now, according to the Russian you picked up, thirty men were stationed at the fort. Yet your men buried only twenty-three bodies. We know your man survived, but that leaves six men unaccounted for, plus the women.'

'Who were Aleuts and half-breeds,' Caleb said of the latter.

'Nevertheless,' Ebbets continued, 'it is entirely possible captives were taken. We cannot allow these savages to believe that we will permit such atrocities. I propose that we take joint action and demand they surrender all survivors to us.'

'And if they refuse, I would delight in blowing those devils straight to bloody hell,' the English captain asserted.

'When the Tlingits come to trade with us, I suggest we take several of them as hostages, preferably the chief or any other important member of the tribe and refuse to release them until the survivors are delivered to us.'

'If they refuse, all we'd have to do is hang a couple of the bastards from the yardarm. We should do it regardless,' Barber stated, warming to the thought.

'You have said very little on this matter, Captain Stone,' Ebbets observed. 'What are your thoughts?'

Caleb lowered the hand he'd pressed thoughtfully against his mouth. 'I think that it's none of our business.'

'You can't seriously mean that.' Ebbets frowned.

'Of all the bloody damned –' Barber spluttered.

'The way I see it, we buried Russians – not English or Americans. That makes it their affair, not mine,' Caleb stated. 'Unlike you, I don't consider myself to be my brother's keeper.'

'If punitive action is not taken immediately, those bloodthirsty aborigines will turn on us next.' Captain Barber pounded his fist on the table. 'I trade in these waters –'

'That is exactly my point,' Caleb interrupted. 'I do business with these Sitka Indians, and I don't intend to jeopardize my trade with them over this. We have no idea what provoked this attack. For all I know, the Russians may have gotten what they deserved.'

'Then, you will not stand with us.' The stern-faced Bostonian captain regarded Caleb coldly.

'No.' Caleb pushed his chair back from the table and stood up. 'Do what you will, but count me out of it. The *Sea Gypsy* sails in the morning.'

'What about the survivors you have on board? What are your plans for them?' Ebbets goaded. 'Perhaps you intend to turn them over to the heathens so they may finish what they started?'

Aware that the merchant captain was attempting to anger him into agreeing with their plans, Caleb ignored the insulting questions and pulled the brim of his cap lower on his forehead. 'With your permission, gentlemen, I shall return to my ship.'

'I am bound for Kodiak when I leave here, Captain Stone,' Barber stated. 'I shall be glad to return your survivors to the Russian settlement there.'

Caleb paused briefly. They were excess cargo to him. 'I'll have them transferred to the *Unicorn*. By your leave, gentlemen.' He bowed slightly from the waist in mock politeness, then left the ship to return to his own.

Once on board the *Sea Gypsy*, Caleb ordered the transfer of his passengers, then retired to his cabin for a long-awaited drink. Unbuttoning his jacket with one hand, he poured himself a glass of rum with the other, then sat back in a chair. After the first swallow of rum smoothly burned his throat, he idly watched the sway of the brass lamp overhead. He was convinced the retaliatory action planned by his colleagues was wrong, and more likely to inflame the Tlingits' passions against them than teach the savages a lesson. He saw no point in becoming involved in something that didn't directly concern him. The destruction of the fort eliminated the Russians from the area. As far as he was concerned, that meant he would have to compete with one less rival.

A knock sounded on his door. 'Come in.' Caleb sat up and reached for the rum bottle to refill his glass. The door opened and the first mate stepped over the raised threshold, then paused inside, holding the door open. 'What is it, Hicks?' he demanded impatiently.

'It's the Russian Tarakanov, sir.' With a backward motion of his head, Hicks indicated that the man waited outside the door. 'He wants to see you.'

But the Russian didn't wait for permission to enter, and instead stepped through the opening into the cabin. Caleb sharply lifted an eyebrow at the intrusion, then asked his mate, 'Did you explain to him the English ship was going to take him and the Aleut woman to Kodiak?'

'Aye, sir.' Hicks nodded, his bushy muttonchops brushing the collar of his jacket.

The Russian bowed at Caleb, claiming his attention, then began speaking is his own language, accompanying his words with gestures. He indicated the navy wool jacket and seaman's trousers he wore, then rubbed his stomach, conveying his gratitude for the clothes and food that Caleb had provided for him, and thrust out his hand.

Caleb stared at it for an instant, then set down the rum bottle and stood up to shake hands with the Russian. He was conscious of the strong grip of the man's fingers as he studied the Russian's face, taking note of his perceptive blue eyes and angular features. Except for the scratches on his high cheekbones, there was little evidence of his ordeal.

'Good-bye, *Kapitan*.' Zachar Tarakanov offered the last in heavily accented English.

'Good-bye. And God's speed to you,' Caleb replied and watched him leave. As Hicks closed the door behind him, Caleb picked up the bottle again and poured more rum in his glass. He'd picked up the Russian and put him on a ship for home. That was the end of his duty, Christian or otherwise.

22

The salmon were running, answering the ancient breeding call that summoned them from the ocean depths to the bays, rivers, and creeks of the islands and coasts of the Northwest. Relentlessly they came, a silver horde churning the placid waters of the bay where the *Sea Gypsy* lay at anchor. In some places, their large fins cleaved the surface, while in others, they ran deep, a lightning flash of white underbelly and argent sides, their color not yet turned the distinctive pink shade of spawning.

Bald eagles, scores of them, circled overhead and sat in tree perches along the spawning streams, while massive hump-shouldered brown bears waded the rivers and creeks, batting thirty- and forty-pound fish onto the banks with their huge paws or snatching them from the water with their fanged teeth. From their summer camp at the mouth of a salmon river, the Tlingits set their salmon traps to catch their winter's supply of food.

Caleb watched two clear canoes set out from shore toward his ship, slicing through the coursing multitudes of salmon. All was in readiness on deck to begin trading: the hide screens were up, the men armed, the cannon loaded and in position.

Again Caleb followed the routine procedure as the canoes pulled alongside his vessel: only one native was allowed on board; the rules were explained; and the number limited to three at a time. With the acceptance of his conditions, the first party was allowed to board.

The third Indian to climb over the taffrail was a young squaw. As she swung her legs over the rail, his eye was caught by the bright copper bands around her ankles. They clinked together, faintly melodic, when she walked. As his eyes traveled upward, Caleb noticed the rounded curves of her high-breasted figure. Her smooth complexion was no darker than an Italian's or a Spaniard's; her hair was long and straight, black and shiny as polished onyx. Silver rings pierced her ears, but no labret mutilated her lips. They were soft and full.

Boldly she returned his stare. Caleb doubted that she was much more than sixteen. His interest was aroused by the savage beauty of her. It had been a long time since that Hawaiian wahine had entertained him. Or maybe it was simply the urges of a lonely man that swung his thoughts, like the needle of a compass, to a woman. And as captain, he'd known many lonely hours – eating alone, drinking alone, walking the quarterdeck alone, sleeping alone.

'How much Boston man pay for furs?' The chief's demand sharply interrupted Caleb's thoughts, bringing him back to the business at hand.

He swung around to examine the bundle of pelts the Indian offered for inspection. Almost immediately, he sensed something different about them, but it took him a while to detect what it was. These skins had been dressed by an Aleut. They weren't the work of a Tlingit. The pelts were obviously part of the booty from the Russian fort.

He offered a price and the dickering began. All the while he argued with the mustached chief, Caleb was conscious of the Indian girl watching him. The chief wanted a bolt of bright calico that the girl had briefly admired. Caleb found himself wondering if she was the chief's daughter or his squaw.

'Two lengths of the cloth for one skin, no more,' Caleb stated flatly.

The chief started to gather up his pelts, but the girl touched his arm, said something to him in their tongue, then faced Caleb. 'Does Boston man have woman?' It was almost a challenge.

'No.' Although he was aware some merchant captains brought their wives and families along on their voyages, the question faintly surprised him.

'How long Boston man not have woman?' she asked.

'A long time,' he admitted, narrowing his gaze.

'Boston man like have Raven?'

The name fit her, from the shining blackness of her hair to the cunning sharpness of her eyes. Caleb drew his head back and studied her thoughtfully, interested in her proposition despite his better judgment.

'How much?'

'The bundle of cloth.' She indicated the calico. Caleb started to shake his head in refusal, but she continued: 'For Raven and furs.'

He glanced at the two braves with her, but he detected no hint of objection in either of their expressions. 'Agreed,' he said.

'Raven come back night.' She moved toward the bolt of calico, but Caleb moved more quickly.

'No.' He placed his hand on the upright bolt. 'The cloth stays here until Raven comes.' Caleb knew very well that if this calico left the ship, he'd never see her again.

'Boston man have furs and cloth. Maybe he leave and not wait for Raven,' she said.

Not for a minute did he underestimate her cleverness. A pride that was closer to arrogance stamped her features. She couldn't be called beautiful despite the strong sensuality of those lips, Caleb realized. Beauty implied softness, and there was none in this woman. She was striking, yes, but there was also a quality about her that challenged a man, brought out his instinct to dominate and be the master rather than the slave she wanted to make of him.

'You bring the furs when you come back,' Caleb said.

After the trading party had left the ship, Caleb stood on the quarterdeck. Suddenly he was amused by all the things he'd imagined about her, the riddle he'd tried to make of her. He'd been alone too long.

Caleb looked at the wild grandeur of this land. Mountains rose abruptly from the shore, in places forming sheer cliffs. Dense rain forests that had never known the ravages of fire blanketed the slopes in a woolly mantle of deep emerald green. Above the treeline, the mountains climbed to jagged ridges and sharp peaks, some still bearing the drifts of winter's snow. The sea battered this whole long chain of breaker islands, its surf crashing over the rocky shores and pounding at the magnificent cliffs.

Yes, Caleb thought, this land could do things to a man, including filling his head with crazy fancies – like making an enigmatic Indian princess out of a comely squaw. He turned from the view, wryly shaking his head.

'Double the anchor watch tonight,' he told Hicks, then headed below. He didn't know whether or not she'd come, but he'd given permission for a canoe to approach at night and he wanted his ship alert for trouble.

*

Shortly after eight bells sounded, a shout came down the fore scuttle and the aft hatchway. 'All hands ahoy!' In his cabin, Caleb reached for his pistol and thrust it inside the waistband of his trousers. As he moved toward the door, there was a quick knock on it. Caleb opened it.

The second mate stood outside. 'Two canoes comin', sir.'

Caleb motioned him topside and followed him up the narrow passageway to the steps. On deck, the crew were scrambling to their defense positions. Caleb mounted the quarterdeck and looked across the moonlit waters toward the Tlingit encampment. A pair of canoes glided silently toward the ship, dark silhouettes with white flashing from the painted designs along their high prows. All the lights on deck were out, save the one in the binnacle.

As the canoes swung parallel to the starboard side of the ship, Caleb murmured, 'Watch bright on the la'board, lads.'

A blanket-draped figure stood up in one of the canoes. 'Boston man.' It was a low-pitched call, but sound travels easily over water.

'Aye,' Caleb responded in normal voice.

'Raven comes.'

He had doubted she would, suspecting the offer had merely been an attempt to get the calico from him. 'Come aboard.'

The tension in the air was palpable as one canoe came alongside the vessel. But it was a tension of a different sort that claimed the crew when the canoe pulled away and Raven stood on deck wrapped in a blue and white blanket.

Caleb knew what his men were thinking and feeling. He'd lived below deck and knew how long these three-year voyages could seem, and the cravings that could gnaw at men deprived of female company for long stretches of time, with only the white-cheeked bottom of the bucko in the next bunk to satisfy them. Rare was the sailor who hadn't submitted to such desires – on one end or the other – including himself.

Caleb wasted no time taking the Indian girl below to his cabin. As he shut the door, he watched her look around his quarters. Her eyes hadn't been still since she had come on board; they darted everywhere, taking in everything. He removed the pistol from the waistband of his trousers and laid it in its case on the sideboard. She turned at the sound and watched him snap the lid closed.

He stood, making no move toward her, while she regarded him confidently, boldly. The bolt of calico was propped in a corner of the cabin. Her glance strayed to it, then back to him. With a casual lift of her arms, she removed the blanket from her shoulders. Beneath it she wore a creamy-white deerskin garment, and her black hair hung all the way to her breasts.

'Boston man like Raven?'

'My name is Caleb.' Slowly he moved toward her.

'Caleb,' she repeated, not lifting her chin when he stopped in front of her, yet holding his gaze with a look that encompassed all the female wiles he'd ever encountered from a white woman.

She made no resistance as he gathered her into his arms. Automatically she tilted her head up in the age-old gesture that invited his kiss. Caleb took it, covering her mouth and feeling the movement of her tongue against his. She pressed her body against him.

Caleb lifted his head, conscious of the slugging beat of the vein in his throat, and gazed at her upturned face. Her lips lay together in a smugly confident line as she watched him through half-closed eyes. She showed him no artifice of innocence or reticence, nor any of the coyness he frequently encountered from Boston prostitutes.

Stepping back, he pulled off the blanket, loosely hooked at her elbows, and guided her to his bunk. He shrugged out of his jacket and began unbuttoning his shirt. At no urging from him, she pulled the deerskin garment over her head. Caleb watched her body gradually revealed – the long, muscled legs and thighs, the curly, jet-black snatch, the firmly rounded hips, and the full breasts. Naked, she crawled onto the blanket-covered bunk, stretching out like a sleepy cat to wait for him.

As Caleb removed the rest of his clothes, her attention unabashedly focused on his erection. Her bold interest aroused him more. He lay down on the bunk beside her and let his hand play over her body, enjoying the smooth warmth of her skin and the firm mounds of her breasts. She arched into the caress of his hand, responding to its touch. He kissed her lips, then her breasts, savoring the hard nipples while she skillfully fondled him, the stroke of her hand eliciting a groan from her throat. Fully aroused, he shifted position and pushed a knee between her legs to spread them so he could mount her.

Her upraised knee prevented him. 'No,' she said firmly. 'Not white man's way. Indian.'

Slipping her legs free of him, she rolled onto her stomach and drew her knees up under her, presenting him with her elevated bottom. For an instant he could only stare at her hanging breasts and rounded cheeks. Then a hot lust swept over him and he positioned himself behind her, holding her hipbones and pushing his engorged cock into her. He rocked with a primitive rhythm, driving in and out, the tempo building into a final paroxysm of shuddering release that shot his seed into her.

Spent, he sank onto the cot. He felt her shifting movement and turned his head to look at her. A sheen of perspiration coated her upper lip. Her half-closed eyes studied him with a satisfied look that said she knew she had drained him.

'Caleb happy.' It was a purring sound.

Again he felt inexplicably challenged by her. Maybe it was the energy he sensed she still had. 'No.' He snarled his fingers in the black curtain of her hair and pulled her to him, kissing her and roughly pinching her erect nipples. It didn't take long for him to become hard again. This time he rolled her onto her back and levered himself onto her. 'Now white man's way,' he said and invaded her moist opening again.

But he moved slowly, drawing almost completely out before plunging back in, resisting the arching exhortations of her hips. He watched her excitement grow, the pressure build until she strained under it. Her fingers clawed him, raking his shoulders and back. Only then did he allow her to pull him down and grind his hips against hers as she wanted. Seconds after she stiffened under him, straining in little jerks, he came into her.

This time when he moved off of her, he had the satisfaction of seeing that she breathed as hard as he did. Her eyes were closed. He felt as though he'd won something, but he didn't know what the hell it was. He chuckled at the fanciful thought and closed his eyes, feeling fully relaxed for the first time in months.

Something awakened him, some faint sound that wasn't the normal creaking and groaning of the ship. He lay still, listening for it to come again. Then he heard the soft, melodic clinking of metal – the copper ankle bracelets Raven wore. She wasn't beside him on the bunk. Caleb could sense it without looking.

She moved quietly somewhere in the cabin, almost silently, only the soft jingle of the bracelets giving her away. He was fully awake now, suspicion sharpening his senses. He doubted that she was concerned about waking him. Her stealth was motivated by something else.

A long silence followed. Then a board creaked in the passageway, and Caleb realized that she'd left the cabin. Moving swiftly, he swung out of the bunk and pulled on his trousers. All the while he looked about the shadowed room. The blanket was gone; so was the bolt of cloth. The lid to his pistol case stood open. He felt inside; the gun was gone, too. He didn't take the time to discover what else she had stolen, but stepped out of the cabin as silently as she had, only he avoided the creaking board.

The low hooting call of an owl sounded overhead. Or was it an owl? Cautiously Caleb emerged from the hatchway. A thick gray mist enveloped the ship, drifting through the rigging and obscuring the foredeck. He couldn't see any of the deckhands who were supposed to be standing watch. If they'd fallen asleep, he swore he'd see them spread-eagled on the shrouds.

At the moment, he was more concerned with locating Raven. He knew she didn't intend to try to swim ashore, not with that bolt of cloth and his pistol to weigh her down. Again he heard the half-muffled hoot of an owl – or was it a *raven?* He peered onto the quarterdeck and noticed a lumpy shape crouched low beside the taffrail. The raucous cry of some other nightbird broke the eerie stillness of the mist.

Caleb crept onto the quarterdeck, certain it was the Indian girl by the rail, but he angled away from her, heading toward the blunderbuss. The mist condensed on the rigging and fell in scattered droplets. At first, Caleb didn't distinguish its dripping and the lap of water against the brig's hull from the faint watery sound of dipping oar blades. The sound came from several directions. He swiveled the blunderbuss to point its flared muzzle at the closest sound and fired as he shouted. 'All hands on deck!'

Swinging around, he saw Raven rise up from her hiding place. Wild cries came from the water, accompanied by the noisy scrambling of the crew. Caleb started for the second blunderbuss that was swivel-mounted on the taffrail. Halfway there he noticed Raven's arms extended in front of her, pointing at him, with his pistol in her hands. He grabbled up a boarding pike and swung it at her outstretched arms. It struck her forearms just as the gun went off. The bullet sang past his ear.

Caleb charged her and wrenched the pistol from her hands. From somewhere on the port side, a cannon boomed, followed closely by the splashing of an overturned canoe. Raven shouted something in her native tongue. Caleb grabbed her and hooked an arm around her neck to choke off any more of her warnings. She clawed at his bare arm, kicking like a wildcat.

Soon there was no more sound except for the dripping mist and lapping waters. Raven stopped fighting him, but her body remained tense, ready to resume the struggle if he gave her the chance. Hicks approached, warily peering into the swirling mists.

'What do you think, Cap'n?'

'They won't try again, not right away,' Caleb guessed. 'Have the crew stand to just in case. And' – he glanced at his black-haired prisoner – 'send someone to my cabin with a set of chains and manacles.'

'Aye, sir.'

Taking his arm away from her throat, Caleb caught one of her wrists and twisted it high behind her back, then marched her to his cabin. Once inside, he shoved her into the room and shut the door. She fell against the table and quickly turned to face him, pressing herself back against the table like a cornered animal. She glared at him, hatred shining from her black eyes.

Caleb raised the pistol she'd stolen from him, its muzzle pointing up. 'I think you would have enjoyed blowing my head off with this, wouldn't you?' He returned it to its case.

In that brief second she launched herself at him. Out of the corner of his eye, Caleb caught the flash of a metal blade and dodged its downward slice, belatedly remembering there'd been a knife on the table. Its sharp tip cut across the fleshy part of his arm, searing his skin. Cursing, he grabbed her wrist and twisted it, forcing her to drop the weapon.

As it clattered to the floor, he started to relax. Immediately her hands were at his face, scratching at his eyes, and she raked her fingers across his cheeks, drawing blood. The instant he seized them and pulled them down, she started biting at his hands.

'You damned little hellion!' Blood was running from the scratches on his face and the cut on his arm. He grabbed a handful of her long black hair and tugged at the roots, pulling her back and forcing her to her knees. A knock rattled the cabin door. 'Come in,' Caleb snapped. The clank of chains accompanied the sound of the door opening.

The second mate stared at him for a dumbstruck moment. 'You're bleedin', Cap'n.'

'Aye.' Caleb glared at him. 'Put this she-cat in those irons. And watch her claws.' After a brief struggle, she was manacled and chained to a support. Caleb pressed a blue neckerchief on the knife cut. 'Where the hell is Dawson?'

'I'll fetched him for you, Cap'n.' The second mate hurried from the cabin.

Left alone, Caleb walked over to the rum bottle and poured himself a drink. As he drank it down, he heard the clink of the chains and looked at the Indian girl curled beside the post. His throat burned from the alcohol, the sensation feeding his anger instead of soothing it. The anger was partly directed at her and partly at himself for nearly being tricked by her.

Her long black hair fanned over her shoulders and chest, completely covering the upper half of her white buckskin garment. Caleb kicked a chair away from the table and sat down facing her.

'I was wrong about you, Raven.' When he mentioned her name, her head came up and her expression held insolence and hatred. 'You're no hellcat. You're more deadly than that. No, you're more like a black widow spider who kills the male after they've mated.'

'Boston man wrong. People come for Raven. Take to village,' she stated.

'Is that why you tried to shoot me with my own gun?'

'Boston man shoot at people. Raven shoot at Boston man to stop.'

'That's a good tale,' Caleb conceded dryly. 'Why don't I believe you?'

His steward, Dawson, hurried into the cabin laden with an assortment of bandages and medicinal aids, and appeared disappointed by Caleb's minor wounds, but he quickly set about treating them.

As the rising sun penetrated the mists, a dozen canoes set out from shore loaded with glowering warriors. Watching their approach, Caleb ordered the Indian girl to be brought up from his cabin. He stood her on the forecastle deck where she could easily be seen. The Tlingits halted their canoes when they saw her.

One stood up, and Caleb recognised him from yesterday's trading session. 'We come for Raven.'

'Raven stays.' Caleb raised his voice so all would hear him.

'She is my hostage.' The murmur of anger among the warriors quickly became a clamor of protest. 'Last night' – Caleb shouted above it – 'you tried to attack my ship. I thought the Tlingits were my friends. I have always traded fairly with you. Yesterday I agreed to sell you a bolt of cloth for the price of twenty otter skins and the company of this woman for one night.' He signaled Hicks to hold up the calico. 'Here is the cloth. So you will know that I honor my bargain, one canoe may approach my ship.'

Hicks waited until it was alongside the *Sea Gypsy*, then tossed the bolt into the waiting arms of the Tlingits. When it was in their possession, the warriors paddled back to join the semicircle of canoes.

'As long as my ship is in your waters, I will keep this woman,' Caleb stated. 'I will treat her well. And when I leave, I will return her to you. If any of your people attack my ship again, I will shoot her.'

More mutterings came from the Indians, but soon they were turning their canoes around and paddling back to shore. Caleb waited until they had landed on the beach of their summer camp, then grasped Raven by the shoulder and pushed her to the aft rail of the forecastle deck to stand before his crew.

'Now, buckos, have a good look at her,' Caleb ordered, then waited for his crew to gather around on the lower deck.

Many times they had glimpsed her briefly, but now they were invited to look their fill. No doubt, Caleb thought, they saw in her what he had seen. They had been without a woman as long as he.

'When she's on deck, you are not to speak to her. If she speaks to you, you are not to answer – no matter what she promises. If she approaches the rail, you are to shoot her.' He saw their resistance to his orders. 'Do you hear me, lads?'

Reluctantly, they mumbled a disjointed chorus of 'Aye, sir.'

'If you value your lives, you won't trust her.' Caleb surveyed them grimly. 'She'd as soon see your heads drying on stakes like those Russians you saw as look at you. Don't ever forget it.' He paused to let his warning sink in, then issued an order to the first mate, Hicks. 'Lay aloft and loose the topsails.'

The setting sun turned the drifting clouds first golden, then crimson pink, and tinted the canvas sails of the *Sea Gypsy*. All hands were on deck during the twilight dog watch, a leisurely time with the day's work done. The crew sat on the windlass or sprawled about the forecastle, smoking and spinning yarns. Dawson was in the galley having a cup of coffee with Old Swede, the cook. Hicks wandered along the lee side of the quarterdeck, smoking his pipe, while the second mate leaned on the rail of the weathered gangway.

Caleb remained separate from them, standing on the weather side of the quarterdeck, the wind blowing the fragrant fir smell of the islands to him. In the brig's hold, he had a rich cargo of pelts, mainly otter skins. The only market for them was China. As he gazed at the savage wilderness that surrounded him, his mind's eye saw the terraced hongs and their great godowns of the Chinese port of Canton, built on the banks of the Pearl. The river itself was an exotic city of boats – sampans, flower boats, tea-deckers, and mandarin boats. With nearly two thousand otter skins to sell by the end of this voyage, he should have a handy sum to reinvest in silks, nankeens, tea, and crepes despite the duties, commissions, and graft he'd be obliged to pay. He might even enhance that sum by smuggling some of the furs to Macao Roads or Dirty Butter Bay.

Eight bells was struck, the sound rousing him from his thoughts. As soon as the anchor watch was set, Caleb went below to his cabin. His hand touched the door latch at the same instant that he heard Dawson curse from inside. 'Ya little she-bitch, give it to me or I'll lay this strop to you.'

Caleb stepped inside. His slim young steward held a leather shaving strop in his upraised hand. When Dawson saw him, he halted his threatening advance on Raven, who had pivoted to partially face both of them. She held her hands behind her back, hiding whatever object they held. She looked like a caged panther ready to spring.

No manacles or chains restricted her movement. After the first two days, Caleb had removed them and merely kept her confined to his quarters, permitting her on deck only during the early-morning hours – never in the evening when his crew had to face the emptiness of their berths.

'What's the problem, Dawson?'

'When I went to put away the cutlery, there was a piece missin', Cap'n. The thievin' little whore filched one of the knives.'

'Hand it over, Raven.' Caleb extended his hand to her, palm

upward. After a long hesitation, she brought her arms from behind her back. The light from the brass lamp flashed on the metal blade of a knife in her right hand. Without waiting to see if she intended to surrender it, Caleb seized her wrist and twisted it from her unresisting fingers, then passed the knife to Dawson.

Dawson was plainly disappointed by her lack of resistance. 'You should have her whipped for stealin', Cap'n,' he asserted.

Caleb was quite certain his steward would volunteer for the task. 'If I did that, I'd have to punish you as well, Dawson, for leaving the knife within her reach.'

Dawson reddened and quickly bowed his head in shame. 'Aye, sir,' he mumbled, then darted a loathing glance at the woman. 'Is there anything else you'll be wantin' this night, sir?' he inquired stiffly.

Caleb's attention shifted to the Tlingit girl. The memories of Canton were fresh in his mind, especially the slant-eyed Oriental women in their brilliant silks embroidered in silver and gold threads.

'Check the trade goods and find something for her to wear. I'm tired of seeing her in that shapeless piece of buckskin.'

'No matter what she's wearin', she'll still be a heathen savage,' Dawson sniped.

'That was an order, Dawson!'

The steward quailed slightly under his glowering look. 'Aye, sir. I was –'

'If you don't like the job any more, Dawson, I'll be happy to break you to a common seaman and put you in the fo'c'sle with the others,' Caleb threatened.

Tears trembled on the fringes of Dawson's long lashes as he answered stiffly, 'I like my job well enough, sir.'

'Then do as you're told.'

'Aye, sir.' This time Dawson was very careful not to look at Raven as he turned away and left the cabin.

Out of the corner of his eye, Caleb watched him leave while continuing to face Raven. When the door latch clicked shut, he let all his attention center on her, and her loosely closed left fist.

'What else did you take, Raven?'

Her lips thinned to a tight, angry line. A second later, she hurled two buttons at his face, ones that had come off his shirt that he'd left for Dawson to sew back on. He dodged one, but the other stung his cheek. She turned her back to him and rigidly folded her arms in front of her.

'Caleb has sharp eyes.' It was a condemnation rather than a compliment.

He chuckled and stepped up behind her, sliding his hands up her arms and under the wide sleeves onto her shoulders. 'If I didn't you would have buried a knife in my back long ago, Raven.' Her lack of response was a rejection of his caress and his smile lengthened at it. He applied pressure to turn her around, but she shrugged free of his hands with an angry twist of her shoulders.

'No. I don't want Caleb.'

A part of him recognized how much her English vocabulary had improved during the last ten days, but it didn't matter in the least to him. Her refusal mattered even less.

'That's what you always say,' he mocked, and pulled her into his arms, ignoring her stiffnes as he always did.

He kissed her roughly, forcing her lips apart. Without warning, she bit him, sinking her teeth into his lower lip. Cursing, he drew back and licked at the cut with his tongue, tasting the blood in his mouth – his own blood.

'You little bitch,' Caleb muttered as she looked back at him, unafraid. He smiled. Any contact with her involved an element of danger. 'I like it when you fight me. You do, too, don't you?'

The initial battle always seemed to arouse his passions more fully. He had no desire to break her wild spirit, merely to bend it to his will.

'I like to go outside.'

'I'm sure you would, but you'll have to wait until tomorrow morning.' He dabbed his kerchief against his smarting, swollen lip.

She glanced toward the door. 'Your slave comes.' Her announcement was followed by a rap on the door.

'Come in.'

Dawson entered the cabin carrying a colorfully striped banian. 'This is all I could find that I felt would be what the captain had in mind, sir,' he stated.

Caleb frowned at the robe, noticing the signs of wear in the threadbare sleeve cuffs. 'Where did you find this?' To his knowledge nothing of this sort was included in the trade goods or the slop chest.

255

'It's mine, sir. Or more correctly, my father's. I have no use for it. When he ordered me out of the house, I took it with me because I knew it was his favorite article of clothing. It's fitting that a savage should wear it,' he declared.

'Very well.' Caleb took the long robe and turned to Raven. 'I want you to wear this. Take off that buckskin.'

'It is mine?' Her dark eyes glittered as she stroked the velvet fabric.

'Yes.'

Immediately she grabbed the skirt of her garment and began dragging it up to pull it over head. Distaste stiffened Dawson's expression as he turned from the sight of her naked body. 'If there is nothing else, sir?'

Caleb nodded a dismissal as he held out the banian so Raven could slip her arms into the sleeves of the kimono-styled garment. Buttons closed the front, fitting the material to her waist and letting the rest flare into a long skirt that brushed the floor. She reveled in the texture of the velvet, feeling it all over with her hands. With the long river of her black hair flowing down her back, she almost looked like a native of India, where the robe style had long ago originated. She looked infinitely more civilized, but Caleb wasn't sure he liked her that way.

'Are you pleased?' He hardly needed to ask. Her hands fondled the gown greedily.

'No man has given me a present like this before. Not even Zachar.' Oblivious of him, she turned to see her reflection in the small mirror fastened to the bulkhead.

'Zachar Tarakanov.'

Her eyes met the reflection of his in the mirror. For an instant she was motionless, betraying the accuracy of his guess. Then she swung around to face him, her expression full of sensual promise.

'I will show Caleb how happy his gift has made me.'

As she moved toward him, he caught hold of her arms and held her away from him. 'Do you know he's alive? He wasn't killed with the other Russians at the fort.'

'I knew this.'

Her indifference was genuine, he realized, and he suspected her reaction would have been no different if Zachar had been killed in the massacre. As visions of those rotting heads flashed through his mind, he hated her violently. If his own head was among them, she wouldn't care either, he thought to himself, then threw back his head and laughed. If the positions were reversed, he doubted that he'd feel any remorse himself. He swept her into his arms and carried her to the bunk.

At the end of another week, Caleb deemed it time to move farther south along the coast. When he'd stopped at the last two villages, both had previously traded with another Boston ship in the area and the few furs they'd left weren't worth the time spent. He put Raven ashore at a village of her clan, as he had promised.

The brightly striped banian she wore stood out vividly against the shoreline. From the quarterdeck, Caleb watched as the natives mobbed her, the robe creating a considerable sensation. She was soon swallowed by the crowd and he lost sight of her. He felt no regrets. South American, Hawaiian, Oriental, African, now Indian, he'd bedded them all and left them all. It wasn't likely he'd look back on this one either – or see her again – or recognize her if he did.

The longboat was headed back to the brig. As Caleb turned from the taffrail, he noticed Dawson standing on the waist deck watching him. Women came and went in his life, but Dawson was always there, it seemed. Caleb paused a moment, wondering on that realization. But it would be another two years before he saw Long Wharf again. Two years of few comforts and little recreation. And Dawson knew his tastes . . . in everything.

Once the longboat was back in its place between the fore and mainmasts, Caleb gave the order to loose the topsails. He watched the men as they scampered up the rigging like so many monkeys. As soon as the sails were freed, one hand remained on each top to overhaul the rigging and light the sails out while the rest of the crew came down to man the sheets, singing out cheerily as they hauled them in.

Within minutes the *Sea Gypsy* was under way, her masts raking, her bowsprit running up. It was down the Northwest coast a few more months, then across the Pacific to Canton, through the dreaded Sunda Strait, and around the Cape of Good Hope across the Atlantic to Boston and home port.

23 *Sitka*
September 1804

After spending the last two years with his family on Kodiak, Zachar stepped once again onto the beach where the settlement of the Redoubt St. Michael had stood, but he could see no trace of its remains anywhere. There weren't even markers to identify the graves of the dead, and now hundreds of newly erected little tents were scattered across the clearing. More than three hundred bidarkas lined the beach. The air no longer smelled of death and charred timbers, but of wood smoke and cooking food. Guards were posted all along the beach and hugged nearly every stump that faced the black forest where he had once taken refuge.

A boat lightered more men ashore from the vessels moored in the harbor that had escorted the bidarka fleet to this site. The *Yermack*, the *Alexandre*, the *Rotislav*, and the *Ekatrina*, on which Mikhail had sailed, were all there, lanterns shining from their topgallant mastheads to light the way for stragglers of the bidarka fleet. But all the ships were dominated by the massive 450-ton frigate *Neva* from the Imperial Russian Navy.

Oblivious to the crackling flames, the hammering of tent stakes, and undulating voices, both Russian and Aleut, Zachar thought of Raven and the last time he'd seen her – here on this beach. He wondered if he would ever know whether she had deliberately betrayed him or innocently told her clan of their plans for a feast day. As long as the doubts remained, he couldn't bring himself to hate her. The guilt for the deaths of his comrades was his; he could not blame her for them.

The crunching of footsteps on the gravel made no impression on him until a hand warmly clasped his shoulder. Startled, he turned. 'Zachar.' He recognized the familiar voice and shadowed face of his brother, Mikhail. 'I didn't think it would be so easy to find you.'

During the voyage from Kodiak, they'd had no contact with

each other. The last time Zachar had seen him, they'd been at the cabin taking leave of their mother and the lovely stranger who was his fourteen-year-old daughter, Larissa. Then, as now, he'd been conscious of the difference in their stations – Mikhail the navigator, with his seaman's clothes and smoothly shaven face, and he the hunter, with his kamleika-covered parka and coarse beard.

'How was your journey?' Zachar asked.

'Without incident.' Mikhail looked around him. 'This land is just as you described it to me. Even without the charts to guide me, I think I would have found this bay.' He surveyed the crowded camp filled with men who were tending fires, pitching tents, standing guard, hanging wet clothes out to dry. 'It may have taken him two years, but Baranov has assembled quite an army.'

'Yes.' The retaking of Sitka had become an obsession of their leader, the newly appointed governor of Russian America. Zachar didn't share his thirst for vengeance, partly because of his own sense of guilt. The back-glow of a campfire lit the thin, wizened figure Zachar recognized as Baranov. With him was a man wearing the uniform and gold braid of an officer. 'Who is that with Baranov?'

'Captain Lisianski from the *Neva*. The frigate was here when we arrived.' Reports had reached Kodiak that two English-built naval ships had sailed from St. Petersburg the previous year carrying the Russians eagles on a round-the-world ambassadorial mission to Japan. The mission was headed by His High Excellency, Imperial Chamberlain Nikolai Rezanov, who had married Shelekhov's youngest daughter, written the company's charter, and obtained from the Tsar a trade monopoly for the Russian American Company. No one, not even Baranov, believed the Navy ships would stop at their colony, and they certainly didn't expect any assistance from them.

'I was told that when the high chamberlain learned about the massacre here at Mikhailovsk from the Hawaiian King, he ordered the *Neva* to come to Baranov's aid while he continued to Japan.' The large triple-masted warship in the harbor dwarfed the crudely made vessels moored near it that had been built at the shipyards of the colony's Yakutat settlement at the Alaskan mainland. 'The frigate makes our sloops look like fishing smacks.'

'Yes.' But Zachar could summon little interest in the frigate.

Tommorrow the combined forces would confront the Kolosh, and he had ambivalent feelings about that. He didn't notice his brother's silence or the way Mikhail studied him.

'I hadn't realized how painful it would be for you to come back to this place,' Mikhail observed. 'So many of your friends were murdered here. It's a miracle you were spared.'

'Yes.' The Russian priest Father Herman, who ran the school on Kodiak that his daughter, Larissa, attended, claimed it was God's will that he had survived. But Zachar had often wondered. Had it been God's hand that protected him – or Raven's? Had it been mere chance that the Kolosh had attacked the fort when he was away from it, or had they waited, at Raven's insistence, until he left? Did he owe his life to her – or to God? But he couldn't tell his brother of any of the questions that plagued him without admitting his betrayal.

'I heard Baranov plans to assault the main village tomorrow, the one along the bluff.'

'He will parley for peace with them first,' Mikhail stated.

'They'll never accept his terms. He wants all the Kolosh to leave Sitka Island. They won't leave.' Zachar's sympathies were not with the Kolosh, yet concern for Raven always clouded his thinking.

Somewhere in the large camp, a bow touched the strings of a guzla and scattered voices began to sing the song Baranov had composed that summer, called 'The Spirit of Russian Hunters.' Other voices joined in and Zachar paused to listen to the growing chorus.

> 'The will of our hunters, the spirit of trade,
> On these far shores a new Muscovy made,
> In bleakness and hardship finding new wealth
> For Fatherland and Tsardom.
>
> Sukharev's towers old Moscow adorn,
> The bells ring at evening, the guns boom at morn;
> But far off's this glory of Ivan the Great –
> We have naught but our own bravery.
>
> Our Father Almighty, we pray for Thine aid
> That Muscovite arms may here be obeyed,
> That we may dwell in amity and peace
> Forever in this region.'

As the last note faded, a hush settled over the camp. Exchanging a few quiet words, Mikhail and Zachar parted company. Mikhail was worried. Lately, it seemed his brother preferred to be alone. He'd been like that ever since the British captain had arrived at Kodiak with the survivors of the massacre and forced Baranov to pay a ransom for their return. Zachar had given a full accounting of all that had happened at Sitka, but rarely ever spoke of it again.

In the beginning, Mikhail had been willing to blame his older brother's moodiness on the dreadful experience. Now he was less sure that was the reason. His brother seemed reluctant to fight. Mikhail was beginning to wonder whether his older brother was a coward.

A long row of native log dwellings lined the shore beyond the tideline. Low openings were cut in their gabled ends, which faced the water. Pillars carved with heraldic symbols that identified the clan house flanked the doorways. Planks hewn from spruce framed the walls, and split logs formed the sloping roofs of the buildings, which averaged thirty feet in width and forty in length. Gravehouses, miniatures of the dwellings, sat atop poles and contained the ashes of the dead.

Raven stood on the planked platform outside the doorway to her clan house, not far from the steps leading to the ground. Word of Nanuk's return had spread quickly through her village. All day she and her people had watched the strange canoes of the Aleuts tow the tall ship with the big canons close to the shores of their village. Now her attention was centered on the canoe carrying the village chief, her brother, and her husband, Runs Like a Wolf. The chief had gone to the ship to demand that Nanuk explain his action.

As the canoe pulled away from the ship to return to the village, a cannon boomed, belching a puff of smoke. Raven flinched at the loud sound and saw the splash of water well beyond the canoe's bow. Several babies in the village started crying, although not a whimper of alarm came from the toddler at her feet as he tried to climb up her leg. Raven quickly reached down and picked up her young son, ready to run for safety, but the ship's cannon wasn't fired again.

Satisfied there was no imminent danger, Raven relaxed slightly and looked at her year-and-a-half-old son. She smiled proudly at the absence of any fear in Gray Wolf's expression as he gazed with wide-eyed curiosity in the direction from which the loud noise had come. His hair was black and straight, its texture soft and silky, his complexion was swarthy and ruddy-cheeked. But his eyes – their dark centers were ringed by a color that was neither gray nor blue, but a combination of both.

Young Gray Wolf pointed toward the shore and jabbered excitedly. The canoe had landed. Raven waited impatiently as her husband made his way to the clan house where they lived. He walked past her without saying a word and ducked to enter the dwelling. Quickly she followed him inside.

The interior was built on three levels, descending to a center floor with a dirt hearth. Runs Like a Wolf turned and walked along the upper level that was partitioned into sleeping quarters and storage areas. Raven caught up with him before he reached the corner post with its totemic carvings.

'What happened?' she demanded.

'Nanuk demanded hostages before he would speak with us, and refused to give hostages in return. He said he did not trust our people.'

Raven stiffened at the insult. She knew it was useless to ask her husband what he thought the chief planned to do. He may have the legs of a wolf, but in her opinion he had the mind of a turtle. There were times when she doubted that he even realized he wasn't the father of her son. Impatiently she turned away from him just as her brother, Heart of the Cedar, ducked through the low opening. Quickly she went to him.

'Does the chief think Nanuk will attack the village?'

'Night comes soon,' her brother answered. 'Nanuk will wait until the sun rises again. The chief is calling a council of the clan. I think he will advise that everyone leave the village when it grows dark and go to the stronghold by the river.'

Raven smiled. 'Not even the cannon on the big ship can shoot that far.'

'No.' His warm look held approval both for the quickness of her thinking and the recollection of that strategic detail.

'Nanuk still has many men and many guns.'

'We will send messengers to other clans and ask them to give us more guns and warriors with which to destroy the Russians. In three days, maybe four, they will come.'

It was as her brother predicted. Under the cover of darkness, they slipped away from the village that lay exposed to the guns of the Russian ships and went to their stronghold that was located near the mouth of a river farther up the bay. Erected on a small bluff, it was surrounded by a breastwork two logs thick and roughly six feet high, with small brush piled around that. On the long side facing the bay, there were two embrasures for the small cannon they had obtained from the Boston man. Two gates were located on the forest side of the stronghold, and fourteen dwellings provided shelter within the fortified compound.

At midday, Raven saw a scout who had been sent to observe the movements of the Russians enter the stronghold. He wouldn't have returned unless there was something to report.

'Is Nanuk coming?'

Slightly winded, he shook his head. 'No. Nanuk and his men landed at the village and climbed the hill behind it. They tied one of their red cloths with the picture of the two-headed eagle on it to a pole and put it in the ground. Now they drag cannons and timbers up the hill.'

That afternoon, her brother added a war design of red paint to the black that always covered his face to protect it from the insects and the glare of the sun off the water in the summer and the snow in the winter. He donned his vest of wooden armor and his shield, then joined the escort of roughly sixty warriors accompanying the chief. They left the stronghold to seek out Nanuk again and learn his intentions.

When the band arrived at the village site, Heart of the Cedar saw for himself the eagle cloth that fluttered from the pole atop the bluff. A breastwork of timber was already partially completed, and the cannons pointed their long snouts at his warrior band. As they halted beyond musket range of the Russians, the chief called for Nanuk to come speak with them.

A handful of men accompanied Nanuk down the slope. The wise leader of the Russians had not changed much since Heart of the Cedar had last seen him. Hair still did not grow on top of his head, and the pale fringe below the shiny top seemed no lighter. His expression was stern and unforgiving as he faced the chief.

'Nanuk tell the meaning of the guns placed above our village,' the chief demanded.

The answer came through an interpreter. 'The Kolosh burned Nanuk's village. Nanuk is going to build his new village in this place. He says that you must bring to him every Aleut you hold as slave, and all Kolosh must leave Sitka Island and never come back unless Nanuk requests to see you.'

Angered, Heart of the Cedar stepped forward. 'Since first Kolosh came, this land has been the home of the Sitka clan. Our spirits live here. We will not leave.'

'When the Russians came, we asked to live in peace with the Kolosh. We built our village in one small place on land the Sitka kwan sold to us. We did not raise our hands against you. We always traded fairly with you. But you made war on us, and I no longer trust the Kolosh. Therefore, I say you must abandon your stronghold on the river and leave the island. If you refuse, our cannons will blow you into the sea. Give me your answer when the sun comes up.'

The chief hesitated. Heart of the Cedar knew that help could not arrive from the phratries by morning and guessed the chief was thinking that also. 'We will give you our Aleut slaves and let you build your new village. We will not make war on you. We will agree to that and no more,' the chief stated.

Nanuk would not accept that. 'Leave or I will drive you from the island.'

The chief glared at the short, wizened leader, then pivoted sharply and walked through his quickly parting warrior escort. They closed ranks behind him and followed him into the dense forest.

The following day, the command of the *Ekatrina* was given to the Cossack Lieutenant Arbusov. Several cannons from the Navy frigate were mounted on the *Ekatrina*'s decks. Under the Cossack's orders, Mikhail sailed the vessel farther up the bay and anchored it close to the Kolosh stronghold. The three other colonial-built ships joined them to form a line, but the frigate *Neva* remained at the village site.

Not a single Kolosh showed himself, but Mikhail knew they were there. All the previous night an eerie chant had come from the stronghold, the wavering singsong cry working on his nerves – and everyone else's – and depriving him of sleep.

The singing had continued into the early-morning hours. It hadn't ended until a short time ago, after the sun was well up in the sky. Now the stillness was filled with a tension that came from the ranks of men crowded together on the deck, a kind of battle-ready eagerness that hardened their features.

'Fire!'

A second later, the air vibrated with the thundering boom of the cannons, and the deck shuddered beneath Mikhail's feet. As men scrambled to reposition the cannons and reload, Mikhail observed that most of the shells fell short of the timbered breastwork surrounding the Kolosh stronghold. A few struck it, but their force was spent and the impact caused little damage.

All up and down the line of ships, the cannon barrage continued. The deafening roar of the guns assaulted his eardrums, and the acrid smell of powder smoke burned his nostrils. Through the layers of drifting gray smoke, Mikhail could see that the stronghold remained intact. Baranov called a halt to the futile pounding that had succeeded only in wasting valuable ammunition, and approached Mikhail.

'Is it possible to maneuver the ship closer to shore, Tarakanov?' Baranov demanded, his frustration showing.

'No, sir.'

As Baranov turned to confer with Arbusov, Mikhail was close enough to hear their plans.

Not a single answering shot came from the stronghold. Encouraged by this lack of resistance, the Cossack officer recommended to Baranov that the native fort be stormed by land, since the ships' cannons had been unable to level it. The decision was made to transport some of the lighter fieldpieces ashore and assault the bluff from two sides. Baranow would lead one group of a hundred and fifty men, and Arbusov would command the other.

As the boats were lowered over the side, Mikhail spied his brother standing on the fringes of one of Baranov's landing parties. He hadn't spoken to Zachar since that first night. Mikhail hesitated, then wound his way through the throng of heavily armed men to his brother's side. Zachar didn't notice him; all his attention was centered on the timbered palisade of the native fort. He looked worried. Or was it fear? Mikhail wondered.

'Zachar.' He watched his brother turn with a guilty start, then quickly avoid his gaze. 'I wanted to wish you luck.'

He nodded stiffly. 'Thanks.' Ahead of him, the men began climbing over the side into the waiting boats that would take them ashore. Zachar shuffled forward to wait his turn.

'Tonight, you can give me a complete account of what happened.' Mikhail made an attempt to remind Zachar of their younger days when he had listened so enviously to his older brother's stories about his adventures.

A smile tugged at the corners of Zachar's mouth as he glanced over his shoulder at Mikhail. A moment later, he was crawling over the rail and climbing down the ropes to the boat.

As he helped row the heavily loaded boat toward the beach, Zachar stared at the brushwood piled around the log breastwork. No matter how he tried, he couldn't forget that Raven was hiding somewhere behind those walls. He looked at the small cannon in the boat, knowing how indiscriminately its shells selected its victims.

The boats landed on the beach without incident. As the force, mainly composed of Aleuts, disembarked, there wasn't a sound or a movement from the native fort. Baranov assembled his force on the beach and prepared to advance in coordination with Arbusov's assault. But the land between the narrow strip of graveled beach and the Kolosh stronghold on the bluff was clogged with a dense thicket of brush and towering berry bushes. They plunged into the wet undergrowth, but the going was hard and slow as they labored to drag the small cannon through the slippery tangle. They lost sight of Arbusov's party almost immediately.

By late afternoon, they were halfway up the slope of the bluff. Zachar leaned his shoulder against a wheel of the cannon and threw all his weight into it, straining to push it another centimeter closer, but the wet footing gave him little leverage. It seemed to take all his strength to keep the cannon from rolling backward. The others around him were having the same problem. He stole a quick look at the log ramparts. The closer they got to the stronghold, the more unnerving the silence became. Bending his head, Zachar redoubled his efforts to budge the cannon.

Suddenly the wild yells of the Kolosh ripped the air, instantly followed by a barrage of musketfire from the breastwork. A rain of lead hammered down on them from above. Zachar crouched behind the cannon and tried to bring his musket up, but all around him the Aleuts were breaking and running, abandoning the more than two dozen Russians in Baranov's group. Immediately, painted Kolosh warriors began streaming over the parapets, howling and screaming war cries. Zachar fired without bothering to choose a target. There were too many.

'Retreat!' Baranov shouted.

Zachar joined the mad scramble down the brush-covered slope, pulling the rolling, rattling cannon behind him. He saw Baranov fall and grabbed him by the arm, dragging him along. The air was filled with flying lead as the guns on the ships provided a fusillade of cover fire, and ultimately forced the Kolosh to turn back.

Safely aboard the ships again, the cost of the abortive charge was tallied; the total came to ten dead and twenty-six wounded. Baranov was among the latter, suffering an arm wound. Conceding failure, he turned command over to Captain Lisianski. The next day, the frigate *Neva* was towed alongside the smaller ships, and a relentless bombardment of the enemy stronghold began. All morning and afternoon, the forest and the bay reverberated with the unceasing roar of the cannons.

Twice the Kolosh waved a white flag from the ramparts. The first time a messenger from the stronghold promised to furnish Nanuk with hostages if he would allow them to remain on Sitka Island. Baranov refused, insisting the Kolosh must leave. On the second occasion, the messenger promised the Kolosh would leave the following day at high tide, and the siege was lifted.

High tide came and went the next day and nothing happened. Lisianski ordered a log raft constructed and mounted several of his heavy cannons on it. At a closer range, the guns began pounding the enemy fort again, at last inflicting damage on the log breastwork. An old man appeared on the beach at twilight waving a white flag. This time he promised the Kolosh would leave. The battery ceased firing.

Unable to sleep that night, Zachar walked the deck of the *Ekatrina*, his gaze continually drawn to the dark mass of the stronghold. When he'd been at Kodiak, distance had made it easier for him, but now to be so close to Raven and not see her was painful. He wanted to believe that she had cared for him, that he hadn't been wrong to trust her.

From the Kolosh fortress came a wailing chant. Zachar paused to listen to the mournful song. The heavy beat of a drum echoed the dirgelike rhythm of the song. Other voices joined in, lifting to a crescendo, then falling away to a near silence, only to have the pattern repeat itself. Zachar couldn't understand the words, but the grief the voices contained needed no translation. The sound chilled his skin.

All through the night, the eerie chant continued without let-up.

An hour before dawn, it finally stopped. The unearthly silence that followed was almost worse. Zachar waited for the sun to come up, but the pink dawn revealed only winged scavengers soaring in slow circles above the stronghold.

There was no response when they hailed the fort. Zachar volunteered to go ashore with the armed party being sent to investigate. When they landed on the beach, everything seemed deathly still. They approached the stronghold cautiously, circling around through the forest. The gates stood open. There was no sound, no movement inside.

With his musket at the ready and his finger close to the trigger, Zachar entered the stronghold with the others. Warily they fanned out, but the place appeared deserted except for the flock of carrion birds that hovered about a pile in the center of the compound. Zachar approached the strange-looking mound. As he neared it, he saw it was a pile of dead bodies, and he quickened his steps, breaking into a run for the last yards.

Death's rigor had already claimed many of the bodies as Zachar searched through them, frantically looking for Raven, terrified he would find her among the dead. But there was only one female adult among the heap of corpses, an old, almost toothless woman. The majority were warriors, showing battle wounds. The rest of the bodies belonged to young infants or the very old. Zachar sank to his knees with relief, certain that Raven was alive – somewhere.

24 *Sitka*
August 1805

On the site of the former Kolosh village, the Russian settlement called Novo Arkhangelsk, New Archangel, now stood. A bastion, mounted with twenty cannons, crowned the broad knoll and commanded the harbor below. A set of steps led down to the main settlement where once the Kolosh log dwellings and totemic gravehouses had lined the shore. Now there were eight buildings – a bunkhouse, commissary, a storehouse, a few cabins, and a barn for the livestock, which consisted of black and white spotted cows, some pigs from the batch King Kamehameha had sent the previous winter, and two goats from a Boston ship. A stockade protected the landward side of the settlement and enclosed more than a dozen vegetable patches within its walls.

The Navy frigate *Neva* was once again moored in the habor after wintering at Kodiak. Alongside her was the brig *Maria*, on which the high chamberlain, Nikolai Rezanov, had recently arrived, the ship guided to its safe anchorage in the bay by Mikhail, now stationed at New Archangel and assigned the inglorious duty of habor pilot.

As Mikhail emerged from the small cabin atop the knoll, he spied Zachar standing guard at the bastion wall. He slogged across the rainsoaked ground to the cannon embrasure where his brother stood gazing seaward. Zachar turned at the sound of Mikhail's footsteps, then glanced at the letter in his hand.

'The *Maria* brought mail from Kodiak. A letter from your daughter, Larissa.'

Zachar stared at the folded sheet of parchment, but made no attempt to take it from his brother's hand. Unlike Mikhail and his daughter, he could neither read nor write. 'What does she say? How is our mother?'

'She is in good health.' Mikhail read aloud the short letter from Larissa in which she told about the continued instruction she was receiving from Father Herman and the help she gave Tasha in her work at the household of Ivan Banner and his Russian wife, the man Baranov had placed in charge of the Kodiak settlement. The last paragraph of the letter dealt with the high chamberlain's visit to Kodiak, and the empty building he filled with hundreds of books, large maps, beautiful models of ships, and strange instruments. ' "I hope that you and Uncle Mikhail are both well and that soon we may be together again." It's signed "Your faithful daughter, Larissa." '

Mikhail offered no comment on the latter wish that she'd expressed. In the foreseeable future, it was unlikely that the company would be sending either Zachar or himself back to Kodiak, and as yet it was unsafe for his mother and niece to be brought here to New Archangel, surrounded as it was by hostile Kolosh with the threat of attack ever present.

When he had returned to Russian America as a trained navigator, Mikhail had thought his trade would enable him to visit many distant shores. Instead, he'd been made a harbor pilot and rarely ventured beyond the waters of this bay. It was a continual source of frustration to him, especially when there were letters to remind him of his static life. He handed the letter to Zachar and watched as his brother folded it and slipped it into his pocket, then glanced toward the crude cabin.

'I heard that Baranov gave his excellency his resignation.' Zachar repeated the current rumor.

'I don't think the high chamberlain has accepted it yet.' Mikhail smiled faintly. 'The large collection of books and pictures that Larissa mentioned in her letter – the ones Rezanov left at Kodiak – supposedly, Baranov told him that he wished his excellency had brought something to fill our bellies instead of our minds.'

Zachar chuckled, although the shortage of supplies was hardly laughable. The camp dogs started barking near the base of the knoll, then ran in a pack toward the beach. Turning his head, Zachar saw a half dozen Kolosh canoes wending their way through the garland of islands toward the settlement. Both men and women were in the boats. The wind blew snatches of the song they sang.

Short of the beach, they halted their canoes. One of the warriors – Zachar suspected the man was a chief – stood up and began to speak. Zachar was able to understand most of what he said.

'We were your enemies,' he called. 'We injured you. You were our enemies. You injured us. We want to be good friends. We want to forget the past. We do not seek to injure you again. Do us no more harm also. Be our good friends.'

The same message was repeated over and over again through different phrases. Already several chiefs from various clans had come to make peace with Baranov and resume a friendly trade relationship.

'I'll tell Baranov he has visitors,' Mikhail volunteered.

Zachar waited outside the cabin while Mikhail summoned their leader. Baranov came out, his black wig fastened to his head with a scarf. The hard life, his advancing years, and the wet climate were all beginning to take their toll on him. His fingers were gnarled and stiff with arthritis, and he limped from the same problem, walking with the aid of cane. Yet his eyes remained bright and his mind quick, belying his nearly sixty years of age.

Together Zachar and Mikhail escorted him down the stairs to the tent that had been erected on the beach for the purpose of entertaining the Kolosh peacemakers. When they reached it, the native interpreters had already ushered the Kolosh into the tent to await their audience with Nanuk. Zachar walked in ahead of Baranov.

His eye was caught by a Kolosh woman dressed in a brightly striped robe. Something inside him seemed to freeze as he stared at her face. It was Raven. Disbelief held him motionless until he felt the prod of Baranov's cane urging him out of the way. As he stepped to the side, he noticed the young boy standing next to her. He looked to be about three years old. And his eyes – his eyes were a light shade of blue! Zachar stared at the child, who was definitely not a fullblooded Kolosh. The boy was the right age to be his son. Was he? His glance darted back to Raven.

If anything, she looked more beautiful to him. Her eyes were as dark as he remembered them, and they still glowed with an inner fire. She studied him in that intent, close-watching way she had always had. Zachar felt the familiar rush of intense pleasure he'd always experienced when in her presence. Any doubts he'd had about her no longer seemed important. She was here and he still wanted her. Nothing else mattered.

He smiled at her and watched her eyes darken and her lips curve faintly in response. The years seemed to fall away from him. Unconsciously he stood taller, threw his shoulders back, and pushed his chest out. Inside he was all eager and excited, filled with an intensely sweet happiness he'd never expected to know again.

The ceremonial formalities were lengthy as Baranov and the clan chief both made several long speeches, professing their desires for friendship and peace. At last, Baranov ordered the feast that had been hastily prepared at the cookhouse to be brought in. The food was accompanied by a brandy keg, and a round of toasts were drunk. Zachar tasted neither. Feasting his eyes on Raven was sufficient nourishment for him, and drinking in the sight of her intoxicated him.

After an agony of waiting, the Kolosh began to dance in celebration and Zachar had his chance to seek out Raven. As he sat on the ground beside her, his tongue suddenly refused to function. None of the things he'd planned to say to her would come out. All he wanted to do was touch her and feel her in his arms again. Raven watched him while she chanted the song to which many of her people danced, leaping nimbly in the air. The boy peered around her to stare curiously at Zachar.

'Is this your son?' And mine? he wanted to ask, but couldn't.

Raven nodded once and dropped out of the singing. 'He is Gray Wolf.'

'He's a fine-looking boy.' Zachar felt certain he saw a resemblance to himself in the child's features, especially his light-colored eyes. 'How old is he?'

'He was born two winters ago at the time when the bear has young.'

By Kolosh reckoning, Zachar believed that was roughly the month of February. The boy was unquestionably his son. His son. The knowledge seemed to swell inside him, filling him with an overwhelming joy and pride.

The tribal dance was approaching some climax, the singers lifting their voices in a crescendo, the whirling dancers yipping shrilly. Zachar became irritated by the bedlam that intruded on his meeting with Raven.

He leaned closer to her to make himself heard above the noise. 'Will you come outside with me?'

Her glance flicked over his face as she hesitated momentarily. 'You go. I will come soon.'

Briefly Zachar wondered at her response, but it was enough that she had agreed to meet him privately. Eager to be alone with her, he rose to his feet and headed for the open tent flap, hugging the canvas sidewalls in an effort to slip away unnoticed.

Outside, twilight purpled the clouds and the distant slopes of Mount Edgecumbe. The salt breeze blowing off the water was cool and kept the swarms of gnats and mosquitoes confined to the muskegs·in the wet forest. Zachar moved away from the tent toward the tall prows of the beached canoes along the shore.

All his senses were sharpened in anticipation. When he heard the sound of a footstep behind him, he pivoted sharply, surprised and elated that Raven had followed him so soon. But it was Mikhail, not Raven, and Zachar struggled to conceal his disappointment.

'Is something wrong?' Mikhail frowned.

'No. Nothing.' Zachar smiled, because things hadn't been so right in a long time, not since last he'd been with Raven.

The furrows creasing his brother's brow deepened in puzzlement. 'Why did you leave? Was it something that Kolosh woman said to you? You seemed to know her.'

'I do.' At that moment, Zachar saw Raven glide through the tent opening with her young son in hand. Nodding his head, he directed Mikhail's attention to her. 'She's meeting me here. Did you notice the little boy? He's my son.'

'Your what?'

But Zachar didn't hear his incredulous response as he stepped forward to greet Raven. This time it seemed the most natural thing to do to take her in his arms and kiss her, to feel the softness of her lips beneath his and the pliant yielding of her body to his embrace. A powerfully tender emotion swelled inside him, and he trembled when he finally lifted his head and gazed down at her face. He thought he had loved her before, but that couldn't compare with the passionate adoration he now felt. It was all-consuming and all forgiving.

Her dark gaze strayed to a point beyond him, reminding him of Mikhail's presence. He turned while keeping an arm around her. 'I want you to meet my younger brother, Mikhail Tarakanov. This is Raven.' Reaching down, he scooped the boy into the hook of his arm and picked him up. He smiled at the child, who seemed so fascinated by this closeup look at him. 'And this little fellow is Gray Wolf.'

Mikhail had the distinct impression that he was looking at a family portrait: the boy with his father's eyes perched on his arm, and the loving husband gazing adoringly at the mother of his son. Only one image didn't ring true to him, and that was the woman who looked at him instead of Zachar.

'I thought I'd never see her again,' Zachar was saying. 'Now I'll never let her out of my sight.'

A quiet seemed to spread over the island. It took Mikhail a moment to realize the dancing inside the tent had ceased. As his attention shifted to the canvas structure, a Kolosh warrior paused in the opening, looking into the darkening shadows as if searching for someone. When his head stopped its slow turning, it was pointed directly at them.

Recalling his brother's last words, Mikhail said, 'I think *he* might have something to say about that.' He nodded to indicate the warrior striding toward them.

Raven stiffened when she recognized Frog of the Forest. In utter loathing, she curled her tongue inside her mouth, then felt the pressure of Zachar's encircling arm increase slightly.

'Who's he?'

'He is Frog of the Forest, the brother of my dead husband. He has taken me to be his second wife.'

During the Russian siege of the stronghold, Runs Like a Wolf had been struck in the legs by grapeshot. Crippled by the wounds, he had been ritually killed by the shaman so he wouldn't slow the clan during their flight. According to the custom of her people, his brother was obligated to take Raven as a wife, even though he already had one. Try as she might, Raven had not been able to usurp his first wife's position as the favored wife. That he preferred that flat-nosed woman over her proved to Raven that he was even more stupid than his brother. And that he thought he could order her around like a slave increased her contempt for him.

He halted in front of her, his blackened face shining in the half-light of dusk. The red painted circles that ringed his eyes made him appear all the more menacing as he glared at her, angry that she had failed to seek his permission and that she had shown her unfaithfulness to him and shamed him in front of the Russians.

'You go back to the tent,' he ordered in their tongue.

'You go back to the tent.' She could feel the hilt of the knife that was strapped to Zachar's side and shifted slightly to bring it more easily within her reach.

'You will do as I say.' Infuriated by her defiance, he grabbed for her arm to force her into obedience.

But Raven eluded his grasp and snatched Zachar's knife from its sheath, then flashed its blade in front of her toad of a husband. 'I will stay with Zachar.' This time she spoke in Russian.

After drawing back in surprise, he took a threatening step forward, cursing her roundly. But Zachar intervened, as she had known he would. 'Leave her alone.' He pulled his pistol and leveled the barrel at him.

'Zachar. In the name of the Holy Saints, what do you think you're doing?' The one Zachar had called his brother laid a restraining hand on Zachar's arm. 'They have come in peace to treat with Baranov.'

'I have no more wish to live with you,' Raven declared contemptuously. 'It shames me to be called the wife of one who is no more than frog's water.'

'I have no wish for you to be my wife.'

'Then I am no more your wife and you are no more my husband.' She lowered the knife, satisfied now that she had provoked that admission from him. The gifts exchanged at marriage wouldn't have to be returned as long as the desire to separate was mutual.

He pressed his lips grimly together, realizing how she had trapped him into it. Then he looked at Zachar with narrowed eyes. 'You want this woman?' he asked in Russian.

'Yes.'

'Give two chisels and one blanket. She yours all time.'

'No.' Raven angrily protested. 'He agrees the marriage is no more. You have to give him nothing.'

'I will pay what he asks.'

'No.' She turned on her former husband and shouted accusations and insults at him. Soon he was yelling back, calling her a witch and other equally vile things.

Within minutes, their loud voices had attracted the attention of those in the tent. Zachar had mixed feelings when he saw Baranov emerge. Nothing he'd tried had been successful in stopping this argument. Neither had allowed him to get more than two words in.

'What is going on here?' But not even Baranov's initial demand gained their silence. He took the pistol from Zachar's hand and fired it into the air. The explosion had the desired effect. 'Now what is all this about?'

Zachar told him, then Raven attempted to give her side of it, only to be interrupted by her warrior husband. Baranov held up the gun, once again demanding silence, then looked at Zachar. 'You want this woman?'

'I want her. This is my son.' He held the child more closely in his arms, confident Baranov would understand. After all he had two children by the Indian woman he lived with whom he greatly adored. 'I am willing to pay the price he asks for her, although Raven claims he isn't entitled to it.'

Baranov made a slight bow in Raven's direction. 'I compliment the lady for so stridently protecting your interests. However, in the name of peace and good will, the price will be paid.' While the interpreter translated his answer for the benefit of the surrounding Kolosh, Baranov murmured to Zachar, 'The items will be charged to your account with the company and the amount deducted from your earnings.'

Not even Raven chose to argue with Nanuk's decision, and the matter was settled. Frog of the Forest was presented with two chisels and one blanket, and Raven became Zachar's woman.

Later that week Baranov performed a crude baptismal ceremony, christening Zachar's son Vasili Zacharevich Tarakanov, but no one ever called the boy by that name. Instead they called him Wolf. An exceedingly clever boy, within a month at New Archangel his vocabulary had become liberally interspersed with Russians words.

In October it began to rain – endlessly, it seemed to Mikhail as he splashed across the sodden compound toward his brother's hut. Cold weather was rarely a problem in this region of Sitka Sound, but the sluicing rains and thick fogs were a constant source of discomfort.

Mikhail turned a weather eye to the west. Heavy clouds completely hid Mount Edgecumbe's island and blurred the others in the bay. The frigate *Neva* no longer loomed in the harbor. A fortnight after the high chamberlain arrived, she had sailed, carrying a cargo of furs valued at 450,000 rubles to Canton, and the *Elizaveta*, one of the small company ships, had been sent to Kodiak for supplies.

The heavy rain had halted work on the keel of a new ship that High Chamberlain Rezanov had ordered to be built and called the *Avoss*, the *Perhaps*. Insulted by the Mikado's treatment of him during his ambassadorial mission to Japan, Rezanov intended to send a naval force there and punish the island nation.

The *Avoss* would be part of that flotilla. He had also ordered Baranov to prepare living quarters on the island in the harbor for the 'compulsory immigrants,' as he called them, that would be brought back from Japan at the conclusion of his military expedition. Now everyone referred to the island as Japonski.

Mikhail didn't share the high chamberlain's enthusiasm for the plan; no one did. The Russian American Company didn't have enough ships to keep its settlements provisioned with supplies, patrol its territories to prevent foreign ships from trading in their waters, and escort hunting expeditions for sea otter. That they should attempt to mount an offensive was ludicrous. Yet, no matter how reasonable Rezanov was on other issues, such as the establishment of medical care, native schools, and a pension fund for the old and disabled, he wouldn't be swayed from his planned Japanese campaign. However they might disagree, the word of the forty-two-year-old plenipotentiary was obeyed.

Arriving at his brother's log hut, Mikhail paused outside the door and knocked. Once he would have simply walked in, but Raven's presence had changed that. Twice he had walked in unannounced and intruded on an intimate scene. Now he knocked first.

No sound came from inside. All he could hear was the hammering of the rain on the roof. He waited, hunching his shoulders against the downpour, then knocked again. But there was no response. Turning, he scanned the other buildings of the settlement, not relishing the idea of tramping through the rain and mud to find Zachar. Rezanov, who had taken over the active command, had called another council of the navigators and chief hunters as well as Baranov and his second, Ivan Kuskov. He and Zachar were to be at Rezanov's cabin within an hour. More than likely he'd find Zachar at the commissary buying more trinkets for Raven.

He heard the splat of footsteps coming around the cabin and turned as Raven walked around the corner carrying an armload of firewood. A blanket was draped over her, hooding her head. Although she walked swiftly, the picture was not one of a woman scurrying through the rain. She carried herself with too much dignity for that. More than once Mikhail had been struck by her pride, which occasionally bordered on insolence.

There was the smallest hesitation in her stride when she noticed him waiting by the door. 'You are wet,' she observed and

277

managed to make him feel foolish for standing outside in the rain when he could have been inside where it was dry.

'I was looking for Zachar.'

'He will return soon.' She walked past him and pushed open the cabin door.

Belatedly he noticed how awkwardly she managed it, hampered by the armload of wood. He followed her inside and shut the door for her, then turned around. The blanket had fallen from her head, revealing the shiny black hair that framed her face. He purposely avoided looking at her.

'Let me take that firewood.'

As he reached to take it from her, his arm grazed her breast. He jerked away, nearly dropping the split logs, as if the contact had burned him. She wore an amused smile on her lips. It was the sultry fullness of her lips that altered the whole effect of the strong bone structure of her face and created an image of compelling beauty – that and the unfathomable blackness of her eyes. He felt the tightening in his loins and abruptly turned away to carry the logs to the woodbox by the fireplace.

'It is long since you were with a woman.' The nearness of her voice told Mikhail that she followed him.

All his senses seemed to clamor for his attention at once, making him aware of the smell of wood smoke permeating the musty air, the plop of water dripping from a leak in the roof, and the cot sitting in the corner of the single-roomed cabin.

'There is a shortage of woman here.' Mikhail was more than willing to blame his reaction on his recent forced celibacy, at the same time recognizing that she had the kind of looks that turned a man's thoughts to sex. He dropped the logs into the box, letting their thumping clatter fill the silence, then moved to stand in front of the fireplace flames. 'You said you expect Zachar back soon?'

'Yes.' She removed the blanket and laid it across the woodbox to dry. 'You want a woman to lay with. Why do you not ask me?' She stood at his side, facing him, almost taunting him. 'Or do you think me ugly?'

'No.' The truth came quickly. 'You belong to Zachar.'

'But you are his brother. It is acceptable to my people for a woman to have two husbands if they are brothers.'

Mikhail laughed harshly. 'Russians don't find such heathen practices acceptable.'

'Why? A woman needs sons. Zachar is too old. More often now his organ is limp in my hands. You are yet strong. You could give me many sons, I think.'

Her remarks generated a heat that filled him. He stared at the yellow flames of fire, inwardly cursing her for doing this to him. 'Zachar isn't too old,' he asserted. 'Baranov is sixteen or seventeen years older than my brother and he has a three-year-old child.'

'He is Nanuk,' she said, as if that explained it all. 'Would you not like to lay with me?'

Mikhail swung angrily around, but he didn't have a chance to speak as the door burst open and Zachar came charging in, the sound of his laughter mixing with the high-pitched giggle of his son. Suddenly Mikhail wasn't sure how he would have answered Raven's question. Troubled by the guilt that followed his uncertainty, he felt uncomfortable facing his brother.

'I didn't know you were here, Mikhail.' Zachar smiled as he lowered his son, Wolf, to the floor. The boy vigorously shook his wet head, shaking himself like a dog and scattering a spray of droplets in every direction.

'I just got here.' The need to establish that he hadn't been alone with Raven for long merely increased his sense of guilt. He hadn't betrayed his brother, but he had wanted to. 'Rezanov has called another meeting.'

Self-consciously, Mikhail moved away from the fireplace – and Raven – to head for the door. 'Wait,' Zachar said. 'I'll walk with you.'

'I go.' The boy darted to Zachar's side as soon as he realized he was going to leave.

'No.' Zachar gave him a little shove toward Raven. 'You stay here and look after your mother. I'll be back later.' There was a pleased smile on his face as he followed Mikhail out the door, then paused to turn his collar up against the rain. 'He's a good boy,' he remarked to Mikhail. 'I think he's becoming fond of me.'

'Yes.' Mikhail couldn't remember ever seeing his brother so happy, practically bursting with pride over his newly found family. They were all too new and shiny for Zachar to see any flaw in them, Mikhail realized.

With heads bent against the pouring rain, they started across the settlement grounds toward the stairs that led to the bastion atop the broad, flat knoll. 'What is this meeting about? Were you told?' Zachar asked.

'No.'

They walked several paces in silence, then Zachar spoke. 'I like this Rezanov. He is a wise man. I know that many of the promyshleniki on the seal islands – the Pribilofs – were unhappy with his order to slaughter no more seals this year, but it must be stopped or there will be no more left where once there were millions swarming over the rocks like bees in a honeycomb.'

'You have been there?' Mikhail frowned.

'Once, long ago,' Zachar admitted as he started up the steps. 'I have heard the raids of the Boston ships killed more than a millon seals this year alone.'

'We lose a lot of furs to them, and the Kolosh obtain many guns from them. Sometimes I think the Kolosh are better armed than we are. At least Rezanov agrees with Baranov, though, that we must trade with the English and the Boston men for supplies. We cannot depend on the company ships sailing from Okhotsk. Look at our situation now. Our flour ration is down to one pound a month per man, and winter is coming.'

As they mounted the last step, Zachar nodded a confirmation of their straitened circumstance. 'The *Elizaveta* should return from Kodiak soon with supplies.'

Nikolai Petrovich Rezanov was a tall, handsome man of forty-two. Clean-shaven and dressed in one of his less ornate military uniforms, he carried himself erectly, naturally commanding the attention of the men who had crowded into his small cabin. His thin lips were drawn together as his pale blue eyes surveyed them, his manner one of grimness.

Mikhail glanced at a wigless Baranov, his bald crown fringed by flaxen hair. Years of gazing at far horizons had etched lines into the old Russian's face that gave him a perpetually quizzical expression. But the look in his eyes was one of sadness and resignation. Mikhail guessed the news wasn't good. Any minute he expected Baranov to lift his hands and offer the usual declaration: 'It's in God's hands.'

Rezanov spoke, not mincing any words. 'We have received word, as yet unconfirmed, that the *Elizaveta* was lost at sea in a gale. There will be no supplies from Kodiak. In addition, the native flotilla of hunters sank in the storm with the loss of two hundred men and the season's largest catch of furs.' All around Mikhail hands were lifted in gestures of resignation, but there was more. 'A message has also been received which contained an unsubstantiated report that the convict settlement at Yakutat has been wiped out by the Kolosh.' The agricultural and ship-building outpost built on the Alaskan mainland had been an experiment modeled after the colonization of Botany Bay by the British. 'The Kolosh have also attacked other redoubts to the north but were repulsed. However, I believe we can count on increased hostilities in our area.'

A few mumbled their remorse over the deaths of men they knew, but Rezanov discouraged any discussion of the news. He signaled for his personal manservant to bring the charts and books to the table, then spread them open for all to study. They were the records of the explorer George Vancouver.

As Mikhail listened to Rezanov expound on his plans for the future expansion of the Russian American Company's territories, he had the distinct feeling that the two recent disasters had only made the high chamberlain more determined to forge ahead. Rezanov strongly recommended that the company abolish its practice of depending solely on the fur trade and engage in the merchant business as well. Mikhail's lust for faraway places was aroused by Rezanov's list of exotic foreign ports as he talked about establishing consuls in the company's name at Burma and in the Philippines, building more settlements first along the Columbia River, then at California and Hawaii. Soon, he claimed, the Peace of Amiens would be broken and Europe would go to war against the belligerent Corsican Napoleon. That would leave the company free to solidify its holdings in Alaska and expand into new territories.

'Look at the map.' He punched a finger at the chart on the table. 'The one who holds Alaska can control the Pacific.'

A drop of water splashed on Mikhail's cheek and broke the spell woven by Rezanov's grandiose dreams of an empire. The reality at Sitka was leaking roofs, lurking Kolosh, and dwindling supplies.

The arrival of the Yankee schooner *Juno* at Sitka provided a temporary solution to the provision problem. Rezanov purchased the vessel and its cargo, which consisted of a large quantity of trade goods, including tinware, pottery, utensils, hardware, muslins, and a variety of implements. More importantly, the ship had nearly two thousand gallons of molasses, nineteen casks of salt pork, four thousand pounds of rice, eleven casks of wheat flour, and other food stores, enough to last several weeks.

For a while, they had plenty to eat and there was music in the settlement, furnished by a duet of clarinet and violin played by a Yankee seaman who had signed on with the company and the high chamberlain himself. But a combination of unusually heavy rains and sleet and thick fogs during the latter months of the year and the constant menace of Kolosh prevented the Russians from supplementing their food supply with fresh game and fish. It was forbidden to leave the fort, and they were forced to begin eating the Aleuts' supply of oil and dried fish.

The *Juno* was dispatched to Kodiak to obtain whatever provisions the Russian village could spare, but all she brought back was more whale oil and dried fish. By February, scurvy was rampant at Sitka. Out of the nearly two hundred Russians at the redoubt, eight were dead and sixty were completely disabled by the debilitating disease.

The situation was dire. A winter sea voyage to Hawaii was out of the question; crossing the storm-riddled Pacific was too lengthy and too risky. At another meeting, Rezanov proposed sailing the schooner down the coast, exploring the mouth of the Columbia River for a future site, obtaining fresh game and fish, and trading at the small Spanish presidio of Los Farallones del Puerto de San Francisco for foodstuffs. Although all Spanish ports along the California coast were closed to foreign ships, he intended to gain admittance by using his credentials as Russia's ambassador to the world. A minimum crew of twenty was required to sail the *Juno*, but the weakened condition of the men at the settlement made it mandatory that she carry a full complement of thirty in the event of illness.

Mikhail immediately volunteered to go on the voyage, but Baranov banged his fist on the table in protest. 'You cannot weaken this garrison by taking all of our able-bodied men! The Kolosh are a constant danger. We must be able to defend ourselves should they attack!'

After considerable dissension, a compromise was reached. Rezanov agreed that part of his crew would be made up of men showing the early signs of scurvy, Mikhail's petition to join the expedition was refused. His disappointment quickly turned to resentment when Zachar was selected to go.

'Why do you take my brother and not me?' he protested. 'He is older and has a family. I am an experienced navigator. I can be of more use to you than he will. He is a hunter.'

'There are other men with families who will be going. And we will have need for an experienced hunter before we reach the Spanish port,' Rezanov asserted sharply, making it plain he would tolerate no more questioning of his decisions.

Trembling with anger, Mikhail fell silent and heard little of the ensuing conversation. Inwardly he railed. He was the navigator; he was the one who longed to see new places. Yet it always seemed to be his older brother who ventured into unknown territory first – his brother who had no desire to go. All he had ever traveled was the old routes – Sitka to Kodiak, the Pribilofs, Unalaska, or mainland redoubts and back. Now he was stuck here, serving out his required enlistment in the company as a harbor pilot.

When the meeting ended, Mikhail left without speaking to his brother. His resentment and disappointment were too keen. At the moment he was so angry that he even blamed Zachar for being chosen instead of him.

Time was critical, and none was wasted as the schooner was hurriedly readied to sail. Little food could be spared from the settlement's meager supplies if those remaining at Sitka were to survive until the *Juno* returned. But the cargo hold was loaded with trade goods – wearing apparel, fine English cloth, leather goods and shoes, tools ranging from axes to gimlets, plus bundles of cloth-of-gold, elaborate muskets, and other items originally intended as gifts for the Japanese Mikado.

Mikhail avoided the harbor area while the preparations for the voyage were under way, only grudgingly taking part when he had no other choice. The bitter knowledge that tomorrow the *Juno* would weigh anchor and sail without him, gnawed at him as he entered his private quarters in the company barracks where he had closeted himself much of the time. He walked directly to the cot and pulled a jug of kvass from beneath it, one of two he'd secreted away as protection against scurvy. But it wasn't for medicinal reasons that he filled a tin mug to the rim with the home-brewed liquor, then drank half of it down. He carried both the cup and the jug to the table and sat down in a crudely finished chair. At Sitka they had only axes and chisels with which to hew the logs into board planks.

He stared morosely at his cup, resenting the clouds and the cold, and remembering the tales he'd heard about the California sunshine that he was never going to see. He dreaded the day Zachar returned and he'd have to listen to all his stories about the place he should have visited. He downed the rest of the liquor and refilled the tin mug.

'Mikhail.'

He stiffened at the sound of his brother's voice, belatedly realizing that the click he'd heard had been the lifting of the door latch. 'Yes, what is it?' he demanded tersely, not looking around.

'I need to speak to you.'

'No doubt you've come to say good-bye.' He had expected this visit and tried to smother his irritations, aware they were childish.

Mikhail stood up and turned to face his brother, gathering his pride so Zachar wouldn't see how much he envied him. Raven and her son, Wolf, stood next to Zachar. Those disturbing black eyes boldly stared at him, and Mikhail immediately felt uncomfortable.

Ever since she had made that initial overture, he'd done his best to stay clear of her, and for the most part he'd succeeded. Yet, like all women, she had a way of making it clear whenever he saw her that she would welcome his attention. He'd often wondered if his brother noticed.

'It's true, I didn't want to leave without telling you good-bye. But there's also something I'd like you to do for me while I'm gone.' Zachar laid his hand on top of the boy's head. Mikhail became tense. 'I don't like the idea of Wolf and Raven staying alone at our cabin.'

'What do you mean?' He looked at Raven, wondering if she'd put Zachar up to this.

'I'd like you to stay there and look after them while I'm away.'

'I can't.' Mikhail was shocked into the strangled protest.

'You are my brother. I have no one else to ask.' Zachar appeared hurt and confused by his refusal. 'I know how you tried to take my place so I wouldn't have to leave them.'

'I don't think you know what you're asking,' Mikhail declared tightly.

Zachar's frown deepened. 'That they receive their share of food, that they have wood for their fire, that they will have someone to protect them if the Kolosh attack – is that too much to ask for my family?'

'No.' Mikhail couldn't tell him what he really meant.

'Then you will stay with them?'

It seemed the final irony. Zachar was making the voyage Mikhail wanted and was leaving him to care for the woman Mikhail desired, however reluctantly.

'Yes, I'll stay with them,' Mikhail agreed.

The *Juno* sailed with the tide the next day, and Mikhail moved his things into Zachar's cabin. With the number of healthy men reduced, he arranged to stand guard on the first shift of the night watch. When he returned to the cabin at the end of his watch, Raven was in the cot asleep. He made himself a bed on the floor in front of the fireplace, but he slept little, spending most of the night staring at the tongues of flame that licked over the red-white logs and listening to the sounds that Raven made as she turned in her sleep.

The daytime hours when he wasn't working at jobs around the settlement, he spent with Wolf. Twice during the week, he shot a bald eagle that had foolishly soared over the garrison. Its meat provided a welcome change from their monotonous diet of dried fish and oil.

Raven set a dish of it on the table in front of him. Neither the sight nor the smell of the fish and oil was appetizing to him any more, but Mikhail knew he had to eat it. There was nothing else. And his trousers were already loose on him. He got his jug of kvass and set it on the table so he could wash down the meat, but it didn't help much. Instead he became fascinated by the greedy way the boy devoured his food.

'You wolf that down like your namesake.' He smiled as he said it, then pushed his dish over to the boy. 'You can have the rest of mine, too.'

'You are not hungry this night,' Raven said.

He looked at her, something he usually avoided. The yellow light of the oil lamp played across her face, shadowing her deep-set eyes and accenting her high cheekbones. He noticed the new gauntness that indicated her loss of weight. The only thing about her that didn't look thinner to him was her lips. They remained lusciously full.

Half angrily, Mikhail grabbed the jug and poured more kvass into his cup. At that moment, Wolf dug into the dish Mikhail had given him. 'I guess I'm not hungry for that,' he said.

'Do you desire something else?'

The tone of her voice coupled with the phrasing of her question caused him to stiffen. Both implied many things to him, all of them arousing. Mikhail wasn't sure whether she intended them to or not. Not once had she made any suggestive move toward him since he'd been here. But neither had she had the opportunity.

'No.' He got up, taking the jug with him, and crossed to the fireplace.

'Do you walk with the guards tonight?'

'No.' A rotation of shifts had put him on the day watch.

'Mikhail must be tired from so many nights. You should sleep in the cot.'

'No.'

'I think this is the only word you know.' Her soft laugh mocked him. Mikhail swung around and found he couldn't meet her taunting look. 'I think Mikhail is afraid to say anything else.'

'I wish my brother were here so he could see what you are really like.' He trembled with the violence of his emotions, hating her and wanting her with equal fury.

'But Zachar is not here.'

'I should have told him why I didn't want to stay here.'

'It is because you wanted this.'

'No!'

Raven responded to his vigorous denial with a shrug of her shoulders and turned back to the table to finish her meal. A burning log popped in the fireplace, its crack sounding loud in the silence. He stared at the glowing embers, gnawed by her accusation, and frustrated by the suspicion it was true. Perhaps he had kept silent because he wanted something to happen. He drank to kill the doubts she had raised.

Sometime in the night Mikhail dreamed about her. She stood before him, the yellow firelight playing over her naked body, revealing to him the fullness of her breasts, the flatness of her stomach, and the black wool of her pubic hair.

The golden vision sank to the floor beside him and melted against his body, engulfing him in a wave of heat. He stared at her face, the black eyes closed, the dark head thrashing from side to side, the heavy lips open and emitting soft moans. His hips pumped with seemingly tireless energy, plunging his cock deep into her moist cavity, then drawing it out and plunging it in again while he floated above her. Everything spiraled together, soaring higher and higher into a brilliant burst of glory.

When Mikhail awoke the next morning, his head throbbed dully. He turned and felt a body beside him. Raven lay snuggled under the blanket with him. The dream hadn't been a dream at all.

'No!' he cried.

She opened her eyes slowly and looked at him, faintly flexing her bare shoulders in a stretching motion. Her full lips curved in a satisfied smile. 'It is what you wanted,' she murmured.

He knew it was true. And he also knew he should leave – walk out the door and never return. If he stayed he would only compound the sin of betrayal he'd committed by laying with his brother's wife. But what if his brother never returned from the voyage? Even if he did, what if all the supplies had run out in the meantime and everyone here died? What if the Kolosh attacked and massacred everyone? Why should he deprive himself of the company that Raven was so willing to give him?

Mikhail stayed.

In the ensuing months, new graves were dug in the settlement as the scurvy claimed more victims and weakened the rest. The death toll would have been higher, but a large spring run of herring in the sound gave everyone at New Archangel new life.

In June, the blockhouse cannon boomed a salute to the returning *Juno* as it was towed into Sitka Harbor. Her hold was loaded with nearly seven hundred fanegas of wheat, almost one hundred and twenty fanegas of oats, one hundred and forty of peas and beans, as well as flour, salted meat, tallow, and salt.

As Zachar stepped from the schooner's yawl, his young son ran to greet him on spindly legs. Compared to Wolf's bone-thin body, Zachar felt exceedingly fat. Tears welled in his eyes as he stared at the boy's face, made gaunt from lack of food. Swinging the bag off his shoulder, he crouched down and hugged the child tightly, then looked beyond him at his wife.

Raven made no move to approach him as she stood beside Mikhail. His brother's arm was curved around her shoulder, silently claiming possession. Zachar knew. In his heart he knew what had transpired between his brother and his wife during his absence. A tightness choked his throat. He bowed his head and blinked rapidly to clear his eyes of the stinging tears.

Covering the action, he opened the bag and pulled out a present he'd brought for Wolf. The Californians had been eager to trade their foodstuffs and homemade goods for anything foreign-manufactured. His bag was filled with items he'd acquired. After giving Wolf his present, Zachar pulled out a brightly embroidered lace shawl and a fancy tortoiseshell hair comb, gifts for Raven.

Out of the corner of his eye, he saw her move away from Mikhail and toward him. With sadness, Zachar realized that Raven hadn't changed. Her loyalty and her company could still be bought. As she moved, Mikhail turned and walked slowly away. Zachar couldn't find it in his heart to be angry. He felt too much pain – for himself and Mikhail.

25 Sitka
Late Spring 1808

Fire belched from the cannon barrels atop the fortified knoll; their salute to the American ship entering the Russian port thundered over the full-fledged town below. But Zachar wasn't interested in the new arrival. In the last two years an increasing number of foreign ships had put in to Sitka, making it a port of call second in importance in the Pacific only to the Sandwich Islands.

Pausing on one of the board sidewalks that lined the streets, Zachar squinted to peer at the blurred figures around him. His eyes were failing him, damaged by too many years of facing the sun's glare off water and snow. A frightening thing for a hunter. None of the shapes resembled Raven, and he hurried on, passing the bakery and its yeasty aromas. He touched the colorful silk scarf in his pocket, unconsciously reassuring himself of its presence. As long as he gave Raven pretty things, he knew she would stay with him. If he ever stopped, she would leave.

As he approached the row of cabins brightened by spring flowers growing around them, two figures emerged from the second structure, the cabin belonging to his brother. Both women wore loose-fitting sarafans over their long-sleeved muslin shirts. Only a handful of women in New Archangel affected the Russian style of dress, other than Baranov's native woman, Anna Grigoryevna, who had recently been given the noble title Princess of Kenai by a special imperial ukase. The birth of Baranov's half-caste daughter, Irina, along with her brother's, had been legitimized by the same ukase.

Zachar hesitated, looking around the other cabins without sighting Raven, then angled reluctantly toward his mother, Tasha, and his daughter, Larissa. They had arrived a month ago from Kodiak. It had been Mikhail's idea to bring them here to live. Their mother was getting too old to do the heavy work demanded of her in the Banner household. Zachar was forced to agree that it was time she led a less arduous life, but he had quickly pointed out to Mikhail that his small hunter's cabin could provide neither the comfort nor the privacy that the two were entitled to have. He had carefully avoided mentioning the awkwardness that would result from having Raven and Wolf living there, too. Instead, he had suggested to Mikhail that Larissa and their mother live with him, since, as navigator, his higher status in the company meant his cabin was larger and better furnished. Makhail had agreed that his place was more suitable, and that his position would give them a better status in the community than that of a mere hunter. But both knew that Raven was the reason behind the living arrangements.

'Where are you going this fine morning?' Zachar forced a heartiness into his greeting.

'We're on our way to the harbor to see the ship that arrived.' Larissa was aglow with excitement.

Zachar stared at this stranger who was his daughter. At eighteen, she was in the full bloom of womanhood. Finely featured with dark, long-lashed eyes and sleek black hair, she attracted considerable notice from the men at New Archangel, accustomed as they were to the less refined – both in manner and looks – Aleut and Kolosh women. But few Russians made any advances toward her. Her trusting look of virginal innocence gave them pause.

That reticence was not fully shared by the nearly twenty Yankees who worked for the company in the shipbuilding yard at Sitka. Although she rarely ventured onto the streets without her grandmother, the Americans took advantage of any opportunity to speak to her, delighting in her accented English and her beautiful smile.

'Do you know what country she is from? Is it an English ship?'

'Yankee, I believe,' Zachar replied.

'I know you are used to ships coming here, Papa,' Larissa said, 'but I find it all very exciting.'

'I know you do.' His attention started to stray to the other cabins, with Raven still uppermost in his mind, when a coughing spasm shook his mother's frail body.

He didn't like the sound of it, nor the flecks of blood in the spittle that she quickly wiped away. She hadn't looked well when she arrived, but she had blamed her weakness on the seasickness she'd suffered during the voyage from Kodiak. Since Sitka was still without a company physician, Zachar couldn't dispute her claim. A month of good food and rest had brought some color back to her cheeks, but she was still very thin.

'How are you feeling?' He felt guilty that he hadn't spent more time with her since she'd come to Sitka, especially in the light of his recent decision, but he was no longer comfortable in his brother's cabin, knowing what he did about Mikhail's past association with Raven.

'Much better. The sun feels good today, doesn't it?' But its light didn't give any luster to her dull and coarse gray hair. She no longer stood tall and straight; her shoulders were bowed from constant coughing. The strength was gone from her face, replaced by an aura of fragility.

'Are you busy, Papa? It would be wonderful if you could walk to the harbor with us,' Larissa suggested hopefully.

Zachar hesitated and glanced anxiously down the row of cabins. 'She isn't there,' Tasha told him quietly. He was immediately uncomfortable at the way she had instinctively known who was on his mind, wondering what else she knew or guessed about his relationship with Raven. 'I saw her walk by a little while ago.'

She tilted her head to indicate the direction Raven had taken toward the main buildings along the harborfront. He should have seen her unless she had ducked out of sight to avoid him, a possiblity that further unsettled him.

Rather than comment on her observation, Zachar turned to the side. 'Shall we go?'

Together they walked toward the harbor. Zachar strained his eyes for a glimpse of Raven, but he didn't see her on any of the streets or sidewalks. As they passed the shipbuilding yard, there were breaks in the rhythmic rasp of a whipsaw cutting logs into boards and the clank of hammers striking anvils. More than one man paused in his labors to stare appreciatively at Larissa.

When they reached the shoreline, Zachar first scanned the small crowd that had drifted to the harbor, then gazed dispiritedly at the brig limping into the bay with a broken foremast. The knowledge that his brother, Mikhail, had been assigned to pilot incoming ships into the harbor that day gave him little consolation. It only meant Raven could be with anyone.

'Her name is the *Sea Gypsy*, Babushka,' Larissa said to her grandmother.

The ship's name struck a familiar chord in Zachar's memory, but he didn't try to recall why, dismissing it as just another ship that had previously visisted Sitka. He was too preoccupied with his own personal problems. He absently stared at the brig, his poor eyesight making its lines indistinct. Soon he'd be sailing away on a vessel not much different from this one. He didn't see that he had any other choice.

'The vessel interests you,' Tasha remarked.

'No, I –' Zachar halted his ready denial, deciding he could no longer postpone telling her his plans. Soon she would have to know anyway. 'I have been assigned to another post. I will be leaving within the month.'

She looked away and blinked at the tears that sprang into her eyes. 'I had hoped to have my children around me when I grew old. But it is in God's hands,' she declared, adopting the Russian philosophy. 'Where will you go?'

He dreaded telling her. 'My eyes are failing me, but all I know is hunting and furs.' After being a hunter all his life, the prospect of being reduced to doing menial chores such as working in the rope-walk or picking oakum was a wound to his pride. Worse, it would mean he wouldn't earn enough to keep Raven content. 'There is one place where a hunter doesn't need keen eyes.' He glanced at Larissa, but she was absorbed with the sailing vessel in the protected bay. When he looked back at his mother, the beginning of dismay had already formed in her expression, indicating that she had already guessed where he was going.

'Zachar, no,' she murmured.

'I am going to the Pribilofs.' He had made up his mind. The company had declared a two-year moratorium on the killing of fur seals to give them a chance to breed and increase their dwindling numbers.

Tasha breathed in sharply, triggering another coughing spasm. When it was over, she barely had the strength to stand. Zachar led her to a large boulder along the shoreline so she could sit and rest.

'Don't go there.' She clutched at his hand.

'I must.' He couldn't look at her haunted eyes. He didn't want to remember his uncle, Walks Straight, or his madness.

As the men rowed the yawl toward the shore, Caleb Stone studied the formidable bastion atop the knoll. Its cannons commanded the harbor and the forest and protected a two-storey building that was crowned with a beacon tower.

'You have built a veritable kremlin on the Pacific,' Caleb remarked to the pilot who had guided his vessel into the harbor. Although he'd been told the Russians had rebuilt their settlement, nothing had prepared him for this.

'It is the headquarters of the company now,' Mikhail Tarakanov replied in his stilted English.

Briefly, Caleb noted the blue and white flag flying smartly above the bastion, then the shipyard and the large hull of a nearly completed three-masted ship. He had hoped for some help in repairing the damage done to his vessel during a storm. It was obvious Sitka had the facilities.

'I had understood that Baranov had resigned.' The old wizened man in his black wig waited on the shore to welcome Caleb.

'The High Chamberlain Rezanov died while crossing Siberia in the winter. The directors asked Baranov to stay. There is much confusion in St. Petersburg because of Rezanov's death and the war in Europe.'

'I see.'

When the yawl landed on the beach, Caleb stepped out to greet Baranov. The Russian governor attempted a few remarks of welcome in broken English and after that relied on his interpreter, a Yankee in the company's service, roughly twenty-five years old, named Abram Jones. From the educated tenor of Jones's voice, Caleb suspected the man would have been more comfortable dressed in the snug dress coat, silk cap, and kid gloves of an undergraduate at Cambridge. He'd sailed on a ship once that had a supercargo from Cambridge. He'd never particularly liked the scholarly kind since then. It seemed that Baranov's former interpreter, the Bengalese Richard, had left two years ago with Baranov's permission to return to his home.

After accepting Baranov's invitation to come to his office, Caleb turned to take his leave of the harbor pilot, intending it to be no more than a perfunctory gesture, but he saw the young woman – barely more than a girl – standing beside Tarakanov. So lovely and innocent, she possessed an almost genteel quality that seemed out of place in this wild country. Although she returned his look, it was not done boldly. Nor did those incredibly long lashes lower in a look of coy flirtation.

With difficulty, Caleb managed to tear his gaze away from her and glance questioningly at the harbor pilot. 'I should thank you for your services this morning, but I find I am more inclined to beg an introduction.'

Tarakanov's hesitation was momentary. 'My niece, Larissa Tarakanova.'

'Captain Caleb Stone of the *Sea Gypsy* out of Salem.' He took her slender hand and bowed over it, raising it to his lips and pressing them against it for a lingering second while she curtsied gracefully.

'It is a pleasure to make your acquaintance, Captain.' Although it was evident the formal response was something she had learned by rote, her delightfully accented English more than compensated for the artificial wording.

'The pleasure is all mine, I assure you.' Caleb straightened, wishing he could tell Baranov to go to hell, but duty came first. 'Perhaps we will meet again.'

As he accompanied Baranov to the steps leading to the fortress built on top of the bluff, his thoughts remained on the young woman Larissa, who was so unlike the Indian squaws and half-breeds who usually cohabited with the Russian hunters. Distracted by his thoughts, he failed to notice the raven-haired Kolosh woman who stared so intently at him when he walked past her.

If it was a surprise to find a lovely, genteel woman like Larissa in Sitka, the governor's residence was an even greater surprise to Caleb, situated as it was thousands of miles from civilization. Constructed out of giant square-hewn timbers, the two-storey building was both a residence, with sleeping quarters upstairs, and an administration center for the Russian American Company, with an office that overlooked Sitka Sound. Besides the kitchens and reception rooms, there was a large banquet hall complete with a huge stone fireplace and a dais at one end of the room for musicians.

Most unexpected of all was the library. In addition to a collection of fine paintings, it housed twelve hundred volumes. The books, some richly bound, covered such subjects as theology, history, astronomy, navigation, mathematics, and metallurgy, as well as some literary works. Half were in Russian; the rest were in French, German, Latin, Spanish, and Italian. An interesting assortment of ship models shared the shelf space with the many books, and framed letters hung on the walls with the paintings.

The library also contained a pianoforte, shipped all the way around the Horn.

Caleb was very impressed with the progress the Russian American Company had made in such a short period of time. Although he had stopped at Sitka for repairs, he requested Baranov's permission to trade in the area. In actuality, Baranov couldn't prevent him from doing so, which Caleb knew, but to do so without his permission would mean Baranov would never grant him any special favors, such as contracting to use his Aleut hunters on a share basis to poach sea otter off the California coast, a highly lucrative enterprise.

Two days passed before Caleb was able to complete the arrangements for the repairs to his vessel, negotiate a fair price for a portion of his cargo that Baranov wanted to buy, and obtain permission to trade in the Russian territory. During that time, Baranov kept him constantly entertained, introducing him to the questionable pleasure of a Russian steam bath and continually plying him with liquor.

Finally their business was concluded. Caleb left the harbor area and wandered through the main section of town that spread out from the base of the knoll. Baranov had told him the combined population of Russian, Yankee, Aleut, and Creole was roughly a thousand people. Caleb could believe it as he passed the commissary, bakery, storehouses, barracks, and kitchens. A high palisade surrounded the town, broken only by imposing gates. Military discipline was evident everywhere. The guard was changed regularly and each man saluted smartly.

As he wandered into the residential area, he noticed the patchwork of vegetable plots, the young plants shooting up in the long daylight hours of late spring. Flowers bloomed in front of nearly every cabin, vivid against the lush green of the land.

His steps slowed when he noticed the girl working in the garden. He'd known he would find her sooner or later. For a while, Caleb simply watched her. She wore a Russian costume similar to the one she'd had on when he first met her. This time, however, the long sleeves were rolled back a few turns and the voluminous material of the loose apronlike dress was belted at the waist, giving him a clearer idea of her shape.

Bending at the waist, he reached down and snapped the stem of a large yellow poppy, then he walked across the blossom-strewn ground to the garden, indifferent to the plants he trampled along the way. She didn't notice him until he was only a few feet away. After her initial start of surprise, she appeared pleased to see him. She quickly smoothed the sides of her dark hair that was pulled back in a bun.

'You look lovely, Miss Tarakanov,' he assured her. 'There's just one thing wrong.'

He displayed the poppy in his hand as he reached up and tucked the stem behind her left ear. Somehow he had known she wouldn't flinch at his touch. She appeared as pure as all the prim and proper Boston girls back home, yet he knew she wasn't the kind to giggle or feign a swoon. As he took his hand away, she reached up to touch the soft petals.

'I stole that just for you.' Caleb smiled. 'The Hawaiian girls wear flowers in their hair like that. And they string them into necklaces, too.'

'Why?'

'It's a custom. Something about if they wear a flower over their left ear, they are married. The right ear means they are not. Or maybe it's the other way around. I always get it confused.' He watched her lips curve into a smile, liking the shape of them.

'Someday I should like to see this place Hawaii. Other Yankees have told me it is very warm all the time. Is this so?'

'Yes'

'It must be like California,' she decided. 'Are the women of Hawaii as beautiful as the women of California?'

Caleb wondered if her question was an attempt to elicit another compliment from him, but her curiosity appeared to be genuine. 'I wouldn't know. I have never met any California women.' The Spanish ports along the southern coast were still closed to all foreign ships. 'Who told you about them?'

'My father. He journeyed on the ship of the high lord chamberlain to the village of San Francisco. He spoke to me of the beautiful California lady the high chamberlain was to marry.'

'No foreign ships are allowed there. How did he get permission to land?' Caleb frowned.

The blank look in her eyes told him she had not known entry was forbidden. There was a faint lift of her shoulders. 'He was the high chamberlain.'

The title meant nothing to him, although the Russain must have been someone of importance. For a minute, Caleb had

296

wondered whether California was being opened up to foreign trade, offering another market for his goods, but apparently the Russian's visit to San Francisco was an exception – unless an exclusive trade agreement had been reached. These damned Russians are so close-mouthed, Caleb thought, and remembered the way Baranov had pumped him for information about the coast to the south, asking about California and the New Albion area around the mouth of the Columbia River.

'How often do Russian ships go to California?'

She shook her head. 'This I do not know. I have heard only of this one. Is it not as you said ships are not permitted there?'

'Yes, it is.' Caleb smiled, pleased to discover she wasn't stupid.

Suddenly she became very alert and looked toward the cabin. As Caleb turned to locate the cause of her distraction, he caught the muffled, rasping sound that came from inside the log dwelling – a sound that vaguely reminded him of someone sawing wood.

'It is Babushka. She is not well.' She looked at him apologetically, then ran toward the cabin, the long, voluminous skirt of her overdress swirling about her legs.

The sound he heard was coughing, Caleb realized. He hesitated, then followed Larissa to the cabin, more out of curiosity and reluctance to have their meeting end so abruptly than out of a desire to help. The door stood open and Caleb walked in. Larissa sat on a cot in the corner of the room close to the fireplace, supporting an old woman whose body heaved with a racking cough.

Idly he inspected the interior of the snugly built cabin. The few pieces of furniture in the room appeared to be hand-hewn. Yet there were touches that softened the crudeness of the furnishings. A muslin cloth, artfully embroidered with bright flowers, covered the table on which a dented samovar sat. Another embroidered scarf lay over an old, scratched sea chest. Ivory carvings, some of the finest Caleb had seen, occupied little niches in the room. A variety of grass baskets, small and large, were put to utilitarian uses, intricate native designs woven into them in bright colors. His trader's eye noticed that the utensils and tableware appeared to be of European or American origin. All in all, the impression he gathered was one of homely comforts, a blend of primitive and civilized.

As the coughing subsided, Caleb returned his attention to Larissa and the old woman. He noticed the red stains on the rag

Larissa took from the woman's spindly hands. Coughing up blood was a sign of consumption. Knowing the old woman would slowly waste away, he viewed her with a detached kind of pity. Larissa started to lower her onto the cot so the old woman could lie down.

'It would be better if she could sit up a little,' Caleb said.

Ignoring the girl's startled glance, he walked over to the cot. There were no pillows, so Caleb gathered up the fur robes that were piled at the foot, absently noticing the needlework stitching around the lining. He used the folded robes to prop the old woman in a semi-reclining position. Although she was a tall woman, her body felt almost weightless as he gently lowered her shoulders and back onto the fur cushions. Despite the exhaustion etched in her face, her dark eyes inspected him. As he straightened, she said something in Russian to Larissa.

'Babushka . . . Grandmother thanks you for your kindness.'

'Babushka is welcome.' Caleb bent slightly at the waist in a semblance of a bow, then straightened, continuing to study the old woman's parchment-like skin. 'How long has she been sick?'

'The cough grows worse for two years now. She works when she is tired.' Her hand indicated a bowl of half-crushed berries on a wooden chair. 'I make her rest. Soon she will feel better.' Caleb doubted that simple rest would cure the old woman's malady, but he kept his opinion to himself. After another brief exchange with her grandmother in Russian, Larissa turned to him. 'Grandmother asks if you would drink tea with us.'

'I would like that.' Caleb smiled.

While the water heated in the samovar, they talked. Caleb made sure that Larissa did most of the talking, prompting her with questions when necessary. He enjoyed listening to the musical lilt of her voice and the charming accent of her English.

By the time the tea was ready to serve, he had managed to learn that her grandmother had raised her after her mother had drowned during a tidal wave at Kodiak, that she had attended a school at Kodiak run by a Russian priest named Father Herman, and that the wife of the company manager at Kodiak had trained her in the womanly arts of cooking, sewing, and homemaking. It explained much of the refinement – the air of convent-raised innocence and high moral character he detected in her.

'What about your father? Is he alive?' Caleb had noticed the carved pipestand by the chair, yet she hadn't mentioned any man other than her uncle – the harbor pilot who had guided his ship into port.

'Yes. He lives here in Sitka, but he's a hunter and away much of the time. That's why Babushka and I live with my Uncle Mikhail.' She was sensitive to the fact that Zachar obviously hadn't wanted her to live with him. It had been that way all her life, and all her life she had yearned to be close to him, yet she had seen more of her uncle than she ever had of her father.

When she'd arrived in New Archangel, she had hoped things would be different, but nothing had changed. Right from the start, she had sensed an estrangement between her father and uncle and suspected that her Uncle Mikhail disapproved of her father living in sin with that Kolosh woman. She knew it was wrong, yet she loved him anyway. And if sometimes it hurt to see the affection he lavished on his son, Wolf, she forgave him. But she didn't know Caleb Stone well enough to confide any of that to him, so she spoke of other things, steering the conversation away from the subject of her father.

An aromatic blend of China tea scented the air, triggering thoughts of Boston in Caleb's mind. Just for a minute, he allowed himself to picture Larissa sipping tea in the parlor of a house in the Bulfinch-designed Tontine Crescent and to imagine the stir she would create. Even in those peasant clothes, she radiated a beauty and dignity that few of the supposedly aristocratic ladies he'd met could match. With a wife like her to ornament the mansion he intended to build on Beacon Hill someday . . . Caleb laughed when he realized he was contemplating marriage.

'Why do you laugh?' Larissa stiffened self-consciously. 'The wrong word I used, perhaps?'

'No. I was laughing at something else entirely. It had nothing to do with anything you said or did.'

She studied him for several seconds before accepting his assurances. The long skirt made a swishing sound as she walked to the cloth-covered table. The teapot sat atop the samovar, kept hot by the rising steam. As she reached for the pot, Caleb noticed the long slanting rays of sunlight that came through the window.

'More tea?' she asked.

'No. I'm afraid the time has slipped away from me.' Caleb stood up and walked over to set his empty cup on the table. It brought him beside her. 'I didn't intend to stay so late. I guess I can blame it on your charming company.'

'I had pleasure, too.' She didn't attempt to hide the regret she felt at his leaving.

'May I have your permission to come again?'

'Yes, that would please me.' Her quick smile soon assumed a wistful quality that Caleb found appealing, yet sad.

'Is something wrong?'

'I feel sad that it will take only a week to make the repairs to your ship.'

Her candor charmed him; she had been sufficiently interested in him to inquire about the length of time it would take for the repairs to be made to his ship, because he certainly hadn't told her.

'Maybe I can arrange for it to take longer.' He winked at her, and she laughed.

She stood at the door as he walked away from the cabin. When he turned down the street toward the harbor, Caleb saw her take the flower from her hair and inhale its sweet fragrance. As he struck out for the harbor, his rolling seaman's gait became a proud swagger.

Larissa waited until he was out of sight, then slowly closed the door and leaned against it. Closing her eyes, she carried the yellow poppy to her bosom and held it there. The handsome, clean-shaven Yankee captain, Caleb Stone, was the most exciting man she had ever encountered. Certainly there was no one in Kodiak who could compare to him. Others had stared at her with that hungry look before, especially some of the Yankees. She was not so naive that she didn't know what it meant. But none had ever produced this warm, tingling sensation inside her.

And he'd asked to come back. She covered her mouth with her hand, trying to smother the laughter that rippled from her throat. She spun into the room, hugging her arms tightly to her chest, feeling she was going to burst inside.

'He has gone?'

'Babushka.' Abruptly, self-consciously, she halted her gay dance. 'I thought you were asleep.' Quickly, she turned to the samovar. 'There is some tea left. Shall I pour you a cup?'

'Yes.' Tasha waited until Larissa brought the cup to the cot and sat down beside her. 'Do not let yourself care for him, my child. He will leave soon. They always leave.'

'I know.' Larissa avoided her grandmother's pleading look. She didn't want to upset her by arguing that she knew it wasn't going to happen to her.

Again Caleb dined at the governor's residence with Baranov. It was a sumptuous feast – roasted wild geese, venison, halibut, Russian bread, pickles, cakes, and the famous bowl of hot spiked punch sitting in the center of the long banquet table. But Caleb had difficulty concentrating on the old Russian's company. Over Baranov's objections, he called an early end to the night and took his leave of the Russian American governor who had dressed for the occasion in a black silk waistcoat, silver-buckled slippers, and a black dress wig that didn't fit him much better than the old one.

A heavy fog rolled off the sound and swirled over the veranda, concealing the top of the flagstaff that stood in the center of the knoll's parade ground. High overhead, the beacon light pierced the gray layers to throw out its signal. The sentry's call, echoing from post to post, sounded hollow and eerie in the fog-wrapped stillness.

At the top of the steps, Caleb paused to look around. It occured to him that Larissa had probably gone to sleep hours ago. He sighed and started down the stone stairs.

The dinner with Baranov had started him wondering if there might not be an advantage to having a Russian wife. Thus far, no merchant, not even John Jacob Astor, had succeeded in persuading Baranov to sign an exclusive contract to buy supplies only from him. A contract like that would be a coup for any trader. With it, he could buy a fleet of ships. Baranov just might look favorably on a man who married a Russian woman.

The idea appealed to Caleb, more so because it provided justification for the strong attraction he already felt towards Larissa. It wasn't enough to have a beautiful, exciting wife. A man must choose wisely as well. He was whistling a tune as he headed for the strip of beach where his boat crew stood by the yawl.

'Boston man.' A low voice called softly to him. 'Caleb Stone.'

He halted and peered into the swirling mist. A figure appeared – a Tlingit woman dressed in some strange faded robe that seemed oddly familiar.

'What do you want?' He was in no mood to be solicited by some native whore.

Instead of answering, she walked closer. Caleb frowned,

301

knowing he had seen those black, black eyes somewhere before but unable to identify her. A boy about five or six years old leaned heavily against her side, almost too tired to stand.

'Do you not remember Raven?' she murmured.

The named finally jarred his memory. He smiled without humor and rubbed his left arm. 'I still carry the scar of your knife,' he said.

'Is that all you remember?'

'No.' But he hadn't the slightest desire to resume their past relationship. 'Is that why you wanted to see me?'

'Maybe.' She shrugged. 'Maybe I think you want to see your son.'

'My what?'

She tipped the boy's chin up so he could see the child's sleepy face. 'See his eyes. They are like yours.'

'That proves nothing. Just because your bastard has blue eyes doesn't make me his father,' Caleb scoffed.

'Maybe that Larissa woman will think it does. I see you with her today, putting flowers in her hair. Your son grows all the time. He needs food, clothes. Caleb has many things on his ship. Keep son a long time.'

'Are you trying to blackmail me?' He took a threatening step toward her.

A sudden shout in Russian distracted Caleb. A man loomed out of the fog. Moving quickly, he planted himself between Caleb and Raven.

'What happens here?' the Russian demanded.

'That Indian bitch is trying to convince me I fathered that bastard of hers so I'll pay her off.'

A look of shock widened the Russian's eyes. Caleb saw their blue color and instantly recognized the man as the survivor of the massacre he'd picked up that same summer. Zachar Tarakanov was his name. He remembered it all clearly now – even Raven's admission that she'd been the Russian's woman.

'You?' The man's voice wavered.

'It's a lie, Zachar. Yes, I remember you.' Caleb guessed the man believed the boy was his son. 'She's probably played this trick on a half dozen men. If anyone's likely to be the father, you are.'

Zachar stared at him, his eyes clouded with doubt. At last, he turned away and scooped the child into his arms, holding him tightly. He muttered something to Raven, then reached out and shoved her toward the village after she failed to move on her own. The fog quickly swallowed them. As his anger faded, Caleb felt the first pang of worry that Raven might carry out her threat to tell Larissa. Larissa. Her last name was Tarakanov, too. And he started wondering whether she was related to Zachar.

In the cabin, Zachar laid the boy on the cot. Wolf was asleep almost as soon as Zachar tucked the blanket around him. For a long time he stood by the cot and stared at the boy he'd grown to love so deeply.

'Is Wolf my son?' He could barely get the words out. His mind echoed and re-echoed with the tormenting question. He turned to face Raven, tortured by doubt. He vibrated with the hate he felt for her. It consumed him as love once had. 'Am I his father?' Zachar demanded hoarsely.

She turned her back to him. He charged across the room, grabbed her by the shoulders, and spun her around. She offered no resistance as he violently shook her.

'Answer me!'

But no sound came from her. His chest hurt so much it felt an invisible hand was squeezing him. Each breath was a half-sob of pain. He stopped, although he unconsciously continued to dig his fingers into her flesh. Her head was thrown far back, exposing her throat. He longed to choke the answer out of her. The defiant contempt in her face mocked him, dared him to try.

Her silence defeated him. Zachar let her go as his lower lip quivered and tears stung his eyes. He felt impotent, stripped of pride and honor.

'You are a stupid man,' Raven jeered. 'I could have got many things from that Boston man.'

'Why? Is Wolf his son?'

'If I say no, how will you know that is truth?'

He stared at her as the cruel realization hit him. No matter what answer she gave him, the doubt would always be there. He could no longer believe her. Wolf might be his son, but he'd never know for certain, because he couldn't take her word for it and no one else could give him the answer.

'The Yankee denied he was the father. He wouldn't have paid you anything,' Zachar retaliated, trying to undermine her confidence.

'He has eyes for the daughter of your dead wife.'

'Larissa?'

'I could have had many pretty things – pretty like this robe he gave me once.' She rubbed her hand over the worn and faded garment, stained and shabby from wear.

'He gave you that?' Zachar stared at the damning evidence that she had been with him that summer of the massacre. In a fit of rage, he ripped it off her, the rotting threads tearing easily, and threw it on the smoldering logs in the fireplace, indifferent to the rake of her nails as she tried to stop him.

Smoke billowed thickly around the torn robe. An instant later, flames exploded to blacken forever the brightly striped cloth. The sudden flare of light illuminated Raven's now naked body, but the sight of it no longer aroused his lust.

'I can get others. I can get many others,' she announced defiantly. 'Caleb will give them to me or I will tell her.'

This time he grabbed her by the throat. 'No, you won't. From now on you will be satisfied with what I give you, because if I ever learn that you have tried to get presents from another man – or if I hear that you have spread this lie about my son to any member of my family or my friends – I will kill you.'

He flung her away from him. Raven stumbled sideways, crashing into the fireplace and striking her cheek against a rough stone. For a moment the whole room went black in front of her eyes. She cupped her hand against her cheek and felt the warm blood running from the cut. Loathing and contempt rose within her as she watched the stupid Russian walk to the cot.

26

Larissa and Caleb strolled along the shore path that was so often frequented by Baranov. They walked close together, their arms occasionally brushing, the fullness of her long skirt sweeping against his leg. The smell of rain was in the air. Already they could see the gray sheets falling on the slopes of Mount Edgecumbe.

'I suppose we should hurry,' Caleb suggested reluctantly. 'Those clouds are going to let loose any moment.'

'We should.' But she slowed her steps.

Caleb watched her push the near side of the loosely hooding wool scarf away from her face. She smiled at him, her dark eyes shining. She looked so beautiful to him.

It had been something of a shock to him when he'd learned earlier in the week that Zachar Tarakanov was her father, but he'd been reassured by the fact that she had very little contact with him. Knowing Raven as he did, Caleb was glad Zachar kept the two apart. It lessened the chances of Raven causing trouble.

In the last week, Caleb had spent every possible hour he could courting her more ardently than he had any woman in his life. Larissa exhibited a rare combination of serenity and vitality that was like a heady wine to him. She soothed and excited him at the same time. With each passing day, Caleb had become more convinced of her suitability, both practically and passionately.

'Soon the repairs to your ship will be finished.' The regret in her voice was unmistakable.

'I've nearly run out of things to have fixed,' he admitted. 'Three days. Maybe I can stretch it to four.'

'Then you will leave to trade with the Kolosh for furs.' She kept her head down as she walked two more steps. 'I will miss you.'

Caleb halted. 'Larissa.' She stopped as well and gazed longingly at him. 'I never realized how very lonely my life has been until I shared this last week with you.' He hesitated. 'Am I speaking too soon?'

'No,' she said quickly, unconsciously straining toward him.

Not once had he dared any more than a lingering kiss on her hand. Now he kissed her lips. He felt their tremor of innocence and uncertainty. But her hesitation was fleeting as she responded with warm, eager pressure. He forgot his restraint and kissed her hard, gathering her tightly into his embrace.

She arched back from him, her hands pushing at his chest. Caleb immediately released her, angry with himself for having frightened her with his passion. A pelting rain struck before he had a chance to apologize and beg her forgiveness. She turned and started running toward the settlement.

'Larissa, wait.' Caleb ran after her.

The rain came down hard. The muslin shirt under her sarafan was already drenched by the time Caleb draped his coat over her head and around her shoulders. They ran together toward her cabin.

As they arrived there, she reached for the latch. 'Larissa, wait.' Rain ran down his face and plastered his shirt against his skin. She paused without turning from the door. Her grandmother was inside, maybe her uncle as well. He couldn't tell her the things he wanted to say in front of them. Abruptly, she swept off his coat and pushed it into his hands. 'I didn't mean –'

Her fingers touched his lips to silence him. Just as quickly she raised up on her toes and kissed him, giving him a taste of her own passion. Her action stunned him. By the time he reached for her, all his hand touched was the slippery cloth of her wet skirt as she darted inside the cabin.

Caleb stared at the door for a minute, then he smiled widely, his spirits suddenly soaring. He hadn't frightened her after all, he realized, and walked away from the cabin chuckling to himself, indifferent to the drenching rain and his wet clothes.

'She will not be good for you. She will never please you the way I have.' Raven's taunting voice caught him in midstride.

The laughter died in his throat as Caleb turned toward the blanket-wrapped figure huddled in the narrow space between two buildings. After a quick glance over his shoulder at the cabin to make sure he wasn't observed, he stepped off the planked walk into the open passage.

'What are you doing here?'

Raven lifted back the hooding blanket and turned her head to show him her right cheek. A purpling bruise radiated from the angry red cut on her cheek. 'Zachar did this.'

'You deserved it. I would have done more than that.'

'Yes.' She turned, showing him the perfect side of her face, her black eyes glowing, her lips curving in a near smile. 'You are the only man to fight me and win. You made me cry out in pain – and in pleasure.' She moved toward him, her tawny face shining with the rainwater. 'I know your ship will be finished in two days. Take me with you.'

'No.'

'We are alike, Caleb. You wish to trade for furs. I will show you the villages that have many.'

'Which villages?'

'They trade only for guns. Do you have guns?'

'Yes.' Caleb had no intention of complying with Baranov's edict against selling them to the Indians. 'Where are the villages?'

'I will show you.'

'I don't need a guide.'

'I can trade for you. Get many furs for one gun,' she reasoned, then quickly switched to another tactic when she saw the first wasn't working. 'Zachar is leaving soon to go to some island far to the north. He wishes to take me. But I have no wish to leave the land of my people. I go with you. You take me from here.'

'No.' Caleb shook his head. 'If you want to leave Zachar, go back to your people. Or don't they want your kind either?'

Her expression grew cold. 'Maybe I talk to Larissa.'

'That boy isn't mine. But if you open your mouth to her I'll tell the first shaman I meet that you're a witch and that it is you who keeps your people from taking this land back from the Russians.' He watched the color drain from her face as fear leaped into her eyes.

Once he'd seen a Tlingit medicine man expose a witch to the tribe. She had confessed her guilt only after he'd held her under water until she'd nearly drowned, then set her naked on a bed of hot ashes. The tribe had hanged her.

Raven's silence satisfied Caleb that she wouldn't carry out her threat. He left her and walked back to the boardwalk. There was no one on the street as he stepped from between the two buildings and headed toward the harbor.

*

The shipbuilder informed Caleb that the *Sea Gypsy*'s repairs would be completed on the morrow, a day earlier than he'd originally thought, and exactly when Raven had claimed. He spent an idle moment wondering how she had known before dismissing it as unimportant.

At best he could stall another day. After nearly two weeks in port, the novelty of the place had worn off for his crew. They were getting restless. This was the trading season, and other merchant ships were getting the jump on them, while they didn't have a single pelt in their hold. He'd have trouble with the crew if he tried to delay any longer. In truth, he couldn't afford to lose more of the season, not on his first voyage as skipper and owner of the brig.

Resolutely he pushed off and started across the street. Everything glistened in the sun-dazzled morning. The rain-washed clarity of the air gave a jewel-like sparkle to the sapphire waters of the bay and the emerald forests of the islands. Even the timbered buildings in town had a polished look to them.

The Russian town bustled with activity. It seemed everyone was eager to be outside in the sunlight after yesterday's confining rain.

Old Tasha Tarakanov sat on a chair in the front yard of her log home letting the sunlight warm her frail bones. Caleb was conscious of the way she watched him. He suspected she disapproved of him, althought she had said or done nothing to indicate it. And it was her approval that he needed. He'd known all along that she played the major role in Larissa's life. Her father was of minor importance. In the little time he'd had, he'd done his best to win the old woman over, but he wasn't sure he'd succeeded.

Caleb spied Larissa hoeing out the weeds in the vegetable garden, a task that earned her a ruble a day from the company. The bright silk scarf covering her head was tied at the nape of her neck, and a belt girded the loose-fitting sarafan at her waistline. She looked up as if she'd been expecting him and dropped the hoe to come hurrying to meet him.

'I hoped you would come.' Her eyes sparkled.

'You knew I would,' Caleb mocked lightly.

Her smile widened. She made a small movement toward him, then hesitated and glanced over her shoulder as if suddenly remembering her grandmother. She took him by the arm and led him up the path to the old woman.

'Good morning, Babushka.' From the start, he'd taken the

liberty of calling her by the Russian word for grandmother, hoping to endear himself to her. 'You look like you are enjoying this fine weather. The sunshine will do you good.'

Larissa began a translation before he finished speaking, then did the same when her grandmother replied. 'She greets you and agrees it is a fine morning.'

Taking the soft package from under his arm, Caleb presented it to the old woman. 'This is for you, Babushka.' He laid it on her lap. Each time he'd visited the cabin, he'd brought a little gift – some tea or sugar, and once some tobacco for Larissa's Uncle Mikhail. This time the occasion was more momentous and he'd increased the value of the gift accordingly. The bundle contained several yards of fine English cloth. He waited for her to unwrap it, but she made no move to do so. 'Tell her to open it.'

Larissa passed on his message. The old woman tipped her head back to look at him, her gaze steady. As she began speaking, Larissa started the translation a phrase or two behind. 'She thanks you for the gift, but she wonders why you bring her presents. She asks – *Babushka!*' Larissa's cheeks reddened.

'What did she say?' Caleb frowned.

Obviously embarrassed, Larissa hesitated over her answer. 'In the Aleutian Islands . . . where my grandmother was born . . . when a man wishes to . . . to take a woman to his home, he gives . . . presents to her parents. If the gifts are accepted, she goes to live with him. That is the custom.'

'And she thinks I'm trying to buy you.'

She lifted her gaze to examine his face. 'I have been baptized into the Holy Faith. To live with a man without God's blessing would be a sin.'

'Tell your grandmother that it is true I do love you and want you to be my wife, but I bring her presents only out of admiration and respect,' he said. 'It is also true that I came today to seek your family's permission to marry you. If there was a priest at Sitka I would ask him to perform the marriage sacrament, but there is none. Ask your grandmother what I should do.'

The wondrous joy that radiated from her expression left no doubt that she accepted his suit. Her lips parted speechlessly. Turning, she sank to her knees beside her grandmother's chair. A torrent of Russian spilled from her, eager and entreating.

As Tasha listened to her granddaughter, a chilling emptiness crept into her body. She suddenly felt very old and very tired.

309

'You would leave with him to go to this place called Boston?'

Dim was her memory of the day she sailed from Massacre Bay at Attu with Andrei Tolstykh, never again to see her mother, Winter Swan, her uncle, Many Whiskers, or old Weaver Woman. She gazed at the dark green mass of spruce and cedar towering beyond the stockade walls, growing thickly like so many stalks of grass. How she missed her treeless island and its ever-blowing wind.

'Caleb says we will come back often.' Larissa's voice roused Tasha from her time-misted thoughts. 'This is where he trades for furs. He says maybe he will also build a cabin here. When we come back, that is where we would live.'

'Come back.' The phrase reminded Tasha that Andrei had also promised her mother that he would bring her back to Attu. She had believed. She couldn't have known the Russians would alter forever their way of life. Now the Yankees came. Tasha folded the wool shawl across her chest, feeling so cold.

'Babushka, I love him. He leaves soon.'

'And you would go with him?' She stared at her granddaughter.

'It's not that I want to leave you, Babushka, but I love him.'

Tasha shook her head tiredly. 'I must think.'

'Babushka,' Larissa pleaded.

'Tell him I will speak to my sons.' She rose from her chair and walked slowly to the cabin, her steps as heavy as her heart.

A tear slid down her cheek as Larissa watched her grandmother go. She felt torn. So blinded by happiness, she had not considered the pain of leaving until she'd seen it in her grandmother's eyes.

She felt the warm pressure of Caleb's hands on her shoulders and turned. 'She wants to talk to my father and uncle. Caleb, she is so ill.'

'And you are young. It isn't as though you are all the family she has. She won't be alone. She has her sons. If it worries you, I will make provisions to see that she is cared for.'

'I wish –' But she was confused, uncertain of what she wished.

'Come walk with me,' he urged.

But she felt the tug in the opposite direction. 'Perhaps I should go to her.'

'Larissa, we may have so little time.'

Swayed by his appeal, she let herself be led away from the cabin.

Caleb paused beside the large flat-topped rock that lay on the curved beach and gathered Larissa into his arms, kissing her with a restrained ardor. When he lifted his head, he continued to hold her, conscious of the disturbed rush of her breathing.

'I can't bear the thought of leaving you, Larissa,' he murmured against the smooth skin of her temple. 'You do love me, don't you?'

'With all my heart,' she whispered fervently.

'What will we do if your family refuses us permission?' He wanted this alliance to cement his trade relationship in Russian America, not create a rift.

'I don't know.'

'Somehow you must convince them to give consent. I promise you I'll see that your grandmother lives comfortably the rest of her days.'

'I –'

'Captain! Praise be to Saint Patrick that I found you!' His second mate, O'Shaughnessy, hurried toward them, out of breath, his cheeks as red as his flame-colored hair. Caleb immediately stepped backward, putting a proper distance between himself and Larissa. 'By your leave, miss.' The Irishman belatedly doffed his hat to her before continuing. 'I searched this Rooskie town from stem to stern for you, Cap'n.'

'What do you want?'

' 'Tis the first mate what wants you, Cap'n. He sent me t' fetch ya' double-quick.'

'Why? What's wrong?'

'It's the Rooskie governor, Baranov. He comes out and boards the *Sea Gypsy* without so much as a 'by-your-leave.' When Hicks questions him, he demands to see the manifest.'

'Hicks refused, didn't he?'

'Baranov brought his soldiers with him. T'was show him the manifest or fight. With half the crew ashore, t'wouldn't ha' been much of a fight, sir. He had me get the manifest, then ordered me t' find you.'

Caleb swore under his breath. 'He'll see the damned guns and ammunition listed.'

'Aye, an' I tole Hicks there'll be the devil to pay and no hot pitch when he does.'

'Come.' Caleb took Larissa by the arm.

'What is wrong?'

'I don't have time to explain. I must return to my ship.' But he sensed he had offered her little reassurance. 'It's nothing for you to worry about.'

When they reached the harbor area, Caleb gratefully accepted Larissa's assurance that he didn't need to escort her back to the cabin, and he climbed into the waiting boat to be rowed to the *Gypsy*. He studied the cluster of men on the brig's deck, recognizing Baranov among them. He knew Baranov would be angry. His hope for a trade alliance or, at the very least, favorable trade concessions was in jeopardy.

As he boarded the ship, Caleb assumed an air of congeniality. 'This is an unexpected visit, Aleksandr Andreevich. You have hardly given me a fair chance to return your generous hospitality.' He didn't give Baranov a chance to reply, fully aware the Russian understood more English than he let on. 'I hope my officers have treated you well in my absence. Let's go below and have a drink – away from all this noise.' He waved a hand to indicate the carpenters, who were more interested in watching the confrontation than they were in finishing the repairs to the ship. 'I have a bottle of very excellent brandy that I've been keeping for a special occasion such as this.'

'The governor is not here on a social visit,' Baranov's translator stated.

Caleb feigned surprise, then smiled. 'Ah, the governor has learned I've been calling regularly on one of his young Russian maidens, Larissa Tarakanov, and has decided to intercede to make certain my intentions are honorable. Let me assure you, my intentions are more than honorable. I'm totally smitten with the lady in question. As a matter of fact, I intended to come to see you in the hopes of enlisting your support on my behalf to convince the girl's grandmother to give us her permission to marry.'

Nothing he said seemed to make any impression on the Russian governor. His expression remained aloof and forbidding. When he spoke through his interpreter, it was not in response to Caleb's personal declaration.

'It has come to the governor's attention that one hundred and thirty muskets are listed on your cargo manifest.'

'That's correct.' Caleb nodded.

'Why was this information deliberately withheld from the governor?'

'It wasn't. With all due respect to the governor, I wasn't asked whether I carried any guns.'

'You are aware that the sale of guns to the Kolosh is forbidden in Russian America.'

312

'I am.'

'And you saw what can happen when the Kolosh have such weapons in their possession. You witnessed the result of the massacre at the Redoubt St. Mikhail and still you bring guns to trade.'

Caleb chose his words carefully. 'I must confess that I didn't consider it to be my problem until very recently. Now, with my future bride's family living here at Sitka, I have naturally become concerned about the safety of those who live here. If the governor would be interested in purchasing the guns and ammunition to supplement the weapons in his arsenal, I would be more than happy to sell them to the company.'

The Yankee-born interpreter appeared hesitant about translating Baranov's reply. 'The governor . . . instructs that you order your crew to unload the illegal goods from your cargo hold. There will be boats alongside shortly to take them ashore.'

'And the terms?' Caleb demanded warily.

'Captain Stone, the governor is seizing the weaponry.'

He stiffened. 'On what authority?'

'He is seizing your illegal cargo on the grounds that you have committed an act unfriendly to the Russian government. I wouldn't protest too strongly if I were you, Captain Stone,' the interpreter cautioned. 'I think he believed part of your story about having a change of heart, but if you argue with him, he's likely to seize your ship. You know how violently opposed he is to the sale of guns to the Indians.'

'Such a seizure would be illegal,' Caleb insisted, clenching his jaw to control his anger.

'Illegal or not, you would be hard put to do anything about it. Washington is a long way from here. If he takes your ship and places you under arrest, it would be a long time before they could do anything about it.'

Ultimately Caleb had to agree that his position was untenable. He bowed stiffly to Baranov. 'Tell the governor that I am delighted to donate the weapons to the defense of Sitka. My crew will have them on deck within the hour.'

'The repairs to your ship will be finished before nightfall. I suggest you sail with tomorrow's tide. You are no longer welcome in this port, Captain.'

All his conciliatory verbiage had gone for naught, Caleb realized. His most valuable trading commodity was about to be taken with no compensation and his ship ordered out of port. Since he'd failed to talk his way out of this, he'd take a new tack and fight. Not now, though. Of the eight crewmen on deck, he counted only three who were armed. There were fifteen soldiers with Baranov, and no doubt the carpenters from the shipyard would side with him in a fight. He unconsciously doubled his hands into fists at his side, rigid with anger and aware he must bide his time. When Baranov sent his soldiers back to offload the guns, he'd have his crew armed and waiting for them.

'Whatever it is you're thinking, Captain' – Baranov's interpreter eyed him with a mixture of understanding and suspicion – 'may I remind you that there are twenty cannons trained on this ship. If you attempt to resist or slip anchor and escape, you'll be blown out of the water.'

Caleb was trapped like a fish in a net. With difficulty, he controlled his rage, too aware of its impotency. 'With your indulgence, may I ask if I am permitted to leave the ship? One way or another, I intend to see Miss Tarakanov again before I sail.'

Baranov curtly nodded his permission without waiting for all of the request to be conveyed to him. Larissa was his one remaining chance, and Caleb intended to use her. When Baranov disembarked with his interpreter, the contingent of Russian soldiers was ordered to remain on board and make certain all the guns and ammunition not required for the defense of the *Sea Gypsy* were removed from the cargo hold by his crew. Within minutes after Baranov had left, Caleb climbed into the yawl tied alongside the brig.

'How can Baranov do this? It is not fair!' Larissa protested. Now she understood why Caleb had insisted that all her family be present before he explained what was wrong, so he could face them and clear his name for her sake.

'Nothing I said made any difference to him.' As he turned to face the window, she noticed the dejected droop of his shoulders that indicated more clearly than his words the helplessness and frustration he felt.

Speaking in Russian, she appealed to her father. 'We must go to Baranov and make him understand that Caleb was not going to sell those weapons to the Kolosh.'

'Why would he listen to us?' Zachar argued gently.

'Because he knows us. Babushka, you must talk to him.' She went down on her knees beside her grandmother's chair. 'He will listen to you. You cannot let him send Caleb away.'

'He has made his decision, my child. Aleksandr Andreevich is a stubborn man. He will not change his order because an old woman asks,' she said, then covered her mouth to suppress a wheezing cough.

'If he leaves, Babushka, I will go with him.'

'No.'

'I thought and thought about this even before today. I decided that if he asked me to go with him, I would.' She picked up her grandmother's thin hand and pressed it against her cheek. 'I have no wish to hurt you, but I love him.'

'That would be a mistake, Larissa.' Her Uncle Mikhail frowned in disapproval.

'Why?' She rose to her feet. 'Explain to him, Father, how it feels to care about someone so much that life has no meaning without them. You would not go to the Pribilofs without Raven. It is the same for me. I want to be with him. I remember the story you told about the high chamberlain and the beautifuly lady from California; how much they loved each other. But she listened to her family and stayed when he left to obtain permission from the Tsar for them to marry. He died. She still waits for him to return, when she could have gone with him. I will go with Caleb.'

'What about Father Herman's teachings? You would be committing a grave sin.' Again it was her uncle who challenged her decision, while her father remained silent.

'Papa is not married to Raven.' She suspected his silence meant support and tried to force him to speak out for her.

But Zachar could say little, pulled as he was in two directions. Part of him violently opposed the idea of his daughter marrying the man who might be the true father of Wolf. Yet he knew, too, that if Caleb Stone married Larissa, it was unlikely he would ever claim Wolf as his own. But Zachar couldn't bring himself to endorse the idea of going to Baranov and appealing to him to reverse his decision to send the Boston man away. He wanted him gone – never to return. If it meant losing his daughter as well, then so be it. Better his daughter than his son.

'Raven has not been baptized. You have,' Mikhail replied sharply.

'It is possible that we can be married,' Larissa stated, aware that this was her last hope of gaining her family's support in Caleb's cause.

'How?' her father asked hesitantly. 'There is no priest.'

'Caleb says that Baranov could perform the ceremony. He is the governor. His word is law. He is the one who baptizes the babies and reads the prayers on the Holy Days.'

She observed the questioning look Mikhail directed at her grandmother. She knew how much store her grandmother put in the opinion of her youngest and favorite son. If Mikhail doubted, she doubted. Encouraged, Larissa immediately pressed her slim advantage. 'Please Babushka, speak to Baranov. If he will consent to nothing else, have him perform the marriage rite.'

Larissa held her breath for what seemed an eternity. Then her grandmother patted her fingers against her gray hair. 'Where is my scarf? Aleksandr Andreevich prefers that a woman's head is covered in the Russian fashion.'

'Here it is, Babushka.' Silently laughing and crying at the same time, Larissa retrieved the silk scarf from the table behind her grandmother and gave it to her, then gaily swept across the room to Caleb's side. 'We are going to see Baranov,' she announced in English. 'All of us.'

Baranov's nephew and secretary ushered them into the office that overlooked Sitka Sound and commanded a view of the Pacific beyond. Taking up his cane, Baranov rose from his chair and hobbled around his large desk to greet them.

He pointedly ignored Caleb, but he was most solicitous of her grandmother, Larissa noticed, making certain she was comfortably situated in a chair that received the warming rays of the sun. Even though Mikhail had carried her up the long flight of steps, the exertion of the walk had left Tasha winded and plagued by a small persistent cough.

'We are both getting old, Tasha Tarakanova.' Baranov lowered himself slowly onto a chair his nephew held, then dismissed the man with a motion of his hand. 'Age has gnarled my fingers like the knobby roots of a fallen tree and made my joints ache. To you, age has given a nagging cough to remind you how precious breath can be. On days like this, one feels how sad it is to become old and tired.'

'Perhaps the years bother your eyes, Aleksandr Andreevich.' Tasha drew attention to the square-lensed spectacles lying on top of his desk. 'Maybe you cannot see as well as you once did and misjudge things.'

'Are we discussing my vision of things, or my perception of them?'

'My granddaughter believes that you have been too harsh with Captain Stone, that maybe you saw the guns and nothing more.'

'This is interesting.' Baranov leaned back in his chair. 'The Tarakanov family comes to plead for clemency on behalf of the Yankee captain. Yet, it was from the Kolosh woman who lives with you, Zachar, that I learned of his treacherous intentions.'

'Raven.' Larissa turned to her father, but his expression was a mirrorlike reflection of her own stunned and disbelieving look.

'She came to me this morning and said your good captain had asked her to relay the word to her people that he had guns and ammunition to sell them. She was afraid there would be more fighting if that happened.'

'What is he saying?' Caleb demanded in English. After Larissa told him, he sprang to his feet. 'That's a lie!'

Baranov shrugged. 'The cargo of the *Sea Gypsy* included a large quantity of weapons. She knew that.'

'She could have learned that from any of the sailors on the ship,' Larissa insisted. 'Caleb – Captain Stone made no secret of it.'

'A woman has the luxury of blindly believing what her heart says, but in my position I must look at the facts and judge accordingly. My opinion is unchanged, and my orders stand.'

No amount of appeal on Larissa's part succeeded in dissuading him. Her grandmother laid a hand on Larissa's arm to silence her. Caleb came back to sit in his chair after pacing to the window and staring at the harbor vista.

'We have known each other many years, Aleksandr Andreevich,' Tasha said. 'When you first arrived at Kodiak, you were ill with a fever and I looked after you. My sons have fought at your side. My daughter-in-law pushed her little girl into your arms before she drowned in the tidal wave. Larissa was that baby girl. She has strong feelings for this Yankee captain. She told me she will leave with him. It is their request that you marry them.'

'Ask the captain if this is still what he wants now that he knows my orders are unchanged,' Baranov instructed Larissa.

She translated Baranov's Russian into English and Caleb's English into Russian. 'The captain says he did not speak idly when he told you he wished to marry me. He says he would be honored to have me as his wife. And as he bowed to your authority earlier, he bows to it now. He binds himself to the vows we will make,' she asserted proudly.

'And you, child?' He squinted narrowly at her.

'I want to be his wife.'

'You would marry him knowing that my orders will then apply to you as well, that you will not be welcome in Sitka, that it is possible you will not see your family again?'

She felt the sting of tears in her eyes. 'Yes, I would.'

They were married in the office by the windows overlooking the bay. The ceremony was conducted in Russian, and Caleb understood none of it, making the responses Larissa prompted him to say. During the prayer, his gaze strayed to the window and the tall bare masts of his ship in the harbor.

Raven. He might have known Baranov hadn't come out to inspect the manifest on mere speculation. He had been so concerned about Raven telling her lies to Larissa he hadn't considered the damage she could do to him with Baranov.

There was a break in the drone of Russian. Caleb glanced at Larissa to see if there was something he was supposed to say. She gazed solemnly at him. 'It is over. We are married.'

He forced aside his preoccupation and smiled at her. She was a lovely bride, even if she wasn't bringing all that he had planned to their marriage. She had fought for him, but there simply wasn't any antidote to Raven's poisoning of his plans.

'You and your bride are to sail with the morrow's tide,' Baranov stated in heavily accented English, and walked to his desk, relying heavily on his cane.

'One moment, Baranov.' Angered that the Russian wouldn't relent and allow them an extra day, Caleb crossed the room. He reached into his pocket and took out a leather pouch, held it a moment, then tossed it onto the open journal on Baranov's desk. 'There's five hundred dollars there in gold. It's all for Madame Tarakanova. See that she wants for nothing.'

'A noble gesture, Captain.'

'She is part of my family now. I think you misjudge me,' Caleb asserted stiffly.

'So I have been told. But it is better, I feel, with your muskets in my arsenal.' Baranov didn't even pick up the bag of coins.

318

It had been a desperate ploy to make himself look good in Baranov's eyes. Its failure made all the previous ones that much more intolerable. Damn Raven and damn Baranov, Caleb thought bitterly as he left the governor's residence with his new in-laws.

At the bottom of the steps, Caleb suggested to Larissa that she accompany her grandmother back to the cabin and pack her belongings, explaining that he needed to return to his ship. He promised to send a couple of men from his crew to the cabin to carry her things to the ship.

As Zachar lingered by the steps, Caleb recalled that Larissa's father had said little during all this.

'Were you aware Raven had gone to Baranov? Or maybe it was your idea so you could get me away from here in case I started believing her lie that the boy is my son.'

'I knew nothing of it.' He looked beaten, as if he rather than Caleb had been the one who had lost so much today. 'She tells me nothing any more.'

No matter how much Caleb wanted a scapegoat, he believed him. 'I wish I could get my hands on her.'

'You could have told Baranov the way she tried to make you give her presents because of the boy. It would have explained why she would make up a lie to hurt you. I am grateful that you kept silent.'

Caleb nearly laughed. He hadn't kept silent to spare Zachar any shame or humiliation, as the Russian seemed to think. Unless he denied outright ever knowing Raven in the past, he would have had a hundred explanations and justifications to make. His past didn't stand up well under close inspection. It would have been twice as hard for him to convince Baranov – and possibly even Larissa and her grandmother – that he had turned over a new leaf.

'There was nothing to be gained by spreading her lies. More people would simply be hurt, including Larissa,' he stated righteously.

'Has Larissa told you I leave soon?'

'No.'

'I go to the Pribilofs, the islands of the fur seals.' Zachar appeared to be troubled, yet hesitant, too. 'You have helped me twice, Captain Stone. You rescued me after the massacre and you told no one that Wolf may not be my son. It is not fair that I should ask you to do more when I have been unable to help you.'

'What are you talking about?'

'So many seals have been killed in the Pribilofs during these last years, especially the pups, whose coats lose their black color and become soft silvery gray fur in September, and nursing females, too. No attention was paid to the age, sex, or quality of the fur. Sometimes thousands of bulls were slaughtered and left to rot with their pelts intact, and only their sex organs taken to be dried and made into a powder. The powder is highly prized in China. Last year, the company ordered the killing stopped to give the herds a chance to replenish their numbers.'

'And?' Caleb raised an eyebrow, not certain exactly what Zachar was suggesting.

'Since there is no more killing, most of the Aleuts and their families have been sent home to Unalaska. There will be only a few of us there to keep watch on the rookeries and guard the company buildings.'

'I see,' Caleb murmured.

'Raven does not wish to go with me to the Pribilofs. She says she will return to her people.'

'You're lucky to be rid of her. She's nothing but trouble.'

'I think you do not understand.' Zachar shook his head sadly. 'If she leaves, she takes my son with her. Once I thought I could not live without Raven. Now I know I cannot live without my son.'

'Take him. How can she stop you?' It seemed simple enough to Caleb.

'Baranov will stop me. It is the law here. A child belongs to its mother. There is nothing I can do. If I could give Raven presents, I could have my son, but already I owe the company more than I can repay.'

'How much would it take – What would you have to give Raven to persuade her to abandon her son?' Considering the value of the information Zachar had so generously given him, he was willing to spring for a few yards of cloth and some copper kettles or trinkets. 'Come on board the *Sea Gypsy* with me and look over the merchandise I have.'

'You would do this?'

'We are family now.' Caleb clamped an arm around the older man's shoulders and walked to the yawl with him.

27

Larissa gathered her skirts more tightly around her with one hand, leaving the other free to hold the cup of steaming coffee as she started toward the stern of the ship. She nodded briefly to the sailor who stood beside the scuttlebutt slowly sipping at the ladle of fresh water.

All hands were at work on this fine morning in early July. Some were in the rigging mending the chafing gear, some braiding sennit or picking oakum. The ship's carpenter labored at his workbench.

Larissa had had a little over two months to adjust to the sights and sounds of her new domain. As she mounted to the quarter-deck, her gaze went automatically to her new husband. The very word filled her with a sense of pride – and a yearning as well to play a larger role in his life than the one he'd thus far permitted.

The old sailmaker looked up from the topsail he was mending as she walked past him, but he offered no greeting. It was the same with the helmsman leaning lazily against the wheel. No one talked – to her or each other – when Caleb was on deck. This past month Larissa had noticed that everyone gave him a wide berth. She smiled at her use of the latter phrase, pleased at how quickly she had learned some of the seaman's vernacular.

In the beginning it had sounded like a whole new language. Now she knew the difference between skysails and topgallants, clewing and reefing, halyards and landyards. Right now, the *Sea Gypsy* was 'under a cloud of sail,' her studding sails spreading beyond the ship on either side, canvas rising in a pyramid to royal studding sails and skysails.

Caleb stood with his feet braced to the roll of the deck, his brow furrowed with that troubled, brooding scowl he so often wore of late. All had not gone smoothly since they had left Sitka, although their marriage was not at fault. Trading had been poor along the coast. For all the time Caleb had spent haggling with the Kolosh, he had barely fifty pelts to show for it. Now he raced the brig north-northwest, risking every inch of canvas she could carry in fair wind or foul.

'Coffee.' She offered him the cup.

Preoccupied, he took the cup from her hand, grunting an absent acknowledgment as his attention returned to the clouds and horizon, watchful for some sign of a weather change. The brisk breeze had a bite to it. Gripping the edges of her shawl, Larissa crisscrossed the corners in front of her.

'Will we be there soon?' she murmured.

'Aye,' Caleb answered, then looked sharply at her. He had kept their destination secret, although she had guessed, and suspected the crew had as well, since much of their initial grumbling had stopped.

'The weather stays good,' she remarked.

'Aye.' A heavy sigh accompanied his response as he turned and looked again at the high, occasionally broken clouds.

'It will not stay,' Larissa assured him. 'The wind will change. The thick fog will come. Landing the boats will be difficult if the winds and currents are bad.'

'What are you talking about?' His tone of voice was wary.

'The Pribilofs.' She faced him calmly. 'I know you plan to raid the seal rookeries there.'

'How –' He broke off the question, half angry and half guilty.

'The chart was left unrolled on the table. Earlier I noticed fur seals feeding in the waters. They would not journey long distances from their islands at this time of year.' She smiled gently at his grim expression. 'You cannot hide things from me, my husband.'

'Larissa, I can't afford to spend two years on the coast to accumulate enough furs to go to Canton the way some merchant ships can. I have to show a profit on this voyage – a big profit.'

'There is nothing you must explain. I made my vows to you.' She would not let herself judge his actions.

During the times they spent alone in the captain's quarters, Caleb had frequently talked about his dreams and future plans and she had come to understand the scope of his ambition. Once, after a particularly frustrating week of trading, Caleb had drunk excessively after dinner and told her about his dashed hopes for a trade alliance with Baranov and the Russian American Company.

She had glimpsed the bitter disappointment that ate at him. While there was no doubt in her mind that his driving need to succeed was his prime motive in making this raid on the Pribilofs, she suspected the act was also a vengeful one, a means of paying Baranov back for ordering him out of Sitka.

'Your father – Zachar – suggested this to me,' Caleb stated.

That she would never have guessed. Somehow it didn't seem right that he was involved in this.

'He will be on the island,' she said.

'Aye.'

There was a tightness in her throat and she coughed to clear the minor irritation. She noticed Caleb's worried look and hastened to assure him. 'It is nothing.'

'There's a nip in the wind. Maybe you'd better go below before you get chilled.'

Larissa didn't argue with his suggestion. She was feeling a little tired. According to Caleb, the sea air did that to a person.

By late in the day, a heavy overcast darkened the sea. A multitude of seabirds wheeled above the waters, filling the air with their lonely, mewing cries. Soon a bawling roar could be heard in the distance, coming from the island rookeries hidden by a shrouding fog. The brig stayed on a steady course toward the fog bank. Gradually Caleb was able to distinguish the crash of the breakers from the loud seal roar.

While the long daylight of the northern summer kept the darkness at bay, they entered and anchored offshore at a place Caleb judged to be on roughly the opposite side of the island from the Russian encampment that Zachar had indicated on his charts. He informed the crew they'd have four hours of sleep, save for the anchor watch, and that would be the last they'd have for forty-eight hours.

The first pearl of dawn came in the small hours of the morning. Only four experienced sea hands were left on the *Sea Gypsy* with Larissa. The rest, including the 'idlers' – the steward, sailmaker, ship's carpenter, and cook – piled into the boats and rowed for the beach. Although many had pistols shoved in the waistbands of their duck trousers, all were armed with clubs or belaying pins and sharp knives.

They landed on the rock-strewn beach amidst a harem. The men scrambled out of the boats, barely taking time to haul them ashore, and charged into the mass of hundred-pound female seals with black pups, swinging their clubs, stunning many of the thin-skulled mammals and crushing others. The killing orgy spread unchecked from one harem of cows to the next. The challenges of the massive six-hundred-pound harem bulls, the agressive beachmasters, were futile, usually stopped by a shot fired into the brain, but with some, the sailors simply poked their eyes out and laughed at the blind charges and frustrated roars. More than a hundred seals died in the first hour.

But too many seals stampeded into the sea and escaped. Caleb called a halt to the chaotic slaughter and divided his men into groups, assigning each to a task to create a more efficient killing operation. Most he set to work skinning the already dead or unconscious seals, with instructions not to waste time on any with scarred or damaged pelts, but to remove the penis bone and sex organs of any of the males. The remaining handful of men he let loose on the seals, ordering them to concentrate on the young males.

All morning and all afternoon the killing, skinning, and castrating continued unabated. Through the night they skinned, scraped, and salted hides by torchlight. Come morning, Caleb detailed a party of men to begin transporting the pelts to the *Sea Gypsy*. A morning meal of salt beef and sea biscuit was distributed among the crew with a mug of rum-laced, molasses-sweetened coffee to wash it down. Caleb ate as they ate, worked as they worked, lending a hand wherever one was short, and roved constantly back and forth among the various operations. As the furs piled up, he drove the men harder, ignoring his fatigue and theirs.

His clothes were blood-caked, blubber-greased, and sweat-stiffened. The shadow of a beard darkened his cheeks. The stench of the bloody carcasses strewn in piles along the beach was all around him, but he was oblivious to everything but filling his hold with the thick glossy pelts.

The killing was amazingly easy. Already he was considering the possibility of letting his men rest in shifts and extending the operation another twenty-four hours. Why leave with five thousand pelts when he could take ten or twenty thouand? There were more than a million seals on this island. Why should he let the Russians have all of them?

*

Zachar walked, holding on to the legs of the boy who straddled his neck. Every now and then, he'd hold his hand up high so Wolf could take a few more crowberries from the pile cupped in his palm. The tundra grass came to his knees, and he waded through the lush tangle of stalks. The island was abloom with wildflowers, blue lupine, and white gentian.

A patchy, swirling fog drifted over the treeless island, here and there obscuring a hill or blanketing a hollow as he headed toward the beach with his son. The pandemonium grew louder with the scream of the seabirds – the red-legged kittiwakes, tufted sea parrots, red-faced murres, and seagulls by the thousands – the pounding of the surf on the rocky shores, and the deafening roar of the fur-seal masses.

Zachar wanted his son to see this awesome sight of the seething mass of fur seals – to see it and remember it always. That's why they repeatedly made the long trek to this spot away from the encampment where they wouldn't be disturbed by the others. He longed to tell Wolf the way it had been when he'd first seen it, to explain that the numbers had been reduced by ninety percent in his lifetime. He wished he could tell him about Walks Straight.

Quickly he shook off the melancholy that tried to claim him and stepped up his pace. It wasn't good to look into the past. Today he had his son with him.

Wolf leaned over his right shoulder, laughing as he grabbed at the berries clutched in Zachar's fist. 'More, Papa.'

Zachar opened his hand. 'There are only a few left.'

'I will eat them all.' With both hands, Wolf plucked the berries from his palm and stuffed them into his mouth until his cheeks bulged, then chomped happily on their sweetness.

'You have the fat cheeks of a pig,' Zachar teased him, and gripped the boy's ankles to hold him securely in place as they neared the rocky terrain of the beach.

'Seals,' Wolf said, spitting berry juice from his full mouth, and pointed to a boulder-strewn area ahead of them.

Out of the mist came a half dozen seals, propelling themselves forward with their flippers in their awkward, humping gait. Zachar sensed their panic and halted, half expecting to see a huge harem bull lumbering after them, but none came. The young bachelor males stampeded into the tundra in obvious confusion; the sea was their natural refuge.

Alerted by their display of fear, Zachar heard the whistles and loud cries – sounds, he realized, that didn't belong to any bird or beast on the island. Reaching up, he lifted Wolf off his shoulders and swung him astraddle of his hip, then walked swiftly to the boulders where the land sloped away to the beach.

Suddenly he noticed the tainted smell on the mist. When he breathed in the stench of blood, Zachar knew what he would find on the beach. Seal carcasses, piled three and four deep, littered the surf-washed rocks along the shore. The obscuring fog hid the end of them.

'Walks Straight,' he moaned, aching inside.

This was the place they'd come ashore. Here, the friendly sea otter had sniffed them curiously. No more sea otter lived in these waters; all of them had been killed or driven off by the carnage. Now the teeming swell of fur seals – bulls, cows, and pups – lay lifeless, grotesque piles of bloody blubber.

Then he heard the shouts – the Yankee voices. He turned and looked up the beach. Two boats with furs stacked higher than their gunwales breasted a wave's curl. On the beach were more men, their faces, hands, and clothes dark with blood, some busy making the slices to free a pelt from its body, others pulling the ropes clamped onto the hide and stripping it off.

A promyshlenik at the Russian outpost on the island had described the procedure to Zachar, boasting of the numbers that could be killed and processed. The images hadn't repulsed him. He was a hunter. But this carnage wasn't hunting.

Not far from him, three men with clubs waded into a herd of young bulls milling in confusion. He watched them swing their wooden sticks, felling the nearest ones while the others barked in fear. One brave young seal tried to attack, charging as ferociously as any beachmaster, but a blow to the head ended his valiant defense.

Zachar set Wolf on the ground next to a large boulder. 'Stay here.'

Trembling with rage, he walked swiftly toward the Yankee raiders. The only thought in his mind was to stop them. 'Look what you do here!' he shouted.

Suddenly a figure stepped out from behind a boulder and leveled a pistol at him. Zachar halted. The Yankee was only five steps from him, close enough for Zachar to make out his features despite his failing vision. The man's eyes had a wild, glazed look, as if he was possessed by a madness for killing. A scraggly beard covered his gaunt cheeks and darkened the hollows under his eyes. Zachar waited for the flash of gunpowder and the impact of the ball. Instead the muzzle dipped toward the ground.

'Zachar.' The man took a step closer, his mouth crooking in a smile.

'Caleb Stone.' Shock flattened all feeling from Zachar. 'You.'

'I hope you weren't expecting someone else.'

Numbly Zachar looked around at the bloody scene. 'How could you do this?'

'You sound surprised. You knew when you told me the Pribilofs were virtually unmanned –'

'I told you?' The conversation came back to him. 'I told you.' Groaning, he turned and staggered blindly into the fog. Tears rushed into his eyes. 'Not for this. No.'

'Zachar!' Caleb instinctively tightened his grip on the pistol butt and frowned as he looked behind him at his sealing crew, debating whether to order them to abandon the operation and return to the brig or to pursue Zachar. The man was crazy.

His side vision detected movement. Turning, he saw the young boy Wolf plowing through the tall tundras grass in the direction Zachar had taken, his short legs stepping high in an effort to avoid the tangling stalks. Caleb hesitated, then gave chase.

Instead of fleeing inland, Zachar was taking an erratic track that paralleled the shore. Wisps of fog swirled in his wake. Caleb shouted to him again, but he knew he couldn't be heard above the bawl of the seals. As Zachar swung drunkenly toward the rocks, a large boulder appeared to move. Then Caleb realized it was a harem bull, one that his men had blinded. Enraged to the point of charging any sound, it went for Zachar, moving with amazing swiftness.

Caleb shouted a futile warning as the massive bull struck Zachar broadside, knocking him to the ground. Caleb tried to run faster, but his legs felt strangely leaden and unresponsive. The bull fell on Zachar, seizing hold of the body with his large canines and shaking it ferociously as he would do with any male seal caught trespassing on his territory. No resistance was offered by Zachar.

The little boy stopped and started picking up rocks and throwing them at the bull seal, trying to drive him away from the body. His aim was poor and the rocks were small. Those that did hit the seal bounced off the thick cushion of fur and blubber with no more effect than a raindrop.

Five yards from the seal, Caleb stopped and took aim with his pistol. Suddenly the little boy ran into his line of fire, armed with a piece of driftwood. 'Get away, son!' Caleb yelled.

The beachmaster swung its small head toward the sound of his voice, bloody gaping holes where its eyes had been. As the boy backed up, Caleb stepped forward and grabbed him by the scruff of the neck, yanking him backwards. The roaring seal made a lumbering move toward them. Caleb sighted quickly and fired. The bull collapsed with a thud.

The boy dashed past him to Zachar's motionless body and knelt beside him. Caleb walked slowly to them and crouched down. Zachar's left shoulder was mangled, blood flooding from the ripped flesh. Caleb noticed the bloodstained rock near Zachar's head and guessed the Russian had been knocked unconscious when he fell. He felt for a pulse in the man's neck but could find none. Warm, sticky blood was on his fingers when he took his hand away. He tried to wipe them clean with the fog-wet grass.

The boy put his hand on the peppered gray head, nudging it as if to waken Zachar. He said something in Russian, which Caleb didn't understand, but it sounded like another attempt to rouse him.

Caleb took him gently by the shoulders and pulled him away from the body. 'He's dead, son.' The boy glared at him, then with a sudden twist jerked free and ran, disappearing almost instantly in a wall of thick fog.

After making a brief attempt to locate the boy, he gave up the search. It was time to leave the island. Already he had been here a day and a half longer than he'd originally planned.

28 *Sitka*
January 1818

Mikhail listened to the muffled peal of the church bell as it proclaimed the news of the marriage that had taken place between Baranov's Creole daughter Irina and the naval lieutenant Semyon Ivanovich Yanovskii, the man named to succeed Baranov as governor of Russian America. He concentrated on the rhythmic clangor, trying to use it to block out the sound of the quick, labored breathing of the old woman lying on the bed – his mother, Tasha. But it was no use. Nothing could mask the desperate attempts she made to suck air into her congested lungs.

He hunched forward in the chair positioned by her bed and stared helplessly at her. She had grown so thin and frail that it was difficult to distinguish the outline of her body beneath the layers of blankets covering her. Consumption had ravaged her body, leaving it vulnerable to the pneumonia that now claimed her.

Her face looked sunken and hollow, her skin a sickly gray. Her eyes were closed. Mikhail wanted to believe she was asleep, resting peacefully, but those rapid wheezing gasps for air told him of her struggle for life. He remembered how much she had wanted to attend the wedding of the daughter of her old friend Baranov, and to see the eucharistic vessels that, as an apprentice to the smithy, her grandson Wolf had helped fashion out of Spanish silver. Instead she lay on her deathbed while the church bell tolled.

A hand touched his shoulder, and Mikhail glanced up, looking straight into a pair of eyes as blue as his brother Zachar's had been. But they belonged to a strapping youth of fifteen who had Raven's black hair and strong-boned features.

'The tea is hot,' Wolf said. 'I will sit with Babushka if you would like some.'

Mikhail nodded and pushed to his feet, glad to relinquish his vigil despite the pang of guilt it brought. As Wolf took his place in the chair by the bed, he walked over to the samovar and half filled a cup with tea, then poured in some rum to fill it within a centimeter of the rim. He took a long sip of the hot, potent brew, then glanced toward the bed.

But Wolf claimed his attention, Wolf and the memories of that rainy night nearly ten years ago when he'd piloted the mail boat from Kodiak into the harbor, the mail boat that had brought the word of Zachar's death – and his son, Wolf. He'd had no choice but to bring the boy to the cabin.

When he'd broken the news to Tasha about Zachar, she hadn't seemed surprised, only emotionally drained. 'I think I knew he would not return from the seal islands,' she'd said. 'I begged him not to go, but he said it was in God's hands.'

Then disguising his bitter frustration so well, Mikhail had drawn the five-year-old Wolf out of the shadows where he'd been hiding like some frightened and wary animal. 'Zachar left someone in our care.' He'd nearly choked on the words, then pushed the boy toward her. 'Go to your babushka.'

After some cajoling, she had persuaded the small boy to climb onto her lap. Her long, thin fingers had touched his rain-flattened black hair, glistening in the lamplight. 'We will get along, you and I,' she'd said. 'I wish only that I were a little younger that I might live to see you grow up.'

Mikhail remembered how he had protested that statement. 'You have many years ahead of you, Babushka.'

Then she had started coughing from the consumption that had now so completely depleted her strength. He'd helped her to bed, insisting she must rest.

That night, too, he'd drunk tea heavily laced with rum and tried to drown the angry resentment he felt that he alone was responsible for the care of his sick and aging mother and young nephew. Zachar was dead; never would he return to shoulder any of the burden. Larissa was gone, banished forever from Sitka with her Boston captain. He, Mikhail, was the only one left.

How he'd railed against the unfairness of it that night, knowing that it meant he couldn't be a member of any of the three expeditions Baranov was sending out that fall to locate sites for future settlements – one to Hawaii, one to California, and one to the mouth of the Columbia River in New Albion, the latter despite a report brought back by Rezanov two years earlier that an expedition headed by two men named Lewis and Clark was at the Columbia. His dreams of traveling to faraway shores had died that night, buried forever by the burden of his family – a burden that rested solely on his shoulders.

For ten long years he'd listened to the stories told by people who had been to the places he'd dreamed of seeing, and heard the reports brought back from the settlements that had been established on the island of Kauai in Hawaii and at Fort Ross in northern California. For ten long years he'd resented the responsibility that had chained him to Sitka like an anchor around his neck. And for ten long years he'd lived with the guilt of that resentment.

He loved his mother. He truly loved her, which made him all the more ashamed that he could look at her coming death as a means of setting him free.

Wolf stared at the face of his dying grandmother, then slowly and gently lifted her hand from beneath the covers. It was all bones, skin, and nails with little flesh to soften it. Yet as he held it, he remembered the many times it had stroked him with affection. The love his father had shown him was a dim memory, kept alive by the stories his babushka had told him about Zachar.

In the last few weeks, though, she had talked more and more frequently about the Aleutian island of Attu, where she'd been born, wishing she could go there before she died. As her thoughts turned back to the past and her childhood on that far island, she remembered in detail the baskets Weaver Woman had made, her mother sewing the fine bird-skin parkas, her uncle, Many Whiskers, sitting on the lee side of the barabara watching the sea, the festive dances, the story-telling times. It was as if she could see more clearly into yesterday than the shadows of tomorrow.

He held tightly to her hand, not wanting death to steal her from him as it had taken away his father. But the whiteness of her hand reminded him of the fog that day on the seal island. The blurred image of the wild-eyed, smelly-clothed man with the pistol swam before his mind's eye, and the voice, that Yankee voice: 'He's dead, son.'

On the heels of that memory came another. He'd been seven or eight when his mother had come for him. Babushka had argued with her, refusing to let him go with her, and Raven had declared, 'I never say Zachar his father. Zachar say it.'

In the end, he had gone with his mother, sometimes living in the log houses of her people, sometimes in Sitka, where Babushka's cabin became a refuge from his confusion. Many times he had asked his mother whether Zachar was his father. Usually he received no answer. Once when she was drunk on the Yankee firewater, she had claimed his father was the Boston man Caleb. In all his life, he'd heard of only one man with that name.

Three years ago, when he was twelve, his mother had contracted syphilis, the white man's great pox, and no Russian or Yankee would give presents to lie with her any more. Mikhail had treated her with mercury and made her well, but still men shunned her. Mikhail had helped him and arranged for him to learn the smithy trade because he was Zachar's son.

Zachar's son was how Babushka thought of him. Raven often lied, but Wolf had never known his babushka to lie. Slowly over the years he had come to think of himself as Zachar's son, too, and pushed aside the doubts Raven had raised in his mind.

Suddenly the rhythm of Tasha's breathing changed, slowing from its fast, wheezing pace to a calmer rate. It sounded so peaceful that Wolf turned eagerly toward Mikhail, certain his uncle was wrong, that Babushka was not going to die – not this day.

'She is better.' He spoke quickly and softly, directing his uncle's attention to his dear babushka. 'See how she rests.'

Mikhail hesitated, then walked over to the bed. As he stood beside Wolf's chair, old Tasha took a deep breath and released it in a long sigh. Then, there was only silence. So calmly, so quietly, she had died.

Wolf stared at her motionless body in disbelief, mentally straining, trying to will her to breathe again. She had left him, as his father had left him. Anger and pain flashed hotly through him as he clenched his jaws together so tightly that his teeth hurt.

Unbidden came the words he'd once heard her say: 'They always leave.'

The anger drained from him. He knelt beside the bed, then made the sign of the cross and tried to pray. He heard Mikhail turn away and stagger to the table. There he collapsed on a chair and buried his face in his arms to smother the slobbering sounds of the sobs that racked his body.

29 *Sitka*
Spring 1836

A young man of twenty-five, dressed in the clothes of a Yankee first mate, walked slowly up the street taking in everything that went on around him with an interest that was more than curiosity. The noise of hammers and saws used by the carpenters building the new three-story mansion on the knoll overlooking the bay, made a steady din in the background. From the smithy came the ring of hammer on iron as plowshares and spades were shaped, bound for the Russian settlement of Fort Ross near Bodega Bay in California.

The Russian Orthodox Church stood on the south side of the street. Twenty years before, Baranov had ordered an old ship hauled on land and remodeled into a church, the first to be built at New Archangel. The seaman paused opposite the square and gazed at the flame-shaped steeple topped by the distinctive Greek cross with its crooked lower bar. Then he continued up the street.

As he passed the shop of a silversmith, his eye was caught by the sign overhead. He stopped and turned back to read it, frowning at the Russian script as if he was having trouble deciphering it. His expression cleared. After hesitating momentarily, he went inside.

Seated at his workbench by the window, Wolf Tarakanov glanced up as the man entered his shop. His coarse black hair and light bronze skin indicated his Indian ancestry, but the gray-blue eyes and Slavic features revealed the mixture of Russian blood. He set aside the silver bracelet and etching tool, then straightened from his stool, absently brushing his hands on the front of his leather apron. A frown flickered across his forehead as he gazed curiously at the seaman. The man's black hair and blue eyes and his facial features were vaguely familiar.

In bad Russian, the man asked, 'I look for Tasha or Mikhail

Tarakanov. The shop sign say your name Tarakanov is. Can you tell where find I them?'

Wolf stared at him intently and responded in English, 'You are Yankee.'

'Yes.' The man appeared relieved that Wolf could speak his language.

'Mikhail Tarakanov lives in California at our settlement there. Tasha Tarakanov died nearly twenty years ago. She is buried in the cemetery.' Wolf hesitated, still trying to identify the reason the Yankee seaman looked so familiar to him. 'I am her grandson, Wolf Tarakanov.'

'I am Matthew Edmund Stone of New Bedford, Massachusetts, the son of her granddaughter, Larissa.'

Wolf blinked in surprise. 'I thought you looked familiar to me. Now I see –' He abruptly checked himself. It was almost like looking into a mirror. 'You are the son of Caleb Stone.'

'Yes.'

A cold feeling ran through Wolf's veins. For a moment he stared at the hand thrust at him in greeting. The name conjured up painful memories and a long-ago question in his mind. He forced himself to shake hands with the man roughly eight years his junior.

'I am the son of Zachar Tarakanov,' Wolf asserted. 'My mother is the Kolosh woman called Raven. She lives in the Ranche,' he said, referrring to the Indian village that had been built in the shadow of the town's log stockade, but his mother's name appeared to have no meaning to the man. 'I was but a boy when your mother left New Archangel. Unfortunately I have no memory of her, and it has been many years since any communication was received from her. I hope she is well.'

'She died almost fifteen years ago from consumption.'

'I am sorry to hear that.' He wanted to ask about Caleb Stone, but he couldn't make the words come. 'Your vessel is newly arrived in Sitka?'

'Aye. She's the whaling bark *North Star*.'

Wolf glanced sharply at the seaman. 'Hell-ships,' he'd heard them called, commanded by notoriously brutal tyrants and crewed by murderers and thieves. He wondered if that accounted for the steely look in the man's eyes and the sternness around his mouth.

'You do not follow your father in the merchant trade?'

'I follow my father. He is captain of the *North Star*. He took to whaling shortly after the close of the War of 1812 with England.' But Matthew Stone didn't explain that the British embargo and blockade had severely damaged Yankee trading in the Pacific or that his father hadn't possessed the resources to recover from it and had lost virtually everything. 'There's a considerable profit to be made in whaling. Some are saying sperm oil will go back over a dollar a gallon. Working on shares, a man can make himself a tidy sum. That's part of the reason we put in here at Sitka. Some of our crew jumped ship in Hawaii. We're short-handed. Your Aleuts are supposed to be good with a harpoon. We thought we might contract with the company for their services – the way ships used to do in the old days hunting sea otter along the California coast.'

'You have had no success,' Wolf guessed, and nodded in understanding when Matthew shook his head. 'The Aleuts prefer their old way of hunting whales – to harpoon them, then wait for the dead whale to wash ashore. The company tried whaling a few years ago, but the experiment was not successful.'

'So I was told.' He shoved his hands in the pockets of his monkey jacket.

Wolf nervously cleared his throat, then asked, 'Is your father also in town?'

'No, he's on the bark. He . . . isn't well.'

'We have a physician here at New Archangel, as well as an apothecary shop. I would gladly arrange for him to –'

'It isn't necessary,' Matthew Stone interrupted. 'It's some fever he picked up in the tropics. It will pass in a few days. We won't be in port long. For my mother's sake, I felt I should try to find some of her family.'

'Perhaps you could come to my home for dinner tonight and meet my wife, Marya, and our three children.'

'No, I . . . can't.' He tempered the quickness of his refusal, but didn't offer an excuse. 'It was a pleasure meeting you . . . Wolf, but I'm afraid I must be getting back to the *North Star*.'

In truth, Wolf was relieved that his invitation to dinner had been turned down. 'I hope your father's fever passes quickly.'

'Thank you.' He nodded to him, then left the shop.

Wolf walked back to his workbench and picked up the silver bracelet, pretending to examine the detail of the totemic design he was etching onto its surface. He picked up the polishing cloth and began rubbing the shiny metal. It flashed in the sunlight coming through the window. But his mind wasn't on the work at hand; instead his thoughts drifted into the past.

For so long he'd thought of himself as Zachar's son that he'd let the doubts about his parentage die. He had thought them dead until today when Caleb Stone's son had walked into his shop, looking enough like himself to be his brother.

Long after Matthew Stone left his shop, Wolf sat on his stool and rubbed the silver bracelet, wondering and telling himself it didn't matter. At last he put down the bracelet and removed his apron, then grabbed his hat and coat and left the shop.

The log palisade that separated the town of New Archangel from the adjoining Kolosh camp known as the Ranche was heavily reinforced, and its portcullised gate strongly guarded. No one challenged Wolf as he passed through the gate. The guards were accustomed to the regular visits he paid his mother; their duty was not to keep their people out of the camp but to restrict the number of Kolosh coming into town. Camp dogs ran alongside him, barking and wagging their tails.

Lost in thought, he paid no attention to them and didn't stop until he was inside the log dwelling of his mother's family. There he paused to adjust his eyes to the gloom, the smokehole in the roof admitting a spray of light. The stale air smelled of fish oil, body odor, and smoke from the center fire that was never extinguished. Meal preparations were under way, as they always seemed to be; food was eaten several times a day.

No one spoke to him. Greeting was not the custom of the Kolosh. Nor was he entirely welcome, Wolf knew. He had chosen the way of the Russian, a way his mother's people continued to reject.

When he saw she was not among the women preparing food, he walked around to her sleeping corner. The Kolosh disdained the use of furniture, so there were no chairs or cots. His mother lay on a sleeping mat, covered with a trader's blanket.

The years had not been kind to her, grizzling her coarse hair with dull gray and jowling her cheeks and eyes. Her slim waist had disappeared under the accumulation of fat and her breasts had become pendulous. As he crouched down, sitting on his heels beside her, Wolf noticed the beads of sweat on her flushed skin.

'Why did you not send word you were ill?'

'I am hot,' she said, as if denying any sickness, and pushed down the blanket.

Deep red splotches dotted the flesh of her inner forearm. Wolf took hold of her wrist to examine the rash more closely. 'Are there more of these red marks on your skin?' he demanded grimly.

She nodded and turned her face away from him.

He straightened to his feet and looked down at her. 'I will bring the physician.'

After the German doctor had examined her, he informed Wolf that Raven was not suffering from a recurrence of syphilis; she had contracted smallpox. The disease had been reported in the villages south of Sitka in the Tongass region. His diagnosis of Raven's illness meant the smallpox had spread; the feared epidemic had reached Sitka.

The Tarakanov family were among the first to be inoculated with the smallpox serum from the apothecary's supply. Vaccinations were ordered for everyone in the settlement of New Archangel.

But the vast majority of Kolosh in the adjoining Ranche encampment and the surrounding island villages refused the white man's medicine, and the plague spread rapidly. Despite Wolf's repeated persuasions, his mother wouldn't allow the doctor to treat her, and the doctor denied Wolf's request to move Raven to his cabin, where he could look after her, insisting on isolating the smallpox victims.

Wolf sat cross-legged on the planked floor and spooned water into her mouth. Never motionless, the shaman leaped wildly about her, singing incantations to the spirits. Bending low, he shook his gourd rattles over her body and twisted his painted face into hideous expressions, running out his tongue and hissing loudly.

But his powers couldn't banish the smell of death in the air. Angered by the futility of both their efforts, Wolf flung the carved-handled spoon aside, then clasped his hands tightly together, trying to contain the rage he felt. He stared at Raven's barely recognizable features, the smallpox pustules covering every inch of her face. He realized she was going to die and he would never know the truth about his father.

A hatred, violent and consuming, took hold of him. He

grabbed her shoulders and shook her roughly, determined to rouse her from the plague's stupor. 'Tell me, you witch!' he raged hoarsely. 'Tell me as you die the name of my father!' Her eyelids moved. 'Am I the son of Zachar Tarakanov or Caleb Stone?'

A weak, cackling sound came from her throat. As her eyes opened to mere slits, an old insolence flared, then regret dulled them. 'The son of Caleb Stone would not have to ask.' Her whispered answer drained the anger from him. Wolf sat back, oddly emotionless. The shaman danced with renewed vigor, his chant increasing in tempo to the beat of the drums and the rattle of his medicine gourds.

In the night, Raven died.

That same night, the whaling bark *North Star* violated the quarantine and slipped out of the harbor under the cover of fog. Later it was reported that a Yankee ship raided a village up the coast and captured four Kolosh braves. Shortly afterwards, smallpox broke out in the village.

Supplies of the smallpox serum were rushed from Sitka to all the Russian stations from Cook's Inlet and the Aleutians to Bristol Bay and Norton Sound and the Yukon in an effort to prevent the disease from reaching the Tlingits to the north, the Athabascans of the interior, the Aleuts of the islands, and the Eskimos of the Arctic coast. Only the Aleuts submitted to the company-ordered inoculations. Like the Tlingits, the other tribes resisted the white man's science.

Wolf witnessed the cremation of many members of his mother's clan. By the time the Kolosh tribe was convinced of the vaccination's worth, half of its adult population was dead.

30 *Sitka*
Easter 1864

The pealing of the bronze bells, cast in Russia and presented by the Orthodox Church at Moscow, rang continually from the tower of the Cathedral of St. Mikhail, which was located almost directly opposite the site of the original church. Their clarion tones signaled the end of Lent's strict observances and the start of Easter's festive celebrations. Atop the flamelike copper spire on the bell-tower cupola, the Orthodox cross gleamed golden in the sunlight.

In the ornate gold and white interior of the cathedral, built in the shape of a cross, fragrant clouds of incense drifted toward the rounded dome of the transept. Wolf Tarakanov stood in the congregation, a black silk cravat tied around the collar of his linen shirt, his black frock coat unbuttoned. At sixty-one, he carried his years with grace and dignity, standing tall and erect, his thick hair the color of tarnished silver. His blue-gray eyes were undimmed, their keenness still enabling him to inspect the skilled repoussé work of the twelve silver-plated ikons that ornamented the Royal Gates. As always, he looked with pride on the silver eucharistic vessels that long ago he'd helped to fashion.

On this Holy Day of Christ's resurrection, the priest appeared wearing the Easter vestment made from the cloth of silver instead of the high-feast-day vestment made from the cloth of gold given to the church by Baranov and beaded by the Aleuts into an intricate mosaic painting. As the priest read the Easter service, a choir of boys chanted the chorus *a cappella*, their young melodic voices blending sweetly. Wolf's attention drifted to the choir.

An elbow nudged his ribs. The gentle reminder to direct his attention back to the service came from his wife, Marya. Instead it served to direct his thoughts to his own family: his lovely daughter, Anastasia, marrying so well to a lieutenant in the Imperial Navy, Nikolai Ivanovich Politoffski; his second son,

Stanislav, a coppersmith, and his wife, Dominika, a Creole of Kolosh blood, and their fifteen-year-old son, Dimitri, whose black eyes often reminded Wolf of Raven; and his eldest son, Lev, a mining engineer; his blond-haired wife, Aila, the daughter of a Finnish military captain, and their two daughters, Nadia, aged thirteen, a pupil at the school for girls founded by Lady Etolin, looking very much the young lady in her muslin dress and ruffled pantalettes with the silk ribbons in her hair, and four-year-old Eva, so plain-looking and serious.

Yes, he could be proud of his family, Wolf concluded; and for a time he paid attention to the liturgy. After a while his legs began to ache from standing so long. He shifted his stance to ease the strain, wondering if the Lutherans in their church across the way had a better idea with their long benches on which the people could sit. He smiled, knowing he didn't dare suggest that to his wife.

Finally it was time to file, one by one, past the priest and kiss the jeweled cross he held in his hand. Outside the church, the clamoring of the bells filled the air, competing with the resonant tones of the pipe organ in the Lutheran Church.

With the somber days of Lent behind them and the religious observance over, the day took a festive turn. All was laughter and gaiety. Individual gifts of eggs, boiled hard and dyed, painted, or in the case of silversmith Wolf Tarakanov, gilded and presented to friends.

Everywhere the greeting 'Christ has risen' was answered with 'He has risen, indeed.' And every salutation was followed by a kiss – or two. It was a mad, merry whirl, with barely time for a breath between kisses.

Late in the afternoon, the entire Tarakanov family gathered at Anastasia's home for an Easter feast. They ate and drank until they could hold no more. The men retired to the parlor to partake of tobacco and brandy; the children were sent outdoors to play; and the women did whatever it is women do when they are separated from the menfolk.

Nadia sat on the front stoop and carefully arranged her skirt so it was spread evenly over her legs and covered her knees. Ignoring her cousins playing in the street, the majority of whom were boys, she picked up the painted egg from her lap and turned to her little sister. 'Cup your hands and I'll let you hold it.'

Conscious of the rare privilege being granted, Eva held her

hands together on her lap, palms upward, and waited while Nadia placed the brightly decorated egg in their small hollow. 'It's beautiful,' she declared solemnly.

'Don't drop it,' Nadia admonished. 'It will break into a thousand pieces if you do, and I'll never forgive you.'

'I'll hold it tight,' Eva promised.

'Nadia.' Fifteen-year-old Dimitri trotted up to the stoop, his cropped black hair falling across his forehead. 'Come play blindman's buff with us.'

She shook her head firmly. 'I might get my dress dirty. Besides, I'm supposed to watch Eva.' She grimaced slightly, tired of always having her baby sister for a shadow.

'What are you going to do, just sit there?' he taunted.

'Maybe.' She shrugged, determined this time not to let him bait her into an argument the way he usually did.

His mood turned sullen as he glanced briefly at his laughing, shouting cousins in the street. 'It is a game for children,' he declared with sudden contempt.

Nadia felt a twinge of sympathy, something he rarely aroused in her, but she was caught in the same trap herself – too old to play with children and too young to be accepted by adults in their conversations.

'What do you think the men talk about?' she asked

'I don't know.' He shrugged diffidently, then a dark gleam appeared in his eyes. 'Let's listen in and find out.' He stole over to the side of the house and slipped up close to the windowsill.

'Dimitri Stanislavich, you –'

'Hush. They'll hear you.' He glared, then motioned quickly for her to join him. 'Come on.'

She hesitated, but her own curiosity was aroused. 'You stay here,' she whispered sternly to her baby sister, then snuck over to the window by her cousin.

Settled comfortably in a handsomely carved parlor chair, Wolf puffed on his pipe, savoring the flavor and aroma of the tobacco smoke, finding renewed pleasure in it after Lent's long abstinence. With an effort, he centered his attention on the stocky, barrel-chested man now speaking, his eldest son, Lev.

'According to the reports that arrived on the last ship from California,' Lev was saying, 'the people there still believe that when this internal strife in America is over and the Union armies have won, the sale of Russian America to the United States will take place.'

Even though the Russian colony of Fort Ross in California had been abandoned and its lands and holdings sold to a man named John Sutter in 1841, a trade was maintained with the southern coast. With the onset of the gold rush in '49, San Francisco had proved to be a lucrative market for the Russian American Company. One commodity was in constant demand – ice. And a new industry had been born in Russian America. In the winter, blocks of ice were chopped from the frozen lakes around Sitka and on Kodiak, then stored in rows of icehouses for shipment to California.

'For three years, they have been talking about a sale. It is only talk,' Wolf's son-in-law, the Navy lieutenant Nikolai Politoffski, scoffed. 'The Tsar will never sell this land to America. It is unthinkable. Never in all her history has Russia voluntarily given up a centimeter of land she occupies.'

'Then explain why the Tsar has not renewed the company's charter giving it exclusive rights to this territory,' Lev challenged. 'For three years we have operated with temporary powers. Three years, the same as these discussions of sale. Do you claim that is coincidence?'

'Yes,' Nikolai snapped, pulling himself up to his full height, every inch the officer, even though the coat of his dress uniform was unbuttoned. 'Land is ever to the glory of the Tsar. The farther from St. Petersburg, the more glorious.'

'Perhaps' – Stanislav began calmly, rising from the horsehair sofa – 'perhaps we are too far from St. Petersburg. Perhaps the Crimean War has shown the Tsar that his Navy could not defend us. The Navy can do nothing to protect the Aleutains and the Arctic coasts from the Yankee whaling fleet. They land all the time to render their whale blubber into oil and spread disease and corruption among the natives. They make the men work on their ships and carry off the Aleut and Innuit women to commit their debauchery. If the Navy cannot stop unarmed whalers, how could they defend us if we were invaded by foreign armies?'

'England would not dare to invade. It is true she holds Canada on our boundaries, but she would not attempt to extend them. It would mean war with the United States.' Nikolai reacted strongly to this attack on the Imperial Navy. 'America is our ally. Look how she helped us, supplying arms and munitions during the Crimean War. Even now our entire Pacific fleet is in the San Francisco harbor, and the Atlantic fleet anchors in New York.'

'I was not thinking of England,' Stanislav replied, 'but of America and her belief in "Manifest Destiny." Look at what happened in California when gold was discovered. The Spanish could not keep the Americans out. They swarmed over the land like bees to honey. And you, Lev' – he waved a hand at his brother – 'you have reported that you have found indications of gold on your mining expeditions.'

'That's true.' Wolf's oldest son nodded.

'Already the wealthy businessmen in San Francisco look north at our furs with envy,' Stanislav stated. 'What will they do if they hear the word "gold"?'

'The word should not be spoken,' Nikolai stated, displaying the arrogant and patronizing attitude so typical of officers in the Imperial Navy – an attitude that seemed to be issued along with the uniform. However proud Wolf might be that his Creole daughter had married so well, he sometimes wearied of the lieutenant's condescension. 'If there are the indications of mineral wealth in this country that you claim, Lev Vasilivich, they should be developed for the company. If our ports were closed to all but Russian ships, as the Navy has recommended, America would not learn of our discoveries. Did we not keep the fur wealth of this land a secret from the world for fifty years? Even the charts of these waters that were published by the Imperial Naval Academy contained deliberate errors. It is unfortunate the Navy was not in charge when the British Captain Cook ventured into these waters. We would not have permitted him intercourse with the natives, and thus would have prevented him from trading for furs. These supposed mineral resources of yours can be protected.'

'It is possible that the Tsar has not granted a new charter because he plans to declare this country a province of Russia and bring it under his sovereignty,' Lev suggested. 'It should be done, so that no more would we be subject to the dictates of the company and forced to buy goods and provisions at the company prices.' His opinion was shared by many of the colony-born who had been educated at the Colonial Academy in Sitka and graduated as navigators, engravers, accountants, or surveyors, obligated to enter the company service to ten-or fifteen-year terms at a nominal salary.

'Then why does the Tsar delay if that is his plan?' argued his brother, Stanislav. He shook his head. 'No, he plans to sell this land to America. He waits for a Union victory. I say we should concern ourselves with what will become of us when this occurs. When they take possession, are we to stay or be sent to Russia? Since we have sworn allegiance to the Tsar, we may have no choice but to go to Russia. It is well for you, Nikolai Ivanovich. It is where you were born and raised.'

'Yes,' Lev agreed quickly. 'But what of us? This land is our home. We know no other. Our father has lived all of his sixty years in this place. Are we to be uprooted? How would we live? Where would we work? This is the only way of life we know.'

'And if we stay, might it not be worse for us?' Stanislav ventured, apprehensive about the strain of Indian blood in their ancestry, especially his wife and his father, Wolf, who were both half Kolosh. 'We have all seen or heard how the Americans treat those of another race.'

In the heavy silence that followed, Wolf studied the carved bowl of his pipe and the dead ashes inside it. This uncertainty about the future had disrupted the entire colony for three years now. No one dared make plans or start new businesses. With the exception of the tea trade, which continued, everything else had come to a standstill. Wolf knew this couldn't continue.

As the discussion wore on, Nadia became bored with it and abandoned her eavesdropping post under the parlor window. Reluctantly Dimitri followed her.

'That is all anyone talks about any more,' she complained. 'I wish America's Unionist armies would win the war and end all this fuss.'

'Do you want the Americans to rule here?' A frown creased his forehead.

'Do you?' Nadia didn't like arguments. She had discovered very early in her life that the smoothest way to avoid them was never to disagree. If it meant pretending something, she would do it to avoid unpleasantness.

Dimitri shrugged. 'The Americans are rich.'

'Yes,' Nadia responded. She, too, had heard the stories that there were homes in San Francisco more opulent and grand than Baranov's Castle, as the governor's residence at Sitka was known. Returning to the stoop, she sat down on the step next to her little sister. 'I'll take the egg back now.'

344

But Eva had sat in that one position for so long with the precious egg cradled in her hands, afraid to move even one finger, that her arms and hands had grown stiff, almost numb. Anxious to be relieved of her burden, she tried to pass it too quickly and dropped it. The brittle shell cracked, splintering the intricate design.

'How could you?' Horrified, Nadia stooped to retrieve her ornamented egg. 'I told you to be careful! Look what you've done! I should never have let you hold it. You're always ruining my things! I'm going to tell Papa about this. You'll be sorry.'

Tears welled in Eva's eyes. As Nadia started up the steps, gently carrying her broken Easter egg, Eva darted into the house ahead of her. She dashed directly into the parlor and sought refuge on the lap of her grandfather, Wolf.

'I didn't mean to drop it,' she sobbed. 'I didn't mean to.'

Nadia followed her into the room and went straight to her father. 'Look, Papa.' Her chin quivered. 'Just look what she did. I hate her.'

'Now, now,' her father admonished gently.

'Let me see it.' Wolf motioned for Nadia to bring him the egg. She walked over to his chair, refusing to look at Eva, who buried herself in the protective crook of her grandfather's arm. After examining the egg, he smiled reassuringly. 'It looks worse than it is. You give me the egg and I think I can fix it for you so you will never see the cracks.'

'I am not a little girl any more, Grandpa.' Nadia held herself stiffly. 'You will make me a new egg and do it so it looks like this one, then pretend it's the same. But it won't be. It won't ever be the same.' She turned with a whirl of petticoats and flounced from the room.

It was still early afternoon when Wolf locked the door of his shop and headed up the street. Rarely did he work a full day in his shop any more, preferring to spend the afternoon hours with his family or visiting friends – or simply by himself.

The afternoon sun was bright, but the air was crisp. Autumn made little visual impack on the evergreen forests of spruce and hemlock that blanketed the mountain slopes and islands. Snow crowned the peaks of the Sisters and Verstovia and frosted the cratered top of Mount Edgecumbe. Wildfowl on their migratory path south flocked in the sky.

Wolf watched the geese flying overhead in a perfect vee formation as he walked along the nearly deserted boardwalk. Earlier in the day the town's batteries had boomed a salute to the Russian vessel entering the harbor. Its arrival had drawn many of the townspeople to the wharf. Some had friends or family among the crew, others hoped for mail, and many were simply curious.

The quiet of the street now was a pleasant change from its usual bustle. There were times when he felt the crowding of twenty-five hundred people on the town's peninsula. It was always spreading, growing. Four cots in the back room of the apothecary shop had grown into a forty-bed hospital. There was a public library, a bowling alley, four lower schools, an academy, and two scientific institutes, one for the study of zoology and the other for terrestrial magnetic phenomena and astronomy. In addition, the third floor of the governor's residence had been converted into a theater for the performance of plays in Russian and French.

As Wolf approached the little teahouse in the town's public gardens, he spied a grizzly bearded Russian in the unfamiliar garb of a promyshlenik. It reminded him of the days when these rough fur hunters, such as his father, Zachar, had dominated the town scene. Otter, seal, fox, and other valuable pelage were still hunted by the Aleuts under Russian supervision, but not in the numbers as before. In an effort to conserve the fur resources of Russian America, a policy instituted under the governorship of Baron Ferdinand von Wrangel several years ago had restricted hunting in a given region to every other year to allow the fur-bearing animals to repopulate unmolested. Furs continued to be the backbone of the Russian American Company's business, but were no longer the only enterprise in which it engaged.

Times change, and Wolf had seen many of the changes. He paused outside the teahouse, studying it for a minute, then walked inside. He sat alone, aware of his oddly contemplative mood. He blamed it on the unsettled mood of the colony, this unanswered question about the future. For himself, he didn't care so much. He was sixty-one years old. He had lived his life.

Yesterday evening his oldest son, Lev, had stopped by to visit, yet they'd talked very little. Wolf sensed his son's frustration and disappointment. Only a few years earlier he'd been excited about the company's plans to begin exploiting the mineral wealth of Russian America, plans they'd followed up by appointing a

Finnish-born mining engineer, Ivan Furguhelm, as the new manager. Then the company's charter wasn't renewed and word came of the negotiations to sell the land to America. Everything came to a stop. The plans were shelved and virtually forgotten.

As Wolf had worked in his shop this morning, he tried to imagine how he would feel if he was deprived of silver – his work medium – if he had to make do with something else that did not have silver's properties, its texture, or its shine. His skill was in shaping and carving this metal, making it come alive under his hands. He understood the loss and frustration that his son must feel to have a skill and no outlet for it.

Distantly he heard the excited shouts coming from the town square, the sound rousing him. Everywhere he looked people were rushing about, laughing and calling to one another. Wolf wandered out of the teahouse as the excitement spilled into the public gardens. He did not hear enough of any one conversation to learn anything beyond the fact that the ship had brought news. Then he saw his son Lev, all smiles, walking quickly toward him.

'What has happened?'

'Have you not heard? Prince Dimitri Maksutov has returned from St. Petersburg. He has been appointed the new governor.' Lev's smile grew wider. 'And he brings news that the Tsar's brother, the Grand Duke Constantine, has signed a pledge to grant the company another twenty-year charter.'

'Another charter.' It took a minute for Wolf to absorb the significance of that. 'Then . . . there will be no sale.'

'No. He has given his word.' Rich laughter broke from Lev. Wolf joined in with him as they clasped each other by the shoulders, rejoicing in the news. 'Tonight there is to be a praznik, with music, dancing, and singing. And the rum is to flow – at the company's expense!'

'And we shall sing Baranov's song,' Wolf vowed, and he began the hymn, his voice raspy with age; but Lev's stronger baritone voice soon joined it as they sang together: 'The will of our hunters, the spirit of trade, On these far shores a new Muscovy made, in bleakness and hardship finding new wealth for fatherland and Tsardom . . .'

Before they finished, a chorus of voices joined them in the patriotic anthem of their land. At the conclusion of the impromptu rendition, there was a poignant silence. Wolf was the only one present who could remember the man who had written the song, the man considered by most to be the father of their country. He'd been sixteen years old when Baranov left. In his mind's eye he could see the short, bald man standing on the deck of the ship, old and tired and sick, gazing one last time at the town he'd built. Baranov had died at sea, near Batavia.

'I never believed for one minute that the Tsar would sell Russian America,' someone declared.

'Nor I,' another insisted.

Suddenly they all claimed they had never believed the rumors. It was unthinkable. The laughter and shouting started again as everyone rushed to spread the news. Arm in arm, Wolf and Lev started for their homes to share the good tidings with their families.

Halfway to Lev's house, they were overtaken by Nadia. She spun to a halt in front of them. 'Have you heard?' She was out of breath, her dark eyes glittering with excitement.

'Heard what?' Lev asked indulgently, holding in his smile.

'Prince Maksutov has come back.'

'He has?' He winked at Wolf.

'Yes, and he has a new bride. Her name is Maria – Princess Maria Maksutova. She's the daughter of the governor general at Irkutsk.' Nadia rushed on: 'She's young, almost my age, and –' Lev started to chuckle, and she stopped in mid-breath, then quickly came to the defense of her statement. 'She's nineteen, and nineteen is close to thirteen.'

'Is that your news?' Wolf asked, trying not to laugh at her.

'Yes, but you see, I saw her,' Nadia hurried to explain. 'She is beautiful, and she has the prettiest smile. Do you think they will have a ball at the castle for her? Do you think Aunt Anastasia will be invited? Do you think she might take me? I would love to go. Mama will probably say I'm too young. Papa, you must talk to her. Just imagine meeting a real prince and princess.'

'We shall see,' he promised.

31 *Sitka*
June 1867

'Grandpa, why does Prince Maksutov want everyone to come to Castle Hill?' Seven-year-old Eva stared at the growing stream of people around them, all headed for the small throng that had already gathered at the foot of the steps. The Greek-styled silver cross danced at the end of the chain around her neck as she bounced alongside her grandfather, Wolf, unconsciously swinging his hand in a wide arc.

'I imagine he has some important news to tell us.'

'But what could it be? Do you think the Tsar has died? Or maybe the Kolosh are going to attack us? Maybe they're hiding in the forest this minute, all painted and wearing their ferocious masks? Do you think Aunt Dominika's relatives will kill us? Would yours?'

'Your imagination works too hard,' he chided gently. 'If the Kolosh were going to attack, the Prince would order the soldiers to the stockade walls, but you see they are here, too.'

'Eva, you are such a chatterbox.' Nadia carefully lifted her crinoline skirts to keep the hem from dragging in the muddy street. 'I expect the Prince has some wonderful news for us and intends to declare a holiday. I wonder if there will be a ball tonight.' She fervently hoped so. She so enjoyed dancing. Glancing over her shoulder, she observed the less than proper comportment of her younger sister. 'Do stop hopping like a frog, Eva. And don't be jerking your grandfather's arm that way. It isn't a pump handle.'

Her excitement subdued by the criticism, Eva stopped skipping and walked sedately beside her grandfather. Sometimes it seemed to her that she never did anything right. She felt the reassuring squeeze of her grandfather's hand and smiled up at him gratefully. He never seemed to mind how much she talked or how plain she looked. He loved her anyway.

The Tarakanov family stood together in a group at the base of the Castle Hill steps. Only Wolf's spouse, Marya, was absent. An illness confined her to bed, and an Aleut woman looked after her. Like those around them, they speculated among themselves about the possible cause for this summons by Prince Maksutov.

It was most unusual. Only the privileged set, composed mainly of officers or managers within the company and their wives and their families, were invited to the balls, plays, or fetes given by their titled governor. The Tarakanov family was on the fringe of that set. Anastasia's marriage to a naval officer had gained her entrance to such festivities. The family connections, coupled with Nadia's natural beauty and aristocratic behavior, occasionally allowed her to be included in the charmed circle.

Soldiers in red-trimmed dark uniforms came smartly to attention at the head of the kremlin steps. A hush settled over the curious crowd below as Prince Maksutov appeared in full dress uniform. His medals for bravery earned during the Crimean War were pinned to his chest for all to see. A Byzantine-styled beard fringed his jaw and chin, giving him a long-faced look. He descended the steps to a midway point, then grimly faced the throng.

'It is my unpleasant duty to inform you that I have received official word from St. Petersburg that Russian America has been sold to the United States.'

Stunned by the totally unexpected announcement, Wolf turned to his children and saw the same shock on their faces. A murmur of dismay ran through the assemblage, followed by a protest.

'What of the pledge to sign a new charter?' someone shouted.

When the Prince failed to respond and offer an explanation, Wolf realized the Tsar had broken his word to them. There could be no other interpretation. He could understand the bitterness he saw in Prince Maksutov's expression.

'They are to take possession in October of this year,' the Prince continued. 'Under the terms of the sale, those of you who wish to remain in the ceded territory are free to do so – with the exception of naval personnel, who will return to Russia. If you choose to stay, the treaty of cession provides that the inhabitants of the ceded territory, "with the exception of uncivilized native tribes, shall be admitted to the enjoyment of all the rights, privileges and immunities of citizens of the United States and shall be maintained and protected in the free enjoyment of their liberty, property and religion." ' The last he read from the paper in his hand.

There was no restriction of race. Only the uncivilized were denied citizenship, Wolf realized, relieved to learn he would not be forced at his age to leave the land of his birth. None of his family need fear their mixed Russian and native ancestry. Then he noticed the apprehension in his daughter's expression and felt the first pang of separation. As the wife of a Russian naval officer, she had to leave with her husband.

'If, within a three-year period, any of you who have chosen to stay should change your mind and wish to move to Russia, the Russian government will provide transportation for you and your families. For those who stay, title will be given to the homes and land you presently occupy. The company will also sign over the various shops, mills, and equipment so that you may carry on your trade or profession. It is hoped that the men in San Francisco who are interested in furs will obtain a franchise from their government so that those of you who work in the peltry will continue to have employment.'

Prince Maksutov explained at length the provisions of the treaty of cession signed in Washington, D.C., and the options available to them. At the conclusion of his address, the crowd was slow to disperse, unconsciously clinging together. So much of their lives had been controlled by the company that this freedom of choice was new to them. There was no one telling them what to do.

'Perhaps it won't be as bad as we feared,' Stanislav suggested, looking to Wolf, his father, for an opinion.

'They cannot claim we are uncivilized.' His Creole wife, Dominika, glanced anxiously at their grown son, Dimitri, who had recently graduated from the navigators' school.

'It isn't a decision we must make hastily.' Lev thoughtfully stroked his mustache. 'We have the opportunity to see what it would be like to be ruled by Americans. It is my feeling we should wait. What do you say, Father?'

But Wolf was watching his daughter as she turned silently to leave, linking her arm with her husband's, her head tipped down. For them there was nothing to decide, no alternative to consider.

Nadia darted quickly to her aunt's side. 'Where are you going?' Anastasia was her favorite aunt, the one who had introduced her to the festive parties and balls.

'There is much to do. Three months will not be as long as it sounds.' Although she appeared calm and poised, Anastasia's eyes looked wet. The prospect of listening to her family discuss whether or not to stay when she must go was too painful to her at the moment, so she grasped for an excuse. 'Everything has to be packed. And I must decide which household items to take and what to do with the rest.'

'Oh, but . . .' The protest died on her lips as Nadia glanced at her uncle, the sight of his uniform recalling the Prince's order that all naval personnel were to return to Russia. For a frantic instant, she wondered how she could obtain invitations to the balls if Anastasia wasn't here, then whether the Americans held such gala affairs. 'I don't want to stay. I want to go, too.'

'That is a decision for your father to make,' Nikolai stated and firmly guided his wife past Nadia.

Nadia turned to appeal to her father. 'We aren't going to stay, are we, Papa?'

'I haven't decided what we will do.' There was a sharpness to his response; he hadn't as yet determined what was best.

'But we are Russian, Papa,' Nadia reasoned. 'How can we stay when the Americans come? It would be disloyal.'

'The Tsar betrayed us,' her cousin Dimitri argued. 'Why was the pledge to grant a new charter not honored? Why was this country sold so secretly? The Tsar does not care what happens to us. I say we owe him no loyalty.'

'Grandpa.' Eva tugged at his hand. 'What are you going to do?'

Wolf shook his head. 'I must go tell Marya what has transpired.' He knew his wife would feel the same as he did and prefer to live out the remainder of their lives in the only land they knew as home. Yet he dreaded telling her that their only daughter would be leaving with her husband.

32

Emerging from the govenor's mansion, Ryan Colby strolled to the top of the veranda steps, then halted and drew a long panatela cigar from his inside jacket pocket. Using the small knife that he kept in the pocket of his brocade vest, he deftly snipped off the closed end of the cigar. Unhurriedly, he returned the knife to his pocket and placed one end of the cigar in his mouth, then reached in another pocket for a match, all the while idly studying the castlelike fortifications atop the knoll and the harbor scene beyond the batteries.

Besides the two American gunboats riding at anchor in the harbor, the *John L. Stevens* was moored in the bay. American troops from the Ninth Infantry and the Second Artillery lounged on the decks. Landing permission had been refused by the Russians until the territory was formally turned over to the United States, an event that waited for the arrival of the official representative from the American government, General Lovell Rousseau, who was en route to Sitka on the U.S.S. *Ossipee*.

Ryan Colby raked the match head across the back of his trousers and cupped the fire close to the cigar tip. His hands and fingers were spotlessly clean and free of calluses. Sunlight showed the copper glints in his light brown mustache and hair, both neatly trimmed. His face rarely revealed what he was thinking unless he wished it. For most of his twenty-five years, he had lived by the quickness of his wits and hands, mostly in the mining camps of California, and of late in San Francisco's Barbary Coast. Experience accounted for the cynicism that was permanently etched into his angular face and made his hazel eyes appear old.

As he shook out the match flame, the door behind him opened. He half turned, leisurely removing the cigar from his mouth, and studied the sandy-haired man coming toward him. He smiled crookedly, briefly commiserating with the eager young attorney over the deal they'd both lost out on.

'I could have saved my breath,' Gabe Blackwood declared, halting beside Ryan. He buttoned the jacket of his three-piece brown tweed suit, but it didn't greatly improve its fit. 'The Prince wasn't even interested in hearing the offer I was authorized to make. I think he'd already made up his mind to sell the company's stock of goods to Hutchinson.'

Ryan shrugged off the loss, too accustomed to luck sometimes sitting on someone else's shoulders to let himself be upset by it. 'And Hutchinson bought it for a song. A mere sixty-five thousand dollars.'

'How do you know that?' Gabe Blackwood frowned.

'I know. It doesn't matter how. He can sell it in California and turn a quarter of a millon dollars in profit. Of course, that shrewd New England trader has convinced Maksutov that most of it will stay here.' Personally, Ryan admired the feat.

'It's obvious Maksutov wasn't doing the negotiating when the Russians got Congress to pay seven millon two hundred thousand dollars for this Alaska Territory.' The attorney donned his derby hat, then started down the steps. Ryan accompanied him.

The two men had met aboard ship en route to the newly purchased territory. In the beginning, Ryan had been amused by the idealistic lawyer who was roughly his own age. His own life had left him with few illusions. Countless times on the voyage, he had marveled at how naive and gullible Blackwood was, always ready to believe the best and certain that right would prevail. The man was intelligent, but he didn't have a grain of common sense. To some things he was as blind as the lady holding the scales. Still, Ryan rather liked the fellow, even though he felt sorry for him.

'What are you going to do now?' Blackwood eyed him curiously as they descended the fortress stairs to the town. 'Head back to California?'

'Me? Not a chance. If Alaska is an iceberg as some of the newspapers claim, then the money Hutchinson just made is only the tip of it. I intend to get my share of the profit, then get the hell out.' Ryan stuck the cigar in his mouth, holding it between his teeth.

'Do you mean you're going into business here? What kind?'

'Look at that town.' Ryan waved his cigar in a sweeping gesture that encompassed the buildings and streets spreading out before them. 'Show me where a man can go to quench his thirst. All you see are churches, a blacksmith shop, bakery, tailor, schools, but not a single saloon or gaming hall. The town could use a few.'

'But' – Blackwood frowned at him – 'territorial laws forbid trafficking in liquor. It's illegal to import it.'

Ryan laughed and shook his head. 'It isn't under territorial law yet. Legal or not, there'll be saloons. And I'm going to have one, if not more. I didn't come here early to buy the Russians' stock of sheepskin coats, hardware, or dry goods. As far as I'm concerned, Hutchinson is welcome to them. I wanted to purchase the company's barrels of rum and casks of wine, its supply of sugar, molasses, and grain to distill my own liquor. If I can, I'm going to buy it from Hutchinson now. If not, I'll have it shipped in.'

'But it will be against the law.'

'Who's going to arrest me, Gabe?' Ryan mocked. 'The Army's going to be in charge after the takeover, at least to start with. You show me a soldier who doesn't like his liquor. The Army isn't going to close down a saloon. But I tell you what – if I get arrested, I'll send for you in California to defend me.'

'I won't be there,' Blackwood replied quietly, appearing subdued and a little hurt by the way Ryan had poked fun at him. 'I'm going to stay here and open a law office.'

'The hell you say.' Ryan had never pegged him as the pioneering sort.

'You saw what it was like in San Francisco before we left. Everyone was talking about Alaska and the opportunities here. It's the same in Seattle and Portland, I've heard. People are going to be coming here. Someday Alaska is going to be a state, and I'm going to be part of making that happen.'

Ryan had heard a lot of big talk in his life. But the determination in Blackwood's voice and the visionary look in his eyes struck Ryan. 'Maybe you'll even be the first governor,' he murmured.

Blackwood glanced sharply at him to see if he was being mocked again. 'Maybe I will,' he asserted defensively.

However idealistically motivated, the man had political ambitions, Ryan realized. And he also knew that more than one man's hide had been saved by influential friends. Blackwood just might be more useful to him than he'd first thought.

'If you're going to open an office, we need to find you a place.

Location's important in any business or profession. Let's take a walk through town.' Ryan directed him up the one and only business street in Sitka. 'I've already picked out the location I want for my saloon. I'll tell you what.' He slapped the hand holding the cigar on Gabe's shoulder, knocking off the buildup of ash. 'I'll be your first client and you can handle all the legal work on the land I want to purchase.'

'I'd like that.' Gabe's sudden grin was almost boyish.

'You're an honest man, Gabe Blackwood.' But Ryan didn't believe for a minute that he would remain so. Nor did he dwell on the thought, his attention moving to assess the town and the various potentials for quick gain. He decided if he had any cash left over, he'd buy up some land on speculation. If Blackwood was right and there was a large influx of Americans following the transfer, property values were bound to rise.

Ryan took a last puff on his cigar, then tossed the smoldering butt into the street. He noticed the small store they had just passed, tucked between two larger buildings on the boardwalk, yet in the center of everything.

'What about this shop?' He motioned the attorney to come back and look at it. Although he couldn't see anyone inside, he tried the door anyway, rattling its hinges, but it was locked. He knocked, ignoring the gabble of Russian he heard coming from the street.

'Ryan.' Gabe Blackwood tapped his arm and motioned toward the young woman and little girl facing them on the boardwalk. 'Do you understand Russian? I think she's talking to us.'

'*Nyet*.' Which was the limit of Ryan's conversational Russian.

But Gabe didn't hear him as he stared at the young Russian woman cloaked in a burnous. Her hair was a shade of golden chestnut, parted in the middle and swept away from her face, framing its perfect features. To Gabe, everything about her was perfect, from the gentle curve of her lips to the delicate blush of her cheeks and the liquid softness of her brown eyes. He wished fervently that he had the Russian dictionary he'd bought at the bookstore in San Francisco, but it was in his trunk.

'Are you Americans?' The little girl's voice jarred him, her English strongly accented but still understandable.

'Do you speak English?' he blurted in astonishment.

'I speak English, German, and French,' the young woman asserted, smiling faintly.

'You are lovely,' he murmured, then realized what he'd said.

At the same instant, he became aware of his lack of manners and swept his hat off his head, simultaneously bowing to her. 'Forgive me. I didn't mean to be rude. Permit me to introduce myself. I am Gabriel Blackwood, a lawyer. I plan to establish a practice here in Sitka. This is my friend, Ryan Colby.' He hardly noticed when his companion bowed to her.

'My name is Nadia Levyena Tarakanova.' Her curtsy was smooth and graceful, confirming his suspicion that she came from a family of some standing in the Russian community. 'This is my little sister, Eva. And this is the shop of my grandfather. It is closed.'

'Is it closed permanently?' Ryan asked. 'What I mean is – does he intend to leave Sitka after the Americans take possession?'

'No.'

'Will *you* be leaving?' Gabe knew that some Russian families had elected to return to their homeland.

'My father chooses to remain for a time.'

Although it was obviously not her desire to stay, Gabe smiled. 'I'm glad,' he said, gazing at her in open adoration. A hint of an answering smile touched her lips. He thought her expression delightfully demure.

'We'd like to see the inside of the shop,' Ryan stated. 'Is it possible to have your grandfather show it to us?'

'My grandfather mourns the death of my grandmother. He had not said when he plans to open the shop.'

'I am sorry to hear of your grandmother's passing.' Gabe hurried to offer his sympathy. 'Please extend my condolences to your family, Miss Tarakanova.'

'You are kind.'

'Not at all. Under the circumstances, this would not be a proper time to speak to your grandfather, but would you tell him that I may be interested in buying his shop if he wants to sell it?' It gave him the perfect excuse to become acquainted with the Tarakanov family – and the lovely Nadia. 'Perhaps I might take the liberty of calling on him next week. Does he speak English as well as you do?'

'He speaks a little English,' she said.

'Maybe you or your father could arrange to be present in the event I have any difficulty making my offer understood.'

'Perhaps.'

'How may I contact you? Where do you live? I could come by

your home.' Gabe wasn't willing to let her get away without knowing where to find her.

She hesitated, as a proper lady should, then gave him directions to her home.

'Are you buying this land?' Nadia's sister tipped her head to the side and studied him with a thoughtful frown.

'Maybe.' It was difficult for Gabe to believe this homely child was Nadia's sister. The washed-out brown of her hair didn't have that golden sheen to it. Her nose was too straight and her mouth too wide. 'Why do you ask?'

'You are American. And everyone is sad because Americans are buying this land. The Kolosh say this land belongs to them,' she stated importantly.

'The Kolosh?' Gabe arched an eyebrow.

'I think she's referring to the Indians,' Ryan said.

'You mean the savages living outside the stockade in those filthy hovels.' He'd noticed the Ranche beyond the gates and the small market area where the local Indians sold fish and game as well as a few wood carvings.

'They say the Americans should pay the money to them,' Eva said.

'The Army should herd them onto a reservation, them and their half-breeds.' Gabe's voice quivered on a note of hate that was buried deep inside him – a hate born at the death of his missionary parents. He'd only been six years old when they'd left him in the care of an aunt in San Francisco and gone to live among the filthy savages to save their heathen souls. Gabe still had their letters that spoke of their love for their red brethren – the same ones who rose up and killed them, led by a half-breed they'd trusted and called son.

'Half-breed,' Nadia repeated cautiously. 'What does this word mean?'

'Someone who is part Indian and part white.'

'Oh. We call them Creole. Many live here and go to our schools and work for the company.'

'I see.' Gabe had his own opinion, but he didn't consider it an appropriate topic of discussion.

Her sister started to say something else, but Nadia quickly shushed her. 'Forgive Eva. She thinks everyone wants to talk with her, too.'

'I understand.' Gabe smiled.

358

'We must leave now. It was a pleasure meeting you, Mr. Blackwood, and Mr. . . . .' she hesitated over Ryan's name.

'Colby.' He nodded to her.

'Mr Colby.' She cast another glance at Gabe, then ushered her sister past them.

Gabe turned to watch her walk away, observing the faint sway of the tassel that weighted the hood of her burnous.

'You didn't waste any time staking your claim,' Ryan observed dryly.

Turning, Gabe looked at him. 'You aren't the only one who knows what you want. Remember when you said I might become the governor of Alaska someday. Well, I think you just met the woman who is going to be the governor's lady.' The more he thought about it, the more auspicious it seemed. 'It would be fitting, a marriage between the old Alaska and the new.'

33 *Sitka*
October 18, 1867

The Tarakanov family walked down the streets of New Archangel, a silent procession led by the family patriarch, Wolf. The
recent death of his wife had aged him, taken the spring from his
step and the light from his eyes. Yet death was a part of life and
life a part of death. And he knew he must carry on.

Despite the urgings of his family to remain at home, Wolf had
insisted on attending the ceremonial transfer of ownership. The
ship carrying the Russian and American commissioners who were
to officiate at the ceremony had arrived in the harbor that very
morning. Through his daughter's husband, Nikolai Politoffski,
they had learned the transfer was to take place at three o'clock
that afternoon at the parade ground atop the knoll.

Wolf believed that his family should be present when the new
regime took power. After all, since they intended to remain and
live under the dominion of the United States, then out of respect
they should be there when the transfer occurred. But his opinion
wasn't shared by most of the townspeople, who preferred not to
witness it.

But already the town that the Americans persisted in calling
Sitka was feeling the pangs of the coming of the Americans. More
changes would occur as soon as Prince Maksutov completed the
process of deeding title to homes, lands, and shops to their
various occupants and tradesmen. Even Wolf had agreed to sell
his shop to Nadia's young American.

At the bottom of the steps leading to the kremlin, Wolf paused
and looked back to make sure all the family was with him. Only
his son's wife, Dominika, was absent. She had remained at home,
fearing her strongly Indian features would arouse the Americans'
prejudice. But Stanislav had come, along with his son, Dimitri.

Shallow puddles were scattered over the parade ground in front
of the governor's residence, but no rain fell. The sun occasionally

broke through the thick white clouds to warm the cool afternoon. The Imperial flag of Tsarist Russia fluttered atop the ninety-foot pole that stood in the middle of the parade ground. Now and then the light breeze whipped the ensign of the double eagle fully out.

The harbor was choked with craft as the Kolosh, who were not allowed in town that afternoon, positioned their canoes amidst the Russian ships and American naval vessels anchored there so they could observe the proceedings, curious about the event to which the white men attached so much importance. The Kolosh had mixed feelings about the coming of the Americans. Their experience with the Yankee whalers who raided their villages, capturing their men and carrying off their women, made them wary. Yet they knew, too, that the Americans sold liquor, which the Russians had always denied them.

Standing close to her Aunt Anastasia, Nadia tightly held the woman's gloved hand. She was emotionally torn, grasping to hold on to the past with its parties and balls, and reaching out at the same time for the reassurance of Gabe Blackwoods's flattering attention. He stood with a small group of Americans, mainly San Francisco merchants. Since she'd met him, Nadia hadn't been so eager to leave once the Americans took possession.

She felt a tremor of excitement when he smiled and nodded to her. No one had ever made her feel quite so beautiful or important as he did. Sometimes, when he looked at her a certain way, she felt all warm inside. She wanted to see more of him, yet she didn't want to appear disloyal to her aunt.

The measured beat of drums signaled the start of the ceremony. Soon Nadia could hear the tramp of marching boots on the fortress steps as the Russian soldiers from the Siberian regiment stationed at the garrison, along with the eighty sailors and officers of the Imperial Navy, climbed the stairs. They were led by the Russian commissioner, Captain Alexei Peshchurov, the official representative of the Tsar.

As the soldiers in their red-trimmed uniforms and glazed caps lined up facing the flagstaff and stood stiffly at attention, Nadia glanced at the governor of Russian America. On this day, Prince Maksutov was strictly a spectator. His expression was impassive, but his young wife, Princess Maria, appeared to be near tears. Looking at the beautiful princess who had been responsible for the gaiety and laughter, the music and the balls that had dominated the social scene for the past three years, Nadia wanted to cry, too.

Distantly came the rumble of more drums. The American soldiers were ashore. The sound grew steadily louder as they approached the hill. At the head of the column, cresting the stairs, marched two generals, heavy gold epaulets on their shoulders, gold sashes across their chests, and polished swords hanging at their sides. The light breeze ruffled the dark feather boas that crowned their Napoleonic hats.

Behind her, Dimitri leaned forward to whisper near Nadia's ear, 'The nearest one is General Lovell Rousseau, Peshchurov's counterpart. The one with the beard is Major General Davis, who will be in command of the American troops. Before he was sent here, he was fighting Indians in the American West.'

'How do you know?' she asked over her shoulder, wishing he hadn't mentioned the word Indian. Since she'd met Gabe Blackwood, she didn't want to remember that anything other than Russian blood flowed in her veins.

'I talked to the pilot that brought the American ships into the harbor.'

Sunlight broke through the clouds and flashed on the gold-spiked helmets worn by the American soldiers as they marched across the parade ground and lined up at attention before the flagpole. Nadia stared at their strange uniforms of dark blue jackets and light blue trousers, and the long rifles they carried.

Her attention was diverted by the Russian color guard as they marched to the base of the flagpole. According to her uncle, the ceremony was to be a simple one: the lowering of the Russian flag and the raising of the American, each accompanied by a cannon salute by the fortress batteries and the guns of the American ships in the harbor.

As one of the soldiers loosened the ropes to haul down the Imperial ensign, the wind suddenly picked up and whipped the flag around the pole. The soldier attempted to tug it loose, but it curled tighter around the staff and became tangled in the ropes. Another soldier came to his aid, but the flag resisted their efforts and clung to the pole. Tension mounted at the unexpected delay. Advice began to come from all sides, but nothing worked.

'The flag doesn't want to come down, does it, Grandpa?' young Eva remarked loudly.

Nadia had the same impression. The flag's resistance to all

attempts to haul it down seemed symbolic, as if it too wanted to continue its reign over this land. Tears pricked her eyes. Beside her, Anastasia cried softly.

After a nerve-racking delay, a Russian sailor was ordered aloft to cut the flag free. On the last breath of a dying breeze, the Russian flag floated down. As it came to rest on the bayonets of the Russian soldiers, Princess Maria fainted.

When it was rescued, Captain Peshchurov made a brief declaration on behalf of the Russian government, making the territory over to the United States of America. The order was given to present arms, and the cannonade salute from the Russian batteries and the American warships began, the thunderous booms vibrating all around Nadia, leaving her shaken when it ended.

Immediately after General Rousseau accepted the delivery of the territory, the American flag was hoisted to the top of the pole. It hung limp and lifeless. With the first salute from a Russian cannon, the flag appeared to shudder. As the firing of the second cannon echoed and re-echoed against the mountains, the flag unfurled its red and white stripes and blue field of stars.

Aunt Anastasia bowed her head and covered her tear-stained face with her hands. Nadia wrapped a comforting arm around her shoulders, crying softly, too. The rousing cheers of the Americans seemed heartless and cruel. As their last jubilant 'hip-hip-hoorah!' faded, the new commander of the military in the territory that the Americans called Alaska stepped forward to make an announcement.

'I am Major General Jefferson C. Davis. I am in sole command of this garrison and this territory. Quarters for myself and my wife are to be immediately made available in the former governor's residence. The barracks are to be vacated and made available for immediate occupation by the troops of the United States Army. All buildings are now the property of the United States government.'

'No,' Anastasia murmured, clutching at Nadia's hand. 'The ship taking us to Russia is not to leave for a month yet. All my things are not yet packed. They cannot turn us out of our home. Where will we go?' Panic-stricken, she turned to her father. 'Papa, what are we to do?'

'You and Nikolai will move in with me. There is plenty of room in my empty house for your belongings,' Wolf assured her, but the general's orders made it clear to everyone that there

363

would be no gradual transition of authority. The Americans were in charge now, and the Russians were literally tossed out in the street.

Within a month the face of Sitka had changed drastically. No more were the guard beats walked by soldiers from the Siberian regiment. Now the sentries who patrolled the palisade and stood watch at the fortress wore the blue uniforms of the United States Army. The Russians had never bothered to name the town's streets, but the Americans quickly remedied that. The main thoroughfare became Lincoln Street, and the two cross streets were called Russia and America.

Everywhere there was overcrowding as the town first had to absorb the Russian families from outlying settlements on the mainland and the Aleutian Islands then had to make room for the Russian soldiers and sailors from the garrison taken over by the American Army, most of whom were waiting to depart on ships bound for Russia. The crowding was compounded by the arrival of several hundred American settlers who jammed the streets. Stakes dotted the town and extended its previous limits for miles, plotting out home-steads. Crude shanties were thrown up, then sold to newcomers for exorbitant prices.

The two commissioners, American Rousseau and Russian Peshchurov, had remained at Sitka for a week, working together to deed title to lands, shops, and homes to Russian individuals. With the exception of the homes, most of the property had changed hands almost overnight, and continued to be bought and sold, each time at a higher price.

Late morning on a bleak and gray day in mid-November, Ryan Colby strolled along the boardwalk, his hands thrust in the pockets of his black cloth redingote, the cigar in his mouth tilted at a jaunty angle. The streets and sidewalks were crowded with bustling people, but he didn't mind the occasional jostling of his elbow.

The steady din of voices – Russian, American, and one or two languages he didn't recognize – was a sound as pleasant as the clink of coins in his cash box. Like the hammering and sawing in the background and the almost constant activity at the wharf, it all meant business and profits for him, both at his saloon and in land sales.

Taking the cigar from his mouth, he nudged his companion.

364

'Look at this, Gabe.' He gestured at the throng of people and the horse-drawn drays rattling up and down the street. 'It's a boomtown, and it's just the beginning. We have storekeepers, homesteaders, prospectors, shipowners, cooks, bakers, a few squatters, real estate dealers, promoters, speculators, gamblers, and whores.' A new sign was going up on a building across the street. Signs seemed to be always coming down and new ones going up as businesses changed hands sometimes twice in one week. This one caught Ryan's eye, and he stopped. 'Now we're getting a barbershop. I tell you, Gabe, this town is busting wide open.'

'Which is exactly why it was so important to draw up a town charter, establish some ordinances, and elect a mayor and city council so we can regulate some of this growth. Granted, we don't have the legal authority to do this yet, and we can't legally transfer title to the various lands that have been sold, not until Congress enacts legislation officially granting us territorial status and bringing us under territorial government.' Gabe had been in the thick of all the organizing, and Ryan had stayed well clear of it. He and the law had never gotten along.

'You're saying that the town ordinances are invalid and your regulations can't be enforced.' Ryan started walking again.

'Technically that's correct. At present, we're under military rule, which means General Davis is the only authority. But it's only a matter of time before Congress makes Alaska a territory. Right now, they're still arguing over the appropriation bill authorizing the seven-million-plus dollar payment to Russia. Our situation is only temporary.' The attorney's optimism was unflagging. 'Even General Davis agreed to the formation of a city council and mayor and gave them authority in town matters.'

'The general was probably glad to have problems like sanding pavements this winter taken off his hands,' Ryan suggested dryly, then paused in front of the door to the newly built restaurant. 'I haven't had breakfast yet. The saloon business doesn't allow me to be an early riser like you. Come and have a cup of coffee.'

'I –' Hesitating, Gabe Blackwood glanced up the street as if he had somewhere else to go. His expression suddenly brightened. 'Isn't that – Excuse me, Ryan.' He moved off, quickly sidling his way through the pedestrians on the boardwalk.

Ryan hardly needed to look to know who the man had seen.

Sure enough, when he glanced up the street, he saw Nadia Tarakanova, accompanied by her grandfather and younger sister, approaching.

'Miss Tarakanova.' Gabe halted in front of her, blocking their path. He removed his hat, indifferent to the chilling breeze that ruffled his sandy hair. He would have taken her hand and kissed it, but the empty market basket she carried made such gallantry awkward. 'What a delightful surprise to see you in town this morning. And you, too, Mr. Tarakanov.' Belatedly he acknowledged her grandfather. 'Forgive me if I find it difficult to take my eyes off your granddaughter. I have never known a lovelier woman. The sight of her is like food to a starving man.'

So captivated was he by the wholesome beauty of her rosy-cheeked face framed by a fur-lined hood, Gabe didn't notice her agitation. 'I am so glad to see you, Mr. Blackwood.' He heard the anxiety in her voice. 'We have just come from the market. We tried to purchase some fresh meat, but the Kolosh – the Tlingits as you call them – refused to accept our money.'

'Your money . . .' Gabe hesitated, searching for a delicate way to phrase his question. 'Is it the parchment paper that the Russian American Company formerly used as currency?'

'Yes.'

'I'm sorry, but few tradesmen are accepting it in payment for goods any more, then only at a heavy discount.' He hated to see her look so stricken.

'But I have no other currency. What am I to do?'

'Now you're allowing yourself to become upset over nothing. It's really a very minor problem, merely a matter of exchanging that old currency for American coin.' Gabe glanced over his shoulder, relieved to see Ryan still standing by the restaurant door. If he'd had the money, Gabe would gladly have changed her currency on the spot, but he was confident his friend would help her out. 'Mr. Colby may be able to help you. Let's go have some tea and talk to him.'

She spoke to her grandfather in Russian. Although Gabe had learned a few Russian words, his grasp of the language was still woefully inadequate. Her grandfather nodded, appearing to consent to Gabe's suggestion.

'We will have tea with you and speak with Mr. Colby,' she said.

'Good.'

366

Gabe led the way to the restaurant entrance where Ryan stood. After an exchange of greetings they went inside. The busy restaurant was noisy with the clatter of dishes, food orders shouted back and forth between the cook and the servers, and the steady chatter of voices. Gabe guided Nadia to an unoccupied end of a long table and waited until she was seated on the bench with her long skirts properly arranged, then sat down beside her. Ryan and her grandfather sat opposite, with seven-year-old Eva between them.

Gabe explained the Tarakanovs' currency plight to Ryan. Although he knew as well as Ryan that the company scrip was almost as worthless as Confederate money, he silently appealed to his friend to be generous, as a personal favor. Ryan obliged, exchanging the two-inch-square pieces of parchment for considerably more than they were worth.

'Didn't I tell you that it was nothing to trouble yourself over?' Gabe watched as Nadia pushed the black fox-lined hood off her head. Her every movement, her every gesture, was a thing of grace to him.

'I can never thank you enough for this.'

'Forgive me for speaking so boldly, Miss Tarakanova.' Gabe spoke with all the volubility of a lovesick swan, and Ryan dipped his chin, hiding the smile that twitched the corners of his mouth. 'But you remind me of a Russian princess.'

'I know all about princesses,' young Eva piped up. 'We had more than Princess Maria. Anna, the Kenai woman who was the mother of Baranov's children, was made a Russian princess.'

'You mean she was an Indian princess,' Ryan corrected, indulgently responding to the child's attempt to take part in the adult conversation.

'No.' She shook her head in a vigorous denial. 'The Tsar made her a real Russian princess. Her name was Anna. Grandpa told me. Didn't you, Grandpa?'

'Yes. She lived to be an old woman,' Wolf Tarakanov confirmed.

'Do you mean the Russians actually gave a noble title to an Indian?' Gabe looked skeptical.

'Yes. It has been the custom of the Russian Tsars to bestow the titles and privileges of nobility on certain persons of a conquered race,' Nadia replied, but Ryan noticed how uneasy she appeared to be with the subject under discussion.

'Making a princess out of an ordinary savage is carrying the custom a bit too far, I would say,' Gabe stated. 'But it shows you just how meaningless titles are and the incompetence of a monarchy. In a democracy, a person achieves importance based on skills or intelligence, not at the whim of some king.'

'The daughter of Princess Anna and Baranov married a man who became one of the governors of Russian America.' Gabe's critical comments had gone over Eva's head. But the subject had gained her the attention of the adults, and she intended to pursue it.

'One of your governors was married to a half-breed?' Gabe frowned and shook his head. 'I suppose in those times there was a shortage of decent women here, just as there is on most frontiers.'

'Grandpa has been telling Eva many stories about the early days,' Nadia offered, almost as an apology. 'She spends many afternoons with him now that the school is closed. I have tried to spend time with her as well and teach her the things that I learned at Lady Etolin's school. It is difficult without the books on history and geography, but she does well with her needlework and languages.'

'Well, you needn't worry about her education much longer, Miss Tarakanova. The school will be open soon. We have a school board now and we're in the process of hiring a teacher,' Gabe assured her. 'Soon you will see a new Sitka, an American Sitka.'

'I have seen a new Sitka,' Wolf Tarakanov inserted dryly.

Ryan studied him curiously. 'Something in your voice tells me that you don't care much for the changes around here.'

The old man shrugged his shoulders. 'Perhaps the changes come too quickly for us. There has always been a pattern to our lives. Every day we knew what to expect. Now all is different. Our pace was slow, but all you Americans hurry, hurry everywhere. It confuses us.'

'You are used to an autocratic rule where nearly every facet of your life is controlled by someone in authority. It will take you time to adjust,' Gabe said. 'But soon you will see how much better the democratic form works. You are your own man now. Nobody tells you what to do.'

'That is so. Once we had to buy all our goods from the company at the prices they set, but they gave us all the fish we could eat. Once we had schools for our children. We had doctors and a hospital. We had to work every day except Sundays and Holy Days.'

'You have that now.' Gabe looked quizzically at the old man.

'Ah, but now this is America and we must pay for everything. But you won't accept our money and we have no work.'

'Well put, Mr. Tarakanov.' Ryan laughed. 'But the American way of doing things is called the free enterprise system. Everybody is free to make as much as they can – and spend as much as they want – and work as much as they have to. You can't sit back and wait for the other guy to pass you the plate. You've got to go out there and grab for yourself. That's how you get rich.'

'There is much more to democracy than merely the commercial gain,' Gabe hastened to add. 'It's a very civilized form that protects the rights of the individual. We have the opportunity here in Alaska to impove the social and economic conditions for everyone. Someday this territory is going to become one of the states in the republic. It's a new land. Its very name Alaska means "great land". Why, we can make this the greatest state in the whole United States of America.'

'And, Mr. Tarakanov, this man hopes to be governor of the great state of Alaska someday.' Ryan gestured toward Gabe. 'I say that in case you didn't guess from that speech he just gave.'

'Is this possible?' Nadia wondered, staring at Gabe with new interest.

'It's possible. In America a man can hold any office. I could even be elected President. I do have some friends in Washington, D.C.' Gabe attempted a diffident shrug of his shoulders. 'Maybe in a few years I might even get appointed territorial governor.'

'I think you would make a wonderful governor, Mr. Blackwood. I hope I will be there the day it happens,' Nadia murmured.

'I hope you will, too.'

Demurely she lowered her lashes under his ardent gaze. 'By then you will have forgotten about me.'

'No. I shall never forget my Russian princess. It is my fondest wish that you would be there at my side.' Which was the closest Gabe had come to openly declaring himself since he'd been seeing her during the last month.

Aware that Gabe's interest was solely for the young woman at his side, Ryan engaged her grandfather in conversation, questioning him about the old days. He feigned interest, nodding and tossing in an 'Is that right?' or 'You don't say' here and there, but he followed little of the old man's lengthy ramblings. His Russian-accented English was much too thick to be easily understood.

369

By the time Ryan's breakfast order was slapped onto the table in front of him, the Tarakanovs had finished their tea.

'Nadia Levyena, I know you have no wish to deprive your young man of your company, but your mama will worry that we are so long away, and I have bored Mr. Colby enough with my talk,' her grandfather announced. 'There is still the marketing we must do.'

'Grandpa is right. It is time we went,' Nadia admitted reluctantly, rising from the bench and stepping clear of the table. As Ryan politely stood, Gabe quickly came to his feet. Nadia turned to Gabe, her market basket in hand. 'I must thank you for the tea.'

'Your smile is all the thanks I need,' he insisted. 'With your permission, I would like to call on you this evening.'

'Your company would be most welcome.' She inclined her head in a graceful nod, but her proper reply couldn't mask the quick glow of pleasure that came to her face.

After the Tarakanovs had taken their leave, Ryan sat down to begin eating his stack of molasses-covered sourdough pancakes, but Gabe was slower to return to his bench seat. As the bearded, aproned man came around with the coffeepot, Ryan held out his tin mug for a refill.

'Ain't you Colby what has the Double Eagle saloon up the street?' the man asked.

'The same,' Ryan acknowledged.

'I'm a miner by trade. Had me some claims along the American River. You can take it from a professional, this here is gold country. Come first melt, I figger to get out in these mountains an' find jest where it's hidin'. I'm just killin' time workin' here in this hash house o'er the winter whilst I put myself together an outfit. S'not, ya understand, that I'm greedy. If'n I wast' have a pardner that'd back me, I'd be gen'rous 'bout givin' him a cut in the mine, 'specially if'n he was someone like you, Mr. Colby.'

'I don't throw my money away grubstaking prospectors.' Although a gambler, Ryan considered the odds being offered too long.

'I'm an experienced miner,' the man protested indignantly.

'Not interested.' Ryan set his cup on the table and picked up his fork, giving his attention to the plate of flapjacks.

'When I make my strike, you'll remember this day an' kick yourself for the chance ya lost.' The has-slinging prospector stalked away from the table.

370

'Everybody's out to strike it rich,' Gabe declared with a shake of his head.

'You make it sound like a crime, barrister.' Ryan shoveled a forkful of pancake into his mouth.

'Everyone's looking to see what they can gain from this territory. They don't seem to realize the opportunity we have to build something here. There's more to life than profit.' He sat hunched over his coffee mug, a troubled frown clouding his face.

'It's for sure no one can accuse you of being a shyster, but I'm beginning to wonder if you're a fool.'

'Why would you say that?' Gabe demanded.

'How many offers have you had to buy that office of yours on Lincoln Street?'

'A few.'

'And each one higher than the last.'

'Sure, but I have my office there and I sleep in the back room. You were the one who urged me to buy it. You claimed it was an ideal location.'

'Because the property fronting the main street in town was bound to rise in value. And the prices have soared. But you'd better think about unloading it before they drop.'

'I didn't buy it with the intention of selling it.'

'Then you are a fool.' Ryan grimaced in wry disgust.

'Why does it make me a fool because I plan to hold on to it?' Gabe challenged.

Ryan leaned forward. 'This place is booming right now, but it isn't going to last. One of two things is going to happen. Either it's going to level off or it's going to go bust. Why take a chance? Make your money while you can.'

'That's what you're doing, I suppose.' Gabe Blackwood struggled to control his anger.

'You're damned right. I'm going to make my fortune and get the hell out of here. You wanta stay, then that's your choice. But take my advice and make youself some money while it's to be had. You can still do your good deeds, like helping those squatters and not charging them a fee.'

'They weren't squatters. They were homesteaders. What this town needs is fewer people whose only interest is in getting rich quick, and more God-fearing people like the Johnsons and the Tarakanovs.'

'The Tarakanovs?' Ryan arched an eyebrow in vague surprise.

'Yes, the Tarakanovs.' Gabe bristled at the inference, his fair skin reddening with anger. 'I suppose you think Nadia's grandfather is a fool as well, simply because he doesn't endorse your particular brand of aggressive commercialism.'

'Not at all,' Ryan replied, stabbing another bite of pancake with his fork.

'Well, I should say not. You have only to look at old Mr. Tarakanov to know that he comes from a fine, upstanding family. Those proud Slavic features of his say it all.'

Ryan halted in the act of raising his fork, letting it pause midway to his mouth. It occurred to him to correct Gabe's obvious misconception as to Wolf Tarakanov's origins. The blue eyes might be Russian, but his features were unquestionably those of a breed. He carried the forkful of food to his mouth, electing to remain silent, deciding that if Gabe wanted to believe the Tarakanovs were pure Russian, that was his business. He had tried to help the man before, but it was evident Gabe didn't appreciate it. And he had nothing to gain by straightening him out on this point.

But he was mildly amused at how Blackwood's infatuation with this Nadia had blinded him to the extent that he saw what he wanted to see and nothing more. The man was a dreamer, and Ryan wondered if maybe that wasn't worse than being a fool. Reality had a way of shattering dreams.

Nadia bent close to the mirror, turning her face this way and that, searching for imperfections with the help of the high flame of the lamp wick. Straightening a little, she licked her fingertips, then slicked the sides of her golden brown hair, flattening them more closely to her head.

But she was still dissatisfied with her appearance. She wanted so much to look beautiful for Gabe Blackwood when he came. Just thinking about him, she experienced a little rush of excitement that quickened her pulse.

All afternoon she'd been recalling his remark that maybe someday he'd be governor here and trying to imagine herself as his wife, presiding over the dinners and fetes as she'd seen Princess Maria do. The prospect thrilled her. And he had called her a princess, she remembered, and said he wanted her at his side.

Feeling terribly daring, she took out the small wooden box that she kept secreted away in the second drawer. She removed the drawstring pouch hidden inside. In the pouch was a square of wool saturated with white lead and chalk. Carefully Nadia dusted her face with the 'Spanish paper,' using it sparingly so it wouldn't be too noticeable.

'What are you doing?'

Nadia jumped guiltily, her heart seeming to leap into her throat as she jerked her hand downward, trying to conceal the patch of whitened wool, but if left a faint powdery trail in the air. Some of her panic eased as she realized it was only her sister.

'You shouldn't sneak up on people, Eva. You startled me.' Hurriedly she tried to stuff the Spanish paper back in its pouch.

'What have you got there?' Eva peered around Nadia before she could get it back inside. Her little sister gasped loudly. 'You powdered your face. Mama says only bad women paint their faces.'

'That's nonsense. Aunt Anastasia powders her face, and she isn't a bad woman.' As Nadia pulled the drawstrings taut, a little puff of white came from the bag.

'Is that who gave it to you?' Eva asked, wide-eyed.

'If you must know, yes!' Nadia returned the pouch to its box, then hesitated before returning the wooden box to its hiding place in her drawer. 'Don't you say a word about this to Mama. She wouldn't understand.'

'Can I wear some?'

'When you are older, you may.' She tucked the box in a corner of the drawer, then hesitated and turned to her sister. 'When Mr. Blackwood comes tonight, I don't want you to say one word to him about the Kolosh or any of the Indians. He isn't interested in your silly stories.'

'Why?'

'Because he doesn't like Indians.' She studied her reflection in the mirror and adjusted the drape of the shawl on her shoulders.

'Doesn't he like you?'

'Of course he does.'

'But you are part Indian like me.'

Nadia whirled away from the mirror and caught her little sister by the shoulders, bending at the waist to stare her in the eye. 'I am Russian. So are you.'

Eva cringed. 'But Grandpa says –'

'I don't care what Grandpa says,' Nadia declared angrily. 'He is old and he doesn't know what he's talking about. Indians are those natives who live in the Ranche. They don't believe in God, and they don't know how to read or write. Their houses have no furniture. They don't have beds; they sleep on the floor like animals. We are not Indians, and don't you ever say that again!'

'I'm sorry.' Eva contritely bowed her head.

'Nadia?' As her mother appeared in the bedroom doorway, she released Eva and straightened quickly. 'Mr. Blackwood has arrived. I beleive he wishes to see you.'

For an instant she stared at her mother's faintly teasing smile, conscious of the wild fluttering in her stomach. She swung back to the mirror for one last inspection. 'Do I look nice?'

'I am certain Mr. Blackwood will think you are beautiful. Come. He is waiting.'

As her mother retreated from the doorway, Nadia said to her younger sister, 'Mind what I said.' Then she hurried after her mother, furiously biting her lips to make them appear red.

34

A March wind prowled outside the wood-frame house, seeking a crack in the mortises and howling its frustration. A heavy cloud cover created a false twilight, necessitating the early-afternoon use of oil lamps. Their yellow flame-glow cast an amber light on the window-panes.

A fire burned in the parlor hearth, radiating heat into the room. From his chair positioned close to the warming blaze, Wolf stared at his sons and their families, all gathered together in this one room, some sitting, some standing, the younger ones perched on laps or squatting on the floor. Only his daughter, Anastasia, was missing. She had sailed with her husband this past December on a ship bound for Russia.

That almost forgotten need to belong was suddenly strong within him again. He was a Tarakanov. He belonged to the family. His strength came from their numbers. A voice from the past echoed in his mind.

'They always leave.' He murmured the words old Tasha had whispered long ago.

'What did you say, Papa?' Stanislav's voice dispelled the poignant recollection.

'Nothing.' He shook his head, trying to shake off his melancholy and rouse himself. 'Your news saddens me, Stanislav Vasilivich.'

'It is not a decision that I make without sadness. It does not fill me with joy to take my family and leave here. But neither do I wish to remain,' his son stated. 'There is no order here under the Americans. Twice my wife has been accosted in the street by drunken American soldiers. Is anything done about it?' No. When the soldiers are off duty, they drink. No one controls them. It accomplishes nothing to complain to their general. He reprimands them but takes no steps to stop the disorder. The sale of liquor is not illegal, he says. It is only illegal to import it. It is no longer safe for our women to walk alone on the streets.'

'You have decided so much.' Wolf sighed heavily. 'Yet never have you spoken a word of this to me.'

'You have said many times that this is where you will stay,' he reminded him.

Wolf looked at his two sons. Both were silent. Both sat with bowed heads. 'Lev, have you known of this?'

After a moment's pause, Lev nodded a confirmation while Stanislav stared at his clasped hands. Once no decision affecting the family would have been made without consulting him, but Wolf realized that the coming of the Americans with their ideas of individual freedom had changed even that.

'Papa.' Stanislav flexed his fingers to tighten the grip of his hands. 'We said we would wait and see how it was with the Americans. But a man cannot live here and take care of his family. The prices the Americans charge for everything are high. The workers in my shop, even the Aleuts, demand that I pay them five dollars a day in Yankee gold. It is too much. I cannot pay this and feed my family. I must think of them.' He pleaded for Wolf's understanding. 'You know how it is for my wife – the way the Americans treat her, the names they call her.'

But this blow was almost more than Wolf could absorb. There seemed so little left for him to say . He reached for the pipe in his pocket, seeking its comfort and attempting to cover his own bewilderment, but his hand was shaking.

'So you leave,' Wolf murmured.

'Yes. Next week there is a ship that leaves for Russia.'

For Wolf, there was pain in knowing that this was a decision Stanislav had been contemplating since before his sister left in December, yet he had been unaware his son was so dissatisfied here.

'And you, Lev.' Wolf looked to his eldest son. 'Will you be deserting me, too?'

A protesting cry came from Nadia as she sank to her knees beside her father's chair. 'Papa, you cannot mean to do this. I want to stay.'

At almost the same moment, eight-year-old Eva flung herself onto Wolf's lap, clinging to him and crying, 'I don't want to leave you.'

Emotion choked his throat as he patted the brown head

pressed against his chest. 'I don't want you to go, my pet.'

'Have no fear,' Lev assured them all. 'We are not leaving. We will stay here.'

'So will I,' asserted Stanislav's son, Dimitri.

Tears welled in his eyes, and Wolf sniffed self-consciously, unable to speak for fear of his voice breaking. He simply nodded instead. When a knock at the front door distracted his family's attention, Wolf took advantage of the diversion to wipe the moisture from his eyes.

The front door opened and a blustering wind whooshed into the room. Gabe Blackwood darted quickly through the opening and stepped to one side, stamping the snow off his boots. His nose and cheeks were reddened from the cold.

'Hello, everyone.' He pulled the fur cap off his sandy hair, smiling broadly at all of them.

Recovering from her surprise, Nadia rose to her feet and went to meet him. 'Mr. Blackwood, welcome.' But her greeting wasn't as warm as it might have been. She was too aware of the other family members in the room and the reason they had all gathered.

'Forgive me if I'm intruding. I can come another time,' Gabe suggested uncertainly.

Before answering, Nadia glanced at her grandfather, hoping he would invite him to stay. He nodded, granting his permission for her young man to remain. 'Please come in, Mr. Blackwood.'

As Gabe started to unbutton his fleece-lined coat, Wolf Tarakanov said, 'Mr. Blackwood must be chilled after his walk. Take him into the kitchen and fix him some tea.'

'I'd like that, Mr. Tarakanov. Thank you.'

Although Nadia noticed how quickly Gabe took advantage of the opportunity to be alone with her, she was too troubled by the recent discussion to feel pleased. She had caught the note of regret in Lev's voice when he had agreed to remain in Sitka. She suspected that he had decided to stay not because it was his wish but because he felt it was his duty to look after his father.

In the kitchen, she busied herself with filling the samovar with water and lighting its fire. As she took the teapot down from its cabinet shelf, her hand lingered on the cedar door. Her uncle Stanislav had built these cabinets for her grandfather.

'You are troubled about something, aren't you?'

Nadia half turned, smiling quickly to conceal her concern from him. 'No. It's just that Grandfather has no sugar for your tea. He has only honey to sweeten it.' She reached for the small crock on the cabinet shelf.

'Something is wrong. I sensed it when I arrived. Your family looked so solemn. Has there been bad news?'

First she said, 'Yes.' Then she said, 'No.' Finally she told him while staring at the honey pot she'd set on the counter. 'My uncle has decided to leave Sitka. He is taking his family to Russia. They say there is too much disorder here for them.'

'But things will get better. This situation is only temporary. The soldiers from the fort have been unruly, I admit, with their off-duty drinking and carousing, but it won't continue. Surely they aren't judging all Americans by the misbehavior of a few?'

'I don't know.'

He turned her around to face him, his hands still cool from the chill of the outdoors. His earnest expression commanded her attention.

'I can't deny there is an unsavory element here in Sitka, but all that will change as soon as the Congress grants Alaska territorial status. There won't be any more military rule. We'll have a territorial government and the soldiers will be gone. Once that happens we'll have a court system that can punish wrongdoers. Presently, the criminal element, or at least the less reputable element, knows that we can't legally enforce our ordinances, so they disregard them, but they won't get away with it for long. This is going to be a decent, law-abiding town where a man can raise a family and feel secure about the future.'

Nadia barely listened to his oratory. She studied his face, the intelligence of his high forehead, and the strength of his angular cheek-bones, their lines emphasized by the long sideburns he wore. The weakness of his chin was a minor flaw in her eyes. Yet as she gazed at him, Nadia could think only of her fear that she might never see him again if her father should decide to leave, too.

'Papa says he is staying, but I know he does so only because of Grandpa. He is unhappy here. Grandpa is old. I worry that if he should die, then Papa would feel there is no more reason to stay. If that should happen, Gabe, I don't know what I would do. I don't want to leave.' Although she had summoned enough boldness to address him familiarly, she hadn't enough to declare that he was the one she didn't want to leave.

'You can't go.' He appeared stunned by her suggestion. His

fingers curled into her shoulders as if to prevent her from moving.

'If my parents leave, I will have no choice. I cannot remain here alone.' The possibility that she might be separated from him was so painful for her that it seemed imminent rather than mere conjecture. 'I shall miss you.'

'No, I won't let it happen.' Infected by the contagion of her fear, he pulled her into his arms and held her close, pressing his lips to her hair. 'I won't let you go, Nadia,' he murmured. 'You are my princess.'

The ardent pitch of his voice thrilled her. Yet there was poignancy in the moment, too, as she wondered if this first embrace might also be their last. She closed her eyes to memorize the sensation of his arms around her, the smell of his wool tweed jacket, and the rough texture of it against her cheek, so she might recall them all at some future time.

'I wish there was something you could do – something you could say to Papa so this awful thing would not happen,' she declared.

'There is.' He sounded so positive that Nadia lifted her head to look at him.

'What?'

'I can ask his permission to marry you. That is . . . if you want to become my wife.' His fingers touched her cheek in a loving caress while he gazed at her with adoration.

Her lips parted, but no sound came out. She was so incredulous she couldn't give voice to her joy.

'It is what I've wanted from the first day we met outside your grandfather's shop.'

'I have also, more than anything in the world.'

'I wonder if you know how happy you have just made me,' he murmured thickly, cupping the side of her face in his hand. 'I love you, Nadia – my princess.'

'And I love you.'

When he kissed her, Nadia felt certain she must be dying and approaching the heaven that the priests described. Surely there could be nothing to equal this glorious bliss she was experiencing. Her lips clung to his an instant longer as he drew away.

'Our marriage will be a symbol for everyone in Alaska,' Gabe declared. 'A union between the old and the new. You and I will show the Russians and the Americans how we can live together and work to build a better place.'

'Yes.' She didn't understand half of what he said, but it sounded important. Everything he said always sounded so important and meaningful. She was convinced that was why he would be governor someday. And she would be his wife. The thought was still enough to take her breath away. But it couldn't happen soon enough to suit her. 'I am so happy that I am almost afraid something will happen to ruin this. Gabe, when will you ask my father for his permission?'

'I would go to him this minute, but from what you have said, I don't think this is the time to talk to him about us.' Letting go of her, he took a step backward, putting a discreet distance between them. Nadia was proud that he was such a gentleman, always so respectful of her reputation. It pleased her that he didn't take advantage of her and behave in a manner that might compromise her. 'I will come to your house later tonight when I can speak to your father alone.'

'He will give his consent. I know he will,' she declared.

As she readied the teapot, Nadia realized that soon she would be doing many such things for him, in their own home, as his wife.

An April rain pelted the windows as Nadia, garbed in the traditional headdress and embroidered bridal gown, knelt at her father's feet and begged his forgiveness for all her sins. Wolf stood to one side watching the ritual that always took place at the bride's home before the wedding ceremony at the church. His heart felt heavy that so few family members were present to witness it.

As Lev gave his daughter a peice of bread and a grain of salt, Eva tugged at Wolf's hand. He bent down to hear her curious whisper. 'Why did Papa do that?'

'So that Nadia knows he will never allow her to go hungry even though she no longer lives in his house.'

Her husband-to-be, Gabe Blackwood, knelt beside Nadia. She ceremoniously presented him with a little whip of braided hair. 'She made that from her own hair,' Eva informed Wolf. 'She snipped off a lock of hair last night. I watched her plait it. Why is she giving it to him? Is he going to beat her with it?'

Wolf patiently shook his head and murmured, 'It is a sign of her submission to his authority. Sssh, now,' he admonished and bowed his head as Lev began reading the prescribed prayers.

The prayers concluded the traditional ceremony at the home of the bride's parents. It was time to make the long walk to the Cathedral of St. Mikhail. The bridegroom helped Nadia into her long burnous so her gown would be protected from the steadily falling rain. Each carried an umbrella as they left the house.

The rest of the family followed. Lev Tarakanov didn't close the door when they left, symbolically leaving it open as a sign to his daughter that his house was always open to her if her husband was ever unkind to her.

Halfway up the walk, Eva noticed the front door was still open. She let go of her grandfather's hand and ran back to the house. As soon as she had pulled the door shut, she dashed back to her grandfather's side and once more slipped her hand in his.

'Papa forgot to close the door and it was raining in. Won't he be glad that I saw it?' She smiled up at Wolf, proud of her deed.

He started to explain the reason it had been left open, then hesitated. The patter of rain on his umbrella seemed to reaffirm the wisdom of her action; and the open door, after all, was only a symbol.

'Come.' He smiled at his well-meaning granddaughter. 'We must catch up with your parents and Dimitri or we shall be late for the wedding.'

From the window of his saloon, Ryan watched the wedding procession making its way toward the church. He hadn't been invited to the ceremony, which hadn't surprised him. He and the idealistic Gabe Blackwood had come to a parting of the ways some months ago.

Ryan had grown weary of the continuous lectures from the righteous, upstanding attorney regarding the corrupting influence of his saloon on the boomtown of Sitka. Blackwood blamed him for the drunkenness in the streets. More than once Gabe had charged him with breaking the law by illegally bringing liquor in, and insisted that, for the good of the community, Ryan must stop, thereby setting an example for other saloon-keepers to follow.

Ryan had laughed at such idealistic notions. 'If anything, the others would cheer if I shut down – and privately have a good laugh over my stupidity,' he had told him. 'If I don't sell it, somebody else will. You can make all the laws you want, but a man's going to have his liquor. Instead of talking to me, go see General Davis. He's the only authority around here. And while you're there, ask him if that last case of Tennessee whiskey I sent him was satisfactory.'

'You and your kind are destroying this town. You're driving away the decent folk.'

'Like the Russians, I suppose. You're a fool, Gabe,' Ryan had declared in disgust. 'The general and his soldiers know damned well what's in the crates being shipped to the saloons in this town, and they turn a blind eye. This is a military town, and a soldier is going to have his rum. Blame Davis or blame Congress for what's happening in the streets, but don't condemn me for making a dollar by supplying what's in demand.'

'But it's against the law,' Gabe had protested.

'Then get somebody to enforce the damned law. You are a fool if you think I am going to throw away a fortune by voluntarily obeying it!'

At that point, Gabe had lost his temper and attacked him, wading into him like a raging bull. Ryan rubbed his jaw, remembering that last punch Gabe had landed before Lyle, the bartender, pulled him off. The attorney unquestionably had a violent side.

That incident had put an end to their friendly relationship, but Ryan had seen it coming. Starting with the first influx of new settlers, Gabe had begun cultivating associations, the more respectable merchants and homesteaders among them. At times, he'd even appeared self-conscious about being seen in Ryan's company, obviously believing Ryan wasn't the right sort for a man with political ambitions.

Ryan smiled to himself. It was money that bought votes. All of Gabe Blackwood's good will and high-sounding ideals would count for nothing without it.

'Any sign of that rain lettin' up?' The bartender, Lyle Saunders, wandered over to the window where Ryan stood, and folded his arms in front of him, resting them on his protruding stomach. His dark hair was slicked down with grease and parted in the middle. Bushy muttonchop whiskers emphasized the jowling of his fat face.

'Doesn't look like it.' Ryan commented.

'There goes Blackwood and his bride.' the bartender observed, then inquired, 'Ever been to one of those Orthodox weddings?'

'Nope.'

'Long-drawn-out affairs they are. Them altar boys or whatever they call 'em, are gonna have a lot of candle grease on their robes before the March of the Three Crowns is over.' He watched them a minute, then pointed a pudgy finger at the trailing party of family members. 'See that young fella. If you still are lookin' for someone who knows these waters, he might be the man for you. Born an' raised here, he was. An' trained as a navigator, too, I understand. He speaks that Indian gibberish, too.'

Ryan made a closer study of the younger Tarakanov walking ahead of the old man and the little girl. He seemed to recall his name was Dimitri. 'Thanks, Lyle,' he said. 'I'll keep him in mind.'

Running feet thudded on the boardwalk outside the saloon. Two soldiers charged past the window, their shoulders hunched against the rain. The bartender took a last look at the wedding party, then turned from the window with a shake of his head.

'Never thought Blackwood would marry a breed,' he muttered to himself.

Ryan doubted that Gabe knew that Nadia was part Indian. Blackwood tended to take things at face value and rarely looked to see what might lie underneath. Sooner or later, he'd learn the facts. While Ryan wouldn't go so far as to claim that the mixed ancestry of the Tarakanov family was common knowledge in Sitka, there were enough people who knew or guessed it. Maybe someone should have told Gabe, but as far as Ryan was concerned, it was a case of 'let the buyer beware.'

The two off-duty soldiers entered the saloon, making enough noise for a whole troop as they stamped the mud from their boots. Ryan turned toward them, recognizing two of his more regular customers, privates Kelly and Wheeler. They swept off their caps and shook them to get rid of the rainwater, then wiped the moisture from their faces.

Wheeler, the shorter and burlier one of the two, with an unruly thatch of straw-colored hair, gestured over his shoulder toward the street. 'Hey, barkeep, where're them folks goin' all gussied up? Is there a party er some'in goin' on that nobody saw fit to tell us about?'

'There's a wedding.'

'The hell you say.' Wheeler and his buddy Kelly sauntered up to the bar. 'Pour us some a' that rotgut.' Wheeler slapped the money down, then leaned on the counter. 'Who's gettin' hitched?'

'That attorney Blackwood.' Lyle set two shot glasses on the counter, then pulled the cork from a whiskey bottle to fill them.

'Ain't he the one what's been sparkin' that Russkie gal?' Without waiting for a confirmation, he turned to his soldier buddy and lifted his glass in a saluting toast. 'I sure as hell envy him poppin' her t'night. You seen her, Kelly? She's the one with the hair like burnt gold, all dark an' shiny an' purty like.'

'The only gold what interests me is hidin' up there in them mountains,' Kelly declared in a disgruntled voice, then bolted down a swallow of the cheap liquor. 'I'll be glad when spring gets here an' this damned weather clears up so I can get out an' start huntin' some of that shiny yellow stuff.'

'Hell, the weather ain't never gonna get no better in this miserable place,' Wheeler complained bitterly. 'How is it that we got stuck in this Godforsaken hole at the top of the world? There ain't a god-damned thing for a man to do in this town 'cept to go drinkin' an' whorin'.'

'Shame on you, Nate Wheeler.' Big Molly came sauntering out of the back room, her hands resting on her tightly corseted waist to emphasize the exaggerated sway of her hips. 'You always swore to me those were your two favorite pastimes. Now I find out you been lyin'.'

With each stride of her leg, the skirt flared to provide a glimpse of her low-topped boots and black tights. Her artificially darkened hair was a mass of ringlets piled on top of her head and secured with a gaudy Spanish comb. The darkness of her heavily kohled eyes contrasted with the white mask of her face, thickly covered with layers of the toxic powder that had already scarred her cheeks. The spots of rouge on her cheeks gave her an almost garish look.

But Wheeler's attention wasn't focused on her face or legs. 'I didn't say they wasn't my favorites, Big Molly. I jest said there weren't no other choice.' He stared at the mountain of flesh that threatened to spill out of her low-cut gown.

'I grant you, Nate, bein' sober in this town ain't much of a choice.' She rested a forearm on the counter, then leaned her weight on it, angling her body to give him a better veiw down her front. 'You just gonna stand there gawkin', Nate, or are you gonna buy a thirsty lady a drink?'

'Give us a bottle an' 'nother glass.' Wheeler dug in his pocket and pushed more money onto the counter, then nudged his buddy. 'Come on, Kelly. Let's go sit ourselves at a table.'

Almost reluctantly Dan Kelly pushed away from the bar and followed after Wheeler as he grabbed up the bottle and glass and headed for one of the tables. Instead of dragging a chair around to sit close to the saloon girl and flank her other side, Kelly chose a chair on the opposite side of the table and slumped his body in it.

'What's the matter with yore friend, Nate?' Big Molly curiously studied the tall, lean private.

'Don't pay no mind t' him. He always sits for a while an' moons over that gold mine he ain't found yet. After he's had a few drinks under his belt, he livens up some.' Wheeler poured her a shot from the bottle, then turned in his chair and draped an arm across her shoulders, letting his hand hang low. 'Right now you an' me can talk.'

'You just mind where that hand of yours goes,' she warned. 'You know the rules. I don't go in for no free fondlin'.'

'Ah, Molly,' he protested.

'Business is business,' she reminded him. 'If you don't like it, take your bottle an' go get some squaw from the Ranche liquored up. Then you can have all you want for free – includin' sores all over ya.'

'Yo're a hard woman, Molly.'

'Now, Nate, you know I'm soft. How many times this past winter have you wallowed in my softness?' she chided him.

Ryan had seen Big Molly work too many times to be interested in watching her hook another customer. He walked over to the bar. 'I'll be in the back office if you need me, Lyle.'

35

After their marriage, the Blackwoods set up house in a sparsely furnished cabin, mainly with cast-off furniture. Nadia took pains to create an attractive setting for her beloved husband.

Her needle was always busy fashioning doilies to cover the marred surfaces of tables and bureaus and embroidering scarfs to hide the threadbare arms and backs of the sofa and chairs. But each time she looked about the rooms, she saw so much more that needed to be done – new curtains for the windows, samplers for the walls, hooked rugs for the floors – the list seemed endless.

Hearing the scratch of pen on paper, Nadia looked up from the needlework on her lap. Gabe sat at the table he used for a desk, bending over the letter he was writing, a study in concentration. Even if it took her a lifetime to turn this home into one in which he could take pride, she'd do it gladly for him.

He paused in his writing and ran his fingers through his hair, then he rubbed his eyes in a gesture indicative of weariness. Quietly, Nadia set her needlework aside and crossed the room, walking softly on the balls of her feet so the click of her heels on the bare floor wouldn't disturb him. In the kitchen, she fixed him a pot of tea and set it along with two teacups and a pot of honey on the silver tray that had been a wedding gift from her grandfather.

She carried the tea tray into the parlor and set it on the table where he was working. He glanced up with a preoccupied frown. There was something so boyish about that expression that, even after two weeks of married life, she still had the urge to reach out and smooth those furrows from his forehead.

'I thought you might like some tea,' she murmured.

'I'd love it.' He sighed and straightened in his chair, arching his back and flexing the cramped muscles in his shoulders.

After filling his cup, Nadia added the amount of honey he liked, then carried the cup around the table to set it in front of him. He hooked an arm around her waist and pulled her close to him.

'What are you writing?' She glanced curiously at the paper that was nearly covered with his elaborate handwriting.

'A letter to Congress urging them to give us the right to a form of civil government. They must be informed of the present conditions – and the potential for sound growth and development here. We can't continue with no law here. They must pass some legislation to end this intolerable situation,' he declared.

'You will convince them.' She pressed her hand on his shoulder in a gesture of both affection and faith.

'Some husband I am.' His smile held a trace of chagrin. 'I've barely said two words to you all evening. Soon you'll accuse me of neglecting you.'

'Never.' She blushed when he slid his hand higher on her rib cage, nearing the swell of her breast, and lifted her hand to kiss its palm. Gently she extricated herself from his embrace and moved back to the tea tray to pour herself a cup. She was still not comfortable with the intimacies of the marriage bed. She enjoyed his kisses, but the rest seemed so brutish to her. 'Did I tell you my cousin Dimitri has found work?'

'That's wonderful news. Where's he working?'

'Mr. Colby hired him –'

'Colby? That blackguard?'

Shocked by his sudden anger, Nadia wavered uncertainly. 'I . . . I thought he was your friend.'

'Him? Never.' Gabe pushed his chair back with a loud clatter and began striding about the room, gesticulating wildly as he spoke. 'That saloon of his and the others are responsible for half the evil in this town! They are houses of sin and corruption, and they should not be allowed to operate!' He stopped, confronting her with his anger. 'What possessed your cousin to go to work in such a place? He'll be violating the law. Here I am fighting to make this town a decent place to live, and one of your family does a foolish thing like this. How is it going to look?'

Nadia cringed slightly from him. 'Dimitri isn't going to work in the saloon. He's a navigator,' she explained hesitantly. 'Mr. Colby has hired him to sail his ship.'

'His ship? What ship?' He drew back, no longer looming over her. 'What's Colby going to do with a ship?'

Sensing the break in his anger, she hastened to assure him that her cousin would be committing no wrong. 'Dimitri said Mr. Colby bought one of the company sloops so he can begin trading with the Kolosh villages in the area for furs. That's what Dimitri is going to do. He's a trained navigator and familiar with these waters and the location of the different villages. He knows about trading, and he can speak the Kolosh tongue very well.'

'Those savages.' Gabe pushed the condemnation through his clenched teeth, then pressed his lips together so tightly they appeared to quiver. 'No man should have to get within a mile of them and their carved wooden idols.'

'Their totems aren't idols of worship. They tell stories and legends of their clans.'

'How would you know?' he challenged.

'That is what I was told,' she murmured uneasily.

'Whatever they are, they're heathen objects and should be burned. No decent person should have to associate with the likes of them – furs or not. If the Army had any sense, they'd clean out that pigsty they call the Ranche, with its disease and drunkenness, and ship all those filthy Indians off to some remote island.' With his diatribe finished, he stalked back to his chair and began writing furiously.

Nadia's hand shook slightly as she lifted her teacup. But the tea was cold. She returned the cup to its saucer, wishing fervently that she had never brought up the subject of the Kolosh. From now on, she must remember how sensitive Gabe was and avoid any mention of them. It was all her fault that he'd become so angry. She should have known better.

A year and a half later the Stars and Stripes waved over the citizenry of Sitka who had gathered on the parade ground in front of Baranov's Castle, now the residence of Alaska's military commander. Ryan Colby stood on the fringe of the crowd, a thumb hooked in the watch pocket of his brocade vest. Nursing his customary cigar, he studied the slender, slouch-shouldered speaker standing on the veranda steps.

There was little about the older man to command such attention. His suit looked rumpled; the wavy locks of his gray hair were inclined to disorder. His high forehead and shaggy eyebrows emphasized his beak nose and receding chin. Yet this man was the former Secretary of State, William H. Seward, the man responsible for Alaska's being purchased from Russia.

388

'Mr. Sumner, in his elaborate and magnificent oration,' Seward continued in a naturally hoarse voice, referring to the Massachusetts senator who had championed the purchase of Alaska, 'although he spake only from historical accounts, has not exaggerated – no man can exaggerate – the marine treasures of the territory. Besides the whale, which everywhere and at all times is seen enjoying his robust exercise, and the sea otter, the fur seal, the hair seal, and the walrus found in the waters which imbosom the western islands, those waters, as well as the seas of the eastern archipelago, are found teeming with the salmon, cod, and other fish adapted to the support of human and animal life. Indeed, what I have seen here has almost made me a convert to the theory of some naturalists, that the waters of the globe are filled with stores for the sustenance of animal life surpassing the available productions of the land.'

Seward was indirectly defending the purchase of the land that had been sarcastically referred to as Seward's Folly, Walrus-sia, and Seward's Icebox in the nation's capital. Ryan's attention wandered to the select group of townspeople attentively standing to one side of the veranda. All but one were members of the de facto city government, composed of the mayor, who was also the government's customs collector, and the councilmen. Ryan wondered how Gabe Blackwood had managed to get himself included, then supposed it was the letter campaign he had waged on Congress, agitating for some form of civil government to replace the present military rule in Alaska.

A black-haired man wearing the billed cap and pea jacket of a seaman was working his way around the outer edge of the crowd, pausing now and then to crane his neck and scan the onlookers as if searching for someone. Recognizing the young skipper of his fast sloop, Ryan stepped back from the crowd and motioned to Dimitri Tarakanov. As the young man joined him, Ryan was struck again by the hard and knowing look of those black eyes that belied the relative youth of his twenty years. In their first meeting in the spring of the previous year, Ryan had concluded that what Dimitri Tarakanov lacked in experience was made up for by his cunning intelligence and casual disregard for danger. He had not regretted his choice.

'Lyle said you were here.' Dimitri spoke *sotto voce*.

'Any problems?'

A smile lifted the outer corners of Dimitri's spiky black

mustache. 'None. The furs are sitting in your shed and the whiskey is stashed on the island. As soon as it gets dark, we'll bring it in.'

'Good.'

Ryan stuck his cigar in his mouth and chewed thoughtfully on it. He had quickly learned there was little profit in the fur trade any more, but it provided the perfect cover for his rum-running activity. Although the Army gave tacit approval to trafficking in liquor, they occasionally confiscated incoming shipments. Ryan considered smuggling the obvious choice to prevent a possible interruption of his supply.

'What's going on here?' Dimitri indicated the speaker with a nod of his head.

'The good people of Sitka are hoping there's something Seward can do for them in Congress,' Ryan answered dryly.

Hope was a mild word to describe the desperation he smelled in the crowd. Most of the people had become disheartened, doubting that their pleas would ever be heard by the government in Washington. Alaska was considered a customs district. There was no law, no legal conveyance of property title, no courts to legally try and punish the guilty, no legal tax levies except customs tax, and no right to vote.

Within a year after the purchase, more than seventy vessels had entered the port and left with their cargo holds loaded with nearly all the metal, equipment, furs, and stores that the Russians had in Sitka. The ships that didn't carry those supplies hauled Russian passengers. The town had already been looted of everything of value, but most of the townspeople didn't realize it.

The boom was over for most of them – the speculators and promoters who could no longer buy and sell land to which they could neither get nor give clear title, the merchants and tradesmen like the barbers and tailors and family men who could not tolerate the lawlessness and disorder. But it was a situation just made for saloonkeepers, gamblers, and prostitutes.

Sitka was literally a military town. Additional troops had been brought in, raising the number of soldiers in Alaska to five hundred, all but a few stationed right in Sitka. Their barracks were in the heart of town, and when the soldiers went on drunken rampages, which they often did, they ruled the streets and terrorized the population.

But the soldiers were Ryan's main source of business – the soldiers and the Indians, both the Tlingits at the Ranche and the ones in outlying villages to whom he traded liquor for furs. Not that he didn't have some competition, and not just from other saloons in town.

Some of the more enterprising soldiers had begun distilling their own brew. Supposedly it had all started at a Tlingit village called Hoochinoo, where a soldier showed the Indians how to take the simple brew they made from bark and berries, add some molasses and yeast, then distill the mixture. The process had since been slightly refined, but molasses remained the main ingredient, with additions of flour, dried apples or rice, yeast powder, and enough water to make a thin batter. The mixture was allowed to ferment to a highly alcoholic state, then distilled. The end product was referred to as 'hoochinoo,' a potent, head-splitting molasses rum that tasted as bad as it smelled.

In the Ranche, hoochinoo sold for ten cents a glass. Ryan had his own still to make the liquor, which he sometimes used to cut his whiskey and stretch the supply, or else he sold it when his whiskey ran out, as occasionally happened in the winter.

'I'll need you to transport some kegs of molasses out to the still for me,' he told Dimitri.

Dimitri nodded, his gaze directed at someone in the crowd. 'My grandfather just saw me. I will have to go speak to him.'

'I'll see you at the saloon sometime after midnight,' Ryan said.

Again Dimitri nodded affirmatively as he moved away to join his family.

At the conclusion of the speeches, the crowd milled around the former Secretary of State, their voices clamoring for order and justice and illustrating the many problems they faced because there was no jurisdiction in the land. Nadia Blackwood stood off to one side with her family and proudly watched her husband, who was in the center of it all next to Mr. Seward.

'There is no more to be learned here,' her father, Lev Tarakanov, stated. 'I think it is time we walked home.'

'He says that because his stomach is hungry,' his Finnish-Creole wife, Aila, teased.

'I need to prepare an evening meal for my husband as well,' Nadia replied dutifully.

'Dimitri and I will escort you safely home if you don't wish to wait for your husband,' her grandfather volunteered. 'I have the feeling he is not eager to leave soon.'

'No. I'm sure he'd like to spend as much time as possible with Mr. Seward.' Nadia knew there was nothing she could contribute to his discussion with the American statesman, and the prospect of waiting here until he was through didn't appeal to her. The idea of having a meal ready for him when he returned home sounded much better. 'Excuse me while I tell him that you are taking me home. I don't want him to worry about me.'

'We will wait for you,' her grandfather promised.

With difficulty she made her way through the crowd and reached her husband's side. He was speaking to the politician. This was the first time since the famed Mr. Seward had arrived that Nadia had been this close to him. It seemed to her that his face resembled that of a very wise parrot. She stood quietly next to Gabe, hesitant to interrupt him when he was speaking.

'. . . are intolerable. Congress has bought and paid for Alaska. It can no longer neglect our needs simply because we sit off here by ourselves. This land is bigger than Texas. You've seen its wealth. Congress must be made to understand that they cannot leave us here alone and forgotten.'

'I couldn't agree with you more . . .' Seward hesitated over his name.

'Blackwood, Gabriel Blackwood,' he quickly supplied.

'Mr. Blackwood. When I return, I intend to speak to my friends in Congress, but you understand I have very few of them. I am not exactly a popular figure in Washington. But someday Congress will recognize the wisdom of this purchase and applaud my foresight.' He used the cigar in his hand to punctuate his comments, then he noticed Nadia hovering at Gabe's side. 'I believe there is a lovely young woman who's trying to gain your attention.'

'I don't wish to interrupt,' Nadia said quickly as Gabe glanced at her in surprise. 'I only wanted you to know that grandfather is walking me home.'

'Mr. Seward, may I have the privilege of presenting my very own Russian princess.' He tucked his hand under her elbow and drew her forward. 'My wife, Mrs. Nadia Blackwood, the daughter of a very old Russian family here in Sitka. The Honorable Mr. William H. Seward, one of America's foremost statesmen.'

'This is a privilege, sir.' Nadia gave him her hand and curtsied as he bowed gallantly over it.

'The pleasure is all mine,' Seward insisted, then turned to Gabe. 'May I say that you are a lucky man to have so comely a wife.'

'I know.' Gabe smiled at her.

'You will excuse me. I am certain there are many important things the two of you wish to discuss.' She backed away, adding softly to her husband, 'I shall be at home.'

'I will be along directly.'

But he wasn't, and the sumptuous meal she had taken such pains to prepare for him was cold by the time he finally arrived. He didn't seem to notice. He was filled with the excitement of his meeting with Seward, the long discussions that had taken place, and the support that had been voiced.

Seward's visit in early August raised hopes but not sufficiently to stimulate the town's declining economy. September came with its depressing rains, and more and more people talked about pulling up and leaving.

As nine-year-old Eva lay awake in her bed, she listened to the voices of her parents in the next room. The dividing wall between the rooms muffled the sound, preventing her from catching every word, but she'd overheard enough similar conversations to enable her to fill in most of the blanks. It was always the same – her father worrying that he'd made the wrong decision by staying in Sitka and her mother doing her best to reassure him that the situation would improve. But she didn't sound very convincing any more.

Eva couldn't see how her father could even think about leaving Grandpa here all alone, but her father kept saying that his first consideration should have been what was best for his own family and talking about how he might be able to find work in the gold mines of British Columbia. She wished one of them would ask how she felt. But no one ever paid any attention to what she thought except her grandfather. Eva suspected it would be different if she were pretty like her older sister. Her grandfather insisted she was getting prettier every day, but she looked and looked in the mirror and knew it wasn't true.

She pulled the blanket up to cover her ears and shut out the low voices in the next room. When that didn't work, Eva tried to concentrate on other sounds, but the faint patter of the rain on the roof was a poor distraction. From the street came raucous laughter and loud voices. Probably American soldiers from the garrison, Eva guessed. She didn't like them. They weren't nice men. They were always drinking and fighting, saying bad things, and making fun of people.

Their noisy voices grew louder until Eva was sure they were right outside her house. Suddenly there was a loud banging on the front door. Eva jumped at the sound, then froze and clutched at the blanket. For an instant there was stillness in the house as the talking in the next room stopped.

The pounding came again, followed by a slurred voice shouting, 'Anybody home? Hey, let us in! Don'cah know it's rainin' out here!'

A second later, someone tried the door. Eva heard it thudding against the bar drawn across it, and sat up in bed, pulling the blankets around her.

'They got it barred,' one of the soldiers complained.

'That ain't at all neighborly.'

'Somebody needs t' teach these breeds some manners.'

The subsequent thud seemed to shake the whole house with its force. She could hear her father's footsteps as he left the bedroom and passed her door. Throwing back the blanket, Eva climbed out of bed and hurried to the door in her bare feet. It sounded to her like those soldiers were trying to break down the door. She was frightened but not so frightened that she didn't want to see what was going on.

As she left her room, wood splintered under another heavy blow to the door. Her father shouted at them to go away. Eva crept quickly and silently along the wall until she could see the front door. Her father stood before it, holding an iron poker in his hand. As the door shook under a battering blow, she heard the cracking of wood and saw the exposed seam of yellow-white wood in the thick board that barred the door shut.

When the soldiers rammed it again, the heavy plank snapped and the door burst open. Three soldiers tumbled through the opening, staggering to regain their balance. Their clothes were wet and splattered with mud. Their dark beards were matted and stringy like the hair sticking out from under their caps. As Eva stared at their reddened eyes, she thought they looked like maddened animals and ran to her father's side for protection.

'Eva, no.' Her father glanced down at her in alarm and quickly shoved her behind him.

'Hey, looka' that li'l girl in her pink nightdress. Ain't she ugly.' One of them pointed at her.

'Hey, li'l girl, you gotta purty older sister a-hidin' back thare somewhares?'

'Leave her alone.' Her father brandished the fire poker.

'Listen t' him,' the first soldier jeered, baring his yellowed teeth.

'Yeah, it sounds like he don't think we's good enough fo' the likes of his kind.'

'Leave my house at once,' her father ordered as Eva cowered behind him.

'Least you could do is offer us some'in' to drink fore ya send us out in that cold and rain. He ain't very hospitable, is he, Nate?'

'Yeah, where's yore liquor?' the one called Nate demanded, drunkenly swiveling his head around to look about the house. 'I know ya got some. Neve' knowed a breed yet what didn't like his firewater.' He took a step into the room and her father quickly moved to block his way. 'Mister, you best get outa my way afore you make me mad.'

'Lev?' Her mother called to him from the rear bedroom.

'Ya hear that? There's women in the house.' The one called Nate gleefully rubbed his hands together. 'I knew it. I knew it. I tell ya, boys, I can smell 'em.'

'You go now and leave us alone,' her father ordered. 'You are not welcome. Go.'

'He's a'mighty anxious for us to leave,' remarked the first solider, the one with the yellow teeth.

'Yeah, if'n he likes it out there in the rain so much, why don't he go?' suggested the other.

The first one grabbed her father. Before he could defend himself with the poker, the other two soldiers ganged up on him and heaved him outside.

'Papa!' Eva screamed and darted toward the door.

A soldier grabbed for her and missed. She ran out into the rain, reaching her father as he slowly picked himself up off the muddy ground, holding one arm against his ribs.

'Did they hurt you, Papa?'

As he shook his head, she heard her mother's voice anxiously calling for him. About that same instant, Eva heard the one called

Nate declare, 'Well, looky here. We got us a yeller-haired squaw.'

A wild, panicked look came into her father's face. 'Eva, run to your grandfather's house.' He seemed not to notice that she was in her nightdress and barefooted, or that the rain was already soaking her.

'But –'

'Go!' He pushed her angrily away from him. 'For your mama's sake be quick!'

Her mother screamed. Her father charged back into the house, leaving Eva alone in the rain and the dark. Her feet seemed rooted to the wet ground. She stared at the open doorway through which her father had disappeared, hearing the lusty, laughing voices of the soldiers, the protesting outcries of her mother, and the angry shouts of her father. Something awful was going to happen, she just knew it. She was frightened. She had never been more frightened in all her life.

She started running in the direction of her grandfather's house, but she couldn't seem to make her legs go fast enough. The muddy ground sucked at her feet, slowing her down, and her long, wet nightgown kept tangling around her legs making her stumble.

No light showed in any of the houses along the street. They loomed dark and tall on either side of her, silent unfriendly shapes in the rain. To Eva, it was like being in a nightmare where she ran and ran and could never get where she was going.

In the dark, she almost ran past her grandfather's house but recognized it at the last second and turned up the path. She stumbled up the steps to the front door, her bare feet numbed by the wet, penetrating cold. She flung herself at the door, pounding on it with her fists and sobbing for her grandfather. Her own cries deafened her to any sounds coming from inside the house.

When it seemed she had no more strength left in her arms, the door opened and her grandfather stood before her, a lighted candle in hand and a pair of trousers pulled on over his red flannels, the suspenders hanging.

He frowned at her. 'Child, what are you doing out at this hour?'

She was shivering uncontrollably and her teeth were chattering from the combination of fear and damp cold. For a full second, she couldn't answer him. He started to pull her inside, out of the cold and the rain, but Eva jerked away from him.

'No. It's Mama.' She tried to talk between her hiccoughing sobs. 'The soldiers . . . They broke the door. Papa . . . he sent me for you. You've got to help. I'm . . . scared, Grandpa. I'm so . . . scared.' She couldn't hold it back any more and began crying in earnest, blubbering out the rest. 'What are the soldiers gonna do to them, Grandpa? What are they gonna do?'

'Crying will not help them, Eva Levyena.' He crouched down, thrusting his arms through his suspenders, pulling them high on his shoulders and shifting the candle from one hand to the other. 'You must be brave. Do you understand? You must go to your sister's house and tell her of this. Tell her also that I have gone to your home. Can you do this last thing?' Eva nodded, her body still trembling wildly. 'Then go while I fetch my musket, and be swift as the wind.'

Her sister lived only three houses away. Eva turned and jumped off the stoop. At first her numbed legs didn't want to function properly as she broke into a staggering run. She cut across the front yards of the intervening houses. She lost her footing on a slippery patch of oozing mud and went sprawling face first in the watery muck, but she scrambled to her feet, driven by her father's admonition for haste that had been reinforced by her grandfather.

A light moved in her sister's house, its glow passing from one window to the next. Eva pounded frantically on the front door. Almost immediately she heard a man's voice demand, 'Who's there?'

'It's me! Let me in. I must see Nadia!' Then she glanced over her shoulder, looking down the rain-blurred street. In the dark, she could just barely make out a man's figure hurrying in the direction of her house. She was certain it was her grandfather.

The door bar made a grating sound as it was slid back. A second later the door was opened and her sister's husband stared at her with doubtful recognition. Eva briefly noticed that he was still dressed in his day clothes. Then her glance went past him to the yellow flame of an oil lamp that her sister held, her face illuminated by its outreaching light.

'Nadia,' she cried and quickly dodged around Gabe Blackwood to run to her sister, unaware of the muddy tracks she left or the water that dripped from her.

'Eva, look at you!' her sister exclaimed in shock. 'Whatever possessed you to go traipsing around in this weather without dressing properly. Why, you're soaked to the skin and you look like some homeless little mud urchin. Let's get these wet clothes off of you. What was Mama thinking when she let you go out like this?'

'Wait,' Eva protested. 'It's Mama.'

'What's wrong? Has she taken ill?'

While she had the chance, Eva blurted out the whole story, the words tumbling over themselves in her haste to get them all out before Nadia could interrupt her again. Her fear increased when she saw the look of horror and distress that spread across her sister's face.

'Gabe, you must do something,' she cried.

His jaws were grimly taut as he snatched his coat and hat from the wall hooks and headed toward the front door. 'I'm going to the mayor's house. I'll drag him out of bed if I have to.' He paused on the threshold, pulling on his coat. 'Bar this door when I leave.'

'Hurry, Gabe.' As soon as Nadia had secured the door behind him, she turned to Eva, who was so cold she couldn't stop shaking. 'Let's get you into the kitchen.'

An hour later, Nadia had rekindled the fire in the iron cookstove, stripped Eva's wet and muddy clothes off her, taking care not to soil her own dress, scrubbed away the mud, wrapped her in a blanket, and plunked her on a chair in front of the glowing stove. All the while Nadia had plied her with questions, making Eva repeat everything that had happened, the things the soldiers had said, and the reaction of her parents.

Although the warmth made her limbs tingle again, Eva felt little comfort. She was too conscious of the agitation her sister couldn't completely conceal, the way she started at every sound and kept looking apprehensively in the direction of the front door, as if anxious for her husband to return. She poured tea into a cup and heavily sweetened it with honey, then gave it to Eva.

'Drink it,' she urged, but her attempt at a reassuring smile appeared brittle. 'We need to warm you inside as well as out.'

'Why hasn't Gabe come back? He's been gone a long time.' Eva was feeling scared all over again. 'What do you suppose has happened?'

'I don't know,' her sister retorted sharply, her own nerves wearing thin from the strain of waiting.

'Grandpa knows I'm here. Why doesn't he come?'

'Drink your tea and hush.' Nadia sipped at the tea she had poured for herself, but Eva noticed the faint tremor of her hand as she lifted the cup to her mouth.

'Something bad has happened. I just know it,' Eva declared. 'Maybe Mama and Papa are hurt. Maybe they need us. Don't you think we should go find out?'

'No, I don't. Gabe said to stay right here until he came back, and that is exactly what we're going to do. Besides it's still raining outside. It would be foolish to go out when we have only now gotten you dry.'

Stung by the curt reproval, Eva hung her head. Sometimes it seemed that she never said or did anything right. 'I'm sorry. It's just that I'm . . . scared.'

'There is no reason for you to be scared. Everything is going to be all right,' Nadia insisted. 'You must stop letting your imagination run away with you. If something terrible had happened, somebody would have already been here to tell us. As it is, the men are obviously handling whatever the trouble is.'

The sudden pounding on the front door caught both of them off guard. Eva nearly jumped out of the chair, but the blanket that was wound around her restricted any movement and caused her to spill most of the tea down the front of her.

After an initial start of alarm, Nadia set her cup on the table and smoothed the front of her dress in an attempt to regain her calm. 'You stay right here, Eva.'

'But what if –' It was no use. Her sister had already left the kitchen. Eva listened tensely to the soft rustle of her long skirts and the quiet, even tread of her footsteps. She heard her sister's inquiry, and a man's muffled answer, then came the sliding of the bar in its grate. One set of booted feet stamped into the house.

Certain that her sister wouldn't have admitted anyone except her husband, Eva wiggled off the chair and rearranged the enfolding blanket to waddle into the front room. She just had to know if her parents were all right.

'. . . mayor and I got there, it was too late.' Gabe shrugged out of his wet coat and hung it on the wall hook along with his hat, all the while speaking in low undertones. 'We found your grandfather lying unconscious. One of the soldiers had hit him over the back of the head. His head hurts, but that appears to be about the extent of it. He had tried to scare the soldiers off with that old musket of his, but the powder was wet and the gun wouldn't fire.'

'What about Papa and . . .'

As Eva watched from a few yards away, Gabe took Nadia by the shoulders and held her in front of him. 'Your father is a very brave man. He must have put up an admirable fight, but he was outnumbered. Those . . . soldiers gave him a brutal beating. Nothing serious. His only injuries appear to be a few cuts and some severe bruises, maybe a couple of cracked ribs.'

'Mama? Did they hurt her?' Nadia clutched at his jacket lapels.

Gabe hesitated a long moment. 'I'm sorry,' he murmured at last, faintly shaking his head. 'I'm afraid they violated her.'

'Oh, no.' Nadia pulled back from him, covering her mouth with her hand.

'I swear to you they'll pay for committing such an unspeakable act.' His voice vibrated with anger.

'I must go to her.' Nadia started to turn away.

'No.' Gabe checked her movement. 'She doesn't want you there.'

'But I must,' Nadia protested. 'She needs me.'

'When I mentioned I would bring you back to stay with her, your mother almost became hysterical. She doesn't want to see you – not now, at any rate,' he explained reluctantly. 'At the moment, your father is the only one she wants with her.'

'Poor Mama,' she murmured, and Eva heard the little sob in her voice. 'I hope you locked those vile men in irons and threw the key in the harbor.' As her remark was met with silence, she stared at her husband, searching his shadowed face. 'You did, didn't you?'

'Nadia, you know the mayor has no authority over the military. He had no choice except to turn them over to the sergeant of the guards. But I am personally going to see General Davis in the morning and demand that these men be court-martialed and imprisoned for their crimes. I promise you they will be brought to justice.'

'I hate that man. I hate those soldiers.' She pressed her knuckles to her temples. 'I just know I should be with Mama.'

'Believe me, it's best that you stay here. Your little sister is going to need you. I think it would be better if you explained to her what happened. Where is she? Did you put her to bed?'

'No. She's –' Nadia turned and saw her standing there silhouetted by the long pool of light from the kitchen. 'Eva, I told you to wait.'

'But I wanted to hear.' She took a quick breath, gathering her courage. 'What does violated mean? Is it something very bad? Is my mama going to die?'

'No! . . . No, she isn't going to die.' Nadia added more calmly, 'It only means she was hurt, but she'll be all right.'

'What did they do to her?' Eva frowned.

'They . . . hurt her.'

'You mean they hit her like they did Papa?'

'Something like that, yes.' Her sister nodded.

That was the only explanation Eva was given. Within minutes, her sister bundled her off to the spare bedroom, insisting that she go to sleep.

36

The morning sunlight filtered through the thinning layers of fog, giving an iridescent shimmer to the mist that drifted outside the windows of the military commander's office in Baranov's Castle. Gabe brushed past the orderly who held the door open for him and walked briskly to the massive desk. It, like most of the other furnishings in the house, was a holdover from the Russian administration and, like everything else, showed signs of neglect.

The chair behind it creaked as the general dragged his booted feet off the desktop and sat up straight, but he didn't bother to stand when Gabe stopped in front of his desk. Nor did he make any attempt to button his uniform. Despite the sweeping brush of his mustache, there was something Lincolnesque about his narrow, gaunt-cheeked face with its full brown beard. But from the way the general had winked at the drunkenness, brawls, and thievery of his men in the past, Gabe knew the resemblance to the dead President was purely physical.

'I understand there was some pressing matter you wished to discuss with me, Mr. Blackwood,' the general stated, then sighed heavily as if his tolerance was being tested.

'Indeed, sir.' Gabe came straight to the point of his visit. 'Last evening, three of your soldiers broke into the home of the Tarakanov family, severely assaulted Mr. Tarakanov, and forced themselves on his wife.'

'The incident was reported to me.'

'It was hardly an incident, General,' Gabe retorted. 'It was a felonious assault.'

'The soldiers in question are presently in the stockade sleeping off last night's drink. When they are sober, appropriate disciplinary action will be taken. Is that all, Mr. Blackwood?' The general made it clear that he didn't wish to continue this discussion of a military matter with a civilian.

'I shall put the question to *you*, General Davis. Is that all?' Gabe challenged. 'Is the extent of their punishment to be a few days in the stockade? This, sir, is not the first time such an 'incident' has occured. In the past, your men have broken into homes and molested the occupants. Their previous victims have always been of Indian extraction, but this time they have gone too far. They have attacked the home of a decent family and I demand that they be punished for this despicable crime.'

'*You* demand.' The general rose to his feet and leaned his weight on his fingers pressed on the desk. 'I don't give a damn what you demand. I am in command here. I shall determine what punishment is to be meted out, if any.'

'Then I say that, judging by the lawlessness and disorder of your troops, you are not fit to command!'

The general straightened, squaring his shoulders as he narrowly studied Gabe. 'Blackwood. Ah, yes, I remember you now. You married one of those Russian breeds, didn't you? Tell me, were last night's so-called victims members of your wife's family?'

Gabe stiffened at the vile accusation. 'They happened to be her parents. But they are Russian, one of the few families who chose to stay.'

'They might be half Russian, maybe more, but there's Indian in them. Aleut, Tlingit, or Eskimo, it doesn't really matter.'

'That's a lie.' A muscle jumped convulsively along Gabe's tightly clenched jaw.

'Is it? I have a full and complete roster of all the families living here at the time America took over the occupation. I checked this morning, and the Tarakanovs appear on the *Creole* side of the list,' the general asserted smugly.

Something seemed to explode inside Gabe's head. Vaguely he could hear the general shouting. The next thing he knew his fingers were buried under that dark beard, digging into the man's throat, and three soldiers were struggling to pull him off the general. He felt stunned – dazed – as if he was in some kind of shock.

'Throw him out,' the general rasped hoarsely. 'Throw him out before I forget he's a civilian!'

The soldiers bodily escorted him all the way to the bottom of the steps, roughly manhandling him, then released him with a shove. Gabe staggered away, his mind still reeling from the general's outrageous lies. They couldn't be true. He couldn't have married a breed – not him. He hated Indians. Those butchering savages had murdered his parents.

Like a blind man, he headed up the street, not knowing where he was or where he was going. He was confused and outraged, his thoughts spinning so crazily, chaotically that he couldn't think straight. He needed to clear his head and somehow sort this thing out.

He spied a saloon and tried the closed doors, but they were locked. First he pounded on them, then rattled them loudly. Finally he heard a voice on the other side. 'We ain't open yet.'

'Open this door.' Gabe didn't give a damn whether they were open for business or not; he wanted a drink.

After the loud click of a lock, the door was opened a crack. 'Oh, it's you, Mr. Blackwood. Sorry, but –' The whisker-jowled bartender never had a chance to finish his sentence as Gabe shoved the door the rest of the way open and shouldered his way into the saloon.

All the chairs were turned upside down on top of the tables and the room had the sour, stale smell of bad whiskey and tobacco. Gabe bypassed the tables and walked straight to the bar.

'What's all the ruckus, Lyle?' Ryan Colby stepped out of the back room wearing a long dressing gown of navy blue velvet lined in a cream silk that was extended to the collars and cuffs of the garment.

'It's Blackwood. He just barged in. I told him we were closed,' the bartender explained.

'I want a drink.' Gabe leaned on the bar.

'Put on some coffee, Lyle.' Ryan walked behind the counter.

'If I wanted coffee, I would have gone to the restaurant,' Gabe snapped. 'This is a saloon and I want whiskey.'

'Whiskey we've got.' Ryan smiled as he uncorked a bottle from the shelf and poured a shotful. 'But you won't mind if I drink the coffee. For me, it's a little early for whiskey.'

'Leave the bottle sit,' Gabe ordered when Ryan started to return it to the shelf.

'Are you sure?' He arched an eyebrow. The Gabe Blackwood he knew rarely imbibed.

'I can pay for it.' Gabe dug in his pocket and slapped the money on the counter.

Ryan left the whiskey bottle where it sat and moved a little way down the counter to light a cigar. He'd seen that wild-eyed look in customers' eyes before, ready for an excuse to start a fight. He held the match flame to the end of his cigar and sucked on the cigar to light it, studying the attorney through the rising screen of smoke. There was no mistaking that belligerent gleam.

'What are you staring at?'

'Nothing.' Ryan shook out the match.

'What's that supposed to mean?'

'It doesn't mean anything.' Ryan didn't intend to be the one to provide Blackwood with the excuse he was seeking. He wasn't one of those men who got a kick out of fighting. Still, curiosity kept him from moving away and leaving Blackwood to nurse his own ill-temper.

Ryan dealt out a game of solitaire, glancing now and then at his lone customer. Blackwood stood hunched over the bar, swigging down his whiskey in gulps, then refilling the glass.

'I should have called him out,' Blackwood muttered and bolted down another swallow. 'I should have.'

'Pardon?' Ryan pretended he hadn't heard.

'I said I should have called the son of a bitch out. That'd stop him from spreading his lies.'

'Which son of a bitch is this?'

'The corrupt little general occupying Baranov's Castle. That bastard isn't fit to command, and I told him so.' He folded his hand tightly around the small shot glass in a throttling gesture. 'It was a damned lie!'

'What was?'

'None of your business,' Gabe snarled.

Ryan shrugged, stuck the cigar back in his mouth, and went back to his card game. The whiskey was loosening Blackwood's tongue. The cursing by a man who normally watched his language was always the first sign. Sooner or later he'd confess what was bothering him. Ryan wouldn't have to pry it out of him.

'I can't let him get away with it,' Blackwood mumbled to himself, then straightened. 'Colby, you got a pistol I can use?'

'What for?'

'So I can shoot the son of a bitch. I can't let him get away with sayin' those things about my wife. My beautiful Russian princess. Anybody that's ever seen her knows that she hasn't got any Indian blood in her. You can tell that, can't you, Colby?'

'Whatever you say.' Ryan made a show of studying the cards

spread on the counter, at last understanding what this was all about.

'No, damn it!' Blackwood slammed his fist on the bar top. 'I wanta hear what you say!'

'I say' – Ryan paused – 'that it's nothing to me one way or the other.'

'That's no answer.' Gabe pushed away from the bar and moved down to where Ryan was playing his solitaire. The slight stagger to his step after only three drinks betrayed his low tolerance of alcohol.

'It's the best I can give.' Ryan moved a black nine onto a red ten.

With a sweep of his hand, Blackwood swept the cards off the bar top, scattering them onto the sawdust-covered floor. 'I want the truth, damn it. Do you think my wife is an Indian?'

'The truth?' Ryan breathed out a silent, humorless laugh. 'I think maybe she is, but I don't know it's so. I'm not the one you should be asking. Your wife is the only one who can tell you the truth. Before you borrow a gun and kill somebody, why don't you ask her?'

Blackwood swayed slightly as he thought over the suggestion. He nodded slowly. 'I think I'll do that.' He turned from the bar and lurched across the saloon to the door.

As it was slammed shut behind Blackwood, Lyle emerged from the rear of the saloon. 'Coffee's ready, boss.'

Ryan took the mug from the bartender and cast one last glance at the door. Blackwood was such a fool. Money was the only dream a man should pin his hopes on. Ryan had never known money to disappoint a man.

Outside the saloon, Gabe turned up the street. Ryan was right; the thing to do was confront Nadia with the general's accusation. She'd be able to give him the answer to clear this whole mess up. Ryan – and probably everybody else – thought he'd married a breed.

But he would never have made that kind of mistake. His parents' murder had taught him better than to ever trust an Indian – any kind of Indian, full-blooded or not. His mother's scalp had hung from the belt of the half-breed whom his parents had loved and adopted as their son.

His hate toward the Indians encompassed more than the death

406

of his parents at their hands. He hated them because his parents had chosen to leave him and live among the Indians, because they had left him – their own flesh and blood – to give their love to some half-white savage. Indians had stolen a great deal from him.

As he charged down the street, driven by anger, he tripped over a loose board and sprawled headlong onto the wooden sidewalk. A grunting oink came from the muddy street as a startled pig scrambled to its feet and trotted away, splashing through the wet mire. Shaken by the sudden fall, Gabe lay there for a minute trying to gather his scattered senses.

As he started to bring his legs under him and push himself upright, a rotten board cracked under his weight, nearly pitching him forward again. Regaining his feet, he roundly cursed the condition of the sidewalk.

Months ago people had stopped paying the taxes levied by the city to maintain such things as the boardwalk. Everyone knew the city didn't have the legal right to levy taxes. Taxes couldn't be levied unless the people voted for them, and they didn't have the legal right to vote in this land. The city government, the town plat, property titles, mortgages – nothing was legal.

Signs of neglect and disrepair were everywhere, especially among the newer, shoddily constructed buildings that had been hastily erected to take advantage of that initial boom. The doors and windows of several were boarded up, crudely lettered with signs that stated CLOSED or OUT OF BUSINESS. One said CALIFORNIA HERE I COME. Everywhere there was garbage, broken crates and staves, rusting barrel rings, and scraps of wet paper. There were more swine wallowing in the street's muck than there were people moving about.

This filthy broken-down town was supposed to be the capital of Alaska someday. And he wanted to be governor of this pighole. As the realization hit him, Gabe started to laugh. It rolled from him, harder and harder, until he was forced to lean against the building behind him for support. Tears ran down his cheeks. He never knew when he stopped laughing and started crying.

For a long time after the sobbing ended, he stared brokenly at the town. Then he pushed away from the building and moved to the edge of the boardwalk. 'Why?' he shouted. 'We could have been something!'

Someone tugged at his coat sleeve. Gabe swung his head around to see who it was. A blanket-wrapped squaw from the

Ranche hovered beside him, her darks eyes avidly watching him.

'Mister, you buy.' She held up some trinket for his inspection. 'Sell cheap.'

'Get away from me.' He jerked his arm away from her.

But the Indian woman persisted, thrusting the trinket closer to his face. 'Sell very cheap.'

'I said to get the hell away from me!' Angrily, he shoved her into the muddy street.

She slipped in the muck and fell, breaking the fall with her outstretched hand, but she lost her carved curio in the mud. She frantically searched for it, burying her hands in the chocolate mud and stirring them around in a desperate attempt to locate it. Gabe watched it all with contempt.

When she found it, she clutched it to her breast and looked back at him. Gabe stared at her round face. His wife had cheek-bones like that. 'Oh, my God,' he groaned and swung away from the sight, trying to deny it in his mind. Then he clamped his jaw tightly shut and gritted his teeth. The rage of betrayal and hate trembled through him.

With her cloak hung on the wall hook, Nadia moved away from the front door and slowly untied her bonnet. She removed it from her head and absently patted her hair back into its proper place.

Gabe had advised her not to go to her parents' home until he had returned from seeing the general, but Eva had been so anxious about them that she had gone anyway. She had been worried, too, and nagged with guilt, certain that regardless of what Gabe had said, she should have gone to her mother last night.

But Gabe had been right. Her mother hadn't wanted to see her. She could still remember the look of horror on her mother's face when she had entered the bedroom. Immediately, her mother had turned her face to the wall and pressed a trembling hand to her mouth. She hadn't responded to a single thing Nadia had said, simply lain in the bed, cowering in terror and shame.

Wisely she hadn't taken Eva in to see their mother. She wished she hadn't taken her little sister at all, but no one had warned her that their father looked so bad. His face was bruised and swollen, his lip cut, his eye blackened. At first she hadn't even recognized him. Poor Eva had stared, never saying a word.

He had looked so broken and lost; the soldiers had beaten more than his body. Last night their mother had made him promise that he would reveal to no one what had happened to her, he had told her. He had given his word, and made both of them swear the same pledge of secrecy. None of their friends or neighbors were to know. If any of them had heard the commotion, they were only to admit that the soldiers had broken into the house and ransacked it looking for liquor. Nadia had done her best to put the place to rights while she was there.

Her father had been so adamant that no one should know the whole truth that Nadia hadn't been able to tell him that Gabe had gone to see the American general. She hadn't wanted to cause him more anguish.

Her poor little sister was so confused by everything. Nadia simply hadn't been able to explain to her, in terms she could understand, the terrible degradation their mother had suffered at the hands of the soldiers. How could anyone explain such a vile thing to an innocent nine-year-old? It was something she couldn't even discuss with her husband. She could empathize with her mother's profound dread that their friends and neighbors might learn of the rape. If it had happened to her instead of her mother, she knew she wouldn't be able to bear having other people look at her and know what those soldiers had done to her. She'd die of shame.

She was relieved that her grandfather had taken Eva home with him. She simply couldn't have dealt with all her sister's awkward questions. The more she thought about the vow of silence she'd taken, the more she thought it would be best for everyone to pretend that nothing had ever happened. Surely when she explained it to Gabe, he would see the sense of it. Why bring unnecessary embarrassment to the family?

She recognized the familiar tread of Gabe's footsteps as he mounted the steps to their house.

'Gabe, I'm so glad you're home.' She moved forward to greet him as he walked in, then noticed the odd look on his face.

'Are you now?' he taunted and kicked the door shut with his foot.

He appeared to sway a little, but Nadia couldn't be sure of it. 'Let me help you take off your coat so we can sit down and talk.' But he didn't move. Instead he stared at her as if he had never seen her before now. Nadia became uncomfortable. 'Is something wrong?' She touched her cheek, wondering if she had smudged it.

'What could possibly be wrong?' he challenged.

'I don't know. You're looking at me so strangely.' She laughed nervously.

'Am I?'

Unable to fathom his peculiar mood, Nadia turned away to move back into the room, twisting her clasped fingers together. 'What did the general have to say?'

'The general had a great deal to say, my little princess.' His voice sounded so harsh and sarcastic that Nadia half turned to glance back at him. She felt frightened without knowing why. 'In fact, that was the question he raised. Whether you are a Russian princess – or an Indian one?'

'Whatever are you talking about?' She swung away from him and searched wildly for another topic that would lead their conversation away from this subject before he went off on another of his tangents about Indians. 'I went to see –'

He grabbed her arm and roughly jerked her around to face him. 'Answer my question, Nadia. Are you Russian or Indian?' He pushed his face close to hers.

She drew back, frightened by his angry look, and strained against the painful grip he had on her forearm. 'Why on earth would you ask such a thing, Gabe?' she murmured lamely, and immediately gasped in pain as he brutally twisted her forearm.

'Damn it, you answer me.'

'You're hurting me,' Nadia whimpered as the pressure increased, intensifying the pain shooting up her arm.

'Are you part Indian?'

It felt as if her arm was going to break at any second. 'Yes,' she gasped, then cried out when he twisted it harder.

'How much?'

'My . . . great-grandmother was half . . . Aleut,' she admitted. 'And my grandfather . . . is half Kolosh.' She didn't get a chance to tell him that her mother's ancestry was mixed as well, half Finnish and the rest Russian, Aleut, and Kolosh.

'You bitch!' He slaped her across the face.

The force of the blow knocked her to the floor, briefly stunning her. She was conscious of the ache in her arm from the wrenching he'd given it. One whole side of her face felt as if it was on fire. She propped herself up on one arm and gingerly touched her cheek and jaw, tasting the blood from the cut in her mouth.

'You lied to me!' he bellowed at her.

410

'I didn't.' She hurried to her feet, anxious to appease his temper. 'I swear I didn't, Gabe.'

'The whole damned town knew I took a breed for a wife – everyone except me! You left out that little piece of information.'

'You never asked.'

He slapped her, striking the same area as before and sending fresh explosions of pain through her head. 'I should have expected an answer like that from you,' he jeered. 'Even if I had asked, you would have lied. You tricked me into marrying you.'

'I swear I didn't.' She cowered from him, shielding her throbbing face with her hand. 'I love you. I wanted to be your wife and help make all your plans and dreams come true.'

'You've ruined them! You've destroyed every chance I had! Don't you see, you stupid little slut! They'll never appoint me governor when this becomes a territory! I'd be lucky if they'd give me an appointment as postmaster – not a man with a wife who's part Indian!' As he raged at her, Nadia started backing up, sensing the explosion that was to come, but he followed her, shouting louder and louder with each step. 'I'm finished! You have ruined everything for me! And you've made me the laughing stock of this whole stinking town! I must have looked like a fool parading around the streets with you on my arm. How could I have been so blind all this time?'

'Gabe, please –'

'Shut up!' He hit her and kept on hitting her.

Nadia tried to run, but that only seemed to incense him more. He grabbed her by the hair and pulled her back. She raised her arms, trying to ward off the blows to her face and head as he pummeled her unmercifully. When she managed to break away from him again, he chased her through the house, overturning furniture and knocking dishes and vases to the floor, and finally trapped her in a corner where there was no escape. Nadia sank to the floor and curled herself up in a protective little ball while he kicked and hit at her until she was insensitive to the pain. She kept sobbing and begging for him to stop, certain he intended to kill her.

She wasn't even aware when he stopped until she heard the slam of the front door and realized she was alone. For a long time she cowered in the corner, crying softly, bruised and battered from head to foot.

When night came, Nadia was petrified at what he might do to

her when he came home. She barricaded herself in the bedroom, then sat up to wait for him, every bone and muscle in her body throbbing with pain.

But Gabe didn't come back that night or the next day, or the next, or the next. Gradually Nadia became less frightened that he might return and more afraid that he wouldn't. By the fifth day, the meager supply of food in the house was gone. She let another day go by, telling herself that Gabe had to come back. His clothes were still here and many of his papers and books. She went another day without eating, certain that someone from the family would stop to find out why she hadn't been at church or gone to visit her parents. No one came.

Finally she admitted to herself that she could wait no longer. Most of the bruises on her face had faded to a faint discoloration easily hidden by several layers of powder. Although the two or three severe bruises were still visible, their violet hues were toned by the application of the Spanish papers. Her coat, gloves, and long skirts hid the rest.

The walk to town seemed exceptionally long and tiring. Picking her way carefully over the rotten boards in the sidewalk, Nadia approached Gabe's office with great trepidation. Outside his door, she hesitated and almost turned away. She couldn't help remembering that this was the very spot where she'd first met him. Gathering her courage, she opened the door and walked in.

At first glance, the office appeared deserted. It seemed her worst fear had been realized and he had truly left. 'Gabe?' she called hesitantly. Nothing. Then she heard a crash followed by a cursing that came from the back room. Nadia shrank from the anger in that voice, but it was too late to flee as Gabe appeared in the doorway.

His disheveled appearance shocked her. His face bristled with the pale stubble of several days of beard growth. The dark hollows under his eyes gave them a sunken look. His suit was badly rumpled and stained, and much of his sandy hair stood on end. He had the pale and drawn look of a man who had suffered through a terrible ordeal.

'What are you doing here?' The anger and bitterness hadn't gone from his voice, yet Nadia heard the pain in it, too.

'I've been worried about you,' she replied hesitantly.

'Well, don't,' he snapped. 'Because I don't want some squaw worrying about me. You've destroyed everything, so just get out!'

412

'I should have told you. I see that now. I shouldn't have kept it from you, but it was easier to pretend that you already knew, so I kept silent. And that was wrong. It's just that I loved you so much and I was so afraid of losing you. I don't blame you for being angry. You had every right to be. I deserved every bit of it and more. Please give me a chance to make it up to you for all the wrong I've done,' she begged. 'Let me try to show you how sorry I am. Please, Gabe, I want you to come home.'

'Home to what? You?' His lip curled in a sneer.

'It is your home.' In her heart Nadia knew she had destroyed whatever love he'd had for her. She would never be the reason he returned. Her only hope was to appeal to his sense of ownership. If he came back, maybe in time, by showing him complete devotion, she'd be able to earn his respect and some of the affection she'd once known from him.

'Get out! Get out of my sight!' He took a threatening step toward her.

Instinctively, Nadia backed up and felt the door behind her. 'I will do whatever you want,' she murmured, bowing her head and blinking rapidly at the hot tears that stung her eyes.

She left his office and turned up the street, keeping her head down so others couldn't see her face beneath the concealing brim of her bonnet. She felt faint and breathed in deeply to drive away the sensation. Now that Gabe didn't want her, there was only one place she could go. Nadia set out for her parents' home.

When she found the front door locked against her, she had to fight tears again. She knocked loudly and waited, then tried again. The third time she finally heard footsteps approaching the door. Her younger sister opened it.

'You should be in school.' Nadia would have preferred that Eva wasn't present when she talked to her father.

'Papa wanted me to stay home and take care of Mama.' Eva cocked her head to the side and stared at her intently. 'What happened to your face?'

Nadia hesitated, but she couldn't bring herself to admit to Eva that her husband had beaten her. 'I fell.' She moved past her into the house. 'Where is Papa?'

'In the parlor.'

Again she faltered. It wasn't going to be easy to admit to her father that her marriage had failed – that she was at fault. She touched one of the sore bruises on her heavily powdered face,

413

knowing how angry he'd be when he saw how Gabe had abused her, and knowing she must convince him that she had deserved it.

Eva followed her into the parlor. Lev sat slumped in an armchair beside the fireplace, staring vacantly at the smoldering log. Most of the swelling was gone from his face, and the bruises had changed color. Nadia paused, waiting for him to notice her, but he seemd completely unaware of her presence.

'When he isn't with Mama, he always sits there like that,' Eva told her..

'Why don't you go check on Mama. I want to speak to him privately.' There was no need to lower her voice. Her father appeared totally oblivious of them.

'She doesn't like to have me in the room. She doesn't want me to look at her. Why is she like that, Nadia?'

'Not now, Eva, please,' she begged, so near the breaking point. Sheer nerve was the only thing that kept her going.

'Everybody says that,' her sister murmured, dragging her feet as she left the parlor.

Slowly Nadia crossed the room to her father's chair. She stood beside it for several seconds, but his blank gaze never wavered from the nearly dead fire. 'Hello, Papa.'

He stirred vaguely, as if rousing himself from a great distance. He looked at her, but his expression was empty of recognition. She fell to her knees beside the chair and clutched his arm, feeling for a minute like a child again.

'Nadia.' Lightly he stroked her cheek, running his fingers over a faint purpling bruise. 'My baby.'

'I had to come, Papa.'

Suddenly he crumpled and buried his face in his hands, his whole body heaving with sobs. 'What have I done?' he murmured over and over. At first Nadia thought he was referring to her tragic plight. 'It's all my fault.'

'No, it isn't, Papa.' She couldn't let him blame himself for the failure of her marriage or for the beating she'd endured. He couldn't have known Gabe would do this to her.

'It is.' He lifted his head, tears streaming down his cheeks, and clasped his hands tightly together. 'We shouldn't have stayed here. We should have left with the others. None of this would have happened. Your mother would be –' He broke down, sobbing loudly.

414

Stunned, Nadia realized that he hadn't noticed her bruises at all. He was too overwrought with his own grief and guilt. 'Don't cry, Papa,' she begged.

He made a concerted effort to control himself, drawing in a deep sniffling breath and wiping the tears off his cheeks. Leaning forward, he rested his elbows on his thighs and bowed his head, clasping his hands together in a prayerlike attitude.

'I know you wish to comfort me, but my conscience allows me no peace.' He shut his eyes, squeezing them tightly. 'A man's first responsibility is to his family – his wife and children. But I put my duty to my father before them. I put all of you in jeopardy by staying in this place, and look what has happened. Your mama never said it, but I know she wanted to leave here. Now –' He choked up again.

Seeing how tortured he was with guilt, Nadia couldn't add to it. It would only bring more pain to tell him what had happened with Gabe.

'Papa, you mustn't do this to yourself. I'm sure Mama doesn't blame you for what happened.'

'Have you seen her today?'

'Not yet,' she admitted.

The shake of his head seemed to indicate utter defeat. 'I don't know what to do. I have tried. I asked Father Herman to come see her, but she wouldn't pray with him. She wouldn't even kiss the cross. I cannot work. She becomes terrified if I leave the house. I –'

'Papa.' Eva came to the doorway. 'I took Mama the broth, but she won't eat it.'

'She must eat.' As her father started to push out of his chair, Nadia checked his movement with a restraining hand on his arm. 'I will go to her.' She stood up, fighting her own weakness that came from lack of food.

He showed a mixture of gratitude and apprehension as she backed away from his chair and turned and walked from the room. Nadia smelled the chicken broth before she reached her parents' bedroom, and her stomach contracted with hunger pangs.

As she entered the bedroom, she looked first at the bowl of rich broth that sat on the table next to the bed. She was conscious of the extra saliva in her mouth and absently moistened her lips while keeping them pressed together. With an effort, she forced her gaze away from the soup to her mother.

A little shock went through her when she saw the drastic change in her mother. Her eyes appeared sunken and darkly hollowed from lack of sleep. Her yellowing gray hair that she had always worn neatly braided in a coronet was snarled and bushed in a hundred different directions. Her once strong and dexterous hands trembled noticeably as she nervously plucked at the bed covers as if wishing to draw them higher.

'Mama?' To Nadia, she looked like some crazy woman.

Fear lurked in her white-ringed eyes as Aila Tarakanova stared at her. 'Where is Lev?' she murmured, then grew panicked. 'Where is Lev Vasilivich? Lev!'

'Papa is resting,' Nadia tried to explain, but she couldn't make herself heard above her mother's frantic screams. Despite Nadia's attempts to restrain her, she clambered from the bed, clawing and shrieking. Nadia was too sore and weak to stop her as she ran to the door.

At that moment, the door opened and her mother ran straight into her father's arms. He held her, crooning softly to reassure her while Nadia stood helplessly by. He led her back to the bed and tucked the covers around her as one would with a child.

'I am sorry, Papa,' she murmured lamely. 'I couldn't stop her.'

'It is all right.' But he looked haggard and drawn as he sat down on the edge of the bed and picked up the soup bowl to begin spoon-feeding her mother, freshly stirring up the delicious aroma.

'Please, Papa, let me do it,' Nadia offered quickly. 'You must rest.'

He hesitated, then set the bowl down, and affectionately patted the nervously plucking hand. 'Nadia will stay with you, Aila, but I will be in the next room. I will not leave you, I promise.'

Although agitated by his departure, her mother seemed to accept that he was close by. Nadia removed her outer garments and laid them across the foot of the bed, then took his place on the edge. Her hand shook slightly as she cupped the bowl in the palm of her hand and breathed in the mouth-watering aroma. Dutifully she fed her mother the first spoonful, but at the next her mother turned her head away in refusal.

'Is it too hot?' Nadia intended to take only a small sip of the broth in the spoon to test its temperature, but it tasted much too delicious and she took it all. 'It isn't too hot, Mama. It's just right. Here, try another spoonful.' But her mother kept her head averted. 'Please, Mama. We will share. You fake some, then I will,' Nadia coaxed.

When her mother refused the spoon again, Nadia let the broth trickle into her own mouth. Nothing had ever tasted so good to her before. She didn't have to fake the smacking of her lips nor the relishing sounds she made.

'It is so good, Mama. Just taste it.' She tried to force a small spoonful into her mouth, but her lips were pressed so tightly together. Some of the precious broth ran down her mother's chin. Nadia swallowed that spoonful of broth as well.

Before she knew it, she had consumed all but two spoonfuls of it. She rationalized away the vague feeling of guilt by telling herself that her mother wouldn't have eaten it. For the first time in three days she had food in her stomach.

'Let me brush your hair, Mama,' Nadia offered. Doing her mother's hair was a task obviously beyond her father's and sister's skill, or she was certain they would never have let it get in such a state. 'A person always feels better when they look nice.' But the minute she tried to touch her mother's hair, she shrank from her and cowered in the bed. 'I'm not going to hurt you, Mama. I just want to fix your hair.'

'No.' Her mother sobbed and started screaming again, then pressed her hands on her head as if protecting it.

Nadia tried to quiet her, but nothing she said made any difference. As her father came charging into the room again, she turned to him in confusion. 'I only wanted to brush her hair.'

It took him several minutes to calm her down before he could explain to Nadia. 'She will let no one touch her hair. I think . . . *they* were fascinated by its light color. Three days ago I caught her trying to cut it all off with the scissors. We have had to take everything sharp away from her.'

Nadia stared at her mother lying in the bed and clutching the Holy Bible that her father had finally given her to quiet her sobbing cries.

'She should not be upset any more. I think it's best that you leave now,' he said. 'You can come visit her another day. Perhaps by then she will be better.'

He sat down on the bed and stroked Aila's arm, crooning to her in a low, soothing tone. Nadia wanted to scream at him to look at her – to see the bruises beneath her powder mask, to hear her confess that her husband didn't want her any more – but he was oblivious of her. Moving numbly, she collected her coat, gloves, and bonnet from the foot of the bed and left the room.

There was nowhere for her to go except back to her own house. She noticed the damp chill in the house when she entered and discovered the fire had gone out in the fireplace. After she got the logs burning again, Nadia sat in the rocking chair beside it, where she had so often sat and watched Gabe as he worked at the table.

The loneliness closed in on her. She hugged her arms tightly around her waist, suddenly very frightened of being alone for the rest of her life. She didn't care how badly Gabe might treat her as long as he came back. After all, she'd brought all this on herself by not telling him the truth. Even though she hadn't deliberately set out to trick him, she had. How could she blame him for reacting the way he had?

The door opened and Gabe walked in. Relief leaped through her. She clutched the arms of her chair, afraid to move, afraid to speak in case he hadn't come to stay.

'What are you doing here?' He glared at her.

'Where else would I go?' She couldn't admit that her father's house was virtually closed to her. 'I am your wife. This is where I belong.'

For a long moment he said nothing. She held her breath, afraid he might turn around and leave. Instead he kicked the door shut. She jumped at the loud bang it made. 'Fix me something to eat.'

'We have no food or I would gladly fix you a meal.'

He hesitated, then reached in his pocket and threw a few coins at her. 'Go buy some and be quick about it – before I trade you to some soldier.'

37

The Double Eagle saloon was jammed with blue-coated soldiers from the town's garrison, their raucous voices drowning out the tinny music from a piano. Smoke layered the room, creating a blue-gray haze, and spittoons dotted the floor, occasionally hit by the streams of yellow tobacco juice spat in their direction.

Dan Kelly stood with his back to the bar, one elbow resting on the counter to support some of his weight while he stared glumly at the front windows. Frost rimmed all but the centers of the panes, and the room's heat steamed over the rest of the glass, blocking out the sight of the snowflakes that drifted outside the saloon. Winter had come, covering the mountains with a blanket of snow and hiding that elusive gold strike from him for another season.

'Kelly!' A hand pounded his shoulder in a back-slapping gesture of greeting.

The blow jarred his arm and nearly sloshed the beer over the rim of his mug. Kelly quickly steadied the glass. Beer was almost always in short supply, since all of it was shipped in to Sitka from the States.

'What the hell you doin' standin' here all by yore lonesome? You look plum' pitiful. Why don't ya come celebrate with us?' Nate Wheeler swayed against him, blinking to focus his alcohol-glazed eyes. 'I'll buy ya a beer. Me an' Gus an' Corky h'been gettin' the shit duty fer better'n two months now – all on account a' havin' some fun with a yeller-haired breed. An' we're gonna tie us on one t'night. Ain't we, boys?'

Kelly glanced at the two louts standing behind Wheeler as they chorused an agreement. 'Some other time.' He turned and leaned on the bar.

But Wheeler paid no attention to his refusal. 'Hey, barkeep! Another beer for my friend here.' He slapped the money on the bar to pay for it, and shouldered another soldier aside to stand next to Kelly. 'I ain't seen you in a coon's age. I'd ask where ya been keepin' yoreself, but I reckon I already know.' He snickered and glanced at his two buddies. 'Ya ever see a man look so sorrowful on a Satu'day night? Reckon he ain't found that mother lode he keeps a-huntin' fer.'

'Not yet,' Kelly admitted. 'But it's out there.'

After more than two years of tramping over the wild terrain in the blazing sun or sluicing rain, panning the mountain streams and chipping ore samples from rocky ledges, he'd found enough traces of gold to convince himself that there was a big vein of it somewhere.

'What's he lookin' fer? Gold?' The soldier named Corky draped himself on Wheeler's shoulder. 'Hell, I know whare there's a bunch of it. An' silver, too. Lots of it.'

'Where?' Kelly challenged contemptuously, and the man started giggling and leaned closer to share his secret.

'It's right here. It's been right under yore nose all this time.' He tittered gleefully. 'I bet we ain't standin' a hundred yards from it.'

'Yeah, it's probably in somebody's safe,' Kelly jeered, then took a swig of his beer and wiped the foam from his upper lip.

'Naw, it ain't. It's layin' right out in the open.'

'Then how come you ain't picked it up?' Wheeler taunted.

' 'Cause it's more'n one man can tote.'

'Bullshit,' Kelly snorted.

'Hey, I can prove it!'

Restlessly, Aila Tarakanova turned her head from side to side on the bed pillow, groaning softly at the hot, stifling weight that pinned her to the down-filled mattress. In a frantic attempt to free herself she flung out an arm. Then she felt the sudden draft on her skin and awakened in a cold sweat, her mind filled with the nightmare of the rape and the echoes of her screams. She jammed a fist in her mouth to silence the shrieks before they hit her again, unaware that she had made no sound louder than a moan.

She lay motionless, casting wild glances about the dark room and listening for the faintest sound, conscious that her night-gown was wadded under her hips but afraid to pull it down – afraid they'd spring on her from the shadows. All she could hear was the sound of her own breathing. She wondered if they'd gone.

Tears began to roll down her cheeks as she clutched the Bible tighter to her breast.

Her terror-warped mind was no longer capable of separating nightmare from reality. Fear came back to grip her in its icy talons. Whimpering for her husband, she crawled cautiously from the bed, panic rising in her throat when there was no response. She crept through the darkness into the parlor.

'Lev.' She sobbed his name, so soft yet so loud to her ears.

She found him lying slumped on the sofa motionless, the way they'd left him that night. Suddenly she heard a noise outside and whirled around to face the front door, panicked by the thought they were coming back.

Terrified, she turned and ran, fleeing the house by the back door and running into the snow-speckled night, mindless of the snow beneath her bare feet. Certain she was being pursued, she searched for a place to hide. Houses weren't safe. They had broken into her home. 'Where?' she sobbed brokenly, both arms clasped across the Bible, hugging it to her chest.

Then she saw the spires of the cathedral silhouetted against the beacon atop Baranov's Castle. She'd be safe in God's house. She ran toward it, slipping and sliding on the slushy street.

Her lungs felt as if they were about to burst, and her heart was pounding so loud she could hear nothing else by the time she reached the cathedral steps. She stumbled and clawed to the top of them, never losing her grip on the Bible. She barely had enough strength to open one side of the heavy double doors, but she managed it and staggered into the sanctuary of the church.

A candle flame flickered near the altar. She moved toward it, tears of relief blurring her vision, her bare feet making no sound. Then she noticed a cloaked figure by the altar and halted abruptly, believing him to be a priest. An overwhelming sense of shame filled her with an abject dread of facing a man of the church. As yet he hadn't noticed her. She darted a quick glance at the adjoining small chapel, then began to inch her way toward it.

Suddenly, off to her right came a hoarse whisper in English. 'All right, which one of you damn fools forgot to make sure the door was shut tight? Corky, you were the last one in. Go shut it before someone outside notices it.'

'Who the hell's gonna see it?' The hissed answer came from the robed figure by the altar. 'I ain't never heard a' nobody comin' t' church in the middle of the night to pray. Hey, Kelly, come'ere an' look at these chalices – or whatever the hell they are. I'll betcha' they're solid silver. Didn't I tell ya' this stuff was jest layin' aroun'.'

Another figure moved in the shadowed darkness of the church. Aila noticed a fourth. There were four men – four Americans. None of them wore the cassock of the priest. They had on dark blue cloaks – Army blue. They were soldiers, she realized and gasped in fear.

'What was that?'

The candle was lifted to throw a wider circle of light. Its faint glow reached her as she stared in horror at the soldier with the shock of straw-colored hair sticking out from under his cap. He was one of them! One of the men who had raped her! Wildly, she wondered how he had gotten here ahead of her. She raked her fingers through her hair, snagging them in the snarled tangles.

'Would ya look at that crazy ole witch?' The one holding the candle took a step closer.

The movement seemed to break the grip of fear that had temporarily paralyzed her. No, she thought, they weren't going to do it to her again – not in the church! She turned and ran to the front door that she had unwittingly left standing open.

'Stop her!' one of them yelled.

Aila screamed when she heard the heavy clump of footsteps pursuing her. 'Forget her. Let's grab the snuff and get out of here!' another shouted.

But the sound of the footsteps didn't abate. 'Hey, lady! Wait,' came a husky, low-pitched call. 'You can't go out there.'

Dan Kelly saw the look of stark terror on her face as she darted through the open door. He had seen such unreasoning fear once before in a homesteader's wife after some Indians had murdered and mutilated her husband, then had their fun with her. He ran after her.

At the top of the church steps, he paused to look down the street, half expecting to see her running down the middle of the main thoroughfare shouting the alarm to the soldiers in the saloons and the barracks and guardposts beyond. The street was empty except for a handful of half-drunk soldiers and a couple of Tlingit prostitutes from the Ranche. No one was showing any interest in the church. The old woman's one short scream wasn't likely to rouse attention. In this town at night, women screamed all the time, sometimes with cause and sometimes without.

There was a movement in his side vision. Turning, Kelly saw a wraithlike figure flitting close to the buildings along the street on his left. He ran down the steps and took out after her, muttering to himself, 'Where the hell is she going? There's nothing this way but the sound.'

As the buildings thinned out, he briefly lost sight of her, the white of her long gown and the paleness of her wild hair blending into the backdrop of the snow-covered ground. But she left tracks in the newly fallen snow. Kelly followed them at a loping run, puffing slightly from the sharp cold that burned his lungs.

As he scanned the area ahead of him, the old woman seemed to materialize before his eyes. It took him a second to realize that the black waters of the sound outlined her pale figure. The watery expanse checked her headlong flight. She paused, appearing to hesitate as she glanced frantically to the left, then the right. Considering all the chances she'd passed up to seek the safety of other people, Kelly doubted that she'd turn right. The main part of town lay in that direction. Slowing his steps, he angled to the left, cutting off that avenue of escape. She appeared to panic when she saw how close he was.

'Don't run, lady,' he called to her softly, trying to calm her fear. The hem of her gown was crusted with snow. As she backed away from his approach, he wondered how she could stand walking in that ankle-deep snow without any shoes, yet she seemed immune to the cold. She wasn't even shivering, although her arms were crossed in front of her as if protecting something. 'It's all right, lady. I'm not going to hurt you. Don't be frightened.'

He crooned to her, hoping that if she didn't understand English at least his tone of voice might make an impression on her, but she continued to back up with each step he took toward her, retreating ever closer to the water's edge, all the while slowly moving her head from side to side in some silent denial.

When she reached the ice-crystaled shore, she stopped. Kelly relaxed and smiled a little, confident that she would listen to him now that she could retreat no farther. He held out his hand to her, continuing to talk to her in low, soothing tones, repeating the same phrases over and over again.

'It's all right, lady. Don't be frightened. I'm not going to hurt you.'

Without warning, she turned and ran into the water. Kelly yelled and started to run after her, then stopped, thinking she

423

would halt if he didn't chase her. But she waded in deeper, her flight impeded only by the increasing depth of the water and the tangling weight of her wet gown. She slipped and went under. Kelly splashed in after her, but she surfaced, flailing to get away from him.

The water flowing over the tops of his boots felt like liquid ice. A man wouldn't last three minutes in water this cold, Kelly thought and stopped. The crazy old woman was a good thirty feet from him, a pale blot in the dark water. As panicked as she was, she'd fight him even if he was able to reach her. There was a good chance both of them would drown.

With a sickening feeling in the pit of his stomach, Kelly slowly backed toward the shore. He could hear the panicked sounds of her breathing, yet she didn't cry out for help. He could barely see her. His wet feet felt numb, mere stumps attached to his legs. He wondered if she was losing the feeling in her limbs, too.

The white patch he was watching in the black sea suddenly disappeared. There was no more sound except the quiet lapping of the water on the shore and the distant revelry from town. Kelly turned and walked slowly in the direction of the barracks. He avoided the church that the others had stayed behind to loot. He didn't know where they were now – and didn't care.

The body of Aila Tarakanova washed ashore the next day. It was found by her distraught husband, who had begun searching for her in the predawn hours when he had discovered she was missing from their home. The townspeople paid little attention to the death. They were all in an uproar over the looting of St. Michael's Cathedral. The theft had been discovered early and the culprits had left a clear set of tracks in the fresh snowfall, leading to their apprehension and the recovery of the stolen items.

Because there was still no civil law to prosecute the guilty, the townspeople's only recourse was to appeal to General Davis. The commanding general seemed to be of the opinion that perhaps this time his soldiers had gone too far. In punishment for their offense, he ordered privates Nathan Wheeler, William 'Corky' Travers, and August 'Gus' Miles drummed out of the service and sent back to the States on the first available Army transport.

Kelly was one of the guards assigned to escort the three men, now dressed in ill-fitting civilian clothes, on board the ship bound for home. None of the three had implicated him in the robbery in which he had taken no active part other than to enter the cathedral with them.

Their faces were all smiles. They'd been kicked out of the Army, all right, but they'd also been kicked out of this Godforsaken northland called Alaska. The lucky bastards were going home. Most of the other soldiers viewed them with envy, but not Kelly.

He felt confused and guilty. A woman had died that night, the same woman, it turned out, that his buddies had recently spent time in the stockade for molesting. It explained why she had been so terrified that night. In a sense they had killed her. Yet he had played a role in her death, too. He reminded himself that she'd been an old woman, another of those Russian breeds, yet that didn't ease his troubled conscience very much.

He glanced at the chain of snow-covered mountains that rose dramatically from the island's shore. The sight of them spurred thoughts of gold. Kelly had no desire to leave this country until he'd found it. Maybe, come spring, he'd take a look around the Silver Bay area.

Winter had barely begun, and already he was looking forward to the spring melt and the fresh outcroppings the thaw would create. Gold was a subject that always took his mind off his troubles.

On a typically mild January afternoon, the sun sat low in the west, its soft rays pinking the white cone of Mount Edgecumbe and pearlizing the wispy trails of mist that blanketed the waters of Sitka Sound. Eva hugged both arms around the pouch containing her schoolbooks and her mother's Bible. She always carried it with her even though the sea water had smeared the ink and dried the pages together. It had been her mother's most treasured possession, especially during these last months. Now it was Eva's.

A group of soldiers lounged idly at the street corner ahead of her. She walked slower, hoping they'd move on before she got there, but they didn't. They were a scraggly, unkempt lot – dirty and smelly. Steadfastly, Eva kept her gaze glued to the ground in front of her as she approached them. She trembled inside with a rage born of fear and hatred.

'She's wearin' skirts. Ya reckon that's a girl?'

"Bout as homely as a mudhen, ain't she?'

Tears burned the back of her eyes. She wanted to scream at them and hurl their insulting remarks back at them; but as violently as she hated them, she was frightened of them, too. She broke into a run, and the awful sound of their mocking laughter gave added impetus to her flight. She didn't slow down until she was nearly home, but she couldn't face the thought of going there. She hated it. Ever since her mother had drowned, it seemed that death lived in the house. Her father just sat around, waiting to die.

Even though she was not quite ten years old, she had tried to assume the role of woman of the house – cooking and cleaning and caring for her father. But the meals that she labored so diligently to prepare usually went untouched by her father. Even the times that he changed into a clean shirt, which were rare, he never noticed how carefully she had ironed it. Nothing mattered to him any more, not even her.

She didn't want to go home. She knew she shouldn't feel that way, but she did. Although her grandfather had always listened sympathetically, Eva wasn't in the mood to hear more of his assurances that in time her father would get over his grief. Nobody seemed to understand that she missed her mother, too – nobody but her sister. She remembered how Nadia had held her and cried the last time she'd come to the house. That had been two weeks ago, before Nadia had broken her arm when she slipped on some ice and fell. Eva decided to visit her sister and make certain she was getting along all right.

Finding the front door of her sister's house unlocked, Eva walked in without knocking. Almost immediately she heard the approach of footsteps coming from the kitchen. An instant later, Nadia came into view, her left arm cradled in a sling, a strained and anxious expression on her face.

'Eva.' She sounded relieved as she nervously wiped her right hand on the front of her apron. 'I thought maybe Gabe had come home early. What brings you here? Did you just get out of school?' She glanced apprehensively at the door, then at Eva. 'Why don't we go into the kitchen? I was just starting to make some *kulich*. I thought I'd surprise Gabe.'

She started for the kitchen without waiting to see if Eva followed her. After that initial barrage of questions, Eva didn't know which to answer first. As she walked slowly into the kitchen, she wasn't even certain Nadia cared to hear her answers.

'I didn't feel like going home, so I thought I'd come by to see you.' She laid her pouch of books on the table, where Nadia had set out all the ingredients for the Russian holiday bread.

'How's Papa?' Nadia added some flour to the nutmeg and vanilla-spiced mixture of butter, eggs, and sugar in the large crockery bowl, then picked up a spoon to start stirring it in, awkwardly attempting to hold the bowl steady with her left hand.

'The same.' Eva slumped onto a chair. 'He just sits in his chair and hardly ever talks.'

'He's taking Mama's death very hard.' After thickening the butter with flour, she added a cupful each of currants and nuts. 'I knew he would.'

Eva stared at the wooden spoon in her sister's hand, watching its circular motion as Nadia attempted to fold the ingredients together. 'I hate him.'

The statement had the desired effect, as her sister finally took notice of her and let the spoon handle rest against the side of the bowl. 'Eva! How can you say that?'

'It's his fault Mama's dead. Even he says so. He shouldn't have let those soldiers hurt her. He should have stayed in the room with her and not left her alone. She wouldn't have gotten frightened and run out of the house if he'd been with her.'

'That isn't fair, Eva. He did everything he could for her. He couldn't sit with her every minute. He needed his rest, too.'

'He could have asked me to stay with her if he wanted to sleep.'

'You know she only wanted Papa with her.' She picked up the spoon and started stirring the batter again. 'What happened to Mama wasn't his fault, and I don't want to hear you say such a thing ever again.'

'After the Americans came, we should have left with Uncle Stanislav, like Papa said.' She stuck her finger into the rich bread batter when Nadia paused to add more flour to the mixture, then slowly licked it off.

'Maybe we should have.'

Nadia's unexpected agreement took Eva by surprise. Always before, her sister had denied such a suggestion, with the explanation that she never would have married Gabe if they had left.

'But we didn't go with Uncle Stanislav or Aunt Anastasia, so there's no point in talking about it.' Her sister's tone seemed unnaturally brittle. 'You should be old enough to understand that we can't change the past. If we could, there might be a lot of things we would do differently.'

'What would you change?' Eva had always thought her beautiful

427

older sister had everything. Everyone had always liked her best, with the possible exception of their grandfather. Otherwise she'd always been the favorite daughter, favorite niece, favorite cousin – favorite everything. She'd gone to the balls and concerts given at the governor's mansion when Princess Maria had entertained there. She had married a handsome and important American. Nobody had ever laughed at Nadia, made fun of the way she looked, or called her names. She had never suffered the agony of not being liked the way Eva had.

Nadia hesitated over her answer. 'I would change what happened the night the soldiers broke in. I would have Papa make them leave.'

Eva thought about that for a while, then nodded slowly. 'That's when everything went wrong. Nothing was the same after that night, was it?'

'No. Nothing.'

'I hate them,' she declared vehemently.

'Who?'

'The soldiers.' She hated them for what they'd done to her parents and for the way they made her feel with their hurtful remarks. She hated all the soldiers. 'Somebody should make them pay for what they've done. What about Gabe? Can't he see that they're punished?'

'There's . . . there's nothing he can do.' Nadia added the last of the flour and tried to work it into the stiffening dough.

'He could try, couldn't he? He could talk to the general and –'

'No!' The suggestion obviously upset her, although she tried to conceal it. 'I told you there isn't anything he can do. Please, let's not talk about it. And don't suggest it to him either.'

'How can I?' Eva muttered. 'I hardly ever see him any more. How come he was too busy to come to Mama's funeral?'

'Because he had important things to do.' But she didn't say what they were.

For some reason, Eva didn't find that excuse very convincing. 'He never comes over to see Papa.'

'He's been very busy.' Despite Nadia's attempts to hold the bowl steady while she worked the flour into the dough, it kept shifting. Eva observed the wince of pain that flashed across her sister's face as a sudden movement of the bowl sideways jerked at her injured arm.

'Would you like me to do that for you?' she offered.

428

'Yes, thank you.' Nadia willingly relinquished the bowl of bread dough and moved away from the table, gently holding her sling-wrapped arm as if it pained her. 'It's surprising how difficult it is to do simple things when you have only one good arm.'

'It must hurt.' Eva abandoned the spoon and began kneading the flour into the dough with her fingers.

'Sometimes, but it's getting better.' Her smile seemed strained. 'You'll have to take some of the kulich home to Papa.'

'He won't eat it,' Eva replied glumly. 'He hardly eats anything. It doesn't matter what I fix.'

'That will change in time. His appetite will come back.'

'No, it won't. He doesn't care about anything any more. If I didn't come home tonight, he wouldn't even miss me.'

'You don't believe that, do you?'

'Yes. Mama didn't want me in her room. Now Papa doesn't even care if I'm there or not.'

'He does care. He may not show it, but that's only because he misses Mama so much right now. But . . . if he knew . . . you were hurting, he'd do something about it. Papa would. I know he would – if he knew.'

'Are you crying, Nadia?' She thought she saw tears in her eyes.

'My arm hurts a little, that's all.' She turned away so Eva couldn't see her face.

From the front room came the sound of the door opening and a man's heavy footsteps walking in. Eva frowned at Nadia's visible start of alarm. She looked so frightened that for an instant Eva thought maybe some soldiers had come. But her sister turned and bustled quickly to the table.

'I'll finish that.' She moved the bowl away from Eva's flour-and dough-sticky fingers. 'You'd better go home before Papa wonders where you are and starts worrying.'

'But who came in?' Eva didn't understand why she was suddenly being sent away. 'Is it Gabe?'

'Yes.' She lowered her voice to a whisper and pleaded urgently, 'Please, just do as I ask and leave. And don't forget your school books.'

'But –' Eva was confused.

'Woman! Where the hell are you?'

Surprised by the anger in the demanding voice, Eva turned toward the connecting door just as her sister's husband appeared in the opening. His expression looked harsh and forbidding, his eyes small points of blackness. The smile, the engaging twinkle of his eyes, was nowhere to be seen.

'What's she doing here?' He glared at Eva.

'She stopped by on her way home from school,' Nadia explained anxiously. 'She was just leaving.'

'Have I interrupted something?' His gaze narrowed suspiciously, darting back and forth between the two of them. 'I'll bet you didn't expect me home so early.'

'I wasn't certain what time you'd come home.' Her sister tried to sound very calm and unconcerned, but Eva heard the faint waver in her voice. She moved cautiously closer to the table, inching toward her book pouch. 'I know how much you like kulich. I thought I'd bake some to surprise you.'

'Now I see.' His glance fell on the tins of flour and sugar sitting on the table. 'You're making a surprise for me. I wonder if I had come home later whether there would have been any left for me – or would you have given it all to that half-breed family of yours? That's what's been going on, isn't it? You've been slipping food to them behind my back. That's why we never have any sugar or flour or anything else to eat in this house!'

'No! I was making this for you, Gabe.'

'Liar!' With an angry sweep of his arm, he knocked everything off the table. Eva jumped at the loud clatter of bowls, tins, cups, and pans as they fell onto the floor, scattering their contents amidst a rising cloud of flour dust. She heard her sister's half-smothered shriek of alarm and turned, her eyes widening as she saw him spring on Nadia and grab the wrist of her broken arm.

'Don't hit me. Please, don't hit me,' her sister sobbed.

He slapped her across the face, then jerked her back to him with a hard yank on her wrist. 'Don't you lie to me, you little bitch.'

'Don't you hurt my sister.' Eva flung herself at him, trying to pull his hand loose from its grip on Nadia's injured arm. 'You let go of her.'

She didn't see the backhanded swing of his arm. Pain exploded in her head as its force catapulted her backward. She fell, striking the juncture of the kitchen wall and floor. For an instant she was too stunned to move.

'Eva!' Distantly she heard her sister call out her name before the outcry of alarm was choked off by a sharp groan. Gradually the pain began to center on one side of her head, leaving a bruised soreness to claim the rest of her. 'My arm!'

'I'll break it again if you don't tell me the truth.' Gabe's threatening response dimly penetrated Eva's consciousness. She tried to sit up. 'You were going to give that kulich to her, weren't you?'

'I was going to . . . send one loaf home . . . for Papa.' Her pain-strangled answer broke on a sob. 'Only one, Gabe.'

'I'll bet it was only one.'

Eva heard the strike of another blow and looked up as the force of it knocked her sister to the floor. She fell on her broken arm and cried out sharply. Eva wanted to go to her, but Gabe was standing over her sister. She was frightened of what he might do to her if she tried to come between them again. The excruciating throbbing in her head hadn't abated from the last time.

Her sister cowered on the floor, protectively hunched over her arm, her body shaking in silent sobs, but she made no sound. Eva wanted to cry, but she was afraid of drawing attention to herself, afraid of incurring his wrath.

'I warned you about lying to me again. Maybe now you'll remember.' He stalked out of the room, grinding his feet in the flour and sugar and crunching the shards from the broken crockery bowl. Huddled against the wall, Eva didn't move until she heard the slam of the front door. When she tried to stand, she felt dizzy, and gingerly touched the side of her throbbing head, her fingertips encountering a lump about the size of a goose egg.

As soon as the dizziness passed, she picked her way through the mess on the floor to her sister's side and carefully helped her sit up, propping her back against a wall. Nadia's face looked ghostly white except for one swollen, purpling-red patch along her jaw where Gabe had hit her. Eva looked at her worriedly, noticing the way she cradled the sling that supported her broken arm.

'I'd better get Grandpa.'

'No.' Nadia's thready voice called her back when Eva started to rise. 'You mustn't . . . tell anyone.'

'But you're hurt.'

'I'll be all right.' Slowly she opened her eyes and reached to take hold of Eva's hand, squeezing it tightly. Eva cried at the pain she saw in her sister's pinched face, and tears rolled down her cheeks because she didn't know what to do.

'He hit you.' It was difficult for her to comprehend that, even though she'd seen it.

431

'It was my fault. I shouldn't have lied to him. I . . . Eva, you'd better go. He might come back.'

'You come with me. I don't want him to hurt you again.'

'I can't go. Papa . . .' Again she faltered. 'This is my home. He is my husband.'

'But he beat you.' Eva suddenly recalled other times recently that she'd noticed bruises on her sister. She stared at the sling, the incidents finally connecting. 'You didn't fall on the ice. He broke your arm, didn't he?'

'Yes,' Nadia admitted, bowing her head. 'I made him angry.'

Eva couldn't imagine her sister doing anything that would warrant such an awful punishment. She stared blindly at the door through which Gabe had disappeared. She kept remembering the way the soldiers had hurt her mother and the cruel remarks they'd made to her. Now Nadia had been beaten by her husband. She trembled with anger and confusion, wondering why men did these awful things.

38

Within a year of his wife's drowning, Lev Tarakanov was dead. Some said he died of a broken heart. But his young daughter Eva regarded his death as an act of abandonment, and she hated him for it. She had needed him. Her abused and battered sister had needed him. But he had forsaken them and she would never be able to forgive him for that. Her grandfather and sister wept at his funeral, but she did not shed a tear.

The creditors took the house and all its contents and sold them to satisfy her father's debts. Neither she nor her sister received any portion of the proceeds. Even Gabe Blackwood was upset about that, but there was no recourse. Theoretically, the confiscation and sale of the property was illegal. However, since Alaska was without civil law, there was no legal basis for the probation of wills or the inheritance of property. Penniless, Eva went to live with her grandfather, bringing with her only the few clothes she possessed and her mother's Bible.

Life went on almost the same as before. There were still few nights when her sleep wasn't disturbed by the carousing of drunken soldiers from the garrison. Her grandfather seemed to require little sleep and sent most of the nights sitting up with his old musket across his lap.

The years of 1871 and 1872 brought little change, except that the trickle of merchants and tradesmen leaving Sitka became a steady stream of disillusioned and disheartened families. A few prospectors arrived to take their place, drawn to Baranof Island by the discovery of gold-bearing quartz ledges in the area of Silver Bay. But the hard-luck miners couldn't bolster the sagging economy. After braying the ore in a mortar, they usually obtained only enough gold to keep them in a grubstake.

Numerous claims were staked, but without law no legal claims could be filed. All the gold found was in hard rock, which required a sizable amount of capital to mine it and a stamp mill to crush the gold from the ore. Investors were leery both because of the absence of any legal claim to a mine and the cost of obtaining the gold from an almost inaccessible area where nearly all the supplies and equipment had to be shipped in.

But, lured by the rich specimens of gold-bearing quartz they had found, the prospectors searched the mountains, seeking that elusive ledge with a vein of pure gold that might open the palms of the tight-fisted investors. Sitka was the place they went to obtain supplies and let off steam after weeks, sometimes months, alone in the mountains.

It was virtually impossible for Eva to step outside the door of her grandfather's house without seeing a drunk staggering down the street, whether it was a soldier, Kolosh, or miner. To venture beyond the doorstep invariably meant subjecting herself to their derisive hoots and insulting remarks. When the school closed its doors in the spring of 1873 because of a lack of funds to pay the teacher, Eva was glad, because it meant she no longer had to walk daily that gauntlet of verbal abuse. By then, her hatred of the soldiers had expanded to include all men except her aged grandfather and the church priest.

As she reached puberty, she learned the meaning of the word 'fornication.' Exposed as she was to the soldiers, miners, and prostitutes who frequented the saloons, she gradually came to understand what the soldiers had done to her mother. Eva could imagine nothing worse. The very thought filled her with revulsion and increased her loathing of men.

She was glad she didn't have her mother's blond hair that had so fascinated the soldiers. Her older sister, Nadia, did, and Eva had seen the bruises she received from her husband. She was glad her face was all broken out with pimples, that her mouth was too wide, her lips too full, and her eyes too close together. She was glad they called her 'frog face' and left her alone. Being pretty was a curse, and she was lucky that she wasn't damned with it.

Late one spring night Eva lay awake in bed watching the dancing northern lights perform their magical ballet in the sky beyond her window. The shimmering blue and green colors of the aurora borealis reminded her of Nadia's satin brocade ball gown – a gown that her husband had ripped to shreds during a recent rampage. As she watched the undulating waves of turquoise lights, they became the brocade material being violently

434

torn into strips of ragged cloth. She turned from the sight and stared at the dark shadows of her room, preferring their empty blackness to the savage beauty outside.

When she heard the faint scrape of a footstep at the back stoop, she stiffened tensely. Her grandfather was *inside* the house. She had heard him moving around the parlor only a moment ago. Soldiers. It had to be, she concluded. No one else would be sneaking about behind the house. Knowing that her grandfather's hearing wasn't as keen as it once had been, she scrambled out of bed, grabbed up her robe from the foot, and ran to warn him.

'Grandpa.' Calling softly, she darted to the chair where he sat dozing and gently shook his shoulder to waken him. Startled, he snorted and came instantly alert.

'What is it?'

'I heard something behind the house,' she whispered. 'I think someone's out there.'

Just then they both heard a sound at the door. Her grandfather rose from the chair holding the long musket in both hands. He moved to the kitchen doorway.

'What is there?' he demanded gruffly in English. 'Speak or I will shoot.'

'It is I.' The reply was made in Russian. 'Dimitri Stanislavich. Open the door.'

Eva dashed past her grandfather and unbarred the back door to pull it open, shaken by the fright her cousin had given her – and angry, too. 'Why do you come sneaking around in the middle of the night?' It didn't matter that it was usually the hour he came, or that it had been months since they'd seen him. 'We thought you were soldiers trying to break into the house. Grandpa could have shot you. It was a stupid thing to do, Dimitri Stanislavich, coming here in the middle of the night. He should have shot you just to teach you a lesson.'

'Is this how a man is to be welcomed home by his family?'

'How were we to know it was you?' She smelled the liquor on his breath and stiffly moved away from him.

Her grandfather struck a match and lit the oil lamp. Its flare of light reached out to embrace her cousin in his seaman's clothes as he shut the door and stepped into the kitchen.

'We received no word that your ship was in port, so I was not expecting you,' her grandfather said, then gestured toward the table and chairs. 'Come and sit down.'

'I forgot to send the message.' As Dimitri swaggered over to a chair, he noticed the ancient musket that stood propped against the wall. 'If you had fired that thing, I wonder which of us would have been more severely hurt. Let me get you a new rifle, Grandpa.'

'That one I know how to use. It is good enough.' With hands braced on the table, he lowered himself onto a chair, betraying the brittleness of age in his slow and careful movement. 'We should have *petnatchit copla* to celebrate your safe return from the voyage. Eva Levyena, bring us glasses and the bottle of vodka from the cupboard.'

If her grandfather had asked, Eva could have told him that her cousin had already celebrated his return. But the customary 'fifteen drops,' which usually meant half a tumblerful, was a Russian gesture of welcome and hospitality, commonly extended to all who entered the household. So she fetched the vodka and glasses from the cupboard and brought them to her grandfather.

She noticed the way his hand trembled as he poured a healthy portion of liquor into each glass tumbler, and realized that Dimitri's arrival had left him shaken. Eva had always viewed her grandfather as a strong, stalwart protector, afraid of nothing; but watching him now, she realized he was a weak old man. Next to him, her cousin Dimitri looked incredibly strong and vital.

Dimitri seemed to notice the haggardness, too. 'You look tired, Grandpa. You should be in bed sound asleep.'

'It isn't wise to sleep too soundly.' He darted a glance at Eva, then lifted his glass to take another drink of vodka. 'Now that you're home again, perhaps I'll be able to rest a little easier,' he said to Dimitri, then carried the glass the rest of the way to his mouth.

Ever since she had moved in with her grandfather after her father's death, he had sat up nights. She had never questioned it, because it made her feel safe and protected, knowing he was on guard. She suddenly realized that her grandfather didn't stay up out of concern for his own safety. He did it to protect her. Eva had never really perceived his action in that light before. Now that she did, she felt bad about it. She realized that, although her grandfather was old and tired, he was willing to sacrifice his rest, maybe even his life, for her safety and well-being. He was doing it for her.

Before he died, her father had sat up many a night, but his

436

sleeplessness had been casued by feelings of guilt and remorse over her mother's death, not by any desire to protect her from harm. By example, her grandfather had shown her the true meaning of family responsibility and devotion. More clearly than before, she saw how selfish her father had been. She moved to stand behind her grandfather's chair, deeply touched by his sacrifice.

'You'd better rest while you can,' Dimitri said in response to her grandfather's comment. 'Because I won't be here very long.'

'You will be leaving again soon?'

Eva heard the note of regret in her grandfather's question, yet it seemed to make no impression on Dimitri as he nodded affirmatively and then explained. 'Colby is closing down his saloon here and moving to Fort Wrangell on the Stikine River. I'll be sailing out of there from now on.'

The announcement was made so carelessly that for an instant Eva couldn't actually believe he meant he was leaving. Then she noticed the rounded droop of her grandfather's shoulders and knew it was so.

'Then you won't be coming back here.' Whenever her grandfather spoke in that emotionless voice, it was a disguise for something that deeply affected him. Eva realized how much he had counted on Dimitri, even though he was away most of the time.

'I might run a shipment of liquor in now and then.' Dimitri shrugged.

Eva clutched the chair back, her fingers tightening on the wooden slat. 'How can you just go off and leave us here alone like that? Don't you care what happens to us?'

'Now, now, Eva.' Her grandfather tried to calm her. 'Dimitri is a navigator. That's how he makes his living.'

'He makes his living by smuggling liquor in for the Americans and by poaching otters and seals. He doesn't even trade with the Kolosh any more.' Everyone thought she was too young to know what was going on, but she did.

'It is his business, not ours,' her grandfather reproved gently.

'He has worked for that man Colby for so long he's become like the Americans.' Eva was angry and refused to be silenced. 'He thinks only about making money and doesn't care what happens to his family. Grandpa is getting old, Dimitri. He needs you here.'

As she gripped her grandfather's shoulder, he reached up and patted her hand. 'We will manage – just as we have whenever Dimitri was away. And we are not alone. Your sister, Nadia, is here.' He smiled wanly at her cousin. 'Take no notice of her.'

But she could see that Dimitri chose to believe what her grandfather said. He did it because he was selfish, and believing it allowed him to do what he wanted. But in effect he was deserting them, just as her father had. And for all the help Nadia could offer them, they might as well be alone. But Eva seemed to be the only one who understood that.

'It is late, Eva.' Wolf affectionately squeezed her hand. 'You must get your sleep.'

'What about you, Grandpa?'

'Dimitri and I haven't finished our drinks yet.'

Reluctantly she left them.

Glass from a broken whiskey bottle in the street glinted in the light of the noonday sun as Gabe Blackwood stepped out of his office. He paused and absently moistened his lips, longing for a taste of the whiskey that had been in that bottle. He glanced back inside his nearly bare office. There wasn't anything of value left to sell. He'd pawned his law books last month. In a land with no law, they weren't any good to him. He couldn't even sell the building. There was nobody interested in buying it.

The pounding of hammers came from the nearly deserted street. It was now a rare sound in a town that had once boasted a population of almost two thousand people and now could muster less than four hundred inhabitants, excluding the Indians, whom Gabe never counted. He hesitated, then closed the office door and wandered down the boardwalk to see what was going on.

A group of workmen were in front of the Double Eagle saloon. Gabe stopped in surprise when he saw they were lowering the big sign to the ground. He'd heard rumors that Ryan Colby was pulling out of Sitka, but he'd discounted them. Obviously he'd been mistaken. He spied Ryan standing to one side, wearing his customary black waistcoat and brocade vest and chewing on a long cigar.

'So you're really pulling out?' Gabe asked him.

'Yep.' His lips moved to form the answer, but the cigar remained clamped between his teeth.

'I've heard the rats are always the first to leave a sinking ship.' There were many things about Ryan Colby that Gabe had grown

438

to dislike intensely, not the least of which was that Colby had known all along that he had married a breed.

Ryan chuckled, then removed the cigar from his mouth, his attention not straying from the workmen carefully lowering the sign. 'I'd rather be the rat than the noble fool who goes down with it.'

'What makes you think it's going down?' Gabe retorted.

'Take a look around and what do you see? A lot of buildings boarded up or standing empty. Surely you've noticed them.'

'The Army's still here in force. The soldiers are your main customers anyway, so why should it bother you if a few decent people leave town?'

'A few? It's been considerably more than that.' The military payroll from that garrison wasn't enough to sustain the town's economy. 'Three years ago this town had thirty-four prostitutes. I'd bet there's fewer than eighteen now. The town's dying.'

'Maybe we're just getting rid of the trash.'

Ryan's mouth was quirked at an angle as he thoughtfully studied Gabe. 'When was the last meeting of your town council – your attempt at a provisional government?' Gabe pressed his lips tightly together. 'Since you seem to have forgotten, there hasn't been a meeting since February. What's the use of one? Nobody's paying their taxes. The town's broke. The school is closed. It's all over here but the shouting – and even that's fading to a whimper.'

One end of the sign thudded onto the ground as one of the workmen let out too much rope. Made top-heavy by the large carved replica of a twenty-dollar gold piece, the sign tilted precariously forward, straining the ropes that held the opposite end upright.

'Careful with that sign!' Ryan called sharply.

'What do you plan on doing with it?' Gabe glanced at the empty horse-drawn dray that waited in the street.

'I'm going to take it with me and put it up over my new saloon in Wrangell.'

'Wrangell?' He was taken aback by the answer. He'd been expecting to hear Ryan say that he was heading for San Francisco. 'That's just another military post. It's no different than Sitka.'

'It's no different in the summer, but come autumn it fills up with miners from Dease Lake and the Cassiars in British Columbia. They can't work their claims in the winter, so most of them spend it – and their gold – in Wrangell. The town is about to boom.'

'You always go where there's easy money, don't you, Colby? You're only interested in how much money you can make from a town, not what you can build.' It was greed pure and simple, and Gabe despised him for it.

'I came to make money.' Ryan's smile was cold and thin-lipped. 'That's what I'm doing. What about you, Gabe? You're a lawyer in a land with no law. Why in hell do you stay?'

Gabe stared at Ryan's tailored waistcoat, the fine linen of his shirt, and the expensive cigar in his hand. His own clothes were shabby and threadbare. Money jingled in Ryan's pockets, but Gabe didn't have two coins to rub together. He didn't have enough money to pay the fare on a ship back to the States. He was barely able to scrape up enough to keep body and soul together. Hell, he didn't even have the price of a much-needed drink. But he was too proud to admit that, like the town, he was busted flat.

'It won't always be like this. Sooner or later, Congress is going to have to give Alaska the right of self-government.' He went back to his old standby answer, but he'd said it so many times now that it rang hollow in his ears.

'It'll be a hell of a long time before that happens.' Ryan watched the workmen loading the sign onto the dray. 'Now that the Alaska Commercial Company has been given a monopoly on harvesting the fur seals in the Pribilofs, they have formed a powerful lobby in Washington. They aren't about to allow the formation of any local government that might tax the money they're making out of the furs. They're going to do their damnedest to kill any measure that would create one.'

Gabe knew it was true. Alaska sat off by itself. Few Americans knew what this vast territory was like. And the big money men were protecting their profits by perpetuating the image of Alaska as one giant iceberg incapable of supporting a permanent white population. People listened to such men. He cursed their stupidity and their deafness that didn't hear the small voices like his own crying out with the truth.

Things never change, he realized bitterly. Once he'd thought that in Alaska things could be different. It was new and fresh, the perfect place to build a better democracy. But he had never considered that those on the outside weren't going to let it happen. They were the ones with the money, the power, and the influence.

Once the heavy sign was tied onto the wagon bed, the driver clucked to the team of horses and flicked the whip across their backs. As the wagon drew level with the two men, Ryan flagged it down.

'I'll ride with you to the wharf.' He walked over to the wagon and climbed onto the seat next to the teamster, then glanced back at Gabe. 'You should have taken my advice, Blackwood. I tried to tell you to make your money while you had the chance. Now you'll be lucky if you can squeeze a dollar out of this town – unless you strike gold,' he added and chuckled as he stuck the narrow cigar in his mouth once more and signaled to the driver to move on.

'Giddyup there! Hah!' The teamster slapped the reins on the horses' rumps.

The wagon rumbled on past Gabe, the trace chains rattling, the shod hooves clopping, and Ryan's parting shot echoing in his ears. It brought home to him all that he'd lost. Even if he was able to practice his profession here in Alaska someday, he'd never be able to realize any of his dreams. Nadia with her Indian blood had ruined that for him. No one would ever appoint a squawman as territorial governor. She had destroyed him with her lies and trickery. He'd lost at every turn.

He'd had plenty of chances to make money – he could have been as rich as Colby, richer maybe – but he hadn't taken advantage of them. Now he was broke, trapped in this stinking town and shackled to a woman he couldn't stand. He'd been a fool.

One way or another he vowed he was going to get the money to get out of here and away from her.

39 *Sitka*
May 1877

From the dirty-paned parlor window, Nadia watched as her husband approached. Nervously she moistened her dry lips, but on this day she was more excited than fearful about his return. He weaved slightly coming up the path, a sure sign that he'd been drinking; but considering how hard he'd worked these past years, turning his hand to any enterprise that would keep food on their table, she understood his bouts with the bottle.

Men drank. They always had; they always would. If Gabe drank more now than he had during the early years of their marriage, Nadia believed it was because he had more cause. There had been too many disappointments over the years. Nothing had ever worked out for him.

He'd tried prospecting for gold, but all he'd ever found was fool's gold. He'd convinced several miners to grant him an interest in their claims in return for his services to protect their titles once the American government made provisions for the legal filing of claims. Even though that wasn't forthcoming, he'd tried to put together a group of investors to develop the claims – without success. And when he'd attempted to sell his interests, no one wanted to buy.

After that, he'd been discouraged, almost desperate. One winter he'd tried gambling, spending the bulk of his nights at the gaming tables of one of the saloons on Lincoln Street. For a while, he'd won, but his luck had quickly changed. Before the winter was out, he'd sold every one of their possessions of any value, from the silver tray her grandfather had given them as a wedding present to her small collection of gilded Easter eggs – all in an effort to win back what he'd lost. But he'd lost that, too.

Last year he'd tried trading goods to the Kolosh for furs, convinced that with his superior intellect he'd be able to make a sizable profit by trading cheap goods for valuable furs, but he'd been the one who'd gotten rooked in the bargaining by trading large quantities of goods for pelts he believed to be otter and fox only to learn they were skins of less valuable animals dyed and stretched to look like the purported peltry to an inexperienced eye.

Invariably he'd taken out his frustrations on Nadia, blaming her for his many failures and seeking solace from a cheap bottle of rum or a cheaper jug of hoochinoo. So many of his efforts had been in vain that it was no wonder he'd become so angry and bitter. Nadia understood why he lashed out at her, and considered the bruises she received from his abuse as a way of sharing his suffering.

The situation wasn't improved by Sitka's steady decline. People left by the scores, turning the once-thriving city almost into a ghost town. Less than two dozen families remained in the community where once hundreds had lived. The Army was still there, but there was a rumor that soon they'd be pulling out, too. No one was quite sure what change that might portend. Strangely, Gabe didn't seem to care one way or the other.

Nadia's nerves felt all on edge as the door opened and Gabe stepped over the threshold. She pressed a reassuring hand to her stomach, feeling the small, barely perceptible mound, convinced that her news would cheer him. She couldn't imagine any man not being overjoyed to learn he was about to be a father for the first time. She had wanted a baby for so long, certain that by giving Gabe a child she could heal the rift between them. Now she could barely contain her happiness.

Gabe glared at the faint smile on her lips. 'What the hell is so amusing?'

'Nothing.' Quickly she lowered her glance and took the hat and coat he shoved at her and hurriedly hung them up.

'Where's that jug of hooch I had last night?'

'In the kitchen. You told me to leave it there.'

'I know what I told you.' He followed her into the kitchen and spied the jug sitting on the table where he'd left it. Before he could ask for one, she set a clean glass tumbler on the table.

'Gabe, I have something to tell you,' she said as he reached for the jug. 'I have some good news to tell you.'

Gabe snorted his disbelief. She'd been nothing but poison to him from the beginning. Everything had started going bad the

443

day he'd married her. He uncorked the jug and poured the potent brew into the glass.

'We're going to have a baby, Gabe.'

The announcement seemed to reverberate through his head like a gunshot. He stared at her, dumbstruck. She was going to have a child. His child. He was revolted by the thought of an offspring of his having Indian blood in its veins, and the prospect of having an Indian son who could rise up and destroy him someday.

'I know you're surprised. So was I.' She smiled tremulously. 'After all this time, it's finally happened. I only hope you're as happy as I am.

'Get rid of it.' He bolted down the slug of alcohol.

'What?'

'You heard me. Get rid of it.' Gabe picked up the jug and poured another shot of hooch into the tumbler. 'Get one of the medicine men in the Ranche to give you a potion to drink. I don't care what you do. Just get rid of it. I want no child that's got Indian in him.'

'No!' Protectively she covered her stomach with her hands, a look of stunned horror on her face.

'Damn it! You do as I say!' Infuriated by her refusal, he hurled the glass at her. She dodged it and it hit the wall behind her head, shattering and spraying glass and liquor in all directions.

'No. No, I won't!'

'Then, by God, I'll beat it out of you!' In one long stride, he was within striking distance. She tried to elude the backhanded swing of his hand, but he managed to land a glancing blow to the side of her head. He'd put his strength into the swing, and the force of it sent her staggering against the cookstove.

He grabbed her by the arm so he could turn her around and hit her again. But as he pulled her around, he had a brief glimpse of a large iron skillet in her hands. The next thing he knew, pain exploded alongside his face and head. He reeled from it, his head ringing, white spots flashing before his eyes. As he tried to shake off the dazing effects of the blow, he saw Nadia bolt out the back door and staggered after her.

With a rhythmic swing of her hoe, Eva weeded between the rows in the vegetable garden behind her grandfather's house. Her face was hidden by the long straw brim of her poke bonnet, shaped like a coal scuttle. Few thoughts crossed her mind when she worked with the soil. In the garden, she forgot all her cares and worries, and all the deep-seated rancor she'd accumulated in her relatively young life.

Somewhere down the street, a door slammed. She heard it slam a second time. The noise was almost immediately followed by a cry of alarm – a woman's cry. Eva straightened, frowning as she turned to look in the direction of her sister's house. It had sounded like Nadia's voice. She wondered whether Gabe was beating her again, and unconsciously tightened her grip on the hoe's wooden handle.

At first she didn't see the woman running across the backyards of the abandoned houses between them, her view obstructed by the tunnel-like sides of her bonnet's long brim. Then Nadia ran into her vision and cast a frightened look over her shoulder. Eva turned her head slightly and saw that Gabe Blackwood was chasing her sister. She had never known Nadia to run from him before. But she'd never been pregnant before, either, Eva remembered, and dropped the hoe to run to her sister's aid.

'Help me, Eva,' she sobbed. 'He wants to kill my baby.'

Aware how rapidly Gabe was closing, Eva grabbed her sister's arm and pushed her toward the back door. 'Quick. Into the house!'

She followed on Nadia's heels. As she dashed through the opening, she heard the thud of his footstep on the first step. Nadia didn't stop running once she was inside but continued on through the kitchen, heading toward the front of the house. Eva turned to shut and bar the door, but she didn't get it closed in time. Gabe pushed on it from the outside while Eva strained, throwing all her weight against the door to keep him from opening it.

'Grandpa!' she yelled.

The sudden hard shove from Gabe was more than Eva could withstand. The door burst open, its force almost catapulting her backwards. Behind her Nadia screamed as Gabe came charging into the house, one side of his face all red and swollen. Eva quickly placed herself in his path.

'No! Leave her alone!' When she tried to stop him, he shrugged her aside as easily as he'd shoved open the door.

He charged by her into the front parlor after Nadia. Eva ran after him, reaching the doorway as he caught up with her sister.

Nadia cried out in fear and struggled to break free of his hold. It was all happening too fast for her aged grandfather, who was only now pushing out of his chair.

'Here! What is this?' he demanded.

But Gabe took no notice of him as he slapped Nadia across the face. 'You'll never run from me again,' he growled and lifted his hand to hit her again.

Eva saw the blood that trickled from a corner of her sister's mouth. 'No!' she cried, but her feet seemed to be rooted to the floor.

Her grandfather grabbed Gabe from behind. With his height and weight, he couldn't be so easily shrugged aside. Gabe was forced to release Nadia and turn to meet this new opposition. 'Stay out of this, old man,' he warned as Wolf grappled with him, straining valiantly to match Gabe's strength.

'You will not strike my granddaughter when she is in this house!' he shouted, his face reddening with the effort of the struggle.

'I'll do as I damn please.'

Suddenly her grandfather's mouth opened in a gasp of pain and shock. He clutched at his chest and turned his blue gaze on Eva in a wide-eyed plea. She didn't know what was wrong. She hadn't seen Gabe strike him. His legs seemed to give out as he slowly crumpled to the floor. Gabe stood over him, his expression registering surprise as well.

'Grandpa!' Seeing him lying motionless on the floor seemed to break the paralysis that had gripped her. Eva ran to where he lay and knelt beside him, impatiently loosening the bonnet ribbon and pushing it off her head. 'Grandpa, what's wrong?' She touched him, but he didn't move.

Nadia crept up beside her, and Eva was vaguely conscious that his collapse seemed to have checked Gabe's attack. 'What happened?'

'I don't know.' Eva gazed bewilderedly at her grandfather, unable to find a mark on him, although his lips were turning a funny shade of blue.

Nadia held her hand close to his nose and mouth. 'He isn't breathing.' Hurriedly she searched for the pulse in his neck, then turned her glance at Eva. 'I think he's dead.'

'No.' Eva pressed an ear to his chest and listened intently for the faintest sound, but Gabe chose that moment to walk away from the body, and the sound of his footsteps drowned out any other. Then he halted, and there was stillness once again in the room. But Eva could hear no heartbeat. Pain choked her throat. She straightened and gazed at her sister, tears welling in her eyes.

'Is he dead?' Gabe asked.

Stung by the indifference in his voice, Eva glared at him though her tears. 'You killed him.' Her hoarse accusation seemed to ring through the room.

The one man who had been good to her, who had never cared how homely she was but loved her anyway – the one man who had sacrificed so much for her – was dead. There would be no others like him. A hatred for all men was now firmly embedded in her soul.

With a shrug of his shoulders, Gabe Blackwood dismissed the possibility that he was to blame for Wolf Tarakanov's death. 'I didn't lay a hand on him. He was an old man. His heart probably just gave out on him.' In his hand, he held a silver egg that he'd taken from the curio cabinet on the wall. Its glass door stood ajar. He glanced at the other gilded eggs displayed in the case. 'Did these belong to your grandfather?'

'Yes. He made them.' Eva rose angrily to her feet, resenting that he would handle any of her grandfather's possessions.

'That's right. He was a silversmith,' Gabe mused and glanced thoughtfully around the room, taking in the silver ikon of the Holy Virgin, the silver candleholders on the mantel, and the shiny silver samovar on a side table – a few of the countless items her grandfather's hands had wrought for his own personal enjoyment and never offered for sale in his shop, items that Eva had faithfully kept polished and gleaming as a way of showing her love and devotion to her grandfather. 'My God, there's a fortune in this room.'

Her fear of him was forgotten as she stalked across the room and grabbed at the egg in his hand, but he pulled his hand back before she could snatch it from him. 'It doesn't belong to you. Put it back,' she ordered.

'Don't be a fool. We have to get everything of value out of this house before anyone finds out your grandfather's dead,' he snapped impatiently. 'You know what happened when your father died. His creditors took everything and left you with nothing. Do you want that to happen again?'

Hesitating, Eva turned to look at all the things that had meant so much to him. 'Grandpa would have wanted me and Nadia to have them,' she murmured.

'If you leave them here, it isn't going to matter what he might have wanted, because there isn't any law to see that you get them,' he reminded her. 'Unless we get them out of here now, somebody else is going to take them.' He began grabbing the gilded eggs off the shelves of the curio cabinet and stuffing them into his pockets. 'Don't just stand there,' he snapped. 'Get busy.'

'But . . . what about Grandpa?' She couldn't argue with his logic. Yet what he suggested seemed so callous and greedy, especially when her grandfather's body was still warm. She stared at his lifeless form, aware that her sister knelt beside it, her face shiny with tears.

'He's dead,' Gabe replied coldly. 'There's nothing more you can do for him now.' He turned from the glass-encased curio cabinet, its shelves now bare and his pockets bulging with the eggs. His glance settled on the framed ikon. 'We'll need something to put all this in. Get some burlap bags or the casings off the pillows. We can't waste time. Get busy, both of you!'

For Eva, every item had some special significance or precious memory attached to it. She couldn't bear the thought of any of them falling into the hands of a stranger whose only interest would be in their monetary value. That possibility, more than Gabe's urgings, pushed her across the room to her sister.

'Come, Nadia.' She avoided looking at her grandfather as she took Nadia by the shoulders and encouraged her to stand up. 'You've got to help us gather everything up.'

Reluctantly, Nadia let herself be led into the kitchen. They emptied the sacks of flour and potatoes and took them to Gabe in the parlor. Then the three of them, working separately, went through every room in the house collecting everything of value, and a few things of sentimental importance, into the cloth sacks. When they had finished, they combined the items and filled two sacks.

Gabe hefted one onto his shoulder and lifted the other in his hand. 'Both of you stay here. I'll go out the back way and stash all this at my house. Then I'll go into town and get Simms the undertaker so he can get your grandfather laid out.' He took a step toward the kitchen.

'Stop at St. Michael's and ask the Father to come,' Eva said.

'I will.' He paused at the kitchen doorway. 'I'm not sure how long this will take me. Don't worry if I'm not back right away.'

The sound of the door closing behind him seemed to signal the closure of another chapter in Eva's life. She turned to her grandfather and encountered the sightless stare of his blue eyes. There had been so much commotion, everything happening so fast, that she hadn't had time to think, only to react. Now the full impact of his death and all it portended for her future was finally sinking in.

She sank to her knees beside his body and wept softly as she gently closed his eyes. No more would she spend her evenings in this parlor listening to his stories of the old days. No more would she hear him tell about Zachar, Raven, and old Tasha – about Larissa and Caleb Stone, or about Baranov and his half-breed daughter Anna, and High Chamberlain Rezanov. No more would she live in this house that had been filled with so much warmth and love, and been more of a home to her than that of her parents.

'Do you think we should put his good suit on him?' Nadia wondered.

Eva agreed, deciding it was better to do something than to dwell on what was going to happen to her. Together they dressed him in the suit he always wore to church and laid him out straight on the floor, folding his hands across his chest. After that there was nothing left to do but sit and wait for Gabe to return.

The time passed slowly, and Eva spent most of it in silence, unwilling to share her deep sense of grief. She had lost so much more than her sister. As she idly stared at Nadia, she noticed the way her sister held her stomach, as if cradling and consoling the infant inside. The sight started Eva thinking about the sequence of events and Gabe's threat of violence that had precipitated her grandfather's demise. Gabe was to blame for her grandfather's death as surely as if he'd killed him with his bare hands. She felt the hatred building inside her again.

'Where is he?' She pushed impatiently out of the chair, suddenly conscious of the darkness that invaded the house as dusk robbed the sky of its light. 'He should be back by now.'

'Maybe he hasn't been able to find the undertaker.'

'Simms would be home for supper by now.' Eva lit the oil lamp and put the glass chimney back in place, then adjusted the wick so the smoke from the flame wouldn't soot the glass.

Something about Gabe's absence didn't feel right to her. Considering all the grief he'd caused, she wondered why she had let

449

him be the one to notify Simms, the local blacksmith and part-time mortician. Gabe hadn't liked her grandfather – or her, either, for that matter. He despised anything that was Indian in origin. So why had he been so anxious to help? she wondered.

'What if he's still at your house?' she said to Nadia. 'What if he's never left there?'

'He wouldn't do that – unless . . .' Her sister paused, frowning thoughtfully.

'Unless what?'

'Unless he was drinking.' She chewed on the inside of her lower lip. 'There was still some liquor left in the jug on the kitchen table.'

'Come. We're going over there.' Eva took her shawl off the wall hook and draped it around her shoulders.

But the house was dark and silent when they walked in the back door. As Eva waited for Nadia to light the kitchen lamp, she stepped on a piece of glass. It crunched beneath the hard sole of her shoe. As the wick flame flared brightly, Eva saw more pieces of broken glass on the floor.

'Gabe threw it at me,' Nadia explained self-consciously. 'He'd been drinking. I shouldn't have told him about the baby when he was drinking.'

Her sister always seemed to find some excuse for his violent behavior, but Eva didn't choose to comment on it this time. She merely glanced at the iron skillet on the floor, then at the empty table.

'The jug's gone.'

'Maybe he fell asleep in the other room.' Nadia picked up the lamp and held it in front of her as she headed toward the front room. Eva followed.

But Gabe wasn't in the front room, nor was there any indication that he'd been there. Nadia led the way to the bedroom, but halted abruptly in the doorway gasping. Eva crowded close to her so she could see into the room.

It looked as if it had been ransacked. The lid to an old trunk stood open, its contents strewn over the sides and onto the bed. All the dresser drawers were open, and it looked as though someone had pawed through them.

'Who could have done this?' Nadia murmured.

Eva spied the jug sitting atop the dresser and pointed to it. 'Gabe was in here. You'd better check and see what's missing.'

450

Nadia entered the room, skirting the piles of clothing and linen lumped together on the floor, and set the lamp on the dresser, then began sorting through the scattered belongings. Abruptly she stopped, as if suddenly realizing something.

'What is it?' Eva watched her closely.

But Nadia looked under the bed first. A lost and bewildered look came over her face as she straightened. 'Gabe's clothes are gone . . . and the carpetbag is missing.'

'He's left,' Eva said. 'Grandpa's things – where would he have hidden them? Quick. We must look.'

But even before the search of the house was over, she knew they wouldn't find them. He'd stolen them. Everything was gone. She should have known she couldn't trust him. Eva saw that now, now that it was too late.

Still, there was a chance he hadn't left town yet, a chance she might be able to get her grandfather's things back. Either way, it was certain he hadn't notified the undertaker or told Father Stephan. Without stopping to tell Nadia where she was going, Eva left the house and hurried into town.

But luck was against her. The proprietor of the trading post informed her that Gabe had left on the mail boat, and remarked how anxious he'd been for the boat to leave. 'Didn't say when he'd be back either,' the man recalled.

Eva knew the answer to that – never. But she wasn't about to confide that, not to a man. If he knew that she and Nadia had been abandoned, he'd try to take advantage of them in some way.

Before she went back, she fetched the priest and stopped by Mr. Simms's house to tell him about her grandfather and make arrangements for the funeral.

They buried him a day later in the cemetery alongside his wife's grave. That night, Eva gathered her few meager possessions from her grandfather's house and moved in with Nadia.

In June, the Army pulled out of Sitka and Alaska, the troops summoned back to the States to assist in quelling an uprising of a band of Nez Perce Indians led by Chief Joseph. Eva was glad to see the last of the blue-coated soldiers. No more would she have to endure their foul language and insulting jibes.

The military rule was over, and the customs collector was left in charge. To protect his 586,400-square-mile area, he had two cases of rifles and two cases of ammunition that had been shipped to him by mistake. The end of the military presence in Sitka caused many of the townspeople to fear an attack from the Indians and half-breeds who lived in the Ranche, and who now drank and caroused unchecked. Eva loaded her grandfather's musket and propped it against the wall beside her bed. She didn't need anybody to protect her or Nadia. She'd do it herself.

As summer left and autumn came, Nadia grew large with child. More and more of the responsibility fell to Eva. With the money she earned cleaning the church once a week, she managed to keep food on the table, but she had to chop and haul firewood from the forest. The hardships were many, but Eva never complained.

Shortly after the start of the new year, Nadia went into labor. The water boiled in the kettle on the stove, and a clean knife lay by the bedstead to cut the umbilical cord. Eva sat with her sister, wiped the sweat from her face with a damp cloth between contractions, gave Nadia her hand to squeeze when they came, and closed her eyes at the agonizing cries.

After two days of labor, Nadia was in a state of exhaustion, yet the baby still hadn't come. No one had ever told Eva that a woman could suffer so giving birth to a child. Her only previous experience of the birthing process had come from watching little piglets being born and baby chicks pecking free of their shells. She decided that surely Nadia hadn't known it would be like this. She could not imagine any woman knowingly going through this torture.

As the hours wore on, she began to fear that something was wrong. Her sister could not endure much more of this. She hated to leave her, but she had to find someone to help or her sister would surely die. There was no doctor in Sitka. But Eva remembered that Mrs. Karotski had given birth to seven children and had been present during the confinement of several pregnant women in town.

'Sounds like that baby's coming backwards,' the woman declared when Eva told her of Nadia's difficulties. She wasted little time gathering her coat and hat, then accompanied Eva back to the house.

With Mrs. Karotski's assistance, Eva had her first lesson in a breech birth. In a few short hours, she was holding a red and squalling baby girl in her arms. The baby's wet hair was so flaxen that she appeared to be bald. She was quite the ugliest thing Eva had ever seen – and she loved her. With great reluctance, she gave her to Nadia so the baby could nurse.

As she watched the infant girl suckling at her mother's breast, she was awed by the miracle of birth. Then Eva noticed how completely exhausted her sister looked, the ghostly pallor of her face, and the straggled, dull locks of her rumpled golden brown hair. The wan smile Nadia so briefly directed at her newborn daughter seemed to take a great deal of effort. Eva inwardly cringed from the memory of all the pain her sister had endured during those endless hours of labor. She could still hear the echoes of her horrible screams.

'We'll leave them to rest now.' The stoutly built Mrs. Karotski touched her arm to draw her away from the bed where the mother and baby lay. 'Bring that pan with you.'

The midwife indicated the pan of blood-soaked rags that contained the afterbirth. Her own hands carried a basin of pink-tinted water that had been used to wash baby and mother. A toweling cloth was draped over her shoulder to hang down the front of her heavy bosom. Eva hesitated, then picked up the pan, making an immediate and unconscious attempt to tighten her nostrils and breathe shallowly so she wouldn't inhale the peculiar smell of the expelled placenta. She tried to hide the revulsion she felt as she followed Mrs. Karotski out of the room.

'That's a fine baby girl your sister has.'

'Will Nadia be all right?'

'I'm sure she will. She did have a very difficult time of it, but she'll get her strength back.'

'I didn't know women went through so much pain having babies,' Eva murmured.

'It always requires some suffering to bring a new life into the world. It's a good thing your sister's husband wasn't here. He couldn't have stood it. A man can't take much pain.' Her mouth quirked in a wry smile. 'If it was up to men to have the babies, none would be born. As it is, they have the pleasure of making them and none of the pain of birthing them.'

Suffering. That's all a man brought a woman, Eva thought and loathed them all.

On a clear, blustery Sunday in February, Eva and Nadia emerged from St. Michael's Cathedral. Muffled wails came from the swaddled infant in Nadia's arms. Nadia paused at the top of the steps and lifted a corner of the blanket to gaze at her newly christened daughter, Marisha Gavrilyevna Blackwood. Eva had objected to the use of the Russianized version of Gabe's name, but Nadia had insisted that tradition be followed and their daughter's middle name should be this.

Everyone in the small community of Sitka was aware of Gabe's continued absence. Too few people lived there any more for it to be a secret. Through the postmaster, they were also aware that there had been no word from him. There was considerable speculation that he had died. Eva encouraged such rumors.

'I wish Gabe were here so he could see our beautiful daughter,' Nadia murmured.

'Be glad you're rid of him,' Eva snapped, irritated that her sister was so stupid as to want him back after all he'd done.

Surveying the town from the steps of the church, she saw the decay and ruin of abandoned buildings, the emptiness and neglect of a deserted town. She was old enough to remember how it had been. Men had built it, and men had destroyed it. Ultimately, in their greed, they always destroyed. As she started down the steps, Eva resolved that her young niece would know the truth about them.

The old beacon atop the castle on the bluff had once guided many a ship to the port formerly known as New Archangel. Now it turned crazily in the wind.

Part Three

Alaska Mainland

40 Sitka
Summer 1897

Since the steamer was expected to be at dockside for several hours offloading cargo and taking on more fuel, Justin Sinclair took advantage of the opportunity to look around the old Russian town and stretch his legs a bit. Lord knew, he'd had few chances to see much of anything in his twenty-two years. What sights could a man see from the deck of a fishing boat?' He swore that when he struck it rich in the goldfields of the Klondike, he was going to eat nothing but meat. He never wanted to smell another fish again. He hated fish and he hated the sea. His father was welcome to both, but he wasn't about to spend the rest of his life stinking like a fish.

Other passengers aboard the steamer had disembarked ahead of him, obviously sharing his intentions. A group of Indians, mostly squaws, crowded around them trying to peddle their goods that ranged from miniature totems carved from wood to silver bracelets and Indian blankets. Justin Sinclair shouldered his way through the bodies firmly shaking his head in refusal at every object thrust in front of him.

Once free of the throng, he paused to look around and get his bearings. A perfectly cone-shaped mountain rose in the distance. Snow still frosted the cratered peak of the extinct volcano, making it stand out that much more sharply against the cloud-studded blue sky.

'Could you tell me where that ship is going?' The question was asked by a woman, her voice oddly accented.

Justin vaguely recalled that there had been a woman standing on the fringe of the crowd at the wharf. He'd noticed her mainly because she had looked so dowdy, wearing a drab dress, a dark wool shawl around her shoulders, and a dark kerchief tied under her throat, completely covering her hair. But this woman's voice sounded young. Justin turned curiously, surprised to find the voice belonged to the woman he'd noticed earlier.

'It's headed for Mooresville.'

'Have you heard they've discovered gold on the other side of White Pass in the Klondike region of Canada?' Again the voice betrayed a youthful vigor.

'Yes, I know.' Justin took another look at her, but it was difficult to see her face.

The scarf that covered her hair was pulled forward, obscuring her eyes as she gazed at the vessel tied up to the dock. Then she turned her head to look at him. He was startled by her face. Her complexion was smooth and shone with the luster of an abalone shell, and her eyes were like large nuggets of shiny black coal.

'Is that where you're bound?' she asked.

'Yes.' He would have stared at her much longer, but she turned away again to gaze at the steamer.

'I wish I were going.' She spoke so softly that Justin knew she hadn't intended him to hear, so he pretended he hadn't.

'Do you live here?'

'Yes.' She pulled the shawl more tightly around her shoulders and seemed to withdraw into herself.

'I have a few hours to pass before the ship sails. I thought I'd look around the town. One of the hands on the ship told me this used to be the old Russian capital of Alaska before we bought it. Maybe you could show me around.'

'There isn't much to see.' The shrug of her shoulders seemed to express her dislike. 'Some broken-down old buildings, a church, and a cemetery. There is little else.'

As he glanced toward town, he noticed the green-painted spire of a church, topped by a peculiarly shaped cross. 'I've never seen a cross like that. What kind of church is it?'

'That is St. Michael's Cathedral. It is of the Russian Orthodox faith.'

'Why do they have that slanted bar at the bottom?'

'When the Christ Jesus was put upon the cross, His feet rested on the lower bar. At the moment of His death, His weight tipped it to one side.' Her dark eyes gleamed like obsidian. 'You should go inside the church. All the gold ornamentation and silver ikons are very beautiful.'

Justin noticed the suggestion was not offered with any religious fervor. 'Why don't you show me the inside of the church?'

Again she drew back. 'No, I couldn't go there with you.' She shook her head.

458

'Why?' His curiosity was aroused by this unusual young woman. She had such an extraordinary face that he wondered why she dressed in such homely attire.

'My aunt might see me with you.'

'Naturally she wouldn't approve of you being seen with a strange man,' he guessed. 'We can correct that situation. My name is Justin Sinclair, formerly from Seattle. And you are . . .?'

An impish light danced in her eyes. 'Marisha Gavrilyevna Blackwood. And I'm afraid you don't understand.'

'Marisha Gavrilyevna. Are you Russian?' He wondered if that was the source of the faint accent that gave her speech its distinctive sound.

'Russian, American, Indian – I'm a little bit of everything.'

He was a little surprised by the open admission of her mixed ancestry, although it certainly made the situation easier for him. At least now he knew what kind of woman he was dealing with.

'It was a pleasure meeting you, Mr. Sinclair, but I must go.'

As she took a step away from him, he laid a restraining hand on her arm, feeling the coarse texture of the wool shawl. 'Why? We aren't strangers any more. I'm Justin and you're Marisha. How could your aunt possibly object now?'

'My aunt objects to all men. She says they can't be trusted, that they only bring pain. My father ran off before I was born and took everything my family had. She insists that all men are tarred with the same brush.'

'What happened to your mother?'

'She died when I was eleven.'

'How old are you?' It was impossible to judge her age – all he could see was her face.

'Nineteen. Already I'm an old maid – like she is.' Bitterness flashed across her face, hardening the set of her lips. 'There aren't many bachelors in this town, and she's managed to chase away the few that have come calling.'

'Where is she now?'

'At St. Michael's, cleaning. I'm supposed to be working in the garden, but I slipped away to come down here.' The corners of her lips twitched with a smile as she made the admission with no hint of remorse. 'She'll be furious when she finds out.'

'Is this where you usually come?'

'No. I just wanted to see the ship and find out where it was going.' She gazed longingly at the steamer.

459

'Since I'm not doing anything and your aunt is already going to be mad at you, why don't you take me to the place where you usually go when you sneak off from your aunt?'

She studied him for a minute, as if assessing the degree of risk. Justin didn't doubt for an instant that this aunt of hers had practically kept Marisha under lock and key, but she obviously had a rebellious spirit.

'This way,' she said and started off.

Walking swiftly, she skirted the edges of town and led him along the southern shoreline facing the sound and its scattering of small islands. Most of the time she kept her head down, avoiding eye contact with anyone who might be watching. Only twice did he notice her glance around to see if they were being observed. They were on the outskirts of town and nearing the forest when she finally slowed down.

'They call this path the Governor's Walk,' she told him. 'Supposedly Baranov used to walk along here.'

'Who's Baranov?'

'Aleksandr Andreevich Baranov was the first Russian governor of Alaska. Actually he built Sitka. There used to be a big old mansion on that knoll we passed. It was known as Baranov's Castle, but it burned down three years ago. Do you see that big rock by the shore just ahead of us? During his last days here, they say he used to spend hours sitting there gazing out at the Pacific. Guess what it's called?'

'Baranov's Rock.'

'Yes.' She laughed and ran ahead to the boulder.

There, she stopped to lean against it and gaze out to sea. Stare as he might, the heavy shawl and the voluminous material of her dress made it impossible for Justin to tell if she was plump or if her clothes merely made her look that way.

As he approached the rock, the beach gravel crunched underfoot. Although she didn't turn, a slight movement of her head indicated her awareness of his presence while she continued to look at the wide stretch of island-studded water.

'In the spring, when the herring come into the bays and inlets to spawn, the Tlingit Indians wait until low tide, then spread hemlock boughs on the exposed beaches, and fasten them down. The herring deposit their eggs on the branches. You should see it,' she murmured. 'The boughs look like they're covered with thousands of pearls.'

460

'It must be something.' But fish was about the last subject that interested him.

'It is.' She sighed and pushed away from the rock. As she turned toward him, she reached up and began tugging at the scarf knot at her throat. 'I hate this babushka. It makes me feel like a babushka.'

'What's a babushka?'

'It's a scarf old women in Russia wear. So the word means both "scarf" and "old woman." It's also a word for "grandmother" – which I'm never likely to be.' The knot initially defied her attempts to loosen it. Using both hands, she finally managed to free the ends and pull the scarf off her head.

'Glory be.' Justin stared in surprise.

Her hair was a bright yellow gold that glistened in the sunlight; it was neither brassy nor tarnished with dark streaks, but pure and rich. The contrast between her dark eyes and brows and her golden blond hair was striking and dramatic. The feeling of shock was slow to leave him, even though he noticed how amused she seemed to be at his reaction.

'You're beautiful,' he murmured, unable to get over it.

She smiled wryly and moved away from the rock, absently swinging the scarf in her hand. 'Beauty is a curse. That's what Aunt Eva says.' Despite her attempt at lightness, Justin detected an underlying bitterness in her tone. 'A girl shouldn't be concerned about her looks. She should dress plainly. Wanting to look pretty is vain, and vanity is a sin. These are the only kind of clothes I have, but someday I'm going to have beautiful gowns to wear. Someday,' she repeated with a determined lift of her chin.

'I don't care what your aunt says, she's wrong. Nobody with hair like yours should cover it up. My mother always said a woman's hair is her crowning glory.'

Marisha touched her hair, smoothing the strands back to the golden knot at the nape of her neck. 'Her crowning glory. I like that,' she murmured thoughtfully, then seemed to dismiss it from her mind. 'Let's walk this way. There's something I want to show you.' She followed a faint trail that paralleled the shoreline for a way, then led into the woods. Justin was too intrigued by her to care where they were going.

Huge trees towered all around them, their overlapping branches shutting out any direct light from the sun. A high humidity made the air seem heavy as they walked along the path through the forest, their footsteps making hardly any sound, cushioned by the soft, composted soil.

'Have you ever seen gold? Real gold, I mean.' She didn't wait for his answer. 'I saw some once. Blue Pants Kelly – he's an old prospector from around here. He used to be in the Army, but even after he got out he still wore the blue pants from his uniform. That's where he got his name. One time he showed me a piece of ore that had thin slivers of gold running through it.'

'They've found gold around here?'

'Some.' She nodded. 'There are a couple of miners over on Silver Bay and a stamp mill, but I guess they haven't recovered any large quantities of gold.' She walked a few steps farther in silence. 'I'd like to find some gold.'

'It's up there in the Klondike. Only there it's placer gold – loose gold. All a man has to do is pan it out of the streams. You don't have to dig tunnels or have a lot of machinery to crush it free from the rocks. You just put some gravel in your pan and pick out the nuggets. It's so easy a child could do it.'

'Or a woman,' she murmured as if to herself.

Through a break in the trees just ahead of them, Justin saw the shimmer of sunlight reflected off the surface of water. The towering spruce thinned out where the ground sloped down to the water's edge, the finger of land claimed by a tangle of tall brush and bushes. The graveled shoreline was strewn with huge drift logs, some almost as tall as a man. As they rounded the point of land, Justin saw the mouth of a river.

'That's the Indian River,' Marisha Blackwood stated. 'The Russian name was Kolosh Ryeka. See that bluff of land back in the forest?' She pointed it out to him. 'The Kolosh, or Tlingit Indians as everyone calls them today, had a large fort there. This is the site of the big battle between the Russians and the Tlingits. The Russian ships anchored in this bay to bombard the fort with their cannon. My great-great-grandfather, Zachar, was married to a Tlingit woman. Her people had attacked the first fort the Russians built on Baranof Island and killed all but a few men who managed to escape. My great-great-grandfather was one of them. He was on one of the ships in the bay when the Russians came to retake the island. He didn't know it, but my great-great-grandmother – his wife – was in the fort with their young son. They escaped into the forest before the Russians overran the fort. It was several years before she and my great-great-grandfather were reunited.' She turned, looking into his face, then gazing again at the water. 'I find it interesting to know that if her son had died that day – my great-grandfather – I wouldn't be here now to tell you about it.'

'Are you the last of your family?'

'No. I have a cousin, Dimitri. He's a fisherman out of Wrangell. From things my aunt has said, I think he does some smuggling, too.' Her faint smile seemed to indicate approval of his illicit activities, no matter what her aunt thought. 'Most of my aunts and uncles left Alaska shortly after the Americans took over. Nobody's heard from them in years. I guess in the Russian days Sitka was quite a city. When I was a little girl, my mama used to tell me about the fancy dress balls they had at the castle. And the concerts and the plays.' Pausing, she crooked her mouth in a wry slant. 'My aunt says that the minute they raised the American flag over Alaska, everything here changed for the worse.'

'It doesn't sound like she has a very good opinion of Americans.'

'She doesn't. A few years ago someone suggested to her that she should apply for citizenship papers. I though she was going to explode. She still considers herself to be Russian. I don't think she likes that I was born an American.'

'And a very beautiful one.' He still marveled over that, and he suspected that the trace of Indian in her ancestry was responsible for her incredibly dark eyes and well-defined cheekbones – maybe even the recklessness he sensed she felt.

'Now you're trying to flatter me.' She gave him an accusing look, then quickly turned away. 'I shouldn't have done that.'

'What?' Justin frowned.

'A girl shouldn't look a man in the eye. My aunt says that's brazen.' She cocked her head in his direction. 'Is it?'

'I don't know.' He was slightly taken aback. It was something he'd never really thought about. 'Some might consider it bold.'

'I don't see how you can talk to somebody without looking at them once,' she declared, then smiled. 'Of course, my aunt doesn't want me to talk to men.'

'I'm glad you don't do everything your aunt tells you.'

'I know she has her reasons for feeling the way she does. She's told me some of the things that happened. But sometimes I think she's just jealous because she's so homely no man would want to

463

talk to her. She won't even let me plant flowers in the garden. Vegetables, that's all we've got. "You can't eat flowers, so why waste the time and space growing them," she says. Someday I'm going to have a garden and grow nothing but flowers in it. I'm so tired of everything being so ugly and drab and never being able to talk to anyone. I hate it!'

'That's the way I felt about fishing,' Justin said. 'Ever since I was eleven years old I worked on my father's fishing boat. I got sick of the smell and the slime – of my clothes being so stiff and caked with ocean salt that they could walk without me, of working a run until you dropped, then unloading your catch at a cannery and going back out for another.'

'And you left – walked out just like that?' She snapped her fingers.

'Yup. I happened to be down on the waterfront when the *Portland* docked in Seattle. I saw them unload the shipment of gold from the Klondike – seven hundred thousand dollars' worth – a ton of gold. And I knew I wanted to get some of it. Right then and there I booked passage on the first ship I could get sailing north. Once I made up my mind, I just did it. There wasn't anything to think about. I wanted to go, so I left.'

'I want to go, too,' she stated. 'Will you take me to the Klondike with you so I can pan for gold? I swear I'll do whatever you tell me if you'll only let me go along with you.'

Justin was momentarily stunned. 'Hey, you're welcome to come along, but you'll have to pay your own way. I've got a little money with me, but that has to buy supplies for the trek over the pass and on to Dawson City. The trail is going to be rough.' He doubted that it was something a woman could tackle, or that he wanted the burden of a female, no matter how pretty she was.

'I'm strong. I won't slow you down,' she assured him as if reading his mind. 'I've got a little money put by. I've been thinking about taking the mail boat to Juneau and seeing if I couldn't get a job there. But I've heard that unless you work for the Treadwell Mining Company there aren't many jobs to be had. If all you have to do in the Klondike is pick nuggets out of a gold pan, then I wouldn't have to worry about a job.' She paused, but he could see her mind was still working. Her tension was almost palpable. 'How much do you think a ticket on your ship would cost?'

'I don't know.'

'I wouldn't need a place to sleep. I can take a blanket with me and sleep in a chair or some corner. And I can bring some bread and food from home, so I won't have to pay for any meals. What else will I need?'

'You'll need warm clothes and a heavy coat. The Klondike's cold in the winter.' Part of him was excited by the possibility of having Marisha Blackwood accompany him, even though he knew it was no place for a woman.

'Some sturdy shoes, too. How soon before the ship sails?'

Shielding his eyes, Justin tried to gauge the sun's angle in the sky. 'A little more than an hour,' he guessed.

'I have to go home and pack my things.' Quickly she began tying the scarf over her hair once more. A smile broke across her face. 'Only it's not going to be my home any more. Will you wait for me at the wharf?'

'Sure.'

'I'll be as quick as I can,' she promised and took off running along the path back through the woods, her long skirts flying.

Justin stood at the bottom of the gangway and scanned the town's nearly deserted streets. Behind him, the steamer's whistle blasted its final call to board ship. The girl was nowhere in sight. He felt a little disappointed, although he was convinced it was for the best. From all the stories he'd been hearing, life was pretty rough in the Klondike. There was no sense adding to the problems by having a woman along. Maybe she'd had second thoughts, too. Or her aunt could have caught her. There was no telling.

'Wait!'

He heard the distant shout and turned, pausing halfway up the gangplank. He spied her running down the street toward the wharf, her arms laden with several large bundles.

'Come on, mate. We're shovin' off.' One of the deckhands standing by the mooring lines motioned Justin up the ramp with an impatient wave of his hand.

'Don't cast off yet. You've got another passenger coming.' Justin ran down the ramp to meet her and quickly relieved her of two cumbersome bundles.

'I thought I wasn't going to make it.' She was panting, her cheeks glowing pink from the exertion of the run, but her smile was wide and shining.

'You almost didn't. Come on. Let's get aboard before they

leave without us.' He nodded for her to precede him up the gangway.

'I haven't paid my fare.'

'They'll take your money on the ship.'

As the vessel steamed out of the harbor, Marisha stood on the stern deck and gazed at the dock, recalling the countless times she'd stood on the old wharf and watched other ships leaving the harbor, wishing she was on board. Leaving Sitka was just about the only thing she'd dreamed about these last few years.

It was barely more than a ghost town. Sometimes when she'd walked along the street, she'd felt like the empty buildings around her – all boarded up and shuttered, alone and forgotten as the world passed by. For so long she'd yearned to escape the strictures her aunt had imposed – strictures that seemed to have only one purpose, and that was to deny her any little pleasure, whether it was a pretty dress, a simple flower, or the companionship of a friend.

Marisha stared at the green-painted spire of St. Michael's Cathedral, where her aunt Eva worked, and wondered if she'd heard the blast of the ship's whistle signaling its departure. She doubted it.

At the very last minute, she'd scribbled a note to her aunt and left it on the table, telling her that she was leaving but carefully omitting where she was going. Not that she expected her aunt Eva to come after her. She didn't. And she knew her aunt wouldn't understand her reasons for leaving. But no matter how much she hated her aunt's oppression, she felt no hate in her heart for the woman herself. Because of that, Marisha hadn't been able to run away without leaving a note for her.

Now she was going. After dreaming about it for so long, she was actually leaving that ugly, drab town with its monotonous rains, that dull, plodding existence, that narrow, lonely life without laughter or beauty. And she was going to have everything she ever wanted – bright satin gowns, pretty trinkets, and beautiful flowers. She was so excited she felt like shouting.

'Having any regrets?' Justin's voice broke her reverie.

Marisha turned and gazed openly at Justin Sinclair, free now from all her aunt's strict rules. Justin's hat was pushed to the back of his head, revealing the dark curly locks of his hair. She like his face, the strength of his heavy jaw, and the way his hazel eyes crinkled at the corners when he smiled – as he was doing now. Constant exposure to the elements had browned his face and burned away much of its youthful softness, but hints of it remained in the smoothness of his cheeks and the gentleness of his lips.

She'd had so little contact with men, especially ones close to her age. Her aunt had seen to that, hardly ever letting Marisha out of her sight when there were men around. But her aunt hadn't been able to watch her every minute, and on the rare occasions when Marisha had been able to take advantage of an opportunity to talk to a man, she hadn't understood what all the fuss was about. Men were human beings, not that much different from herself.

As she studied Justin Sinclair, Marisha wondered how much longer she would have stayed in Sitka if she hadn't talked to him today. The thing that had held her back was not knowing where to go or what to do after she got there. But he'd answered both for her – the Klondike and prospecting for gold. Deep inside, she'd always known that running away wasn't enough, she had to be running *to* something if she was ever going to realize her dreams.

She also realized that she and Justin were a lot alike. Both had been discontented with their former life; both had wanted more than it could ever give them; both had left family behind; and both had embarked on an adventure to the unknown to find their pot of gold.

'Not a single regret,' she declared unequivocally. 'This is the happiest day of my life.' Impulsively she kissed him on the cheek. 'Thank you.'

But as she drew back, his hands caught her. The scarf lay loosely about her neck, letting the sea wind blow freely through her hair. Marisha looked at him curiously, observing the stillness of his expression. Then he bent his head and kissed her lightly on the lips.

She said nothing when he released her, and instead faced the ship's stern. But she was very aware of his presence by her side. She'd never been kissed by a man before. She hadn't found the experience as revolting as her aunt had intimated it would be. In fact, the kiss had been very pleasant. Her lips still tingled with the warm sensation of his mouth on them.

41

As the ship steamed up Lynn Canal, the steep coastal mountains seemed to draw closer and become more jagged and forbidding, like hoary sentinels observing the passage of intruders below. Here and there, blue-faced glaciers lay nestled in the gorges and chasms; an occasional giant ice mass reached all the way to the deep water.

'There it is.' Justin pointed to a long, narrow valley just coming into view off the port bow.

Marisha craned her neck to catch a glimpse of the settlement that had been built on the gravelly delta at the mouth of the river by a former riverboat captain, trader, and prospector named William Moore and called Mooresville after him. She could see the wharf and the long row of buildings that ran parallel to the watercourse responsible for carving out the narrow canyon between the mountains

'I see it.' It looked bigger than she had expected, and her excitement grew in proportion. Until now, she'd never been out of Sitka in her life, but here was a new place with new people. Her old life was well and truly behind her – and this new one was just beginning.

'The trail to the Klondike leads right up that canyon to White Pass,' Justin told her as he pointed it out. 'It's longer than the route over Chilkoot Pass, but I was told this isn't as steep or as treacherous.'

Beyond those snowy crests lay Canada and the Klondike – gold nuggets and all that they could buy her. She pulled the wool scarf from her head and stared for a moment at its coarse, dark threads, remembering all the years it had covered her head and scratched her skin. She hated it and the drab life it represented. She threw it over the side; she felt she was casting off all the strict conventions with which she'd been raised. As she watched it flutter onto the dark waters below, she felt free.

'Why'd you throw that away?' Justin protested. 'You'll need it to keep your head warm.'

But Marisha laughed. 'No, I won't, not ever again.' Tied inside her bundle of clothing was an old hooded cloak of her mother's, lined with black fox. The fur was worn thin in places, but the garment would provide all the warmth she would need.

Justin pushed away from the rail. 'We'll be docking soon. Let's get our belongings together so we can be ready to leave the ship as soon as they lower the gangway.'

The other passengers on the steamer seemed to have the same idea. As the mooring lines were thrown out to tie the vessel up to the wharf, Marisha was pushed and shoved by those behind her trying to get closer to the front of the line.

Standing on the other side of Justin was a dapper-looking gentleman dressed in a dark tweed lounge suit, with a black Homburg sitting squarely on his head, and his handlebar mustache neatly waxed. His suitcase reminded Marisha of the kind that traveling salesmen used to carry their samples. He appeared indifferent to the jostling, but Marisha noticed that he never budged an inch. When his glance strayed to her, she started to look away, then remembered it wasn't necessary. He nodded and smiled to her, and Marisha returned the gestures.

'Excuse me,' he said, shifting his attention to Justin. 'But you have the look of cheechako – a local term for a newcomer to Alaska. I've been here before.' He tapped his suitcase. 'Ladies' corsets. Would you mind a word of advice?'

'No.'

'Before you do anything else, get yourself and the lovely missus a room for the night. Otherwise you're liable to find yourselves sleeping on the ground. There's few beds in town, and they'll be snatched up quick.'

Justin hesitated only an instant, then smiled and nodded. 'Thanks. I'll remember that.'

But he didn't correct the man's erroneous assumption that they were married. Marisha thought the mistake was amusing, and almost laughed wickedly when she imagined her aunt's reaction, then tried to be forgiving. Her aunt couldn't help being the way she was, but Marisha was determined not to be like her.

As the gangway went down, Justin and Marisha were swept along by the press of people anxious to leave the ship and get that much closer to the goldfields of the Klondike. The flow carried them into the town's main street. A sign on one of the many false-fronted buildings that lined both sides of the street proclaimed the town to be Skaguay.

'Skaguay.' Justin saw it, too.

'It's a Tlingit word that means a windy place.' Marisha knew that much. And with the long river valley acting as a channel for the wind, it was probably appropriate.

A stout man in a bibbed apron added more shovels to the barrel that sat in front of the general store bearing the sign. Justin went over to him. 'How come the sign says Skaguay? I thought this place was Mooresville.'

'It was – up until the first of August. A bunch of men off the *Queen*, led by a man named Frank Reid, decided Captain Moore didn't have any right to homestead this valley, so they resurveyed it, laid out this town, and sold the lots. The captain's taking them to court. But in the meantime you're in Skaguay.'

It sounded to Marisha as if the man was being cheated out of his land. At least now they had laws in Alaska. It hadn't always been that way. She remembered her aunt telling her how the creditors had taken everything her parents had owned and she received nothing, simply because there was no law by which property could be passed to a person's heirs. But that had all changed when Marisha was a child back in 1884 when Congress had passed a measure that provided a judicial system in Alaska and brought it partially under the laws of the State of Oregon. There was still no provision for civil government. Alaska still wasn't a territory, merely a district, albeit an enormous district.

A wagon pulled by a team of horses came clattering toward her. Marisha moved quickly out of its path, then hurried to catch up with Justin as he started up the street. After the relative quiet of Sitka, Skaguay was bedlam. Horse-drawn vehicles, people, and pack animals jammed the busy street. Marisha could feel the fever of the town – contagious gold fever that spread everywhere and infected everyone.

All up and down the street men hawked items designed specifically for the gold prospector headed for the Klondike. There was everything from clothing and gear to newfangled prospecting equipment. Several times Marisha paused to listen wide-eyed to the spiels and extravagant promises.

On one street corner, a man in a checked suit challenged the handful of men clustered around him: 'Test your luck. Is the hand quicker than the eye? All you gotta do is guess which one of these three shells that little dried pea is under. That's right. Step right up here, young man. I can see ya got sharp eyes. How much ya wanta bet. Six bits, a dollar? A dollar it is. Which shell do you say it is?'

Marisha didn't think the scrawny youth with the peach-fuzz beard and red and black plaid shirt was as old as she was. He pointed to the middle shell. The man lifted the shell and there sat the pea. The man invited him to try his luck again. Marisha watched while the lad continued to play and win. Finally he walked away with ten dollars jingling in his pocket.

Each time she had known which shell the pea was under. It looked so easy that Marisha dug out the kerchief in which she had tied the few coins she had left. Before she could step forward to answer the man's call of 'Who's gonna be next t' try their luck?' someone laid a hand on her arm.

She turned, her lips forming the first word of protest to Justin, but it wasn't Justin. She stared at the stranger dressed in a severe black frock coat, white shirt, and flat-brimmed black hat. He looked like a preacher. She knew all about the sins of gambling, but this was a game of skill and an alert eye, not chance.

The stranger inclined his head slightly toward her and murmured in a quiet voice so on one else could hear. 'It's all a trick to take your money.'

Stunned by his claim, she didn't object to the firm pressure of his hand on her arm as he drew her away from the men clustered around the shell game. 'But I saw that boy win –'

'But you won't see anybody else win for a while,' he told her. 'That boy was the live bait on the hook that lures the fish to bite. If you look over in front of the store, you'll see him passing the so-called winnings to the shell man's partner; maybe he'll get a couple bits in change for his trouble. He's what's known in the business as a "capper".'

Sure enough, when Marisha looked over at the store the stranger had indicated, she saw something being furtively passed between the boy and another man. Then the boy flipped a coin in the air, smiling widely as he caught it, and went swinging off down the street. She glanced back at the game in progress and heard someone groan.

'Ya gotta watch close. Come on an' try it again,' the shell man urged the loser.

471

She turned back to the stranger, half convinced of the truth of his claim. 'If it's crooked, why don't you tell the others?'

His smile emphasized the deep grooves etched in his face and lit his blue eyes. 'All the others are men. If they're fool enough to be taken in, that's their problem. But it goes against the grain to see a pretty golden-haired lady cheated out of her money.'

Marisha preened slightly at his compliment. She still was unaccustomed to hearing words of praise about her beauty instead of the condemnations she'd heard from her aunt. She enjoyed it. 'Thank you, Mr. –'

'Cole. Deacon Cole.' He touched the front brim of his hat, inclining his head slightly.

'Mr. Cole.' She smiled and shifted a bundle of her belongings to a more comfortable position in her arms.

'Did you just arrive on the steamer?'

'Yes. We're on our way to the Klondike to find gold.'

His faint smile grew more pronounced. 'The color of your hair is probably the closest you're going to come to it, but I don't expect you to believe me. Take my advice and stay away from the shell games, thimble rigs, and three-card monte.' Again he touched his hat brim. 'Good day to you, miss.'

'Good day,' she murmured and watched him stroll away, tall and lean-looking in his preacher's black frock coat. Finally she shrugged aside his disheartening prediction and turned to look for Justin just as he emerged from the semicircle of onlookers at the shell game. He spotted her almost right away and motioned for her to join him.

'Come on,' he said gruffly. 'We've gotta find some place to spend the night.'

As Marisha fell in step with him, she noticed the disgruntled expression. 'Is something wrong?'

'No,' he snapped, then grudgingly admitted, 'Yes. I lost five dollars back there.'

'I was talking to a preacher –' As Marisha paused to point him out to Justin, she saw him wander into the Pack Train saloon. She'd never heard of a preacher going into a saloon before. She was so startled by the sight that she forgot to finish her sentence.

'I wish I'd talked to him,' Justin muttered. 'I'd still have my five dollars.'

While she was still trying to puzzle out what kind of preacher went into saloons, she noticed the two women who were lounging about the saloon doors. She knew the type of women who frequented saloons. But these two didn't resemble the plump and slovenly females she'd seen outside the saloons in Sitka. Their lips were painted a scarlet red, their cheeks were rouged, and their eyes thickly outlined with kohl. One had hair as black as soot; the other's was a bright carrot red, but both wore their hair piled atop the head in a mass of tight curls. Their waists were tightly corseted, which made their bosoms appear unusually large. But it was the bright colors of their satiny skirts that caught Marisha's eye – jewel-bright colors of red and green. After she was rich, all her gowns were going to be brilliant like theirs – no more dark, somber browns and blues for her.

One of the saloon women puffed on a cigar. Marisha had never seen a woman smoke before. She thought it was something only men did. The more she thought about it, the more she thought she'd like to try it sometime and see what it was like.

Her aunt would certainly never approve of it. But her aunt also considered saloon women wicked and sinful. But what did her aunt know about it? She was an old maid; she'd never loved a man in her whole life; she had never so much as even allowed a man to touch her. She couldn't possibly know what it was like. All that fuss she'd made about how horrible kissing was – that hadn't been true at all. Marisha was almost at the point of believing the exact opposite of anything her aunt had told her.

Fascinated by the sights and sounds of this booming, bustling town, Marisha didn't mind that she had to follow Justin over half of it in search of a place to sleep. Every place so far had been full. Outside the last one, Marisha lowered her heavy bundle to the ground and waited while Justin went inside.

Within minutes, he was at the door motioning for her to come in. 'They have some empty beds,' Marisha said as she carried her cumbersome bundles into the small inn.

Justin nodded. 'Your room is down this hallway.' He led the way down the narrow corridor and stopped in front of one of the doors. He set his own pack down, then unlocked the door and stepped aside to let her enter.

The room was small. The bed took up most of the space, leaving little room for moving around. A washstand with a basin and a pitcher stood in one corner. Beyond that, the room was as bare of adornment as her old bedroom at home had been.

Hesitantly she turned to Justin and tried to find something good to say about it. 'It's . . . clean.'

'Yes.' He handed her the key.

'Where will you be?'

'This was the last room they had,' he replied. 'I'll find a place to sleep outside. I might as well get used to it. I'll be doing a lot of it on the trail.'

'I almost forgot.' She dug out her handkerchief with the money and started to untie the knotted ends. 'How much was the room?'

Self-consciously he shifted his weight from one foot to the other. 'I know I said you had to pay your own way, but I don't feel right about taking money from a woman.'

'I can't stay here. Since you paid for it, you sleep here and I'll go outside.' She grabbed up the bundles she'd deposited on the bed.

'I can't let you do that.' Justin stood in the doorway, blocking it so she couldn't get by him. 'It isn't right for a woman to sleep out in the open like that.'

'Like you said, I'm going to be doing a lot of it on the trail, so I might as well get used to it.'

'Pretend this room is a present and just accept it. Instead of buying you candy or some trinket, I got you a place to sleep. Stop arguing and be a little grateful.'

'I am. It's just the money –'

'Forget it. After what I lost this afternoon, I'm going to have to find work anyway to raise some more cash so I can buy the supplies and gear I'll need for the trip. The price of this room isn't going to change that.'

Marisha could tell he was becoming impatient with her, but despite what he said, it still didn't seem fair to her that she should sleep snug and warm while he was out in the damp night.

'The bed's big enough for two people,' she said, then saw his shocked look.

'Marisha, are you saying that I sleep with you? Do you know what you're suggesting?'

For a brief moment she didn't follow his meaning. Then it occurred to her that a bed was a place where people did more than sleep. It was where a man and woman mated. She stared at the bed, wondering about the act her aunt had so reviled – the one that God had designed man and woman to be able to perform.

474

She didn't trust her aunt's word on anything. She wanted to find out things for herself, experience everything and decide for herself if it was good or bad.

Soberly she faced Justin. 'I know what I'm saying. I want you to stay here tonight with me.'

Still he hesitated. 'Marisha, I've made you no promises.'

'I know.'

'I'm on my way to the Klondike as soon as I can get the rest of the money I need.'

'I know. That's where I'm going, too – to find gold.' She opened the bundle in which she'd packed the food she'd taken from the house. 'If you're hungry, I can offer you a cold meal. It isn't much, just some dried salmon, bread, and homemade cheese.'

'The bread and cheese sounds good.' Justin hauled his heavy pack inside the room and shut the door.

Later that night as the wick burned low, the flame sputtered and wavered, throwing out a faint light that left the bed in shadows, Marisha lay in Justin's arms. She was aware that the way he kissed and caressed her had eased much of her anxiety. Still, no matter how much she was enjoying the way he was making her feel now, she didn't know what was to come.

She wished there had been someone she could have asked before she lay with a man for the first time – someone who could have explained things to her.

Her knowledge of the mating act was limited to the most rudimentary level, garnered from observing animals coupling. She had never seen a man's organ – not even that of a baby boy. She could only surmise that it protruded from him the way it did on a dog or a bull. She resented her ignorance and nearly threw back the heavy quilt so she could see him, but that was too bold for even her to countenance.

During the awkward, fumbling moments after he moved on top of her, she didn't know what to do. She could feel something hard probing for her opening, then he found it and pushed into her, but there was resistance from within. It hurt. At the moment of full penetration, a sharp, searing pain ripped through her. As she bit her lower lip to keep from crying out, Marisha was prepared to concede that in this instance maybe her aunt was right and there was nothing enjoyable about the mating act despite the pleasurable kissing and caressing that had preceded it.

Gradually, as he continued to rock in and out of her, the aching began to ease, and the sensation of his rhythmic movement became faintly pleasurable. The tempo increased. Within moments, he began to groan and jerk convulsively. When the last shudder faded, he lay motionless, his weight heavy on her. Then he levered himself off of her and rolled onto the mattress in apparent exhaustion. There was a faint throbbing sensation between her legs. It wasn't so much pain as it was a vaguely hollow feeling.

'Mmm, that was good,' Justin murmured.

Marisha concluded that she must not have been as inadequate as she had thought. When she tried to decide how she felt about it, she couldn't make up her mind. She couldn't truthfully say that she had enjoyed it, but neither could she say that she had hated it.

42

Since Marisha had never slept with anyone before, she hadn't realized another person's body could hold so much heat. It was like cuddling up to a glowing coal stove. If for no other reason, she probably would have considered letting the sleeping arrangement stand for that one alone; but she had found that the second time Justin made love to her was better than the first, the third better than the second, the fourth better than the third. As each time became more pleasurable than the last, her sexual curiosity increased. She became more actively involved – not merely responding to his touch but touching him. Sometimes they had made love twice in one night. Once they had even done it in the morning with the light from the rising sun streaming through the window. After that, Marisha no longer had to guess by feel what his organ looked like. It was as if she finally had an outlet for all the passions that had been repressed for so long, and she had to explore them all fully. The discovery process proved to be highly satisfying.

Not that they were able to spend all their time making love; they couldn't. The Klondike and its gold was still their priority, but the lack of sufficient funds had forced them to delay their departure to Canada's Yukon Territory. First they had to find work to earn the necessary money.

Marisha was lucky. On her second day in Skaguay, she got a job washing dishes at one of the hash houses. Although she was paid very little, she was entitled to a free meal. Plus she always managed to slip out some food for Justin so he wouldn't have to spend his money to eat. Still, her daily wages amounted to little more than the rent they had to pay for the room.

After she had spent three days washing dishes, one of the customers commented to the cook and owner of the eating establishment, 'You're making a mistake, Mabe, keepin' that purty yeller-haired gal hidin' back there in the kitchen, a-slavin' over them dirty dishes. She should be takin' orders out front so the boys can see her. I'd bet you'd do twice the business.'

Just like that, she went from being a dishwasher to a waitress. She not only caught on to the new job quickly, but she also learned to handle the customers, who were almost exclusively male. After a week of being surrounded by men, Marisha couldn't figure out why her aunt had regarded them as crude, objectionable brutes, ready to pounce on the first female they saw. A smile or a kind word was all most of her customers wanted. Some seemed lonely and wanted to talk.

Still all the attention she received from the men was a new and heady experience for her. Now she walked with her head held high, at last taking pride in her looks. 'Glory Girl,' they called her. It all started shortly after she started working in the front. A customer – an old sourdough – who'd been there in the morning came back that noon with a friend and pointed to Marisha, declaring, 'There she is. Ain't she a glory to behold?' The tag stuck. Truthfully, Marisha liked it.

She wrapped a rag around the handle of the coffeepot to shield her hand from the metal's heat, then picked up the pot and began making the rounds of the tables, refilling cups. She paused beside the preacher's chair.

'More coffee, Mr. Cole?' She smiled with practiced ease. Although he'd only been in the restaurant twice since she'd been working there, he wasn't the sort of man a person could forget.

He nodded affirmatively and slid his cup over so she could fill it. As usual he was dressed in his somber black coat and starched white shirt. She'd never seen him wear any other clothes, yet he always looked neat and clean. She especially noticed his hands. They were smooth and pale, not imbedded with grime and roughened by calluses like the hands of most of her customers. There wasn't even a speck of dirt under his blunt fingernails.

'Hey, Glory Girl, bring that pot over here! We need some more coffee.' The request was bellowed across the room. Marisha didn't have to turn around and look to recognize the voice of a leather-skinned wrangler with one of the pack outfits in town.

'Be right there, Curly,' she called back, then inquired of the preacher, 'Need anything else?'

'This'll do.' He picked up the coffee cup and rocked the chair back onto its rear legs as Marisha started across the room.

The preacher always sat at the same corner table in the chair facing the door, and he always sat alone.

When she reached Curly's table, he held out his cup for her to fill. A flop-eared cap covered his head and hid his thin crop of hair. Marisha doubted that Curly was much past thirty, but he was already going bald. She glanced at the two men with him, not recognizing either of them.

'Got a smile to sweeten this coffee for me?' Curly asked.

She smiled at him as she turned to pour coffee into his companions' cups. Although she was conscious of their ogling stares, she was almost used to that.

'You work too hard in this place,' Curly declared.

'A girl has to eat.'

'If eatin's the only thing keepin' you here, we can solve that, can't we, boys?' Curly grinned at his friends.

'You bet,' replied the scraggly-bearded man sitting in the chair closest to Marisha. 'You can move into the shack with us. Why, that way you'd have a place to sleep and plenty to eat, too. An' you wouldn't get lonely 'cause we'd be there t' keep you company.'

'I already have those things. Sorry.' Such suggestions had been made to her countless times already, too many for her to regard them as offensive.

'A purty gal like you needs someone t' look after her and protect her an' keep her safe from harm,' he insisted. 'Someone like us.'

'Sorry, fellas, but I'm already spoken for.' Marisha smiled as she went about filling the second man's cup with coffee.

'Didn't I tell you?' Curly said. 'She's already got herself a man friend.'

The third man held out his cup. As she reached across the table with the coffeepot, the bearded man hooked an arm around her waist and hauled her against him, nearly causing her to miss the man's cup and pour the coffee onto the table.

'He cain't be much of a man if ya gotta work in this place,' he declared.

Somehow Marisha managed to keep her balance. 'You'd better be careful. This coffee is hot.' She reached back to pry his hand from her waist, but he tightened his hold.

'If'n you was to move in with us, you could quit this dump.'

He smiled suggestively. 'Do you know you're even purtier up close?'

'I'm glad you think so. Now will you let me go?' She continued to tug at his hand, firm yet patient, having learned from experience that it was the best way of dealing with this kind of harmless advance. Anger invariably provoked a man into persisting.

'Miss?' the preacher called to her. 'I've changed my mind. I'd like to order some breakfast.'

'I'll be right there,' she promised, then glanced pointedly at the man holding her. 'Do you mind? I have a customer waiting.'

'Ya see, now if you was livin' with us, you wouldn't be jumpin' to every man's biddin'. Why, lookin' after the needs of three of us wouldn't be near as hard as workin' in this place – an' a hell of a lot more fun. We'd see to that, wouldn't we, boys?'

'Yeah, we'd keep ya entertained.' The third man snickered.

'I'll bet you would,' Marisha retorted, guessing exactly what kind of entertainment they had in mind. 'But I'd rather keep my job. Now, will you remove your hand or do I have to scald you with this hot coffee?'

'Now that ain't very friendly,' he scolded.

Across the room, a chair came down on all four legs with a resounding slam. Deacon Cole rose to his feet in a smooth, fluid motion and walked slowly toward them. He halted short of the table.

'Mister, I'll ask you just once to let her go,' he stated.

'I don't recall anybody invitin' you over here.' The bearded man tightened his grip on Marisha. 'Why don't you just go back t' your chair in the corner an' mind your own business.'

'This is my business,' the preacher replied. 'I'm hungry. I want something to eat. And I won't get it until this lady takes my order. You've got your coffee. Now why don't you drink it and let her get back to work.'

'It so happens that I'm gettin' kinda attached to her.' He gave Marisha a little squeeze as if reasserting his claim on her.

Marisha felt this had dragged on long enough. 'Curly, tell your friend to let me go. I have work to do.'

'I suggest you do as the lady says.' The preacher smiled pleasantly. At least, it seemed pleasant until Marisha noticed the small derringer that had appeared almost magically in his hand. 'I tend to become irritable when I'm hungry.'

'There's no need of gettin' testy about it,' the man grumbled uncomfortably and immediately turned her loose.

Marisha quickly moved away from his chair while staring at the snub-nosed gun, shocked to see such a thing in a minister's hand. As he turned from the table, she saw him tuck the deadly little weapon up inside his sleeve. She couldn't help thinking that it was a strange place to keep a gun as she followed him to his corner chair.

Seated again, he smiled faintly. 'After that, I expect I'd better order something. I wouldn't want to be called a liar. I'll take a stack of hotcakes.' Marisha frowned at his inference that it had all been a pretext. Nothing her expression, he cocked his head to the side. 'Did I make a mistake just now?' He spoke in a low voice that didn't carry beyond her hearing. 'I had the impression that you didn't welcome his attentions.'

'I didn't, but he didn't mean any harm. Most of the fellas here will only go as far as a girl will let them.'

He studied her with quiet speculation. 'Could be you aren't as innocent as I thought.'

'There are a lot of things I don't know, but I'm learning fast. Men like to talk. That's one of the first things I found out. But they don't mean half of what they say. It was kind of you to step in, but it wasn't really necessary.'

She wanted to make it clear that she was happy here and didn't care to have any Good Samaritan intervening, however well-intentioned. She liked the men who came in and talked and joked with her. She had never been offended by anything they said or did, nor had she considered their behavior to be out of line.

She walked away from the table still wondering about this preacher who had such peculiar ideas about right and wrong. Obviously he believed that he had rescued her from an unfortunate situation on two occasions – yet he carried a hidden gun and frequented saloons.

'I need a stack, Mabe,' Marisha told the cook and owner, then lingered in the overheated kitchen. 'Do you know a preacher named Deacon Cole?'

'Preacher?' He snorted and turned away from the range, mopping his face with an already damp rag. 'I'd venture to say the only gospel Deacon Cole knows is the one according to Soapy Smith.'

Marisha frowned. Soapy Smith was a name she had heard

481

bandied about by the local townspeople in conjunction with the band of swindlers and con artists who preyed on those passing through with money in their pockets on their way to the Klondike.

'You mean Cole isn't a preacher,' Marisha concluded.

'Hardly. He's a cardsharp – a professional gambler. Anybody who's fool enough to sit in a game of poker or faro with him deserves to lose their money. Folks call him Deacon 'cause of the way he dresses, but gambling is his only religion.'

'What's his real name then?'

'Who knows?' He shrugged. 'Nobody uses their right name up here – or damned few, if any.'

'Why?'

' 'Cause here it don't matter much who or what they were "Below," ' he said, using a local term for the United States. 'Here a man can put distance between himself and the past and make a fresh start.'

The comment started Marisha thinking. She had begun a new life but kept the same old name. Marisha Blackwood was the girl who had worn headscarfs and dowdy clothes, who hadn't been allowed to talk to men or look them in the eye, who had seldom smiled or laughed. What she really needed in this new life was a new name. She had changed, and it was time she changed her name, too. But, to what?

That night she sat cross-legged on the bed and unwrapped the meat scraps that she'd filched from the restaurant and hidden in the large pockets of her old brown skirt along with half a loaf of bread. She spread the paper on the mattress so Justin could help himself. The bed creaked noisily as she shifted to watch him tear the bread in half again.

'I'm going to change my name.' She was barely able to contain the excitement she felt over her recent decision. 'I haven't come up with a new one yet. But it's not going to be anything that sounds Russian. I want a name that's unique. Don't you think?' She picked up a bread crumb that had fallen on the paper and chewed thoughtfully on it, too absorbed by the task of choosing a name to notice his silence. 'Do you have any ideas, Justin?' When no answer was forthcoming, she frowned at him. 'Justin, did you hear me?'

He sat staring at the bread in his hands, not touching it or the meat scraps. Her second question finally roused him from his brooding silence. 'What'd you say?' he grunted, but it was a poor attempt at feigning interest.

'You haven't been listening, have you?' The last two days he'd been extremely moody and depressed over his failure to find a good-paying job. She was getting tired of his silence and inattention that only ended when the lights were out and they were in bed. He dropped the bread onto the paper with the meat and pushed off the bed, then wandered to the window by the washstand. 'After all I went through to get this, aren't you going to eat it?'

'I'm not hungry.' He faced the night-darkened windowpanes, his hands thrust deep into his trouser pockets.

Marisha sighed. 'What's wrong now?'

'Have you noticed the leaves are starting to turn on the trees in the mountains?'

'No. It's dark when I go to work and dark when I get off.' Truthfully she couldn't care less whether the leaves were changing colors or not.

Justin turned to look at her. 'Don't you know what that means?'

'Why don't you tell me?' She folded her arms in front of her in a gesture that was both tolerant and challenging.

'I'm running out of time. If we don't leave for the Klondike soon, it's going to be too late in the season to make the trip. I could be stuck here in Skaguay for the winter.' He faced the window again and stared at the dark panes. 'A whole damned winter wasted.' He slammed the flat of his hand against the window frame. 'I've gotta get the money I need! Somehow I've gotta figure out a way to get there.'

'How much more money do we still need?'

'I could get by with ten more dollars, but at the rate we're going it might as well be a hundred.'

'Maybe I could get another job.'

'Doing what? And when? You work from dawn to dusk as it is,' he reminded her.

'I could work a few hours at night, cleaning or scrubbing floors some place.'

He swung away from the window to face the bed where she sat. 'Let's face it, Marisha. There's only one kind of night work a woman could do that would raise the kind of money we need!' He strode toward the door and grabbed his coat from the wall hook as he passed it. 'I'm going out for some air.' He yanked open the door, then paused. 'I won't be long.'

Sitting alone in the dreary room, Marisha drew her knees up under her chin and tucked her long skirt over her stockinged feet. She knew what kind of night work Justin meant. She knew prostitutes made their living by charging money for their favors. If she hadn't been too certain about what that entailed before, she knew now.

She closed her eyes and visualized what that ore sample had looked like and the shiny, sparkling flecks of gold that ran through it. The streams in the Klondike had gold nuggets the size of pebbles in their gravel beds. In her mind, she pictured the sight and tried to imagine what it would be like to scoop up a handful of gravel and pick out the shiny gold nuggets.

For two days she could think of little else. She listened to every snippet of conversation at the restaurant that mentioned the gold camps of the Klondike. It seemed everyone was on his way there, except her. She worried that maybe they'd find it all before she and Justin got there.

As she left the restaurant, she paused outside the building and heard the sharp click of the door lock behind her. She bunched the fur-lined burnous around her neck but didn't raise its hood to cover her head. Tired and footsore after a long day's work, she started down the boardwalk toward the rooming house.

The long street was without the normal daytime traffic of rumbling horse-drawn vehicles and braying mules and donkeys. Most of the town's bustling activity now took place inside the saloons and gaming halls that Marisha passed. She could hear a tinny piano playing some ragtime song and a man encouraging others to 'Place your bets.' There was a steady hum of voices in the background, sometimes punctuated by laughter or an exultant shout. Through some of the grimy windows she could see saloon girls dancing with customers. Always she could hear the muted clink of coins. Money – the thing she and Justin didn't have, the thing they wanted, needed.

Her footsteps made a hollow sound as she walked along the boardwalk, her way lighted intermittently by the rectangular patches of light that came from the saloon windows. Three men in obvious high spirits came charging out of a saloon door just ahead of her. One of them noticed her. As they all turned to look at her, Marisha recognized Curly and the two companions that had been with him the other day.

'Would you looky there? It's our Glory Girl.' The bearded man immediately doffed his hat in greeting, but he didn't appear quite as scruffy as the first time she'd seen him. His beard was neatly trimmed and his hair parted precisely down the middle. As she drew nearer, she noticed that Curly had on a clean shirt.

'Good evening.' She nodded to them and continued on by the saloon, but they swung around to walk with her.

'Whatcha doin' walkin' the street yourself? Where's that man friend of yores?' Curly demanded. 'He should be here to make sure you don't come to no harm.'

'It seems there's no need for him to be here. I have the three of you to escort me safely to my rooming house.' She smiled.

'If you was our gal, we'd never take a risk like that,' the third man insisted.

'Why not instead of goin' to yore roomin' house, why don't we walk ya to our shack?' the bearded man suggested. 'I guarantee it'll be a lot more fun.'

Marisha started to ignore the remark as she had always done, then in a moment of daring she paused and swung around to face her three would-be escorts. 'Do you really want me to go to your shack?'

'Shore,' the bearded man blurted in surprise.

'And if I went, how much would you pay me?' she demanded. Their mouths gaped wordlessly as they stared at her. In their silence, she heard rejection and pivoted sharply away, feeling a hot flush of humiliation burn her cheeks. 'It was all just more talk, wasn't it? You didn't really mean what you were saying,' she said bitterly and began walking away.

Instantly they hurried after her. 'We meant it. Honest we did. It's just that we never thought you was . . .' Curly faltered in midsentence.

'Yeah. We never suspected you was the kind who . . . well . . .' The third man couldn't get the words out either. 'We jest didn't know.'

'We want ya t' come to our place, don't we, boys?' the bearded one insisted. 'We'd pay ya.'

Marisha halted again and waited for them to flock around her. 'How much?'

'Well.' The bearded man shifted uncomfortably and glanced at his companions. 'The goin' rate is usually three dollars, an' there's three of us, so that'd be nine.'

'I want ten dollars.' Her throat felt dry.

'It's a deal.' Curly wiped the palm of his hand on his pants leg, then thrust it out to shake hands with her.

'Deal.' When she gripped his hand, he gave it an arm-pumping shake.

'Eee-hah!' The bearded man gave a triumphant shout, then turned to the third member of their group and gave him a slapping shove on the back that propelled him toward the door of the nearest saloon.

'Hank, go fetch us a bottle. We gonna have us a high time tonight. Ain't that right, Glory Girl? Why, you know, we don't even know yore name.'

'You just said it. My name's Glory.'

'Glory. Why, I'll be damned. Did you know that, Curly?'

'I surely didn't, but it fits her to a tee.'

Her legs felt a little rubbery and there were nervous flutterings in her stomach. Yet she had no doubts about this decision – no second thoughts, no regrets. It was exactly the same as when she had left Sitka. If she and Justin were ever to get to the Klondike and find that gold, they had to have money. And time was running out. This was the quickest and surest way to get the ten dollars they needed; Justin had said so himself. Now that her mind was made up, Marisha was committed, with no looking back.

Papers were stuffed in the cracks to keep the wind from blowing in the crudely built shack. Its single room measured no more than ten by twelve and had only one window. Curly hurriedly lit the lamp and began stoking the fire in the potbellied stove. Judging by the nearly empty pot of beans and sow belly that sat on top of it, Marisha guessed it was used for both cooking and heating.

Two bunk beds stacked one on top of the other sat along one wall. In the corner next to them stood a narrow cot. A couple of kegs and a wooden crate served as chairs for the crudely made table by the window. All three men stood by the table as the man called Hank uncorked the whiskey bottle and poured a generous shot into each of the three tin mugs lined up on the table.

As she watched them, an inner voice cautioned her. 'I'll take my money first, boys.' She didn't know where the warning came from. Maybe it was left over from her aunt's oft-repeated edict that men couldn't be trusted. Either way, she didn't want to be cheated out of what was rightfully hers.

They hesitated momentarily, then started digging into their pockets. As they pooled their money to come up with the requisite ten dollars, there was a brief debate over which of them had to pay more, since ten couldn't be equally divided by three, but the problem was quickly resolved.

'There you are, Glory.' Curly dropped the coins into her cupped palm. 'Ten silver dollars.'

Clutching them in her hand, she turned away and walked to the corner cot. They had kept their side of the bargain, and regardless of how fast her heart was beating, she knew it was time to keep hers. She removed the warm burnous and slipped the coins into one of its deep side pockets, then laid it on the nearby lower bunk. Keeping her back to the men, she took off her blouse and long skirt and laid them on top of the burnous. As she continued to undress, she added a flannel petticoat and long-sleeved chemise to the stack of clothes. She wore no corset. Her aunt had always regarded that undergarment as figure-flattering, and therefore forbidden. Clad only in a plain camisole and a pair of flannel drawers, she turned around to face the open-eyed men. Determinedly, she ignored the drumming of her pulse.

'Who's going to be first?' She began unbuttoning the front of her camisole.

'That's me,' the bearded man declared. Quickly he gulped down the last of the whiskey in his cup and wiped his mouth with the back of his hand. He hitched up his trousers by the waistband and swaggered toward the cot. A wide grin split his bearded face as he hooted to his companions. 'I'm goin t' glory, boys! I'm a-goin' t' glory!'

The coins jingled in her pocket as she hurried down the hallway to her room. But no sliver of light gleamed under the door. 'Justin,' she called softly, then tried the knob. It wouldn't turn. Aware that it was late, she hoped he hadn't gone out looking for her. She could hardly wait to tell him that they had the money to go to the Klondike. She rummaged through her pockets and found the key, then unlocked the door and entered the darkened room.

A faint light came from the window and revealed a long, lumpy object lying on the bed. Without pausing to light the lamp, she walked to the bed. 'Justin, you scamp, you could have waited up for me.' But when she tried to shake him awake, she encountered only cloth – mounds of cloth and no body.

She turned from the bed, wondering where he could be at this hour. She tried telling herself that maybe he'd found work at one of the saloons as she fumbled in the dark for the matches and lit the lamp. Its light revealed that the items haphazardly strewn on the bed belonged to her. She knew full well that they'd all been stacked neatly in the corner when she'd left for work that morning. Someone must have been in their room. She hurried over to the bed to see if anything was missing.

As she started to sort through the articles, she heard the rustle of paper and uncovered a note. The crudely printed scrawl was barely legible. When she saw it was addressed 'Dear M.,' she quickly glanced at the signature at the bottom. It was signed 'Justin Sinclair.' For an instant she stared at the block letters, then remembered that Justin had once told her he'd never finished his schooling and had instead worked on his father's fishing trawler. She went back to the beginning of the note and began to read it aloud.

' "Dear M. Sorry there was no time to see you before I left." ' Left? She stared at the last word in shock, then hurriedly read on. ' "Got a job taking a pack train to Dawson. Took the place of man fired for being drunk. This my chance to get to gold camps. Knew you would understand." '

Although there was more, she stopped reading and sat down on the edge of the bed, the silver coins clinking together in her pocket. Her fingers tightened on the paper. She understood all right. She understood that he'd left her behind.

She started reading again, her voice wavering with the anger she felt at his betrayal. ' "Needed a blanket. Took yours." ' She searched through her pile of belongings, wildly throwing things aside. The blanket was missing, as well as the sacks of flour, salt, and dried beans she'd taken from her aunt's home. She was raging inside when she picked up the note again. ' "No time to buy supplies. Will pay you. Be back when I strike it rich." ' That was all there was except for his name at the bottom of the sheet. She crumpled the paper in her hand, crushing it into a ball.

He said he'd take me. He said he loved me. Then she remembered: 'They always leave.' Aunt Eva used to say that. After he takes what he wants from a woman, he abandons her.

In a fit of pique, she hurled the note across the room and stood up. The sudden motion jingled the money in her pocket. Reaching inside, she took out the coins and stared at them, remembering what she'd done to earn them. At the time it hadn't seemed so terrible. It hadn't been as wonderful as when Justin had made love to her, but she hadn't expected that it would be. Maybe what she'd done was wrong. Maybe Justin's desertion of her was a punishment. She felt all twisted up inside, angry and hurt, confused about the right and wrong of things.

She let the coins slide through her fingers onto the bed, then removed the heavy burnous and flung it onto the foot of the bed. She stared at the ten shiny silver dollars lying in a scattered cluster on the blanket.

'If you had waited, Justin, you could have had the money, too.' She would have given it to him. She loved him, and they were supposed to be going to the Klondike together. That's why she'd done it.

Maybe if she'd given him the money, he'd have left her anyway. Maybe he hadn't loved her. She wasn't sure about anything any more – except that ten dollars was more money than she'd ever had at one time in her entire life, more than she could have made working at the restaurant for a week. And she'd earned it in less than two hours, with considerably less physical labor. It wasn't enough to get her to the Klondike, but she didn't think she wanted to go there now.

As she lifted her skirt to sit down on the bed, she felt the coarseness of its fabric and realized she did have enough money to buy one entire outfit – corset, camisole, pantalettes, bustle, chemise, petticoats, skirt, shirtwaist – and still have a little left. She could throw these drab, shapeless garments away, these hated clothes that belonged to Marisha Blackwood – the woman she was never going to be again.

Justin was gone, and she vowed she wasn't going to look back. This was a new life. And she was going to have new clothes and a new name. From now on, she was Glory ... Glory ... She paused to think of a suitably unique last name. In deference to Justin for his help in setting her on this new road and for unwittingly providing her with the funds, she decided it was only right that she adopt a variation of his name. From this moment forward she would be Glory St. Clair.

43

Lazily Glory pushed herself into a reclining position on the pillows propped against the bed's headboard, then pulled the blanket up to cover her bare breasts. It was not an attempt at false modesty because of the man busily engaged in pulling his embroidered silk suspender straps onto his shoulders, but rather an attempt to protect herself from the room's drafty chill. Her long hair lay loose and tousled about her neck and shoulders. Idly she twirled a golden lock of it around her forefinger as she watched him shrug into his coat, then reach for his pearl gray fedora hat.

'I'll take that five-dollar piece now.' She held out her hand for the gold coin he had shown her earlier and promised to pay her *after* she had lain with him. His clothes, his jewelry, his manner – everything about him reeked of money. Which was why she hadn't insulted him by insisting that he pay in advance.

'I enjoyed myself, Glory. I truly did.' He took the coin from his vest pocket and held it up. 'But this is all the money I have. I can't very well give it to you.'

'But you agreed!'

'So I did. Unfortunately I shall have to go back on my word. With that tight little glory hole of yours, you have your own gold mine, Miss St. Clair. You aren't likely to starve as I surely will.' He tucked the coin back into his pocket and tipped his hat to her. 'Good evening.'

As he walked out the door, her initial shock at his audacity turned to outrage. She scrambled out of the bed. 'You come back here!' In the two months since she'd quit her job at the restaurant and gone to selling her favors full time, this was not the first man who had refused to pay her.

By the time she reached the door, he was halfway down the hall. She could hardly pursue him into the street, not when all

490

she wore was her bright blue silk hose and the Paris brand hose supporter – articles her now fleeing customer had asked her not to remove. Hurriedly she pulled on her lace-trimmed drawers and corset cover, then slipped her feet into her pointed-toed shoes, and grabbed her old furlined burnous off the wall hook. With the latter to cloak the state of her near undress, Glory ran down the hallway and out of the rooming house.

A layer of newly fallen snow blanketed the street, and more flakes swirled down to speckle the night air. Her customer was nowhere in sight, but Glory saw the fresh tracks he'd left in the snow and followed them like a bloodhound until they were stamped out by other footprints outside Jeff Smith's Parlor. She hesitated only an instant, then walked into the gaming establishment.

Normally she didn't go into the saloons and gambling halls. The girls who worked in them regarded her as a trespasser trying to take their trade away from them. Glory usually sought out her customers in the various restaurants and hotels in Skaguay – or, as the recently established post office spelled it, Skagway.

The parlor's false front artfully concealed the crudeness of the building behind it. The long, narrow room was dingy and drab, its bare walls and floors built with roughly finished planks. Cigar smoke obscured her vision as Glory scanned the crowded room. Amidst the drone of low voices was the click and clatter of poker chips, dice, cards, roulette balls, and spinning wheels.

Her attention was caught by a man's crisp summons: 'Get your bets down, folks. Pick your lucky number and place your money on it.'

The call came from a red-haired man standing in front of a tall wheel of fortune. At almost the same moment that Glory located the source of it, she noticed the man in the gray fedora hat at the table. Although his back was to her, she recognized the hat and doubted there were two like it in Skagway. She pushed through the crowd to the man's side and grabbed his arm.

'I want my money.'

After his initial start, he recovered his poise and gazed at her disdainfully. 'What nonsense is this? I've never seen you before. Kindly remove your hand from my person.'

'That's not what you said twenty minutes ago in my room. In fact, there were plenty of places you wanted me to put my hands,' she reminded him – to the amusement of the onlookers.

'I don't know what you're talking about.' But a telltale flush reddened his neck.

The red-haired operator gave the wheel a spin. It clattered noisily as he made his time-worn pitch. 'Round and round she goes. Where she stops, nobody knows.'

'You owe me five dollars and I want it now,' Glory demanded. 'No man's going to cheat me out of my money and get by with it.'

'Nonsense.' He tried to laugh away her claim and appealed to the onlookers for support. 'Do I look like the sort of man who would cheat someone out of their money?'

Suddenly Deacon Cole appeared by her side. 'I don't know, mister. Are you?'

'Of course not.'

'The lady says you owe her money.'

'I don't care what she says.'

For the second time the little derringer materialized in Deacon Cole's hand. He thrust the muzzle under the point of the man's chin and kept it there. 'Are you calling the lady a liar?' His voice remained as calm and even as his expression.

The gambling hall became unnaturally silent. There was no more talking, no rattle of dice, no rustle of cards or clicking of clips. The only noise was the clatter of the fortune wheel spinning.

'No.' Panic was in the man's eyes. 'I . . . I don't have any money to pay her. Honest.'

'He had a five-dollar gold piece in his vest pocket,' Glory stated. 'He showed it to me.'

As Deacon Cole started to feel the vest pocket, the man quickly confessed, 'I don't have it. It's on the table. I bet it on the wheel.'

The gold coin sat on one of the numbered squares. Glory easily located it among the other chips scattered over the board.

'Pinky,' Deacon Cole addressed the wheel's operator. 'Did this gentleman put that half eagle down?'

'Yes, he did.' There was more time between clicks as the fortune wheel continued to slow. Glory started to reach for the money that rightfully belonged to her. 'Sorry.' The red-haired man stopped her. 'The bet is down. The wheel is turning.'

'That bet belongs to the lady now, Pinky. Any winnings go to her. Isn't that right, mister?' He nudged the man's chin with the muzzle of his derringer, tilting it a little higher.

492

'Yes, yes. It's hers.' Beads of sweat trickled down his forehead as he attempted to nod vigorously.

'Got that, Pinky.'

'You bet.' For a moment, Glory thought the wheel was going to stop, but it continued to turn slowly, numbers ticking by the arrow one by one. Then it stopped.

'Luck smiles on the lady. The winner at five to one.'

The crowd that had been so silent shouted their approval. Glory couldn't believe it. Instead of five dollars, she had twenty-five. The winnings were pushed to her and she gathered up the chips in her hand, cradling them against her old coat. It was almost more than she could hold.

'I'm broke,' the man complained now that the derringer was tucked away in its hiding place.

'Maybe this will teach you a lesson. We don't like cheats in this town,' Deacon told him, then turned and took Glory by the arm and guided her away from the table. 'Let's cash your chips in.'

'But . . . I thought I might play again.' She craned her neck to look back at the wheel of fortune.

'Don't – unless you want to lose your hard-earned money.'

'Why?'

There was hardly any movement of his lips as he answered her in an undertone. 'Because that's the crookedest wheel in town.'

'But I just won.'

'Exactly. Pinky owed me a favor.'

Glory didn't know how his friend Pinky had done it, but she believed Deacon Cole. She no longer resisted, even slightly, the guiding pressure of his hand.

'Where's your uncle?' he asked.

'My uncle?'

'Yes, your boyfriend, partner, or whatever you want to call the man who looks out for you, makes sure you don't get roughed up or cheated. The man you split the money with.'

'The money's mine. All of it. No one looks after me. I look after myself.' She clutched her winnings a little closer to her body. When he halted, she stopped also, feeling defensive without understanding why.

'You haven't been at this long, have you?'

'No.' She lifted her chin.

'I have a feeling there's a lot you don't know about the business.'

'Maybe, but I learn fast.'

'There are always a few things a person has to learn the hard way, but that doesn't mean someone can't pick up a few pointers from those who are . . . more experienced, shall we say?'

'Such as?'

He smiled, and it was the first break in his impassive expression. 'Come to the Golden North Hotel tomorrow, about noon, and I'll introduce you to her. She might even give you a job.'

'I don't need one.'

'If you're in it for the money, there's more to be made in the saloons than there is on the street. I'll be there at noon. Meet me there if you want.'

'I'll see.' She glanced down at the pile of chips in her hands. 'I guess I owe you for helping me get this money. I don't know how I can repay you.'

'That's easy.' His smile widened, reaching his eyes. 'My pockets are empty. I need a ten-dollar stake to get back in that poker game over there.' He indicated the table along the wall where cards were being dealt to the four men seated around it.

'Are you sure it's an honest game?'

'My dear Miss St. Clair, an honest poker game in this town is as rare as a virgin.'

She laughed. She couldn't help it. If it hadn't been for Deacon Cole and the favor owed to him by his friend Pinky, she wouldn't have had this money. She gave him a handful of chips and added one more to make it ten. 'Good luck.'

'Indeed.' Once he had the chips in hand he seemed to forget her. Before he had taken the first step away, his attention was already centered on the poker table.

The horse and wagon traffic had turned the snow-covered street into a mire of slush and mud. Glory lifted her garnet-colored skirt until the hem cleared the tops of her buttoned shoes, then picked her way carefully across the street.

On the other side, the boardwalk in front of the Golden North Hotel had been swept clear of snow. Glory mounted the planked walk, wet with the muddy tracks of many footprints, and let her skirt fall naturally to the break of her kid-leather shoes. She paused short of the hotels' entrance and ran a smoothing hand over the snug-fitting waist of her jacket-coat, elaborately trimmed with gold braid at the waist, yoke, and forearms of its leg-of-mutton sleeves, then edged with plush seal fur. A long-feathered bird adorned the brimless seal hat she wore. She slipped her hands into the seal muff that dangled from the loop around her wrist and walked to the hotel door to keep her noon appointment with Deacon Cole.

On entering, she spied the tall, black-coated gambler perusing some notices tacked to a wall in the nearly deserted lobby. As she walked over to him, the frou-frou of her taffeta petticoats attracted his notice and he turned.

'I wondered if you would come.' He cast an appraising glance over her, but his expression registered neither approval nor disapproval.

'I decided there's no harm in listening. Besides, I had nothing better to do,' she replied, feigning indifference. 'How was your poker game last night?'

'I did well.'

'What does that mean?'

'A smart gambler never brags about the size of his winnings.' He reached into his pocket and pulled out a gold eagle. 'But I did well enough that I can return the money you staked me.'

Glory shook her head in refusal. 'I owed you that.'

'Take it anyway.' He took her right hand out of the muff and pressed the ten-dollar gold piece into its palm. 'I may be in straitened circumstances again someday and I'll know who to see.'

'In that case, I'll hold on to it for you.' She smiled, and he responded with a faint curve of his thin lips.

The tall clock in the lobby chimed the quarter hour. 'I'm sure Miss Rosie is becoming impatient. I'll take you to meet her.'

'Where is she?'

'At the moment, she's waiting in my room.'

Miss Rosie, as Deacon had called her, was a formidable-looking woman, tall and buxom in a stiffly starched white shirt-waist with a navy bow tied around the high collar, and fitted cuffs capping the full sleeves. Her hair was a brassy shade of yellow, piled atop her head in a small crown of curls and waved tightly at the sides with tiny little ringlets for bangs. Her powdered face looked stern, and her blue eyes cold and unforgiving. In a strange way, this madam reminded Glory of her prudish old maid aunt.

As soon as Deacon completed the introduction, Miss Rosie dismissed him. 'I should like to speak privately with . . . Miss St. Clair.' She spoke her name with a trace of scorn. The instant the door clicked shut behind him, the woman asked, 'How do you get your hair that color?' She walked over to take a closer look. For a moment, Glory thought she was going to check her roots.

'It's naturally this color. I don't do anything.'

'It's very pretty, but I expect you know that.' She walked behind her. 'Why don't you take off your coat, Miss St. Clair? It's never wise to get overheated.'

The hotel room was sparsely furnished with a bed, chest of drawers, and a chair. Except for the shaving mug and brush that sat beside the washbasin and pitcher on the chest of drawers. there was no other evidence that a man occupied the room.

Glory slipped off the muff and removed her coat, then laid them both on the bed next to the madam's garment. Like Miss Rosie, she too wore a shirtwaist blouse, only hers was made of silk in a shade of garnet that matched her skirt. Its style was more feminine, with ruffles around the scooped yoke and dainty tucks ringing the high collar. Satin bows banded its leg-of-mutton sleeves.

'Very pretty.' Miss Rosie surveyed her with a critical eye. 'I like my girls to dress fashionably. But you need to pull that corset another couple inches tighter. Men like a tiny waist.'

'I'll try to remember that,' Glory muttered, although the rigid whalebone ribbing was so constricting that she could hardly breathe in it now.

'How old are you?'

'Nineteen.'

'Where have you worked before?'

'At a restaurant down –'

'No, no. What saloon or bawdy house?'

'I haven't.' Glory watched with fascination as the woman deftly rolled a cigarette, slipped an end into a carved ivory holder, and lit it.

'What's your specialty?' She exhaled a stream of smoke through her pursed red lips. When she closed her mouth, twin trails of smoke came out of her nostrils. Glory wondered how she did that.

'My specialty? I don't think I know what you mean.'

'Is there anything you do other than fuck?'

'I can cook and sew –' Before Glory could continue, the woman started laughing.

'Deacon was right. You are new at this,' she declared. 'I meant with a customer – other than kissing and fondling.'

As much as she hated displaying her ignorance, Glory had to ask, 'What else is there?'

'You've never heard of the French trick?'

'No,' she admitted, feeling decidedly uncomfortable.

'That's sucking a man's cock until he comes. Some men like it better than fucking. Others like to screw a girl in the ass.' She flicked the ash from her smoldering cigarette into the brass spittoon that sat on the floor next to the chair. Glory had the distinct impression that Miss Rosie was deliberately speaking bluntly to embarrass her. And she was succeeding. Her face felt very warm indeed. 'Mostly it's the married men who want the other kind of sex,' Miss Rosie went on. 'I need to know what my girls are willing to do, so that my customers are happy and keep coming back.' Her smile became faintly taunting. 'How long have you been in the business?'

'A couple of months.'

'I suppose that explains why you haven't run into any requests like that. What do you use for protection?'

'Protection. You mean, like a gun?'

A raucous laugh burst from the woman. 'I mean to keep from getting pregnant or diseased.'

Glory turned red, again hating to admit her ignorance. 'I didn't know there was anything you could do to prevent it.'

Miss Rosie shook her head. 'You're green. I recommend to all my girls that they insert a sponge inside them. And all of them buy packages of condoms – rubber sheaths for the men to wear over their cocks. Some men object, but most of the time they'll buy them just to be sure they don't catch any disease.' She paused and studied Glory for a minute. 'Didn't the man that initiated you into all this tell you about such things? No, probably not. Was he the reason you got into this business?'

'Not exactly. I needed the money. It just seemed easy.' Glory was discovering that Deacon was right. There was a great deal she didn't know.

'But there was a man. There always is.'

'He went to the Klondike.' Although she was reluctant to discuss Justin with Miss Rosie, she also saw no reason to make a secret of him.

'I suppose he promised to come back after he struck it rich.

That's usually what they say. Was he the first man who made love to you?' Rosie seemed to interpret Glory's silence as one kind of answer. 'You never quite forget the first man, no matter how many men come afterward. I don't know why that is, but it's true. Either way, I'm glad you don't like girls. I have enough problems with Belle and Cheyenne Sue as it is. It's much easier to deal with jealous boyfriends than it is jealous women.'

Glory didn't know what she was talking about, but she decided not to admit it. The madam took a last puff on her cigarette, then extracted the butt from its ivory holder, and dropped it in the spittoon.

'The fee I charge my customers is three dollars. If they want one of my girls for the whole night, it's thirty dollars. I get half and you get half. You keep all the tips and get the commission on whatever liquor or condoms you can persuade him to buy. It will cost you seven dollars a week for your room. As soon as the doc checks you out and assures me you haven't got syphilis or some other disease, you can move your things over to the North Star Dance Hall.'

'I haven't even said I want to work for you.' Glory resented the woman's assumption.

'Do you?'

'No. I'm doing all right. And I certainly don't see why I should give half of what I earn to you.'

'How much do you make a night?'

'I've made as much as thirty dollars.' Only on two occasions, but Glory didn't tell her that.

'You'll make twice that working for me, maybe more if you aren't lazy. And I have men on the payroll who make sure none of the customers beat up any of my girls. There's some who enjoy doing that. You're lucky you haven't run into any of them yet. That pretty face of yours wouldn't be so pretty after they got finished with you.'

The comment prompted Glory to recall the stories her aunt had told her about the way her father had brutally abused her mother – beating her and breaking her arm. She recognized that there were men around capable of committing violent acts on women.

'Perhaps I was wrong about you, Miss St. Clair. Maybe you aren't as intelligent as you appear. You have the looks to attract a steady and wealthy clientele. You might even acquire the skill to

498

keep it. I am offering you a job where you can make twice the money you are earning now with considerably less risk of bodily harm or disease.' She took her coat off the bed, a fine seal jacket trimmed with silk passementerie and fringe. 'The rooming house where you live is not going to allow you to continue your night-time activities much longer. Soon you'll wind up in some one-room shack. Crib whores are the lowest. You may be inexperienced in the trade, Miss St. Clair. That is forgivable and easily rectified. We all began as novices. But inexperience is no excuse for stupidity.'

'I quite agree, Miss Rosie.' Glory walked over to the bed and picked up her own jacket. 'And I don't consider myself to be stupid. How soon can I make an appointment to see the physician you mentioned?'

Glory became one of Miss Rosie's girls and learned the finer points of her profession at the North Star Dance Hall. By springtime, when the first hordes of gold seekers descended on Skagway bound for the Klondike, there were nights when she netted as much as a hundred dollars from her drink commission, fees, and tips. And she was always able to make some money on the side by pointing out a customer with a hefty bankroll to Soapy Smith or one of his henchmen.

Soapy Smith and his gang of con men, gamblers, pickpockets, and outright thieves virtually controlled Skagway. Soapy made sure his men preyed only on those passing through and left the good citizens of Skagway alone. Jefferson Randolph 'Soapy' Smith even helped to build the first church in Skagway. He preached brains, not violence.

His reign of power, however, was short-lived. In July of 1898, he was confronted by a mob of angry citizens and killed in a gun battle, but not before he had fatally wounded the man who'd shot him – Frank Reid, the very man who had led others the previous summer to jump the claim of Captain Moore and sell lots in the renamed town of Skaguay.

The tenor of the town changed after his death. The constant flood of 'outsiders' bound for the goldfields along the Yukon kept business brisk, but money didn't flow as freely. By then there was a steady stream of people returning from the Klondike – most of them broke and disillusioned, with nothing to show for all the hardship they'd endured but calluses and loose belts.

Glory made a few inquiries about Justin, but no one seemed to have heard of him. She didn't know if he'd struck it rich, died on the trail as so many had, or had come limping back with his tail between his legs.

Those who had been there and returned had an older, wiser look about them. She could always distinguish the face of a veteran from that of a fresh, eager man who had yet to make the arduous trek over White Pass along the trail that had been nicknamed 'Dead Horse Trail' for the piles of carcasses and bones of pack animals that hadn't survived it.

Whenever she walked down the street attired in her latest gown, she wondered whether Justin would recognize her now – and whether he'd ever heard of Glory St. Clair and guessed who she was. By the winter of 1898-99, practically everyone who had ever passed through Skagway spread the word about the golden-haired Glory at the North Star Dance Hall. She was in the enviable position of being able to pick and choose whom she wished to bestow her favors on.

She had more clothes than she could possibly wear, all the latest fashions from San Francisco. Men lavished presents on her – everything from jewelry to a huge golden-eyed husky she called 'Nugget.' She received countless proposals of marriage, some from respectable businessmen. Yet she formed a lasting alliance with only one man. She had everything she could possibly want – money, clothes, popularity, and the companionship of a man she genuinely liked – still she felt restless.

Rain hammered at the windowpanes of the hotel suite. She covered her ears, trying to shut out the sound. 'I hate it when it rains.' It always reminded her of Sitka. 'I'd rather have blizzards or sleet than that incessant rain.' She glared at Deacon Cole as he calmly and precisely arranged the ace of hearts on the card trimmer, then pushed down the ivory-handled blade to shave a smidgeon off one side. 'I swear nothing ever bothers you,' Glory complained.

'Rain is a sign of spring.' He ran his thumb along the edge of the newly trimmed card, then inserted it in the deck.

'Spring.' She sighed and wondered if she should blame the season for her mood. 'I wish there was something to do, someplace to go.'

'Come here.' Deacon shuffled the deck of cards several times, then placed it on the table. 'Cut the deck and see if you can find an ace.'

Glory knew he had trimmed the edges of all four aces, making them a hair narrower than the rest of the cards in the deck, but her fingers couldn't detect the difference. Three times she cut the deck and three times she failed to reveal an ace.

'I give up.' She pushed the deck to him. He cut the deck four times in rapid succession, with no perceptible pause to feel the cards, and showed her all four aces.

'Now the kings.' He shuffled the cards again.

'You altered those, too?'

'The corners.' Again he showed her all four cards. Then he shuffled the deck and dealt out five hands, face up. In one were all four kings and another held all four aces. He gathered up the cards and repeated the procedure, this time changing the location of the hands that received the kings and aces.

Over the last year, she had watched him practice for countless hours – sometimes with 'strippers,' cards with their edges altered, or with a 'holdout,' a mechanical device sometimes concealed in a sleeve or a coatfront – until the moves were flawless. Always there was the sandpaper beside him to keep his fingers baby-smooth and sensitive. She stared at those long fingers that were equally sensitive and deft when they caressed her.

'Why do you cheat?' It was something she had often wondered. 'Is it that important to you to win?'

'Gambling is my profession, the way I earn my living. There are too many good players around to rely on skill and luck alone.' He put the four aces on the top of the deck and the four kings on the bottom, then proceeded to shuffle the cards – or appeared to do so as he practised the false shuffle. 'If a gambler doesn't know how to cheat, he's never going to know when he's being cheated.'

He turned over the top four cards and revealed the aces.

She moved to stand behind his chair and idly stroke the slope of his shoulders, feeling his muscles beneath his linen shirt. She watched his reflection in the mirror strategically positioned on the opposite side of the table from where he was seated so he could observe himself while he practised dealing 'seconds.'

But when Glory looked in the mirror, it was her image she studied instead of his. The tea gown was new – a loose, unboned gown of royal blue cashmere that fell in graceful folds from the shirred yoke. Wide malines lace poufed over the balloon sleeves and trailed from the shirred cuffs. Her hair was swept atop her head in a golden halo effect, a single lock drooping in a curl on her forehead. Her face was sparingly powdered to enhance her naturally smooth white skin. A touch of kohl accented the blackness of her eyes and the faintest hint of lip rouge gave color to the pouting fullness of her mouth.

She glanced at Deacon's reflection and saw that he was watching her, his face as expressionless as his hard blue eyes. Absently, she smoothed the crown of his coarse dark hair, wondering what he saw when he looked at her. He'd never given her money or bought her a single present. And she'd never wanted him to – not even the first time. It was crazy, she knew, but she didn't want to put a price on their friendship. She couldn't say that she loved him, but she trusted him. And that was crazy, too. He was a gambler and a cheat.

'I've heard rumors there's been a gold strike on the Nome River not far from Council City on the Seward Peninsula.' Deacon shifted his attention to the deck of cards in his hand. 'Supposed to be a big one. Some miners who lost out on the Klondike are making their way there.'

'Is that right?' She wondered if Justin would be one of them.

She hadn't forgotten him. Maybe what Miss Rosie had said was true – that a girl never forgot the first man. Glory knew she had never tried. In his note, Justin had said he'd come back after he'd struck it rich. Maybe he would. Men were such funny, proud creatures. It wouldn't have mattered to her whether he'd come back rich or not, but the Justin she remembered wouldn't have seen it that way. He'd keep looking for that gold until he found it.

'It looks like Nome City is going to be the next boomtown. Shouldn't be as hard to get to as the Klondike. It's located right on the coast of the Bering Sea. People are already buying tickets to be on the first steamer scheduled to leave in late spring.' He dealt out a hand from the bottom. 'I've got mine.'

'You're going!' The announcement took her by surprise.

'Skagway's becoming too civilized for me. The railroad will be finished soon. The town council's talking about installing electric lights. The Klondike boom is pretty well finished. A smart gambler always goes where the money is. It's time for me to be moving on.'

Glory moved away from his chair and wandered to the window. The rain continued to fall outside, like a thousand drumming fingers pelting the glass. 'It snows up there,' she murmured, then turned back to face the table. 'I don't suppose you'd like some company on the trip, would you? I'm getting tired of this town, too. A change of faces and scenery might be nice.'

As he dealt out the last card, he raised his left hand and wagged two slips of paper. 'I had a feeling you were getting restless so I booked passage for two.' He smiled, ever so faintly, and Glory laughed.

44 Nome
June 1899

The new gold region was located on the southern coast of the Seward Peninsula, the northwesternmost point of land on the North American Continent, which extends into the Bering Sea and forms the strait between Alaska and Russia. The camp itself was situated directly on the exposed seacoast near the entrance to Norton Sound.

The ice that clogged the Bering Sea in winter and isolated the gold camp at the mouth of the Snake River, broke up in June. On the twentieth, the first vessel anchored more than a mile offshore, the lack of a deep-water harbor preventing it from coming closer. All the passengers and freight were lightered ashore on shallow-draft barges, which were towed to within thirty feet of the beach, then allowed to drift on the breakers until they ran aground.

Dressed in her best travelling suit, Glory eyed with misgiving the remaining expanse of water to be crossed to reach the sandy beach. Other passengers, all men, splashed through the waves, wading the last few yards to shore, too anxious to reach the gold camp to worry about wet feet or clothes.

'Do you have any idea how much this suit cost me?' She sat down on the edge of the barge as Deacon hopped into the water. He looked amused as he paused to wait for her. 'I don't think it's funny.'

'Climb on my back and I'll carry you ashore,' he offered.

Struggling with the long skirts that tangled her legs, she finally managed to crawl onto his back and wrap her arms around his neck. He carried her piggy-back, slipping several times and nearly losing his footing in the knee-deep water. When they reached solid ground, he lowered her to the sand.

As she absently rearranged her skirts, she gazed at the pathetic excuse for a town, officially named Anvil City, but universally called Nome. A few cabins were built out of driftwood, but it was mainly a collection of tents. The setting was desolate. The so-called mountains beyond the beach looked to be no more than tall windswept hills, their tundra-covered slopes showing the green of early summer. There weren't any trees – not for a hundred miles.

'You've never been in a rough-and-tumble gold camp before, have you?' Deacon remarked.

His comment made Glory suspect that her expression had revealed her dismay at the surroundings. 'It's hardly a sight to cheer the soul.'

'Let's go look it over.' His hand cupped her elbow.

'What about my trunks?' She glanced back at the luggage being unloaded off the barge and set on the beach.

'Believe me, they aren't going anywhere,' he assured her dryly.

Winding trails weaved among the scattered tents and log shacks. If the town had a center, Glory decided it was well disguised. She didn't know how Deacon knew which meandering trail to take, but she trusted his instincts. Ragged, unshaven men stared at them as they passed dingy canvas tents pitched along the beach. The slop of footsteps in the mud and the low murmur of voices sounded behind them. Glory glanced back at the straggling bunch of men following them.

'Everyone's following us. We must be going in the right direction,' she murmured, holding her skirts high to keep the trailing hems out of the muck.

'They are following you, my sweet,' Deacon dryly informed her. 'Who knows how long it's been since some of them have seen a white woman – especially one such as you.' He paused on the trail, the grip of his hand checking her progress. His attention was centered on a large canvas tent. A carved wooden sign, weather-beaten and worn, was propped against its front wall. Its mud-splattered lettering was difficult to read, but the carved emblem, its yellow paint faded and chipped, resembled a twenty-dollar gold piece. 'The Double Eagle. I wonder . . .' Deacon murmured, then tightened his grip on her arm and propelled her toward the tent flap. 'Let's go in.'

There were only a few customers in the saloon, but they stopped talking when Glory and Deacon walked in. The furnishings were as crude and makeshift as the structure itself. Barrels, kegs, and crates served triple duty as chairs, shelves, and supports for the tables and the long wooden plank that was the bar.

A gray-haired man straightened from the bar, his dark suit and brocade vest setting him apart from the more roughly dressed men in the saloon. His glance shifted from Glory to Deacon and stopped. A frown flickered across his forehead as his gaze narrowed. He took the cigar from his mouth.

'Deacon,' he said hesitantly, then a smile broke across his face. 'I'll be damned if it isn't you.' He strode across the tent with a vigor that belied his gray hair. 'I should have known no one else would show up here sporting a lady like this on his arm.'

'I see you're still carting that sign around with you, Ryan.' Deacon warmly shook hands with him.

'It's my good-luck piece. Haven't gone broke with it yet. Last I heard you were in Skagway.' But his eyes strayed to Glory.

'Last I heard you were in Dawson,' Deacon replied, then turned slightly to include Glory. 'Meet Ryan Colby, proprietor of the Double Eagle saloon. I dealt faro for him in Juneau a few years back. May I present Miss Glory St. Clair.'

'I've heard of you, Miss St. Clair.' Colby bowed slightly, smiling. 'But then, who hasn't heard of Skagway's famed demimondaine. May I say that you are more beautiful than you have been described.'

'You may.' She smiled.

'This calls for a drink – on the house, of course. Let's go over by the stove.' He directed them toward the coal stove near the center of the tent. 'Hey, Pete, bring us some whiskey from my private stock,' he called to the man behind the crude bar. 'And get my chair from the back for the lady.'

Glory stood close to the heavy iron stove, enjoying the warmth it radiated after the briskness of the outdoor air. The number of kegs and crates positioned around the stove indicated the popularity of this particular area of the tent, even though none of them were occupied at the moment. The bartender came with the whiskey, and Ryan Colby passed the glasses to them.

'Welcome to Nome.' He toasted them, and Glory politely sipped her drink, appreciating the fire that warmed her insides, but not liking its taste. She had never quite figured out what men found to like about alcohol. 'Although I admit it doesn't look like much of a town.'

'Let's say it's unusual – like its name.' Glory cupped the small glass in her gloved hands. 'I presume there's a Mr. Nome.' In her experience, new towns in Alaska were always named after someone.

'As a matter of fact, there isn't. The popular opinion around here is that the name was derived from an Eskimo phrase – *Kn-no-me*, which means "I don't know." Supposedly, it was the reply an Eskimo made when someone asked him the name of this area. Actually it acquired the name quite by accident some years ago. An officer on a British ship in the area noticed that no name had been given on the map for a prominent point of land. So he wrote down on the map a question mark followed by the word "name," with the intention of later supplying one. Only he forgot. When a draftsman made a copy of that map, he misread it, thought the question mark was a "C" for Cape, and the "a" was an "o," and wrote down "Cape Nome." '

'That sounds more unbelievable than the Eskimo story,' Deacon remarked.

'The truth usually does, I've found.' The aging saloonkeeper tapped the ash from his cigar onto the tent's dirt floor. 'It won't be long before the name of this town will be on everyone's lips. Those three lucky Swedes struck pay dirt on Anvil Creek. All hell's gonna break loose here – and soon, too. The lumber for my new saloon should be on the ship that brought you here. I'll be needing a good faro dealer again, Deacon. Pay's a hundred dollars a week.'

'It's a generous offer, Ryan, but I have to decline. You see, I've persuaded Miss St. Clair to become my business partner. We're going to build our own establishment here.'

'And I was hopeful that I could convince Miss St. Clair to operate out of the Double Eagle. Considering how many have already shown up just to look at you, you could have been quite an attraction in my place.' He indicated the increased number of customers in his saloon, all standing at the bar and staring in Glory's direction. 'I don't suppose I could talk you into changing your minds.'

'No.' Ever since Deacon had suggested it, Glory had been intrigued by the idea of owning a place of her own. She had learned a lot working for Miss Rosie, and observed a few things she would do differently. Thanks to the big pot Deacon had won at poker and the money she'd managed to save despite her extravagant spending, they had the funds to do it – although she wasn't sure she would have picked Nome as the site if she'd known what it was like. Still, compared to what was here, their place would be a palace. And she'd never yet met a man who didn't like his comforts. If there was as much gold here as Ryan Colby intimated, they were bound to become rich.

'As a matter of fact, our building materials and supplies are being off-loaded from the ship,' Deacon informed him. 'If you have any suggestions on a possible location, we'd be interested in hearing them.'

'Take your pick. Just about every lot in town is up for grabs. There's as much lot jumping going on as there is claim jumping. A man's supposed to have forty days to make improvements on the lot he staked or lose it. But few people check to see if the time's expired. They just build where they want and worry about who rightfully has claim to it later – like any boomtown. You know the way it works – possession is nine-tenths of the law. He who has, usually keeps.'

'I'd rather have title to the land than trust the law to give it to me,' Glory said. There had been too many occasions in her family's past when they'd lost property because of the law – or the absence of it.

'It was just a suggestion.' Ryan shrugged indifferently. 'I know Deacon's a gambler who likes to play the odds. I know a few who've staked out lots on speculation. In the meantime, you'll be needing a place to stay. Nome is short on accommodations. You're welcome to my private sleeping quarters in the back of the tent until you get your place built, Miss St. Clair. You're liable to find it a bit noisy at night, but I expect you're used to it.'

'That's very generous of you. Mr. Colby.'

'Not at all. It won't take long for the word to spread to those women-starved miners in the hills that Glory St. Clair is at the Double Eagle. They'll be coming here to spend their gold. This place is going to be so full you won't be able to turn around.'

'Then Deacon and I will have ample opportunity to advertise our new business.'

'So you will.' He saluted her quickness, then looked beyond her. 'At last, here comes Pete with your chair. A ship's carpenter-turned-prospector made it for me to settle his account. I think you'll find it's very comfortable.' As Glory turned, she noticed a portly white-haired man walking toward them before her attention

508

was distracted by the bartender carrying a finely crafted leather-upholstered chair. 'I'd tell you the man's name, but I'm afraid you'd steal him from me, and I need him to build my new bar,' Ryan said. 'Set the chair by the stove, Pete.'

As Glory admired the chair's intricately carved back, highly polished to bring out the wood's grain, she heard someone speaking to Deacon behind her.

'I don't mean to intrude,' the man said. 'But I'm afraid I've been eavesdropping on your conversation. I heard you mention that you were interested in purchasing a lot on which to build. Permit me to introduce myself. My name's Gabe Blackwood, attorney at law.'

If a thunderbolt had struck her, Glory couldn't have been more stunned. Everything stopped. She couldn't move. She couldn't breathe. She couldn't speak. She was numb with shock, wondering if she had heard correctly. Had he really said he was Gabe Blackwood? Could there possibly be two men with that name? She'd always been led to believe her father had left Alaska and gone back to the States, taking the Tarakanov family treasures with him. Could it be him? Was this man the father she'd never seen?

She turned slowly, tightening her grip on the shot glass of whiskey, surprised she hadn't dropped it. The man wore a billed fur cap with the ear flaps turned up, revealing the white hair she had noticed earlier. His clothes looked well made if slightly soiled, although the latter was to be expected in this town.

Her father would have been in his later fifties. This man could be that – or more. It was difficult to tell. Excessive consumption of alcohol had a way of aging a man beyond his years, and there were indications that this man drank heavily. But, then, her father had drunk a lot, too.

'Excuse me.' Glory interrupted Deacon's conversation with the man. 'Did I hear you say that you knew of some property for sale, Mr. . . . Blackwood, was it?'

'That's correct, ma'am. Gabriel Thornton Blackwood, attorney.' He doffed his hat.

'Miss Glory St. Clair.' She extended her hand, and he bowed over it. Glory recalled that her mother had often remarked about how gallant her father was.

She searched his face, trying to find a resemblance to an old tintype she'd once seen. She'd found it while going through a

509

trunk of her mother's things shortly after she'd died. It had been a picture of her father with Secretary Seward and several townspeople. Her aunt had subsequently destroyed the tintype, but that image of her father – the only one she'd ever seen – had remained in her mind. She tried to match it to the man in front of her.

His fair skin was flushed with drink. She could smell the liquor on his breath. His hazel eyes were bloodshot with wrinkled, saclike pouches weighting the lower lids. A network of blue veins crisscrossed his nose, running close to the surface of his skin. His cheeks were round, and a pointed yellow-white beard covered his chin. Maybe it covered a receding chin, Glory couldn't tell. The man in the tintype had been younger, thinner.

'Are you from Alaska, Mr. Blackwood?'

'No. I've only recently arrived from San Francisco via Council City. I'm representing some clients with mining interests in the area.'

'Then this is your first trip to Alaska.'

His hesitation lasted no longer than it took for him to glance at some person behind Glory. Ryan Colby was the only one it could be. 'No, I've been to this great land before. The Juneau area mainly.'

Something stopped her from asking if he'd ever been to Sitka, even though she was certain in her heart that this man was her father. After all these years, she'd finally met him. But she didn't know what she felt. Confused mostly. Did she hate him? How could she love someone she had never known?

According to her aunt, this was the man who had wanted her dead even before she was born. This was the man who had abandoned her mother, left her penniless and alone with a baby on the way – the man who had stolen all the silver objects her great-grandfather had made, who had never come back to see the child he'd fathered.

Glory remembered her mother's great loneliness, the way she had always blamed herself for his desertion. Glory resented him for that – and for her years of growing up without a father, with little food on the table and clothes stitched from her mother's worn-out dresses on her back. She had hated that life, the starkness of it, the lack of warm, tender feelings, and the misery of not being allowed to love or laugh.

If he had stayed, how different it all might have been. With a

510

father to love and care for her, she'd probably never had come to this Godforsaken place in the wilds of the north.

But, likely as not, she never would have had all those trunks of beautiful clothes or the sack of money tucked in the bodice of her corset. Truthfully, Glory didn't know whether to thank him or to slap him. So she did neither.

'You have already met my partner, Mr. Cole, haven't you?' But she talked right over his affirmative response. 'We are interested in acquiring a lot in Nome on which to build. I think it is very fortunate that one of the first persons we meet turns out to be a lawyer. I feel it is so important to have legal title to land, and who better to insure that than an attorney. You will help us, won't you, Mr. Blackwood?'

'I should be delighted.' He stood straighter, his chest puffing slightly, obviously flattered by the importance with which she regarded him. 'You are very wise to engage legal counsel in this matter, Miss St. Clair, especially here in Nome. As is the case in so many boomtowns, the letter of the law is frequently disregarded. In my opinion, most of the mining claims filed around Nome are invalid.'

'Why?'

'Because the Swedes that supposedly discovered the gold and filed claims on all these gold-bearing creeks in their own names as well as those of their friends and families are not American citizens. They're foreigners and therefore not eligible to locate mining claims on American soil. As I have told many of the American miners here, it is my belief that these aliens have no right to the gold here. The land and its minerals belong to Americans.'

'How very interesting,' Glory murmured. 'Are you married, Mr. Blackwood?'

'Gracious no,' he answered quickly, startled by her question. Then he assumed an expression of deep regret. 'I am a widower. My wife died many years ago. A beautiful woman she was, of Russian descent. God rest her soul.' The words sounded rehearsed to Glory, with no feeling behind them. She wondered if he even knew her mother was dead. 'Why do you ask?' He frowned.

'I wondered if you would dine with Mr. Cole and myself this evening. From what you have said, there is much we need to know about our new town and many matters on which we'll need your advice. Since we have only just arrived and aren't familiar with the dining facilities in Nome, perhaps you would be kind enough to select a place.'

'It would be my pleasure.'

'Good. We will meet you here at seven.' With a half-turn, she smiled at the saloon's proprietor as he rolled the cigar in his mouth. 'Mr. Colby has graciously offered us accommodations here.' She glanced at Deacon. His features were too well schooled to show any expression, yet she knew he questioned her actions and her interest in Gabe Blackwood, but she had no intention of enlightening him. 'I will want to change for dinner, Deacon. Perhaps we should return to the beach and make arrangements to have our trunks transported here to the saloon.'

'Perhaps we should.' His tone indicated a concession to her wishes rather than an endorsement of them.

She faced Gabe Blackwood again. 'Until seven, then, Mr. Blackwood?' She gave him her hand.

'Seven.' He continued to hold her hand as he stared at her with a vague look of puzzlement. 'Have we met before, Miss St. Clair? I have the feeling I've seen you somewhere.'

She experienced a little rush of satisfaction. 'If you've ever been in Skagway, it's possible you've seen me, but I'm sure we haven't met before, Mr. Blackwood. I would have remembered you.' She withdrew her hand from his grasp and turned, setting her drink on top of a wooden keg. 'Gentlemen.' She nodded to both men, then took Deacon's arm and walked at his side to the tent flap.

Everyone watched her leave, including Ryan and Gabe. At the bar, several men gulped down their drinks and hurried after her, not wanting to let her out of their sight.

Ryan lowered his cigar, smiling wryly. 'There goes my business. Not that I blame them. She's quite a beauty.'

'She looks so familiar to me,' Gabe murmured as if thinking out loud. 'It's something in the way she holds her head . . . or carries herself like –'

'– like a princess.' Ryan missed the startled look Gabe threw at him. 'As prostitutes go, I suppose she is a queen of sorts. One thing I do know, though, when the gamblers and whores arrive, that's a sure sign this place is going to prosper.'

He glanced at the man he'd journeyed to Alaska with so many years ago and absently wondered why a woman like Glory St.

Clair had been so captivated by Gabe Blackwood, practically hanging on his every word. He had to concede that neither age nor alcohol had dulled the glibness of Blackwood's tongue. He could still fire a man's sense of injustice with his oratories.

His speeches on America for Americans went over big with the vast majority of miners, who had arrived too late and discovered that a half dozen Scandinavians had staked mining claims on virtually the entire area. To add insult to injury, the Scandinavians weren't even experienced prospectors. A couple of them had been reindeer herders. Yet, in less than a month of prospecting, these greenhorn aliens had found pay dirt. It didn't set well with men who had looked for gold half their lives.

'You've changed, Gabe,' Ryan remarked.

'What makes you say that?' He stiffened.

Ryan knew that while they might be old acquaintances, they were not old friends. If anything, Gabe resented the things Ryan knew about his past.

'There was a time when you wouldn't have anything to do with sin and corruption. Yet tonight you're going to have dinner with a whore and a gambler.' Ryan chuckled to himself as he moved away.

With the assistance of Gabe Blackwood, Glory and Deacon had managed in less than two weeks to acquire possession of a prime lot on the main thoroughfare of Nome, called Front Street. Construction had begun on their building almost immediately. Still, Glory came up with a variety of excuses to seek Gabe Blackwood's counsel, and she conferred with him on nearly every detail, regardless of Deacon's protests.

Summer in Nome brought twenty-four hours of daylight and allowed building to continue around the clock. At half past ten in the evening, Glory stood in front of the building site and inspected the progress being made by the carpenters presently framing in the structure's second story. The high collar of her multi-tiered shoulder cape of shamrock green wool with gold piping grazed her chin as she turned her head to gaze at the elderly man on her right, her arm companionably linked with his.

'I am so relieved that you don't feel the workers should be any further along than they are.' She leaned closer to make herself heard above the pounding of the hammers and the breaking of

513

the surf on the nearby beach. 'I always wonder if they're actually working while I'm sleeping. It would be so easy for them to take advantage of the situation.'

'Well, you can rest assured that this time it isn't the case.' He patted the gloved hand that lay along his forearm.

'My partner knows so little about such things. I confess I didn't know who else I could ask except you.'

'It is my pleasure, as always.' He paused, frowning slightly. 'Where is your partner this evening?'

'In the midst of a poker game at the Double Eagle.'

'For your sake, I hope he isn't losing.'

'When I left, he had a tall stack of chips in front of him. Deacon is very lucky. He rarely loses. Of course, he's an excellent player who believes you don't have to cheat to win,' Glory lied. 'Once the local people realize that he runs honest tables, our place should be very popular.'

'Then this will be a gambling hall and saloon. I was never quite clear on that.'

'No, not exactly. There will be gambling and liquor on the premises, but we intend to operate the Palace as a kind of private club. A place where a man can relax, have a quiet drink or two, play cards or dice, and enjoy the company of a beautiful woman if he chooses. It won't be for the ordinary man on the street. Some I've met haven't bathed in months. That isn't the sort of customer we want,' Glory declared. 'We hope to attract gentlemen such as yourself.'

She'd heard about such clubs that catered to people with money. Whether it was called a club or saloon, the cost of doing business was practically the same. As far as she was concerned it made more sense to call it a club. They could charge more for the drinks; the price for female company would be higher; and more money could be won at the gaming tables. She'd seen some of the gold dust and nuggets the miners were taking out of the mountain streams. A man with money always felt he was entitled to the best. She intended to convince him he was getting it at the Palace.

'You are such a lovely, intelligent girl. You don't belong in this business.' His graying brows were drawn together in an intensely earnest frown. 'A woman like you should be married to a fine, upstanding young man.'

'Unfortunately, the young man I met was neither fine nor

514

upstanding. By the time I realized that, I was ruined. No decent man wants a fallen woman for a wife.' Very early, Glory had learned that men preferred such stories to the truth. 'If I had met someone like you, I wouldn't be here today.'

'Now you're flattering an old man,' he chided, but she noticed he stood a little taller. She had also noticed that lately he took more pains with his appearance – always neatly dressed, his cheeks shaven, his beard trimmed. He was not so old that his interest wasn't aroused by the attention she'd been paying him.

'You're not old,' she protested, hugging his arm a little tighter. 'I never think of you that way. You look much too wise and distinguished, like some important person – a governor maybe.' She laughed softly while closely watching his reaction. 'Imagine me on the arm of a governor.'

His expression softened with melancholy as he gazed at her. 'Any governor would be proud to have you at his side, Glory. May I call you Glory?'

'If I may call you Gabe.'

He smiled. Of common accord, they started walking, moving away from the din of hammer and saw and strolling leisurely in the direction of the Double Eagle.

'I once dreamed of becoming governor of Alaska,' he mused aloud.

'You could still become governor, couldn't you?' She eyed him curiously.

'I don't think so.'

'Now you're being modest. I'm not the only one who comes to you for advice. The miners listen to you as well. I've seen them. No one in Alaska has ever truly emerged as a leader. I've heard that's why Congress has always appointed an outsider to serve as governor.' Actually, she hadn't heard any such thing, but no man expected a woman to know much about politics. 'You could be that man.'

'I'm flattered by your confidence in me, but I'm afraid it will take more than that.'

'Yes, you do need money. It's ironic, isn't it, to talk of money when those mountains are littered with gold.' She gazed at the mountains a short distance from the beach, bathed in the golden light of the midnight sun. Splashes of summer wildflowers created a picturesque patchwork. 'And practically all of it is in the hands of a bunch of foreigners. Surely something can be done about it.

What about that young lieutenant the Army sent here from the military post at St. Michael?'

'I spoke with Lieutenant Spalding shortly after he arrived in Nome. He has only a small squad of soldiers under his command. His sole responsibility is to maintain order. He has no authority to settle mining disputes.'

'If the mining claims of these foreigners are illegal, as you say, why doesn't someone call a meeting of all the miners and declare all previous claims to be voided? Then everyone would have a chance to stake new claims. It seems fair to me, but I'm sure you know more than I do.'

'If such a thing were done, there would be a stampede into those hills. Everyone would be fighting over the same claims.'

'I suppose it would be a matter of who got there first. It's a shame that someone like you never gets the bonanza gold. You would put the money to good use instead of squandering it in gambling halls and sporting houses.' She laughed shortly. 'Deacon is fond of saying that a person makes his own luck. I'm not sure that's true. If it were, I'd be a governor's wife.'

'Speaking of your partner, here he comes now.' With a nod of his head he directed her attention to the tall, spare man in the somber black coat moving toward them with a slow, measured stride. Gabe Blackwood turned back to her and said, 'I shall bid you good night and leave you in his capable hands. As always, the time spent with you has been a joy to me, Glory.' He lifted her gloved hand to his lips.

'For me as well, Gabe.' She watched him walk away, saw him tip his hat to Deacon as he passed.

'You were with him again.' Deacon turned to look at the man's back. 'I'll be damned if I know what you see in him. He isn't rich, so it can't be that. He's a garrulous old windbag, so it can't be his stimulating conversation. So what is it?'

'He interests me.'

'That's obvious. But what isn't obvious is why.'

'Maybe I simply feel sorry for him. After all, he is an old man with no family.' It was something she couldn't even explain to herself, not logically anyway. She hated him for many reasons. Yet she was curious about him, too. She wanted to know what he was like, how he thought, what he dreamed – and where he was vulnerable. She had already discovered he was easy to lead, just like tonight when she'd fed him all that talk about making a good

516

governor and hinting that the miners and their gold could give him the financial backing he would need. Sometimes she wanted to hurt him and sometimes . . . Sometimes she just wished things had been different. A stiff breeze blew in off the sea and lifted the wool layers of her tiered cape as she glanced at Deacon. 'What happened to your poker game? Did your fellow players get tired of losing?'

'Something like that.'

She noticed the Eskimo woman standing patiently behind him. She was a short, stout woman, who was made to look even stouter by the parka-like coat made from striped cloth and a thick pair of mukluks on her feet. Her head was uncovered, the coat's hood lying in thick folds around her neck. The breeze whipped strings of black hair onto her forehead and round cheeks.

'Who's your friend?' Glory smiled wryly at Deacon. 'Maybe you'd like to explain what you see in *her*?'

'Oh, yes. I almost forgot.' He glanced over his shoulder and motioned with his hand for the woman to step forward. She did so, smiling shyly at Glory. 'Actually, I was bringing her to you. This is your new maid. I won her in that poker game.'

'You what?'

'She was part of the winnings. You see, this old sourdough didn't have enough money to call my bet, but he was convinced he had a winning hand. So he put up this Eskimo woman and swore she could cook, sew, and keep house.'

'Do you mean she was his wife?'

'No. He claimed he picked her up in Kotzebue so he could have a woman to do his cooking and sewing through the winter – and keep him warm at night, I suppose, although he didn't say that. Either way, I won her. You're going to need somebody. I thought you might as well train one of the natives here to be your housekeeper, maid, cook, or whatever you want. She does speak some English.'

'That's a relief.' Glory knew that Deacon was right. Eventually she was going to need a maid of some sort. Still she eyed the Eskimo woman uncertainly. 'Does she have a name?'

'Matty,' the woman answered, tapping her chest. 'Me called Matty.'

'Well, my name is Glory St. Clair. Do you think you would like to work for me, Matty?'

'You betcha, Missy Glory. Work hard. Work good.'

45

The white canvas sides and roof of the tent screened out the brilliance of the midmorning sun while allowing the interior to be illuminated by its refracted rays. Glory sat on a pillow-cushioned keg, still dressed in her white linen nightgown, its vee-shaped neckline ruffled with stand-up lace. Her hands lay folded in her lap, nearly hidden by the wide lace trim on the sleeve's snug-fitting cuffs. Her eyes were closed and her head bobbed with the rhythmic strokes of the hairbrush as Matty pulled it through her waist-length hair, brushing out the cornmeal used to clean it.

Her scalp tingled from the raking bristles, yet the brushing was soothing and restful. It seemed to ease the loneliness that had plagued her of late. She thought it strange to feel lonely when she was surrounded by hordes of men anxious to keep her company. And there was Deacon to hold her at night so she wouldn't have to sleep alone – or at least on the nights when he wasn't playing in some marathon poker game. Strong, quiet, undemanding Deacon, always there if she needed him, never judging. Yet there was a void he didn't fill.

It was an ache that wouldn't go away. She'd been conscious of it ever since she met Gabe Blackwood, her blackguard of a father. It was like being homesick, which was ridiculous. She never wanted to go back to Sitka or that life where she had known real loneliness. She sighed wearily.

The brush paused in midstroke. 'I pull hair. Hurt Missy.'

'No. You're doing just fine, Matty.' Actually, the Eskimo woman was more of a help than Glory had first thought possible.

Granted there was much that Matty still had to learn, but after less than a week, Glory wondered how she had managed without her. She was smart and quick to learn. Glory rarely had to show her how to do something more than once. She was easygoing, quick to smile or laugh – even at herself. Glory remembered the day Matty had tried on her Gainsborough hat with the ostrich plumes and spotted veil. She had been such a ludicrous sight that Glory hadn't been able to contain her laughter. But it hadn't mattered, because Matty laughed at her reflection in the mirror, too. By the time they had stopped laughing, Glory had busted the lace of her corset. She had never laughed like that with anyone, certainly never with another woman. Of course, Matty was of the opinion that she laced her corset much too tight, and she helped her with the greatest reluctance, always scolding her in the process.

With the exception of her mother, Glory had never been close to another woman. While she was able to see that her Aunt Eva had loved her in her own perverse way, the restrictions Eva had imposed had been too severe. There had been too much resentment for Glory to feel a strong attachment to her aunt. And Glory hadn't been friendly with any of Miss Rosie's girls. There had been too much rivalry between them.

Deacon was the only person she both trusted and respected. He was her business partner and her bed partner, but they shared little else. Yet she had shared many things with Justin Sinclair – all her dreams and desires, her frustrations and resentments. He had known all about her past – who and what she was, and where she came from. Looking back, she saw the way they had struggled together and huddled close for warmth in the drafty room. In so many ways, he had set her free, shown her a new way of life and taught her the pleasures of her body. There had been a strong bond between them. When he left without her, she'd been hurt, but she'd never forgotten him.

Glory attempted to break out of her self-pitying mood, and she opened her eyes to gaze at the standing mirror. Absently she studied the Eskimo woman's image in the reflecting glass – the flatness of her profile, the pertness of her small nose, the roundness of her plump cheeks.

There were so few details that she knew about Matty. The woman was twenty-five. She'd had a husband and a son. Both had died from the white man's diseases that had decimated the Eskimo population. During the last couple of years, Matty had lived with one white man or another, mostly prospectors looking for gold in the northern streams and tributaries of the Yukon River. Glory realized that Matty was probably lonely, too.

519

'Do you have any family, Matty? Brothers? Sisters?'

'No. Me have none. Mother's people in village way far. Me never see.'

'What about your father and his people?'

'Him white man.'

'Then you're half white.' Glory stared at Matty's reflection, searching her predominantly Eskimo features for some indication of her mixed ancestry, but she found no evidence of it.

'Him a whaler. Him a captain,' she asserted importantly. 'Take many women from village. Him pick mother. Him old man but him good to mother. Her like him much. Her sad when him leave. Her happy when me come.'

'Did you ever see him?' Glory wondered if Matty had grown up as she had – without a father.

'Him no come back. Me named for him.'

'What was his name?'

'Captain Stone.'

'Stone.' Glory turned on her seat to stare incredulously at the woman. 'Not Caleb Stone?' No, it couldn't be, she realized. He would have died long ago. But the name triggered memories of the countless stories her aunt had told her about their family history. Without thinking, she recited the facts she'd been told in connection with Caleb Stone. 'Tasha's granddaughter, Larrisa, married a Yankee captain named Caleb Stone and went away with him on his ship. The family never saw her again.' Possibly she remembered it because it had sounded so romantic or because her ancestor had escaped from Sitka, as she had wanted to do. 'Later they learned she had died. Wait a minute.' She clutched excitedly at Matty's arm. 'She had a son. It was the son who came back and told the family. He was a whaler. His name was Matthew . . . Matthew Edmund Stone.'

'Me Matthew. Same like him.'

'Matthew . . . Matty. My God, do you realize what this means?' Glory laughed in disbelief, then clasped a hand over her mouth to silence it. It was almost more than she could take in at one time. She reached for the hand that held the hair brush and curved both her hands around it. 'You and I are related, Matty. We're cousins . . . three or four times removed, probably, but – Isn't it astounding? I can hardly believe it.'

'You are cousin to me?' Matty repeated uncertainly.

'Yes.' Glory nodded. 'We're family. Your father would have

been my great-grandfather's first cousin – or something like that. I just know that you're Tasha's great-great-granddaughter and I'm her great-great-great-granddaughter.' She laughed again, delighted by the discovery.

It didn't bother her that Matty was half Eskimo. Glory supposed she owed that to her aunt, who had never let her be ashamed of her own mixed blood.

'Your father wasn't white,' she told Matty. 'He was part American, part Russian, and part Aleut. I'm all three of those plus Tlingit.' She moved her head from side to side in a gesture of continued amazement. 'Matty, I'm so glad Deacon won you in that poker game. We might never have met otherwise.'

'Me glad, too,' Matty replied solemnly. 'Have job now. Have family now.'

'Yes.' Although she had said the same before, Glory was moved by the words coming from Matty's lips. Tears welled in her eyes. 'We both have family now.'

The canvas flap was lifted aside and Deacon ducked through the opening. He paused inside, letting the curtain-like partition fall back in place. Glory blinked to clear her eyes. 'Were the workmen on the job?' He had left earlier to check on the building site.

'Yes. They'll be starting the finish work day after tomorrow.' He looked so fresh despite an all-night poker game. Briefly she marveled at the indefatigable energy that allowed him to go so long without sleep and show no ill effects. 'You'll need to meet with the paperhanger this afternoon. I ran into a friend of yours.'

'Who?' She was conscious that Matty had resumed brushing her hair.

'Your Mr. Blackwood. He asked to see you. He's waiting outside.'

She hadn't seen him since the morning before the ill-fated miners' meeting nearly two weeks ago. 'Tell him' – she began stiffly, then reconsidered the refusal she'd been about to make – 'to come in. Fetch my wrapper, Matty. And a ribbon for my hair.'

As Deacon lifted the canvas and stepped through the opening to the other side, Matty brought the amethyst wrapper and helped Glory slip into it. While Glory buttoned the front of it, Matty tied a matching ribbon around her hair.

Gabe Blackwood entered the private quarters and doffed his

521

hat, holding it in front of him. 'Good morning. I hope I'm not disturbing you.'

Leaving the bottom buttons of the wrapper's skirt unfastened, Glory turned to face him. 'You have disturbed me more by your absence. It's been so long since I've seen you I was beginning to wonder if you meant it when you said you enjoyed my company.' After continually making up reasons to see him, she had deliberately stopped the practice to see if he would come to her.

'I thought you had finally tired of mine.'

'That is hardly the case.' She assumed her most charming smile and gestured to the leather-covered chair next to one of her trunks. 'Please, come in and sit down.' He hesitated, his glance darting to Matty, dislike flickering in his expression. Taking the cue that he didn't want her present, Glory suggested, 'Matty, see if Mr. Colby has some coffee, and bring us two cups.'

Gabe watched her leave the partitioned quarters before he ventured over to the chair. 'I don't like the idea of you having that Indian around. You can't trust any of them. They lie and cheat, and they'll steal from you, too, if you don't watch them.'

'Matty is Eskimo, not Indian.' Glory repeated the distinction so frequently made by Eskimo natives.

'It's the same thing.' He did not appear pleased by her defense of the woman.

'Not to an Eskimo.' Long aware of his prejudice, she smiled, pretending to tease him. 'What if I were to tell you that Matty isn't full-blooded Eskimo? Her father was a Yankee whaler.' She was tempted to tell him that she and Matty were related, but she didn't want to reveal her identity to him.

'Breed or Indian, it makes no difference. I have no time for the nonsense preached by bleeding hearts like Sheldon Jackson about the white man's mistreatment of Alaskan Indians. They're a worthless bunch of good-for-nothings that should be shipped off to a reservation somewhere.'

Glory gave him a wide-eyed look. 'I never realized you felt so strongly about it.'

'None of them can be trusted. If we could get rid of them, there would be no more need for the Army to be here. The military's been the bane of Alaska right from the start. We don't need some snot-nosed lieutenant from the Army telling us what we can or cannot do. We are fully capable of governing ourselves without any interference from them.'

'I heard about the miners' meeting.' Glory sat down on the trunk next to his chair.

'Then you know we were ordered to disperse at bayonet point.' His anger over the incident was still fresh. 'That upstart of a lieutenant actually threatened to use force to clear the tent and forbade the holding of any more meetings.'

He omitted mentioning that the purpose of the meeting had been to nullify all existing mining claims in the district and declare the creeks open for restaking. Nor did he tell her that he and a few of his cronies had arranged for some friends to camp on Anvil Mountain and watch for a bonfire signal advising them the deed had been accomplished, so they could stake the best of the claims for themselves. But Glory knew of their plan. She'd made it her business to know about anything and everything Gabe Blackwood was involved in.

'I know the Army has since issued orders that no one is permitted to carry pistols or revolvers,' Glory remarked.

'It's an order impossible to enforce. Broke miners from the Klondike are arriving in Nome by the hundreds. The decks of every steamer coming down the Yukon are packed with them. No one, and certainly not a handful of soldiers, is going to be able to disarm those seasoned sourdoughs. And, believe me, after missing out on the Klondike, they aren't too happy about arriving here and finding that all the paying claims have been staked by some foreigners. They feel they have a right to jump those claims and I don't blame them.'

'You've been very busy lately trying to settle disputes between owners before they erupted into bloodshed. At least, that's what I've been told.' She'd also heard that a lot of the claim jumping was simply a means of blackmail, since the real owner preferred to pay off the jumper rather than have his claim tied up until a judge could hear the case. At the moment, the only judge was in Sitka. No one knew for sure when he'd be coming here.

'Is that why you haven't been by to see me?' he asked.

'When you had so many important matters to occupy your time, it wouldn't have been right for me to force my company on you.' She studied her primly folded hands, avoiding his curious gaze.

'My dear, you have never forced your company on me.' The chair creaked under his shifting weight as he leaned toward her. 'When you come by to see me, it has always been the highlight of my day. I look forward to your coming.'

'You have no idea how much it means to me to hear you say that. I want so much for you to like me.' The quiver in her voice was genuine. Glory knew that what she said was true. Regardless of how much she hated him for the way he'd treated her mother, abandoning her and their unborn child, she wanted him to like her – to truly become fond of her. She wanted to know he could care for her. Yet, crazily, she wanted to see him destroyed, too. She knew it was within her power to do it – if she wanted to.

'I do like you, Glory, very much.' He covered her hands with his own, as if trying to impress upon her the sincerity of his words. 'Almost from the first moment we met, I have felt close to you. You have come to mean a great deal to me. Truly, I mean that.'

Feigning agitation, she pulled free of his hands and rose to her feet, taking a step away and hearing the creak of his chair that signaled he had risen also. 'People in town are talking about us. You know that, don't you?' She paused, conscious of him standing behind her. 'They say we're having an affair.'

'What nonsense! I have never done more than kiss your hand.'

'I know that.' She swung around to face him. 'But remember who I am. If you saw a well-known prostitute in the company of the same man day after day, would you believe their relationship was platonic? No, I don't think so. And neither do they.'

'You mustn't let their wagging tongues upset you.' He gently took hold of her shoulders.

'Don't you see, it isn't me I'm worried about. It's you. The future governor of Alaska shouldn't be seen with the notorious Glory St. Clair. As soon as I heard what the gossips were saying, I realized I shouldn't see you any more.'

'I didn't know you thought so much of me.'

'I do.' She took hold of both his hands. 'I never wanted to hurt you, Gabe. Believe that. I only wanted you to like me as a person, as a human being with feelings and needs like everyone else. You've always treated me with courtesy and respect. You'll never know how much that means to me, Gabe.'

'My sweet, lovely girl. You have not hurt me. You have given me too much joy. Let people talk. I don't care a whit what they say.'

'You're just saying that to make me feel better.' She drew back to look at him, a faint pout on her lips.

'If I were concerned about what people might say, I wouldn't be here now. A half dozen people saw me enter your quarters a few minutes ago.'

'You know what they think we're doing back here, don't you?' She smiled in her naughtiest fashion.

'I believe I do.'

'Why, Gabe, I do believe you're blushing.' She laughed. 'Is that what you'd like to do with me?'

'I believe you are teasing me, Miss St. Clair.'

Although her suggestion had obviously made him a little uncomfortable, she saw the look in his eye – the hesitant desire of an old man uncertain of his ability to perform. She could get him into bed. She had learned her trade too well not to know how to coax a man into bed. With older men, especially the straitlaced ones, it was almost like bedding a virgin; both had to be babied along. Which was why she avoided both when she could.

She let go of his hands before he felt her shudder of revulsion. 'It was naughty of me, wasn't it?' She smiled as she moved away, walking over to the keg by the bed and picking up a pack of Turkish cigarettes. From the saloon side of the tent, several voices were raised in excitement, but Glory was too used to the noisy carrying-on to pay any attention to it.

'What do you suppose all that commotion is about?' Gabe wondered.

'Maybe somebody's winning at the faro table.' Glory shrugged and struck a match. As she held the flame to the tip of the cigarette, Matty returned carrying two tin mugs of coffee. Glory took a puff on the cigarette to light it, then exhaled the smoke to blow out the flame. 'What's the excitement out front, Matty?'

'Man come. Him say him find gold in sand.' She set the coffee on the crate that served as a table.

'Gold? On the beach? Don't tell me people are believing a story like that?' Glory scoffed and at the same moment noticed that the voices had receded.

'Everybody leave, go see,' Matty replied.

Curious, Glory stepped to the opening and pushed part of the canvas back to see into the saloon. It was deserted. Through the raised tent flap of the entrance, she could see a steady flow of people going by, headed in the direction of the beach.

She glanced back at Gabe. 'Do you suppose it could be true?'

'Traces of gold have been found in beach sands in other places along the Seward Peninsula,' he said. 'Prospectors use it as an indication of possible gold locations inland.'

Glory stared again at the miners going by the tent. 'Let's go see what they found.'

She crossed the room, dropping her freshly lit cigarette in the coffee cup as she passed the crate, and grabbed up a shawl from a pile of clothes on a trunk. 'Are you coming?'

She ignored the disapproval in his expression at her failure to dress before venturing into the streets. As far as she was concerned, she was decently clad. She swept the shawl around her shoulders and started for the opening with Matty on her heels. Reluctantly, Gabe followed.

Once on the street, they were quickly swept into the human current flowing toward the beach. The skeptics strolled leisurely, snickering at the believers who dodged and darted through the crowd, rushing to get there first. The ones who were neither skeptics nor believers, but caught somewhere in between, like Glory, walked swiftly, equally afraid of committing themselves in case there was no gold and afraid of missing out if there was. Like lemmings, they never wavered from their course to the sea.

The beach area immediately outside of town was strewn with small tents pitched by destitute miners recently arrived from the Klondike. Their camps were already overrun with people digging in the sand when Glory reached them. She quickened her pace, seeking a less crowded area to avoid the pushing and shoving.

She saw a bearded sourdough scoop up some sand in his gold pan and take it down to the sea's edge. As he crouched down, squatting on his heels to wash the sand in the metal pan, Glory hurried onto the wet wave-packed sand to observe the outcome. She hovered behind him, watching over his shoulder while he patiently sloshed the water back and forth, letting the lighter grains of sand spill over the side with the water, slowly reducing the amount of sand in the pan and allowing the heavier gold – if there was any – to settle to the bottom. It was a tedious process.

Her nerves wore thin with the waiting. 'Is there gold in the sands?' she demanded impatiently.

No answer from the prospector was necessary as she saw the shimmer of gold dust along the bottom edge of the pan – not much, enough to coat the underside of a fingernail. But if that existed in a random scoop of sand, how much more could be found? She grabbed up the skirts of her nightgown and wrapper and ran back to Matty.

'There is gold here.' She spoke in an undertone, as if it was a secret that could be kept from the people swarming all over the beach looking for the same thing. She tightly gripped the woman's arm with both her hands. 'We're going to be rich, Matty.' For an instant, she gave in to the excitement that charged her, and she hugged Matty. 'This gold is ours. For once, the Tarakanovs are going to be rich!'

'Missy Glory okay?' Matty looked at her worriedly.

'I'm okay,' she said and released a short, exuberant laugh. 'You stay here. I'll be back as quick as I can.'

Reports confirming the presence of gold on the beach had spread rapidly. Glory had to fight her way back to town through a headlong rush of prospectors, merchants, bartenders, and gamblers now joining the stampede. Although she watched for Deacon, she didn't take time to look for him. She didn't know where Gabe had gone and didn't care. She bought a shovel, a rusty metal bucket, some mercury, and a crude wooden rocker from a merchant whose clerks had deserted him. With no one to help her transport her newly purhcased equipment to the beach, she had to struggle with it herself.

By midafternoon, she and Matty were working their claim, and the first flakes of gold were wrapped tightly in the lace handkerchief in the pocket of her wrapper. Glory had worked out a system: she shoveled a scoopful of ruby-colored sand into the wooden rocker that resembled a baby's cradle; Matty filled the pail with sea water and poured it over the sand while Glory rocked the 'cradle' back and forth as vigorously as she could; and Matty pushed the tailings out of the way.

The principle of the rocker was simple: the water washed the lighter sand through the hopper and out the bottom; the gold, being heavier, would be caught in the riffles in the bottom of the rocker; the finer flakes of gold would be trapped by the mercury-coated copper plate in the bottom.

Despite the cool breeze blowing off the sea, sweat rolled from Glory's skin. As Matty waded into the surf to refill the metal bucket, Glory propped the shovel against the rocker and straightened, pressing a hand against the ache in the small of her back.

She felt the stiffness of her muscles and realized just how long it had been since she'd worked in her aunt's garden. She wiped at the perspiration trickling down her cheek with her hand and felt the fiery sting in her palm from a broken blister. She tore off a strip of material from the hem of her nightgown and wrapped it around her hands for protection.

'I should have gotten some gloves,' she said to Matty when she returned with a full pail of water. The sight of the water sloshing in the pail made her realize how dry her mouth was. 'I should have brought some water to drink, too.'

'Missy want me get water?'

'No.' Glory swallowed with difficulty. 'We can't stop now.' She wagged her cloth-wrapped hand, motioning for Matty to pour the water into the rocker. 'Later. We'll rest later.'

The summer sun stayed to watch the gold-crazed scramble on the beach below, sometimes hiding behind a cloud to laugh at a world gone mad. All up and down the stretch of coast outside of town, men lined the beach, digging up the sand in their search for gold. Some were wizened, bearded prospectors – sourdoughs – longtime victims of gold fever, experienced and seasoned to the patience and back-breaking labor required to separate the shiny stuff from the sand. Others were merchants, tradesmen, gamblers, professional men – lawyers and the like – men who rarely held a shovel in their hands or got dirt under their fingernails. All manner of tools were employed in their frenzied efforts to extract the gold from the sand. Those without shovels used their hands to scoop up the gold-bearing sand. Large tin cans took the place of buckets to haul the water from the sea. The ones who didn't have rockers used the old standby gold pans or substituted washboards to trap the gold in their metal ripples. A few hammered together sluice boxes.

As the summer sun began its downward slide to the lowest point on the hazy horizon, Glory slumped to her knees beside the wooden rocker. Her arm muscles quivered in exhaustion from constantly shaking the rocker and shoveling sand. Weary and aching, she didn't trust her trembling hands and fingers to remove the gold trapped in the cradle's riffles.

'I need to rest a minute,' she told Matty, who seemed untouched by the fatigue that claimed Glory. She licked her dry lips, her breath coming in deep, labored drafts. 'Matty, why don't you go back to town and get us some food and water. Bring back some blankets, too. We'll sleep here tonight.' She didn't want anyone stealing their equipment in the night.

After Matty had set the bucket by the rocker and left for town, Glory let her body slump onto the cradle's wooden frame, taking a few minutes to catch her breath and get her strength back. Resting her cheek on the rough wood lip of the rocker, she gazed at the gold trapped in the bottom. It glittered and gleamed, almost seeming to wink at her. She dreamed of this from the time she was a child when she'd been awed by the shiny gold and silver ornamentation that gilded the interior of St. Michael's Cathedral, and had heard the prospectors' tales and seen the sample of gold ore.

Straightening, she reached in her pocket and took out the lace handkerchief that held her gold. She laid it in the bottom of the rocker and carefully untied it. Her hands were steady as she painstakingly transferred the grains of gold caught in the bottom creases to the small pile in her handkerchief. When it was once again securely knotted, she held the precious bundle tightly against her breastbone. Tears filled her eyes as she laughed and cried at the same time. She had wanted gold. Now she had it.

A hand clamped onto her shoulder. In panic, Glory grabbed for the shovel propped against the rocker and swung it at the thief who would steal her gold. 'It's mine!' she cried.

The man grabbed hold of the wooden handle before the shovel struck him. 'Glory, for God's sake, it's me!'

'Deacon.' The shovel suddenly felt heavy, and she let him take it from her hands and set it aside. 'I thought –' It was obvious what she thought and she laughed in relief. 'I'm glad it's you. Where have you been?'

'Looking for you. I ran into Matty and she told me where to find you.' He crouched down beside her, sitting on his heels, and brushed the grains of sand from his trouser legs. 'You don't have to worry about meeting the paperhanger. He's somewhere out here in this insanity.'

'There's gold, Deacon. Gold right here in this sand. Do you realize how many times we've walked along this beach? And it's been right here under our feet all this time.'

'Do you have any idea what you look like?'

Glory started to brush at the granules of sand that coated her wrapper, but there was too much. The action drew attention to the soiled strips of cloth wrapped around her hands and the dirty, frayed lace trim of her nightgown that extended beyond the velvet cuffs of her wrapper. Her unbound hair lay about her back and shoulders in a grimy, windblown tangle.

'I am a mess,' she conceded.

'A mess.' He mocked her understatement and lifted one of her hands, drawing a wince from Glory as his grip put pressure on a broken blister. 'Look at your hands. Your fingers are all red and scratched. Your nails are chipped and broken, and no doubt these rags are covering blisters. Your face is wind-burned. I could go on . . .'

'My hands will heal. A bath will take care of the dirt. And *this* will buy all the new clothes I need.' Defiantly she held up the knotted handkerchief containing her gold.

'How much do you have there?' He snatched it from her hand.

She made no attempt to grab it back from him, and instead, watched anxiously as he held it in his palm, testing its weight.

'Fifty dollars, probably less.' He tossed it onto her lap. 'Is that all you've gotten?'

'So far.' Her gold find was a thing to celebrate, but Deacon was ridiculing it.

'How long have you been at this?'

'Since a little before noon.'

'You've labored for more than ten hours for fifty dollars.' He shook his head in disgust. 'Glory, you make more than that a night lying on your back.'

She wouldn't look at him. Suddenly Deacon – who had never treated her roughly before – grabbed her arm and pulled her to her feet, then jerked her around to face the crowded beach.

'If it's gold you want, Glory, there it is – in the pockets of those fools out there digging in the sand like a bunch of crazy clams! Do you know what they're going to do with their gold? They're going to spend it. They're going to have the wildest time they've ever had in their lives – drinking, gambling, and whoring! And when that gold's gone, they're going to come out here and dig some more, and do it all again! I've never met a rich prospector yet, no matter how big his strike. Maybe there's one out of a thousand who doesn't die broke, but the rest do.'

He swung her around, his fingers digging into her aching shoulder muscles. Glory fixed her gaze on his black tie, unable to meet the piercing glare of his hard blue eyes.

'One way or another I'm going to have the Palace open for

business when they hit town to celebrate – if I have to hang the damned paper myself. I'm going to make sure they have a place to spend their gold. It's going to take a hell of a lot of work. Are you going to help me?'

She was conscious of the gold-weighted kerchief in her hand; it was the fulfillment of her dream. 'You don't understand, Deacon,' she insisted. 'It's my gold.'

Abruptly he released her and pivoted away. She fought back the tears of frustration and resentment as she watched him leave. She looked down at the lace handkerchief in her hand and curled her fingers more tightly around it.

46

After a few hours of fitful sleep, wrapped in a blanket on the sand, Glory awakened so stiff and sore that any movement was torture. But the gold waited. All up and down the beach, there was activity, some of the men toiling through the twilight hours of midnight. She wakened Matty. Someone along the beach was boiling coffee and frying bacon. Glory could smell it, but she settled for some stale water and a chunk of sourdough bread left over from last night's meal, and shook her head at the strip of blubber that Matty offered to share with her.

As soon as she had washed down the last of the dry bread with a swallow of water, Glory started to work. Her muscles protested each time she lifted the shovel to scoop sand into the rocker or grabbed the rocker's wooden side to shake it. She finally traded places with Matty and started hauling water for the rocker. For a time that was easier, but eventually the bucket full of water seemed to get heavier and heavier.

The bucket's wire handle cut painfully into her blistered palm despite the rag bandage tied around it. As Glory tried to switch the bucket to the other hand, she accidentally stepped on a trailing piece of her nightgown's torn hem. Her legs tangled and she fell, spilling the water.

Frustrated, tired, and sore, she knelt there. She felt gritty all over. Her clothes were so stained and impregnated with sand that they'd never come clean again, even if the rips could be mended. The sea water had ruined her leather shoes. Her hair was so tangled she knew she'd break half a dozen combs trying to get the snarls out of it.

Matty dropped the shovel and hurried over to her. 'Me help.' She slipped her hands under Glory's arms.

'I can't do it.'

She didn't think she had the strength to stand. All she wanted to do was collapse on the sand and cry. Yet Matty had worked as long and as hard as she had, and never once complained. Driven by guilt, Glory struggled to her feet, aided by Matty's supporting hands. When Matty reached down to pick up the overturned bucket, Glory stopped her.

'Leave it. Let's take out what gold we've gotten so far,' she said and forced her leaden legs to carry her to the rocker.

Yesterday, she had cleaned out the gold in the riffles after nearly every shovelful of sand had been washed through. Today she had done as the miners around her were doing, letting the gold accumulate in the creases. The beach sand held no nuggets, only fine 'flour' gold, as it was called. Carefully, she scraped it from the wooden riffles and added it to the gold dust in her handkerchief.

She stared at the tiny mound of yellow flakes in dejection. 'It's no use. All this work and we've probably got only eighty dollars. Deacon was right, Matty.' She looked at the surrounding strip of beach jammed with men panning, sluicing, and rocking for gold. 'The gold in Nome is in the pockets of these men. That's what we should be mining instead of this sand.' She stood up, cupped her hands to her mouth and shouted, 'Hey! Would anybody like to buy a rocker and a shovel? Mine's for sale!'

Heads turned in her direction. Soon a dozen would-be miners were swarming around her, mostly townspeople without the proper tools, or the knowledge or skill to build rockers or sluice boxes out of the driftwood on the beach. Glory auctioned off everything – the rocker, the shovel, the rusty bucket, the vial of mercury, and even the blanket – getting twice what she'd initially paid for them . . . in gold dust.

As the buyers moved in to carry away their purchases, Glory linked her arm with Matty's. 'Let's go to the Palace. Deacon should be there. Then I want a bath and a hot meal.'

'Hey! Wait a minute.' A shaggy-bearded man ran up to her.

'Sorry, mister. You're too late. Everything's been sold.' She kept walking.

'Marisha, wait.'

She halted at the sound of her given name. No one knew it except – She turned and stared at the unkempt prospector. A dirty and faded slouch hat covered hair that had grown long and curled about the collar of his plaid shirt and dirty jacket; and suspenders held up the baggy trousers, crudely patched at the knees. The full beard and mustache hid most of his face, making his age almost impossible to determine, but there was something familiar about his eyes.

'It is you,' he declared. 'I knew there couldn't be two women in Alaska with hair like that.'

'Justin,' she ventured tentatively. Only the eyes and the voice were recognizable.

He rubbed his heavy beard as if becoming conscious of his changed appearance. 'I guess I'm not a cheechako any more. I look like a woolly old sourdough now, don't I? You live through a couple winters in the interior, and it'll do this to you. You get to where you don't even look at what it is you're eating to stay alive.'

'Yes.' She'd heard some of the stories of hardship told by sourdoughs – so-called because of the homemade starter they used as yeast to make their bread and hooch. Men who were old in experience but not necessarily mature.

Glory continued to gaze at him, conscious of the irony of the meeting. She'd always wondered whether Justin would recognize her. Yet the way she looked now – dressed in these soiled, shapeless clothes, her hair tousled, her face bare of makeup – she probably looked like dowdy Marisha Blackwood. If anything, she looked worse than when he'd last seen her. This wasn't the way she'd imagined their meeting at all.

'I can't believe you're here.' Justin shook his head in amazement. 'I only arrived myself a couple days ago. Did you get my letter?'

'Your letter? No, I . . . I haven't received anything – except that note you left me when you took off for the Klondike.'

His glance wavered briefly. 'I just couldn't take you with me. The way it turned out, that first winter was bad. It wasn't a place for a woman. I was worried you'd come on your own instead of staying in Skagway.'

'I thought you'd probably forgotten all about me.'

'No.' He smiled, the heavy beard and mustache parting to show his teeth. 'I guess it's obvious I never made that big strike. When I heard they'd found gold here, I wrote to tell you I was going to Nome to try my luck. Course you never got that letter.'

'No.' And she wouldn't have, even if she'd been in Skagway, because he'd addressed it to someone who no longer existed.

'Hey, Glory! You gonna work this bit of sand?' The shout came from a grizzled prospector standing with his partners on the strip of beach that Glory had claimed.

'No. You're welcome to it,' she yelled back, then noticed the puzzled frown on Justin's face.

'What'd he call you?'

'Glory. That's my name now. I changed it to Glory St. Clair. I took the last name from you. It seemed only fair, since you took things that belonged to me.' She watched the look of shock and disbelief spread across his face.

'*You're* Glory St. Clair?' His glance swept her snarled hair, her grimy, tattered clothes, and bandaged hands.

She had to smile. 'In a couple of hours I will be – after I've had a bath and a change of clothes.' Suddenly, she didn't want to continue the conversation, not while she looked like this. 'Why don't we meet tonight?'

'Sure.' He was still too stunned to take it all in. 'Where will I find you?'

'Ask anyone in town. They'll tell you where I am.' She smiled as she started to move away from him, now anxious to leave. 'Come on, Matty.'

'I'll . . . see you later,' Justin said, appearing confused and uncertain about everything, in view of her startling revelation.

'Him a friend?' Matty asked, as they plodded through the sand toward town.

'Yes. I knew Justin a long time ago. Or at least it seems a long time ago.' She wished she knew what he'd said in that letter he'd written her.

'Better you see him. Me not like old man,' Matty declared in an obvious reference to Gabe Blackwood.

Glory made no comment, keeping silent about her reasons for seeing Gabe. She guessed that Matty sensed his prejudicial dislike of her or anyone of native extraction, but she didn't attempt to explain his attitude. There were too many other things on her mind just now.

They stopped first at the Palace. From the outside, the building looked complete, even to the gold-painted sign that proclaimed its name in a flourishing scroll. But inside, many finishing touches remained undone. The walls were still in their rough state. The mirrors, paintings, and sconces weren't hung, but the recently arrived gambling tables and chairs were set up in the gaming area, and the mock parlor held the upholstered settees and chairs.

No workmen were about. The place was silent. Glory was

about to decide Deacon wasn't there after all. Then she heard the clink of glass coming from the carved bar they'd imported from San Francisco.

'Deacon?' she called hesitantly.

He straightened from behind the counter, coatless, the cuffs of his white shirt rolled back to bare his forearms. His fingers were looped through the handles of three beer mugs. He did not smile when he saw her. Glory halted, unsure of her welcome.

'I see you finally came to your senses,' he observed dryly and turned to set the beer mugs on the bar's mirrored back shelf. 'You're just in time to lend a hand unpacking these glasses. I can use your help. Matty's too.'

'I can't right now. Neither can Matty. I'm going to need her,' Glory said quickly. 'I wasn't sure whether you'd still want me as a partner.'

'Your money's in this place, too.'

'Before you commit yourself, there's something you should know. I ran into an old friend on the beach. We're going to be getting together tonight. I need Matty to help me get cleaned up so I can look halfway presentable.'

'And that's why you can't help me get ready to open,' Deacon guessed. 'Obviously this "old friend" is a man.'

'Yes.' She didn't want to lose Deacon's friendship. Neither did she want to lie to him. Even though she didn't know how the evening with Justin was going to turn out, Deacon had to know Justin was someone special to her, and she'd rather he knew that from the beginning.

There was a moment when he hesitated. 'I have no private claim on you, Glory.' He shrugged, surprising her with the casualness of the gesture. 'When you're finished with Matty, have her move my things into one of the rooms upstairs here.'

She felt a twinge of disappointment that he would relinquish her to another man so easily. Which was crazy in a way, considering that he'd never objected in the least to her profession. But Justin wasn't a customer.

'I will.' She hesitated. 'Deacon, I –'

He interrupted her. 'You don't have to make any explanations to me. Go meet your friend or do whatever it is you're going to do. The sooner that's handled, the sooner you can get back here and lend me a hand. I want to be open for business by tomorrow.'

'Sure.' There was nothing else for her to say, although Glory wished there was something that might make her feel better about this. Trying to shake off a sense of guilt, she turned and left, accompanied by Matty.

Back at her quarters in the Double Eagle, Glory managed to procure the use of a bathtub. While Matty hauled water from the Snake River, the source of Nome's drinking water, and heated it over a fire behind the saloon, Glory combed her snarled hair, her scalp aching from the constant tugging at the roots. When the tub was filled with water, she stripped off her clothes and ordered Matty to burn them. She soaped and scrubbed until her body felt raw.

Afterwards, Matty rubbed her with perfumed oils and brushed her hair dry, then helped her dress, tightly lacing Glory into her corset and fastening the red satin gown with the scandalous décolletage that Glory had been saving to wear for the opening of the Palace. Despite all the creams and balms she'd applied, nothing could be done for her sore, unsightly hands, so she hid them with a pair of long gloves that extended above the elbow. A layer of powder toned down the redness of her sun- and wind-burned face.

Ready at last, she had Matty collect Deacon's things and take them to the Palace, then sat down to wait for Justin. A hundred times, it seemed, she checked her reflection in the mirror, looking for some flaw in her appearance that could be corrected. She was anxious to make a good impression on Justin and erase his former image of her. Glory was certain she hadn't been this nervous since the first night she'd gone to work for Miss Rosie.

As she reached for the whiskey bottle to fill one of the two glasses on the tray, someone cleared his throat behind her. She pivoted toward the sound. Justin stood a step inside the partitioned room, fingering the hat he held in his hands. Glory stared at him. This was the Justin she remembered. The beard and mustache were gone, exposing his familiar features that now looked oddly pale. The long, shaggy locks of his dark hair had been shorn, returning its natural curl. His shirt, trousers, and jacket were all new.

Justin stared at her like a man transfixed. His lips moved twice before anything came out. 'They . . . said you were in here. I would have knocked, but that's hard to do on canvas walls.'

She smiled, his reaction filling her with confidence. 'Come in, Justin. Would you like something to drink?'

'Yeah, I could use a drink.' He walked over to her and took the glass of whiskey she poured for him, his gaze never leaving her.

'We should drink to something.' She raised her glass and waited for him to make the toast, but he seemed incapable of speech. 'Here's to meeting again in Nome. There's no place like it.' She sipped at her whiskey, but he made no move to follow suit. 'Is something wrong?'

He dropped his gaze, but it fell no farther than the white mounds of her pushed-up breasts. 'I don't know what to call you.' He shook his head. 'You don't even look like Marisha now.'

'I'm not. I'm Glory.'

'I guess so.' He quickly downed a swallow of the whiskey, then studied the glass in his hand.

Glory noticed his troubled frown and felt a twinge of unease. 'What's wrong, Justin? Don't tell me you liked Marisha better?' she scoffed, knowing full well that he had never stared at Marisha the way he stared at her now.

'I knew her.'

'Meaning you don't know me.' She was mildly irritated by his attitude.

'I don't understand. I mean . . . when I left, you had a job.' He gestured wildly, mindless of the hat in his hand. 'You were working at that restaurant. You had a place to eat and sleep. I figured you'd be all right. What happened?'

'I quit.'

'But why? Was it my fault? When I left, you weren't in a family way or anything like that, were you?'

'No. Nothing like that.' It occurred to her that she could have lied, led him to believe that he was in some way responsible for the life she'd chosen. While it amused her that Justin wanted to think that way, she also found it wearisome. 'Do you see this gown I'm wearing, Justin? I had it specially made in San Francisco. No waitress could afford a gown like this if she saved for a hundred years. How else would a woman get enough money on her own to be half owner in the Palace, being built down the street? She either strikes gold or marries some rich man and becomes his chattel. I chose to become my own gold mine.'

'But this afternoon on the beach, you were –'

'– briefly a victim of the gold fever. Just for a little while I was caught up in the dream we had long ago. Remember how you and I used to sit up and talk about the gold we were going to find in the Klondike? I let myself think it was going to come true here in Nome. Luckily, I came to my senses.'

'Didn't you find any gold?' Justin frowned.

'Sure. Eighty . . . maybe a hundred dollars' worth after two days of back-breaking labor.'

'What's wrong with that? If you could average that every day for a year, do you realize how much that would be?'

'And do you realize what I'd look like after a year? My skin would be ruined. My hair would be, too. I'd have muscles like a man, calluses on my hands. I like being a woman, Justin. I like being soft and pretty. I like smelling of perfume instead of sweat. I don't want to be rich and look like some worn-out old hag.' Angry tears stung her eyes as she struggled to make him understand. 'You know what it was like for me growing up – never having anything, not friends or clothes or fun, always being told what to do and how to behave. I'm not going to live like that ever again, and I don't care what I have to do! I thought you more than anyone would understand that.'

'I do. I guess I just never thought about it that way. It's just that I never meant for my leaving to hurt you.'

'It did. But that isn't the reason I became a whore. I'm in it for the money. It's a business to me.'

'I believe you. But where does that leave me?'

'It leaves you wherever you want to be,' Glory replied. 'Maybe I should ask why you came tonight? Was it just to ease your conscience or what?'

'I'm not sure if I know,' he admitted as he continued to study her. 'Curiosity was part of it. Practically every prospector from here to the Yukon has heard of Glory St. Clair. And I wanted to see Marisha again. I never expected to miss her – you – when I left Skagway, at least not as much as I did. Hell.' He laughed, but it was obvious that he was uncomfortable, and a little embarrassed. 'When my partners found out I was meeting you tonight, they made me take a bath and dragged the barber away from his diggings to give me a shave and a haircut. I even bought me some new clothes. I'm not even sure if I know what you expect from me. Talk is that you and that gambler have some kind of arrangement.'

'Deacon is a friend as well as my business partner, but you won't find his things here in this room. I don't have any one special person, someone that I really care about.'

'None?'

She shook her head. 'You were the only one I ever shared anything with – my thoughts, my feelings, my dreams. No one else knows me the way you do. To them, I'm just Glory St. Clair. They don't even know where I got the name.'

'Mari –' He stopped, a boyish smile of chagrin breaking across his mouth. 'Maybe I should get used to calling you Glory.'

She moved close to him and studied the gentle line of his mouth, remembering that long-ago day when she had received her first kiss from those lips. 'Maybe you should.'

'Glory.' He started to touch her, then realized that his hands were full, his hat in one, and the whiskey glass in the other. For an awkward second, he didn't seem to know what to do with them. Then he laughed, and tossed his hat and the whiskey glass in the air. In the next second, she was in his arms and he was kissing her with the thoroughness of a man long hungry for the taste of her lips.

With his head pillowed on the crook of her shoulder, Justin lay alongside her, his hand caressing the roundly firm flesh of a breast beneath the covers. Absently, Glory twirled a dark curl of his hair around the end of her finger. Making love with him had been good. He wasn't as skilled in the art of arousal as Deacon, but he more than made up for it in eagerness and intensity – as if he had to prove he was better than any man she had lain with before. That part didn't matter to her. The others were business and this was pleasure, but she wasn't certain he would understand the fine difference. She kissed the top of his head, then rubbed her chin on it, sublimely content.

'It was a waste buying those new clothes,' Justin murmured, his low voice vibrating against her body. 'I don't think I had them on more than twenty minutes.'

'Maybe. But I'm glad you had the bath and a shave. That's my biggest complaint about Nome.'

'That men don't take baths?'

'No. That getting a bath is such an ordeal – hauling the water, heating it. It's the Russian in me, I guess,' she mused. 'I miss bathing regularly.'

'Baths, huh.' He rolled away from her onto his back, resting his head on the adjoining pillow and raising his arms up over his head, exposing the dark hairy armpits. 'Do you know I haven't slept in a bed since I left Skagway?' He gazed at the water-stained canvas roof of the tent. 'Hell, I'd be satisfied if me and my partners had a tent to sleep in.'

'You don't have one?'

'No. Our boat capsized coming down the Yukon. We lost the tent, most of our gear and equipment as well as our supplies. We were hoping to get a grubstake once we got here, but so far we haven't had any luck. Course we're taking gold out of our claim on the beach, so eventually we'll have our own money to buy what we need. Problem is I'm not sure how long we're going to be able to work it. Some of the owners of the tundra claims are saying that their claims go all the way to the ocean and that we've jumped their claims. Others are saying that the beach is public property and no one can stake a claim on it. Until a court says who's right, we're just gonna stay there and keep working it.'

'In the meantime, you're just going to camp out there in the open?' One night of sleeping on that damp sand with that chilling wind blowing in off the sea had been enough for her. She couldn't imagine anything more miserable.

'Got any better ideas?' he asked.

'Sure.' She rolled onto her side, propping herself up with an elbow. 'You can sleep here.'

'I don't know how well that would go over with my partners – me sleeping on a nice soft bed and them out there in the cold. Not that I don't like the idea, but it wouldn't be fair to them.'

Now that he had turned down her impulsive offer, she realized it was best. The bed wasn't always going to be available when he wanted to sleep, and it might be awkward when she had customers to entertain. Still, she wanted to help him, and there was another alternative.

Glory rolled out of bed, dragging the top blanket with her and wrapping it around her. Barefoot, she padded over to a large steamer trunk and knelt down on the ground to open it. She flipped open the hidden compartment located in an inner wall, and removed the flat leather pouch.

'What are you doing?' Justin sat up, the remaining cover falling down around his waist.

She took out five of the bills in the pouch, then returned it to its secret compartment and rearranged the gowns inside to conceal its location again. With the money in hand, she stood up and walked back to the bed.

'You said you needed a tent, some equipment and supplies. Will five hundred dollars do the job?'

He stared at the bills in her outstretched hand, then looked at her, slowly shaking his head. 'I can't take that from you.'

'Why not? You wanted a grubstake. Well, here it is. It's the perfect solution, because it gives both of us what we want. I've always wanted to own a gold claim, and this buys me part interest in one.'

After hesitating a moment longer, he took the money and counted the bills as if not quite believing they were real. 'With this, I bet I could buy everything we need yet tonight. Hell, they were gonna throw out lines and catch fish for supper. Maybe I could get my hands on some meat.'

Throwing back the covers, he swung out of bed and reached down to pick up his faded red flannel long underwear. Quickly he stepped into it. He was still buttoning with one hand while he was pulling his trousers on with the other. Glory had never seen a man dress so fast in her life.

'I can just see the looks on their faces when I come walking up with all the stuff.' He grinned. 'Damn, are they gonna be surprised!' He didn't bother to button his shirt as he hurriedly tucked the tails inside his trousers. His coat was in his hand and his hat was jammed on the back of his head when he came around the bed and gave Glory a quick, hard kiss. 'I gotta go. Thanks . . . Glory.'

His barely contained excitement brought a smile to her face – a smile that became wistful as he charged out of the tent. It was easy to imagine how excited he would have been if he'd been there that night when she'd come back to their room with the ten dollars needed for their Klondike grubstake. A lot had changed since then, and five hundred was considerably more than ten. She sighed, wishing he'd stayed a little longer, wishing that he hadn't been so quick to take the money and run. He'd just been excited; that's all.

But it was just as well he'd left now. She was needed somewhere else, too. There was a lot of work still to be done to get the Palace ready for business. But, unlike Justin, Glory took her time getting dressed.

Although the Palace was unfinished, Deacon and Glory opened the doors the next day, admitting anyone and everyone with gold dust in their pouches. The place was almost immediately jammed with prospectors ready to celebrate their find. With only the minimum of hired help to run their establishment, they quickly pressed Matty into service, placing her in charge of the gold scales, responsible for weighing a miner's gold and givng him the dollar equivalent in tokens he could spend at the Palace. They were fully aware that a miner was apt to overlook any 'accidental' spillage of his dust by a clumsy Eskimo breed. A blanket lined the shelf below the enclosed counter on which the gold scales sat. Its nap caught the spilled flour gold. On a good night, they could glean as much as a hundred dollars from the blanket.

With the discovery of the gold-bearing beach sands, the economy of Nome boomed. No expensive machinery was required to extract the gold from the sand. This was a poor man's diggings. Every man in town had gold dust in his pockets. People rushed to take advantage of it. Suddenly men who had deserted their trade to mine the sands discovered there was as much money to be made at their old jobs and went back to their former work.

The next weeks were chaotic for Glory and Deacon. The carpenters and paperhangers put the finishing touches on the Palace, working around the steady crowd of customers. The piano arrived from Seattle. A musician formerly with the Philadelphia Symphony agreed to play it for them as long as they kept him supplied with morphine.

Two more prostitutes were hired, bringing the number of Glory's girls to four. Following Miss Rosie's lead, Glory had carefully screened them, requiring that they be free of disease, reasonably clean and neat, and at least capable of good manners. Once those criteria were met, she selected on the basis of personality and looks, wanting to give customers a variety from which to choose. Joining the sultry, copper-skinned French-Indian woman from Saskatchewan with the ubiquitous name of Frenchie, and the plump, hennaed Mad Alice, so called because of her volatile temper, were the baby-faced Gladys, who was quickly renamed Happy Bottom by the miners, and 'Good' Betsy, a former schoolteacher who always praised her customers when they were 'good.'

Glory's arrangement with her girls was the same as Miss Rosie's had been, splitting the fee fifty-fifty, letting them keep the tips, charging them a flat rate for the condoms, allowing them to sell them for whatever they could get, and giving them a commission on the drinks they sold. However, she did charge a higher rent for their rooms. Meals and laundry, with the exception of linens, were extra. In addition, Glory arranged with her dressmaker in San Francisco to allow her girls to charge clothes to her account, and she received a small kickback from the dressmaker for the additional business. Despite the costs for bouncers, domestic help, a kitchen staff, the piano player, and the monthly 'fine' of ten dollars for each prostitute recently imposed by the town's newly formed consent government, the profits were ample.

The Palace was not without competition. By the middle of September 1899, twenty different saloons were in operation, including the Dexter Saloon run by C. E. Hoxsie and the once-famed gunslinger and marshal of Tombstone, a paunchy, middle-aged Wyatt Earp. Behind some of the saloons on the north side of Front Street, rough and hardened prostitutes plied their trade from one-room tents and wooden shanties, some of them as quick to steal a customer's poke as to bed him. It was popularly known as the Stockade for the high fence that was built around it to shield the town's more righteous citizens from its sordid activity.

With Nome's population exploding to five thousand people, business was lively for everyone. But that wasn't what prevented Glory from seeing Justin more than two or three times a week. The ownership of mining claims – both the rich placer deposits in the gulches and creeks of the inland mountains and the gold-riddled sands of the beach – remained in dispute. As far as the beachfront was concerned, the general consensus was that, according to U.S. law, beaches were public property, and therefore open to everyone. As long as a man had a shovel in his hand, he had a right to that section of the beach, an area that was, more or less, agreed to be roughly twenty square feet as measured by a miner's standard long-handled shovel. The tides played havoc with that system.

In an effort to continually occupy the section they claimed, Justin and his partners took turns coming into town, with two of them always remaining at their beach site. Glory didn't really mind the separation. It just seemed to make the time they did spend together that much more special. She had something to look forward to now. Deacon appeared to have taken the change in their personal relationship in stride, although sometimes he seemed more aloof and withdrawn. Yet he'd always been that way, so it was difficult for her to tell if the change was real or imagined. Either way, she could hardly complain.

The September sun was shining brightly, but Glory's gum

boots were weighted down with mud as she picked her way through the mire. Nome's streets were figments drawn on a long-disregarded town plat that bore no resemblance to the winding paths that recent rains had turned into rivers of mud, in some places two feet deep. It was a standing joke that a man never knew when the next step would take him to China.

Buildings went up wherever there was space; sometimes they were built in the middle of where the street was supposed to be. That created narrow trails no more than eight feet wide in places.

An expanse of murky brown water confronted Glory. She stopped to hoist her skirts higher and to try to gauge its depth before stepping into it. Matty bumped into her from behind, nearly knocking her into it, but Glory recovered her balance.

'Why do you stop here?' Matty looped both arms through the curved handle of the market basket mounded with foodstuffs.

'I'm debating whether I have to wade or swim through that puddle,' Glory replied.

Although Matty usually did the daily marketing, Glory went with her whenever there were major purchases to be made. She was often able to persuade the merchants, especially the ones who occasionally visited the Palace, to shave their prices a little. With rumors of a possible food shortage in Nome this winter, Glory was attempting to accumulate a stockpile of non-perishable goods.

She shifted her grip on the heavily loaded market basket she carried, trying to ease the strain on her arm. Normally she loaded her purchases in a wheeled cart pulled by a team of sled dogs that Deacon had bought for her, but this thick mire made the use of such a conveyance impractical. But Glory knew their load wasn't going to get much heavier, since their last stop was the bakery.

'It can't be much farther.' She glanced up the long row of false-fronted buildings, scanning the lettered signs. All around her, men slogged through the river of mud, seemingly indifferent to the slop sucking at their boots. The yammer of sled dogs was an incessant din that competed with the pounding and sawing of wood as carpenters worked busily to slap together another building. 'Wasn't the bakery shop next to the watchmaker?'

There was an empty space where she thought the bakery shop should have been. The spot wasn't completely empty. The framework for a new building now occupied the site.

'It's gone now,' Matty observed. 'This place is crazy. The people are crazy.'

'I agree.' She sighed heavily and retraced her steps to the fruit and cigar store they had just passed. The proprietor was sorting through a crate of apples, turning them so the bruised side wouldn't show. 'Excuse me.'

The man started guiltily, then quickly began rubbing the apple in his hand on the sleeve of his coat. 'Just polishin' these here apples, Miss St. Clair.' There were few people in town who didn't know her on sight. 'Got a new shipment in. Real beauties they are, too. Would ya like some? You know what they say – an apple a day keeps the doctor away.'

'I don't believe so. But maybe you can tell me what happened to the bakery that used to be next to the watchmaker?'

'Somebody hauled it off in the night with poor Mr. Parker still in it. Guess they hitched on to it with a team a' horses an' jest drug it off. It jolted Mr. Parker right out a' bed. Heerd he got quite a knot on his head when he fell. The new place is gonna be a gen'ral store.'

Glory wasn't surprised by the story. Lot jumping was as prevalent as claim jumping in Nome. 'What about the bakery?'

'Can't say as I know where it's located now.' He shook his head regretfully.

'Thanks.'

As she started to turn away, he stopped her. 'Take this apple, Miss St. Clair.' But he checked it for bruises before he gave it to her. 'If anyone was to ask ya where ya got it, you jest point 'em to me.'

'I will.' As she walked back to Matty, she tucked the apple in a corner of her already full market basket. 'Well, now what? We've got everything but bread.'

'I think maybe another bakery is by the picture place.' Matty nodded in the direction of some wood-framed buildings catty-corner from them on a side street.

As Glory turned to look, someone across the street waved to her. The constant coming and going of pedestrians in the street briefly blocked the man from her view. Then she saw him as he moved in and out among the people to cross the muddy trail to her side. His collar was turned up and his hat was pulled low. It was a moment before she had a clear look at his face and was able to recognize Gabe Blackwood. Lately there had been so many demands on her time that she hadn't seen him very often.

'Glory, what luck! I was just on my way to see you.' He smiled widely, looking every inch the distinguished barrister instead of the aging, down-at-the-heels lawyer she'd first met on arriving in Nome. She was well aware that she was responsible for a large measure of his renewed self-esteem, but it had been easy to accomplish; all she'd had to do was reinforce the vainglorious image he already had of himself. All the things she'd ever heard about him were true; she'd seen enough of his pettiness and prejudice to know that. Now she no longer cared whether he even liked her.

'It's been a while, Gabe. How have you been? Very busy, from all that I've heard.'

'I've tried,' he said, feigning modesty while swaggering slightly. 'You know how keen competition is among lawyers in this town.'

'There's almost as many lawyers as there are saloons.' But she noticed he didn't mention the local election held only a few days ago.

It was held to form what was known as a 'consent' government. Which meant the townspeople of Nome 'consented' to be governed by an elected mayor, council, and chief of police; have laws and regulations imposed on them; and voluntarily pay various taxes and licensing fees. The United States Congress had yet to pass legislation that permitted the formation of municipal governments in Alaska with the power to impose laws and levy taxes on its citizens.

In the election, Gabe had allied himself with the ticket that represented the town's business community, including its sixteen lawyers. The miners' ticket had swept the election. The town's few women had been allowed to vote, and Glory had taken advantage of it, but she refrained from telling Gabe that she had cast her ballot for the winning side.

'Well, this winter the city of Nome is going to be short one attorney,' he announced importantly.

'What do you mean? Are you leaving?'

'Yes. That's what I was coming to tell you.' He reached into his inside coat pocket and withdrew an envelope and a steamer ticket. 'I've booked passage on the next ship bound for San Francisco. From there, I'm taking the train to Washington, D.C.'

'Why are you going there?' She struggled to control a rising sense of panic. 'I don't understand. What's this all about?'

He waved the envelope. 'Remember I told you I knew some people in Washington? Well, I hadn't corresponded with them in some time, but I wrote one of my old friends in early summer, telling him about the situation here in Nome. I just heard back from him. It seems there's a bill coming up before the Senate this spring which would provide for the formation of civil governments in Alaska. It also may deal with some of the mining issues we're facing here. Since I have firsthand knowledge about many of the problems here, my friend suggested that it might be beneficial for me to come to Washington and meet with some of the senators to discuss the situation.'

'I think that's very wise of your friend.' She breathed a little easier, and laughed to cover any alarm she might have shown. 'I must admit that when you first said you were leaving, I thought you meant you weren't coming back. I'm glad that's not the case. I would have missed you. I shall miss you while you're gone. The winter's going to seem even that much longer without you here.'

'And I will miss you. You've been good for me. But I'll be back on the first ship that sails next summer.'

'Why must you leave so soon? If this bill doesn't come before the Senate until next spring, surely you could wait.'

'It's too close to the winter freeze-up and I don't want to take the risk of being frozen in here. By ship, I'm only two weeks from San Francisco, if the weather cooperates. But if I'm forced to go overland, it's fifteen hundred miles or more by dogsled to the nearest ice-free port. That's much too grueling a journey for a man my age.'

'Of course, you're right. This will be my first winter this far north. I'm told Norton Sound is solid ice by the beginning of November. I can't imagine what it's going to be like – cut off from the world for eight months. I shall probably besiege you with questions when you return.'

'I hope I'll have some very good news to tell you.' His expression was smug as he tucked the envelope and ticket back inside his pocket.

'What kind of news?'

'If this bill passes, it's quite likely they'll be dividing Alaska into several districts. Which means they'll be appointing more federal judges. It's so impractical now, with only one judge in the whole of Alaska, and he's in Sitka.' He paused and winked at her. 'It could be that you'll have to address me as "your honor" when I return.'

'*Judge* Blackwood,' Glory murmured. In the back of her mind she knew that the higher a man's position, the harder his fall would be from it. It gave her something to think about.

'Mind you, it's only a possibility,' he cautioned, then chatted a few minutes longer before taking his leave from her.

47 *Nome Winter 1899-1900*

Many of the city's inhabitants scrambled for a place on the last ship out of Nome rather than face a winter there, with a threat of food shortages and a possible typhoid epidemic from the grossly unsanitary conditions, not to mention the blizzards and freezing temperatures with only the questionable shelter of tents and crude wooden huts to protect them. Several of the more unsavory characters in Nome were deported by the newly elected 'consent' government, along with many of the destitute who hadn't the means to support themselves through the winter or the funds to purchase a ticket.

Roughly three thousand remained behind in Nome to brave the conditions and protect their holdings. 'Good' Betsy, the former schoolteacher, was the only one from the Palace who refused to stay.

Justin and his partners chose to stay. They scavenged for wood and built a shack on the beach out of pieces of scrap lumber, broken crates, and driftwood gathered from the diminishing piles along the banks of creek mouths. Many of the other prospectors who had mined the 'golden' sands that summer, the so-called beachcombers, elected to live in their tents.

By mid-November, ice five feet thick locked the entire coastline and extended miles into the sea. The Bering Strait, the body of water that separates Alaska from Russia, was rarely covered by a continuous sheet of ice. Open stretches of water existed beyond the ice pack, usually littered with ice floes.

In this tundra region, the entire area was underlain with permafrost. This permanently frozen underlayer of ground created a major problem for the city of Nome. Without water wells, the inhabitants were forced to rely on the Snake River for their drinking water. And the permafrost wouldn't absorb their sewage. Just as they had to haul in all their drinking water, they had to haul out all their excrement. During the summer it had been dumped into the Snake River, a practice that created the typhoid scare because of the potential contamination of the drinking water. As a solution to the problem that winter, the city officials hauled the refuse and sewage far out onto the ice so that when spring breakup came, it would float away and eventually be deposited in the sea.

But the scarcity of public 'facilities' didn't allow the problem of sanitation to be totally eliminated. By the time February rolled around, Glory didn't dare venture down the alleyway next to the Palace. To do so meant skating on a thick glacier of frozen urine. Front Street was almost as bad.

Yet with all the cases of typhoid fever, bloody dysentery, and pneumonia that did occur, Nome's population increased that winter. The absence of a government assay office in Nome made an accurate record of the amount of gold taken out of the immediate area that summer impossible to determine. Too much went out in the pockets and pokes of men who didn't want to brag about how much they'd made for fear of being robbed. But the best guesses estimated that the total amount extracted from the beach alone ranged from a million to two million dollars, and roughly another million and a half dollars had been taken from the inland placer claims along the mountain creeks.

While rumors of the gold strike had lured many prospectors like Justin and his partners from the Klondike to Nome during the summer, the news of the 'poor man's diggings' on the beach brought the rest. Fifteen hundred or so had been lucky enough to crowd onto the last sternwheeler going down the Yukon River from Dawson, arriving in late fall. The majority waited until winter set in and the river froze solid. Then the mad exodus to Nome began down the river's ice road. They traveled by dog team or horse-drawn sled. Some walked all the way, pulling small sleds loaded with their gear. Others strapped on ice skates and skated to Nome. An intrepid few made use of the latest craze and bicycled their way across the breadth of Alaska in the dead of winter. Many called these people 'Nomers,' but a few looked at the madness of their headlong rush to Nome and called them 'Nomads.'

All winter long, they arrived – exhausted, hungry, frost-bitten, or half frozen. It wasn't only the prospectors who came from the Klondike. Many were, as the Canadian Mounties described them, the dregs of Dawson – gamblers, prostitutes, pickpockets, swindlers, confidence men, thieves, and outright felons.

At the end of March, a west wind brought mild weather and a breathtaking display of northern lights, and it blew the snow on the ground into new drifts. The total amount of snowfall in Nome was never great compared to what fell in the interior, but what fell stayed to be blown around.

There were few customers in the Palace that night as Glory wandered over to the table next to the coal stove and sat down in a chair across from the one Deacon occupied. 'It's quiet tonight,' she remarked.

'Mmmm.' He didn't glance up from his solitaire game. 'I think the whole town's at the dance hall down the street. It's a damned shame we didn't see that "Nomad" arrive in town. Everyone could have been here.'

The recent arrival had brought several copies of newspapers from the 'outside' with him. In this isolated community, it didn't matter that the papers were more than three months old. It was still 'news' to them. At the moment, evey column on every page of the newspapers was being read aloud at another establishment down the street.

'I heard the Seattle newspaper carried a story that said there were thousands of people massing in their city to come to Nome as soon as the ice breaks up. They're predicting that the Nome gold rush will attract more people than the Klondike strike did.'

'I wouldn't be surprised.' Deacon placed a red nine on a black ten. 'It's a hell of a lot easier to reach. A ten-day ocean cruise from Seattle gets them here, versus a sea voyage followed by a brutal trek over a mountain pass, then a float trip down a river shot with rapids. It's nearly like taking a holiday.'

As she watched Deacon play, Glory suddenly realized that cards were being turned up from the deck out of order. 'Why in the world are you playing solitaire with a marked deck?'

The corners of his eyes crinkled with a smile. 'You don't think I'm going to let the devil win.'

She sighed. 'You're incorrigible.'

The heavy mahogany door to the Palace swung open. A man bundled to his eyes in layers of clothes walked in amidst the swirl of cold air and snowflakes. Glory recognized him from his walk

552

even before Justin started peeling off his scarf. She pushed out of her chair and crossed the room to greet him.

'I didn't expect you tonight.'

As she reached him, he shoved his fur-lined gloves into his coat pockets, then spanned her tiny corseted waist with his hands and lifted her high into the air, spinning around and laughing as he did so. She braced her hands on his shoulders for balance, conscious of the cold air that surrounded him as they whirled around. Finally he let her feet touch the ground. Before she had time to catch her breath, he kissed her soundly.

'I have come to celebrate,' he proclaimed as he released her.

'Celebrate what?'

'We dug up a whole seam of ruby-red sand today. It's the richest stuff we've panned yet.' Winter's snow and freezing temperatures hadn't halted the beach mining. The sands were dug and bucketed inside the tents and shacks. In the relative warmth of the habitations, the gold was sluiced, rocked, or panned from the sands by the miners. 'Tonight I don't much care how the gold got on the beach. I'm just glad it's there.'

Countless theories had been suggested to explain how the gold came to be in the sand. Some claimed that during the Ice Age a glacier must have swept a ledge of gold-bearing quartz from the mountains and deposited it on the shore. Others were certain an underwater volcano had belched the gold from the bowels of the earth and the tides had washed it ashore. A few believed that meteor showers had rained gold onto the beach. Most people subscribed to the theory that the entire floor of the Bering Sea was covered with gold that was constantly carried ashore by the waves, creating a virtually inexhaustible supply. Only a few sane men discarded such fanciful thoughts for the more mundane probability that the beach gold had been washed there from the placer deposits in the mountains by rains and spring melts.

'For a minute, I thought you'd been down the street at our competitor's, hearing the latest news, and you wanted to toast McKinley's renomination for the Presidency or the U.S. victory over the rebels in the Philippines.'

He hooked an arm around her waist and pulled her against his side. 'You don't really think I'd go anywhere else, do you?' he chided, then glanced around at the number of empty seats. 'You're not very busy tonight. Looks like I'll have you all to myself for a change.'

His coat was damp and cold from the melting snowflakes that clung to it. Glory shrank from the contact. 'You're cold. Come over by the stove and get warmed up.'

'You could warm me up, you know. I spend most of my waking hours, as it is, huddled around a stove. I was hoping for something different to thaw me out tonight.'

'Maybe that can be arranged.' Glory walked over to the carved mahogany bar. 'A bottle of good whiskey, Paddy, and two glasses.' The bartender set them on the polished counter in front of Glory. With the glasses and bottle in hand, she turned back to Justin. 'A little firewater should warm you up.'

'That's not what I had in mind either, but it'll do for a start.' Rubbing his fingers together to restore their circulation, he followed as she led the way to the table by the stove.

She set the glasses on the table and uncorked the whiskey bottle. Deacon continued to play his solitaire game, paying no attention to either of them. 'Are you hungry, Justin?'

'Is a polar bear white?'

'Matty, tell the cook to slice off some of that ham and fry some sourdough pancakes for Justin,' she called over her shoulder, her glance absently lingering on Matty's dark dress with the high lace collar. More than Matty's outward appearance had changed. She practically ran the domestic side of the Palace now, in addition to doing most of the sewing and mending, and she was learning to read.

'Are you going to stand there all night or what?' Justin reclaimed her attention.

'I'm going to sit.' She swept her satin skirt out of the way and sat down in the chair next to Justin. He took a drink of his whiskey, then glanced at Deacon, drawing attention to his silence. She doubted that Deacon was so engrossed in his card game that he hadn't noticed who had joined him at the table. 'Do you see who's here, Deacon?' Glory prodded. 'Our most faithful and loyal customer.'

'Why would he be anywhere else when he can get whatever he wants for nothing right here?' Deacon drew the cards into a pile and pushed back his chair.

Stunned by his sarcasm, Glory stared at him in disbelief as he strode away from the table to the long bar. He leaned his elbows on the counter, his back turned to them, and rested his foot on the brass rail. The more she thought about his insulting remark, the less she liked it. She had no intention of letting it stand unchallenged.

'Excuse me,' she murmured to Justin and rose from her chair. Her satin gown swished about her legs as she crossed to the bar. When she halted beside Deacon, his glance flicked briefly to her, then returned to the glass of whiskey in his hand. He tossed it back, then reached for the bottle to refill his glass. 'I think you'd better explain the remark you just made, Deacon.'

'I don't see what there is to explain. It should be obvious to anyone, even you.' He recorked the bottle and lifted the whiskey glass to his mouth, continuing to face the bar.

'I prefer to hear you say it.'

'All right.' He turned his head to look at her, his hard blue eyes unwavering. 'Since we opened the Palace, he's been coming here two or three nights a week, drinking the best of our whiskey and eating all he wants. And all of it's free – not to mention your company upstairs. He can drink and eat to his heart's content and it doesn't cost him one red cent. It's all on the house. He'd be a fool to go anywhere else.'

'If it's the money that's bothering you, Deacon, you can deduct the price of his meals and drinks from my share of the profits,' she said. 'I wouldn't want to cheat you out of anything. After all, he is my friend, not yours.'

'I'm not the one being cheated, Glory. You are. Can't you see that?'

'No.'

'Then open your eyes, because you're being used!'

She wasn't even aware of raising her hand until she felt the jarring contact with his cheek and jaw. For a moment, he was totally motionless. Carefully, almost too carefully, he set the whiskey glass down on the counter and straightened. Unconsciously, Glory held her breath, expecting some sort of violent retaliation. Instead he turned and headed for the stairs, his stride as controlled as his feelings.

Instantly she regretted slapping him. The last thing she wanted was an open breach with Deacon. She cast a glance in Justin's direction just as Matty set a plate of food in front of him.

'Deacon.' She hurried after him. He paused at the foot of the stairs and waited for her. 'I'm sorry. I didn't mean to hit you.'

'Well, I'm not sorry. I meant everything I said.'

'You're wrong about Justin.'

There was a small shake of his head in disagreement. 'Remember when I warned you about the shell game, and the time I told you the wheel of fortune was rigged. You listened to me then.'

'I know. But this time you're wrong.'

'You grubstaked the man. You pay for his food and his drinks. You sleep with him. Tell me one thing, Glory, one thing that he's given you outside of his company, which you have essentially bought. He has a poke full of gold that he's taken out of that sand, but he hasn't spent a penny of it on you.'

'What could he buy me?' she argued. 'I have everything.'

'And I suppose you wouldn't like a present from him – even if it was something as simple as a pretty ribbon for your hair? Any little something to show he cared? He's a taker, Glory. And if you can't see that, you're a fool.'

She made no move to stop him as he started up the stairs. For several seconds she watched him, then turned and walked back to the table.

'What was that all about?' Justin asked.

'Nothing.' But she knew Deacon had raised questions that couldn't be dismissed so easily.

48 *Nome*
Late June 1900

Glory stood at the foot of the four-poster bed and gazed silently at the motionless baby-faced woman lying before her. Gladys almost resembled a sleeping doll. A yellow ribbon, tied in a pretty bow, was around her loose nut-brown hair. Her extraordinarily long lashes lay softly together. A picture of innocence, except that the rosy color was missing from her round cheeks. She looked ghostly pale.

Two hours ago, Matty had found Gladys lying in a pool of blood, a damning shoe hook in her hand. Glory hadn't even known she was pregnant. She wasn't any more. Once a prostitute in Skagway had bled to death in a botched abortion attempt. Glory had barely known her, yet she had been sobered by her death – the loss of two lives.

Pregnancy could put a woman out of business. Despite all the precautions, it still could happen. It was one of the curses of the trade.

After taking her pulse, the doctor tucked Gladys' arm under the cover, then removed the stethoscope from around his neck and returned it to his black bag on the stand beside the bed. As he snapped the bag closed, Glory started to ask, 'Will she –' But the doctor silenced her with a raised finger and motioned toward the door. Glory followed him out of the room into the windowless hall, lit by newly installed electric lights. 'Will she be all right, Dr. Vargas?'

'She's young and seems quite healthy. I think she'll be fine. Believe me, Miss St. Clair, I have unfortunately seen worse cases,' he said, talking while he walked to the staircase. 'She may run a slight fever for a time. That's to be expected. However, if it should rise, you contact me at once.'

'I will.' Glory accompanied him down the steps.

'I'm sure it will be several weeks before she's up and around again. In the meantime, she's going to need rest and quiet.'

'Rest is no problem. But the quiet? I'm afraid that's an impossibility in Nome.' Glory paused at the bottom of the stairs and glanced pointedly in the direction of Front Street.

Outside, the cacophony never stopped – people shouting, hammers pounding, saws rasping, dogs barking, trace chains rattling, hooves clopping, feet tromping, whistles blowing, wagons rumbling – all against the backdrop of the sea's roar. The predicted invasion of Nome by gold seekers and opportunists had occurred. With the arrival of the first ship in the latter part of May, there had been an almost daily influx of people, an estimated fifteen thousand, and more ships were reportedly on the way. No one had ever seen anything like it. It was a sight that staggered the imagination of even the wildest dreamers.

'Indeed.' The doctor smiled in agreement. 'Well, do the best you can.'

'Naturally.' Glory walked him to the bar and saw that he was paid for his services. He regretfully refused the drink she offered him, insisting he had many patients to see.

After he'd gone, she no longer tried to conceal her troubled thoughts. At this time of year, the sun shone twenty-four hours a day. Usually there were as many people in the streets at one o'clock in the morning as there were at one in the afternoon. Yet only a few customers were in the Palace that morning.

The Palace no longer looked like a fancy saloon. All the new furnishings, mirrors, paintings, and art objects had arrived on the first ships to reach Nome after the breakup. It now resembled an exclusive gentlemen's club where a well-heeled man could drink and gamble at a discreetly positioned faro, blackjack, or poker table. The occasional nude painting and red-globed parlor lamps hinted at the other entertainments provided by Glory's stylishly dressed 'girls.' The price of admission was a mere twenty-five dollars.

Another dealer relieved Deacon at the faro table and he came over to inquire about Gladys. 'She's going to be fine, but she won't be able to work for several weeks,' Glory told him, then sighed. 'And as busy as we are, too. That sounds callous, doesn't it? I didn't mean it that way. It's just that with Mad Alice leaving to marry that photographer, and now Gladys, it leaves only Frenchie and those three new girls.'

'Maybe you can persuade Alice to postpone the wedding,' Deacon suggested.

'I've tried that. And her future husband doesn't want her to continue working after they're married.'

'How narrow-minded of him,' he murmured.

'Yes,' Glory agreed, then realized he was mocking her. 'All right, so maybe he isn't asking too much. But I just wish she wasn't getting married now. It isn't as if she'll never receive another proposal. With the shortage of women in Alaska, any woman can find a husband if she wants one.'

'And you don't want a husband.'

'Not now,' Glory answered a little stiffly, knowing that his comment referred to Justin. 'Maybe never.' She was tired of these subtle jibes he made. As Matty walked toward them, Glory looked forward to a change of subject.

'Is that why Justin hasn't been around for more than a week?' Deacon inquired within Matty's hearing.

'It hasn't been that long,' Glory retorted, then attempted to ignore him.

'Oliver picked up the mail,' Matty said, referring to the ex-prizefighter who worked as a bouncer and errand boy at the Palace.

'Thanks.' She took the half dozen envelopes Matty handed her and began to flip through them. They were mainly bills – one from her dressmaker, another from a wholesale liquor company. The envelope at the bottom of the stack bore Gabe Blackwood's name in the return corner.

'You'd better think again, Glory,' Deacon said. 'It's been at least that long since Justin was here.'

'I see Justin this morning when I go to fetch the doctor,' Matty said.

'He was in town?' The letter from Gabe Blackwood was momentarily forgotten as Glory glanced up in surprise.

'He was at the pie lady's tent when I went by.'

'I understand he spends a considerable amount of time there,' Deacon remarked.

'How would you know?' Glory demanded.

'I've made it my business to know,' he replied evenly.

She chose to ignore his implication. 'What was he doing there, Matty?'

'He was sitting and talking.'

'Sarah Porter is a widow from somewhere around Portland with two young children to feed. Like a lot of others, she arrived broke, thinking she could magically pluck gold from the sand. Now she's baking and selling pies for a living. I'm told she's become quite a pet of the miners since she arrived *two* weeks ago.' Deacon subtly stressed the length of time this woman had been in Nome.

'You seem to know a great deal about her. I take it you've met her.'

'I'd heard so many times that no one in Nome could make an apple pie to rival hers that I had to find out for myself. The pie was good.'

'And Mrs. Porter?' Glory wanted to bite her tongue for asking that.

'Very pleasing to the eye.' He looked so amused and complacent that she wanted to scream.

She ripped open the envelope containing Gabe Blackwood's letter, not wanting Deacon to have the satisfaction of knowing how keenly his innuendos were getting to her. 'If this woman is as popular as you claim, I find it strange that I've never heard of her.'

'Why, Glory,' he chided. 'She's a young mother, all alone, with two little children to raise in wicked Nome. Surely you don't believe a man would tell you about someone like her.'

'Meaning she's decent and respectable and I'm not, I suppose.'

'I didn't say that.'

'You didn't have to.' She turned to Matty. 'Would you please inform Oliver that I'll be needing the buggy.'

'Where are you going?'

'To visit Mrs. Porter and her pies. The Palace has always prided itself on providing our customers with the best Nome has to offer. Perhaps we have overlooked something.' She glared at Deacon, daring him to suggest that she had any motive other than the one she had stated, but he remained silent. He'd achieved his objective and planted the seed of suspicion in her mind that Justin was seeing this young – *respectable* – widow. 'Be sure and check on Gladys for me while I'm gone,' she told Matty, then walked swiftly to the stairs and lifted her skirts an inch to begin her ascent, accidentally crumpling the mail in her hand.

Upstairs, she entered her room and tossed the letters on the bed. She didn't bother to step behind the hand-painted dressing screen in the corner as she began unfastening the crimson gown she was wearing. Within minutes, she had donned a respectably high-necked day dress of blue and gold satin damask and slipped a bolero jacket over the puffy leg-of-mutton sleeves of her dress.

Oliver was standing guard over the buggy when Glory emerged from the Palace a few moments later. Always exceedingly proper and correct in his manners, he bowed to her and offered one of his massive hands to help her into the buggy. The back of his hand was marked with a network of old scars from his years of bare-knuckle fighting.

'Would you like me to ride with you, Miss St. Clair?'

'No, thank you, Oliver.' She picked up the reins and slapped the chestnut horse on the rump with them.

People, horses, dogs, conveyances of every description jammed the street. Everything moved at a snail's pace, but riding in the buggy was infinitely preferable to being jostled, shoved, and occasionally trampled by the mob in the street. A dust cloud two feet thick hugged the sandy street, constantly being churned to powder the air.

New buildings were springing up like mushrooms, most of them knockdowns shipped from Seattle or San Francisco and assembled on the spot. Theaters, banks, newspaper offices, restaurants, and more than a hundred saloons were going up, all on one long main thoroughfare. Nome, which some said had been built with one foot on the beach's sand and the other on the tundra, was two blocks wide and five miles long.

Sometimes Glory wondered if she would ever get used to the stench of so many people massed together in such a small area. The invasion had only compounded the sanitation problem that had previously existed. Public water closets had been built on pilings along the waterfront so the tide could flush them out roughly every twenty-four hours, but they weren't adequate to serve the exploding population.

As she neared the area where Dr. Vargas had his office, Glory began to look for the pie shop. Finally she spied a hand-lettered sign hanging on a tent; HOME-MADE PIES was all it said. Judging by the number of men crowding around the tent, she was certain she was at the right place. She parked the buggy along the side of the street and stepped down.

All the sides of the tent except the rear wall were rolled up. Rough wooden planks supported by wooden crates lined the three open ends serving as counters. Every available foot of space at the counter was taken and men were standing to wait their turn, their heads blocking Glory's view of the person behind the counter.

She picked up the short train of her dress so it wouldn't drag on the dusty ground and walked closer to the tent, where she could smell the aroma of freshly baked pies. A man turned and glanced her way, then froze. It was Justin. She wouldn't have minded his surprise if she hadn't noticed the flicker of guilt and the anxious glance he darted at the person behind the counter. But he was smiling widely as he walked toward her.

'Glory, what are you doing here?' He didn't speak too loudly, and he was careful not to get too close, she noticed.

'Why, I imagine the same reason you are. I've heard the pies here are the best in town.'

'That's true.' He stuck his hands in his pockets as if he wasn't sure what else to do with them.

'What do you recommend?' She walked past him toward the tent. 'I've heard the apple is very good.'

'It is. I kinda like the raisin myself.' He followed her, but he was careful not to let it appear to a casual observer that they were together.

The space at the counter in front of Glory was vacated by an old prospector. She quickly stepped up to fill it. A freckle-faced boy about nine years old paused on the other side of the counter, both hands gripping the wire handle of a large enameled coffeepot.

'Want some coffee, ma'am?'

'No, thank you.'

At the rear of the tent, another boy, probably a year younger, was up to his elbows in dishwater. Then she saw the woman busily slicing a pie into wedges. Her brown hair was swept back in a chignon, revealing her ears, and a mass of curls in front drooped rather attractively onto her forehead. She wore a simple starched white shirtwaist with a dark tie, and a plain dark skirt with a white apron tied around it. She was petite, the image of the 'little woman,' Glory thought scathingly. Homemaker and mother all rolled into one.

Glory had come prepared to dislike Sarah Porter on sight, and she did. Equally irritating was the patience of the miners and the absence of their usual cursing. While part of it might be attributed to the presence of the two young boys, Glory suspected that it was mostly out of deference to the young widow.

When the woman noticed Glory standing at the counter, she

immediately summoned the boy from the back. 'Timothy, will you come serve this pie to Mr. Sorenson?' As the boy willingly left the dishtub, the woman walked over to Glory. 'May I help you, ma'am?'

On closer inspection, Glory was prepared to concede the woman was attractive – in a plain sort of way, although her eyes were too close together. 'I'd like to buy some pie. I've heard that both your apple and raisin are excellent.'

'You must have been talking to Mr. Sinclair.' She smiled in Justin's direction as he stood discreetly to the side of Glory. 'Raisin is his favorite.'

'As a matter of fact, he did recommend it to me,' Glory admitted. 'I think I'll take one of each.'

'Of course.' She partially turned from the planked counter. 'Andrew, bring the lady some coffee. You would like some, wouldn't you?'

'No, thank you. Your son already inquired. He is your son?'

'Yes, I married quite young.'

'A child bride,' Glory murmured. Young, my foot, she thought to herself. She's twenty-eight if she's a day.

'Yes. I lost my husband under tragic circumstances this past winter. We're from Oregon originally. I'm sure you can appreciate how difficult it can be for a woman with two young boys to raise and no man to help. I sold everything we had to pay our passage here, hoping . . .' She paused and smiled apologetically. 'I'm sorry. You didn't come here to hear my sad story. It's just so good to see a woman's face. There are so few of us in this town. Respectable women, I mean.'

'Yes.' Glory wasn't convinced that the woman didn't suspect the nature of her profession, not when she was so aware how few women there were in Nome. 'You seem to be doing quite well for yourself, though.'

'I am. I never guessed I could make a living for my children at something so simple as making pies. Some of these poor men tell me they haven't tasted a real homemade pie in years. I had God's blessing the day I met Mr. Sinclair. There I go, rattling on again. I'll get your pies.' The young widow moved away, leaving Glory to wonder exactly what Justin had to do with all this. Justin shifted uneasily beside her.

'Are you on your way into town, Justin? she asked, fully aware that if he was, he was taking his own sweet time about getting there, since Matty had seen him here almost three hours ago. 'I'll be glad to give you a ride.'

'No. I . . . uh . . . gotta get back to the diggings. I just came to get a pie. Sort of a treat for my partners.'

'In that case, I'll drive you back.'

'That'd be great.' But his reply lacked enthusiasm.

The young widow returned with the pies. 'There you are. Still warm from the oven.'

'How much do I owe you?' Glory unfastened the gold ornamental latch on her flat folding pocketbook.

The woman told her, then added, 'The first time, I have to charge you for the pie tins. After that, you bring them back and I just charge you for the pie.'

'Of course.' Glory noticed that the difference in cost was considerably more than a pie tin would cost even at Nome's inflated prices. The woman was not only making a profit on her pies but also on the pie tins. It was very clever, she thought as she handed over the money.

She watched while Sarah Porter carefully counted out the change. When the woman switched the money to her other hand to place it in Glory's palm, Glory was instantly suspicious. Running a business had made her wise to all the sleight-of-hand tricks to shortchange someone, and switching hands was an easy way to palm a coin. Glory glanced at the change in her hand.

'I believe you still owe me a quarter,' she said.

'I do?' The surprise and innocence in her voice were very convincing. She recounted the money she'd given Glory. 'I just don't have a head for such things, I guess.' As she started back to the cashbox, she glanced down. 'Why, here it is on the ground. I must have dropped it.' She bent down and went through the motions of picking the coin off the ground, but Glory was certain it had been in her hand all the time. 'There you are. I'm so sorry.'

'That's quite all right.' But Glory was convinced it was all an act – the poor helpless female with two little boys and no head for business – and a very convincing act it was – to anyone but another woman.

'I'll take my raisin pie now, Mrs. Porter. It's time I was getting back to work,' Justin said.

'Right away.' But when she turned away, it was to call her sons. 'Timothy, Andrew. Mr. Sinclair is leaving. Isn't there something you want to tell him?'

Both paused to chorus, 'Thank you for the candy, Mr. Sinclair.'

'You're welcome,' he responded, then said to Glory, 'They're really well-mannered kids. If you wait a second, I'll help you carry the pies to your buggy.'

'Of course,' she murmured, aware that he had provided himself with an excuse to leave with her.

Sarah Porter came back with his pie. Justin paid for it, insisting she keep the change. Glory was seething as he accompanied her to the buggy. She climbed onto the seat without saying a word to him. He stowed the pies away and crawled up beside her. Immediately she slapped the reins, urging the horse into the street.

An uncomfortable silence reigned as they traveled over the crowded trail to the beach. The scene there defied description as men and machines gouged up the sand, creating a confusing network of gullies and trenches and towering sandhills of tailings. Every bizarre contraption ever invented to extract gold was in evidence. Pumps of every kind, windmills, steam engines, grizzlies, and gigantic dredges that resembled some prehistoric metal monster were operated side by side with the more conventional sluice boxes, rockers, treadmills, and long toms – and almost everything was brightly painted with all the shades of the rainbow, giving the scene the appearance of some freak sideshow.

'Wait'll you taste her pies.' Justin finally spoke up, competing with the roar and the clatter of the chugging machines. 'They're really good. She's an excellent cook. I've been telling her that she really should open a restaurant or maybe a boardinghouse.'

'Have you?' Glory murmured.

It was obvious to her that Justin had sampled more of the widow's cooking than just her pies. Silently she listened to more praise of the woman's food, as if he were trying to convince her that was his only interest in Sarah Porter.

'You really have to admire her, coming all this way to a strange place to make a new life for herself and her children,' Justin stated.

'She is an amazing woman. There's no doubt about that,' Glory declared dryly. 'And she seems to be very grateful to you for the help you've given her.'

'I didn't really do all that much – just loaned her some money to buy a few of the supplies and things she needed to start her business.'

'How generous of you, Justin.' Exceedingly generous, Glory

thought, considering that he had financed the business, bought candy for her sons, and *paid* for the pies he took; yet in all this time she hadn't received a single thing from him. It was beginning to look as though Deacon had been right about Justin all along. 'I was going to ask you how the beach was paying out, but you must be doing very well if you can afford to loan money to Mrs. Porter. By now, my interest in your claim must amount to a tidy sum of gold.' She had yet to see a single ounce in return for her grubstake the previous summer.

'Actually, we aren't taking out as much as we were. We've tried several new places, but it's beginning to look like the sands might be played out. Most of the beach has been worked over pretty good. With all these people here and their crazy contraptions for getting out the gold, there's hardly an inch of space that isn't being worked.'

Although that was a complaint Glory had heard from more than one prospector who had been at it a year like Justin, this time it seemed more an attempt to make it sound as if her share wouldn't amount to very much. He had gladly taken anything she wanted to give him, and he didn't seem to think he owed her anything in return – not even his loyalty.

Deacon had tried to warn her, but she hadn't wanted to see. She had thought – What had she thought? That Justin loved her? That she loved him? She didn't know any more. She felt like such a fool. It was a repeat of Skagway, and Justin was about to run out on her again.

Justin continued to talk, but Glory stopped listening. She resisted the urge to tell him that his poor helpless widow, Sarah Porter, wasn't as pure and lily-white as he believed her to be. She was hardly able to manage a civil good-bye to him when she dropped him off at his beach claim.

Back at the Palace, Glory informed the bartender Paddy that if Justin Sinclair ever came in again he was to pay for any food or drink he ordered, and she instructed him to notify everyone else of the change. Deacon stood there listening to every word, but Glory was much too proud to openly admit that he'd been right all along. Instead, she walked past him without saying a word and went straight to her room, not even bothering to look in on Gladys.

The mail lay on the bed where she'd left it. For a moment Glory stared at the ripped-open envelope from her father, Gabe Blackwood – the man who had used and abused her mother, then taken her money and deserted her, the same way Justin had planned to do with her. It was time men like that were taught a lesson and made to suffer the way her mother had – and the way she had. Glory had never thought she had a vindictive bone in her body, but she did. She vowed to make them pay for what they'd done.

She picked up the envelope and took out the letter. First she skimmed its handwritten contents, then read it again, more slowly.

My dearest Glory,

By the time you receive this, I shall probably have set sail for Nome. I have booked passage on the steamship *Senator*, which should arrive at Nome in the middle of July.

You have probably heard that Congress has at last passed legislation that allows for the creation of municipal governments in communities with a population of three hundred or more. There were many heated debates over the passage of this amendment which necessitated the delay in my return. But I am pleased to say my lobbying efforts were successful, even though the language of the bill does not contain all that we sought.

I have much to tell you, but I fear I have neither the time nor the space to write it all. Suffice it to say, I shall be sailing with the newly appointed federal judge for Alaska's second district, Arthur H. Noyes; the federal district attorney, Joseph K. Wood; and another influential man from North Dakota, Alexander Mackenzie. He is the president of the Alaska Gold Mining Company, and a truly dynamic individual.

I look forward with eagerness to enjoying the pleasure of your delightful company again. So many exciting things are on the horizon. Soon I will be there to share all the wonderful news with you. Until then, I remain –

Most sincerely yours
G. Blackwood

Even though he hadn't received the appointment to the new judgeship that he had coveted, he was riding high, expecting better things in store for him. And that's just the way Glory wanted it.

49

It was bedlam on the beach. Thousands of tons of freight were stacked along the waterfront, stretching from the very edge of the tide-licked sands back to the bench and for two miles along the shore-line. It was all cargo unloaded from the ships anchored in the roadstead several miles off the coast. Machinery of every description was piled on the beach, from printing presses to monstrous gold-extracting contraptions guaranteed by their makers to dredge the gold from the sand or the sea floor. Pianos, bar fixtures, stoves, sewing machines, and buggies intermingled with thousands of board feet of lumber, tons of coal and grain, crates of canned goods, and other provisions and supplies. Adding to the mass of cargo was the luggage – steamer trunks and duffels belonging to the passengers from the ships.

Once an owner was successful in locating the goods belonging to him, there was still the problem of getting them off the beach. Horse-drawn freight wagons hauled much of it. The lighter loads were pulled by six to twelve dogs harnessed in tandem to a small wagon. The heavier items were usually loaded on lighters – a barge type of conveyance – then towed offshore by steam- or gasoline-driven launches.

The result was an ear-deafening chaos. Shouts of 'Gee!' 'Haw!' 'Giddy-up thare!' 'Whoa!' 'Mush!' mingled with the cracking of whips and the cursing of the drivers. Dog fights were constantly erupting to add their snarls and growls and yips to the reigning noise, while the surf continued its battering of the coast. Occasionally, it was all drowned by the chugging roar of a passing launch. Adding to the cacophony were the whistles from the vessels anchored well off the coast. A ship signaled its arrival in Nome with several loud blasts, and every ship in the roadstead responded in kind.

At the moment, it appeared there was a veritable armada

poised off the coast of Nome. That morning the whistles had heralded the arrival of the steamship *Senator*. As soon as Glory had received word the ship was in port, she had driven the buggy out to the beach to await the disembarking passengers, knowing that Gabe Blackwood would be among them.

She sat in the shade of the buggy's roof, out of the broiling sun, and watched the slow approach of the lighter. As always, its flat top was jammed with people. In that crowd, it was impossible to recognize anyone. Carried by the waves, the bargelike vessel drifted toward the shore and ran aground several yards short of the beach. Some of the passengers were fortunate enough to have on rubber boots, but the rest had to wade ashore in their shoes unless an obliging fellow passenger agreed to carry them on his back.

Glory recognized Gabe Blackwood the instant he hopped into the water. 'Oliver.' Leaning forward, she called to the burly ex-fighter standing by the buggy horse's head. 'Mr. Blackwood is coming ashore now. Please tell him I'm here.'

'Yes, ma'am.' He bowed to her, then set off to plow his way through the stream of arriving passengers already ashore.

From her vantage point atop the buggy seat, Glory was able to observe Oliver meeting Gabe – and the man who appeared to be with him. He was tall – several inches taller than Gabe – and, even at this distance, there was something imposing about him. Glory wondered which of the three men Gabe had mentioned in his letter this one might be. Perhaps the judge. Gabe looked in her direction and waved. Glory waved back.

Parting the way for them, Oliver led Gabe and his companion to the buggy. As they approached, Glory noticed the changes in Gabe. There was a stark contrast between the man she saw now and the one she'd met a little over a year ago. His hair and chin beard were whiter. Instead of the shabby, ill-fitting suit, he now had on a single-breasted sack suit of navy wool flannel with alternating stripes of gray and blue. The pearl-gray fedora hat he wore was made from a good quality felt and banded with gros-grain silk two inches wide. But it was more than his outward appearance that signified the change in him. The confidence he exuded now no longer came from a bottle.

'My dear, what a delightful surprise,' he declared, stepping up to the buggy and taking the gloved hand she extended to him. 'I didn't expect you to be waiting here for me.'

'You've been gone so long, surely you didn't believe I'd not be here to welcome you back to Nome.'

'A man of my age does not dare presume such things,' he said, then appeared to remember his companion from the ship, and turned, directing her attention to him. 'Allow me to introduce Mr. Alexander Mackenzie, the president and general manager of the Alaska Gold Mining Company, who will be setting up his offices here in Nome. Mr. Mackenzie, Miss Glory St. Clair. She and her partner own the Palace, one of the finer etablishments in Nome.'

The face-to-face meeting reinforced her first impression of the man. Over six feet tall with thick shoulders and a portly build, Alexander Mackenzie had a commanding presence. His dark eyes were hard, but not in the same way that Deacon's were. With Deacon, it was more an absence of any emotional expression. With Mackenzie, it was a calculating coldness. He was clean-shaven except for the dark, full mustache that virtually concealed his mouth. He carried his head high, with his chin thrust forward as if daring anyone to take a swipe at it. Glory had the distinct feeling that this man was not only agressively ambitious but that he could also be ruthless.

'Welcome to Nome, Mr. Mackenzie.'

'Thank you.' He touched the brim of his hat. 'It's a pleasure to meet you, Miss St. Clair.'

'I wish you luck finding office space here, Mr. Mackenzie,' she said. 'When you can find it, it's at a premium. A closet-sized space will cost you sixty dollars a month, and that's without heat, light, or a janitor. You're lucky if the walls are plastered. Nome has become very crowded.'

'Your counsel is well taken, Miss St. Clair, but I'm sure I'll find something to suit me.' His confidence was almost scary.

'I must admit that from the deck of the ship it appeared that the entire beachfront was blanketed with snow,' Gabe said. 'When we drew closer to shore, I realized it was tents. We had heard that thousands had come, but the enormity of it didn't really hit me until now.'

'The beach is nothing compared to the congestion downtown. It's packed with people.' Glory paused and let her glance slide to Mackenzie. 'I have to confess that when I first saw you with Mr. Blackwood, I thought you might be the new judge. I understood he would be arriving on the *Senator*.'

'Judge Noyes was feeling slightly indisposed after the lengthy sea voyage. He decided to remain in his stateroom aboard the ship for a day or two.'

'I'm glad to know he has arrived. I know how anxious Mr. Blackwood has been to bring his many cases before a judge so these disputes over ownership of mining claims can finally be settled.'

'Yes, Mr. Blackwood and I have discussed the cases of several of his clients,' Mackenzie stated.

But there had been more than just discussions, Glory learned later that day when she had an opportunity to talk privately with Gabe. He had agreed to turn over his fifty percent contingent fee interest in his claim-jumping cases to Mackenzie in return for stock in the Alaska Gold Mining Company, which had an authorized capital of fifteen million dollars. Another Nome law firm had entered into a similar agreement, Gabe said, then confided that Mackenzie had said he 'owned' Judge Noyes and the new federal district attorney. While Glory was skeptical that anyone – even Alexander Mackenzie – had that much power over federal appointees, she didn't voice her doubts to Gabe.

A short two days later, she discovered how wrong she was. An attorney from the other law firm went before the new judge and asked for an injunction on behalf of his client against several of the original and richest claims filed by the Scandinavians, illegally according to him. The judge not only granted the injunction against Jafet Lindeberg's Discovery claim and several other highly productive claims, but he also named the Alaska Gold Mining Company as the receiver until the ownership issue was settled through a litigation process. He further ordered that all personal property on the premises be confiscated, including any recovery gold, and that Mackenzie post a five-thousand-dollar surety bond per mine. And it was all accomplished within minutes – with no opposition from the original claimants or their counsel. It seemed someone had failed to inform them the request was being brought before the new judge.

After granting the injunction and appointing the receivership, Judge Noyes adjourned the court. Mackenzie had wagons of men waiting outside. They raced out of Nome and took possession of most of the major mining claims on gold-rich Anvil Creek.

Nome buzzed with the news. Mackenzie had not only evicted the miners and taken possession of the mining equipment, gold dust, and nuggets, but he also intended to work the claims. Some claimed Mackenzie hadn't even posted the required bond. Most believed the five-thousand-dollar bond was a farce anyway. Miners had been taking fifteen thousand dollars in gold *a day* out of the Discovery claim.

That night, it was practically the only subject discussed at the Palace. While many had wanted the claims of the so-called foreigners thrown out, most thought the judge had given Mackenzie a license to steal. They doubted there would be any gold left by the time the ownership issue was decided. Everywhere Glory went, the talk was the same. She stopped to watch a high-stakes poker game with a large pot of chips in the middle of the table.

'I heard Jafet's lawyers never got a chance to argue their side,' one of the men said. 'After they found out he'd lost control of his claims, they tried to see the judge, but he wasn't available.' The man tossed in a stack of chips and added an almost disinterested 'I'll see your raise.'

'Yeah, and you know why the judge wasn't available?' The next player flipped over his cards, indicating he was folding, then supplied the answer to his own question. 'The judge conveniently left for St. Michael. Word is he won't be back for two weeks or more.'

Raised voices came from the doorway. Glory glanced toward the entrance to determine the problem. She smiled faintly when she saw Justin at the door, his entry barred by the dark-suited man stationed there to collect the admission fee. As she started toward the entrance, she noticed that Oliver was already on his way to quell the disturbance.

'Oliver.' Justin recognized him with a mixture of relief and exasperation. 'Will you please tell this man who I am? I've tried to explain that I'm one of Glory's friends, but he just won't listen. He keeps insisting I have to pay him.'

'I'm sorry, Mr. Sinclair –' Oliver began.

'It's all right, Oliver,' Glory said as she crossed the last few feet to the doorway. 'I'll handle this.'

'Yes, Miss Glory.' Oliver stepped back, but he didn't leave.

'I'm glad you showed up.' Justin tried his smile on her. 'I was beginning to think I was going to have to fight my way in to see you. This guy didn't believe I was your friend.'

'I don't think it's Hawkins' fault,' she replied smoothly. 'After all, he's been working for us nearly three weeks now. And in all that time, you've never been here once.'

'I know.' He seemed to realize the smile wasn't working. 'I'm sorry it's been so long, but I've been kind of busy lately. The time just sorta got away from me.' He started to take a step in, but the new man intervened to stop him again. Impatient and puzzled, Justin frowned at her. 'Will you tell this guy to let me pass?'

'Have you already paid him?' Glory smiled.

'Of course not.' His frown deepened.

'I'm sorry, Justin. Those are the new house rules.'

'Since when?'

'Since I decided that's the way it would be.' She kept her voice level, enjoying this moment. 'You pay for your raisin pies. Why shouldn't you pay to get in here?'

'Is that it?' He glared at her. 'I never made you any promises.'

'I never made *you* any promises, Justin.' Glory took pleasure in pointing that out to him. 'As an old friend, you're more than welcome at the Palace any time. But from now on, you'll have to pay your way. There won't be any more free rides – if you get my meaning.'

For a long moment Justin didn't move. Not even an eyelash flickered. Then abruptly he swung away and charged out the door, slamming it behind him. Glory lingered an instant, gazing at the door, then turned back to the room. From across the way, Deacon watched her. She thought she detected a smile of approval from him. She smiled back.

In the morning hours, after most of the customers had left, Deacon came to her room. Glory discovered that the old magic they'd once shared was still there. But more important, she was at ease with him. There never seemed to be any need for explanations. Deacon understood the difference between business and pleasure.

August brought rain that turned Nome's sandy streets into a quagmire and seemed to add to the slough of the city's inhabitants. The quantities of gold found on the beach became steadily smaller, no matter how ingenious or expensive the contraptions used to mine it. The 'golden sands of Nome' were golden no more.

The rich placer deposits of the treeless inland mountains continued to yield their nuggets and grains of gold, but most of the claims were controlled by Mackenzie. Nearly everyone was convinced the gold was going into his pockets and not into receivership for the rightful owners. Judge Noyes returned from St. Michael, but refused to hear the protests of the original claimants and summarily denied their motions for appeal to the circuit court in San Francisco. In defiance of his rulings, the attorneys left for San Francisco at the end of the month to directly petition the court of appeals to review their cases.

By the end of the summer, mining in the inland mountains had virtually come to a halt. Any prospector in the hills who unearthed pay dirt inevitably covered it up again, fearing that if the discovery was known the claim would be challenged and wind up – through legal shenanigans – in Mackenzie's hands.

Nome was rife with tension. The crime rate soared. The end of August brought the cover of darkness for the criminal element to commit their robberies, burglaries, and assaults. In early September, Wyatt Earp was arrested a second time for assaulting a policeman, and a grand jury concluded that the presence of women in the city's gambling halls and saloons was the major cause of the lawlessness. An order banning all women from such places with the exception of those engaged to sing or otherwise perform for the customers was passed. At the Palace that night, the piano player accompanied Glory's girls as they sang a collection of songs ranging from 'Just As the Sun Went Down' to 'Because I Love You,' and other popular ballads.

Meanwhile, Nome hovered on the edge of violence. The threat was always there that if the courts failed them, the miners would take the law in their own hands. The result would be open warfare between the miners and Mackenzie's band of toughs.

At midday on the twelfth of September, Glory sat on the chaise longue in the small sitting area off her bedroom. Clad in a loose-fitting tea gown, she idly puffed on the cigarette in her holder and listened to Gabe expound, as he endlessly did, on the vast power and influence held by Alexander Mackenzie. Outside a storm raged, threatening to blow up a gale.

'My stock in the Alaska Gold Mining Company is going to be worth a small fortune,' he declared. 'More, once the judge invalidates the previous claims to the mines and gives legal title to the corporation.'

'You sound so confident that will happen.'

'Those foreigners have no right to stake claims on American soil. Everyone knows that,' he replied with the patience of a parent speaking to a child.

'Perhaps.' She rolled the ash off the tip of her cigarette into a brass ashtray. 'But it's my understanding of the law that the government is the only entity that can question the citizenship of a miner. Another miner doesn't have the right to use a person's citizenship as an excuse to jump his claim. How can you be so sure the judge will rule in favor of the Alaska Gold Mining Company?'

'Because Mackenzie's got the judge in his pocket. The judge will do whatever he tells him. I tell you, Glory, it's going to be a great day when he finally issues his decision. That stock will not only make me a rich man, but with Mackenzie behind me I will be appointed governor of Alaska. You wait and see.'

'Aren't you a little bit concerned about what might be happening in San Francisco, Gabe? The lawyers for both Lindeberg's Pioneer Mining Company and the Wild Goose Mining Company are there petitioning the federal appeals court to overturn Judge Noyes's ruling.'

'Nothing will come of it. When has anyone from the outside given a damn about what happens in Alaska? Never. And that isn't about to change now. And don't forget' – he leaned forward in his chair, assuming a confidential attitude – 'Mackenzie has important friends. That man has personally known every United States President from Cleveland to McKinley. His base of power is unparalleled.' He paused to chuckle. 'They don't call him 'Alexander the Great' for nothing.'

So far, Glory had to concede, Mackenzie appeared to be untouchable. It wasn't that he was beyond the reach of the law, but rather that he controlled it. She didn't care about Mackenzie, but what fascinated her was the corrupting influence he'd had on Gabe. Her mother had frequently mentioned his high ideals and his dream of becoming governor. He'd never lost the dream. Now he'd found a man with the power to make his dream come true. Every day he was getting older, and time was running out. Knowing that, he was letting the ends justify the means. And his lifelong prejudice allowed him to do it with a free conscience.

The howling wind rattled the windows, its fury underscored by the roar of the wickedly pounding surf just yards away from the rear of the Palace. The storm's tumult almost drowned out the knock at her door.

'Come in,' Glory called.

Matty opened her door and walked in carrying a tray laden with a silver coffee service. 'Bring it over here, Matty.' Glory swung her feet off the chaise longue, crushing out her cigarette in the ashtray, then removing the butt from the holder, as Matty crossed the room and set the tray on a low table by the chaise.

'The storm is getting very bad,' Matty told her. 'The waves are coming higher and higher. The sea is angry. Soon, I think, it will come ashore.'

'I hope you're wrong, Matty. All those people living in tents on the beach . . .' She shook her head, not wanting to think about that.

Storms out of the south struck the coast of the Seward Peninsula every spring and fall. In its highly exposed location, Nome invariably took the brunt of these southeasters, properly called equinoctial storms. Many sourdoughs claimed they were called that because they were 'unequaled' and 'obnoxious.'

'When storms like this come, my people always leave the coast and go inland where it is safer.' Matty darted an anxious glance at the ominous gray beyond the rain- and wind-lashed window. 'The signs are bad. Maybe we should go, too.'

'We've been through storms like this before,' Glory said. 'This one may be worse than some of the others, but I don't think we'll have to take such drastic measures.'

'Deacon says maybe we will,' Matty stated, then moved toward the door.

As Glory poured coffee from the silver pot into the two cups, she thought about Matty's last remark. Deacon was not the kind to become unnecessarily alarmed. She passed a cup and saucer to Gabe, then carried hers to the window, vaguely conscious of the sound of the door closing behind Matty. She peered out the water-spattered windowpane and noticed the way the building shuddered under the force of the powerful wind. Faintly she could hear the crash and clatter of debris being blown around outside.

Behind her, Gabe snorted in contempt. ' "The signs are bad." That's a lot of stupid native superstition.'

Below she could just barely make out the towering sea waves as they came crashing down to splash against the rear foundation of the Palace. She hadn't realized the water was that close. 'The waves are already at the back door.'

'What does that mean?' he scoffed. 'These storms have licked at the city's toes before. Don't be taken in by all that nonsense. I wish to God you'd listen to me and get rid of that . . . woman . . . once and for all. Her kind are no good.'

'We've been over that before.' She turned away from the window.

'I grant you, she's cheap labor. But you can't trust her. Those people lie and steal. It's their nature. You simply don't need her kind around here. Believe me, I know what I'm talking about. I've had experience handling Indians. You've gotta keep them in line and teach them their place.'

The longer she listened to his lecture, the angrier she became. She knew just how he had kept her mother in line.

'Just what is their place?' she demanded coldly, but he didn't seem to notice the chill in her voice.

'It isn't living among decent white people. The best thing for you to do is get rid of her.' He jabbed his finger at her to drive home the message. 'Trying to civilize those people the way you're doing with her is a waste of time. They're like a leopard; you can tame them but you can't change their spots. They're always going to be treacherous and deceitful. Let her go back and live in an igloo and eat blubber. It's wrong for you to associate with her kind.'

'What if I told you I *am* "her kind"?' She was sick to death of his prejudice. This time he'd gone too far.

He stared at her for a stunned moment, then laughed shortly to conceal his confusion. 'What are you talking about?'

'What if I said I am her people? Or maybe I should put it another way. She is my people. We're related. Matty and I are cousins.'

'I don't believe that.'

'It's true. What's the matter, Gabe? Don't I look like an Indian princess to you?'

'Hardly.'

After going this far, something goaded her into going the rest of the way. 'What about a Russian princess?'

Taken aback by the question, he appeared suddenly nervous and wary. 'Russian? Why would you say that?'

'I'm known professionally as Glory St. Clair. Would you like to know what my real name is?'

'What?'

'Marisha. Marisha Blackwood, daughter of Nadia Levyena Blackwood – maiden name Tarakanov.' Her announcement shocked him out of his chair.

'That's impossible!'

'Nadia Levyena Tarakanov of mixed Aleut, Tlingit, and Russian extraction was married to American lawyer Gabe Blackwood

577

at St. Michael's Cathedral in Sitka, Alaska. Surely you remember that day.' She walked toward him, watching the shock and disbelief on his face. 'Or maybe your memory is clearer about the day you left – the day Nadia's grandfather, Wolf Tarakanov, suffered a heart attack after he tried to stop you from beating her and killing the unborn child she carried – the same day that you stole all the silver from his house and fled on the mail boat.'

'How – how did you learn that? Where did you find it out?' He backed away from her, involuntarily moving his head from side to side in disbelief.

'Most of it from my mother's sister, my aunt Eva. Mother talked about you, too, about how you wanted to be governor.'

'I don't know who told you all this, but it's a lie,' he blustered. 'Not a word of it is true. You're wrong if you think you can blackmail me with this. I won't stand for it.'

'Blackmail you? Now what kind of daughter would try to blackmail her own father? You are my father.'

'No. It can't be.'

'But it is. Don't you remember telling me how familiar I looked to you? Isn't it possible I remind you of my mother?'

'No.'

'You can deny it all you want, Gabe, but it's a fact. I am your daughter and I can prove it. My mother is dead, but my Aunt Eva is still alive. And there are a lot of people in Sitka who would remember me – poor little Marisha Blackwood. I've only been away three years.' He was staring at her as if looking at a ghost. She stopped in front of him and ran her finger along the rounded lapel of his suit jacket. 'What's the matter, Papa? You don't look happy to meet me.'

He knocked her hand away. 'Don't touch me! Stay away from me, I say!' He half turned from her, a wild panic racing over his features.

'What do you suppose Mackenzie will think when I tell him you're my father? I doubt it will bother him – unlike you – that I have some Indian blood. But for the future governor of Alaska to have as his daughter one of the most famous – or should I say infamous – scarlet ladies in the whole of Alaska, somehow I have the feeling he'll have second thoughts about making you governor.'

'You wouldn't tell him?'

'Oh, wouldn't I?' She strolled away from him. 'Newspapers

love scandal. Can you imagine the headlines? "Notorious Soiled Dove – Daughter of Man Seeking Appointment as Alaskan Governor." ' Glory paused and tipped her head back to laugh. 'You'll never be governor, Gabe Blackwood. I wanted it within your reach. But you'll never have it.' She swung back to face him. 'I'll see to that. You'll never be appointed governor, judge, or garbage collector. Nothing – that's what you are and that's what you'll stay.'

'You deceived me. All this time, you deceived me.' He vibrated with anger. 'Just the way she did. You're all alike. Nothing but a bunch of lying scum!' He took a threatening step toward her, but Glory stood her ground, unflinching. He would not intimidate her as he had her mother. 'I let her destroy my chances once. But I'm not going to stand by and let you ruin them for me this time. I've waited too many years for this. Too many years.'

'And you'll still be waiting on your deathbed,' she taunted.

His hand seemed to come out of nowhere. Glory caught a brief flash of it before it struck her face. Pain exploded alongside her head. She wasn't even aware of the brief cry that came from her as she staggered backwards under the force of the blow, dropping the cup and saucer. As he struck her again and again, she raised her arms trying to fend him off. She kept retreating, suddenly realizing how frightened and helpless her mother must have felt under his battering assault.

She bumped against an object that blocked her retreat. He hit her again and she fell onto the bed. Feeling the soft feather mattress under her, Glory tried to scramble to the safety of the other side. But he caught at her tea gown. She heard the tearing of the fragile fabric as she frantically tried to pull free. Before she could succeed, he was on the bed and his hands were circling her throat.

Glory screamed as loud as she could, doubting that she would be heard above the growing fury of the storm raging outside. Too quickly he choked off her cries. Kicking and struggling, she clawed at his face, ripping the skin with her fingernails and trying to gouge out his eyes. Her efforts succeeded in preventing him from tightening the stranglehold of his hands and choking off all her breath, but her lungs already felt like they were going to burst. Glory knew she couldn't hold him off much longer. If only she had a weapon – something – anything to hit him with, but there was nothing at hand.

Her strength was rapidly waning. She felt herself slipping into the blackening mists of unconsciousness and tried to fight it. Suddenly she was free of his hands. With the first gulp of air, she started coughing. She grabbed hold of her throat and dragged herself over to the nightstand by the bed, intent on getting the pistol she kept in the drawer. She looked to see where Gabe was, but it was Deacon she saw standing by the bed. Gabe was just pushing away from the side wall, his left hand rubbing his jaw.

'Are you all right, Glory?' Deacon turned to her just as she saw Gabe reach inside his jacket and pull out a revolver.

'Look out! He's got a gun.'

Deacon spun around. The spring-action derringer jumped into his hand from its hidden sleeve holster. Before he could aim, Glory saw yellow flame leap from the muzzle of Gabe's gun and a deafening explosion rent the air. Deacon jerked and grabbed at his right arm. The derringer went off, the bullet going harmlessly through the ceiling.

'No!' Glory scrambled off the bed.

She grabbed the pearl-handled pistol out of the drawer and used both hands to point it at Gabe. She squeezed the trigger, shutting her eyes at the thunderous report as the gun bucked in her hand. The shot went wild, striking the wall several feet from him. Shock was in his expression as Glory struggled to cock the hammer. He bolted from the room.

Deacon was on his knees near the bed, his left hand gripping his right arm near the elbow. His face was twisted in pain as he sucked in air through his teeth. Glory hurried to his side, forgetting for the moment the fleeing Gabe and her own aches and bruises. She took one look at the crimson blood seeping through his fingers and streaming down the back of his left hand, and ran to the door.

'Matty!' she shouted. 'Come here! Quick!' She went back to Deacon. Her hands were shaking as she tore a strip of material from the hem of her gown. 'We've got to stop the bleeding.' She tied the cloth around his upper arm above the wound and retrieved a coffee spoon from the service tray to twist the cloth tighter, fashioning a tourniquet.

'Your face,' Deacon murmured.

His remark made her conscious of her swollen lip and the blood that trickled from the cut – and half a hundred other throbbing places. 'I'm all right,' she assured him. Her injuries seemed extremely minor compared to his.

'I came upstairs to tell you the storm's getting worse.' His voice was husky with pain. 'Feel the building rock? That's the waves hitting it. Others along the street are trying to anchor theirs down. We need to do the same. In the meantime, we better get everybody out and save what we can. Glory' – he paused and she could hear the roughness of his breath – 'what happened up here? Blackwood looked like a madman.'

'Sssh, don't talk.' The pallor in his face frightened her. 'I'll tell you later.' She heard Matty's footsteps in the hallway outside and glanced at the open door as the woman appeared. 'Deacon's been shot. We've got to get him to a doctor.'

'It's bad, isn't it?' Deacon said.

She couldn't bring herself to answer him. It wasn't a fatal wound by any means. She doubted that he was in any danger of bleeding to death. But she'd noticed the little bone chips when she'd bandaged it. She was afraid the bullet had shattered the elbow. If it had, his right arm might be permanently crippled. And Deacon was a professional gambler.

Glory donned a long raincoat and a pair of galoshes while Matty fashioned a sling for Deacon's arm and helped him into one sleeve of his rain slicker. As they started to leave the room, Glory picked up the gun she'd dropped on the floor and stuffed it in her coat pocket, rather than take the time to return it to the drawer.

The minute they stepped outside the front door of the Palace, the gale-force winds slammed into them. Debris was flying everywhere. Water flooded the street as the storm lashed the shallow Bering Sea into a fury and drove it ashore. There was hardly a tent anywhere still standing. Some of the flimsier wooden structures on the beach side of Front Street were collapsing, unable to withstand the powerful battering by the sea. A larger, stronger building had been moved off its foundation. Several men were frantically at work trying to anchor it down.

As they attempted to cross the flooded street, fighting the gale winds that tried to flatten them, Glory realized this was no ordinary equinoctial storm. Its destructive force was beyond anything the city of Nome had seen before. Before leaving the Palace, she had passed on Deacon's recommendation to Oliver to evacuate everyone and save what he could. Now she was glad she had.

Anything that wasn't securely nailed down was either flying or floating. As they climbed onto the planked boardwalk on the other side of the street, a large barrel nearly rolled them down. Deacon's features showed the pain that not even his iron command of expression could conceal. Glory realized how far they had to go to reach the doctor's office. In this storm, it would be an ordeal for him.

'The hospital!' she shouted to make herself heard above the roar of the wind and the sea. It was closer, only a couple of blocks. Matty nodded her understanding, and they changed directions, the two of them flanking Deacon.

Within minutes, Glory was soaked to the skin, her clothes plastered to her body, water running into her boots. All her attention was centered on staying upright in the seventy-five-mile-an-hour wind and dodging the flying scraps of wooden crates and pieces of roofs.

A block from their destination, Glory saw a man emerge from a small office and start toward them, hugging the walls of the buildings for support. He had some sort of satchel clutched to his chest as he staggered forward, hunched over to battle the wind. A split second later, Glory recognized Gabe, even though she couldn't see his face clearly. Suddenly, she could feel the sensation of his hands on her throat. The rage and terror she'd felt resurfaced. He would pay for what he'd done.

As she moved away from Deacon, Matty started to pause. 'Go!' Glory motioned for her to continue. Deacon said something, but the storm carried away his words. Glory knew she wouldn't have heeded them anyway.

When Gabe recognized her, he stopped and looked wildly around. She remembered the gun in her pocket and searched the opening in the wet cloth, never taking her gaze off Gabe as she continued forward, constantly buffeted by the wind. At last her fingers located the wet, slick metal, and she pulled it free of the material. She had no conscious intention of killing him. She just wanted to make him pay and it wasn't really clear in her mind what that meant.

Something smashed into a window a few feet in front of her. She lifted her arms to protect her face from the flying glass revealing the gun in her hand. He started to retreat, then abruptly charged into the mud- and water-logged street, awash with floating debris. Glory waded into the street after him, angling on a course to intercept him, but it was hard going with her wet skirts constantly tangling around her legs. She was conscious that he was laboring too, handicapped by his age and the strain of all his recent exertion.

In the middle of the street, he halted and dropped the satchel, then fumbled for something inside his coat. He pulled out the revolver. Glory hesitated, then saw a sheet of tin come flying through the air and strike his arm. It knocked the gun from his hand into the muddy soup near his feet. He started to search for it, then apparently thought better of it, and began running, staggering and stumbling through the muck. Lifting her skirts, Glory hurried after him.

The buildings on the opposite side of the street offered partial shelter from the howling wind. Glory scrambled onto the sidewalk's slippery boards and chased after Gabe. He ducked between two buildings just ahead of her. Afraid of losing him, she sprinted to close the distance.

When she rounded the corner, he had just turned back, the inrushing sea blocking that avenue of escape. There was no place left for him to run. He was trapped. He stood facing her. Slowly, brokenly, he shook his head in some silent denial.

'I'm not my mother.' The wind whipped away her words. She raised the pistol and stared at the sodden, bedraggled, pathetic-looking old man.

Something distracted her, a roar that seemed louder. Her gaze lifted. In shock, she stared at the monstrous breaker rising above him. She couldn't move; she couldn't speak. She watched in horror as the towering wave smashed into the rear of the buildings on either side and came crashing down on Gabe, swallowing him up.

A second later, the flood wave was sweeping into her. She tried to reach the relative protection of the building, then grabbed hold of the corner, clawing frantically to keep the sucking water from dragging her out to sea. The force of the wave lifted the building up and pushed it forward. Glory nearly lost her grip, but she managed to hang on. As soon as she regained her footing, she staggered into the street to escape the next breaker.

Someone saw her and rushed to help her to safety. Glory looked back once. There was nothing but debris and surging water in the place where she'd last seen Gabe.

*

583

The storm raged on, not reaching its peak until that night. Tents by the thousands were ripped apart and blown away. All mining equipment on the beach was demolished and carried out to sea. Four ships, including the mammoth barge *Skookum*, broke apart in the savage surf. Nearly half of Nome's business district, virtually every building on the beach side of Front Street, was destroyed, including Ryan Colby's Double Eagle saloon. Colby himself was missing and presumed drowned. Many lives were lost, but there was no accurate estimate of the number. Soldiers and looters were out in force.

Nothing was left of the Palace except kindling wood. An eye-witness told Glory that the waves had picked it up and smashed it into the building across the street. The girls had thoughtfully grabbed some of her clothes, and Oliver had rescued a few of the more valuable items before they'd fled the storm. Everything else was gone.

As for Deacon, Gabe's bullet hadn't shattered the elbow joint as Glory had feared, but it had chipped the bone and damaged a main trunk nerve. The latter was the cause of his excruciating pain that only regular dosages of morphine could dull. The doctor wouldn't speculate on how much the nerve would heal.

Like thousands of others in Nome, they were homeless. Roughly fifteen thousand people left Alaska for the states that autumn, many of them penniless. But Glory, Deacon, and Matty stayed on, and Glory started rebuilding the Palace, but this time not on the beachfront.

On the fifteenth of October, two deputy marshals from California arrested Alexander Mackenzie on felony charges and transported him on the last ship leaving Nome to San Francisco for trial. Glory almost wished Gabe was alive to see his grand dream dissolve.

50

That winter, Glory discovered she was pregnant. Within minutes after the doctor had confirmed her suspicion, she knew exactly what she was going to do. She would have the child and raise it herself, regardless of the complications he – or she – might create in her life. She had grown up knowing her father hadn't wanted her, that he would have gotten rid of her if the choice had been his to make. Her mother had loved her, but that had never fully compensated for the feeling of rejection she had known. Now a life was inside her, and she wasn't going to reject it.

When Deacon learned of her decision, he insisted they be married. His wound had healed, but the damaged nerve hadn't. He had the full use of his hand and arm, but he'd lost most of the sensation. The sharp, tingling pain stayed with him. More and more he had come to rely on morphine to help him make it through the day.

But he cared for her. Of that, Glory had no doubt. And she had grown to care very much for him. It was love – of a kind – perhaps stronger than the romantic kind she had once dreamed about. His days as a professional gambler were over. While he could still play cards and deal hands, he couldn't handle the holdouts, slip in the cold decks, or recognize the strippers any more because of the accident, because of her. Glory felt responsible for that, but she also felt she owed him so much more.

On February 11, 1901, the same day that Alexander Mackenzie was convicted and sentenced to a year in prison in California, Glory married Robert 'Deacon' Cole. When the spring thaw came, they built a small house with gingerbread trim a few blocks from the new Palace. In her condition, Glory could do no more than supervise, and she left much of the running of the business to Deacon and Matty.

Summer didn't bring a horde of gold seekers to the beaches of

Nome. The sand had played out. More than two million dollars in gold had been taken from it. Now it was gone. And the city's economy had to rely on the inland mines, which was no great hardship, since they were rich and productive. The first ship to arrive that summer brought the news that President McKinley had pardoned Mackenzie on the grounds that his health was 'too feeble' for him to serve the remainder of his prison term. The reports also added that the supposedly ailing Mackenzie had been seen sprinting to catch the train out of Oakland. It seemed to Glory that Gabe had been right, after all, about Mackenzie's connections in high places.

In July, Glory gave birth to a seven-pound boy. Deacon stood beside her bed, the red-faced infant lying in the cradle of his good right arm. Propped up by a half dozen pillows, Glory watched him gaze at the sleeping baby.

'Glory,' Deacon murmured, 'I do believe that we've been dealt an ace.'

That's what they named him – Ace Matthew Cole – the Matthew after Matty, the other person who was dearest to her. Between the three of them, they managed to spoil him outrageously, but Ace was the happy kind of baby who was easy to spoil. Glory was so content with her new family and new life that it didn't seem to matter at all when she heard that the widow Mrs. Sarah Porter who ran a popular boardinghouse in Nome had married Justin Sinclair.

That summer the city council outlawed both gambling and prostitution, but both enterprises flourished openly. The vast majority of the townspeople were not ready to give up their vices. That same summer the streets of Nome were planked with boards three inches thick and a foot wide. Glory and Deacon were able to take Ace out in his baby carriage without getting the wheels mired in the mud.

The following year, Glory went back to work at the Palace full time and left Matty to look after Ace. The times were good those first few years after Ace was born. While the profits they made never did come close to equaling what they had earned during the wild years of the gold rush, they were enough for Glory to hire a Chinese cook, Chou Ling, to fix their meals at home; and to install a piano in the parlor and import crystal and china for their dinner table. If Deacon disappeared more frequently now into the back office at the Palace where he kept his supply of morphine, Glory tried not to notice. After all, how much pain could she expect him to tolerate without seeking some relief?

On the night of September 12, 1905, exactly five years to the day of the disastrous storm, Deacon staged a prizefight at the Palace – illegally, since prizefighting, like gambling and prostitution, was outlawed. People forked over the gate fee just the same and jammed inside to see the sixteen-round fight between the Waco Kid and Bruiser McGee. Every available inch of space was taken as the men crowded around the makeshift ring erected in the center of the Palace and bet their money on their favorite.

Once the bell rang to start the opening round, the shouting never stopped. The excitement was contagious, yet Glory didn't find much pleasure in watching the two bare-chested men in short boxing trunks beat each other to a pulp. Admittedly, she didn't know an uppercut from a kidney blow, but the blood-splattered spectacle of the two men was enough to convince her of the utter brutality of the sport. She was glad she'd insisted on having the Persian carpet taken up when she saw the blood-smeared floor of the ring. Actually she had more fun watching Oliver on the sidelines, punching and jabbing, bobbing and weaving, as if he was in some imaginary fight himself.

The favorite, Bruiser McGee, was knocked out in the fourteenth round, but the crowd didn't seem to mind as they bellied up to the bar. They seemed satisfied that they'd seen a good fight, even though most of them suspected it had been fixed. Actually it had been, but Glory didn't admit that to any of the customers as she circulated and encouraged them to drink.

Fights were a drawing card to bring in business. Tonight the crowd stayed until well after midnight, drinking and gambling and generally having a good time. Sometime after three in the morning, it started to quiet down. Glory wandered over to the bar.

'What'll ya have?' Paddy smiled at her while continuing to polish dry the glass in his hand.

'Coffee, if there is any.' She leaned tiredly on the counter. A little smile stole over her mouth as she thought of her sandy-haired blue-eyed boy, picturing him asleep in his bed, innocent and beautiful as only a child can be.

Deacon came up and stood beside her. 'How's it going?'

'Fine.' She carefully didn't ask where he'd been the last hour or so. 'It's been a good night.'

'A very good night.' He sounded so fresh and chipper.

Glory suddenly noticed the changes in him, changes that had come about so slowly. He'd lost weight, she knew, but she hadn't realized how thin he was until now. His skin looked pale. His eyes weren't the same. They didn't have that sharpness, as if they were permanently dulled by pain or drugs. She remembered the old Deacon and wanted to cry.

Suddenly, from the street came the clang of a fire bell, followed by shouts of alarm. For an instant she stood staring at the door. Those closest to it went outside to take a look.

One of them came running back in. 'Fire!' he shouted. 'Fire in the Stockade.' The news that the fire was so close started a stampede to the door.

'Stay here.' Deacon headed for the exit.

But Glory had no intention of doing anything of the kind. She dashed into the back office and retrieved the fur parka Matty had made her. She threw it around her shoulders and hurried to the door. She pushed her way into the crowd on the board sidewalk and wood-paved street outside, gawking at the billowing smoke and faint glow coming from behind the saloons down the street.

Glory darted onto the narrow street for a better view, but it was difficult to see anything. The two- and three-story wooden buildings, some with protruding second-story bay windows, flanked both sides of the street, creating a narrow canyon. Men gravitated toward the blaze, some to help the firemen, others simply to watch.

'Has anyone heard how bad it is?' Glory asked the man next to her, aware that the close-set cabins in the Stockade were little more than tinderboxes.

The man shook his head. 'That glow don't look good, though. It's gettin' brighter.'

Within seconds a man came running down the street shouting, 'The Alaska Saloon's on fire!'

The saloon was less than a block from the Palace. The fire had jumped the alleyway that separated the Stockade from the main business district of Nome. Suddenly, an explosion shot flames into the air, eerily backlighting the snaking electric wires strung on the staggered line of poles in the street.

'Holy Jeezus, a gasoline tank musta blew,' the man beside her declared.

Practically every building along the street had one. The fire was already out of control. Glory knew that if more gasoline tanks exploded it would spread even faster. The whole block might go up in flames. Maybe even the whole town. Down the street, she could see people carrying things out of the buildings that were closer to the fire, desperately trying to save what they could in case it spread, as it seemed bound to do. Glory ran back into the Palace.

Oliver, Paddy, and one of the dealers were taking down the expensive paintings from the walls. Glory sent the girls upstairs to pack their belongings.

'Where's Deacon?' she asked.

'Mr. Cole is in the office,' Oliver told her. 'Don't worry, ma'am. This time we'll be able to save most of the stuff.'

'I know you will.' She smiled, remembering how guilty he'd felt after the storm because so much had been lost.

Lifting her skirts, she ran to the back office. As she entered the room, Deacon glanced over his shoulder, then went back to removing the cash from the safe and stuffing it in a small satchel. She walked over to him as he put the last bag of coins inside. She had a quick glimpse of his morphine supply in the bottom of the satchel before he closed the bag.

'I want you to take this and go to the house.' Deacon pressed the satchel into her hands.

'But –' There was so much to be done here if they weren't to lose it all.

'I know Matty will look after Ace, but I'll feel better knowing that you're with them and all of you are safe.'

The vibrations of another explosion, closer than the last, shook the building. The fire was spreading, and their house was only two blocks away. She suddenly understood that Deacon feared it was in jeopardy as well as the Palace.

'I'll go.'

But watching the conflagration from the front window of their home as it lit the skies above Nome like daylight wasn't easy for Glory. When she had arrived at the house, there hadn't been any need to awaken anyone. They were all up – Matty, Chou Ling, and Ace, too. As a precaution, she had Matty and Chou Ling pack many of the valuables and the essential things like clothes and toiletries, as well as some sentimental irreplaceable items. She even put Ace to work packing his toys.

Once that was done, there was nothing to do but wait and watch the glow become brighter and spread over a wider area. Ace was fascinated by the fire and shrieked in delight each time he spied yellow flames leaping into the air. He wanted to go see it, too young to understand the massive destruction it was causing or why his mommy had tears in her eyes when the fire's glow encompassed the Palace.

By the time the fire was finally put out, two blocks in the heart of town had been leveled, destroying some fifty businesses, ranging from saloons, restaurants, and hotels to grocery stores and a bowling alley, plus almost twenty cribs in the Stockade. Glory stood beside Deacon, facing the blackened area that spanned both sides of Front Street. The smell of smoke and charred ash was strong. Nothing remained but smoldering rubble, with some pieces of scorched corrugated iron here and there and a few partially burned safes. Matty stood behind them, holding on to Ace's hand with a firm grip.

'We'll have to rebuild again,' Glory murmured, aware that several people were already at work shoveling away the charred remains of their former businessses to clear the sites and start anew.

'No,' Deacon said.

'What?' She looked at him in surprise. 'Why?'

'It's time to move on. They're still taking gold out of these mountains, but the boom is over.' That was a gambler's way – to skim the cream and leave, never staying in one town too long. 'I've heard Fairbanks is growing fast.'

Just as she had trusted his judgement when he had decided they should leave Skagway for Nome, she trusted it now. If they were going to start over, it might as well be in a new place. 'We packed practically everything last night,' she told him.

'I know.'

They sold the house, the lot on Front Street, and many of the items they didn't choose to take with them, then loaded everything up and sailed to St. Michael – all five of them: Deacon, Glory, Ace, Matty, and Chou Ling. From there, they took one of the last riverboats going up the Yukon, bound for Fairbanks and points beyond.

Glory had never ventured into the interior of Alaska before. The wild beauty of it stunned her – the grandeur of its rugged mountain ranges, the vibrant color of whole mountain slopes forested with stands of birch, their golden autumn leaves still clinging to the branches. She hadn't realized how much she missed seeing trees, even though they weren't the towering cedar and spruce of her Sitka home. Wild animals abounded – moose, bear, caribou, wolf. And away from the coast, she discovered, the sky was usually clear instead of shrouded with clouds much of the time. At night, a multitude of bright stars lighted the sky. It rarely seemed dark, and the northern lights frequently performed their dazzling dance. The weather was relatively mild, though the nights were cold, but there wasn't the incessant wind blowing damp and cold off the water.

Fairbanks sat on the flatland along the banks of the Tanana River, a tributary of the Yukon. Glory noticed the first day that it didn't have the atmosphere of the typical gold camp. The saloons, gambling halls, and red-light district were all there, but the usual bands of opportunistic swindlers and thieves were absent. The new town had been settled by experienced sourdoughs, too canny to be taken in by such types.

The gold found in the region wasn't 'poor men's diggings' as in Nome; rather it was 'rich man's placer,' contained in a stratum of gravel some hundred feet down, close to bedrock. Shafts had to be sunk to locate the gold-bearing gravel, then tunnels dug to follow the pay streak. It would take years to get the gold out of the ground, and men would have to be employed.

Judge James Wickersham had chosen Fairbanks as the site for his courthouse. A new two-story schoolhouse had been built. Miners and merchants had brought their wives and families. As Glory and Deacon and Ace walked through the streets of Fairbanks to familiarize themselves with the town, women spoke to her and smiled at the young boy holding her hand, and men tipped their hats to her. Ever since they'd left Nome and boarded the riverboat, traveling as man and wife, she had been treated like a respectable lady by the people she met. No one had familiarly draped an arm around her or made suggestive comments, not even the few who recognized her. She had never objected to such attention in the past. In her profession, it was expected. Now Glory found that she liked the respect being shown her.

In Alaska, as she already knew, people were much more tolerant. When a prostitute married and gave up her old way of life, that was that. She wasn't haunted by her past. As long as she behaved like a proper wife and mother, she was treated as one by those around her. There were simply too few women in Alaska for it to be otherwise.

At the end of the first week, Deacon took Glory to see a saloon he had found that was for sale. 'It's not as big as I would like, but maybe next spring we can enlarge it. We won't have time this year to do it before the snow starts. It's not worth what he's asking. And I know the upstairs isn't what you'd like. But nothing else is available right now. So what do you think?'

'If you're satisfied with it, Deacon, go ahead and buy it. But there's something you should know.'

'What?'

'I've decided I'm not going back to work. This is a new town, a place to make a new start. I've been thinking about that a lot since we arrived here,' she admitted. 'Ace is four years old. Soon he'll be going to school. Deacon, I don't want him to be ashamed of me or what I am.'

'If that's what you want, it's all right with me. But . . . Glory, what are you going to do with yourself?' He briefly shook his head. 'I'm sorry, but I can't see you staying at home cooking and cleaning. What will Chou Ling and Matty do?'

Glory took a deep breath and plunged in. 'I already have that figured out.'

'Oh?' His eyebrow shot up.

'I want to build a boardinghouse. Chou Ling can do the cooking and Matty can help with the cleaning. I'm thoroughly experienced at playing hostess and keeping the accounts. As a matter of fact, I think I've found the perfect location.'

'Where is that?' Deacon smiled wryly, realizing the full extent of her planning.

'There's an old shack on the edge of town that sits right on the pack trail to Valdez. As Fairbanks grows, that trail will become a well-traveled route.'

'How much is it?'

'That's the only thing I haven't found out yet.'

'That's a surprise,' Deacon said. 'For a minute there, I thought you'd already bought it.'

In addition to the saloon, they bought the lot for Glory's boarding-house. All winter long, she worked on the plans for it, deciding on the number of rooms, the size of the kitchen, dining room, and parlor, the arrangement of the living quarters in the rear, and the linen, dishes, cookware, and silverware she'd need. She planned menus, chose wallpaper, and selected curtain materials.

Construction on the boardinghouse began in the spring. By Ace's fifth birthday, they had moved in, and Glory had her first boarder two days later. Ace started school that autumn, and Glory decided it was time they all began attending church on Sundays.

The following year work was begun to install a telegraph line and to improve the trail from Fairbanks to Valdez, south of Fairbanks, a port that was ice-free year-round. Much of the news coming up the trail was for the Alaska Syndicate, a conglomerate formed by J. P. Morgan, the Guggenheim mining family, and others. As the Kennecott Copper Company, they bought the mile-long claim to the copper cliffs in the Chitina River Valley – cliffs that contained sixty to seventy percent copper. Construction had begun on a railroad to carry the mined copper two hundred miles to the sea.

Not satisfied with its rich copper mine and railroad, the syndicate had acquired control of the Northwestern Steamship Company and the Alaska Steamship Company, which gave them a monopoly on all shipping to and from Alaska. Plus they owned a dozen salmon canneries along the coast. Rumor was they had their eyes on the abundant Alaskan coal deposits, even though President Theodore Roosevelt had placed them off limits to private development.

By 1910, the road from Fairbanks to Valdez, called the Richardson Trail after the president of the Alaska Road Commission who had authorized the work, was finished. A regular stage service was in operation, with travel by horse-drawn sleds in the winter and stage-coach in the summer, a journey that took about a week one way.

The Cole boardinghouse was only a block from the stage stop, and Glory's business flourished, rapidly becoming one of *the* places to stay while in Fairbanks. Deacon's saloon was doing well, too. And Ace's teacher told them both what an intelligent son they had. They were respectable citizens of the town now, attending church services regularly and donating to worthy causes. Glory sang in the church choir and Deacon joined the Masonic Temple. Matty had married a half-breed Eskimo whom Glory had hired to do odd jobs, both at the boardinghouse and Deacon's saloon. Matty and Billy Ray Townsend built themselves a small cabin on the back of the property.

Life was good, and it seemed destined to stay that way. In 1912, a bill introduced to the United States Congress by delegate James

Wickersham, the former judge at Fairbanks, was passed, officially making Alaska a territory of the United States, although limiting the power of its territorial legislature. Finally, forty-five years after Alaska had been purchased from the Russians, it was a territory, with the right of self-government and representation in Congress.

The following year, Glory saw the first automobile come up the Richardson Trail, traveling all the way from Valdez, a distance of some three hundred and sixty miles. Then in 1914, the Fairbanks newspaper announced that survey work to select a route for a new railroad had begun.

An ice fog blanketed Fairbanks, reducing visibility to almost zero – a fairly common winter phenomenon that occurred when the temperature plummeted well below zero and the wind was calm. As Glory had learned, Fairbanks was a place of extremes; temperatures in the summer could soar into the nineties, and in the winter fall to sixty below zero.

She had long ago decided there was no such thing as perfect weather anywhere in the world, and if there was, a person would soon get tired of it. Personally, she didn't mind the freezing cold or the occasional ice fog, much preferring them to the depressing rain and constant wind of the coast.

On this dark, gray winter morning, her half dozen boarders had been served their breakfast, the dishes cleared, the beds made, and Chou Ling had begun lunch preparations. This lull in the day's activity was her time to take a short rest. She sat at the walnut dining table in their private living quarters. Yesterday's newspaper was in front of her and a cup of coffee nearby. A cigarette smoldered in the ivory holder between her fingers. Glory confined her smoking and her occasional nip of alcohol to the privacy of their own rooms, never indulging in her little vices in front of anyone outside her small tight circle.

As she absently patted the large amber comb to make certain it still held her pompadour-styled hair firmly in place, she noticed Deacon pace to the window for the fourth time. She started to suggest that he sit down and have some coffee with her, but there was something about his edginess that prompted her to hold her tongue.

Her glance lingered on him as he took out his handkerchief and blew his nose. Although his clothes fit him well, Glory knew how little flesh there was on his bones. His hair was almost all gray now. He looked older, older than he really was. She noticed the sheen of perspiration on his face when he turned from the window, and wondered if he was catching a cold. But her inquiries about his health invariably drew a sharp response, so she didn't ask. She avoided his glance and quickly switched her attention to the newspaper in front of her, skimming the article relating the war news of the European conflict.

'The paper thinks the United States will have to become involved in this war with Germany,' she remarked, although it all seemed much too far away to concern her.

Her comment elicited no response from Deacon. When she looked up, he was back at the window. The connecting door that led to the front of the boardinghouse opened and Ace walked in, a tall, gangly fourteen-year-old with sandy-brown hair and an engaging smile.

'I got that old Victrola working for Mr. Hammermill,' he announced proudly.

'I don't know how you managed it.' Glory marveled at his ability to understand the workings of mechanical things, then fix them. He was always tinkering with something it seemed, whether it was a kitchen gadget of Chou Ling's or a light switch. Every time he saw anything new, he wanted to take it apart and see how it worked. Usually he managed to put it back together.

'It wasn't hard.' He shrugged. 'The arm was broken and I just had to come up with something that would work in its place. If there isn't anything you need me to do, Mr. Cheevers had challenged me to a game of checkers.'

'Go ahead. But try to remember he's a guest and don't trounce him as badly as you did last night.'

'I'll try.' Ace grinned.

As he left the room, she glanced at Deacon. He still faced the window, his shoulders slightly hunched forward and an arm curved around his middle. Glory took a sip of her coffee and went back to reading the newspaper.

'I don't believe this.' She reread the story that had caught her eye. 'According to this report, the route being recommended for the new railroad will use Seward on the Kenai Peninsula for its ocean terminus and extend north only as far as Nenana. They're planning to terminate it some fifty miles short of Fairbanks. How can they do that?' she protested. 'Have you heard about this, Deacon?'

'Yes,' he answered abruptly and swung from the window.

'It doesn't make sense for them not to run it to –' She suddenly realized that he wasn't listening to her as he strode across the room to the back door. When she saw him yank his coat and hat off the wooden coat tree, she rose quickly from her chair in alarm. 'Deacon, where are you going?'

'I need to go to the saloon.'

'Now?' She frowned when he almost doubled over, as if stabbed by some sharp pain that passed quickly. 'It's early. There's no need for you to be there yet. At least wait until the sun comes up. It's foolish to venture out in that freezing cold and fog. You can barely see your hand in front of your face. Later it might improve and –'

'Glory, if it wasn't important, I wouldn't be going,' he snapped impatiently. 'I've waited as long as I can.'

'Deacon, please . . .' She paused as he began buttoning his coat, realizing that none of her arguments were making any impression on him. 'If you must go, at least dress warmly.' She pulled the wool scarf off the coat tree and started to put it around him, but he took it from her and twined it around his neck, raising it to protect his face. 'Do you have your gloves?'

He nodded affirmatively and bent down to pull on his mukluks. He stamped his feet into them, then drew the heavy fur-lined mitten gloves from his coat pockets. 'See you later.'

Glory shivered at the chilled air that swept in from the short passageway to the outer door, a kind of insulating airlock between the frigid outside temperatures and the warmth of the house. She heard the outer door shut, then slowly turned to walk back to the table.

Something wasn't right. She simply didn't understand what could possibly be so urgent that Deacon had to venture out in this weather, especially when she could see he wasn't feeling well. She remembered the rivulet of sweat that had trickled down his temple, and the pain that had shown in his face. She wondered if his arm was bothering him that much. And if he was in pain, why hadn't he taken some morphine before he left?

Unless – the thought suddenly occurred to her – he didn't have any more morphine here. Lately he'd had to take it more often and in larger dosages. She knew he'd become totally dependent on it. She remembered the piano player in Nome and how sick he'd gotten and how much pain he'd been in that time his supply of the drug had run out.

596

She hurried into their bedroom and went through the drawer where Deacon had always hidden his morphine. It wasn't there. She looked in the rest of the drawers and anyplace else she could think, but didn't find any.

Now she was worried and frightened. In his condition, Deacon could become violently ill at any time – the way the piano player had. And the last place he should be was out in that freezing fog. She left the bedroom and hurried to the wall telephone in the parlor. She lifted the receiver and listened to make sure the line was clear, then turned the crank handle.

'Hello, Millie,' she said as soon as the local operator came on the line. 'This is Mrs. Cole. Will you please ring the saloon?'

'I sure will. By the way, Helen Chalmers had her baby last night. Another boy. They so wanted a girl this time. After four boys, I can't blame them. Oh, and old man Devereaux slipped and fell and broke his hip.'

'How awful,' she murmured automatically, silently wishing the woman would shut up.

'It's ringing, Mrs. Cole, but I'm not getting any answer.'

'Let it ring. Papa Tom might be in the back.' Papa Tom was the janitor Deacon had hired to clean up the place after the saloon closed. He lived in one of the back rooms.

'Hel-lo?'

'Papa Tom.' Glory gripped the long mouthpiece of the telephone and leaned closer to speak directly into it. 'This is Mrs. Cole. Deacon just left here a few minutes ago. He's on his way to the saloon. Would you have him ring me as soon as he arrives there?'

'Ya want him to call ya?'

'Yes. The very minute he arrives. It's important, Papa Tom. Will you tell him?'

'Yeah. That all?'

'Yes. Thank you.' She returned the receiver to its hook and rang off.

A half hour later, she still hadn't heard from him. She rang the saloon again, and Papa Tom assured her he hadn't arrived or he would have given Deacon the message. Afraid of waiting longer, she told Matty of her concern, and Matty agreed it would be wise to send her husband, Billy Ray, out to look for Deacon. In the meantime, Glory called various places along the way where Deacon might have stopped. But no one had seen him.

That night, a search party of neighbors found Deacon's body. He had frozen to death, they said, but Glory knew the morphine had killed him as surely as the cold.

Those following months after Deacon's death were the hardest Glory had ever had to face, even though Ace and Matty were always nearby to offer comfort. She had never guessed it was possible to miss a person so much. Deacon had always been there. She realized that he'd never asked anything of her, except to marry him. Other than that, she had been totally free to do what she wanted and never had to be concerned whether she had his approval.

On a hot Sunday in July, Glory stooped down beside his tombstone and laid a bouquet of forget-me-nots on his grave. Straightening, she gazed through the black net of her veil at the inscription etched into the stone: BELOVED HUSBAND – ROBERT 'DEACON' COLE. A sentiment that was so true it brought tears to her eyes.

A pesky black fly buzzed around her face, seeking an opening in the protective net. As she brushed it aside with her hand, Glory noticed the black gloves and the black sleeve of her tunic dress. Once she had sworn never to wear a dark, drab color again. But for Deacon she had donned the black of mourning.

'He wouldn't have liked me in this color,' she said to Matty.

'No, he surely wouldn't. He liked it best when you wore bright, pretty things.'

'Yes.' The black dress absorbed the sun's heat and added to the oppressive warmth that seemed about to suffocate her. 'It's time to start over, I think.'

'Yes.'

She breathed in deeply and released a sigh. 'I've decided to sell the boardinghouse.'

'What will you do?' Matty looked at her in surprise.

'Make a new start. It's time to move on. If Deacon were here, that's what he'd say.'

'Where will you go?'

'They're building a new town on the Cook Inlet where the railroad has its construction camp. They're calling it Anchorage. If Ace and I are going to start a new life, it might as well be in a new town.' She reached out and took hold of Matty's hand. 'Will you and Billy Ray come with us?'

'We are family. Family should stay together.'

51   *Anchorage, Alaska*
May 25, 1923

Glory raked the small pile of chopped underbrush onto the larger stack and paused to catch her breath. She wasn't used to hard physical labor, and turning forty-five years old didn't make the work any easier. Still, it was more fun than work. She looked down the long field at the swarm of people laboring as hard as she was.

Not far from her, men with shovels stepped back from the tree stump they'd been digging and watched while another volunteer fastened a chain around the stump and attached it to the tail brace of his harnessed team of horses. A tractor chugged by her, dragging another tree stump by a chain. As the driver waved to her, Glory recognized her son, Ace, and waved back. Whenever there was a choice between horses and horsepower, he always chose the latter, so she wasn't surprised to see him operating the tractor.

Everywhere she looked, people were at work, the men unearthing tree stumps and chopping out the undergrowth, the women and children raking the brush into piles, all of them swarming over the sixteen-acre tract. It was a scene of confusion and industry – noisy with the roaring chug of tractors, the snorting neighs of horses, the hacking chops of axes, the ordering shouts of men, and the shrieking laughter of children. There was an underlying excitement that, to Glory, was reminiscent of another time and another place.

'Do you know what this reminds me of, Trudy?' she said to her new daughter-in-law.

'What's that, Mother Cole?'

Glory wasn't sure how much she liked being called that. It made her feel so old. But she knew Trudy used the term out of affection and respect. She smiled at the girl Ace had married three years ago. The daughter of a construction worker on the railroad, Gertrude 'Trudy' Hannighan had moved from Seattle with her family four years ago. The day Ace had met her, he'd come home and told Glory that he'd found the girl he wanted to marry.

Glory found nothing wrong with his choice. Trudy was an intelligent, outgoing girl who was absolutely convinced there was nothing Ace couldn't do. Sometimes Glory thought that if her son suggested he and Trudy should go to the moon, Trudy would start packing that very minute.

Trudy was an attractive girl with even features and a ready smile. Her short dark hair was cut in a bob – the latest style on the outside. Taller than average, she had a sturdy look to her that Glory liked. A dark-haired, dark-eyed two-year-old boy came toddling up to her on chubby legs and threw his arms around Trudy's legs. Her son – Glory's grandson Wylie Deacon Cole. A grandmother – Glory wasn't sure she felt *that* old.

'What does this remind you of, Mother Cole?' Trudy prompted again and swung her young son up into her arms.

Glory looked back at the scene. 'Nome. That summer after they discovered gold on the beach and people were scurrying everywhere. The noise and confusion of it.' She altered her grip on the rake handle to let the top rest against her shoulder. In doing so, Glory felt the soreness of a beginning blister in her palm. She glanced down at her work-gloved hand, letting go of the rake to open it, and laughed softly. 'And the blisters.'

'You prospected for gold, too?'

'Oh, yes, I caught the gold fever just like everyone else.'

'It must have been exciting being there when all that was going on.'

'Yes. That summer of 1900 was insanity,' she mused, then shook her head wryly. 'So is this. Will you look at all of us out here clearing land for an airport? I can't figure out why, when there aren't any airplanes in Anchorage.'

'There never will be if we don't have a place where they can land. Ace says that someday aviation will open up Alaska the way railroads never can. It's the way of the future.'

'I've heard him say that.' At least a thousand times, Glory was sure.

Her son had become fascinated by these flying machines during the war years, devouring any and all accounts of the aerial dogfights over the skies of Europe and the World War I aces who fought in them. Last year, his fascination had become an

600

obsession when he had seen his first airplane – some old craft that landed on the water. Glory thought Ace had referred to it as a Boeing amphibian. Ever since then, his dream had been to learn to fly. It didn't trouble him at all that the Boeing amphibian was presently at the bottom of Cook Inlet after an attempted takeoff had failed.

Somehow, Glory knew he'd never be content until he'd flown himself. It worried her sometimes. Mostly because she was afraid it would be these airplanes that would lure him into leaving Alaska for the States so he could learn to fly.

In the States, business was booming, but Alaska's economy was in a slump. Since the end of the war, there had been a sharp decrease in world demand for its principal exports – salmon and copper. Most of the time, the boardinghouse Glory had built in Anchorage was only half full, providing her with just enough income to meet her expenses. She wouldn't have had even that if the Alaska Railroad hadn't made Anchorage its headquarters and the base for its repair shops, where her son worked. And two of the six houses she owned were vacant, with no hope of finding anyone to rent them. Ace and Trudy lived in one of the remaining four, and Matty and Billy Ray in another. But Glory still had a little money saved, and she was able to make a living, although it was hardly what she had once earned. But those were other days, other times – another life. She had no regrets. If she had it to do over again, there was nothing she would change.

Ace came by on the tractor again and stopped, then shouted above the engine's vibrating chug, 'You won't get anything done leaning on those rakes. Get back to work!' He grinned and set the tractor in motion again.

By day's end, the airfield was cleared. To celebrate the town's feat, a bonfire was built and everybody feasted on wieners and washed them down with coffee or lemonade.

A little more than a year later, Glory sat in the rear seat of her three-year-old Model T Ford with her young grandson, Wylie, beside her. Her son, Ace, was behind the wheel talking excitedly to his wife, Trudy, about his favorite subjects – flying and airplanes – as they bounced along the rutted road to the Anchorage airfield. His fascination had become an all-consuming passion. He talked about little else.

Ace could, and did, talk for hours on the scientific principles of aviation. Every conversation was sprinkled with aeronautical terms such as 'lift,' 'drag,' 'stabilizers,' and 'airfoils.' But his excitement really began to build whenever he started talking about the potential benefits aviation could bring to Alaska. The territory was huge, with few of its towns linked by overland routes. To reach Nome, from Anchorage, a person had to travel by ship, or take the train to Fairbanks, then a riverboat on the Yukon, and still be short of his destination at the end of that. And such trips were only possible in the summer. In the winter, travel was by dogsled. Eight months of the year, all mail went to Nome by dogsled.

But airplanes didn't need roads carved through miles of rugged terrain or tracks laid or bridges built. An airplane could fly over all the swollen creeks or snow-choked passes. A trip that would take better than a week by dogsled or horse-drawn vehicle, a plane could make in a day. And Ace was quick to point out that Alaska sat smack in the middle of the great circle route from the United States to the Far East. Soon mail and goods would be sent by air, making the trip in a fraction of the time it would take a ship to cross the Pacific. According to him, Alaska was going to be the crossroads of the world.

As they approached the homemade field, Ace slowed the Model T and pulled it off on the shoulder of the dirt road. Ace didn't wait for the engine to cease its sputtering before climbing out of the car. As he lifted Wylie out of the back seat, his attention was already focused on the airplane at the end of the field preparing for a take-off. Absently he helped Glory out of the car.

'There it is,' he declared with the excitement of a child at Christmas. 'It's a Hisso-powered Standard.'

The airplane had been shipped by steamer from the States to Seward, then come by rail to Anchorage. Ever since it had arrived at the railroad yard, Ace had spent every spare moment he could watching the pilot, Noel Wien, and his mechanic, William Yunker, assemble the plane. He was still upset that he'd missed being there when the plane was taken up for a test flight.

Glory watched with a mixture of skepticism and apprehension as the plane came charging down the field, picking up speed. No matter how many times Ace explained it to her, she didn't understand how such a machine could get off the ground. But just as it drew level with them, its wheels left the ground. The plane was airborne. It roared by them, steadily widening the distance from the ground.

'Look, Wylie.' Ace pointed out the aircraft to his three-year-old son. 'Someday your daddy is going to fly a plane like that.'

But it was five years before he got his wish and found a pilot willing to teach him how to fly. After that, there was no stopping him. He took all the money he and Trudy had saved up to build a house of their own and borrowed the balance from Glory to buy a wrecked Wright-powered Stinson biplane and the parts to repair it. With Billy Ray's help, he worked on it late into the nights, putting it back together. Sometimes, he had only two or three hours of sleep before going to work at the railyard the next morning, then doing it all over again that night. Trudy and young Wylie brought his meals to the shed where he labored on his beloved plane. Trudy often joked to Glory that Ace loved that plane more than he did her or Wylie, but she seemed to understand that at last he was fulfilling his dream, and she never objected to the hours he spent away from his family.

On a crisp autumn day in October of 1929, the stubby red-painted Stinson was ready for its test flight. The whole family turned out for the event, including Chou Ling. At the far end of the field, Billy Ray helped Ace turn the biplane into the wind and set the tail. Glory's heart was in her throat when the plane came rolling down the field. Everyone else cheered when it lifted off the ground, but she breathed a sigh of relief. Twice, Ace buzzed the field, then wagged his wings.

'I wish he wouldn't show off like that,' Glory murmured to Matty after his last low swoop, but there were tears of pride in her eyes.

'I have never seen him so happy.'

'I know.'

Within an hour, he was back, landing the plane as effortlessly as a bird. He taxied over to them and cut the motor. His expression glowed with pride and achievement as he climbed out of the cockpit.

'It handles better than anything I've ever flown before,' he insisted as they all crowded around to congratulate him. Considering his limited experience, that wasn't the highest praise, but since he'd virtually rebuilt the plane from the wheels up, it said a lot for his ability. He singled Glory out from the others. 'Come on, Mama. I'll take you up for a ride.'

'Me?' She hung back, resisting as he tried to pull her closer to the plane. 'No, Ace, you really should take Trudy first.'

'You own part of this plane, too, Mama. I think you should be first.'

'Go up with him,' Matty urged her. 'It will probably be tame compared to other things you've done in your life.'

Glory let herself be coaxed into climbing into the plane, which was not altogether an easy task, her movements restricted by the tubular style dress and coat she wore. Ace made sure she was comfortably strapped in, then advised her, 'Be sure and button your coat. It's a bit nippy up there.'

Truthfully, Glory was nervous and excited at the same time as the biplane began its takeoff run. The aircraft bounced and thumped over the rough ground. It didn't seem to Glory that the Stinson was traveling nearly as fast as when she had watched Ace take off in it alone. Then suddenly, they weren't bouncing any more. She looked down and realized they had left the ground. She was flying. She was actually flying, despite the fact that there was hardly any sensation of speed. It was a peculiar experience to be moving – climbing, watching everyone and everything grow smaller – yet not feeling as if she were moving at all, with only the vibrations of the plane's engine to tell her otherwise.

When Ace banked the plane away from the field, Glory felt her stomach lurch sickeningly. She grabbed hold of her seat, certain she was going to fall out of the plane – or that the plane was going to fall out of the sky. But Ace leveled out the wings and they were flying smoothly again.

'McKinley!' he shouted and pointed to the north.

Far in the distance, the mountain the Indians called Denali, 'the high one,' dominated the sky, dwarfing the peaks that were closer. For once, its towering crest was free of the clouds that usually hid it. Glory was awestruck, never dreaming she would have such a grand view of the majestic mountain from the air. Below were the railroad tracks that led north – as of this year, all the way to Fairbanks.

Then Ace banked the plane in another slow turn and flew over the town of Anchorage. Glory couldn't get over how different everything looked from the air. She didn't even recognize the boardinghouse until Ace pointed it out to her. It was a whole new world – an exciting one. At last she understood her son's passion for aviation. It offered more than a new town and a new start. It gave him an ever-moving horizon; he could never fly to the end of it.

She was almost sorry when she saw the airfield come into view again and Ace set up for his landing and the wheels touched down with a bouncing jolt. When they stopped, Glory climbed out and let Trudy and Wylie take her place in the Stinson. Before the day was out, Ace had taken every one of the family up for a ride in his plane.

A week later, Ace quit his job with the Alaska Railroad, and the Ace Flying Service came into existence. Glory acted as his financial partner, Trudy kept the books, Billy Ray was his mechanic and ground crew. That same month, the stock market crashed and Wall Street was in a panic.

With the 'outside' in the grips of the Great Depression, there was widespread unemployment. People who had left Alaska for the high-paying jobs in the States started coming back. Rising gold prices made small-scale mining operations feasible again. The salmon industry improved.

Almost from the beginning, Ace was kept busy. Somebody always had someplace they had to go – whether it was miners, trappers, fishermen, engineers, or even prostitutes – and they usually wanted to get there in a hurry. Or if they didn't, they had something they wanted to send or have picked up. Or there were supplies to be dropped or a medical emergency that required a doctor to be flown somewhere or the patient flown to the doctor.

In those first years, Ace hauled everything from a small gas tractor, diapers, frozen meat, and mattresses to Victrolas and phonograph records. His passengers were whites, Eskimos, Indians, malamute dogs, and even a corpse or two. Drunk or sober, sick or healthy, crazy or sane, he'd take them wherever they wanted to go – or as close as he could get to it.

But the flights were rarely accomplished without incident. Most of the time, his landing fields were small sandbars in rivers, frozen lakes, or hilltops. He'd knocked off his landing gear, broken propellers, torn wingtips, busted struts, and half a hundred other things. Sometimes the plane was too damaged to fly out, and he'd either have to repair it on the spot with whatever was at hand or walk fifteen or fifty miles through wild terrain that in spring was sometimes a jungle-like swamp to the nearest scrap of civilization and have the needed parts flown in to him, then repair the plane and fly it out.

He flattened his propeller blades for maximum power. On

shortfield takeoffs, he'd learned to wait until the very last second before raising his flaps to obtain maximum lift and angle of climb. In subzero temperatures, whenever the plane's engine wasn't running, the oil had to be drained to keep it from freezing. In the deceptive whiteness of snow-covered landing fields, he'd learned to feel for the ground. Surviving meant learning to crash safely. And like a lot of other bush pilots, as they were called, Ace often joked that his red Stinson was merely a collection of spare parts flying in formation.

Navigating in Alaska was no easy trick either. His plane was equipped with a compass and an altimeter, but he was never too sure how reliable either of them was. For all the beauty of Alaska's mountain ranges, her glaciers and lofty lakes, or the mystical effect of her natural phenomena like shimmering sundogs above the snow or dancing northern lights, she could be cruel with her winds and fogs, her squalls and blizzards that could encapsulate a plane in a white-out that made the earth and sky seem one, with no up or down.

It was a trackless land without vast interconnecting road systems or telephone poles or railroad tracks to use for landmarks. Ace learned to recognize rivers and know one from another – no easy task, considering the thousands of rivers in Alaska and the equal number of streams that during spring thaw ran as swollen as rivers. Since a tree always falls downstream, he learned to tell downstream from upstream by watching for fallen trees. For him, every little twist and bend and branch of a given river was a road sign: Two turns after the fishhook bend and there's Cosgrove's cabin. Odd-shaped hills, distinctive peaks, peculiarly shaped lakes – he knew them all, whether they were on a map or not. There were times when he got lost, but not many. And he was never really lost, because he always knew he was in Alaska.

Part Four

Full Circle

52 *Anchorage*
May 10, 1935

Twelve-year-old Lisa Blomquist looked around the crowded
hall, twisting and craning her neck in an effort to see over and
beyond the heads of people seated at the long tables.

She didn't see how her younger brothers could have disappeared so quickly. One minute they had been playing by their
chairs, and the next they were gone. She had promised Mama
that she'd keep an eye on them and make sure they didn't get into
any trouble. She didn't understand how her brothers could
behave like this when this grand dinner had been given in their
honor.

Well, not exactly *their* honor, she corrected herself, since they
were only children. But it was for the families who had come to
build farms in Alaska at a place called Matanuska Valley. And she
and Erik and Rudy were a part of the family, so it was for them,
too.

The whole town of Anchorage had declared a holiday and
turned out to meet the train when they had arrived that day. A
band had played and everywhere flags had waved. She couldn't
blame her brothers for getting tired of the endless speeches.
That's the way it had been ever since they and the other families
from Minnesota had left St. Paul, traveling by train to Seattle,
then by ship to Seward, Alaska. All along the way, people had
met them and newspapermen had asked them questions. 'Colonists,' that's what the newspapers called them – 'colonists' and
'pioneers' going to the great frontier of Alaska.

It was all a part of Franklin D. Roosevelt's New Deal, a
program of resettlement that would take farmers from lands on
which they were unable to make a living and transport them to
Alaska. Lisa didn't understand it all exactly, although she had
listened when the relief worker had explained it to her parents.
She did know that the government had paid for the trip, provided

the whole family with suitable clothes – the first she'd ever had that weren't hand-me-downs, made-overs, or flour-sack dresses – and supplied needed furniture even to the extent of replacing that which was too old or rickety. Her mother had discovered they had a lot of furniture that wasn't worth moving.

All the attention and excitement had been a little frightening at first. Lisa had always felt very self-conscious among strangers, but everybody she'd met on the long journey had made her feel so important – and brave. All of them were being treated as if they were special. Before they'd left Seattle, she and her brothers, as well as the rest of the children in the group, had been given toys – real toys. Lisa was so glad that her mother had encouraged her father to sign up to come.

As she was about to despair of locating her brothers, nine-year-old Erik came running up behind her and grabbed her hand, then started pulling on it to drag her with him. 'Come, Lisa. I've gotta show you somethin'.'

'What is it? Where's your brother?' Reluctantly she let herself be pulled along while she scanned the area ahead of them, looking for Rudy. 'You were supposed to stay near the table, both of you. Mama's going to be mad and then you'll really be in for it.'

'But we found an Indian,' Erik whispered, his blue eyes rounded and shining with excitement. 'You said there wouldn't be any, but we found one.'

'That's nonsense. I told you there aren't any Indians in Alaska, only Eskimos, and they live way far up north in igloos where there's ice and snow all the time – not down here where there's trees and everything's green.' An instant later, she spied her curly-, flaxen-haired brother rocking back and forth against a side wall, his head slightly turned so he could peer out of the corner of his eye at someone down the way. Erik pulled harder on her arm to hurry her along, although she needed no urging to confront her errant brother. 'Do you realize I've been looking all over for you two, Rudy?'

'Sssh.' Even though he was a year younger than Lisa, Rudy always tried to boss her around.

Erik hovered close to his big brother and snuck a look around him. 'There he is, Lisa.'

'Sssh,' Rudy hissed again. 'He'll hear you.'

'Stop it, Rudy,' Lisa declared impatiently, then looked to see who they were talking about. The boy was tall and broadshouldered, although on the thin side, yet she doubted that he was much more than two or three years older than she was. His hair was black, and a little on the shaggy side. He tugged at the collar of his shirt where it buttoned at the throat as if trying to ease its tightness. 'He's no Indian, Erik. See the way he's dressed in long pants and a jacket.'

'Yeah, but look at his black hair and eyes,' Rudy insisted. 'See how brown his skin is. You don't know everything, Lisa. Alaska's a frontier and Indians live in the frontier and they attack settlers like us.'

'Yeah, they do.' Erik piped in his agreement.

'He's probably here spying on us so he can go back to his tribe an' tell his chief how many of us there are so they'll have enough braves to kill us all when they attack.' Rudy smiled at his brother's frightened look.

'I don't wanta be killed.' There was a slight pout to his lower lip.

'Don't listen to Rudy. He's just being a smart aleck.' She noticed the boy glance in their direction, and decided to put an end to Rudy's scare tactics once and for all before he gave Erik nightmares. She took Erik by the hand. 'Come on. I'll prove it to you.' When Erik realized she was taking him over to the 'Indian,' he tried to twist free but not too wildly for fear of attracting attention. 'Excuse me,' she said to the older boy, indifferent to her brother's struggles. 'But my brothers think you're an Indian.' For a moment, his stony stare unnerved her a little, then he smiled. It was a nice smile.

'My grandmother's great-grandfather was five-eighths Indian, but I don't know if that counts. She says I look like him, though.'

'See. I told you,' Rudy declared triumphantly.

Lisa wasn't sure whether the answer meant he was part Indian or not. It sounded like it. 'Do you live here?'

'Yeah. My dad's a bush pilot.'

'What's that?'

'He flies planes, hauling people and supplies to remote villages, wherever they want to go.'

'Oh. That kind of pilot.' There weren't many planes in northern Minnesota, but she'd seen pictures and newsreels of them.

'Can you fly a plane?' Rudy wanted to know.

'Yeah. My dad taught me.'

'Wow! That's super!' Rudy was roundly impressed. 'How old are you?'

'Fourteen.'

'Wow, I'm going to learn to fly when I'm fourteen, too. Maybe even sooner,' he declared.

'And just where do you think you're going to get a plane to fly?' But Lisa thought better of getting into an argument with her brother, and quickly changed the subject. 'I'm sorry. My name's Lisa Blomquist and these are my brothers, Rudy and Erik. We just arrived from Minnesota.'

'I guessed that. I'm Wylie Cole.' But it was more than good manners that prompted Wylie to tell her his name. Usually he didn't like girls; the ones he knew were always giggling and acting silly. But this Lisa seemed different. He had to admit she was kinda cute with those big blue eyes and hair the color of wild honey, plaited into long braids that hung well below her shoulders.

'Yeah, we're from Minnesota, the land of ten thousand lakes,' Erik inserted importantly.

'We don't have ten thousand lakes in Alaska,' Wylie replied. 'It's more like a couple million. And some of the best hunting and fishing you'll ever find anywhere. There's moose and salmon – and bighorn sheep in the mountains.'

'Are there bears here?' Erik remembered the stories Rudy had told him.

'Yeah, will we see any of those big white polar bears?'

'No, they don't come this far south. Around here, it's mostly grizzlies. I shot my first one last spring.' Wylie saw the way her eyes widened and knew he'd impressed her. 'I go hunting and fishing a lot. This next winter, my dad says I can run a trap line. I figure I'll get enough money from the furs to buy me a new rifle.'

'I got a rifle,' Rudy said, but Lisa noticed he didn't brag about how many squirrels and rabbits he'd shot with it. They hardly compared to a bear.

'Lisa. Rudy. Come here this minute.' At the impatient summons, Lisa turned guiltily. As Wylie followed the direction of her glance, he noticed the woman walking stiffly toward them. A cloche hat hid all but the curly ends of her blond hair and framed her stern expression.

Lisa turned back to him. 'It's my mother,' she explained hastily. 'We have to go now. Good-bye.' But she glanced over her shoulder at him one last time as she started shepherding her brothers toward the woman. 'It was nice meeting you.'

'Same here. Maybe we'll see each other again,' he offered

hopefully and received a quick, wistful smile in response.

When Lisa and her brothers rejoined their mother, Wylie overheard the tongue-lashing she gave them. 'How could you be so rude?' she scolded. 'Now you will go back and you will sit in your chairs until I say you may move.'

'Mama –' Rudy started to protest.

'You will do as I say or I will have your father take you outside and lay a switch to you.' The threat ended any further argument.

Wylie sighed in disappointment. He hadn't wanted to come to this dinner for the colonists in the first place. He never felt comfortable among a lot of people, never knew what to talk about. But it had been easy to talk to Lisa Blomquist. He wished her mother hadn't made her go back to their table. It would have been nice if he could have talked to her a little longer.

Alaska probably seemed strange to her. He hoped he hadn't frightened her when he referred to the grizzlies in the area. But somehow she didn't strike him as being the type who was a scaredy-cat. In a way, she reminded him of his mother and Grandma Glory. Which was kinda silly, because she was just a girl.

He wondered whether she'd like it here. A lot of newcomers to Alaska didn't; they felt too isolated from the rest of the world and endlessly complained about the cold and the mosquitoes. He wished he'd had the time to tell her all the good things about Alaska and convince her that it really was a great place to live.

In hopes that he might have the chance to talk to her again, Wylie moved to the other side of the room, where he could keep an eye on her table. A couple of times during the remainder of the evening, the milling crowd parted long enough for her to notice him standing by the wall. Each time she smiled at him a little hesitantly, and Wylie smiled back. He didn't want her to feel all alone without a single friend in Alaska. But she never ventured from her mother's side and he didn't get another chance to talk to her.

Later, as he followed his family out of the community hall, Wylie reached up and unbuttoned his collar. His mother observed his action with a smile. 'I wondered how long it would take you to do that. I'm surprised you didn't pull the button off.'

'I would have, but I figured you'd make me sew it back on. Then I'd have to wash the shirt 'cause I got blood on it from sticking my finger with the needle so many times. And I'm not very good at that woman stuff.' He shrugged.

'I realized long ago that you were never going to be any help to me around the house, Wylie. I sometimes think if you had the choice you would live outdoors. Most women get married so they won't have to live alone. But here I am with your father flying off for days to parts unknown and you traipsing off to hunt or fish in some forgotten neck of the woods.'

Ace put his arm around her shoulders. 'Just think how fast you'd get tired of us if we were around all the time.'

'The shock would probably kill her.' Glory paused beside the rear passenger door of the closed sedan and waited for them to catch up with her. 'That was quite a dinner. What did you think of these cheechakos, Trudy?'

'I have the feeling that, regardless of what they might have been told to the contrary, they expected to find a land covered with ice and snow. That was my image of it when I was a new-comer, a cheechako. I'm certain they never expected it to be so green or the weather so mild and warm.'

'They probably didn't.' Glory opened the rear door and slid onto the seat. Trudy climbed into the back seat, too, letting Ace and Wylie sit in front. 'I must say they didn't fit my image of farmers. Some of them looked poor enough to qualify for this program, but one of the men I talked to said he'd worked in a sawmill most of his life and farmed a few acres on the side. He said he raised enough to feed his family and keep a cow and some pigs. I wouldn't think that makes him a farmer, any more than playing poker makes a person a gambler. And he thought the stumps on his farm were a problem. Wait until he sees the stands of timber in Matanuska Valley. Turning that land into farms isn't going to be as easy as he thinks.'

'Others have done it,' Ace reminded her as he started the car's engine. 'Some families have homesteaded land in the valley. You ate some of their food for dinner.'

'But look at the number of people who gave up after a couple years,' Glory replied. 'You've flown over that valley many times, Ace. You know how many homesteads have been abandoned as well as I do.'

Wylie remembered seeing them, too, and hoped that Lisa's parents didn't become discouraged and quit. He hated to think that he might never see her again. His father's response offered him some reassurance.

'But the government is behind this project. There's already four hundred transients from the CCC camps along the Pacific

Coast there at Palmer, setting up the main camp and tents for the colonists to live in until houses can be built. The transients are going to help them clear the land, build the houses and barns, make the roads, and build the bridges. These colonists aren't going to be doing the work all by themselves the way the home-steaders before them had to.' Ace rolled up his window to keep the dust from blowing inside the car as they picked up speed on the open street.

'Some of the local people aren't too happy about the transients that have been brought in,' Trudy said. 'A lot of people here depend on the summer jobs they get on the railroad or the road commission crews. They're concerned this cheap labor from outside will take their jobs.'

'It seems to me if the people of Alaska are going to be con-cerned about something it ought to be Japan,' Ace stated grimly. 'I flew a couple of cannery boys to Nushgak on Bristol Bay this past week. While I was there, I talked to one of the hands on a fishing boat. He said they'd spotted a Japanese ship in the Aleutians. He swore they were taking soundings, and he said it wasn't the first Japanese they'd seen in Aleutian waters.'

'I think eveyone in Alaska has been worried about Japan since it marched its armies into Manchuria four years ago,' Glory replied.

'Why shouldn't we be? The western Aleutian Islands are only six hundred and fifty miles away from the Japanese military bases at Paramushiro. When that Naval Disarmament Treaty expires next year, the U.S. better start building some bases in those islands. You mark my words, we'll be going to war with Japan. I just hope before that happens the Congress starts listening to people like General Mitchell or we'll be utterly defenseless in an attack. Right now, all we have is four hundred soldiers sitting in the Chilkoot Barracks. There's no airstrip, no road to it. You can get to them only by tugboat.'

Glory remembered the warning General Billy Mitchell had given when he'd spoken to the House Military Affairs Commit-tee this past February. He had referred to Alaska as 'the key point of the whole Pacific.' 'He who holds Alaska holds the world,' he'd told them. 'Alaska is the most strategic place in the world. It is the jumping-off place to smash Japan. If we wait to fight her in the Philippines, it will take us five years to defeat Japan.'

'Don't worry, Mom,' Wylie spoke up. 'If the Japanese attack

Alaska, I'll take you and Grandma Cole to a safe place in the mountains and teach you how to cook over a campfire.'

It was a comment made half in jest, yet Glory suspected that such a prospect was the sort that appealed to a fourteen-year-old's imagination. She wouldn't be surprised if Wylie could live off the land. More than once Ace had commented after returning from a hunting or fishing trip with Wylie that his son seemed more at home in the woods and the mountains than he did in his own house.

For his age, Wylie was extremely resourceful, and his mind was like a sponge when it came to picking up native survival lore, from making his own snowshoes and snare traps to building a snow cave or stalking game. He'd had Matty teach him how to make his own mukluks and parkas, and Billy Ray had shown him how to utilize bones to make weapons.

Just this past winter, Wylie had gone with Ace on a flight, but a bad storm had forced them to land on a frozen lake. Strong winds had threatened to flip the aircraft on its back and Ace hadn't been able to find any way to tie it down. At that point, Wylie had chopped a hole in the ice, stuck the tie-down rope in it, then urinated in the hole. In that sub-zero cold, it had frozen within minutes, securely anchoring the plane.

Ace was disappointed, although he hid it well, that Wylie didn't share his love of flying. To Wylie, flying was merely a means to get to some remote region.

Wylie showed all the signs of becoming a loner. In that, he reminded Glory of Deacon. Wylie, too, wasn't the kind to indulge in idle conversation. Trudy said that sometimes hours went by without him uttering a word. And he had Deacon's poker face, seldom letting his feelings show.

Even though he wasn't an unruly boy, he had discipline problems in school. If a teacher told him to do something that didn't make sense to him, he wouldn't do it. His resistance grew in proportion to the pressure applied. Glory sometimes wondered if Wylie had inherited that trait from her – and his love of hunting from the blood of the Indians and the Russian promyshleniki. Maybe Wylie was the sum total of all his ancestors mixed together.

'Say, Wylie, who was that pretty girl I saw you talking to tonight?' Ace teased. 'Don't tell me you've got yourself a girlfriend?'

'Dad,' Wylie protested, reddening slightly.

'Would you look at that, Trudy. Your son's blushing.'

'I am not.' But his face felt hot, and growing hotter. He scrunched a little lower in the front seat, hoping his mother and grandmother wouldn't notice his embarassment. 'She was just some girl from one of those colonist families. She was just asking me a bunch of questions about Indians and polar bears.'

'Does she have a name?'

'I guess so.' Wylie pretended that he didn't know it. He just couldn't bring himself to talk about Lisa Blomquist.

In the latter part of May, the other colonists from Michigan and Wisconsin reached the Matanuska Valley, to bring the number of families to the planned two hundred. All had been on the relief rolls in their home states and had some farming background. The government had selected the volunteer families only from the northern tier of states, specifically the so-called 'cutover' region that had been denuded of its forests by lumbering operations and had poor soil unsuitable for farming. The selection was restricted to that three-state area on the basis that its climate most closely resembled Alaska's and the families, mainly of Scandinavian descent, could more easily adapt to the far northern climate.

The forty-acre tracts were chosen by lot, drawn by the head of the family. But very little land was cleared that first summer. The colonists and transients spent most of their time building a community center in Palmer for meetings and church services, and the farmhouses and barns on the individual tracts. But the work was slow, frequently hampered by the heavy late-summer rains typical of the region.

Wylie thought about Lisa Blomquist many times during that first year, wondering how she was getting along, and whether she was liking it there. As he helped his mother in the garden that summer, hoeing out the weeds, he wished he could show Lisa the six-pound turnips, seventy-pound cabbages, and giant-size potatoes they'd grown so she could see how vegetables flourished in the north's long daylight hours. In the fall when he'd killed his first moose of the season, he'd wondered if she'd ever eaten its meat and whether she liked the taste of it.

Many times when he walked his trap line that winter, surrounded by the silence of snow, he stopped and gazed northeastward, toward the valley roughly fifty miles away on the railroad's branch line to the coalfields – Matanuska Valley, closed in on three sides by towering mountain ranges. He hoped she wasn't lonely.

The next year, grumblings of discontent were reported from some of the colonists. Before the summer was out, several of the original families gave up and went back to the States. Soon, more followed. But Wylie never found out whether Lisa Blomquist's family was among the ones that left.

After a time, he stopped thinking about the twelve-year-old girl with blue eyes and honey-colored braids.

53 Anchorage, Alaska
June 1940

Wylie walked behind the pushmower, leaning his weight slightly into the handles to propel it along as the rotating cylinder of curved blades cut the yard's long grass. His blue plaid shirt hung on a fence post, discarded after he'd finished mowing the lawn area in front of the boardinghouse belonging to his Grandma Glory. The afternoon sun was warm on his back. Its heat, coupled with the slight physical exertion, raised a sheen of perspiration on his skin.

There was a certain pleasant monotony in mowing – walking back and forth, back and forth, the air scented with the fragrance of newly cut grass and filled with the droning whirr of the mower blades. He reached one end of the backyard and maneuvered the pushmower around to start back toward the other.

As he turned, Wylie noticed two people coming up the front walk to the boardinghouse. Normally he wouldn't have paid any attention to such a common occurrence. Europe was at war, and most believed it was only a matter of time before the United States would become involved. The first steps in the long-neglected defense of the Alaska territory had begun with a four-million-dollar appropriation to build a cold-weather aviation laboratory in Fairbanks and a new Army post in Anchorage to be called Fort Richardson. Eight hundred troops from the Fourth Infantry Regiment had already arrived in Anchorage, bivouacking on the edge of town until the new fort was built. The military contracts had brought a horde of construction workers to town, all of them needing someplace to live.

It was a common sight to see men coming up the front walk of the Cole boardinghouse, but not two women, especially when one of them was young and pretty. Wylie stared appreciatively at the girl with the page-boy bob until the building blocked his view of her. Then he leaned again into the pushmower, briefly regretting that there were no rooms available.

Lisa Blomquist paused at the front steps and glanced at the large and rambling two-story building with a small picket fence bordering the flower beds in front. After five years of nothing but hard luck on their farm in the Matanuska Valley, her father had finally given up and found a job with a construction crew here in Anchorage. Now Lisa and her mother were house-hunting, trying to find a place to live here in town.

They'd been at it all day long, but something was wrong with every house they saw. Either the monthly rent was more than they could afford, or the house was too small, or too old, or in a bad neighborhood. Finally someone had suggested they go see Mrs. Cole, explaining that, in addition to this boardinghouse, she owned several rental properties in town.

Lisa followed her mother up the steps to the front door. A gray-haired Eskimo woman greeted them as they walked in. Lisa noticed the barely disguised look of dismay that crossed her mother's face. 'Mrs. Cole?' she asked hesitantly.

'No.' The heavyset woman smiled. 'I am Matty Townsend. If you've come to inquire about rooms, I am sorry to say we are filled up at the moment.'

'No, I came to see Mrs. Cole about possibly renting one of her houses.'

'One moment. I will get her for you. Please make yourself comfortable.' She indicated the collection of chairs and sofas in the parlor off the entryway.

When the Eskimo woman walked away, Lisa followed her mother into the parlor. She picked up one of the magazines on the table and started to leaf through it while her mother wandered about the room inspecting its furnishings, enviously touching a porcelain vase and covetously eyeing a crystal lamp.

At the sound of approaching footsteps, Lisa laid the magazine back on the table and turned to face the doorway. A tall, slim woman appeared in the opening, her gray hair swept up and away from her face and coiled in a smooth chignon at the nape. Lisa was struck by the contrast between its light color and the deep black of her eyes. It was hard to guess the woman's age. There was something so youthful about her as she walked into the room, smiling and confident.

'I'm sorry to keep you waiting,' she said to Lisa's mother. 'I'm Mrs. Cole.'

'I'm Mrs. Blomquist and this is my daughter Lisa.'

'How do you do, Lisa.'

Despite the warmth in the greeting, Lisa felt strangely shy and tongue-tied, very much the country hick. She tried standing a little straighter, emulating the woman's erect carriage, a look emphasized by the heavily padded shoulders of the royal blue dress she wore. Not even her clothes had the dowdy look of an old woman's, Lisa realized. Women of comparable age in Palmer were either plump or bags of bones, their skin lined and wrinkled like a prune. She'd never seen anyone like Mrs. Cole before, except maybe in the movies.

Lisa was so intent on studying the woman that she missed the conversation between Mrs. Cole and her mother. She couldn't even remember hearing their voices until Mrs. Cole took a step backwards toward the doorway. 'Excuse me a minute. My grandson is out back. I'll have him take you over to see the house.'

As she left the room, Lisa turned to her mother. 'She seems very nice.'

She sniffed in disapproval. 'She *claims* she's a widow. I suppose she could be.' Her eyes swept the room and its contents. 'But I have my doubts that this was always a boardinghouse.'

'Mama.' Lisa was shocked by the insinuation that this might once have been a house of ill repute, and that Mrs. Cole had owned it.

'I have been told by more than one person that it isn't wise to ask too many questions about a woman's past here in Alaska. It's been said that many men who have become leading citizens in the community married "fallen women." They claim there were so few decent women in Alaska during the early days that the men, in desperation, took the other kind for wives.'

'Mama.' Lisa was embarrassed that her mother would even suggest that Mrs. Cole might have been one of those – and strongly suspected that she was jealous.

When Mrs. Cole returned, she was accompanied by a tall, broadshouldered young man in a blue plaid flannel shirt. His face looked as if it had been chiseled out of bronze. His eyes were almost black, like his grandmother's, but they lacked their warm sparkle. His seemed more guarded and watchful.

'I'd like you to meet my grandson, Wylie Cole. This is Mrs.

621

Blomquist and her daughter Lisa. They presently live in Palmer, but her husband has been hired to help with the building of the new Army fort here in Anchorage. They're looking for a place to live here so he won't have to commute back and forth to work.'

Lisa Blomquist. For an instant, Wylie was too stunned to do anything except stare at the girl. Immediately his mind flashed back to that first meeting five years ago. She was the right age. The pigtails were gone and the color of her hair was maybe a shade or two different, but her eyes were still big and blue. Wylie was sure there couldn't possibly be two girls named Lisa Blomquist living in the Matanuska Valley; she had to be the same one he'd met.

She stared at him intently, but without a flicker of recognition in her expression. She didn't remember him. Wylie felt deflated by the discovery and wished he could jog her memory, but claiming a previous acquaintance was one of the oldest lines in the book. He covered his disappointment, realizing that he'd obviously not made as much of an impression on her as she'd made on him.

'It's a pleasure.' He addressed both Lisa and her mother. 'My car's outside. I'll be happy to drive you over to see the house.'

Wylie. It was an unusual name, yet somehow it sounded familiar to her. Lisa couldn't think why until she was seated in the back seat of the Chevy, then she remembered that the pilot who had been killed in that plane crash near Barrow, Alaska along with Will Rogers, had been named Wiley, too. At the time, everybody had been talking about it. She remembered the pilot's name because it had been the same as that boy she had met – That was it, she realized. She was almost positive his name had been Wylie Cole. But it was so long ago. She leaned foward in her seat, straining for a look at the driver's face. The black hair and eyes, the Indian-like profile – it had to be him.

She wanted to say something, to mention their past meeting, but with her mother sitting there in the front seat beside him she couldn't bring herself to do it. So she sat back in her seat and stared out the window, now and then stealing glances at the back of his head, wishing she had the nerve to speak up.

At the house, Wylie showed the mother and daughter through the rooms. Completing the circuit, they came back to the starting point in the front room. Wylie halted. 'Was there anything else you'd like to see, Mrs. Blomquist? Are there any questions?'

'I think I'd like to take another look at the kitchen. It seemed a little small.'

'Go right ahead. Take all the time you want. I'll wait here for you.' He didn't feel like accompanying her.

'Aren't you coming, Lisa?' Mrs. Blomquist asked as she started toward the kitchen located in the rear of the house.

'No, I . . . I think I'll wait here.' Her back was to him as she spoke. He studied the natural luster of her light brown hair, long and sleek with the ends turning under to brush the tops of her shoulders. He wanted to reach out and touch it to see if it was as soft as it looked. She watched her mother leave the room, then turned and hesitantly smiled at him. 'It's a nice house.'

'Yes.'

'I know this question will probably sound funny.' She seemed very nervous and self-conscious, as if she wasn't altogether sure she should be saying any of this. 'But . . . is your father a bush pilot?'

'Yes, he is.' Wylie frowned at her curiously, wondering what had prompted the question.

'I thought so.' Her lips parted in a wide smile that seemed to light up her face. 'We've met before. I don't know if you remember –'

'– the dinner at the community hall for the colonists on their way to the Matanuska Valley.' Wylie smiled broadly.

She stared at him in amazement. 'You do.'

'As I recall, you had pigtails about down to here.' He drew a line across the top of her collarbone, unable to resist the urge to touch her, however briefly.

'And my brothers thought you were an Indian.'

'That's right.'

She seemed to glow with happiness. 'Do you still like to hunt and fish? I remember you telling me – telling us how you had killed a grizzly bear that winter.'

'I still do.' He caught the sound of her mother's footsteps and Lisa glanced in the direction of the kitchen.

'It's a nice house,' she repeated.

'I hope your parents decide to rent it.'

'So do I.'

'If they do, we'll probably see each other again.'

'We probably will.' She seemed to be as pleased about that as he was.

'Maybe we could even take in a movie some Saturday night,' Wylie suggested as her mother came into view.

'Maybe we could.' She flashed him a quick smile, then turned to face her mother.

Lisa was half afraid her mother wouldn't even consider renting the house because of her suspicions about its landlady. But the very next day, she took her husband to see it. Within a week, they had moved into the house. And two weeks later, Lisa went to the local movie theater with Wylie Cole.

At the movie's end, Wylie and Lisa left the theater through the lobby doors that funneled the crowd into the street outside. The crowd thinned quickly, scattering in all directions as Wylie guided her to his car parked at the end of the next block. The summer sun still claimed the evening sky, spreading its long, golden light over the town.

'It's a beautiful night,' Lisa remarked.

'Yes.' After holding her hand through the entire movie, he missed the feel of its light grasp. He stuffed his hands in the pockets of his jacket so they wouldn't feel so empty. Suddenly she laughed softly, then shook her head. 'What's the matter? Did I miss something funny?'

'No.' She sighed, then shook her head again. 'I'm still amazed that you remembered me. That was a long time ago.'

'I don't see why it's all that surprising. The Matanuska project was big news around here for a couple of years there. Stories were always circulating about what was happening in Palmer. Since you were the only person I'd ever met from there, it was probably natural that I thought of you whenever people talked about it.' Then he grinned at her. 'Beside, not many people have mistaken me for an Indian.'

'Erik and Rudy do have a way of making a lasting impression.' She smiled ruefully, then asked, 'Do you have any brothers or sisters?'

'No. There's just me.'

'It must have been kinda lonely for you.'

'I guess when I was a kid maybe it was.' Looking back, Wylie wondered if meeting Lisa with her two younger brothers, watching the way she looked after them, and observing their private squabbling weren't some of the reasons she'd stayed in his mind all this time. 'But now, for the most part, I like being by myself.'

624

'I think I know what you mean. I am almost convinced that being the only girl is the same as being an only child. Living on the farm the way we did, I really didn't have anyone to talk to or play with. Our closest neighbors didn't have any girls my age, and my mother . . . She isn't exactly the kind you can confide in.'

'I always wondered whether you had a hard time of it.'

'I guess we did. The soil on our tract was too poor to grow much, so we kept dairy cows. My daddy worked really hard, but he just couldn't make a go of it.'

'Are you sorry you came to Alaska five years ago?'

'No!' she shot back in quick denial, then paused. She had too much pride to admit to him that until they came to Alaska and moved into their newly built house on the farm, she'd never lived in a home where the roof didn't leak or the wind didn't blow through the cracks or the plaster didn't fall off the walls. Life here had been a constant struggle, but at least they were better fed, better clothed, and better housed. 'When we lived in Minnesota, that's when we had the hard time of it.' They'd been so poor, with nothing but more days of poverty ahead of them.

'I think Alaska is a great land. Of course, I was born here, so naturally I'm prejudiced, but a lot of people from the outside can't stand our long winters or the mosquitoes.'

'The winters are longer,' Lisa admitted. 'But they aren't nearly as cold as the ones in Minnesota. And the mosquitoes aren't any worse than the black flies that swarm all over Minnesota in the summer.'

'You really like it here, don't you?' Wylie stopped next to his Chevy.

'I really do.'

'I'm glad.' He opened the passenger door for her and waited until she was safely inside, then closed the door and walked around to the driver's side. He almost felt like whistling.

It was just a short drive to her house. All too soon, they were pulling up in front of it. Reluctantly Wylie walked her to the door, wishing there was some way to prolong this time with her.

As she turned to face him, her expression seemed to mirror his own feelings. 'I had a wonderful time tonight, Wylie.'

'So did I. You don't happen to have any plans for next Saturday night, do you?'

'No. None at all.' Her cheeks dimpled with her smile.

'Maybe we could take in another movie.'

'The previews looked good.'

'I'll pick you up at six-thirty, if that's okay.'

'Fine.'

Wylie hesitated, wanting to kiss her good night even if it was only their first date, then cursed the lingering daylight that put them in full view of the whole neighborhood. But what the hell did he care what the neighbors thought. She stood there, looking at him, watching and waiting. He bent slightly and kissed her and felt the warm pressure of her response.

He straightened, breathing a little faster. 'Six-thirty next Saturday?'

'Yes.'

They went out that next Saturday, and every Saturday after that for the rest of the summer and fall, plus a few evenings in between. Lisa was nervous the first time Wylie asked her to have Sunday dinner with his family. Although he'd never actually said that he was interested in establishing a more permanent relationship, meeting his parents seemed to be a possible step to something more serious. In view of that, Lisa was terribly anxious to make a good impression.

But it all seemed to go wrong the minute she arrived at his parents' home. A January thaw followed by freezing temperatures had left icy patches on the front walk. As she stepped out of the car and started to the front door ahead of Wylie, she slipped on some ice and fell before Wylie could catch her. She tore a hole in the only pair of stockings she owned and skinned her leg. It was some entrance she made, hobbling into the house with blood running down her knee.

His mother and grandmother fussed over it, insisting the cut be washed, disinfected, and bandaged, when all Lisa wanted to do was pretend it had never happened. She was grateful when they all finally sat down at the dinner table and conversation turned to something other than her nasty fall.

'Did I tell you, Wylie, that when I was up in Fairbanks this last week, they had that new air base, Ladd Field, finished?' His father scooped potatoes onto his plate, then passed the bowl to Lisa. 'That cement runway they built is supposed to have more concrete in it than we have in every street and sidewalk in Anchorage. They claim it's so thick it won't even buckle at sixty below.'

'They'll have their chance to test it this winter,' Wylie replied.

'I heard one of those Army pilots from outside complain about the flying conditions up here.' His father chuckled. 'He's been "flying the beam" for so long, he's forgotten how to fly by the seat of his pants.'

' "Flying the beam" is pilot talk for navigating by directional radio beams,' his mother explained to Lisa. 'A pilot can tune his radio to the transmitter located at a known airfield and fly to it.'

'You can count the number of transmitters in Alaska probably on the fingers of one hand,' Ace Cole added. 'These Army pilots are finding out what it's like to fly in the north. It gets so cold up here it'll turn your oil into something that resembles Trudy's raspberry jelly, hydraulic systems freeze, and rubber tires can get so brittle, they shatter like glass. That's saying nothing about how quickly ice can accumulate on a plane's wings. They're really putting that test lab in Fairbanks to use, trying to adapt their bombers and fighters to these cold weather conditions. And air bases – I'll bet the Army has a dozen fields under construction.'

'The shiploads of construction workers and soldiers that poured into Anchorage this last fall rival anything I ever saw in Nome,' Wylie's grandmother stated. 'They're sleeping in tents, wanigans – just about anything that has four walls and a roof. Matty and I converted the parlor into more sleeping rooms, and we still have twenty people on the waiting list.'

'All I can say is it's about time Congress woke up to the fact that Alaska needs some military installations. They poured more than four hundred and fifty million dollars into Hawaii, and it's twenty-five hundred miles from the West Coast of the United States. Last spring, like Ernest Gruening said, a handful of enemy paratroopers could have captured Alaska overnight. Now it might take them a week.'

'At least something's being done about it, Ace.' Mrs. Cole didn't appear greatly concerned about her husband's gloomy outlook.

'I suppose we should thank Stalin for that. If he hadn't signed that pact with Hitler, Congress probably wouldn't have done anything. Now they're worried about all the military bases Russia has on the Siberian coast. One of them is only a hundred and fifty miles from Nome. I still say it's Japan we have to worry about. I know General Buckner has ordered construction to go on around the clock to get all these defensive installations in'. I just hope it isn't too late.'

'Dad.' But Wylie glanced at Lisa as he spoke. 'Why don't we talk about something else? You're making it sound as though we're going to war at any minute.'

'We may be. We can't bury our heads in the sand and pretend that what's going on in Europe and the Pacific is not going to affect us – and soon.'

'The President has promised that the United States isn't going to be drawn into another world war.' Glory dabbed at a corner of her mouth with a napkin.

'Japan and Germany made no such promises. Look at the supplies the U.S. is shipping to England now. How long do you think Hitler is going to let that continue?' Ace stabbed his fork into a piece of the moose roast. 'As usual, everyone outside is looking across the Atlantic. That's why they've forgotten about Alaska until this Russian scare came up. Those generals and congressmen in Washington, D.C., ought to be able to look at a world map and see that from Fairbanks it's fifteen hours' flying time for a bomber to Tokyo – or New York City. Fairbanks is only four thousand miles away from every major city in Europe, for God's sake.'

'Ace, calm down,' Trudy Cole said patiently from her chair at the opposite end of the table, then smiled apologetically at Lisa. 'You're not only getting yourself all upset, but I'm afraid you're also upsetting our guest with your war talk.'

'Lisa, I'm sorry.' He looked at her with something akin to surprise.

Again, she was the center of attention, the very last thing she wanted. 'No, it's all right, really.' She smiled nervously.

Truthfully much of what had been said she hadn't known about. At home, when her family discussed what was going on in Alaska, the talk usually centered on the number of high-paying jobs that were available, the way housing and food prices kept rising, the amount of money they were going to make, the things they could spend it on.

'Trudy, I think you're wrong,' Wylie's father stated. 'Maybe it's good for someone like Lisa to be alarmed by what I've said. After all, it's the young people who will have to fight when the war comes. You and I are too old to do more than hold down the home front. But, Lisa and Wylie –'

'Dad,' Wylie interrupted him again. 'You're really making things difficult.'

'Why?'

'Because . . . I received a letter from Uncle Sam that said "Greetings." ' He paused, and a gasp from his mother filled the break. 'I've been trying to figure out how to tell you and decided this would be as good a time as any – with everyone here in one place – to let you know I've been drafted.'

Lisa couldn't say anything. Her mind was suddenly filled with visions of him in uniform and his face in the newsreel films they showed at the movie theater depicting the war scenes in Europe.

'Wylie.' His mother had tears in her eyes, and his grand-mother, seated next to him, reached over and lightly squeezed his hand.

'I knew it was coming.' His father was the only one who seemed to take the announcement in his stride. 'I was hoping you'd sign up for the Army Air Corps before you got drafted. With your flying experience, you still might be able to get in. They need good pilots.'

Wylie shook his head slowly. 'Sorry, Dad, but if I'm going to do any fighting, I want my feet on the ground.'

'When do you have to leave?' his grandmother asked softly.

'Soon.'

'How soon?' His mother seemed to brace herself for his answer.

'This week.'

Lisa couldn't talk at all. She just stared at him.

'Gracious.' His mother laughed suddenly, then stopped before it turned into a sob. Lisa understood. Half the reason she hadn't said anything was because she was afraid if she tried she'd break into tears. 'Do you know I think I left the pie in the oven?' Trudy declared and left the dining room almost at a run to disappear into the kitchen. Wylie laid his napkin beside his plate and started to rise, but his father motioned him back into his chair.

'I'll go see if she's burned the pie,' he said and got up from the table.

Later, after they'd all gone through the motions of finishing dinner, Lisa offered to help clear the table and wash the dishes. But the elder Glory Cole glanced once at Wylie's mother, then gently suggested that it might be better if they did it by them-selves and told Lisa to go into the living room with Wylie.

She couldn't say a word to him as he led her to the big sofa. She felt brittle – as if the least little jar would shatter her into a thousand pieces. She sat down, trying to hold herself together.

'Lisa, I'm sorry.' He sat staring at his clasped hands, his head bowed.

'You should be. That was a terrible way to break something like that to people who care about you.' She was angry with him, angry that he hadn't told her privately, that his whole family had been looking on. Didn't he think the news would upset her? Didn't he know how much she cared?

'I know it was, but I was hoping with you here that my family's reaction wouldn't be quite so emotional. I knew how much this was going to upset my mother. I'm her only son.' He looked at her. 'I didn't mean to hurt you, Lisa.'

She couldn't stay angry at him, not when there was so little time left.

After that disastrous dinner, Lisa saw Wylie one more time before he left. He parked the car in front of her house and let the engine idle. The porch light was on, but Lisa made no move to get out of the car. All evening long, he'd acted as if it were just another date, and not the last one they'd have for a long time. She sat huddled in the passenger seat beside him, bundled in her scarf, coat, and gloves. She wished he'd say something – that he cared, that he loved her – anything that would let her know where she stood with him. But the silence just went on.

'I guess I won't see you for a while,' she said finally.

He half turned toward her and laid his arm along the back of the seat. 'Probably not.'

It was too dark to see his face clearly, but Lisa doubted that his expression would reveal anything anyway. She felt his hand stroke the back of her head and push the wool scarf back to touch her hair.

'Will you write to me?' she asked.

'Sure. Will you write to me?' It almost sounded like he was teasing her.

'Of course.' She'd write every day if he asked. 'I wish you didn't have to go.'

'Hey, I'm not all that happy about going into the Army, but I don't have any choice. Besides, you aren't going to miss me for long. Not in Alaska. I'll bet there's already ten guys standing in line to take my place.'

'It wouldn't matter if there were a hundred. You make me so mad sometimes, Wylie.' She was close to tears. 'Don't you want me to wait for you?'

'Nobody knows what's going to happen. I don't think it is the time to make any promises we may not want to keep tomorrow. A lot of things can change, Lisa.'

'Maybe for you.' She stared blindly at her gloved hands, clenched tightly together on her lap.

'Why don't we just wait and see what happens when I come back?'

'Sure.'

'Lisa. Would you look at me?' Reluctantly, almost warily she lifted her chin and gazed at him. 'I am coming back. You can count on that. And you damned well better not forget me.'

His fingers tunneled under her page boy and gripped the back of her neck, drawing her toward him. He kissed her long and hard, as if determined to leave his mark on her. Lisa clung to him, equally determined that he would remember her, holding nothing back in her desire to show him how much she cared. But it hurt too much inside. In the end, she pulled away and bolted from the car, crying as she ran to the house.

54 *Anchorage*
December 7, 1941

Winter darkness continued to reign over the morning as Lisa approached the church steps to attend the nine o'clock service, accompanied by her parents and, grudgingly, by her younger brothers. It would be another two hours before daylight would brighten the sky. A man stood to one side of the church doors. There was the faintest break in her stride as Lisa recognized him.

'Do you see who's here, Lisa?' her mother murmured, barely moving her lips. 'I'll bet he's waiting for you.'

'Just because he's standing outside doesn't necessarily mean Mr. Bogardus is waiting for me.' But she was afraid her mother was right, and she didn't know what to do about the situation.

It was ironic when she thought about it. Against her mother's wishes, she had quit her clerking job at a local drugstore five months ago to take a better-paying job as a payroll assistant for a construction company from the States that had established a branch office in Anchorage to handle their government contracts in Alaska. Tall, boyish-looking Steve Bogardus was a partner in the company and managed the Anchorage office. He was her boss.

A month after she'd gone to work for the company, he'd asked her out. Naturally she had refused. Then two months ago he'd discovered that she had no transportation and walked the several blocks from her house to the office. He'd offered to pick her up in the mornings and take her home at nights, insisting that it wasn't out of his way and that it wasn't a good idea for a young, single woman to be walking alone down dark streets, not to mention the cold weather. At the time, it had seemed foolish to refuse a ride to and from work, especially with winter on its way. So she had accepted his offer.

Naturally her mother had met him the first time he'd come to pick her up. The minute she found out he was twenty-nine years old, an engineering graduate, unmarried, and a partner in the firm, all her objections to Lisa's new job vanished. Then Lisa had made the mistake of mentioning that he'd asked her out and she'd turned him down. Now her mother badgered her constantly about him and demanded to know why she was throwing her life away on someone like Wylie Cole, who would never amount to anything, when she could have a man who had his own business and a bright future. She didn't see why Lisa sat home every night when she could be going on dates with Mr. Bogardus. It made no difference to her that Wylie was stationed in Alaska and Lisa was able to see him, however infrequently. If anything, it made her more determined. Several times, her mother had taken it upon herself to ask Mr. Bogardus to stay for dinner when he'd brought Lisa home after work. He'd always accepted.

Lisa was in an awkward situation. To make matters worse, she liked being with Steve Bogardus and that made her feel guilty. He was so different from Wylie. His face was so expressive she was always able to tell when he was tired or when the pressure to complete a job was building up or when he was excited about something. He was attentive and kind, always opening doors for her or praising her work or remarking on a dress or her hair – sometimes even flirting with her. Wylie tended to be more aloof, seldom complimenting her and rarely demonstrative in his affections unless they were alone. Lisa knew Wylie wasn't as experienced as her employer. How could he be? Steve Bogardus was older. Sometimes the age difference frightened her as much as his persistence did. And her boss could be very persuasive when he wanted something.

'Good morning, Mr. Bogardus.' Lisa forced a smile as she mounted the steps.

'Good morning, Lisa.' Then he greeted the rest of her family with equal cordiality. 'I didn't see you drive up. Don't tell me you walked to church this morning?'

'It wasn't far, really. Our car refused to start.' With the high wages her father was receiving, they'd finally been able to get rid of the old farm truck this last summer and buy a car. 'I guess it hasn't gotten used to these Alaskan winters yet.'

'Neither have I.' He shuddered in a mock reaction to the cold temperature. In spite of herself, Lisa smiled. 'I wish I had known about your car though. I could have given you a ride to church.'

'We will let you take us home, Mr. Bogardus,' her mother said. 'But only if you say you will stay to dinner.'

'As usual, you've twisted my arm, Mrs. Blomquist.'

Lisa avoided his eyes. 'We probably should go inside. I think we're blocking the door.'

'You're right. It's probably warmer inside, too.' He opened the door and held it while the Blomquist family filed through.

Lisa stepped farther into the lighted vestibule and paused to slip off her gloves and unbutton her heavy coat. She smiled and nodded to the ushers standing at the inner doors to the sanctuary, passing out the morning's programs. As Steve Bogardus walked over to stand with Lisa and the rest of her family, she noticed Wylie's mother and grandmother at the far end of the vestibule.

'Excuse me. I'm just going over to speak to Mrs. Cole for a minute. I'll join you inside.' She moved away from her family and her boss, hoping that Mrs. Cole might have heard from Wylie. More than three months had passed since she'd seen him, and almost that long since she'd had a letter from him, although she had written to him regularly. His warning that he was a notoriously poor correspondent was small consolation. 'Good morning.' She smiled at both women, then belatedly noticed the aging Eskimo woman with them and nodded to her as well. 'Matty.'

'Lisa.' Trudy Cole greeted her warmly. 'I was hoping I'd see you in church this morning. We received a letter from Wylie yesterday. I was just showing it to Mother Cole. He said he might not have time to write you and asked me to pass on his news.'

'His news?' She took the sheet of paper his grandmother offered to her. The letter was short, covering little more than half the page.

'Yes. The Army asked for volunteers with knowledge of Alaska and its terrain to form a group called the Alaska Scouts. I think he gives the full name of it in his letter.'

' "All-Alaska Combat Intelligence Scouts," ' Lisa read.

'That's it. They're going through a lot of specialized training. That's why he wasn't sure he'd have time to write you.'

'He sent along a picture.' Matty handed her the snapshot she'd been studying. 'Wylie's the one in the middle.'

Lisa stared at the three men in the photograph, dressed alike in parkas, each with a rifle slung loosely over his shoulder. Between the parkas' fur hoods and the straggly beard growth, their faces were barely visible. They didn't look like soldiers at all. In fact, Lisa wasn't sure she would have recognized Wylie immediately if Matty hadn't already pointed him out to her.

'He's growing a beard.' She wasn't very thrilled about that.

'Yes.' The tone of her voice seemed to indicate that his mother shared the opinion. 'He says it will keep his face warm.'

'I suppose it will,' Lisa conceded, but she thought it made him look like some wild and woolly mountain man.

The resonating notes of the church organ filled the air as the organist struck the opening chords of the call to worship. 'I think it's time we took our seats.'

'Yes.' Lisa returned the letter and the photograph. 'Thanks for letting me know about Wylie.'

'You don't have to thank me for that,' his mother assured her. 'Some evening when you don't have anything to do, come over to the house. I'm usually there by myself anyway. Between the Army and all the contractors, Ace is flying parts and equipment all over Alaska. I hardly see him any more.'

'I'll do that,' Lisa promised.

Her family was seated in one of the rear pews. She noticed that her mother had conveniently saved her a place on the end next to Steve Bogardus. She sat down beside him and reached for the hymnal. As she listened to the organist play, her thoughts centered on Wylie. He hadn't forgotten her even if he hadn't had time to write. Then the service began and she gave her attention to it.

Midway through the minister's sermon, she heard a distant rumbling that resembled muffled explosions. Others heard it too, and heads turned and ears strained to identify the odd sound. A faint questioning murmur went through the congregation.

For once the minister didn't drone on, and the morning service ended at its appointed time. As Lisa took her place in the long line slowly filing out of the church doors, everyone was asking a variation of the same question: 'Did you hear that noise?'

'At first I thought it was thunder.'

Lisa turned to Steve Bogardus. 'What do you suppose it was?'

'More than likely they were conducting some maneuvers out at Fort Richardson. We probably just heard the echo of their guns.' He smiled to indicate his lack of concern.

The explanation seemed more plausible than thunder in December. After shaking hands with the minister, Steve Bogardus led the family out of the church. 'My car's parked down the street.'

Before they reached the bottom of the steps, Lisa heard the wail of a siren, then realized there was more than one. She stopped. So did everyone else around her.

Then someone came running up. 'It's on the radio. The Japanese are bombing Hawaii.'

'No,' she murmured.

'Come on.' Steve took her arm. 'Let's go to my car. There's a radio in it.'

Lisa broke into a run. All the things Wylie's father had said were running through her mind. She tried to tell herself it wasn't true, that it was all a false alarm. There wasn't really going to be a war.

But the radio announcer confirmed the story that Japanese bombers had struck Hickam Field and the naval base at Pearl Harbor in Hawaii, and he further stated that more than a dozen warships in the harbor were in flames and predicted monstrous losses. All off-duty soldiers in Alaska were ordered to report immediately to their units, all non-military aircraft were grounded, and the streets were to be cleared of all civilian traffic. Everyone was to return home and await further instructions.

When the announcer began to outline evacuation procedures in the event of an enemy attack, Lisa murmured, 'My God, they really believe the Japanese might invade Alaska.'

'Why did we ever come here? I knew it was a mistake.' Her mother panicked. 'Jan, what are we going to do?'

'We are going to do what the man said – go home and wait.'

'Lisa.' Steve Bogardus gripped her hand. 'I'd better go to the office. There might be bulldozers or other equipment the Army will need. Will you be all right?'

'Yes.' At the moment, she was numb with shock.

They abandoned the car and set out on foot, Steve to his office and the Blomquists to their home. The shriek of sirens added to the atmosphere of confusion and panic as transport trucks charged through town picking up soldiers. Military trucks and armed vehicles of every description rumbled through the streets, and bombers and pursuit planes thundered through the air over the city, heading out on patrol.

All day Lisa stayed close to the shortwave radio, as did everyone else. By the door sat the knapsacks, packed with the recommended two-week supply of food and survival gear for a flight into the mountains. Propped beside them were her father's and brothers' hunting rifles in case they had to provide civilian resistance. Heavy curtains and blankets were already in place to observe the strict blackout orders.

When the Alaska radio stations went off the air on orders from

General Buckner to facilitate military communications, the Blomquists tried tuning their radio to a Canadian station. Instead they picked up Radio Tokyo. When its announcer reported that Dutch Harbor in the Aleutians and Kodiak had been bombed to rubble, Lisa started to cry. Wylie was supposed to be based at Kodiak. Then Radio Tokyo claimed Fairbanks had been attacked by air and that Sitka and Anchorage were in Japanese hands. Lisa knew she was in Anchorage and so far the Japanese weren't, which allowed her to doubt the accuracy of the previous report on the destruction of Kodiak.

In that first harried week after Pearl Harbor, the Army's air force in Alaska – which consisted of six obsolete bombers and twelve obsolete pursuit planes – was in the air patrolling eighteen hours a day. On Tuesday, three fighters shot down a U.S. weather balloon. Navy planes out of Sitka bombed a 'submarine' they sighted – and sank a whale. After that, Alaskans seemed to recover both their equilibrium and their sense of humor.

The Japanese threat was real. They had only to look at the Philippines, where the Japanese forces had landed after Pear Harbor and had MacArthur's troops in retreat, to know that. Alaska was too strategically located for the Japanese to ignore for long. They had to be prepared for an invasion. All military dependents were evacuated from the entire territory of Alaska, which had been declared a military area.

The flurry of construction projects that had begun in the fall turned into a full-scale storm that winter, as the threat of invasion lent a new urgency to the need for defensive installations. The increased work-load affected everyone from contractors like Steve Bogardus and construction workers like Jan Blomquist to bush pilots like Ace Cole, who was flying men and supplies to remote sites. Despite persistent rumors that Alaska would be abandoned by the War Department and not receive the additional troops, planes, and naval vessels needed to improve its meager defenses, as had happened in the Philippines, all work was speeded up. Lisa left the payroll department and went to work filing and filling out the numerous forms, putting in long hours in an effort to keep up with all the paperwork created by additional contracts and new deadlines for completion.

It was late afternoon on the first Saturday in March when Steve Bogardus brought Lisa home after working in the office all day.

Lisa was too tired to care when her mother invited him to stay for dinner that night, or when she refused Lisa's help in the kitchen and shooed her into the living room with her boss. She turned on the radio to catch the latest war news, then sank onto the couch, wishing fervently that she could slip off her shoes.

'We really should be celebrating tonight.' Steve Bogardus sat slumped against the back couch cushions, his boyish features with their dusting of freckles looking worn and haggard. 'That contract the government awarded our company for work on the Alaska – Canada Military Highway is going to amount to a lot of dollars.'

A road running through Canada and linking the United States to its Alaska Territory had been talked about for so long that Lisa had never believed it would actually be built in her lifetime. But the war with Japan and the knowledge that its superior naval power was capable of closing the sea lanes to Alaska had changed all that. Construction of the fifteen-hundred-mile-long military road had been authorized and given the highest priority. The massive undertaking was to be a joint effort of civilian contractors and workers and the Army Corps of Engineers and its regiments.

'I'm sure you're right.' Lisa sighed. 'But I keep thinking about the amount of paperwork there will be.'

'Don't worry. We'll be hiring more help in the office.'

'That's the best news I've heard yet, Mr. Bogardus.'

'When are you going to start calling me Steve?'

She became conscious of his arm draped along the back of the couch and the closeness of his hand to her shoulder. 'It isn't really proper to call your employer by his first name.'

'I thought we were friends, too.'

She felt his fingertips brush the ends of her hair and quickly stood up to elude them. 'I never said we weren't, Mr. Bogardus.' In an attempt to cover her agitation, she walked over to the radio.

'You know I should be taking you out to dinner. It's time I started paying back all your generous hospitality.' He pushed himself off the couch and wandered over to the radio.

'My mother would like that.'

'Lisa, you know I meant you – not your family.'

'Yes.' She turned and faced the small snapshot that she'd stuck in the corner of the framed photograph of Wylie. The larger picture showed Wylie in his Army uniform, and the smaller one was more recent, taken after he'd joined the Scouts.

'Is this your soldier boy?' He removed the snapshot from the corner of the frame for a closer look.

'Yes, that's Wylie.'

'His name's Wylie?'

'Yes. Wylie Cole. He's with the Alaska Scouts.' She had never told Steve anything except that she was dating someone in the service.

'One of Castner's Cutthroats,' he murmured.

'I beg your pardon?' Lisa frowned.

'That's the nickname they've given Colonel Castner's hand-picked platoon of commandos. They're supposed to be a rough bunch of men from all parts of Alaska – miners, trappers, hunters, natives, all crack shots able to live off the land. And very deadly, too, from what I've been told. Some claim they're a group of misfits who found Army discipline not to their liking.' He eyed her thoughtfully. 'You didn't know that, did you?'

'Wylie's not like that.' She took the photograph and tucked it back in the frame, angered by his attempt to make Wylie sound dangerous.

'It's probably Army propaganda to create the image of a tough commando unit.' His comment seemed an attempt to satisfy her more than anything else. 'Does he really expect you to sit home every night and never go out and have any fun?'

'Of course not.'

'Then why do you turn me down every time I ask you out?'

'Because'

'Because why?'

'Steve, please,' she protested.

'At last you've said my name.'

Rattled by the slip, she blurted, 'It just came out. I wasn't thinking.'

'What you mean is that you *said* what you were thinking. It's encouraging to know that you do think of me as Steve and not that cold Mr. Bogardus.'

It was true. She did think of him as Steve. She had for some time now. 'It doesn't mean anything,' she insisted.

'It means we can drop this Mr. Bogardus nonsense.'

She heard the tramp of booted feet on the front porch and turned gratefully toward the sound. 'That must be Dad.'

But when the front door opened, a tall, rough-looking man with a heavy black beard stepped inside. Dumbstruck, Lisa stared at the

639

stranger. There was a flash of white in the middle of the dark beard growth as the man smiled.

'Mom said I should call, but I thought I'd surprise you. It took some doing, but I managed to wangle a weekend pass out of the sarge.'

'Wylie.' She recognized his voice, stunned to discover that not even the snapshot had prepared her for the shocking change in his appearance.

He scratched at his beard. 'It's me underneath all this thick fuzz.' He shrugged out of the parka and draped it on the hall tree.

The action seemed to break the spell that had held her motionless. She quickly crossed the room to his side, but when he started to put his arm around her, Lisa drew back. Up close, he looked leaner and tougher than she remembered. She glanced over her shoulder at Steve, trying to blame her reluctance on his presence.

'Wylie, I'd like you to meet my boss, Steve Bogardus.' She led him over to meet Steve.

'I've heard a lot about you, Private Cole.' Smiling warmly, Steve shook hands with him, but Lisa was conscious of the way Wylie coolly studied him.

'I'm afraid I can't say the same, Steve. Lisa hasn't mentioned you at all.'

Lisa flushed guiltily; even though she hadn't actually gone out on a date with Steve, she enjoyed his company. 'Mother invited Mr. Bogardus to dinner tonight, Wylie,' she said.

'I wasn't about to turn down the chance to enjoy a home-cooked meal,' Steve added.

Lisa could have hugged him for the way he backed her up and made it sound very innocent – which it was, she reminded herself. 'You haven't eaten, have you, Wylie? Mama always cooks enough food to feed an army. I know there'll be plenty to eat if you want to join us.'

'Like Steve, I'm not about to turn down a home-cooked meal.'

With seven for dinner, the Blomquists' table was crowded. Wylie found the seating arrangement to his satisfaction, since it put Lisa on his left and her boss, Steve Bogardus, across the table from him, allowing him to observe both of them.

He'd always known Lisa might start seeing someone else. With so many men concentrated in Anchorage and so few women, it was a foregone conclusion that she'd have ample opportunity to date. He'd almost managed to convince himself that it wouldn't be fair

640

to expect her to sit home alone and wait for him, that it would be all right if she dated a few guys. After all, there was a war on, and who knew what might happen to him? When he came back, that was the time to settle things between them.

But every time he saw Bogardus glance at Lisa – even though he believed they weren't actually dating yet – he wanted to reach across that table and mash his face to a bloody pulp. And Lisa's mother didn't help the situation by making her preference for Bogardus very clear by the way she manipulated the conversation to show him in a favorable light. Wylie had always known that she had never really liked him. Now with the pressure she was putting on Lisa and the natural temptation of someone like Bogardus, he knew it was only a matter of time before Lisa gave in.

And there wasn't a damned thing he could do about it. He'd virtually given her permission to see other men while he was away, so how could he object now?

Hell, he wasn't blind. He could see what Bogardus had going for him – he was here, on the spot, in contact with Lisa every day. And the man was probably getting rich off these government contracts. It was obvious he had her whole family wrapped around his finger by the way they all laughed at his jokes. Wylie supposed Bogardus was good-looking if a person liked the Van Johnson type. Although Lisa tried to hide it, he could tell by the way she kept looking at Bogardus then looking self-consciously away that she was attracted to him. And Wylie's frustration mounted because he didn't have a single damned right to condemn her for it.

Lisa's father and brothers practically deluged Wylie with questions about what was going on, but to most of them he had to plead ignorance even when he knew the answers. Attached, as his Scout group was, to Army Intelligence, there were a lot of things he knew – some by rumor, some from reliable sources, and some personally.

But he couldn't talk about the sightings of Japanese ships in Aleutian waters or that their presence and activity indicated they were seeking out landing sites. Nor could he mention that strategists in Washington wanted to launch an invasion against Japan from Nome, Siberia, and Kamchatka, an impossibility without Russian cooperation, and Russia had yet to declare war on Japan. He couldn't discuss the secret bases that had been built at Dutch Harbor and Cold Bay on Unalaska and Umnak Islands under the guise of a fish cannery – bases General Buckner had ordered built without authorization, since they commanded the strait that provided shipping access to Siberia, Nome, the whole Upper Alaskan Peninsula, and the eastern half of the Aleutian Islands.

Earlier that afternoon, he'd aroused his grandmother's curiosity with his questions about their family history, especially about their ancestor Tasha, who had lived not only on Kodiak, but on Unalaska, Adak, and Attu. She'd become suspicious when he'd asked too many specific questions about the islands themselves in an effort to obtain whatever sketchy information she could give him about the terrain, natural harbors, caves, landmarks – anything that might be of use.

Everything seemed to indicate there would soon be action somewhere in the Aleutian chain. He'd talked to a couple of the Aleuts in his outfit who had trapped on some of the islands and learned quite a bit from them. But on the whole, very little was known about the islands. No detailed mapping had ever been done. The pilots were using Rand McNally road maps, and the Navy had charts that were based on a Russian survey done back in 1864.

There were times when Wylie doubted that the War Department realized just how big Alaska was. It had thirty-four thousand miles of coastline, more than the entire United States. On most maps, the Aleutian Islands were never shown to scale. As a result, they usually ended up resembling the Florida Keys. There was a big difference, however. They stretched some twelve hundred miles westward from the tip of the Alaska Peninsula. From Anchorage to the westernmost island of Attu, it was almost two thousand miles.

It was a hell of a lot of territory to patrol, especially when the Army had only five combat squadrons in its air force and five thousand combat troops with twenty thousand support personnel and the Navy had only three cutters, maybe a dozen destroyers – more than half of them World War I class – five cruisers, six antique S-boat submarines, some PBY seaplanes and tenders, and a fleet of Yippee boats, mostly small fishing crafts purchased by the Navy to patrol the waters. And no one knew just where the Japanese might strike.

Wylie had never claimed to be a brilliant military strategist, but even he could look at a map and see that Alaska was a lot closer to Japan than Hawaii was. If the Japanese took Hawaii, they'd still have to cross twenty-five hundred miles of ocean to reach targets on the West Coast. But if they took Alaska, the Bremerton Navy Yard and the Boeing bomber plant in Seattle were only three hours flying time away. All of Canada and the United States would be exposed – and Russia would be at point-blank range. As close as Japan was, a supply line could easily be established.

But Wylie could talk about none of that. He had to act dumb and look like some stupid GI while Bogardus knowledgeably discussed how the military road from the U.S. to Alaska was to be built and how the workers, civilian and military, were to be deployed all along the route to begin construction at several points at once.

Dinner that night was the longest meal he'd ever had to sit through. But it finally ended. Although Lisa's mother urged Bogardus to stay a while longer, he insisted he had some plans to study. Wylie watched silently while Lisa saw him to the door.

'I'll pick you up Monday morning,' he heard Bogardus say.

'I'll be ready.'

Wylie realized that she rode to work with him every morning – and probably home every night, too. And he wouldn't be around to do anything about it. Spring was on its way. The winter storms that plagued the northern seas would be abating. He had a hunch that if the Japs were going to make a move against Alaska it would happen soon. If or when that happened, as a Scout he was destined for the front lines. They were a commando unit, trained to conduct raids and infiltrate enemy positions. He didn't know when he'd have another chance to see Lisa again.

After Bogardus had left, Lisa's father discreetly shooed the boys from the room to give Wylie a chance to be alone with her. She walked over to him, nervously rubbing her palms together.

'Wylie, I'd like to explain about Mr. Bogardus –' she began.

He cut her off. 'You don't owe me any explanations, Lisa.'

'But –'

'Let's just drop it, shall we?' He was angry, and he knew it showed.

'All right.' But she appeared confused and hurt by his attitude.

It was early morning, barely half past five. From the small encampment on the shoulder of Ballyhoo Mountain, Wylie surveyed the mountain-ringed bay below. There was a break in the storm that had plagued the island chain for nearly two weeks, hampering the efforts of the meager air and Navy patrols to locate the Japanese task force that, according to CINCPAC intelligence, was headed for the Aleutians. Heavy clouds lingered overhead, but the driving rain had stopped, and the powerful wind – the dreaded williwaw – no longer roared down the volcanic canyons around Dutch Harbor, flattening tents and anything else in its path. For a change, nothing obscured Wylie's view of the harbor, its naval station, and Fort Mears.

The rising sun made a feeble attempt to penetrate the clouds as Wylie scanned the long fingerlike body of water that was Unalaska Bay, the same bay where Captain Cook had anchored during his search for the Northwest Passage, the same bay along which his ancestor Tasha had once lived at the time of the initial uprising against the Russians. Now here he was, part of a small detachment of Scouts sent to Unalaska to gather intelligence, while others were at Kodiak, the Pribilofs, Cold Bay, and Umnak.

A canvas flap rustled behind him. Wylie turned as Big Jim Dawson stepped out of his tent and paused to yawn and stretch, looking like some big burly bear just emerging from a winter's hibernation. Before the war, he had been a mining engineer turned prospector from up around Circle. A thick-set man of average height, he had a beard the color of dirty snow and hair black as coal. He had joined the Alaska Scouts at the same time that Wylie had. They'd gone through the arduous training together – made the long, grueling marches through the woods in the snow, endlessly sketched and made maps, and practised day after day shooting every kind of weapon that a man could carry either over his shoulder or on his back. They'd gone through hell together and had come out hardened and tough – and good buddies, their friendship cemented by all they'd endured side by side.

'I'm hungry.' Big Jim rubbed his stomach as he walked over to stand beside Wylie. 'I sure could go for a big stack of those sourdough flapjacks of yours. It's your turn to do the cookin' this morning. Remember?'

'I remember.' For the most part, all the Scouts shunned the tasteless Crations. Instead, they carried along their own hip-pocket stove and side meat for frying grease and the precious sourdough starter. They supplemented their diet with whatever game or fish they could catch.

'Anything going on down there?' Big Jim gazed down at the six ships anchored in the harbor.

'It's quiet. They're probably all still in the sack after that air-raid drill they had just before dawn.' Then Wylie stopped and frowned, pausing to listen to the bugling alarm he heard drifting up from the bay. 'Hear that? Sounds like one of those ships is sounding general quarters.'

Before Big Jim could reply, the wail of air-raid sirens echoed across the bay, mingling with deep-throated whistles of the ships at anchor as they summoned their crews to battle stations.

'Somehow, I don't think this is one of their goddamned drills,' Big Jim muttered.

Wylie lifted the binoculars he wore slung around his neck while Big Jim dived back into his tent to get his own pair. In the harbor below, all the ships were getting up steam to flee the port. At the naval station and Fort Mears, men were scrambling to man the anti-aircraft and machine-gun positions. Dutch Harbor had no airfield because of its extremely mountainous terrain. The only aircraft stationed there were a few PBY's tied in some nearby coves.

As he swept the points of the compass, Wylie spotted the Jap Zeros breaking out of the clouds, coming at them out of the south. Big Jim joined him, but Wylie didn't take his glasses off the enemy planes, following them as they peeled off to attack.

'I make it fifteen Zeros.'

'That was my count, too,' Big Jim confirmed.

The first bursts of flak exploded in the sky over the harbor, but the black puffs of smoke were quickly followed by more as the rest of the shore batteries joined in to lay a screen of flak over the harbor. On the bay, the lumbering mail plane was desperately attempting a takeoff run, but it was strafed by two diving Zeros before it could get airborne. On fire, the mail plane careened toward the beach.

'They're after the PBY's.'

Their initial targets did appear to be the seaplanes moored in the secluded coves. 'At Pearl Harbor, nothing got in the air against them either.'

'Well, one's gonna make it.' Big Jim pointed to a Catalina climbing up to meet the Japanese attack.

Spotting it, an enemy plane made a pass at the PBY. As the Zero flew over it, the waist guns opened up on its exposed belly. At the same instant, the Zero was hit by flak. It wheeled over, spewing black smoke and yellow fire, and twisted downward like a corkscrew, crashing into the bay.

Wylie's ears vibrated with the steady boom of the heavy guns, the spitting rattle of machine guns and tracers, and the powerful explosions of bombs – all combining to make a deafening thunder that shook the ground beneath his feet. All the endless training had taught him to observe what was going on, the enemy targets, their strategy, their objectives, but part of him couldn't believe what he was seeing. Those Jap planes were real; so were their bombs.

Four of the enemy bombers swung away from the harbor and headed for the Army fort. Over their targets, they dropped their thousand-pound bombs, reducing the tank farm to flames and blowing up a barracks. As the smoke cleared, the wounded started crawling out of the blackened rubble. Wylie swung his binoculars away from the site, his eyes blurring, his anger impotent.

'Look out!' At the same instant that Big Jim shouted the warning, he slammed into Wylie's shoulder, driving him to the ground.

Instinctively Wylie rolled the minute he hit. Tracers from the strafing Zero chewed up the ground where he'd been standing a second ago. He felt the sweat break out across his forehead, the dryness in his throat, and the tightening in his stomach. But already the rifle he alway carried was in his hands, and his nerves stayed steady enough for him to squeeze off a couple of rounds at the streaking Zero as it peeled away to look for another, more important target.

'The sneaking bastards.' But Big Jim wisely made no attempt to get up and offer them a standing target. Neither did Wylie, choosing instead to watch the fast and furious action below from ground level.

The enemy attack lasted a full twenty minutes. With their bomb supply exhausted, they pulled away and flew back to the south. From Ballyhoo, Dutch Harbor appeared to be practically destroyed – a smoking mass of bombed rubble and debris. But the damage wasn't as bad as it looked. The ships in the harbor were virtually unscathed; the radio shack and its equipment were intact; and the human casualties represented only one percent of the force. Nearly all of the fifty-two casualties occurred when the bomb blew up the Army barracks at Fort Mears.

The following afternoon the Japanese planes struck Dutch Harbor again, scoring two direct hits on an old beached ship, the *Northwestern*, and blowing up four large fuel storage tanks. American patrols still hadn't located the Japanese task force operating in the Aleutian waters.

Far to the south, at Midway Island, a large naval battle was in progress. But it didn't seem very important to the men at Dutch Harbor. The war in the Aleutians had begun. Less than a week later, it was known that the Japanese had captured the island of Attu.

56 *Anchorage*
June 20, 1942

As the twin-engine Lochheed taxied toward the hanger bearing the faded sign ACE FLYING SERVICE, Ace Cole rubbed the taut muscles in the back of his neck. It was the end of a long day for him. Flying wasn't as much fun as it used to be, or maybe it was just that it was getting too tame. With all the instruments and radio beams there wasn't much excitement left.

He taxied the plane to a halt in front of the hanger and automatically began shutting down the engines and switching off the electrical systems. When he glanced out the cockpit window, he noticed the stocky, gray-haired Billy Ray trotting toward the plane, carrying a set of wheel chocks in his hand. For a minute, Ace just stared, unable to remember the last time he'd seen Billy Ray move that fast.

'Something must be wrong,' he murmured to himself.

Just about that same instant, a handful of soldiers emerged from the shadows of the hangar. It felt like his heart took a sickening nosedive into his stomach. Wylie. They hadn't heard a thing from him since the Japanese attack at Dutch Harbor and their subsequent capture and occupation of the islands of Kiska and Attu.

'Sweet Jesus, no.' He wrenched the seat belt loose and scrambled out of the plane faster than he ever had in his life.

But the minute his feet hit the tarmac, his legs seemed to turn to rubber. He was shaking inside, more scared than he had ever been in his life. He paused, trying to get a grip on his usually calm nerves, as the soldiers started walking toward the plane.

Billy Ray walked over to him and pulled a greasy rag out of his dirty overalls, then wiped his hands with it. Despite his age, he was still the best mechanic Ace had ever known. There wasn't any engine he couldn't fix; now it just took him a little longer.

'How long have they been here?' Ace nodded toward the Army lieutenant and his soldier escort.

'They showed up shortly after you called the tower for landing instructions.' He glanced uneasily at Ace.

He took a deep breath, then asked, 'Did they say what they wanted?'

'Nope. But there's somethin' funny going on,' Billy Ray replied.

That remark wasn't the kind Billy Ray would make if he thought Ace was about to receive some bad news about Wylie. Ace frowned and thrust his hands into his jacket pockets, tipping his head back a little to stare at the soldiers.

'Is there something I can do for you, Lieutenant?' he asked.

The officer advanced another two steps, then halted. 'Are you Mr. Ace Cole?'

'That's right.'

'Is this your aircraft?'

'It is.'

'It is my duty to inform you that the Army is exercising its emergency powers and taking over your aircraft for military use.'

'What!' The reaction exploded from him. Of all the things he had braced himself to hear, this was not one of them.

'The Army is commandeering your airplane.'

'To do what with it?' Ace demanded.

'That's Army business, sir.'

'That's my plane. I make my living with it, and that makes it my business.'

'When the emergency is over, the plane will be returned to you, Mr. Cole.'

'What emergency? And in what condition will it be? I've seen some of your Army pilots. I'm telling you right now, nobody flies that plane but me.' Ace punched a finger against his chest to emphasize the point.

'The Army will compensate you for any damages to your property,' the lieutenant assured him.

'Oh, no, you don't.' Ace shook his head. 'If you need planes, then you damned sure need pilots. I've probably got more experience flying in this country than a whole squadron of your Army boys put together. If you need this plane, you've got it, but I'm gonna fly it.' He swung toward Billy Ray. 'Get this plane gassed up and ready to go while the lieutenant and I go talk to somebody in charge.'

'Ace.' Billy Ray motioned for him to come closer. Ace walked over and Billy Ray turned his back on the soldiers and whispered, 'If you don't want these engines to run when you come back, they won't run.'

Ace glanced at the Eskimo's craggy, lined face and carefully hid a smile. 'No.' He laid his hand on the man's shoulder. 'I want those engines roaring strong as a bear when I come back.'

'You got it.' Billy Ray grinned.

When Ace volunteered his services to the lieutenant's commanding officer, they were gratefully accepted. He soon learned that his plane wasn't the only one the Army had commandeered that night. They had taken over nearly every aircraft that had crossed into the territorial border, including forty-six commercial planes belonging to United, Northwest, and several other airlines. The Army had in its possession a fleet of some fifty-five planes – everything from Lodestars, Ford trimotors, and gooneybirds to Army C-53s, not to mention a small collection of bush planes.

At a briefing that night, he learned of the Army's intentions. The scope of it stunned him. What they proposed seemed not merely a logistical nightmare but a virtual impossibility. But the impossible had always intrigued him. He hated to count the number of times he'd landed where he'd been told a plane couldn't land.

Two PBY patrol planes had picked up a large Japanese task force on their radar screens, steaming to the northwest in the Bering Sea between the Pribilofs and St. Lawrence Island. CINCPAC intelligence at Pearl Harbor had intercepted a coded Japanese message which suggested the Japanese were planning to invade the western Alaska mainland, probably at Nome. The Army intended to airlift in the necessary troops, munitions, and supplies to defend the western coast. Speed was of the essence, since no one knew when the Japanese might strike. A massive airlift of this nature had never been undertaken before, but that didn't seem to faze the Army.

Ace called Trudy that night from Merrill Field. 'Hi, Babe Thought I'd let you know I was back.'

'It's about time. What's going on out there? Matty just called to say she'd talked to Billy Ray. He said some Army people dragged you off.'

'They've got some flying they want me to do for them. Some supplies and equipment they need rushed to one of their bases double-quick.' It was difficult to sound casual when inside he was all eagerness to take part in this monumental effort. 'I'm not sure how long it will take. It'll probably be several days before I'm back, depending on the weather. Don't get worried if you don't hear from me for a while.'

'You aren't turning around and flying right back out?' she protested. 'Ace, you haven't had any sleep. What about dinner? Aren't you coming home?'

'No. I'll grab something to eat here and catch a couple hours' sleep while they're loading the plane.'

There was a hesitant pause on the other end of the line, then Trudy spoke, sounding resigned. 'All right. But you be careful, Ace.'

'I will.' He glanced around first to see if anyone was listening, then added, 'I love you.'

'I love you, too.'

In the sub-Arctic daylight of dawn, Ace supervised the loading of the assigned cargo into his plane. A sergeant stopped to check his manifest as two soldiers lifted a crate and shoved it inside the cargo door.

'Wait a minute. Take that back out,' the sergeant ordered.

'Leave it,' Ace said.

'Sir, you're already eight hundred pounds over capacity.' The sergeant started to show him the tonnage total listed on the manifest.

'Sergeant, I've been *twelve* hundred pounds overweight before and still taken off. Take my word that I know how much this plane will carry and still fly.' He smiled as the sergeant hesitated. 'The idea is to get as much there as fast as we can, isn't it?'

'Yes, sir. But if you don't make it there, my ass'll be in a crack.'

'And my body'll be in the wreck.' He took the clipboard from the sergeant and signed his name to the manifest, then handed it back to him. 'Believe me, Sergeant, I'm more worried about my ass than yours. Slide it in, boys,' he told the soldiers.

They waited, but all the sergeant said was 'Good luck,' and walked away.

All up and down the flight line, planes of every description were being loaded with supplies, munitions, anti-aircraft guns, and combat troops armed with enough ammunition to last for three days and food for ten. 'Operation Bingo,' the Army called

651

it. Ace thought the name was appropriate. It was like pulling numbers out of a barrel cage, putting kernels on a square, and waiting for the right combination – and hoping they would get it in time to win.

Once the twin-engine plane was loaded and the cargo secured, Ace and his co-pilot, Skeeter Olson, strapped themselves into the cockpit seats and waited for their turn to take off. As the heavily loaded plane lumbered down the runway, Ace coaxed it off the ground and let it fly straight and level a few feet off the runway to increase airspeed, then put it into a slow climb.

As they achieved sufficient altitude, Ace put the twin into a shallow bank and turned it to a west-northwesterly heading. 'You know, don't you, that this thing should never have been able to get off the ground,' Skeeter muttered.

Ace just smiled and reached down to adjust the trim. In the distance, he could see the airliner that had taken off ahead of him. Most of the other civilian pilots in the planes had never flown this six-hundred-mile air route from Anchorage to Nome. There weren't any accurate maps of the region, no emergency facilities, and no search-and-rescue operations. The Signal Corps was hastily setting out to build radio stations along the route, but it would be several days before they would be in operation. In the meantime, they were all on their own. Some were bound to stray off course and become lost, or develop engine problems and be forced down on some frozen lake. Ace hoped he wouldn't be among them.

Near the Kuskokwim Mountains, Ace noticed a bank of dark clouds stretching across their path. 'Better go back and make sure that cargo is lashed secure,' he advised his co-pilot. 'It looks like it's going to get a little rough.'

'Roger.' Skeeter unbuckled his belt and started to climb out of his seat. 'What are we carrying back there, anyway?'

'Don't ask.'

Within minutes, Skeeter was back. Ace throttled the engines back a little as they encountered their first strong turbulence, then stole a glance at his co-pilot's white face. 'Everything tied down tight?'

'Yeah.' His Adam's apple bobbed as he swallowed and turned to stare at Ace. 'Those are live shells back there in those crates.'

'Were you expecting the Army to lob rocks at the Jap bombers?' Ace mocked.

Skeeter didn't say anything as he faced the front again and

stared out the cockpit window. 'Shit,' he murmured. 'We're flying a fucking bomb.'

Ace said nothing. They were entering the clouds, and at the moment he had his hands full holding the aircraft steady. Unable to climb above the clouds and unwilling to fly under them with mountains all around, Ace chose to fly through them.

For more than an hour the twin-engine plane battled through the weather front, buffeted by strong winds and fluctuating undercurrents that bounced them around until their teeth rattled. The plane groaned and shuddered like a coatless old woman on a cold night.

'Jeezus, when are we gonna get outa this shit?' Skeeter gritted his teeth to keep them from clattering together.

'Do you wanta see if we can get above it or under it?'

'Above it.' Skeeter didn't even have to think about his answer. 'With that load back there, I don't want to go down till we get to Nome.'

'Let's flip a coin,' Ace suggested. 'Heads we go up; tails we go down.'

'Jeezus, Ace, your goddamned father was a gambler all right, but I don't see why you have to take after him.' His voice wavered with the shuddering vibrations of the plane. But he removed the coin Ace always kept in the ashtray and gave it a feeble toss into the air. He couldn't catch it and the coin dropped to the floor.

'Call it as it lays,' Ace said, not taking his attention from the instrument panel.

He heard Skeeter swear under his breath, then announce, 'Heads it is.'

'Liar.' Ace eased the nose of the aircraft down. 'We'll go down to four thousand and set if we can't find a break in the clouds.'

'God damn it, Ace, you couldn't see that coin.'

At forty-four hundred feet, Ace spotted a hole in the clouds and flew through it, then leveled out at two thousand, where the cloud layer was thin and scattered. Below them was a body of water dotted with ice floes.

'Do you have any idea where we are?' Skeeter demanded.

'Unless we were blown farther off course than I thought, that should be Norton Sound below us. Can you see the coastline to the north?'

'Yeah. You figured we were flying over water all the time,

didn't you?' Skeeter accused. 'How come you didn't tell me instead of lettin' me sweat like that?'

'There was always the chance I was wrong.' Ace swung the plane north and followed the coastline until he spied the town where he was born, perched beside the sea.

The airfield sat on the northeast side of town, across the Snake River. A strong crosswind was blowing as he made his final approach for landing. He tipped a wing to the wind, crabbing to hold his course down the center of the runway. At the last minute, he leveled out. An instant later, the plane's wheels touched the runway. He cut power on one engine, but kept the windward engine running to steady the plane in the strong wind while it finished its landing roll and slowed down. Another plane was coming in as he taxied off the runway.

Within an hour, his plane was unloaded and refueled and they were in the air again, heading back to Anchorage for another load. Ace made three trips to Nome that day. In all, the fifty-five planes made a total of a hundred and seventy-nine trips, transported nearly twenty-three hundred combat-ready soldiers, twenty anti-aircraft guns, and tons of supplies and equipment. Within twenty-four hours, the troops were dug in at Nome and their guns were in position.

Ace flew for three more days, shuttling in supplies and equipment. The airlift continued, on a reduced scale, for three more weeks. The welcoming party was ready to greet the Japanese, but they never came. And the patrol planes couldn't find the task force that was supposed to be in the Bering Sea.

Despite the anticlimax, Ace knew the experience was one he'd never forget. He'd been part of something that had never been attempted before and had helped to make it a success. Maybe he was too old to be a soldier, but he'd done his bit for the war.

Inga Blomquist paused in the kitchen doorway, the coffeepot in her hand, and studied the pair still seated at the dinner table. Both rested their arms on the table and leaned slightly forward, their heads turned so they could watch each other while they talked. They were so wrapped up in one another they were completely oblivious of her presence. Inga liked the picture her daughter, Lisa, and Steve Bogardus made. She hoped that it meant that Lisa was at last going to forget about Wylie Cole.

For a time this spring, it had seemed as though she had. Twice she had gone out with Steve. Then all that fuss about the Japanese attack on some Aleutian Island had erupted, and Lisa had gotten all upset and worried that something was going to happen to Wylie. She had started feeling guilty about the dates she'd had with Steve.

Sometimes she wondered why Lisa couldn't see how lucky she was that a man like Steve Bogardus was interested in her. He would make such a good husband. But at Lisa's age, she, too, had been blinded by sentiment. No woman should marry her first love. On the day she and Jan were wed, if she had known about the years of struggle and hardship and hunger that awaited her, she would never have married him. Jan Blomquist had been poor, but she had been so young that she'd thought money didn't matter, that it was enough they were in love – but it wasn't. She hadn't always complained. She hadn't always been unhappy and resentful. Many times she had wanted to explain that to Lisa, but she had never been able to find the right words.

As Steve started to look up, Inga moved briskly forward. 'Here is the coffee, fresh and hot.' She stopped by his chair and filled the cup before him. 'It is so good to have a man around the house. With both Rudy and Jan away all week working at that construction site, the house seems empty.' She smiled warmly at him. 'I am glad you could join us for dinner tonight.'

'There isn't anywhere else I'd rather be, Mrs. Blomquist.' He glanced at Lisa. 'Or anyone else I'd rather be with.'

Slightly flustered by his comment, Lisa picked up her cup. 'I'll have some coffee, too, Mama. And if I were you, I'd be careful what I said in front of Erik. He likes to think he's the man of the house when Papa and Rudy are gone. You'll hurt his feelings.'

'He is hardly ever here since he met that girl.' She poured coffee into Lisa's cup, then filled her own and sat down.

'I was just telling Lisa that I'm planning to fly up to Big Delta and check on the progress of the road construction. Considering all the paperwork she's been handling for our contract on the Al-Can Highway, I thought it would be a good idea if she came along and saw this road that's creating so much work for her. But she's a little reluctant to come with me. I think she's afraid of how it might look.' His smile teased her. 'Or maybe she doesn't trust me.'

'I trust you.' But Lisa's tone was still hesitant.

'I still think you shouldn't turn down a chance to see history in the making,' Steve persisted, then appealed to Inga. 'What do you say, Mrs. Blomquist?'

'I think it is an opportunity Lisa shouldn't pass up.' She stirred a spoonful of sugar into her coffee.

'There. I rest my case.' He leaned back in his chair, lifting his hands in a gesture that indicated there was nothing more to be said. 'Even your mother approves.'

'I don't know,' she murmured.

'You will need to wear trousers and a blouse with long sleeves, and something to protect your face.' Inga Blomquist had no intention of allowing her daughter to pass up this heaven-sent opportunity to spend time alone with Steve Bogardus, away from the office. 'You remember how bad the mosquitoes and flies can be in the interior during August.'

'Better wear some boots, too,' Steve advised.

'I haven't even said I was going,' Lisa protested, but the soft laugh that followed it signaled her agreeement.

From Big Delta, they traveled in an open jeep. An old-style Army hat, with a wide brim suitable for suspending mosquito nets, shaded Lisa's face from the glare of the sun. She had pulled it down tightly over her head to keep the wind from blowing it off, but the hat didn't stop the wind from whipping the ends of her shoulder-length hair or stinging her eyes with the dust from the graveled road.

Dressed in Levi's, a blue plaid shirt, and a denim jacket, Steve had picked her up at the house that morning before it was light. Their chartered plane had taken off at the crack of dawn and winged its way north under clear skies. Lisa had been entranced by the view from the air of the railroad tracks and the new road connecting Anchorage and Fairbanks. Even Mount McKinley had obligingly chased the clouds away and revealed its hoary crown.

While they were still south of Big Delta, Steve had instructed the pilot to make a swing to the east so Lisa could see the new highway from the air. Now they were traveling down the smooth, graded road she'd seen that stretched along the valley of the Tanana River. Mountains rose on either side of the flat alluvial plain. Occasionally they met another vehicle or a convoy of trucks, and the jeep was engulfed in the trailing cloud of their dust.

She could feel dirt caking her skin and her clothes, but strangely she didn't mind. Being out here in all this open country surrounded by magnificent scenery reminded her of when they'd first arrived in Alaska and everything had been so new and exciting. That's the way she felt now – eager to embrace a new experience.

As Steve slowed the jeep, the rush of the wind was replaced by a roar of a different kind. Lisa peered through the haze of the dust-covered windshield, trying to see what was ahead of them. She could make out the vague shape of some big piece of machinery.

'Why are we slowing down?'

'We've reached the end of the finished road.' He shifted gears. 'From here on, it's under construction.'

They swung off the main road and followed a tote road that paralleled the graveled highway, bypassing the heavy equipment that chugged and roared over a long section widening the road, bringing it to grade and finishing the shoulders. Men and machinery alike were half hidden in a cloud of dust.

The tote road was little more than a rutted track, wide enough for one vehicle. Lisa clutched the side of her seat and braced an arm against the dashboard as they bounced over the narrow trail. More than once they were forced off it by an oncoming truck and caromed through the heavy grass, already flattened in places by previous traffic. Ahead she could see the temporary construction shacks of the workers' camp. Some men in hard hats were standing in front of one of them conferring over some plans. Steve parked the jeep a few yards away. Lisa was slow to take her hand away from the dashboard, as if her body was not quite sure the wild ride was over.

'Sorry,' Steve said. 'That last stretch was a little rough.'

'I didn't mind.'

He hopped out of the jeep and walked around to offer her a steadying hand while she crawled out. She brushed at the dust clinging to her trouser legs, then realized it was useless and abandoned the effort. Two of the men walked over to greet them, and Steve introduced her to his project engineer and the foreman of his road crew.

After the usual exchange of pleasantries and inquiries about their journey from Anchorage, the talk centered on the road – the progress, the problems, the projections. Lisa listened attentively,

657

surprised at how much she understood from reading all the reports that crossed her desk, even though she didn't understand some of their technical jargon. But being here made all the reports come alive. They weren't just words on paper or dots on a map or lines on a graph. And the people who had written them had faces, feelings, and frustrations.

'Those colored boys from the Ninety-seventh are really stepping out on these flats. They're making about eight miles a day,' the engineer said.

'According to last night's radio report, the Army's got less than three hundred miles to go and the road will be cut all the way through.' The engineer shook his head. 'I gotta give those soldier boys credit. What they knew about road building you could have written on the palm of my hand. When they started in March, I figured we'd be lucky if the road was cut through by next year. At this rate, there'll be trucks traveling on it before Christmas.'

It was a staggering thought that a fifteen-hundred-mile-long road could be built through a virgin wilderness by some ten thousand inexperienced soldiers and six thousand civilians in less than nine months.

'The Ninety-seventh made it to the river crossing. They'll be ferrying their equipment across today. If you got time, you might want to drive on ahead and take a look.' The engineer glanced at Lisa as he made the suggestion.

'We'll do that,' Steve said. 'I think Lisa will find it interesting.'

An hour later, after Steve had gone over everything with his engineer and foreman, they climbed back into the jeep and headed down the unfinished road. The traffic was heavier as trucks loaded with supplies, machinery, and equipment churned up the soft, dry surface. The strangling and blinding clouds of dust from the trucks, traveling much of the time in low gear, forced Steve to reduce the jeep's speed.

As they neared the site where the road was to bridge the Tanana River, the way became blocked with a jam of machinery, supplies, and men. Steve pulled off the road and skirted the congestion, then stopped the jeep on a small rise that gave them a vantage point.

Lisa stepped out of the dust-coated jeep to watch the activity at the river. Steve came around to stand beside her. A giant twenty-ton caterpillar was being loaded on a makeshift ferry built up from five log pontoon boats. Not far from the loading area of the ferry crossing, the first pilings for a bridge were being driven. Away from the congestion sat a huge stack of fifty-five-gallon oil drums. Lisa had noticed them scattered by the hundreds all along the route. Their presence made it obvious how the road had obtained the nickname, the 'Oil Can Highway.'

'The work never stops,' Steve said. 'As soon as those Negroes get those lead "cats" ferried across to the far side of the river, they'll fire them up and start in. Meanwhile, that Iowa bridge-building crew are sinking their pilings for the bridge, so that when my road crew get this far, it will be a clear shot to the other side.'

The road. That's all they talked about the whole day. It was as if the war didn't exist. Everything seemed to revolve around the road. Having seen it herself, Lisa felt the same way. Nothing else seemed quite as important.

It even changed her perception of Steve. All day she had listened to him discuss the road, speaking with authority about various facets of the work in progress. She had seen him in action, physically directing the work instead of perusing reports or talking on the telephone. The work he did was vital to the whole territory. She was impressed by him, more impressed than she had ever been by him when he had merely been her boss.

At dusk, their plane landed at Merrill Field in Anchorage. Although it had been a long day, Lisa felt strangely rested. She would have said it was the result of all that fresh air if she wasn't so conscious of the film of fine dust that coated her entire body, clothes and all.

As they walked to his car, Steve casually draped his arm around her shoulders. 'Are you glad you went?'

'Oh, yes,' she answered with a rush of enthusiasm. 'I wouldn't have missed it for anything.'

'I was sure you'd feel that way.' When they reached the car, he stopped and started to open the passenger door for Lisa, then paused with one hand on the door grip and the other on her shoulder. 'Why don't we go out and have a late dinner together?'

'I don't think so – not the way I look.'

He drew his head back to study her. 'I don't know. I kinda like the way you look with that smudge of dirt on your nose.' He ran his finger down it. 'Besides, I'm not any cleaner than you are. So, what do you say?'

She hesitated, almost tempted, then shook her head again. 'No. I'd better get home. Mama will be worrying about me.'

'No, she won't. Do you know why? Because you're with me.' He slide his hand under her hair and cupped the back of her neck. 'And if you don't believe that, we'll call and let her know we're back. But I'm not going to accept your mother as an excuse for turning me down.'

His quick kiss took her by surprise. Flustered and self-conscious, she looked away from him. It had never been easy for her to ignore his attentions. Now she didn't think she wanted to.

'Is it that soldier boy of yours again?' But Steve didn't give her a chance to answer. 'Lisa, one of the things I found attractive about you from the beginning was the loyalty you displayed. But I don't think it's justified. I have to be honest and say that I don't feel one bit guilty about trying to lure you away from him, because I don't see that he has any claim on you. He's had plenty of chances to tie you up. But I don't see any ring on your finger, and I doubt if there's been any promise of one.'

'It isn't that.' She hadn't even been thinking about Wylie.

'Look at me, Lisa.' He forced her head up. 'I've done just about everything but stand on my head to persuade you to go out with me.'

'I know you have, Steve.'

'If that's what it's going to take for you to be convinced that I love you, I'll do it.' He released her and started to get down on his hands and knees.

It was a full second before Lisa realized that he really intended to stand on his head. 'Steve, no!'

When she grabbed for his arm to pull him up, her foot slipped on the gravel and she started to fall. Steve tried to catch her. In the next second, they were tangled together on the ground, laughing at the suddenness of it. He rolled onto his side, levering himself up on an elbow to look at her.

'Are you all right?'

'I'm fine.' She gazed at him, her smile softening. 'And you don't have to stand on your head to convince me, Steve.'

For an instant he stared at her lips. Then slowly he kissed her.

57 A Mile Off Adak Island
August 28, 1942

The sea was running heavy. The strong underwater currents constantly buffeted the submarine *Triton* as it ran submerged a mile off the coast of Adak Island, nearing its destination off Kuluk Bay. Wylie glanced at the artificially blackened faces of the other eighteen Scouts crowded together in the narrow confines of the crew's quarters. Nineteen more Scouts were aboard the submarine *Tuna*. The commando group was scheduled to rendezvous outside the reefs of Kuluk Bay.

As the heaving seas tossed the submarine about, the deck pitched violently. Wylie automatically braced himself at the first motion. A few Scouts weren't quick enough. He heard their muffled curses of pain as they were slammed against something. Nearly everyone had bruised some part of his body during this voyage. Wylie had noticed a couple of the crewmen with bandaged ribs, and several sported bruised cheeks or cuts above the eye.

A few minutes ago the sergeant had returned with the word that they were off Adak Island – code name 'Fireplace.' The talking had subsided as they rechecked their packs and weapons. Wylie felt the tension in the air. His palms were clammy, but he wasn't sure how much of that was nerves and how much was the closed quarters of the submarine. At the moment he would gladly face a Jap rather than spend another hour cooped up in this underwater coffin.

The watertight bulkhead door swung open and one of the submarine's officers stepped through. 'The skipper has given the order to surface,' he announced.

'That's the best news I've heard yet.' Wylie straightened, keeping his legs spread slightly apart to brace himself against the roll of the deck. 'These quarters are about as comfortable as a straitjacket.'

661

'You get used to it after a while,' the young ensign assured him. 'It'll seem just like home.'

'Your home maybe, not mine,' he replied dryly.

Moments later the submarine broke onto the surface and the hatch was cracked. Silently, one after the other, the Scouts scrambled up the ladder onto the *Triton*'s sea-washed deck. Surrounded by the inky blackness of a cloud-covered night and the murky dark sea, they swiftly inflated their rubber boats, communicating with hand signals. Not far away, another submarine rode on the surface of the heavy sea, showing no light to reveal its presence to the enemy.

As soon as the boats were launched, Wylie and the other commandos slipped over the side to take their places in the rubber rafts. A mile away, they could barely make out the dim outline of the Adak coast, marked by heavy surf breaking on its shore. They paddled away from the pitching submarine and headed for the mouth of the bay.

Within minutes both submarines had submerged. Wylie felt a tightness in the pit of his stomach. Restlessly, he scanned the area, trying to detect any movement that would betray a Jap position – if there were any Japanese on the island. All the natives and civilians in the island chain had been evacuated within days after the first Japanese attack, most of them to camps in the southeast panhandle.

The War Department had finally authorized the establishment of a new base in the Aleutian chain that would be closer to the Japanese-held islands of Kiska and Attu than the airfield at Cold Bay, which was twelve hundred miles round trip. The Navy had picked Adak Island for the new location.

In two days, an invasion force of forty-five hundred men was scheduled to land on Adak. It was known that the Japanese regularly landed small parties of soldiers on various islands, including Adak. But no one knew if they were still there. The mission of the commando unit, commanded by Colonel Castner himself, was to seek out any Japs on the island and make sure no radio messages were transmitted to Kiska. The long months of training that Wylie, Big Jim, and the other Scouts had gone through were about to be put to the test.

The wind was constant and cold. Hardly anything could be heard above its incessant rush and the roar of the sea. The minute Wylie felt the raft scrape bottom, he clambered over the side and helped drag the boat onto the beach. On land, he didn't feel nearly as vulnerable or exposed. Now he could move.

Stealthily the commandos fanned out under the cover of darkness and began their sweep of the three-hundred-square-mile island. All night long, Wylie crept over the rough terrain and spongy tundra, sweeping his assigned sector. Once, he startled a big black raven – or it startled him. He was never quite sure which of them jumped the highest before the bird took off, cawing loudly in protest.

At dawn, a fog swirled over the island. Wylie rejoined his unit and reported that he'd found nothing, no trace of any Japanese, not even the ash of a campfire. He felt let down and angry, like a hunter who had spent all night searching for game, only to discover there was none in the area. It was small consolation that no one else had seen any Japs either.

'I feel like a groom who's been left standing at the church,' muttered Big Jim Dawson.

'I think we all feel pretty much that way.' Wylie heard the drone of an airplane's engines overhead and looked up, recognizing the PBY as one of their own, scheduled to fly over the island that morning. The colonel set out a cloth strip to signal an 'all clear' to the plane, and the Scouts settled in to wait for the invasion force to arrive at the island, unpopulated except by bald eagles and ravens.

The troops arrived on Sunday, August the thirteenth, along with a storm. High winds and heavy seas wreaked havoc with the barges and lighters that transported the supplies, machinery, and equipment, capsizing several and sending their cargo to the bottom, driving others against one another on the beach, and scattering them along the coast. Yet one way or another, nearly everything made it ashore, including anti-aircraft guns, a variety of heavy construction equipment, and crack units of the Aviation Engineer Battalion.

While the beachmaster organized the storm-strewn landing, the Engineers sought out the Scouts to help them locate a likely place to build a landing strip. They split up in small groups, with Wylie and Big Jim taking one party of Engineers on a tour of the island's mountainous terrain. The storm continued to blow fiercely. The winds were so strong Wylie had to lean into them to stay erect.

'You've got your work cut out for you,' he shouted to one of the Engineers. 'You aren't going to find any flat ground on this island unless you make it flat.'

'If the rest of the island is like this, you're right.'

'It is.'

But Wylie had overlooked one place in Sweeper Cove that flooded every time the tide came in. As a joke, another Scout mentioned it to one of the Engineers, but the Engineer didn't laugh. Within hours, they had their men building a dam, a set of dikes, and a tide gate. At low tide the next day, they shut the gate. Before the morning of September first, graders and weasels were rolling through the mud. The steel matting for the runway was at the bottom of the bay. Bulldozers packed down sand to make a landing strip.

Ten days later, the first plane landed at the new base, code-named 'Longview.' Two days after that, the Thirty-sixth Squadron of B-17s arrived, along with eighteen other planes and another shipment of steel matting, which the Engineers laid overnight. The new base was in full operation, as yet undiscovered by the Japanese.

In the latter part of September, Wylie's commando unit was sent out again, this time on a reconnaissance mission to scout the island of Amchitka, only seventy miles away from the Japanese-held island of Kiska. Again they encountered no Japanese and reported back that the island had the customary volcano; other than that, it was a long, narrow flat marsh.

Then it was back to Adak. Rain, wind, and fog seemed to hang over the island like a pall. It hadn't taken Wylie long to discover that the weather in the Aleutians was anything but agreeable. While the tropical Japanese current that blew warm air up from the south kept the sea ice-free and the temperature mild all year, when it came in contact with the cold Arctic mass of air from the north, storms were the inevitable result. And the long chain of islands was like a buoy marking the site where the two systems clashed.

For pilots, it was a nightmare flying in fog thick as soup and simultaneously bucking gale-force winds. In the Aleutians, there was no such thing as good flying weather. If a pilot could see to get off the ground, the plane took off. But he didn't dare try to climb out of the soup. The higher he flew, the colder the outside temperature became, and ice formed on the wings. Countless planes were lost when their wings iced and they spun out of control into the ocean.

Navigating was no simple feat either. The combination of winds with fog could blow a pilot a hundred miles off course. Radio navigation beams were rarely effective because of the electrically charged air from clashing weather fronts which created a static so loud that it drowned out the radio signals. The constant turbulence threw instruments out of whack, and the heavy mineral deposits in the volcano-born islands affected the compasses.

In an attempt to keep pressure on the Japanese, two or three bombing missions were flown daily – when the planes could get off the ground. Wylie had watched the bombers limp back. If the Japanese fighter planes or their ground flak succeeded in damaging one bomber, the weather usually scored six. They were fighting two enemies – the Japanese and the weather. But the Japanese were in the same position.

Mess call sounded, but Wylie didn't budge from his cot in the small pyramidal tent. Instead he glanced at the can of chili sitting atop the little metal stove that heated the tent, its tin lid pried open. He swung his legs off the cot and stepped on the mud-soaked papers that served as a floor in the tent.

All the mess tent had to offer was C rations. That was hardly worth slogging through the mud and the bone-chilling wind for when he could have hot chili, jam, and crackers in the relative comfort of the tent. With luck, he and Big Jim had enough canned goods squirreled away to last them until they made it back to headquarters at Kodiak.

He pitied the poor guys who were going to have to stay here. The conditions were as miserable as the weather. The Seabees were working like crazy, building barracks, warehouses, hangars, offices – virtually an entire city – but in the meantime the men lived in tents erected on a small bulge of land affectionately termed a hill. All the vehicle and foot traffic had turned the ground into a quagmire.

Wylie stirred the chili, then tasted it to see if it was hot, but it was barely lukewarm. He added two more chunks of coal to the stove's fire and sat back on his cot to wait. The slog of footsteps sounded in the mud outside the tent. He glanced up as the tent flap was lifted aside and Big Jim walked in, giving Wylie a glimpse of the gray, dismal clouds outside.

665

'Brrr.' Big Jim growled and shuddered like a dog shaking off water. 'That's the coldest damned wind I've ever known. Hell, it don't even feel that cold in the dead of winter on the Yukon River.' He stamped over to the stove and held his gloved hands out to the heat, rubbing them together.

'It's the damp.'

Big Jim reached inside his parka. 'You aren't going to believe this, but some of our mail caught up with us.' He tossed a couple of thin envelopes onto Wylie's cot. 'Don't ask me how or why, but there it is.'

Wylie picked them up and glanced first at the return addresses. Once was from his mother, and the other from his grandmother. Nothing from Lisa. He looked at the postmark. 'August. Here it is the last day of September. Why does it take so long to get mail from Anchorage?'

'Hey, I've gotten letters from relatives in the States that have been four months old. I wouldn't complain if I were you. We're lucky to get any mail at all. Sometimes I think people forget we're even up here.'

'Most of them don't know we are.'

There was a virtual blackout of news regarding the campaign in the Aleutians. Two weeks passed before the Navy had even admitted that the Japanese had bombed their base at Dutch Harbor and had taken over the islands of Attu and Kiska. All journalists and members of the press had been 'escorted' out of the Aleutians. Not even the four-page *Military Press*, mimeographed more or less daily at Dutch Harbor, was allowed to print stories about what was going on in the Aleutians without clearance from the Navy Department in Washington, D.C. Three weeks after the fact, the *Military Press* published an article about a bombing attack on Kiska. Any mention of Alaska was clipped out of every magazine and newspaper that came into the Territory. Not even Alaskans knew what was going on here – and that included Wylie's own family.

Wylie could guess the War Department's argument. It would have a demoralizing effect on the American public if it became widely known that the Japanese had seized U.S. soil. When they were forced to acknowledge it, they would prefer to downplay it by saying the Japanese had erected temporary facilities on an undefended island in the Aleutians that had no significant strategic value.

As he opened the letter from his mother, he heard the drone of an airplane, followed by the screaming wail of the air-raid siren. Both he and Big Jim moved simultaneously, grabbing their rifles. The anti-aircraft guns opened fire as they bolted out of the tent and headed for the trenches. Wylie glanced up and identified a Japanese 'Rufe' swooping in, an amphibious plane. The first bomb exploded, its thundering blast joining the boom of the anti-aircraft guns.

Everywhere men were scrambling for cover. Wylie slid into the muddy trench and spun around to bring his rifle to bear on the Japanese plane. He squeezed off a couple of shots at the plane while it was in range, adding his groundfire to the flak of the guns. The 'Rufe' climbed out and banked to make another run at the base. Wylie kept one eye on it while he scanned the cloudy skies, waiting for more Jap planes to emerge.

'Where's the rest of them?' Big Jim wondered.

'I don't know.' Wylie watched their own fighters scramble to get in the air as the 'Rufe' returned to strafe the airfield, flying through the black puffs of flak smoke that dotted the air.

By the time the first American fighter was airborne, the Jap plane had ducked back into the clouds. He didn't come back and no more came. The all-clear signal sounded.

'Well, I shot at my first Jap,' Big Jim said as they crawled out of the mud-slick trench.

'Yep. And now they know where we are.' As Wylie stepped back into the tent, he smelled the scorched chili on the stove and started swearing.

The base at Adak was bombed every day for five days straight, but the Japanese never sent more than three planes at a time, and their bombs inflicted only minimal damage.

At the end of November all the wire services carried the story of the completion of the Alaska-Canada Military Highway on the twentieth of the same month, eight months and eleven days after construction had started. Wylie read the myriad statistics with brooding interest: 1,523 miles long, 200 bridges, 8,000 culverts, 16,000 workers, $138,000,000 cost.

The road was all Lisa had talked about in the last letter he'd received from her in October; nothing else, not even a question when he might get leave again or a reminder that she was thinking of him or looked forward to seeing him. He tried not to read anything into it, but at the back of his mind the possibility nagged that Steve Bogardus was the cause of it.

In the middle of December, orders came through to establish an advance base at Amchitka, virtually in the enemy's backyard. Wylie's unit had already reconnoitered the island in September. A lone bomber was sent over the island to ascertain whether any Japanese troops had been stationed on Amchitka in the interim, and to level the native village.

When Wylie and the Scouts landed on the island, accompanied by a survey party headed by Engineer Colonel Benjamin Talley and Lieutenant Colonel Hebert, the native buildings lay in rubble, including the small Russian Orthodox Church. While they were scouting the island to locate a site for a new air base, one of the Scouts, a Sioux Indian, found indications that the Japanese had been there ahead of them conducting a survey to establish an airstrip of their own.

No one was willing to let the Japanese gain another foothold in the Aleutians. The islands could too easily turn into stepping-stones. Plans were immediately set into motion to gather a full-scale force to occupy the island.

As usual, the Alaska Scouts were assigned to spearhead the landing. On January 5, 1943, Wylie and the rest of his commando unit boarded the destroyer *Worden*, part of the combat task force of four destroyers, three cruisers, and four transport ships. The fleet set sail right into the teeth of a raging blizzard. The storm continued for a week without letup, while the task force pitched about the heavy seas well off the Amchitka coast.

After a week of being confined below deck by the storm, Wylie was restless and edgy. On the night of January 11, he slept fitfully, strapped in his bunk. An instant before a hand touched his shoulder, he came wide awake and stared up at Big Jim's dingy white beard. 'No, I won't lend you any money and I don't give a damn whether you've got a royal flush or not,' Wylie muttered irritably and started to roll onto his side. 'Go back to your poker game and leave me alone.'

'We're going in, Wylie.'

'What?'

'The storm's died down a bit, and the big brass has decided it's now or never. Our supplies won't hold out much longer. So we're going in.'

Wylie sat up. 'What time is it?'

'Somewhere around one in the morning. Does it matter?' Big Jim grinned. 'We're steaming toward the harbor now. We should get there before dawn.'

The sea was still running with better than twenty-foot swells. When the *Worden* entered the mouth of Constantine Harbor shortly before dawn on the twelfth, the surf ran bridge-high on the destroyer. Wylie and the other Scouts negotiated the wave-washed decks and clambered into the whaleboats, then set off for the shore in a blinding snowstorm. Wet, cold, and half frozen, they battled their way through the twenty-foot surf to the beach, landing safely.

Within minutes after they had dragged the boats onto the beach, the storm's roar was pierced by the eerie wail of a ship's whistle signaling its distress. The sound sent chills down Wylie's spine.

'It's the *Worden*,' Big Jim said through cold-stiffened lips. 'It has to be.'

Instinctively Wylie stepped closer to the crashing waves and peered anxiously into the driving snow, straining to see the disabled ship, but the storm obscured it. The eerie whoop of its whistle reminded Wylie of the frantic bleat of a wounded animal being dragged down by a predator. He kept thinking about the crew on board – the men he'd spent the last week with.

It wasn't long before the wind carried the whistle's chilling cry to abandon ship. The *Worden* was going down. 'Damn it,' Big Jim cursed beside him. 'The water's freezing. Those men won't last long in it.'

'Come on.' Wylie started moving along the beach, trying to get closer to the sound.

Everyone in the landing party joined the search for survivors, spreading out along the beach and scanning the waves for bodies in the water. By some miracle, they managed to rescue several of the crew and drag them ashore. From them they learned what had happened to the *Worden*.

As the destroyer had steamed from the harbor, a powerful current had tossed the vessel onto a rock pinnacle. It had pierced the hull, ripping through the steel plates to flood the engine room. The destroyer *Dewey* had steamed to her aid, but the attempt to pull her off the rock had failed when the cable snapped. The *Worden* capsized. The destroyer *Dewey* had managed to pick up most of the survivors, but fourteen sailors had drowned before she could get to them.

But the task force remained committed to a landing. The transport ships carrying the twenty-one hundred troops, composed of soldiers and Engineers, threaded their way into the harbor, carefully skirting the wreck of the sunken destroyer, and unloaded their troops. One transport made the mistake of presenting her beam to the eighty-knot wind when she was leaving. It hurled her onto the reef, running her solidly aground.

The blizzard continued to rage as night fell. Cold and wet, Wylie kept moving to stay warm and guard against the real enemy, which was frostbite. Mentally he cursed the bombs that had destroyed the native village and the shelter its housing could have provided. It was a long night without shelter and only cold rations.

By morning, the storm still raged. But with the Japanese-held island so close, an observation post had to be established and manned. Wylie and Big Jim were among the Scouts picked to form a squad to cross the thirty-mile-long island to its northwest tip. From there, the peaks of Kiska Island were visible – weather permitting.

After a week, the storm finally passed. Assigned to the lonely outpost, Wylie had to daily fight tedium and boredom under miserable conditions. His sleeping bag lay on the mud floor of the tent. His extra pair of shoes and socks were kept atop the stove, so he could change them every half hour to keep his feet from freezing. It was almost a welcome diversion when the Japanese finally discovered the base on Amchitka on the twenty-third of January. At least now when he took his turn at watch there was a chance he'd see something.

During the following two weeks, he had plenty of opportunities as the Japanese 'Amchitka Express' began. Two and three, sometimes as many as six, 'Rufe' floatplanes took off from Kiska and made bombing strikes on the runway under construction. U.S. fighter planes provided some air cover, but the 'Rufes' usually waited until the fighters left to refuel, then took off to make their sorties over the base. As soon as they were spotted from the observation post on Aleut Point, as the northwestern tip was called, a warning was flashed to the base.

Despite the enemy's harassment, the Engineers finished the runway. By the end of the month, Chennault's group of Flying Tigers had landed their squadron of P-40 Warhawks at Amchitka. Now when Wylie signaled the approach of 'Pontoon

Joe,' as they had dubbed the pilot who regularly flew the Amchitka Express, the Tigers went up to form a reception committee. The enemy bombing raids started tapering off after the arrival of the P-40 squadron.

After being stationed at the isolated outpost for a month, Wylie believed he was in real danger of catching the 'Aleutian stare.' He'd seen it in other dogfaces, and among flight crews and pilots, too. It was the vacant stare of a person who no longer cared. Some blamed it on the dismal weather – the constant wind, cold, and fog – the miserable living conditions, the endless monotony of their jobs, whether it was flying in soup, repairing a plane for the hundredth time and knowing it would have to be repaired again, or building things and watching a williwaw roar down from the mountains and level them in seconds, or digging trenches, then filling them up in the Army's endless attempts to keep the soldiers busy at something even if it meant making work.

There was no rotation of troops, and diversions were few, usually limited to radios; a few scratchy phonograph records; and for those stationed at Dutch Harbor, Umnak, and recently Adak, old Hollywood B movies. Liquor was scarce. At Adak, Wylie had once seen a line a block long at the PX after it received a shipment of Coca-Cola.

Apathy, malingering, irritability, insomnia, and disinterest were just some of the symptoms. Some lost their sense of humor and couldn't even joke about sex. Others became homosexuals. Several suicides were committed every month. Some just withdrew completely into themselves and stared. They usually went home – in strait jackets.

Being a member of the Alaska Scouts, Wylie had not only escaped a lot of the Army discipline but also a lot of the boring routine. He knew what was going on, while most of the others didn't. Out of the two hundred thousand troops now stationed in Alaska, most were support personnel, noncombatants who would never see action. Wylie knew that Command was intent on pushing the Japanese out of the Aleutians. It was only a matter of time before an invasion was launched against the two enemy-held islands. In the meantime, though, he was stuck at the observation post on Amchitka.

At the end of January, another squad of Scouts relieved them. They made the trek back to the base camp, where Wylie discovered conditions weren't much better than they had been at the tiny outpost. The most direct route to the tent area went through a series of lake-sized puddles. Beside him, Big Jim cursed as they waded through the mud to their tents. They dropped their bags inside.

'Let's go to the mess tent. I gotta have some decent food,' Big Jim complained.

'Who says they've got it?' But Wylie adjusted the strap of his loose-slung rifle and stepped back out into the cold wind.

Just then the air-raid sirens went off. Automatically Wylie swung around to scan the skies to the northwest, the direction of Kiska. All around him men were scrambling to man the anti-aircraft guns or seeking cover. He spotted a large V-formation approaching Amchitka at a high altitude.

'Hell, they've never sent more than six planes.' Big Jim stared, straining to identify the aircraft. 'There must be thirty of them.'

'Something's not right.' He narrowed his eyes, but the formation was too far away. 'I wish I had a pair of binoculars.'

'We'd better get the fuck out of here. When they drop their bomb-load, there ain't gonna be nothing left of this base.' He started to push Wylie toward the hills. Wylie let Big Jim hurry him away from the tent area, but he kept tracking the formation.

'Hey, where are you going?' someone called to them.

Wylie recognized the Navy pilot insignia the man wore and paused. Along the flight line, the P-40 Warhawks of the Flying Tigers were revving up their engines, the whirling props blurring the snarling Bengal tigers painted on their snouts.

'You'd better get moving, mister,' Wylie advised. 'If you don't, those Japanese planes are going to blow your ass to smithereens.'

'If those are Japanese planes, they're the first ones I've ever seen that flapped their wings,' he jeered.

'Shit, they're geese,' Big Jim said, and he started to laugh.

Wylie joined him and laughed until his sides hurt and tears ran from his eyes. Still laughing, Wylie and Big Jim slogged through the mud toward the mess tent.

'Reminds me of the time those Navy PBY's thought they'd picked up the Japanese fleet on their radar and started dropping their bombs. Turned out, they damn near sank the Pribilof Islands,' Big Jim recalled and broke into a fresh peal of laughter.

672

All along the way they traded stories, trying to top one another by telling the most ludicrous. En route to the mess tent, they stopped to pick up the mail that had been forwarded to them. Both of them were so weak with laughter they could hardly stand up.

When they entered the mess tent, Big Jim paused to wipe his teary eyes. 'I bet everybody's wondering what the hell we've been drinking.'

'Hell, they'll just take one look at us and figure we've been sipping our shaving lotion,' Wylie replied.

About a dozen soldiers were in the mess tent, and more were wandering in. Wylie and Big Jim walked over to take their place in the chow line.

A cook came out of the kitchen area carrying a steaming tray of some unrecognizable dish, and shoved it onto an empty place in the line. A wool scarf was wrapped around his neck and head, a fur cap with ear flaps perched on top of it, and his sleeves were rolled up, exposing his bare forearms.

Big Jim set his tray of food down next to Wylie's, then crawled over the bench seat and sat down.

'Corn-willies, Vienna sausage.' Big Jim stabbed a leathery-looking pancake with his fork. 'What do you suppose this is?'

'I think I heard it called a "manhole cover." '

'Goddamn, but I'll be glad to get back to Circle. I bet the bears wouldn't even eat this shit.' But he dug in just the same. 'I don't know what I'm missing the most – food, whiskey, or women. Do you know how long it's been since I've had a piece of ass? I don't even know if I remember what a woman looks like.'

'What are you talking about?' Wylie mocked. 'Don't you know there's a girl behind every tree in the Aleutians?'

'Very funny,' he muttered, fully aware that there were no trees in the Aleutians. He set his silverware down and pushed up from the table. 'I gotta get some coffee to wash this down.'

The food tasted as bad as it looked. Rather than think about what he was putting in his mouth, Wylie reached inside the pocket of his parka and pulled out the mail he'd picked up. He flipped through the envelopes and saw the letter he'd been waiting to get – Lisa's. He laid the others aside and opened hers.

Dear Wylie,

It's been a long time since I heard from you. I saw your mother at church last Sunday and asked if you had mentioned whether there was a chance you'd be coming home soon. I thought you might arrange to get a weekend pass over the Thanksgiving holiday, but she said you hadn't indicated to her that you'd be home.

I was hoping you would. I've been wanting to talk to you so I could explain some things to you. I didn't want to write it in a letter. But, since I'm not sure when you'll be home again, I decided I'd better not wait to tell you. I'm not sure if you remember meeting Steve Bogardus, the man I work for, but Steve and I are getting married in December. I . . .

December. Wylie didn't bother to read any farther. This was the first of February. She was already married. Unconsciously he tightened his grip on the letter, crumpling the edge of it.

'Hey, Wylie. Look here. They got a magazine filled with pictures of nude women.' Big Jim thrust it in front of him.

The magazine was opened to a page that showed a tawny-haired girl, her naked body arched in a provocative pose. A white-hot fury seared through him. Wylie struck out blindly, knocking the magazine out of Big Jim's hands; and abruptly rising to his feet, he upset the table and the bench. Distantly he could hear Big Jim yelling at him, but the angry and stunned expression on his friend's face didn't mean anything to him. He wanted to hit something – anything – and Big Jim was the nearest. He slammed his fist into the center of that dirty white beard, then dived after him when Big Jim tumbled backward.

The next thing he knew, several pairs of hands were dragging him off his friend. The fight went out of him as he watched Big Jim get up slowly, moving his jaw back and forth to see if it worked.

'What the hell got into you?' Big Jim glared.

'Sorry.' Wylie shrugged off the restraining hands, feeling half sick inside and unwilling to look his friend in the eye. He glanced at the overturned table and the spilled food, then reached down and picked up the bench.

The soldiers who had broken up the fight lifted the table and set it back up. One of them retrieved Wylie's mail from the muddy floor, including Lisa's letter. When Wylie saw him start to read it, he snatched it out of his hands.

674

'That's mine, mister,' he growled.

'I wasn't going to keep it,' the soldier retorted.

One of his buddies spoke up. 'Wanta bet the letter says, "Dear John"?'

Big Jim stepped up to stand beside Wylie. 'It's none of your damned business, soldier, what that letter says.'

But they all knew. The silence of the mess tent told Wylie that. He crumpled the letter into a ball and stuffed it inside the pocket of his parka.

58 *U.S. Submarine* Nautilus
May 10, 1943

A soldier of Mexican extraction accidentally jostled Big Jim's arm, nearly causing him to spill his coffee. 'Watch it, Pedro,' he growled and wedged himself into the narrow space on the bench beside Wylie. 'Did ya ever get the feeling submarines weren't designed to be transport ships?'

'Once or twice.'

The *Nautilus* was one of the largest submarines in the fleet, displacing some twenty-seven hundred tons. But even its accommodations were cramped by the addition of some hundred and twenty-five passengers, part of the ten-thousand-man force distributed among the thirty-four vessels in the invasion fleet. The storm had forced the postponement of the scheduled May seventh landing at Attu, repeatedly pushing it back another twenty-four hours. Now the storm had ended and Operation Landcrab was set to commence in the early-morning hours of the eleventh. Instead of one mass landing, the Army division was split into four segments. The largest contingent of troops, the Southern Force, was to go ashore at Massacre Bay; the Northern Force was to hit the northern harbor and submarine base of Holtz Bay; one regiment was to be held in reserve aboard ship; and the fourth group, made up of a crack combat battalion of four hundred and ten officers and men that had been organized in the last three months by Captain Willoughby, this 'Provisional Scout Battalion,' as it was called, was to land at Scarlet Beach and cut off any Japanese retreat into the mountains. The commando-trained Alaska Scouts were dispersed among the various regiments. Wylie and Big Jim had ended up with Willoughby's Scout Battalion.

A lanky private from Texas started to sit down at an empty place across the table from Wylie and Big Jim, then glanced at the bearded, tough-looking pair and hesitated. 'Is it all right if I sit here?' he drawled thickly.

'Go ahead.' Big Jim shrugged.

The Texan sat down and started pouring sugar into his coffee. 'Most of the fellas are tryin' to grab some sleep before we go in, but I jus' couldn't shut my eyes. Guess you two couldn't sleep neither.' He stuck a spoon in his cup and churned up the sugar in the bottom. 'Do ya think the Japs'll be waitin' there for us?'

'It's hard to say.'

'It's crazy, ya know.' He grinned nervously. 'We been trainin' fer months in those California deserts, learnin' desert warfare. They said we was goin' to North Africa an' face Rommel's bunch. Then three months ago, they started turnin' us into an amphibious outfit. When we marched onto that ship in San Francisco, all of us figured we was headed for the Solomons. Hell, we musta been at sea two days before they told us we was headed for the Aleutians. Shit, I never even knew where they were.'

'A lot of people don't.' Wylie shook a cigarette out of the pack and lit it.

During the week they'd been cramped together on the submarine, Wylie had heard the same story many times. Even stripping every base in the Territory, Alaska couldn't muster enough combat-ready troops to form a full division, and none were trained for an amphibious assault. But the War Department had the Seventh Motorized Division handy, trained for desert tank warfare. Since it was no longer needed in North Africa, they assigned it to the amphibious invasion of the sub-Arctic Aleutian Island of Attu. Then, with the same secrecy in which they had cloaked the whole Aleutian campaign, the troops hadn't learned their destination until they were en route. To call it crazy was almost an understatement. What made it perhaps even more insane was the fact that only the Provisional Scout Battalion had set foot on Aleutian soil, training for one week on the snow and tundra at Dutch Harbor. The rest of the division had almost no knowledge of the terrain or conditions in which they'd have to fight.

A dearth of cold-weather gear had prevented the Army from properly outfitting the invasion force. Willoughby had managed to raid the supply depot at Dutch Harbor and refit his Scouts with proper jackets, socks, and waterproof 'shoepac' boots. Without them, Wylie doubted that his battalion would have had a chance of surviving the overland trek they were going to have to make to be the 'pincer' of the Landcrab operation.

Wylie gave the captain credit for preparing his men the best that he could in the time he'd had. Instead of rifles, submachine guns, and small weapons, he'd armed them with automatic rifles, machine guns, mortars, and demolition equipment. Instead of ball ammunition, they carried tracers and armor-piercing bullets, capable of penetrating ice instead of ricocheting. Their packs were filled with grenades, along with a day and a half's supply of food.

'I'll tell ya one thing I'm glad about,' the Texan said, talking incessantly so he wouldn't have to think about the coming battle. 'That I'm not in that Southern Force that's landin' at Massacre Bay. I mean, that'd be spooky, wouldn't it? Why would anybody ever wanta give a place a name like that?'

'About two hundred years ago some Russian hunters murdered all the men in a native village on that bay. That's how it came to be called Massacre Bay,' Wylie stated.

'It'd give me the fuckin' willies if I had to land there,' the private declared.

The alarm rang, summoning the submarine's crew to their battle stations. The skipper came on the address system. 'We have picked up an unidentified vessel on our radar screen.'

'Jeezus, I'll bet it's a Jap submarine!' The Texan's nervous exclamation drowned out part of the explanation the submarine commander offered to his passengers.

'We're closing in on the target now.'

Everyone fell silent. Wylie waited tensely for some sound, some vibration of the vessel that would indicate the torpedoes were away.

Moments later the crew was ordered to stand down. The unidentified vessel had turned out to be the *Nautilus*'s sister submarine, the *Narwhal*, with its contingent from the Scout Battalion. The torpedoes had been ready to fire when the skipper recognized the vessel.

'I don't like it,' Big Jim muttered under his breath to Wylie. 'First those two destroyers run into each other in this fog. Now we damned near torpedo one of our own submarines. I tell you I don't like it.'

'I didn't know you were superstitious.'

'Hey, you guys!' A soldier burst into the galley. 'They just picked up Walter Winchell's broadcast on an Alaska radio station.

678

He said, ' "To Mr. and Mrs. America and all the ships at sea. Keep your eye on the Aleutian Islands." '

'Shit.' Big Jim set his cup down in disgust. 'Why don't we just send up flares so the Jap'll know we're coming?'

One hour after midnight, Wylie and Big Jim stood near the front of the line that formed to the hatchways as the submarine ascended toward the surface. Ahead of them, the lieutenant turned and looked down the line.

'Remember, move as quiet as you can and as fast as you can,' he instructed again. 'If any enemy ships are sighted, this submarine will dive, whether we're all on board the rafts or not. So we have to move out. Got that?'

Heads nodded. As the submarine surfaced, a crewman simultaneously spun the wheel, cracking the hatch cover. Wylie pulled back, avoiding the cold sea water that spilled through. He scrambled up the ladder ahead of Big Jim and barely squeezed through the narrow hatch hole with his full combat pack.

Moving swiftly, they inflated the rubber rafts on the submarine's afterdeck and climbed into them, crowding together. The lieutenant signaled the conning tower. A moment later, the hatches were closed. Wylie watched the black waters of the sea sweep over the deck of the submarine as it started to submerge. An instant later, he felt the surging water lift the raft and carry it away. They were three miles off the western coast of Attu, code-named 'Jackboot.'

It took them two hours to reach the small stretch of beach on the western side of the island. A gentle surf ran them aground in the dawn light. Wylie and Big Jim quickly scrambled over the side and plowed into the heavy snow that reached all the way down to the tideline. Mountains walled in the strip of snow-covered beach, rising sharply from the sand. The beach appeared to be undefended.

The temperature was below freezing as Willoughby assembled his officers and men on the beach. A muscular six-footer, he was a commanding figure with belts of machine-gun ammunition crisscrossing his broad chest. Instinctively, Wylie and Big Jim kept watching the thinning mists of the mountains while the captain ordered the rubber rafts hauled inland beyond the tideline and a signal flashed to the submarines waiting at periscope depth offshore.

As the sun climbed above the horizon, the fog started to lift. Willoughby walked over to Wylie and eyed the mountain walls that hemmed in the beach. 'If the Japs have any lookouts posted in these mountains, the fog isn't going to hide us from them much longer. Let's find a way up.'

'A creek has cut a steep ravine over there.' Wylie gestured in the direction of the gulley. 'Looks like it will take us all the way to the top.'

'Let's move out.'

Wylie and Big Jim took the lead up the snow-packed ravine while Willoughby and the Scout Battalion strung out behind them. Three men were left at the beach to guide the rest of the battalion scheduled to land soon from the destroyer. The air was cold, burning his lungs as Wylie struggled up the steep incline. The sun was up, but so was the wind.

He couldn't shake the feeling that the enemy was just behind the next snowdrift. Continually he scanned the windswept snow ahead of him, tinted blue by the clear skies above. Under other circumstances, he might have seen the beauty of the light play, but at the moment he was more concerned about where the Japs might be.

The droning hum of airplane engines rose above the sound of his own labored breathing and snow-crunching footsteps. Wylie paused and glanced seaward, spotting a group of F4F Wildcats from the aircraft carrier in the invasion fleet. As the fighters swooped toward the beach, others in the long straggling line turned to watch them.

'What the hell are they doin'?' someone asked.

Wylie heard the explosive bursts of their guns an instant after he saw the flash of their tracers as they strafed the beach, riddling the rubber rafts with their bullets and sending the three men Willoughby had left behind scrambling for cover. The boats were destroyed.

'One damned thing's for sure, we can't retreat now,' Big Jim observed cynically. 'Makes you wonder whether they did it on purpose.'

Turning their backs to the sea, they struck out again for the high ridges above them, plodding through the snow and the spongy tundra. Wylie could hear the thundering report of Navy guns bombarding the beaches where the other two assault forces were to land.

The sun continued to shine on the island's heights, but fog hung in the valleys like cottony clouds. With the snow, the cold winds, and the soft ground, it was slow going even for men in top physical shape. Wylie's beard was crusted with icicles from the moisture in his breath. Late in the afternoon, Wylie and Big Jim topped the crest of a ridge in advance of the battalion. From the high ground, they could see in the distance Holtz Bay, where the Japanese rear defenses were supposed to be located. They crouched low in the howling wind and waved Willoughby up to show him their position, then waited there, scanning the terrain, while he went back to bring up his men.

'I haven't heard any enemy fire yet.' The wind tore at Big Jim's voice, trying to carry it away. 'S'pose the others made it onto the beaches?'

Wylie shook his head, reluctant to speculate, and flexed his numbing fingers to keep them supple, then tightened his grip on the automatic rifle. 'I heard General DeWitt claimed we could take this island in three days. One's almost gone by, and we haven't seen any sign of the Japs.'

A pair of American bombers rumbled through the sky overhead, then banked to circle their position and make the scheduled airdrop of more ammunition, medicines, and food to replenish their meager thirty-six-hour supply. Wylie watched the bundles fall from one of the B-24s, the attached parachutes billowing and filling with air. As they drifted earthward toward their position, the high wind caught them and carried the parachutes past the steep ridge. Wylie swore bitterly as he watched the chutes come down in a deep fissure, completely inaccessible.

As the bombers continued to circle overhead like a pair of giant vultures, Big Jim muttered angrily, 'Whose fucking side are they on? If the goddamned Japs didn't know we were here before, they sure as hell do now!'

Not far away, their captain was furiously waving his arms, trying to signal the bombers to leave before they gave their position to the enemy. Wylie wiped at his runny nose with the back of his gloved hand, conscious of the mucus freezing on his nose hairs. 'Maybe there aren't any Japs on the island.' So far he'd heard no sound of resistance, presuming the other landings had taken place as scheduled. He couldn't help wondering if this was going to be like all the other missions where they had landed, expecting trouble and finding none.

'They're here.' Big Jim gazed out across the steep ridges and fog-filled valleys. 'I can smell the slant-eyed bastards.'

As Willoughby gave the order to move out, Wylie glanced one last time at the supplies in the bottom of the crevasse, then pressed forward. He knew if they weren't able to link up with the Northern Force, they'd have some hungry times ahead.

The Scout Battalion spent their first night on Attu trapped atop a mountain by darkness and a blinding fog, and blasted by an icy wind. Barely able to see a hand in front of the face in this treacherous terrain, they were forced to camp. With no fires to warm them, Wylie and Big Jim kept moving, despite their exhaustion, and joined their commander in exhorting the rest of the soldiers to do the same. Some didn't. By dawn they were suffering from severe frostbite.

At first light, they headed southeast, forcing their half-frozen limbs to carry them over the western mountain summit. They overlooked the enemy's defense positions along the ridges west of Holtz Bay. Wylie no longer had to wonder whether there were any Japs still on the island. At the moment, the enemy appeared unaware of the Scout Battalion at its rear.

Moving quickly while they were still undetected, they descended the steep slopes, literally sliding down them. Suddenly the Japanese artillery opened up. Wylie scrambled for cover behind an ice boulder. Below, the Jap soldiers abandoned their ridgetop trenches and attacked up the slope. Wylie started shooting at the moving human targets, his rifle joining the clatter of machine guns returning the enemy fire. A big mortar from the rear forced the Japs to retreat to their ridge entrenchments. Wylie and the others dug in on the cold, snowy slopes.

Coordinates of the enemy artillery positions were radioed to the Navy battleship lying off the coast. When its shelling proved ineffective, the Air Corps was called in to bomb the targets. By day's end, the Japs still had them pinned down on the slopes. They'd fought to a draw. Under the cover of darknesss, Wylie helped some of the wounded to a ravine in the rear area where a makeshift clinic had been set up by the battalion's doctor. It kept his body moving and kept his mind off the numbing cold and the gnawing hunger in his stomach. Their food supply had been exhausted that morning.

The next day started off as a repeat of the previous afternoon's fighting – no food, no rest, no warmth, and still pinned down by the Japs. Wylie heard a plane fly over, but the clouds were too thick and low for it to be seen. The captain couldn't raise anybody on the radio, so the situation of the other assault forces was unknown. Their own was pretty dire.

That afternoon, Willoughby led an attack against the enemy ridges. Running from ice clump to ice clump with machine-gun fire kicking up snow and tundra all around him, Wylie advanced on the enemy position, shooting at anything that resembled a target. On his belly, he crawled across a stretch of ice toward an enemy machine-gun nest while Big Jim gave him cover fire. As he looped his finger through the icy cold ring of the grenade pin, he was conscious of the battle sweat that dampened his clothes and absently marveled that he could be bone-cold and perspire at the same time. He pulled the pin and lobbed the grenade at the Jap nest, then hugged the slushy ground as the explosion shook it. Then it was up and over, firing as he went into the smoking hole.

After several hours of fierce fighting, they dislodged the Japs from their high ground. By the time darkness came, they were firmly dug in. Wylie retreated into a cave that had been hollowed out of a snow-drift and crept close to the tiny fire that had been built. After warming his hands over the small flames, he pulled off his boots and changed to a dry pair of socks, aware how quickly wet things could freeze in these temperatures. If that happened, frostbite – or worse, a frozen limb – was guaranteed.

Wylie glanced up as Big Jim crawled into the snow cave, a hoary apparition with his beard, eyelashes, and eyebrows crusted with snow and ice. Wylie knew he didn't look any better. With hands shaking from the cold, Big Jim lit a cigarette, then crumpled the empty pack and nudged it onto the small fire, fueled by empty ration boxes and anything else they could find that would burn.

From beyond the perimeters of the summit, a Japanese voice, amplified by a megaphone, taunted them in English: 'American dogs! You die! Tomorrow we kill you!'

'Hell,' Big Jim muttered. 'All they have to do is sit out there and wait for us to either freeze or starve to death.' He took a drag on the cigarette, then offered it to Wylie.

'Thanks.' His lips felt so numb that he could barely feel the cigarette between them as he inhaled. The smoke made him a little dizzy, and he passed the cigarette back to Big Jim. 'How far do you figure we are from the mountain pass between Holtz and Massacre Valley?'

'Two miles, more or less.'

They were supposed to link up with the Northern Force at the pass. They'd been two days without food. Both their ammunition and medicine were running low. At the moment, their only hope of obtaining the needed supplies lay in reaching their own lines. But there was an obstacle in their way.

'Yankee! You die!' their Japanese tormenter shouted again.

Wylie gritted his teeth. Under the circumstances, it was difficult to argue with his prediction. He rubbed his feet, feeling the needle-sharp stings tingle through them as he tried to stimulate the flow of blood. Finally he pulled on his boots.

'Hey, the fire's getting low. Anybody got anything they can throw on it?' Big Jim glanced at the other soldiers huddled in the snow cave taking their turn at stealing a little warmth. They dug into their pockets, but all they came up with was a chewing gum wrapper.

Wylie stared at the dwindling flames a couple of minutes longer, then unbuttoned his parka and reached inside. He pulled out the last letter that he'd received from Lisa – the one he'd read so many times that he almost had it memorized. He smoothed out the wrinkles, then laid it gently on the fire. He watched it char and curl as the flames shot around it. For a brief moment, the writing stood out clearly, then the paper blackened. He refastened his parka, wrapped his arms around his loose-slung rifle, and huddled forward, staring at the flames.

'Wylie.' Big Jim spoke hesitantly, his voice pitched low. 'I've got a favor to ask you.'

'Ask.' Wylie watched the ash from his letter crumble and break off. 'Steve and I are getting married' – the words seemed burned into his brain.

'Do you remember me mentioning that I had this woman who cooked and kept house for me up at my cabin outside of Circle?'

'Yeah. What about her?' Wylie grunted.

'If . . . if anything happens to me, Wylie, would you kinda look out for her? You know, make sure she's all right.'

Roused from his own private reverie by the unexpected request, Wylie lifted his head. 'What are you talking about? Nothing's going to happen to you or me – unless you count freezing your balls off. You're talking crazy and you know it, Dawson.'

'I know. But just the same, if anything happens, will you go see her?' Big Jim persisted. 'Her name's Anita Lockwood. She's staying at my cabin on the Yukon. I told her she could till I came back.'

'Damn it, will you stop it, Dawson?' Wylie was angry with him for talking like this.

'Will you check on her?'

'Yes,' he snapped.

In the brief silence that followed, two of the soldiers inside the cave traded places with two from outside the snow shelter. They hovered next to the fire, their teeth chattering. Reverently one added torn pieces of a ration box to the greedy flames.

'Wylie.' Again Big Jim hesitantly claimed his attention. 'She's . . . a breed – part Athabascan Indian.'

For an instant Wylie was motionless, recalling the number of times he'd seen signs stating NO NATIVES ALLOWED. There were many business establishments Matty wasn't allowed to enter, which meant his grandmother had to do most of the shopping for the boardinghouse. Nearly all public places, such as movie houses, had separate sections for the natives. Eskimos, Aleuts, and Athabascans weren't allowed in the USO's. Now Wylie understood why Big Jim hadn't talked very much about this woman before and why he thought it might make a difference to Wylie.

He glanced at his friend. 'So?'

Gratitude flashed across Big Jim's expression before he averted his face and mumbled, 'I just wanted you to know that.'

'You've told me, so let's just drop it. There isn't going to be any reason for me to go see her anyway.' He paused and stared at the fire. 'And for your information, my ancestors were Aleuts, Tlingits, and Russians.' The captain ducked inside the snow cave. 'While you're all sitting there warm and toasty by the fire, make an ammunition count.'

'Hey, Joe!' The Japanese shouted from the darkness. 'Tomorrow morning you die!'

'I wish somebody would shoot that fucking bastard,' Wylie growled.

On the fourth day of battle, their fifth on the island, exhaustion, hunger, and killing cold claimed more victims than the enemy did. Men hobbled on frozen feet and vomited in the snow. Yet they successfully fought off a Japanese counterattack, but the last of the mortar ammunition was used doing it. Wylie knew it was desperation that drove all of them forward, even if it meant they had to crawl because they were in no shape to walk. They couldn't retreat; there was no place to go. Their only salvation lay in reaching the American lines.

When the sun went down that night, enemy bullets, illness, or frostbite had incapacitated half the battalion. From the radio reports Willoughby received, neither of the other two forces of the three-pronged invasion were faring much better. The Southern Force at Massacre Bay, the main assault group, hadn't advanced ten yards from their first position. The enemy held the pass and the high ridges overlooking the valley, and the Southern Force was suffering heavy losses from its repeated assaults on the pass. Massacre Valley was living up to its name. And the Northern Force had advanced little more than a mile.

Willoughby ordered a continual harassment of the enemy that night, determined not to give them a chance to rest or to move reinforcements to face the Northern Force. Wylie spent the night in a cold ravine, sheltered from the wind, stamping his feet and flaying his arms to keep warm and stay awake. Periodically, he'd crawl to the crest of the ravine and fire at the Jap positions.

Early the next morning, the Japs stopped returning their fire. By radio, Captain Willoughby informed the commander of the Northern Force that the battalion was moving out. As they advanced – walking, hobbling, and crawling – it quickly became apparent that sometime in the night the Japanese had pulled back. The way was clear.

When they staggered down to Holtz Bay, Wylie knew they were a pathetic-looking sight. Out of the three hundred and twenty men who reached Holtz Bay, he and Big Jim were among the forty who could walk without pain. The battalion had lost eleven men, and counted twenty wounded. All the rest were suffering from severe exposure, mainly to their feet. Gangrene had already set in for some. The hospital cases were evacuated, leaving behind a force of a hundred and sixty-five men out of the original four hundred and twenty.

As they sat down to taste their first food in nearly six days, in a heated tent no less, Wylie clamped a hand on Big Jim's shoulder. 'I told you, you son of a bitch, nothing was going to happen to us.'

Big Jim grinned tiredly, then glanced toward the distant sound of battle and sobered. 'The Japs aren't off the island yet, Wylie.'

The previous day, the Navy ships lying off the coast of Attu had used up all their bombardment ammunition. They could no longer shell the enemy positions. If a Japanese task force should appear, they were helpless to defend even themselves. The ground troops had to rely on air support from the carrier planes and the land-based bombers on Amchitka. Most of the time, heavy fog and solid clouds kept them grounded. But the battle raged on. The Southern Force remained trapped in Massacre Valley, uselessly flinging its men at the impregnable Japanese lines, but the Northern Force attacked the enemy-held ridges above Holtz Bay, gaining the crests in savage hand-to-hand combat. Wylie slept through most of it, too exhausted to care.

Shortly after midnight on the morning of the eighteenth, Wylie and Big Jim emerged from their tent and joined the remnants of the Scout Battalion assembling outside. With two days of rest and a full stomach, he felt fit and revived. The captain had called for volunteers to go out on a patrol to scout the pass leading to Massacre Valley. It was a job Wylie had been trained to do. Everyone knew the hell the Japs had been giving the guys on the other side of the pass. If there was a chance of breaking through the enemy lines, Wylie wanted to be part of it.

Wylie and Big Jim were assigned to the advance platoon. They set out ahead of the main patrol to scout the northern approach to the mountain pass. Before they reached the top, they heard the muffled crunch of footsteps in the snow and the muted clatter of equipment. Assuming it was an enemy patrol, they fanned out and took cover. As the figures emerged out of the fog, Wylie curled his finger against the trigger of his automatic. Then he caught the murmur of voices talking in American.

'Halt! Who goes there?' the platoon leader demanded.

The oncoming squad stopped and quickly identified themselves as a detachment from Colonel Zimmerman's outfit in Massacre Valley. The Japs had pulled their troops out of the pass. After a week of bloody fighting, the American forces had finally achieved their objective and linked up at the mountain pass between Holtz Bay and Massacre Valley.

59 *Attu*
May 26, 1943

Inch by bloody inch, they had driven the Japs backward, taking the mountaintop of Point Able, then Sarana Nose, steadily pushing the enemy toward the sea and their main camp at Chichagof Harbor. The long Chichagof Valley lay open before the American forces, but that avenue was an invitation to death. The tenacious Japanese were dug in along the ridge that overlooked the length of the valley. There was no alternative. They had to root the enemy soldiers out of Fish Hook Ridge.

Three days before, the order had come down through the chain of command to take the ridge. For three days they'd been trying. But the snow- and ice-encrusted hogback presented the soldiers with some of the wildest terrain they'd had to face. And the remaining Japanese were concentrated all along the steep, ragged heights of the ridge's back.

Yesterday it had snowed. And the Japs had used the snow to camouflage their positions by lying motionless under the white stuff, holding their fire while an American squad advanced, then unleashing it with devastating effect or else rolling grenades down on them.

The morning dawned cold and relatively clear. Wylie sat in a fox-hole, his rifle comfortably cradled in his arms, almost a permanent extension of his body. The blade of the fixed bayonet gleamed coldly in the morning light. Big Jim was next to him, huddling deep inside his parka for warmth, his breath vaporizing into a thin white cloud as he peered at the jagged summits of the razorbacked ridge. They were some two hundred feet from the top – not far, but they all knew they'd have to fight every inch of the rest of the way.

'According to those two Jap prisoners they captured yesterday, there's less than a thousand Jap soldiers on that ridge.' Big Jim turned his head to look at Wylie, the wolverine-lined hood of his non-regulation parka covering half of the near side of his face. 'We must have fourteen thousand troops on the island now. Don't those fucking bastards know they can't win?'

'Somebody must have forgotten to tell them.' Wylie kept his chin tucked deep inside his collar and the encircling hood of his parka, letting the fur warm his cold mouth. 'Just like somebody forgot to tell those Jap prisoners not to talk. I hear they never figure on being taken alive, so they aren't instructed against revealing the strength and position of their troops.'

'But less than a thousand.' Big Jim shook his head.

Wylie glanced at the other GI's huddled in the foxhole with them – haggard, cold, and hungry, waiting for the dreaded order that would send them up that ridge in a coordinated assault on the enemy positions. They were wrapped in Japanese blankets. Most of them wore caps, hoods, or waterproof boots they had scavenged off the bodies of dead Japanese to replace or supplement their inadequate Army issue, even though it could mean they would be mistaken for the enemy and shot by their own troops.

'I don't think they feel any better knowing they're facing less than a thousand Japs.' Wylie nodded in the direction of the teeth-chattering soldiers.

Big Jim studied them for a moment. 'Yeah, I guess we're all gettin' tired of the fightin' and the killin'.'

'Just don't get so tired you let your guard down, because I guarantee you, the Japs aren't going to give you any breaks.' Snow crunched under a set of scurrying footsteps as someone approached the foxhole. Wylie's attention was already shifting toward the sound as he added, 'And I'm not particularly interested in looking after your woman.'

A sergeant appeared, running in a low crouch, and slid quickly into the protection of the foxhole. 'All right, boys, we're gonna be movin' out. An' I wanta hear your guns chatter instead of your teeth. All set?' At their affirmative nods, he swung his attention back to the other soldiers as they reluctantly unwrapped their blankets and draped them around their shoulders Indian-style. 'And remember – any dead Japs you find, if they don't stink, stick 'em.'

'Yeah, Sarge. We hear ya,' one grumbled at the oft-repeated order.

'Let's find out where they are today.' With a pump of his arm, the sergeant gave the signal to attack.

Wylie and Big Jim charged out of the foxhole together, firing up at the last known enemy position as the three-sided assault on the head of the ridge began. Wylie had barely taken three steps when machine-gun bullets began marching downhill through the snow, seeking his range. He flung himself the opposite way and rolled behind a snow-drift barely a yard in advance of the foxhole. All along the line, the deadly Jap barrage forced the attacking soldiers to seek cover, reducing the charge to a yard-by-yard advance.

'Looks like they've got a nest in that snowdrift on the right!' Big Jim shouted.

Wylie wiggled into position for a look, then studied the limited approaches to it. 'I'll try to make that crease on the left. Cover me.' He squatted behind the drift, then nodded to Big Jim that he was ready to make his try.

The crease in the steep slope was little more than a shallow depression, but any cover was better than none. As Big Jim opened fire, Wylie sprinted from the dubious protection of the snow hump, darting and weaving on a line to the crease, firing as he went. Bullets whined and chewed up the snow all around him. One tugged at the sleeve of his parka. But he made it and flattened himself into the hollow, listening to the splat of bullets in the snow searching for the place he had gone to ground. He was breathing hard and his heart felt as if it were pumping like a steam engine.

Careful not to show himself, Wylie looked over the shallow gully. Partway up, it made a jog to the right. From there it looked like he might be able to work his way around and come up on the Jap position on their blind side. He started crawling on his belly.

The rattle of machine guns and rifles exchanging fire was all around him, punctuated by the explosions of grenades. In the distance, heavy bombers thundered through the sky, dropping their payloads on the enemy headquarters at Chichagof Village. The low rumble of their exploding bombs reverberated over the island. The air reeked with the acrid odor of powder smoke.

Yet all of Wylie's senses were keenly tuned to his immediate surroundings. When he heard the faint clink of metal against ice, followed by a soft thump muffled by snow, he froze instantly. A second later an enemy grenade tumbled past him, rolling down the slope.

'Grenade!' He shouted the warning to those below and pressed himself flat against the slope, hugging the cold, wet ground.

A deafening explosion rent the air. The snow-covered tundra shuddered beneath him as pieces of snow, mud, and ice pelted his back. He waited a moment, then started climbing again. He heard someone scrambling up the slope behind him. When he reached the log in the shallow ravine, he glanced down and saw Big Jim. Wylie smiled faintly, then pushed on.

It took the better part of an hour for them to work their way, unseen, to the curling snowdrift where the enemy machine gun chattered at the company of soldiers below. Wylie inched as close as he dared, then plucked a grenade from his string and grabbed the pin. He signaled to Big Jim that he'd go first. In perfectly synchronized rhythm, they rose, one after the other, and lobbed their grenades at the nest, then ducked back to cover. The screams and explosions sounded as one as chunks of flesh, equipment, and snow hurtled through the air. When the debris stopped falling, Wylie and Big Jim scrambled onto the drift.

Four Japs had been in the nest. There wasn't much left of two of them. Two more were sprawled on the high side of the drift surrounded by blood-splattered snow and charred mud. The hand of one twitched. Wylie fired four rounds into him.

Suddenly bullets whined around their heads. They dived into the debris-littered trench that led to the enemy nest as the GI's started scrambling up the slope to join them. They waited until several soldiers had slithered into the wet trench, then crept forward to locate the next Jap position.

The trench ran fairly straight for twenty yards, then took a sharp turn along the jagged ridge. Wylie inched up to the corner and cautiously peeked around it. He looked straight at the muzzle of a Jap rifle ten yards away and jerked back as a hot flame stung his cheek. He reached up. When he took his hand away, there was blood on his glove. The bullet had cut a furrow through his beard and scratched his cheek. Wylie ignored it. In this cold, blood coagulated quickly or froze over.

They made a few attempts to bounce grenades down the trench, but the enemy soldier was untouched. Finally Big Jim took two soldiers and climbed out of the trench in an attempt to slip around behind the Jap while Wylie and the other soldiers kept him occupied.

Minutes later, Big Jim sent one of the soldiers back with word that the Japs had two separate machine-gun emplacements ahead.

There was no way to take one without being exposed to the fire of the other. They'd have to attack both simultaneously. To do that, they had to dislodge the sniper in the trench, and Big Jim couldn't get behind him because of the machine guns.

'All right.' Wylie leaned his back against the trench wall and studied the three shivering soldiers, all with hands tucked under armpits trying to keep them warm. 'We're gonna throw our grenades around the corner, then follow them. Just be damned sure you get them well around the corner or they'll blow up in our faces.'

They tossed the grenades around the corner in rapid succession. As the first one exploded, Wylie sprinted after them and sprang toward the far side of the trench, slamming his shoulder against and firing into the exploding dirt, snow, and mud as he hit. The others followed him, taking whatever was left of the narrow space, one flopping down on his belly in the icy slop and firing blindly into the erupting shower. As the air cleared, there was no answering fire. They crept cautiously forward in a crouch until they could see the first machine-gun emplacement. Wylie sent the soldier back to Big Jim with the message that they were in position and would wait for his signal.

The hoot of an owl was the most bizarre sound Wylie had ever heard on a battlefield. He was chuckling as they launched their attack on the Jap position, crossing the open stretch that was exposed to the machine guns in the next several yards ahead and above them. But those guns were busy with Big Jim.

Within minutes, they had silenced the machine guns and Wylie had plunged his bayonet into the spine of the last Jap who looked like he might be still breathing. He turned and looked to see if Big Jim needed any help, but all appeared quiet there. He recognized Big Jim's snowy beard and parka as a figure waved to him, signaling his success. Wylie started to wave back. As he raised his hand, the ground behind Big Jim exploded. For a split second, Big Jim seemed frozen in position, then he pitched forward, falling across the bunkered rim of the machine-gun nest.

'No!' Wylie shouted, then recklessly scrambled and clawed his way across and up the rough ridge.

The other soldiers reached Big Jim before Wylie did. He pushed them out of the way and crouched beside his friend. With difficulty, Big Jim focused his eyes on him and smiled faintly.

'I . . . thought he was . . . dead.' The death rattle in his throat was unmistakable.

'You stupid son of a bitch, why didn't you stick him?' Wylie bawled angrily, tears running down his cheeks and into his ice-crusted beard. Blindly, he looked up and yelled, 'Medic!'

'Anita. Will . . . you . . .' A loud sigh cut off the request. Big Jim never got the rest of it out.

'Hell, yes, I'll look after her, but you're not going to die, Jim. You can't die.' Wylie sobbed. 'Damn it, I told you nothing's going to happen to us!'

'I think he's dead, sir,' one of the soldiers ventured.

'Shut up!' He looked wildly around. 'Medic! Where's the fuckin' medics?'

The soldiers pulled back and left him kneeling there alone in the snow with the body of his buddy. They'd willingly tangle with the Japs, but none of them wanted to lock horns with one of Castner's Cutthroats. They pushed on to continue their attacks on the Japanese positions along Fish Hook Ridge.

Unable to sleep, Wylie lay awake staring at the dark ceiling of the tent. He listened to the snores of the other men, like himself scheduled for evacuation. They were all frostbite victims. With Wylie, the diagnosis was battle fatigue.

He had no idea how long he'd sat and talked to Big Jim, but it was dark when they'd hauled him down off that ridge. After that, he'd just sat. These last sixteen days he'd seen so much misery and death – guys with their feet frozen black and their knees all bloody from crawling, bodies blown apart by enemy grenades, or men with their guts hanging out. Most were strangers; some he'd known by name; some he'd fought beside; but with Jim, it was different. Maybe they hadn't been as close as brothers, but Wylie had thought of him like a brother.

Why did Jim have to die? Why was he still alive? Jim had someone waiting for him to come home. He had no one except his parents. It wasn't fair.

Wylie closed his eyes, trying to shut out the guilt and grief. It was becoming painfully clear to him that he could escape from the world, but he couldn't escape from the thoughts in his head. He sat up, fully dressed, and pulled on his parka. The sleeves and front were crusted with dried blood from holding Jim's body in his arms. Now they felt useless and empty.

He slipped out of the tent, moving with quiet stealth, and wandered into the fog, missing the familiar weight of his rifle slung across his shoulder. The smell of coffee and breakfast cooking drifted on the cold night air. He stared in the direction of the fog-wrapped mess tent, knowing the troops were being rotated back from the front lines to have a hot meal before going into battle at dawn. He'd heard them talk about the morning's planned offensive to finish off the Japanese, although he'd given no sign he was listening. It wasn't his battle. He'd done his share of fighting. Like Big Jim had said, he was tired of it.

A shrill wailing cry floated out of the night. At first Wylie thought it was the wind howling down a ravine, but it sounded more like voices, a whole chorus of voices. He turned to face the crest of Engineer Hill, wondering if he was going crazy. Suddenly soldiers – American soldiers – started pouring over the top, running as if the devil were after them.

'The Japs!' a panicked soldier yelled at him. 'They're coming! They're right behind us! A whole damned army of Japs!' He threw a frightened look over his shoulder and continued to run, stumbling forward as if he couldn't make his legs move fast enough. 'Run! It's the Japs! Run!'

More streamed over the hill with the same cry. With a strange feeling of detachment, Wylie walked to the top of the hill and looked down through the wispy fog. In the faint light of predawn, he could see Japanese soldiers massing below. With the calmness of a disinterested observer, Wylie estimated there were at least several hundred of them.

Farther along the ridge of the hill, an American officer started shouting orders. Wylie couldn't make out his rank, but he guessed he was from the command post erected on the hilltop to direct the morning's artillery fire. Soldiers, responding to the shouted orders, scattered along the rim. As Wylie stared at them, he realized they were all noncombatants, support personnel – cooks and kitchen staff from the mess tents, medic, and stretcher bearers from the evac center, road builders and heavy-equipment operators from the Engineer units, staff officers and radio operators from the command posts. He couldn't identify one combat soldier among them.

Slowly it hit him that the Japanese army had broken through the front lines. There were no fighting units to stop them. It had taken sixteen days of brutal, bloody fighting to corner them in that valley. Now they'd broken out of the trap. There was nothing standing between them and the tons of supplies and ammunition behind him except this motley collection of service personnel who'd probably never been in combat in their lives. Those sixteen days of hell had been for nothing. He refused to accept that Big Jim had died for nothing. He couldn't let that happen.

'Somebody give me a rifle, grenades – anything!' he shouted.

Someone shoved an M-1 rifle in his hands along with a bunch of ammunition. Quickly he wedged himself between two soldiers hunkered down along the brow of the hill, and assumed the prone firing position. The soldier on his left pushed a small pile of grenades to him.

'Have some,' he urged nervously. 'I haven't handled any since I got out of basic.'

Screaming like banshees, the massed Japanese charged up the hill, their war cry of 'Banzai!' echoing eerily in Wylie's ears. The officer Wylie had seen earlier on the hill turned out to be the artillery commander. From his vantage point, he called out targets for the grenades as calmly as if he were directing an artillery barrage. Wylie pulled the pins and threw his grenades at the onrushing Japs until his supply was exhausted. But the holes blown in the massed front were quickly filled. The fanatical charge didn't break.

Wylie picked up the M-1 and began squeezing off round after round at the massed targets. Still they came on. Even those who were hit staggered forward. Sweat poured down his forehead. He'd never seen anything like this. The fire from the hilltop was mowing them down like rows of cornstalks, yet nothing seemed to stop them. They were so close now he could see their faces, their mouths open with the cry of 'Banzai!'

He used up his clip and shoved another one in, hurrying frantically. As he took aim again, he saw the front line falter. It was point-blank range now. He added his rifle's voice to the thunderous report of the other small-arms fire from the shoulder-to-shoulder men on the ridge. For a brief moment, it appeared that they were turning back the Jap charge.

But as the Japs fell back, they seemed to gather the needed momentum and hurtled themselves forward again in a maniacal rush. Wylie kept firing, his body vibrating with the constant recoil of his weapon as he pushed to his feet, realizing they couldn't stop the Japs now. Their momentum was going to carry them over the top.

As the Japs crested the hill, some Engineers rushed up from

the rear to meet them. Wylie was firing into their slant-eyed faces. Four fell at his feet before he ran out of ammunition. There wasn't time to reload. He cursed the lack of a bayonet and used the rifle as a club, desperately swinging at them as they swept over the rim. Suddenly he was facing a Jap with a scar on his left cheek, his mouth twisted in a sneer. Wylie saw the bayonet coming at his stomach, but he couldn't seem to get his rifle-club around fast enough. At the last second, he managed to knock the point of the bayonet down. It stabbed into his thigh like a hot iron. As the Jap soldier yanked it out, his leg collapsed under him and he fell, waiting for the killing thrust in his back that never came.

The Engineers behind Wylie broke the enemy's charge. The remnants of the Japanese Army fell back and regrouped on the lower slopes, then tried again to gain the summit without success. Faced with the dishonor of defeat at the hands of the Americans, some five hundred Japanese held grenades to their chests and pulled the pins, choosing death. As the Japanese proverb proclaimed, 'It is simpler to die than to live.'

Anchorage
September 1943

As Wylie gazed at the walls of his old bedroom, they looked familiar yet different somehow – like something out of the distant past that didn't seem quite real to him any more. He'd been back only two days. The Army had let him come home on leave now that his leg had sufficiently healed. It had been a long, slow process. He still didn't have the full use of it and needed a cane to get around. In time, he'd be able to dispense with it, too.

The injury had kept him out of the Kiska invasion, but that had turned out to be little more than an exercise. The Japs had abandoned their Aleutian stronghold and withdrawn their troops, somehow managing to sneak out through the Navy blockade of the island. Most of the casualties had come from soldiers shooting each other by mistake, although he'd heard that Japanese mines and booby traps had taken their toll, too. Wylie wasn't sorry he'd missed it.

There was a knock at his bedroom door. He guessed his mother had come to tell him they were ready to leave for church. He wished he could tell her to go away. Grudgingly, he answered it without budging from the bed. 'Yes?'

'It's your grandmother. May I come in?'

The bed creaked under his weight as he pushed higher on the pillows, wincing at the pull on his stiff leg muscles. 'Sure.'

The door opened and she walked in, then hesitated a moment before closing the door behind her. Idly, Wylie wondered how it was that his grandmother never seemed to age. Except for her blue-gray hair and the few lines in her face, she didn't really look old. He glanced at the royal blue dress with white polka dots and mentally added that she didn't dress old either, although her shoes were slightly more sensible than what she might have worn in her youth.

'I'm glad to see you're all ready for church.' Her glance

skimmed his sharply creased uniform and smoothly shaved face. She was struck by how thin and pale he looked – and how much he'd aged. The ordeal had stolen his youth, Glory realized. He would never be young again. She walked over to the straight chair and moved it closer to the bed. 'I was hoping we'd have a chance to talk before it was time to leave.'

'Grandmother Cole, I really don't feel like talking about the war just now.'

'I know.' She sat down. 'You've had to answer more than your share of questions about it since you've been back, haven't you? But you mustn't mind all the questions your parents have been asking you. They mean no harm. It's just that the reports we received about the fighting were so sketchy.' She opened her pocketbook and took out a poem that she'd cut from a paper someone had sent her. 'Have you seen this, Wylie?'

She handed it to him and watched him read the short poem written by Warrant Officer Boswell Boomhower this past summer. Glory already had it memorized by heart.

> *A soldier stood at the Pearly Gate;*
> *His face was wan and old.*
> *He gently asked the man of fate*
> *Admission to the fold.*
> *'What have you done,' St. Peter asked,*
> *'To gain admission here?'*
> *'I've been in the Aleutians*
> *For nigh unto a year.'*
> *Then the gates swung open sharply*
> *As St. Peter tolled the bell.*
> *'Come in,' said he, 'and take a harp.*
> *You've had your share of hell.'*

When Wylie said nothing, Glory began to speak again. 'I had a boarder staying with us recently who'd fought in Europe during the First World War. When the Depression came, he moved to Alaska and trapped for a while on some of the islands in the Aleutians. He talked a lot about the war and his experiences on the islands – enough for me to know that only those who have been through it can appreciate what it was like. Even then, it can affect each one differently.'

He gave her back the poem and frowned as he shook his head. 'I don't understand how you could know.'

698

'I may be a woman, Wylie Cole, but I've seen a lot and done a lot in my time,' she chided gently. 'Besides, you're supposed to be wiser as you get older.'

'I suppose.' However faint, it was the first genuine smile she'd seen from him since he'd been home.

'Wylie, all of us have endured things in our lives. When we try to talk about it, we can't seem to express the agony, fear, and grief of those moments – yet they live in our minds.'

'Yes,' he murmured. 'They do.'

'The past will always be with us, Wylie. We'll never forget the things that happen in our lives, and I don't think we should, no matter how painful some of the memories might be. But there comes a time when we must start over, when we must pick up the pieces of our lives and go on.'

'I know, but there's still a war on.'

'And your job isn't done.'

'I guess it isn't.'

His mother tapped on the door. 'It's time to leave for church.'

'We'll be right there,' Glory answered, then smiled at Wylie. 'Well, you've already heard one sermon this morning. Are you ready for another?'

'No.' He made no move to get up.

'You can't lie in that bed forever.'

'I suppose I can't,' he muttered. Reluctantly he lifted his bad leg and swung it off the side of the bed, then reached for the wooden cane propped against the nightstand.

The slopes of the Chugach Mountains outside of Anchorage wore their autumn cloaks of gold, the rocky summits thrusting their heads against the September sky. Dry brown leaves swirled in the dusty street as Ace stopped the car in front of the church and let his passengers out.

Wylie walked slowly with the aid of his cane. Beside him, his mother practically beamed with pride as people began to notice them. Laboriously he climbed the church steps, dragging his leg up one step at a time, as all along the way family acquaintances eagerly welcomed him home.

Until his grandmother had spoken to him this morning, he'd been dreading this predictable gamut of questions and comments that sounded so trite and meaningless. Now he listened to them, smiled, nodded, and offered some appropriate reply.

'It's so good to see you again.' 'I'll bet you're glad to be home.' 'When did you get back?' 'When do you have to report?' 'I heard it was bad.' 'You were in my prayers.' 'My sister's nephew is stationed in the Aleutians, too.' 'You are such a brave boy.' 'Some of your mother's good home cooking will put that weight back on you in no time.' 'I'll bet you showed those Japs a thing or two.' 'God bless you, Wylie.'

Someone opened the door for him. He stepped inside and paused in the vestibule, leaning heavily on his cane while his eyes adjusted to the relative gloom of the church after the brilliant sunshine outside. His mother and grandmother joined him.

'We probably should wait here until your father comes,' his mother said.

'That's fine.'

Several more people came up to speak to him. Then, over their heads, he saw Lisa. No one had mentioned her since he'd been back, and he hadn't asked about her. He realized that he'd known all along he'd see her at church this morning. That was the biggest reason he hadn't wanted to come. He wondered if his grandmother had been talking about the war or Lisa when she'd urged him to accept the pain of the past and start over.

Lisa looked different to him, more mature and sophisticated. Part of it was the fur hat and coat she wore, an obvious indication of her new affluence. Her dark blond hair was still cut in the long page-boy bob and her features were the same, but she didn't look like the shy, quiet girl he remembered.

She noticed him, hesitated, then said something to the man standing next to her. It was Steve Bogardus. Wylie recognized him instantly. Just for a minute he felt the flare of jealousy. He stiffened as they started toward him. His mother touched his arm. As he turned to her, he realized that she'd seen them, too.

'Maybe we should go sit down so you can rest your leg.'

But he knew there was nothing to be gained by postponing this meeting, however much he might wish to. 'I'm fine, Mom.'

Then she was there. 'Hello, Wylie.'

'Lisa.'

'You remember my husband, Steve Bogardus, don't you?' Self-consciously she included him.

'Of course.' Wylie shifted the cane to the left side so he could shake hands with her husband. 'Hello, Steve. Congratulations, a little late.'

'Thanks. It's good to see you in one piece. I heard you had a rough time of it.'

'No rougher than anyone else had.'

'I'm glad you're back,' Lisa said.

'So am I.' Wylie didn't know what to say to her. He didn't even know what he wanted to say to her. He wondered if anything should be said once a thing was over. Regrets? He had some. And there was no denying he still wanted her. But she was married now. It still hurt, but time had lessened the sharpness of it, as well as the bitterness.

A vague frown flickered across her face. 'You've changed.'

'It's the beard.' He stroked his smooth jaw. 'It'll grow back.'

'I guess that's it.' But she didn't sound certain.

'Your father's here, Wylie,' his mother interrupted. 'I think we should take our seats now.'

'Okay.' This time he took the excuse she offered. He'd never been any good at small talk.

'It was good seeing you again, Wylie,' Lisa said.

'Yeah. Same here.' He switched hands with the cane to properly support his leg and started forward in his usual gimpy gait.

As he moved past Lisa, she asked, 'Is it bad?'

Wylie paused, leaning on the cane. 'Nothing that won't heal. It just takes time.'

His mother took his arm and walked with him as he moved away. 'I'm sorry, Wylie,' she murmured.

'There's no reason for you to be sorry.'

'I know, but –'

'No buts, Mom. I never asked her to wait for me.'

At the conclusion of the morning service, they left the church ahead of Lisa. Wylie didn't speak to her again. During the drive home, he was silent. He spent most of it staring out the window, noting the changes in his hometown. Even on Sunday morning the streets were crowded. There were soldiers everywhere he looked. Fourth Avenue was crowded with bars. There was no shortage of liquor in this town. If Anchorage had been experiencing a boom before the war started, now it was fairly bursting at the seams. He guessed that nobody could come back to a place and find things the way he'd left them. Places changed as well as people.

As they neared the house, he glanced at his father. 'How busy are you going to be next week, Dad?'

'Not busy at all. I arranged for Skeeter and Sledge Chadwick to do most of the flying this week so I can have some time to spend with you. I thought we might see if the trout are biting.'

'I'd like you to fly me up to Circle the first part of the week. There's somebody I have to see.' But he knew more explanation than that was needed. 'A buddy of mine who got killed on Attu asked me if I'd go see his girl. I promised him I would.'

'If that's what you want, sure we can go. Just name the day and I'll have the plane ready.'

The log cabin was nestled in a stand of birch. The sunlight filtering through the yellow leaves cast a golden glow over the small clearing as a whispering breeze stirred through the branches. A thin trail of wood smoke spiraled from the cabin's chimney, adding its scent to the crisp autumn air.

Wylie leaned heavily on his cane, breathing fast. His leg throbbed from the half-mile walk. He was beginning to realize that he was more out of condition than he'd thought. While he paused to catch his breath, he studied the cabin. It was easy to picture Big Jim in this setting – out back somewhere chopping wood. The place looked like his home, rugged and strong, basic and honest, with no frills.

A pair of huskies were chained near the front of the cabin. The big gray one stood up and stared at Wylie, then lifted its nose, trying to catch his scent. The dog walked stiff-legged to the end of its chain. Even from twenty yards away, Wylie could hear the low rumble of its growl. The chain on the second one rattled as it trotted forward for a look. The first one started barking and the second one joined in.

Out of the corner of his eye, Wylie caught a movement at the cabin window. He ignored the ache in his leg and pushed off with the cane. The dogs went into a frenzy, leaping and running to the ends of their chains, barking ferociously. The cabin door opened and a dark-haired woman stepped onto the small porch. She wore trousers and a man's plaid shirt. Her hair was black and straight, the blunt ends brushing the top of her shoulders. But the sight of the black-haired toddler in her arms almost stopped Wylie in his tracks.

'Stony! Rocky!' the woman yelled at the dogs. Their barks turned to excited yips as they wiggled and hopped like young pups.

Wylie paused at the bottom of the planked steps. 'Are you Anita Lockwood?' She wasn't at all what he'd expected. The high cheekbones, the black hair and eyes, and the strong nose, they looked Indian, but there was no coarseness in her features. And her skin was more the color of rich cream than dull bronze.

'Yes.' She jiggled the child in her arms as she watched him with a guarded look.

'I'm Wylie Cole. I wrote you a letter a couple months ago about . . . Jim.'

She seemed to relax a little. 'Yes. I received it. Thank you. I'm not sure if I –' She stopped self-consciously, and quickly changed what she'd been going to say. 'I sent your letter to his parents in the States. I thought they would like to know.'

Wylie knew that she wondered whether she would have been notified of Big Jim's death. It was the reason he'd written her, because he didn't think she would have. 'That's fine,' he said.

'You said you would come, but I didn't think you would.'

'I promised Jim.'

'How did you get here? You didn't walk all that way, did you?' She seemed to be groping to make conversation. He felt the same awkwardness.

'My dad flew me in from Anchorage.' He saw her glance back along the trail. 'He's doing some fishing. I caught a ride from Circle.'

'I see.'

'Do you mind if I sit down?' Wylie shifted more of his weight onto the cane and eased the strain on his leg. 'My leg's kinda tired after hiking that half mile from the road.'

'Of course. Forgive me and please come inside.' She hastened to open the door for him as Wylie negotiated the steps. 'I'm afraid we don't get many visitors.'

The interior of the two-room cabin was snug and compact, every inch of space utilized. Wylie thumped into the main living area and paused to look around at the simple furnishings. The tables, chairs, cabinets, and cupboards all looked homemade yet well crafted, with the exception of one stuffed leather chair by the wood stove. The padded armrests were worn and cracked, and he suspected the old blanket folded on the seat cushion covered a tear in the leather. He knew without asking that it had been Big Jim's favorite chair.

'Sit down.' Anita Lockwood gestured toward the chair and set the boy on the floor. 'I'll make some coffee.'

Unwilling to take Jim's place, even figuratively, Wylie hesitated and watched her go to the cupboards and take down a tin of coffee. He had a brief glimpse inside the cupboard when she opened the door. There were few supplies on the shelf. He wondered how she was getting by now that Jim was dead and she no longer received money from him each month. He'd already checked and found out she hadn't received Jim's insurance money. He limped over to the chair and sat down, wincing as he stretched his sore leg out.

The cushions were all hollowed out to comfortably fit a man's shape. Wylie settled back into them and leaned his cane against the armrest. The little boy came toddling over, a finger hooked in his mouth. He stared first at Wylie, then at the cane. He looked to be about two or three years old. Wylie wondered why Big Jim had never mentioned the child.

'Hello.' Wylie smiled at him. 'What's your name?' The boy jabbered something unintelligible, and pointed with his wet finger at the cane. 'You're kinda fascinated by this, aren't you? I'm afraid it's bigger than you are.'

After quickly setting the coffeepot on the wood stove, Anita scooped the boy up with an apologetic glance at Wylie and plunked him down on the floor a few feet away amidst some wooden blocks. 'Play here,' she said firmly, then she moved back and sat down on the edge of a wooden rocker. 'The coffee will be ready in a few minutes.'

'The boy wasn't bothering me.' Wylie studied her curiously.

She lowered her head and chewed at the inside of her lip, then looked at him squarely. 'His name is Michael. Jim named him after his father but most of the time he just called him Mikey. When he was a baby, Mikey became very sick and ran a high fever. It took us three days to reach a doctor. We did all we could, but Jim always felt bad, especially after we learned that now Mikey is backward. Jim always worried that people would make fun of him because his mind is so slow.' She glanced at her hands. 'That's probably why he didn't tell you about Mikey. He wasn't ashamed of him,' she added defensively. 'It was just his way of protecting him.'

'I see.' Although the boy explained why Jim had been so anxious for Wylie to look after this woman, it made him wonder why Jim hadn't married her – a breed or not. 'This is a nice place,' he said.

'Yes. Jim built the cabin himself and he made all the furniture, too. He was good with his hands.' The pride and deep love she'd had for the man were clearly visible in her expression. There was a kind of radiance to her face when she talked about him. Then it faded. 'I wrote his parents and asked if I might stay here. But I haven't heard back from them yet.'

'Do you have any family, Anita?'

'My mother is still living, but she is very old now. My younger brother, Joe, is away at the native boarding school at White Mountain.'

Since the turn of the century, there had been two separate educational systems in Alaska. One was for natives and the other for whites and those of mixed blood who led a 'civilized' life. Wylie wondered why Anita's brother hadn't chosen the latter, but maybe it was easier not to fight the existing prejudice.

'Is that where you attended school?' It was obvious to him that she had received an education beyond the normal elementary level of most rural natives.

'No. I went to the Sheldon Jackson School in Sitka. I wanted to become a teacher, but . . . I was needed at home after my father died.' She gazed at a built-in cabinet; its glass doors revealed shelves lined with books. Her face softened again. 'Jim went to college. In the winters we used to read a lot and talk about the things we read. He was very intelligent. He taught me a lot. I probably should pack up all his books and send them home to his family with the rest of his things.'

'I think Jim would have wanted you to keep them. He would have wanted you to keep a lot of this,' Wylie stated.

The coffee started boiling atop the wood stove, its aromatic steam spreading throughout the small cabin. Anita poured a cup for each of them. Wylie wasn't sure whether the coffee deserved the credit or not, but the initial awkwardness passed and they talked freely. Wylie hadn't been able to talk much about Big Jim to anyone. With her, he could open up about his buddy. The time passed all too quickly for him. Before he knew it, he had to start back to meet his father.

He gave her some money, insisting Big Jim had left it with him to give to her. He suspected that she knew it was a white lie, but he also knew it was what Big Jim would have done if he'd thought of it. Then he left, promising he'd be back to see her and little Mikey again.

*

During the month that he was home recuperating, Wylie managed to make it back up there once a week. He found himself looking forward to the visits and the chance to get away from the hustle of Anchorage. He'd never been one who found much enjoyment sitting in bars and drinking, or standing in line at a whorehouse. And Lord knew, there were plenty of both in Anchorage. At Big Jim's cabin, he found a measure of peace and contentment. He didn't know if it was the setting or the company. He thought it might be a bit of both.

With a swing of the axe, he buried the blade in the halved log. The wood splintered as it split into quarters. Wylie chopped the two pieces the rest of the way apart, then spiked the axe blade on the flat top of the dead tree trunk and reached down to pick up the chunks of firewood, with no protest from the muscles in his leg. He was conscious of the blood rushing through his veins and heating his flesh. He'd worked up a sweat and it felt good.

A jay chattered at him from a bare branch overhead as he added the armload of wood to the long stack that represented a winter's supply of firewood. There was a crackling rustle of dry leaves behind him. Wylie glanced over his shoulder as little Mikey came scurrying up, grinning widely and proudly clutching some large splintered chunks of wood in his gloved hands. He hurried to the woodpile and stretched as tall as he could to stack his wood on top the way Wylie had.

'Let me give you a lift up there, Mikey.' Wylie picked him up and held him over the woodpile so he could deposit the small sticks on top, then swung him onto his hip. 'You're quite the little helper.'

His cap was askew and Wylie straightened it for him. The boy laughed. He was always laughing. Wylie had never seen a child so happy all the time. To Mikey, the world was filled with joy. Maybe it came with being retarded. Wylie didn't know, but he hoped that Mikey never found out he was different from other children; he hoped that smile of his would never go away.

The hinges on the cabin door creaked shrilly. Anita stepped to the end of the porch, hugging her arms around her to ward off the sharp nip in the air. 'If you two are finished, why don't you come inside? I just took the bread out of the oven and the coffee's hot. I thought we might sample some of that jam your mother sent.'

'Sounds good.' Wylie carried Mikey to the door, striding easily, hardly favoring his leg at all. As Anita opened the door, he made a mock shudder at the screech of the hinges. 'I've been meaning to oil that door.'

'That's the last thing Jim said before he left.'

Wylie glanced thoughtfully at the door as he closed it behind him, then turned. Anita reached to take the boy from him, but Wylie shook his head. 'I can manage.'

She didn't argue. 'I'll pour the coffee.'

He set Mikey on the floor and crouched down beside him to remove his cap, overcoat, and gloves, then shrugged out of his own and hung them all on the wall hooks by the door. He walked to the table and sat down, absently running his hand over the smoothly planed top.

'You know I loved Jim.' He smiled crookedly. 'I've never said that about another man before.'

She glanced up from the loaf of fresh bread she was slicing, her look one of understanding. 'He was a good man.'

Mikey came over and crawled onto Wylie's lap. 'I think he likes me.' Wylie affectionately rumpled the top of the boy's hair. Mikey mimicked the action and laughed.

'I know he does.' Anita smiled.

'Maybe this won't sound right, but . . .' He paused, trying to find the words that would make what he was about to say not sound stupid. 'Neither of us has anyone except family. The man you loved is dead, and the girl I loved married someone else. I think we get along pretty good together. Jim is something we have in common. Maybe it's a lousy reason for two people to get married, but . . . I guess that's what I'm proposing. Mikey here needs a father, and you could use a man around to look after things. Course, the Army still has first claim on me, but I am available on a part-time basis to start out.'

He kept talking because she wasn't saying anything. She wasn't even looking at him. She wiped her hands down the sides of her pants. 'Wylie, I'm not sure your parents would like the idea of you marrying me. Jim's parents were really upset when he told them about me. I don't want to cause any problems between you and your family. I –'

Wylie stopped her. 'Why don't you and Mikey fly back with me this afternoon and meet my family? You don't have to make any commitment. Afterwards, if you still think it's a bad idea, we'll drop it.'

She hesitated, then nodded cautiously. 'Okay.'

*

The meeting went better than even Wylie had expected. It turned out that his mother had asked Billy Ray and Matty to dinner that night, providing Anita with an opportunity to see the way they were treated. He'd already told his parents a little about Anita's situation, and they knew how close he'd been to Big Jim. When he introduced them, he indicated that the trip was an opportunity for Anita to do some shopping and didn't hint there was anything more to it than that.

Later that evening after his mother had gone upstairs to help Anita put Mikey to bed and Matty had stepped outside to see how much longer Billy Ray and his father were going to be tinkering with the car, Wylie sat alone in the living room with his grandmother, listening to the radio. He watched her slip a cigarette into an ivory holder, then light it.

'What do you think of Anita, Grandma Glory?'

'She's a pleasant, intelligent girl,' she answered readily. 'It's easy to see why your friend was so taken with her.'

'What if I said we are considering getting married?'

'Are you?' Her expression never changed.

'I've suggested it,' Wylie admitted.

'Is it because of Lisa?'

'No. It's because of Jim, although I admit if Lisa hadn't gotten married, I probably wouldn't be asking Anita. But like you told me, it's time to start over – for Anita, too.'

'There will be some who won't accept her. You know that,' she said and rolled the tip of her cigarette in the ashtray. 'In the old days, it was different here. What you were or what you'd done in the past didn't matter so much. Now we're more civilized. That makes certain people feel superior to others in some way.'

'That's their problem.'

'Perhaps. But you must be prepared to deal with it.'

'I think I am.'

'So do I,' Glory said, then smiled. 'I just wanted to hear you say it.'

'Anita's concerned about how Mom and Dad will accept her.'

'Your father isn't going to think a single thing about it. However, if the choice was your mother's, I don't think she would pick Anita to be your wife. Mothers always want more for their children. They're rarely happy with their children's choice for a mate. But I doubt that she'll ever let you or Anita see that.'

'And you, Grandma?'

'Pain, happiness, sorrow, and contentment – you're going to experience all those feelings. It will never be all one or all another. I've lived my life without regrets. That's the one wish I've always had for you and your father – and all the people I love.' She studied the ivory holder of her cigarette. 'In all the years we were married, Deacon never told me what to do or how to behave. He let me decide for myself and accepted whatever I chose without judging. It was perhaps the greatest gift he ever gave me. That's the way I've tried to be with you and Ace. If Anita is your choice for a wife, Wylie, then she's mine as well.'

'She's my choice, but I'm not sure yet whether she agrees.'

Matty's return to the room ended the conversation. Minutes after she came back, his mother and Anita came downstairs. Dressed in a plain blouse and skirt, Anita somehow looked more womanly to him – and more vulnerable.

'Did you get Mikey to sleep?' he asked.

'Yes.' She still wasn't very talkative in the presence of his family, but she appeared more relaxed and less defensive than she'd been earlier.

'I got that old teddy bear of yours out of the closet. Mikey latched onto it like it was gold,' Trudy said, laughing. 'He was asleep in minutes.'

'I'm afraid he isn't going to give it up very willingly,' Anita said.

'That's all right. Teddy bears shouldn't sit in closets when there's a child around who will love them. Mikey can keep him,' Wylie said.

'Would anybody like some coffee?' Trudy asked. 'I already have some made in the kitchen.'

Ace walked in just then, still wringing his freshly scrubbed hands. 'Sounds good to me.'

'Me, too,' Billy Ray chimed in, a step behind him.

'Please, let me get it for you, Mrs. Cole,' Anita volunteered.

His mother hesitated, then smiled. 'All right. The cups are in the right-hand cupboard –'

'Never mind, Mom,' Wylie interrupted. 'I'll give her a hand.' He followed Anita into the kitchen and got the cups from the cupboard, then leaned sideways against the counter to watch while she filled them with coffee. 'What do you think of my family?'

'They're very nice.' Her smile came quickly, then faded just as quickly. She set the coffeepot on the counter and turned to him, her dark eyes earnestly searching his. 'Wylie, are you sure you want to marry me? I mean, it's not just me. It's Mikey. He's never going to be a normal boy. He's always going to need care. I don't think you're aware of how much responsibility you're taking on.'

'No more than what you were prepared to shoulder alone,' he reminded her. 'I considered all that before I ever suggested marriage to you. Believe it or not, I think I know what I'm doing.'

She shook her head, the gesture a mixture of vague amusement and amazement. 'I think I know why Jim liked you so much.'

'Is that a yes or a no?'

'Yes. If you still want me and Mikey, I'll marry you.'

Hesitantly, Wylie bent toward her, then paused inches away and lifted her chin with his fingertips. He kissed her with tentative pressure and felt the uncertainty in her response.

Yet the first kiss made the second one easier. Each of them had a wealth of love to give and a need to share it with someone. It was going to be all right.

They kept the wedding simple, with only the family in attendance, then returned to the cabin for a few days to pack Anita and Mikey's things and move them to Anchorage so his family could look after them while Wylie was gone. With the housing shortage that existed, they accepted Glory's offer to let Anita and Mikey stay in the small one-room apartment in the rear of the boardinghouse that had been Chou Ling's. The old Chinese cook had passed away the previous spring, and the new cook already had a place to live. The solution seemed ideal, since it not only gave Anita and Mikey a place to stay, but it also meant Anita could help Matty with the work at the boardinghouse and earn some extra money. The prices for everything in Alaska were high, but at least the Territory wasn't under the rationing program that had been instituted in the Lower Forty-eight.

Wylie reported back to duty, fully recovered from his wound. With the Japanese pushed out of the Aleutians and losing ground elsewhere in the Pacific, the threat to Alaska appeared over. There was talk for a while that the Chain would be used as a staging area for an invasion of the northern Japanese islands of the Kuriles sometime in June of 1944, but Russia still hadn't declared war on Japan. With the Kamchatka Peninsula so close to Japan, Russian cooperation was needed. The plans were put on the shelf until Russia joined the war in the Pacific.

That spring, the Alaska Scouts were assigned to new duties that would put to use their combined extensive knowledge of the territory. Wylie and several other Scouts were sent to the Arctic desert of the far north. Initially Wylie accompanied a team of geologists sent to the area by the War Department to explore the large area of land, roughly the size of Indiana, that had been set aside back in 1923 as Naval Petroleum Reserve No. 4 – Pet 4 they called it. As far back as 1886, oil seepages had been reported in the area. An exploration in the 1920s had confirmed the existence of an oil-bearing area of unknown volume and the federal government had reserved the land for future needs.

Faced with the possibility of a long war, the War Department had decided they had better determine the potential at Pet 4. Geological studies of the North Slope were to be made and test wells drilled. While a permanent base camp was being built at the Eskimo village of Barrow, the northernmost point on the continent, to handle the incoming drilling equipment, men, and supplies, Wylie went with the geologists to a site on the Colville River some eighty miles from a place called Umiat.

Erosion had cut away a part of a hill, creating a bluff. Oil dripped from the exposed sedimentary layers and polluted the river. The geologists swarmed all over the bluff, examining the exposed strata and using them as a blueprint to understand the rock layers that formed the North Slope.

During the Arctic summer, the sun never set for thirty-six straight days. The tundra's brown vegetation that was swept with snow and freezing winds in the long winter burgeoned with life. A brilliant, multicolored array of wildflowers burst into bloom to carpet the land and provide fodder for the herds of caribou. Hundreds of species of birds came by the thousands to nest in the area and feast on the black clouds of mosquitoes and gnats that swarmed over the tundra. For the geologist party, head nets were the only protection from the hungry insects, but there were times when they were so thick on the protective netting that Wylie couldn't see out. Birds soon flocked to the camp just to gobble up the mosquitoes.

Full-scale drilling operations were scheduled to begin the following year – 1945. That winter, Billy Ray died after suffering a massive heart attack while shoveling snow. Wylie managed to make it home for his funeral. When he reported back to duty, he found himself assigned to a party of Scouts whose task it was to survey a pipeline route from Barrow to Fairbanks.

The war was winding down in Europe. Hitler's defeat appeared to be a matter of months. But there was no such optimism in the Pacific. By now, thousands of soldiers and Marines had heard the dreaded cry 'Banzai' and learned that the Japanese soldier preferred death over defeat.

The route of the proposed pipeline ran right through the heart of the Brooks Range, the formidable and forbidding barrier mountains that separated the North Slope from the interior of Alaska. Wylie had flown over their jagged peaks before, but from the ground they were even more awesome. It quickly became apparent to him why they put the 'wild' in 'wilderness.' The violent upheaval of brown rock and boulders created a terrain of incomparable, cruel beauty.

In the middle of August, in the Brooks Range, the news reached him that American planes had dropped an atomic bomb on the Japanese city of Hiroshima. Two days after that, the Russians had finally declared war on Japan. The Soviet armies were invading Japanese-occupied Manchuria. For Wylie, there was more good news – of a personal nature. He was a father. Anita had given birth to a baby girl.

On August 15, 1945, Japan surrendered, although the official ceremony didn't take place until September 2. The war, at last, was over. By the end of September, Wylie was home and held his two-month-old baby daughter, Dana Marie Cole, in his arms for the first time.

But the joy of his homecoming was short-lived. Matty, in her early seventies now, took ill. Glory told him that since Billy Ray had died, Matty hadn't been well. In less than a month, she joined him.

At the gravesite, Wylie stood beside his grandmother. Her eyes were bright with unshed tears, her posture erect, her shoulders squared and straight. Yet she looked brittle to him, like a fragile porcelain figurine that needed careful handling or it would shatter. She had shunned the wearing of black, insisting Matty wouldn't have wanted it. The coat she wore against the autumn chill was ten years behind the fashion, the wool material a shade of bright rust and trimmed with a wide, thick gray fox collar. The brisk wind constantly stirred the ruff, creating an ever-changing pattern of furrows in the thick hairs and blowing them against her jaw and cheek, but she never seemed to notice.

After the services concluded, the family, lingered at the gravesite to speak to the handful of Matty's friends who had attended. Once Wylie saw his grandmother dab at her eyes with a lace handkerchief. Then his father came up and gently took her by the arm to guide her to the car. Wylie followed with his mother. Anita hadn't come to the cemetery. She had decided it wasn't wise to bring either their infant daughter or Mikey to the services, and there was no one outside the family to care for them.

Wylie drove while his parents sat in the back seat. His grandmother sat in front with him. She barely spoke, merely gazed out the window at the passing scenery. Wylie doubted that she saw any of it, but he was wrong.

'It's all changed so in the last few years,' she murmured. 'Buildings and houses springing up everywhere like the weeds in my aunt's vegetable patch back in Sitka. There are streets now that I've never even seen before.'

'It's not a town any more. It's a city,' Ace replied from the back seat. 'There were four thousand here in 'thirty-nine. Now they're saying the population of Anchorage is around forty thousand.'

'Yes.' Glory sighed heavily. 'It isn't fair that Matty had to die now after the territorial legislature just passed that new law prohibiting segregation. There were so many stores that Matty longed to enter, just to browse through the merchandise. She never had the chance.'

'It was a stupid practice to begin with,' Trudy declared. 'It's time they abolished it.'

'I know. I wish they'd take all those signs that hung in the windows saying 'No Natives Allowed' and 'Coloreds Need Not Apply' and build a big fire with them. So many feelings were hurt by them.' A quiet anger vibrated through Glory's voice. 'Whenever I saw those signs in front, I hated to go in those places, especially when Matty had to wait for me outside. What fun we would have had going into those stores today.' She ended on a sad note and lapsed into silence.

A week later, Glory called and asked Wylie to come over to the boardinghouse. After he'd been discharged, he'd rented one of the houses his grandmother owned and moved his small family into it. With all the confusion of coming home, moving, and Matty's death, he hadn't had time to look for a job. Mostly he'd been helping his father out at the flying service.

Glory barely gave him a chance to sit down before she announced, 'I've decided to close down the boardinghouse. With both Matty and Chou Ling gone, it's not the same any more. I'm too old to run this place myself.'

'You're not old, Grandma Glory.'

'You were two years old when you first called me grandma. That was what? Twenty-two years ago? Well, I didn't feel old then, but today I do,' she said decisively. 'But old or not, it's time for me to change and begin a new life.'

'What do you plan to do? Sell out?' He didn't try to talk her out of the decision. He'd learned long ago that once she made up her mind about something, that was it. She forged straight ahead and never looked back. 'Where will you live? Are you planning to move in with the folks?'

'No, I'm not so old that I can't look after myself,' she chided. 'Do you remember that four-room log cabin I own? Well, the present tenants are moving out. That will be my new home. But I don't intend to sell this place. Although with property being as high as it is, I probably should. What I plan to do is convert the boardinghouse into small apartments.' She handed him a sheet of paper that had a rough sketch of the proposed layout. 'I thought you might be able to oversee the remodeling work for me. I don't feel up to the task of arguing with carpenters and plumbers.'

'If that's what you want.'

'That's what I want.'

'How will you keep busy? I can't imagine you doing nothing,' Wylie said.

'Now you sound like Deacon.' She laughed. 'Between managing my various properties and playing with my great-grandchildren, I expect I'll keep adequately busy. And this spring I intend to plant a large flower garden, the likes of which Anchorage has never seen. I've always planned to have one. Now I'm going to do it. And mind you, there won't be a single vegetable anywhere in sight. It'll be strictly flowers.'

Wylie spent the bulk of that winter moving his grandmother to her new home, selling the excess household goods, furniture, and linens, and remodeling the boardinghouse. All the new apartments were rented by the time the last strip of wallpaper was hung. That spring, Glory planted her flowers over the entire front yard of the rustic log cabin.

61 *Anchorage*
June 30, 1958

Wylie threaded his way through the thousands of celebrants who had jammed into Delaney Park, locally known as the Park Strip. Now and then he stopped and scanned the crowd, trying to locate his family among the horde of people. He'd been en route to Anchorage late that afternoon on a routine cargo flight when the radio had crackled with the news.

He'd never intended to get into the family flying business. It had simply happened. The summer after he'd gotten out of the service, his father had been injured in a plane crash. Wylie had filled in for him – temporarily. He was still there, gradually running more and more of the company's operation.

A half hour ago, he'd landed at Merrill Field and seen the seven-inch-high headlines in the *Anchorage Times*, confirming the news in two words: 'WE'RE IN.' He'd fought his way through the bumper-to-bumper traffic of horn-honking cars to his house, found the note Anita had left for him, and hurried on foot over to the Park Strip to join the celebration of Alaska's statehood.

After six days of debate, the Senate had finally passed the bill at eight o'clock in the evening, Washington, D.C., time, that would allow Alaska to become a state. Now it was only a matter of two thirds of the states ratifying the bill. And the ratification was already assured. Everywhere cars honked, sirens wailed, and church bells rang with the news. In the park a bonfire roared, flames leaping high, fueled by fifty tons of lumber, forty-nine of those tons honoring Alaska as the forty-ninth state in the Union. The extra ton was for Hawaii, a gesture of optimism for its statehood battle.

Again, Wylie paused, trying to identify Anita or his parents among the sea of faces. He thought he recognized Dana's dark head amidst a group of young people on the far side of the blazing fire. He started to work his way around for a closer look. A serpentine chain of dancers blocked him.

'Wylie.'

He heard his name above all the noisy jubilation around him. He stopped, already recognizing the familiar voice as he turned in its direction. Lisa stood several yards away, wearing some simple blue dress that looked both casual and elegant. Or maybe it merely looked expensive, he decided.

It had been a while since he'd seen her, usually at church, and he'd been too busy lately to attend regularly. But her husband and two sons had always been with her and he'd been surrounded by his family. Now she stood alone. There was no one between them.

Slowly he crossed the space, taking the time to notice all the little details that he hadn't dared study before. If it was possible, she had grown more beautiful. He'd never pretended to himself that he'd forgotten her. He hadn't – any more than Anita had forgotten Big Jim.

'Hello.' Her voice had a breathless edge to it.

'Hello.' He smiled.

'It's been a while since I've seen you,' she said.

'I was just thinking the same thing.' Then he pulled his thoughts back from the wayward direction they were taking, and glanced around. 'I was trying to find my family. They're all supposed to be here somewhere. You haven't seen them, have you?'

'No, but a person can get lost easily in this crowd. Steve's off looking for the boys now. One minute they were here with us and in the next they were gone. They're worse than Rudy and Erik ever were.' She laughed nervously. 'This is quite a celebration.'

'It is.'

'It's hard to believe Alaska will be a state now. It doesn't seem so long ago that I was climbing off the train with my family here at Anchorage on a frontier adventure – and my brothers were mistaking you for their first live Indian.'

'I have to admit it doesn't seem very long ago that I showed you and your mother the house my grandmother had for rent.' For a poignant instant, Wylie felt the years in between dissolve. He had an urge to suggest that maybe they could take in a movie some Saturday night as he had then, but he didn't.

A wistful expression flickered across her face. 'It may not seem very long to either of us, but I have two teenaged boys to prove it.'

'My daughter is thirteen now, too.'

'I'm glad I had this chance to see you again before we left, Wylie.' She tried to smile, but there was sadness in it, maybe even a little regret.

Then he realized what she'd said and frowned. 'You're leaving?'

'Yes.' She made an attempt at brightness. 'Steve has been transferred back to the company's main office in San Francisco. Some junior vice president is taking over the branch office here in Anchorage. The general consensus is that the construction boom is pretty well over in Alaska, at least for a while.'

'So you'll be living in the Lower Forty-eight from now on.' For some reason, the phrase came to him: 'They always leave,' but he couldn't remember where he'd heard it before.

'Yes. My parents are excited about it. You know they moved back in 'fifty-two. Mother finally got her way,' she added wryly. 'Of course she's been complaining because they live so far away she doesn't get to see her two grandsons as often as she'd like.'

'She always was a hard woman to satisfy.' Even with the high cost of living in Alaska, Wylie suspected the Blomquists had managed to save a tidy sum out of the high wages Jan Blomquist had earned during the war and postwar boom. But the story was typical. Few who came to take advantage of the high-paying jobs ever stayed once they'd made their money. They came, made their money, and left with it to buy some retirement home in the Lower Forty-eight.

'I'm glad I was here almost long enough to see Alaska become a state, though,' Lisa said.

'Yes.' He realized that Steve might return at any minute, and he didn't want to see him, not this time – this last time. 'Well, I ... I'd better hunt up my family. Good-bye, Lisa, and good luck.' He didn't trust himself to touch her, not even to shake hands, so he gave her a vague one-fingered salute and began backing away.

'Good-bye, Wylie.' As he turned away, he heard her add, 'I'll miss you.' But he pretended he hadn't heard and walked blindly into the crowd.

He let himself become lost in the noise and mass of people, paying no attention to where he was going or who was around him as he tried to shake off the ache for something he couldn't have. Sometimes he wondered if Anita didn't have it easier. At least Big Jim was dead, leaving her with nothing but memories. For him, Lisa existed in the flesh, still out of reach but very much alive. Now that she was leaving, she'd be out of his sight – maybe even out of his mind – but he doubted that he'd ever get her out of his heart. Maybe that's the way it always was with the one a person loved and lost, always making a person wonder, What if?

Suddenly he saw Anita standing almost directly in front of him, facing the fire. His parents were there, too. They'd brought a lawn chair for his grandmother Glory to sit in, but she was standing beside it, still very active for her age. Mikey stood next to Anita and gazed round-eyed at the giant bonfire, enthralled by the leaping flames. At fifteen, he was nearly as tall as Anita, but functionally he had the mind of a six-year-old. He could dress himself and tie his shoes now. He knew his name and address. All those little accomplishments were milestones in his life.

Dana, Wylie's thirteen-year-old daughter, was standing off to one side of the family, giggling with a girlfriend. It was difficult to say which of them she resembled most, since her black hair, dark eyes, and strong features came from both of them, but she was more out-going than both of them put together. She had on a pair of blue jeans and one of his old shirts. It was the 'real cool' way to dress, or maybe it was 'hip.' Wylie had trouble keeping up with all her slang words. She was really just a tomboy making the awkward transition to a young woman. Sometimes he wondered whether the transformation would ever take place. Not that he minded. He enjoyed having someone to take hunting and fishing with him, even if sometimes he felt as if he needed a translator.

His attention swung back to Anita. Her black hair was softly curled by a permanent wave. The dress she wore was simple and attractive, not nearly as expensive as Lisa's. The flying business was good, but not that good. And Anita hadn't retained her youthful figure the way Lisa had. Some padding had been added to her waist and hips over the years. But she was a good woman. And they'd had a damned good marriage. In some ways, they were perfectly suited to each other. Whatever passion might be lacking in their marriage, they more than made up for it with the deep respect and genuine affection they shared.

Wylie felt calm inside again as he walked up behind her and put his arm around her. 'You found us!' Anita exclaimed after an initial start of surprise. 'Did you see the note I left you?'

718

'Yes, but I was beginning to think I'd never find you in this crowd.'

'I know. Isn't it exciting? We've finally won statehood after all these years.'

'And it's been a good many years, too,' Glory inserted. 'I remember when Judge Wickersham proposed admitting Alaska into the Union back in 1912 or maybe it was 1911. Of course, he wasn't a judge then. He was a delegate to Congress. He did manage to make us a territory that time.'

'I told Dana to be sure and remember everything that happened today,' Anita said, flushed with the excitement of the occasion. 'It's an event she can tell her grandchildren about.'

'Well, I can tell ours that I was at four thousand feet, flying over the Tanana River, when I picked up a radio transmission from Fairbanks saying that Alaska was now the forty-ninth state. I admit I did a little rocking of the wings.' Wylie smiled. 'I might have tried a victory roll if I'd been sure there was nothing breakable in the crates I was hauling.'

A large piece of lumber at the top of the blazing fire collapsed in a shower of sparks. Mikey clapped his hands in excitement and started to move closer to the bonfire. Anita caught his arm as a string of firecrackers tossed into the blaze went off.

'I want to see, Mom.' He pulled away from her, trying to get loose.

'It's too hot. You'll get burned. Just stay here by me.' She grabbed him firmly and pulled him back, but he was getting almost too big for her to manhandle.

'I wanta go.' But he quickly forgot his disappointment to watch the roaring blaze.

'He is so fascinated by the fire.' Anita warily kept an eye on him.

'He reminds me of Ace when he was four years old,' Glory declared. 'Half of Nome was on fire, and there he was, watching from the window of our house, clapping his hands and laughing with glee every time one of the gasoline barrels blew and shot flames up in the air.'

'That was a long time ago, Mother.' Affectionately Ace put his arm around her slim shoulders.

'Yes, it was.' But she started remembering back to that crazy summer in Nome when people had poured onto the beaches by the thousands – fortune seekers all of them, whether they were prospectors, peddlers, gamblers, pickpockets, swindlers, prostitutes, or would-be kings. Looking back, Glory could see more clearly the jealousy, resentment, greed, and even hatred that had warped the lives of so many people. This land and its riches seemed to have a way of bringing out the worst and best in people.

Glory gazed at all the unfamiliar faces around the giant bonfire and recalled the days when she had been the center of attention wherever she went. Her family were the only ones who took any notice of her now. To the rest, she was just a decrepit old woman. None of them would ever guess that she had once been Glory St. Clair. Then she laughed under her breath, realizing they'd probably never even heard of Glory St. Clair.

'What's so funny, Mother Cole?'

'I was just thinking about something that happened a long time ago.' Glory suspected that Trudy thought it had become a habit of hers. 'Do you remember when we helped clear this park so Anchorage could have an airfield. Wylie, you were just a little tyke then. The whole town declared a holiday and turned out to help. We had a bonfire that night, too.'

'It was some airstrip, wasn't it?' Ace chuckled. 'There was a road running right through it. Of course, in those days, there weren't very many cars to worry about.'

'I'm glad they made it into a park,' Trudy said.

'It's all changed so much.' Glory waved her age-spotted hand at the skyline of the city, the bracelet around her wrist jingling faintly. 'Look at all those tall buildings. On a clear day, I used to be able to see Mount McKinley from the back door of my cabin. Now there's a five-story office building blocking my view.'

Nearly all of the construction had been done within the last twelve years, a result of the cold war with Russia, which had caused the Department of Defense to engage in a massive buildup and modernization of military installations in Alaska.

'I keep telling you, Mother Cole, that you really should move in with us. There's certainly enough room in our new house and we have a spectacular view of Cook Inlet and the mountains, including McKinley.' Trudy was proud of the retirement home they'd built in the new housing development on a bluff overlooking Cook Inlet, called Turnagain-by-the-Sea. 'And it's so peaceful. I'd think you'd want to get away from the hustle and bustle of downtown.'

'I happen to like the hustle and bustle, as you call it. And I am not yet so old that I can't take care of myself.'

Ace had heard the argument between his wife and mother too many times to pay any attention to it. 'We can't say Alaska's been forgotten any more, not with the millions and millions of dollars the Defense Department has spent here.'

'But how much of it stayed?' Glory challenged. 'Most of the contractors, equipment, and workers came from the outside. They spent some here and took the rest home, without paying any taxes. During the gold rush, they think seven hundred and fifty million dollars was taken out of Alaska. That doesn't count the millions in copper the Morgans and Guggenheims took out of the Kennecott operation. A great part of our wealth was taken from us, and we couldn't even tax those doing it until 1949.'

'I read in the paper that Alaska Salmon Industry, out of Seattle, managed to keep the fisheries out of our control in the statehood bill,' Ace said, then grinned. 'But I think that oil strike they made last year in the Kenai Peninsula south of here will more than make up for it. The geologist who kicked the tree and said "Drill here" – the Chamber of Commerce took his boot and had it plated with gold. Can you imagine that?'

'I remember when I was up on the Arctic slope, north of the Brooks Range back in 'forty-four and 'forty-five. It was really something to see that green oil tinged with red dripping out of the sands of the bluffs.' Wylie absently rubbed Anita's shoulder as the talk of oil turned his thoughts back. 'I understand some oil companies have geologist teams up there looking it over now that the Navy pulled their drilling teams out of the area back in 'fifty-three. With this oil strike in the Kenai, a lot of the major companies are taking a real serious look at Alaska. I think they're certain there's more to be found.'

Oil. They called it black gold, Glory recalled, and gold always started a fever. The symptoms of it were always the same – the claim jumping and lot jumping, the suits and receiverships, all the grabbing and pushing, the hordes of people and piles of equipment. She wondered if she had the energy to go through another boom. Booms were for young people.

'Grandma Glory.' Dana sauntered over to join them, her hands thrust in the back pockets of her jeans. 'Is it true that you were once a dance-hall girl in Nome?'

'How old are you?' Glory didn't blink an eye.

'Thirteen.'

'When you get a little older, I'll answer your question and tell you all about it,' she replied.

'Then you can tell us, Dana.' Wylie winked.

'But Grandma Glory, you're already old. You might not be alive by the time I'm older,' Dana protested.

'Dana, what a thing to say!' Anita declared in sharp reproval.

'The child has a valid point,' Glory insisted. 'Lord knows, I am old. But don't worry, Dana, I have every intention of living to be a hundred.'

Epilogue

Anchorage
March 1974

Glory Cole survived the Good Friday earthquake on March 27, 1964 – the one that rocked Alaska and destroyed so much of Anchorage. She lived to read about the huge oil strike at Prudhoe bay on the North Slope of Alaska and experienced the initial boom as other oil companies, drilling crews, suppliers, construction workers, prostitutes, and related fortune seekers converged on Alaska to take part in the oil rush. She observed all the bitter wrangling over the proposed pipeline – the injunctions and lawsuits that were filed, the hatred that grew toward the conservationists, the prejudice that surfaced toward Alaskan natives, the greed and the struggle for something better.

On the very day authorization was given for the construction of the pipeline from Prudhoe Bay to Valdez – four years short of her hundredth birthday – Glory Cole died quietly, peacefully in her sleep, surrounded by all the members of her family. She died as she had lived – with no regrets and no looking back.

Ace claimed that she hadn't really died, that she'd simply moved on to a new place to start over.

☐	Heiress	Janet Dailey	£5.99
☐	The Glory Game	Janet Dailey	£4.99
☐	Rivals	Janet Dailey	£4.99
☐	Masquerade	Janet Dailey	£4.99
☐	Aspen Gold	Janet Dailey	£4.99
☐	Tangled Vines	Janet Dailey	£5.99

Warner Books now offers an exciting range of quality titles by both established and new authors. All of the books in this series are available from:

Little, Brown and Company (UK),
P.O. Box 11,
Falmouth,
Cornwall TR10 9EN.

Alternatively you may fax your order to the above address. Fax No. 0326 376423.

Payments can be made as follows: cheque, postal order (payable to Little, Brown and Company) or by credit cards, Visa/Access. Do not send cash or currency. UK customers and B.F.P.O. please allow £1.00 for postage and packing for the first book, plus 50p for the second book, plus 30p for each additional book up to a maximum charge of £3.00 (7 books plus).

Overseas customers including Ireland, please allow £2.00 for the first book plus £1.00 for the second book, plus 50p for each additional book.

NAME (Block Letters) ....

....

ADDRESS ....

....

....

☐ I enclose my remittance for _____

☐ I wish to pay by Access/Visa Card

Number ☐☐☐☐☐☐☐☐☐☐☐☐☐☐☐☐

Card Expiry Date ☐☐☐☐